Benjamin Silliman

First Principles of Chemistry

Benjamin Silliman

First Principles of Chemistry

Reprint of the original, first published in 1861.

1st Edition 2022 | ISBN: 978-3-37505-717-6

Verlag (Publisher): Salzwasser Verlag GmbH, Zeilweg 44, 60439 Frankfurt, Deutschland
Vertretungsberechtigt (Authorized to represent): E. Roepke, Zeilweg 44, 60439 Frankfurt, Deutschland
Druck (Print): Books on Demand GmbH, In de Tarpen 42, 22848 Norderstedt, Deutschland

FIRST PRINCIPLES

OF

CHEMISTRY,

FOR THE

Use of Colleges and Schools.

BENJAMIN SILLIMAN, JR., M.A., M.D.

With Four Hundred and Twenty-three Illustrations.

FIFTIETH EDITION.
REWRITTEN AND ENLARGED.

PHILADELPHIA:
H. C. PECK & THEO. BLISS.
1861.

TO

Benjamin Silliman,

FOR FIFTY YEARS PROFESSOR OF CHEMISTRY IN YALE COLLEGE,

This Volume,

DESIGNED TO PROMOTE THAT SCIENCE, TO WHICH HE

HAS DEVOTED HIS LIFE,

IS RESPECTFULLY DEDICATED,

BY HIS SON,

THE AUTHOR.

PREFACE TO THE THIRD REVISED EDITION.

During the five years which have passed since the second edition of this work was prepared, intense activity has prevailed in all departments of chemical research. Any attempt to preserve the stereotype plates of that edition in the present was found to be quite impracticable. The whole work has been entirely revised, rewritten, and so far rearranged, as experience has shown to be desirable. Some parts have been enlarged, and some have been contracted, so that on the whole the size of the volume remains much as before. A great number of new illustrations have been added, more than doubling the number in the former editions. A considerable number of wood cuts have been taken from Regnault's excellent *Cours de Chimie*, and many new ones have been drawn from the author's apparatus. Every important fact, formula, and number in the work has been carefully compared with the most recent and valued authorities. The changes made in the atomic weights of elementary substances, during the last five years, have been numerous and important; and in most cases these changes have added simplicity to the science. The new facts and principles gleaned in no inconsiderable numbers for this edition, have been woven into the text in such a manner as to present, it is hoped, an uniformity of design.

In the Organic Chemistry, greater simplicity and unity has been given to the principles involved in the almost unwieldy mass of facts which have accumulated so rapidly during the last ten years. The author has again to acknowledge his obligations to his friend and former associate, Mr. Hunt, for his lucid and original exposition of this part of the subject.

The adoption of this work by many of the first seminaries of learning in this country, is a gratifying evidence to the author that his design has been appreciated; and he trusts that those who gave their confidence to the two first editions, will find the present one, in many important respects, superior to them.

New Haven, September 30, 1852.

FROM THE PREFACE TO THE FIRST EDITION.

THE object of this work is sufficiently indicated by its title. It has grown out of the exigencies of teaching, and has been received as the text-book in the public lectures at Yale College.

It is important that a work of this kind should contain only such matter as is actually taught to a class by recitations and lectures. All fulness beyond this is unavailable to either teacher or pupil, and serves often to embarrass the one and discourage the other. This is, perhaps, the reason why several works, otherwise excellent, have failed to answer the purpose for which they were written. The science of Chemistry has now reached the point where its first principles can be presented by the teacher with almost mathematical precision.

Chemistry has attractions of an economical and experimental character, which will always secure for it a place in every system of education. Without wishing to diminish its claims to attention on these grounds, the author urges the paramount advantages possessed by his favourite science, as a study peculiarly fitted to train the mind to a methodized and logical habit of thought. If nothing more is to be derived from its study than the entertainment offered by brilliant phenomena, and a knowledge of convenient economical processes, the pupil will fail of its most important advantage. The beautiful philosophy, the perspicuous nomenclature, and lucid method of modern chemistry, are so obvious that they cannot fail to awaken the attention of every intelligent pupil, and carry him on his course of intellectual culture with rapid progress.

The author has consulted all the best authorities within his reach, both in the standard systems of England and France, and in the scientific journals of this country and Europe. The works of Daniell, Graham, Brande, Kane, Fownes, Gregory, Faraday, Mitscherlich, Berzelius, Dumas, Liebig, and Gerhardt, have all been used, as also the treatises of Dr. Hare and Prof. Silliman.

The Organic Chemistry is presented mainly in the order of Liebig in his *Traité de Chimie Organique*. The author takes pleasure in acknowledging the important aid derived in this portion of the work from his friend and professional assistant, Mr. THOMAS S. HUNT, whose familiarity with the philosophy and details of Chemistry, will not fail to make him one of its ablest followers. The labour of compiling the Organic Chemistry has fallen almost solely upon him.

If it shall be found to meet the wants of both teachers and pupils, and to promote the progress of Scientific Chemistry in this country, the author will feel that he has not laboured in vain.

NEW HAVEN, December 30, 1846.

TABLE OF CONTENTS.

PART I.

PHYSICS.

PART II.

CHEMICAL PHILOSOPHY.

PART III.

INORGANIC CHEMISTRY.

PART IV.

ORGANIC CHEMISTRY.

FIRST PRINCIPLES

OF

CHEMISTRY.

PART I.—PHYSICS.

INTRODUCTION.

1. OUR knowledge of nature begins with experience. While this teaches us that like causes, under similar circumstances, produce like effects, we recognise also, as inseparable from our experience, the great principle that every event must have a cause. Man, "as the priest and interpreter of nature," seeks to extend his experience by experiment. Every experiment is but a question addressed to nature, asking for an increase of knowledge; and if we question her aright, we may be sure of a satisfactory answer.

2. *Observation* instructs us in a knowledge of the external forms of nature, and we thus acquire our first impressions of the various departments of Natural History. Our knowledge would, however, be very limited, without a constant effort to extend our experience by experiment. The nations of antiquity excelled greatly in many branches of human knowledge, and their skill in the arts of design remains unequalled. Their ignorance, however, of natural phenomena, and the laws by which they are governed, was remarkable; because they overlooked the true connection between cause and effect.

---

1. What is the beginning of our knowledge of nature? What great principle do we recognise in connection with experience? What is an experiment? 2. What does observation teach? How does it extend our knowledge?

The ancient philosophy abounded in plausible arguments regarding those natural phenomena which could not fail to arrest the attention of an intelligent people; but its reasonings were based on an *à priori* assumption of a cause, and not upon an inductive inquiry after facts and their connections. It failed to apply itself to the careful collection and study of facts *in order to* science. Facts in nature are the expression of the Divine will in the government of the physical world. The universe of matter is made up of facts, which, observed, traced out, and arranged, lead us to the knowledge of certain laws and forces which proceed directly from the mind of God. These are the "laws of nature:" science is but the exposition of them and of science based upon such grounds, the ancient philosophy was completely ignorant.

3. It is important to distinguish that knowledge which is purely intellectual in its character, from that which results from observation and experience. Speaking of this subject, one of the most learned of living philosophers remarks: "A clever man, shut up alone, and allowed unlimited time, might reason out for himself all the truths of mathematics, by proceeding from those simple notions of space and number, of which he cannot divest himself without ceasing to think; but he could never tell, by any effort of reasoning, what would become of a lump of sugar if immersed in water, or what impression would be produced on the eye by mixing the colors yellow and blue."—(*Herschel.*) We may, however, with propriety doubt, whether there is any knowledge or philosophy so purely intellectual, or absolute, that it does not imply some previous recognition of physical facts.

4. The *observation* of facts forms only the foundation of science,—an isolated fact has no scientific value. The knowledge of physical laws deduced from the study of observed facts will enable the philosopher to foretell the result of the possible combination of those laws, and to assign reasons for apparent departures from them. In this way discoveries are predicted and detailed; observation is anticipated, and called

---

Characterize the ancient philosophy. How did it fail? What are facts? What are laws of nature? What is science? 3. What convenient distinction is named? What remark is quoted in illustration of this? 4. What is said of observation? What of an isolated fact? What does a knowledge of natural laws enable the philosopher to do?

on to verify the alleged discovery. The perturbations of the planet Uranus indicated the existence of some body in space heretofore unknown. When Le Verrier had reconciled these disturbances with the supposed influence of a new planet, and determined its elements of motion, he had as truly discovered the remote sphere, as when the German astronomer, by pointing his telescope to the precise place in the heavens which Le Verrier had designated, announced to the world that the stupendous prediction was verified by observation. In like manner, a familiarity with chemical laws enables the chemist to foretell the result of combinations which he has never investigated, and in some cases to assign with confidence the constitution of bodies which he has never analyzed.

5. Our knowledge of Natural Science is conveniently classified under the three great divisions of Natural History, Physical Philosophy, and Chemistry. The first teaches us the characters and arrangement of the various forms of animal and vegetable life and minerals, giving origin to the sciences of Zoology, Botany, and Mineralogy. *Physical Philosophy* explains the forces by which masses of matter are governed, and unfolds the laws of Light, of Electricity, and of Heat.

Chemistry teaches us the intimate and invisible constitution of bodies, and makes known the compounds which may be formed by the union of simple substances, the laws of their combination, and the properties of the new compounds. It investigates the forces resident in matter, and which are inseparable from our idea of molecular action,—forces whose play produces the phenomena of Light, of Heat, and of Electricity. Chemistry also unfolds the wonderful operations of animal and vegetable life, so far as their functions depend upon chemical laws, as in the processes of respiration and digestion, giving the special department of Physiological Chemistry.

Illustrate this in case of the perturbations of Uranus. 5. How is our knowledge of nature classified? What does the first teach? Physical philosophy teaches what? Define the province of Chemistry.

I. MATTER.

General Properties of Matter.

6. *Experience*, founded on the evidence of our senses, convinces us of the existence of matter. We feel the resistance which it offers to our touch; we see that it has form, and occupies space, and hence we say it has extent; and, lastly, we attempt to raise it, and we find ourselves opposed by a certain force which we call weight.

Matter possesses extension, because it occupies some space. It is impenetrable, because one particle of matter cannot occupy the same space with another at the same time. It has gravity, because it obeys the law of universal attraction. Whatever, therefore, possesses these three qualities, is matter.

7. All the changes of which matter is capable may be referred to one of three great principles or forces, and to their modifications or combinations. These are ATTRACTION, REPULSION, and VITALITY.

Attraction is divided into Mechanical and Chemical.

8. *Mechanical Attraction* is divided into, 1. *Gravitation*, acting at all distances, and between all masses. 2. *Cohesion*, acting between bodies or particles of the same kind only, and at immeasurably small distances. To this power are referred all the phenomena of solidification and crystallization. 3. *Adhesion*, acting between bodies of unlike kinds, at immeasurably small distances, and forming mixed masses. *Chemical Attraction*, or *Affinity*, exists only between molecules or particles of unlike kinds, acts only at immeasurably small distances, and produces homogeneous masses which have properties unlike the constituent elements. In a word, gravity acts on all matter and at all distances. Cohesion acts only on the same kind of matter at insensible distances. Chemical affinity acts only between unlike particles at insensible distances.

Repulsion is a force seen in the impenetrability of matter

---

6. Whence our knowledge of matter? Define its properties. 7. Name three forces governing matter. 8. Subdivide mechanical attraction. How is chemical distinguished from mechanical attraction? What of repulsion? Define vitality.

and in its power of expansion. It is the antagonist of cohesion, or, as it is sometimes called, the attraction of aggregation. *Heat* resolves the several forms of mechanical attraction, and surrenders matter to the dominion of repulsive force, by which its particles or molecules are widely separated.

Vitality rules superior to all the laws of mechanical and of chemical attraction, suspending, modifying, or applying them for the production of those complicated results which are seen in the organized structures of plants and animals.

9. Such are the great forces to which matter is subject. All the changes resulting from the operation of the forms of mechanical attraction belong to *Physics*. Those referable to vitality fall within the province of the *physiologist*.

The consideration of the changes produced in matter by the exertion of affinity, or chemical attraction, constitutes the appropriate business of the *chemist*.

All that relates therefore to physics might be properly dismissed from a manual of chemistry; but it is usual for the chemical student to devote a share of his attention to those departments of physics, some knowledge of which is essential to a correct understanding of chemical phenomena.

Of Mechanical Attraction.

10. *Gravitation* is a force measured in any particular case by *weight*, whether we speak of a movable mass capable of equipoise in our balances or of the weight of the planets as deduced from their observed motions. It acts at all distances upon all matter, and is directly as the mass and inversely as the square of the distance. The weight of a body is therefore proportioned to the number of molecules or particles which it contains.

11. *Cohesion*, is seen alike in solids, in fluids, and in gases—three states of matter incident to the equilibrium of the forces of repulsion and cohesion, and modified by the laws of heat. Those who regard light, heat, electricity, and magnetism as imponderable bodies, refer their properties also to the antagonistic power of repulsion, by which these manifestations are so controlled that we have no proof of the existence of mutual cohesion among their particles.

---

9. What does physics include? 10. How is Gravitation measured? Define its law. 11. What of Cohesion?

In the force of cohesion, or attraction of aggregation, as manifest in solid bodies, we recognise a power which opposes the division of matter.

12. *Divisibility of matter.*—The question of the infinite divisibility of matter has in past times been the subject of most animated discussions, and until the discoveries of modern chemistry, no satisfactory solution was reached. We know that the largest and most solid masses of matter, even entire mountains, may be ground down by mechanical force to dust so fine that the winds will bear it away, but each minute particle still occupies some space; and we may imagine that a great multitude of smaller particles may be formed from its further division. A grain of gold may be spread out so thin as to cover 600 square inches of surface on silver wire, and one ounce, in this manner, be made to cover 1300 miles of such wire. One grain of green vitriol, (sulphate of iron,) dissolved and diffused in 20 million grains of water, will still be easily detected by the proper tests. The delicate perfume of musk and the aroma of flowers are remarkable examples of minute division in matter.

The organic world also presents us with beautiful examples of the great divisibility of matter, in the remarkable forms of animalcules revealed by the microscope, many millions of which can be embraced in a single drop of water. Yet each of these inconceivably minute organisms has its own muscular, digestive, and circulatory systems. How minute, then, the ultimate particles, of which many myriads must be contained in each animalcule!

Chemistry has happily resolved the question of infinite divisibility, by proving that all matter consists of certain particles of definite values, whose relative weights and bulks may be precisely determined. These particles are called—

13. *Molecules,* or Atoms.*—Ultimate chemical analysis has demonstrated that matter consists of many distinct varieties, called elementary or simple bodies, and that

---

12. What degree of divisibility exists in matter? Give some illustrations. 13. What is said of molecules?

---

* *Molecule*, a diminutive of *moles*, a mass. This term is preferable to 'atom' or 'ultimate particle,' as implying no theory, which both the others do. Atom is from *a*, privative, and *temno*, I cut, signifying their supposed indivisibility.

these several separate sorts of matter possess each its own combining quantity, from which it never varies, and this quantity, called its equivalent, atomic, proportional, or combining number, is susceptible of accurate determination by the balance. The molecules of simple bodies are necessarily simple themselves, while the molecules of compound bodies are, on the contrary, complex. Whatever size these molecules may possess, they are the centres of all the forces and qualities whose united effects and activity give matter its physical or chemical properties. Although we may never know the absolute weight of any molecule, we do know with much certainty the *relative* size and weight of the molecules of over sixty sorts of simple matter, which chemistry has revealed to us. The laws of crystallogeny also inform us that these molecules have an inherent difference of form; some being spherical, while others are ellipsoidal.

Of Cohesion in reference to the three states of Matter, the Solid, the Liquid, and the Gaseous.

14. *Properties of Solids.*—It is a distinguishing property of solids to have their particles bound together by so strong an attraction as in a great measure to destroy their power of moving among each other.

No solid, however, not even gold and platinum, which are the most compact solids known, has its particles of matter so aggregated as to be incapable of some condensation. Blows, pressure, or a reduction of temperature, will condense almost all solids into a smaller bulk. Water may even be forced through the pores of gold, by very great mechanical pressure. All solid bodies are, therefore, considered as porous, and their particles are believed to touch each other in comparatively few points.

Cohesion in solids may be destroyed either by mechanical violence, as in pulverization; by solution, as in the case of saline bodies soluble in water; or by the agency of heat, as in the fusion of wax or lead. The mobility of the particles in solid bodies is shown also in the elasticity, malleability, ductility, and laminability of many metals, which are among their most useful properties. *Hardness* is a quality having

---

What forms have the molecules? 14. What mobility have particles in solids? What of pores in solids? How may cohesion be destroyed?

no relation to the preceding, and is possessed by solids in very various degrees, and apparently without reference either to the density or chemical nature of the substances,—for gold and platinum, among the heaviest of known bodies, are comparatively soft, while the diamond, which is only about one-sixth part as heavy as these metals, is the hardest of all known substances. Cohesive attraction, when once disturbed by mechanical violence, is not usually brought into exercise again by mere approach of the separated particles. The broken fragments of a glass vessel or portion of stone do not reunite at ordinary temperatures. Nevertheless, we have some examples of a contrary nature.

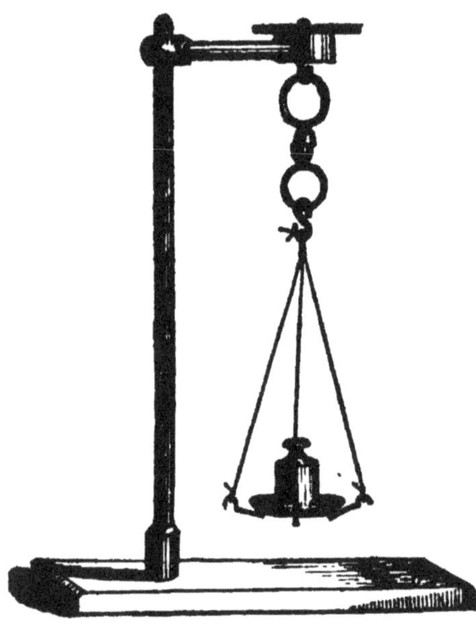

Fig. 1.

If we press together two smooth surfaces of lead, clean and bright, as, for example, the halves of a leaden sphere, (fig. 1,) cut through, they will adhere or unite together so firmly as to require the power of several pounds weight to draw them asunder, as shown in the annexed figure. The plates of polished glass, also, which are prepared for large mirrors, if allowed to rest together with their surfaces in close contact, have been known to unite so firmly as to break before they would yield to any effort to separate them. In these cases, actual contact of contiguous particles is effected, and thus the conditions of cohesive attraction are fulfilled. We may regard the welding of iron and the cohesion of masses of dough or putty as examples of a similar kind. The casting of metals by voltaic electricity, from cold solutions of their salts, also affords us elegant examples of adhesive attraction.

What of hardness? Give examples of cohesion at common temperatures.

15. *In fluids*, the particles have perfect freedom of motion among themselves. They are either inelastic liquids, like water, or elastic gases or vapours, like air and steam. A gas is a permanent elastic fluid: a vapour is such only in certain conditions of temperature and pressure. In water we have a familar example of a body, presenting the three conditions of matter, in the ordinary changes of the seasons.

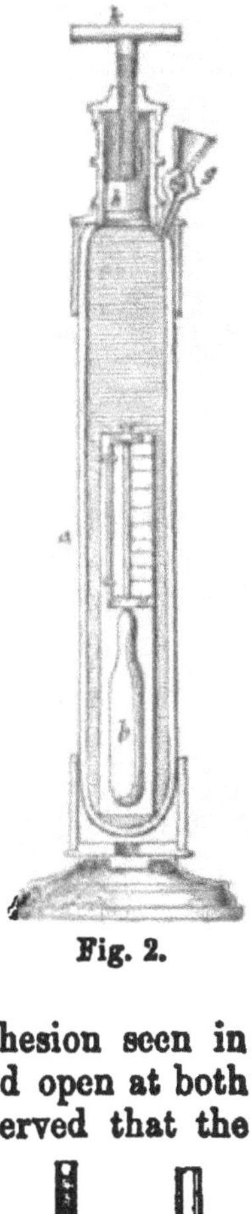

Liquids are not completely inelastic, but are compressible to a very slight extent by pressure, as is shown in the apparatus of Oërsted, fig. 2. A small glass bulb *b*, with a narrow neck, is filled with water lately boiled, and placed in the glass vessel *a*, also filled with water by the funnel *g*; a metallic plug *h* is forced down by the screw *k*, producing any required pressure. A small globule of mercury in the stem of *b* by its descent notes the amount of condensation which the water in *b* suffers. No change of dimensions in the glass *b* can happen, because it is equally compressed from within and without. In this way the compressibility of water has been shown to be equal to one part in 22,000 for each atmosphere of 15 pounds pressure. Alcohol has about half this degree of compressibility; ether about one-third more, and mercury only about one-twentieth as much.

Fig. 2.

16. *Capillary attraction* is a form of cohesion seen in liquids. If a tube with a very fine bore, and open at both ends, is immersed in water, it will be observed that the liquid rises, as seen in fig. 3, to a certain elevation in the tube, and to a less degree also on the outer surface. In mercury, (fig. 4,) on the contrary, which does not moisten the glass, there is a depression of the column in the tube, and the surfaces of the mercury are convex. The height to which a fluid will rise in a tube by capillarity is inversely as the diametor

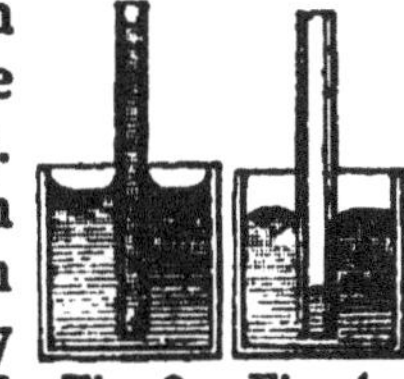

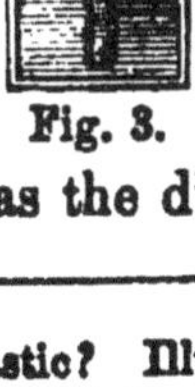

Fig. 3. 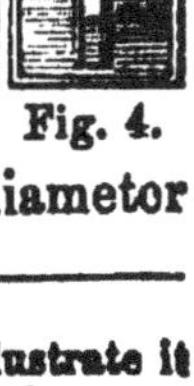 Fig. 4.

15. How are the particles in fluids? Are fluids elastic? Illustrate it by the case of water? 16. What is capillarity? What relation has diameter to capillarity?

of the tube. Two plates of glass held as in fig. 5, opening like the leaves of a book, and their lower edges immersed in a fluid, show this law by the curve which the liquid assumes. By the power of capillary attraction, the wick supplies fuel to the lamp or candle. Plugs of dry wood driven into holes bored in granite, and then saturated with water, swell so much by the water taken into their pores by capillarity that the rocks are split open. Even a bar of lead or tin, bent like the letter U and placed by one end in a vessel of mercury, will, after some time, convey it out of the vessel drop by drop. Two small balls, one of wax and one of cork, (fig. 6,) thrown upon the surface of water, manifest repulsion at first, for the water not wetting the wax while it does the cork, causes an elevation about the latter, from which the former, so to speak, rolls off, and the balls separate in the direction of the arrows. Two balls of cork, for a like reason, attract one another. Hence the familiar fact that chips on the surface of quiet water always crowd together, and gather about a log or larger body on the surface. The wetting of surfaces by a fluid is perhaps a sort of chemical affinity. Iron, glass, the skin, or a piece of wood are not wet by mercury; while gold, silver, lead, and many other metals are so. Oil spreads itself in a thin film on the surface of water, and by its cohesion quiets the agitation of moderate waves.

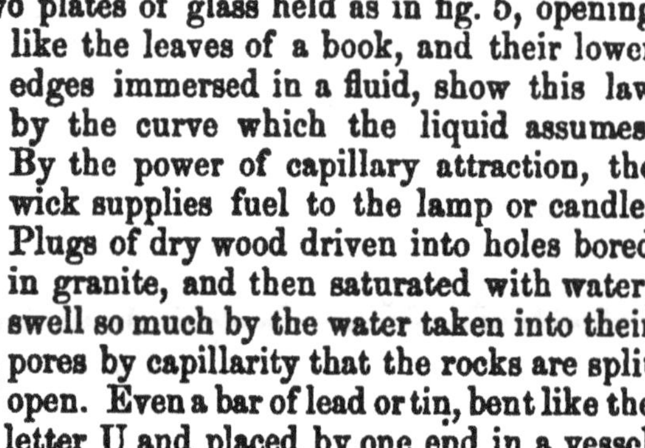

Fig. 5.

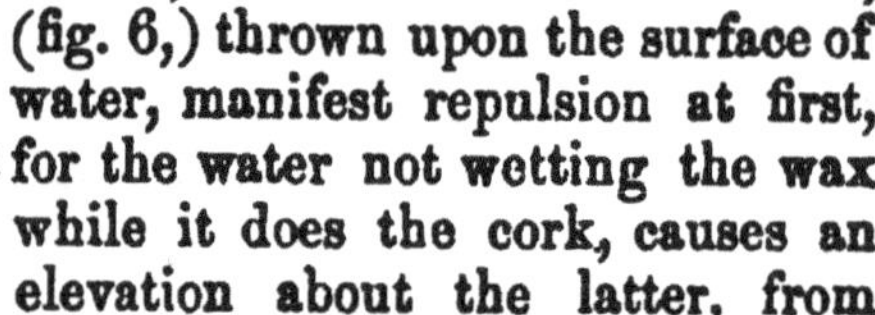

Fig. 6.

17. The cohesion in liquids is much greater than is commonly imagined. A disc of glass suspended from the beam of a balance over a surface of water will adhere with a measurable force to the water when brought in contact with it. The force required to withdraw it is that which will rupture the cohesion of the outer row of particles at the edge of the disc, then the next row, and so on to the centre *a*, as shown in the circles on fig. 7. In the soap-bubble we see a thin film of water,

Fig. 7.

Illustrate this by fig. 5. Explain the action of light bodies on water. What is wetting? 17. What of cohesion in liquids? Explain the adhesive disc and the soap-bubble.

giving us a beautiful example of the cohesive power of water. It is a great hollow drop of water. The cohesive power in the film of the bubble is so great that if the pipe be taken from the mouth before the bubble leaves it, a stream of air will be forcibly driven from the bore by the contraction of the film, which will deflect the flame of a candle. To the same cause is ascribed the spherical form of the dew-drop, the cohesion in the outer row of particles.

18. In the structure of plants and of animals, capillary attraction performs functions of the highest importance in the economy of life. Animal membranes possess the power of exuding or of absorbing fluids from their surfaces. This power has by several authors been considered as a special attribute of animal tissues, and as such has received the name of *endosmose* and *exosmose*, or the inward and the outward force of membranes. These actions are generally regarded as modifications of capillarity, and may be well illustrated by the *endosmometer*, (fig. 8.) An open glass *b* has it lower end tied over by a bit of bladder *c*, and its upper opening elongated by a narrow glass tube *a*, this apparatus is filled with weak sugar-water, and is placed in an outer vessel *n*, filled with strong syrup of sugar. Soon the column of fluid is seen to mount from *a* to *o* or out at the top, from the penetration of the denser fluid through the membrane. The power which plants possess of absorbing the nutritive fluids from the soil through the delicate bulbous ends of their spongioles is supposed to be identical with that force shown in this instrument.

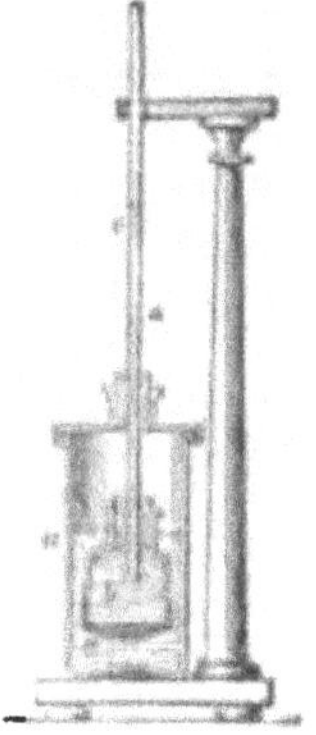

Fig. 8.

19. *In gases*, the force of cohesion among the particles is entirely subordinate to the repulsive action by which they are expanded. The physical properties of gaseous bodies are best understood when we study

The Mechanical Properties of the Atmosphere.

20. We on the surface of this earth are at the bottom of a vast aerial ocean, in which we live and move and have

---

Whence the form of the dew-drop? 18. What is endosmose? What exosmose? Explain the endosmometer. 19. What of cohesion in gases?

our being. From its chemical influence we cannot escape, nor free ourselves from the vast load of its mechanical pressure which we unconsciously sustain. It penetrates deeply into the crust of the earth, and is largely dissolved in its waters. All that relates to its chemical history will be given in its appropriate place. Its mechanical properties demand attention now. What is true of the mechanical properties of air is also true of the gases.

21. *Elasticity.*—Vessels filled only with air we call empty; but it is obvious, when we plunge an empty air-jar beneath the surface of water, that it contains an elastic and resisting medium, which must be displaced before the vessel can be filled with water. Elasticity is the most remarkable physical property of the atmosphere and of all gases. Upon this property depends the construction of

22. *The air-pump,* an instrument in principle like the common water-pump. It depends for its action on the elasticity of the air. Suppose two tight-bottomed cylinders, *a* and *b*, (fig. 9,) to be filled with air. If a solid plug, or piston, is fitted to each so tightly that no air can pass between it and the sides of the vessel, we shall find it impossible to force down the piston to the bottom of the cylinder. It descends a certain distance with an increasing resistance, and is again restored, as with the force of a spring, so soon as the pressure is removed. If we suppose one of the pistons to be in the position shown in *b*, and the air beneath it of the same *tension* or density as that above, and we attempt to draw out the plug by its stem, we also feel a continually increasing resistance, and the piston returns forcibly to its former position when we release our hold. We thus demonstrate the elasticity of the air, and also its weight and pressure. Such an arrangement of apparatus, slightly modified, is an air-pump. If each of the pistons is pierced with a hole, over

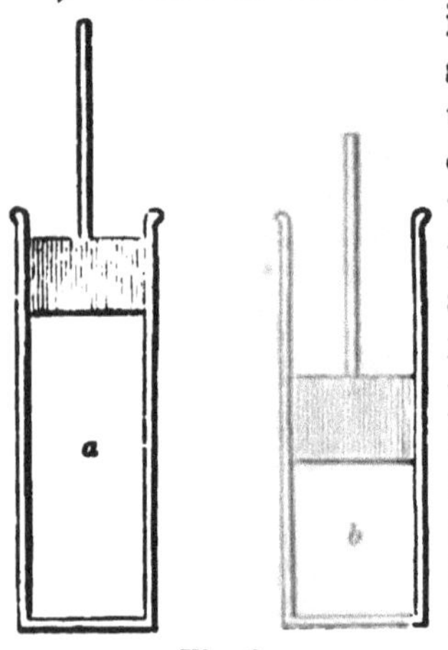

Fig. 9.

20. What is said of the aerial ocean? 21. Demonstrate the elasticity of air by an empty vessel. 21. What is the air-pump? How does it employ elasticity? Illustrate this by fig. 9.

which is a flap, or valve, of leather or silk *v*, opening upward, and closing with the slightest downward pressure, and a similar opening, or valve, be provided in the bottom of each cylinder *v*, we have an air-pump. (Fig. 10.) It remains only to connect the cylinders by a duct with the plate on which the air-receiver R is placed, and to provide suitable movements for the pistons by a lever or otherwise, and our instrument is complete. The plate and receiver are accurately ground to fit air-tight, and great pains are taken to have all parts of the apparatus as perfectly air-tight as possible.

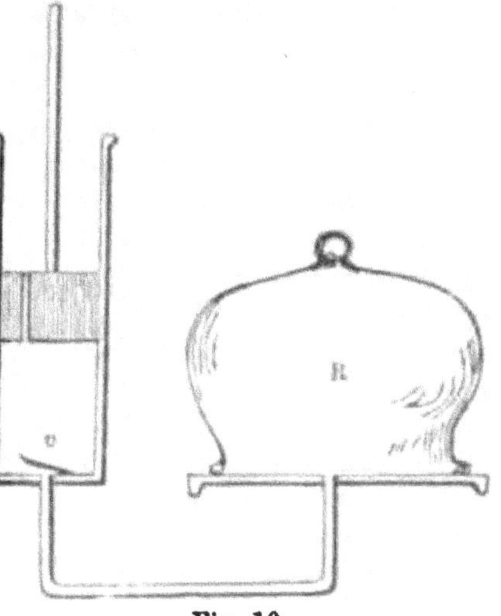

Fig. 10.

23. *Vacuum.*—It is obvious that the air in the receiver will, by virtue of its elasticity, rush into the cylinders alternately as these are moved; the valves in the cylinders preventing the return of the air to the receiver, while they permit the escape of the successive portions *from within*, and those on the piston closing the access of the outer air. Thus, with each movement of the lever, fresh portions of air from the receiver, more and more rare each time, will find their way to the cylinders and be pumped out, while the space in R becomes constantly more void, until the vacuum is completed. This happens whenever the weight and resistance of the valves in the cylinders is greater than the elastic force of the rarefied air in the receiver. And hence it is obviously impossible to make a *perfect* vacuum by mechanical means. There will always remain a certain very tenuous atmosphere in even the most perfect and delicate air-pump, unless, indeed, it be removed by *chemical* means. This may be done by employing a bell-jar filled with carbonic acid, the last portions of which may be removed by potassa or caustic lime—pre-

---

How are the valves of the pump arranged? 23. What is a vacuum? Why is a perfect vacuum impossible? How may the last portions of air be removed?

viously placed for that purpose in a vessel on the pump-plate. The French instruments often have the cylinders of glass, to expose the mechanical movements of the valves and pistons. Excellent air-pumps, with only one cylinder, on the plan proposed by Leslie, are furnished by the instrument-makers in Boston and New York.

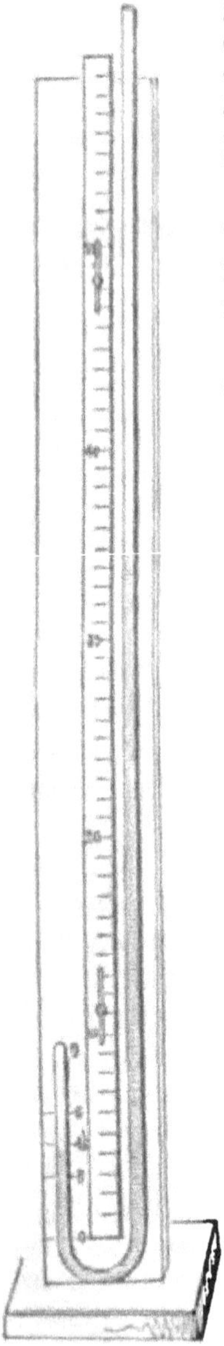

24. *The bulk and density* of the atmosphere varies with the mechanical pressure to which it is submitted. This inference is drawn from what has just been said regarding the theory of the air-pump. The volume of the air is inversely as the pressure to which it is subjected, while its density is directly as this pressure. This is known as Mariotte's law, from its discoverer, an Italian philosopher of that name.

Fig. 11 shows the simple apparatus used for demonstrating this law. It is a glass tube turned up and sealed at the lower end: a graduated scale of equal parts is attached to it. Mercury is poured into the open end of this tube so as to rise just to the first horizontal line; a portion of air of the ordinary elasticity is thus enclosed in the short limb of 9 inches. Now if mercury be poured into the longer leg, so that it may stand at 30 inches above the level of the mercury in the shorter leg, it will press with its whole weight on the included air, which will then be found to occupy 4½ inches, or only half of its former space. If, in like manner, the column of mercury be increased to twice this length, its pressure on the included air will be tripled, and the space occupied by it will be reduced to one-third, and so on in simple proportion. It consequently happens that at a pressure of seven hundred and seventy atmospheres, air would become as dense as

Fig. 11.

24. What is the relation of volume to density in the air? What is the law of Mariotte? Explain figure 11. When is air as dense as water?

water. The terms *tension* and *density*, as applied to gases, have the same meaning.

25. *The weight of the* atmosphere is of course shown by the air-pump. The receiver is fixed by the first stroke of the pump, and if we employ on the plate a small glass, open at both ends, (fig. 12,) and cover the upper end with the hand, we shall find it fixed with a powerful pressure. This is vulgarly called *suction*, but is plainly due only to the weight of air resting on the surface of the hand, and rendered sensible by the partial withdrawal of the air below. Hence, all vessels of glass used on the air-pump are made strong, and of an arched form, to resist this pressure. Square vessels of thin glass are immediately crushed on submitting them to the atmospheric pressure, or exploded by the removal of the surrounding air while they are sealed. The weight of the air is also well shown by the bursting of a piece of bladder-skin tied tightly over the mouth of an open jar on the plate of the air-pump. As the pump is worked, the flat surface of the bladder becomes more and more concave, and at length bursts inward with a smart explosion.

Fig. 12.

Fig. 13.

26. Numerous common facts and experiments illustrate the same thing. Were the atmospheric pressure removed from under our feet, we should be unable to move; and the difficulty we experience when walking on clay is due to a partial vacuum formed by the close contact of the foot to the plastic soil, excluding the air. Boys raise bricks and stones by a "sucker" of moist leather, on the same principle. The power of the atmospheric pressure to raise heavy weights is well shown in the

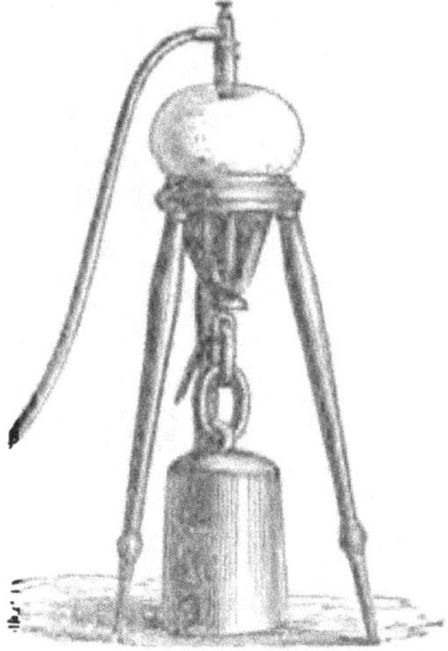
Fig. 14.

---

25. What illustrations of the weight of the air are given in figs. 12 and 13? 26. How is the weight raised in fig. 14?

annexed apparatus, (fig. 14.) A glass jar, having an open bottom, is covered with impervious caoutchouc. When a vacuum is produced in the jar, the yielding cover rises, carrying with it a weight which is below. This is sustained in the air, as by an elastic spring. The amount of the atmospheric pressure has been experimentally determined as equal to fifteen pounds on every square inch of surface. This fact is demonstrated by the

27. *Barometer.*—This instrument (as its name implies) enables us to weigh the air. It was discovered by Torricelli, an Italian philosopher, in the year 1643. When a glass tube, (fig. 15,) sealed at one end, and about 36 inches long, is filled with mercury, the open end closed by the finger, and inverted in a vessel containing mercury, so that the open end may be beneath the surface, so soon as the finger is withdrawn the mercurial column is seen to fall some distance, and, after several oscillations, to come to rest at a certain point, where it is apparently stationary. At the level of the sea, this point is found to be about 30 inches above the surface of the mercury in the basin. The empty space above the mercury is the most perfect vacuum that can be produced; and, in honor of its discoverer, is called the Torricellian vacuum.

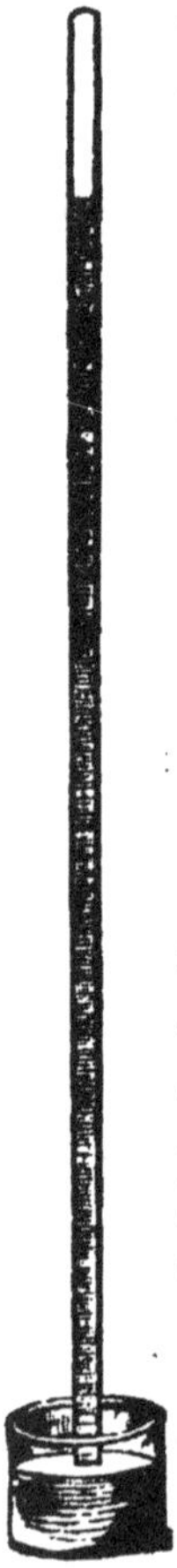

The mercury is sustained at this height by the pressure of the atmosphere on the surface of the fluid in the basin, and the height of the column varies with the atmospheric pressure, and with the elevation of the instrument above the level of the ocean. Had water been the fluid employed, it would have required a tube more than 34 feet long to accommodate the column. If the experiment be tried above the ocean level, as on the top of a lofty mountain, the column of mercury will be found of a less elevation in proportion to the height of the mountain. It was the distinguished Pascal who first, in 1647, suggested this experiment on the top of a mountain in France, as conclusive proof that

Fig. 15.

---

27. What is the barometer? Describe its principle? What is the Toricellian vacuum? Why is 30 inches the height? What was Pascal's suggestion?

it was the weight of the air which sustained the mercury in the barometer.

28. The principle of the barometer is beautifully shown in fig. 16. A large bell-glass, with a wide mouth *c*, has two syphon barometer tubes attached. One *a* has the mercury standing at the proper height at *a*, while its cistern enters the bell. The other tube at one end also enters the bell, but, bending upon itself, it holds a portion of mercury in the outer cistern *b* on its other extremity. When this apparatus is placed on the air-pump and exhausted of air, the mercury *a* falls in proportion to the vacuum produced, while that in *b* mounts in like proportion. In *a* we see the effect of diminished pressure, as on a mountain or in a balloon; in *b* the pressure of the external air causes the mercury in it to mount, forming a gauge of the exhaustion.

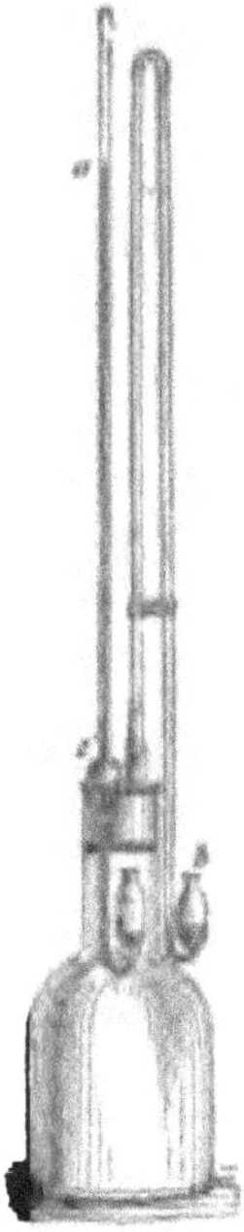

29. If the tube of the barometer has an area of one inch, and the height of the column is 30 inches, the weight of the mercury sustained in it is by experiment found to be *fifteen pounds*. And this is the pressure which the atmosphere exercises on every square inch of the earth's surface. A column of atmospheric air one inch square, and reaching to the uppermost limits of the aerial ocean, will also weigh, of course, just fifteen pounds. We thus come to regard the mercury in the barometer as the equipoise on one arm of a balance, of which the counterpart is the atmospheric column. As the latter varies daily from meteoric causes, so also does the height of the mercurial column oscillate in just proportion. Hence the barometer is properly called a "weather-glass," and by its movements we judge of the approach of storms. These changes of level sometimes amount at the same place to 2 or 2½ inches, although usually they are much less.

Fig. 16.

Various forms of the barometer are in use: those for measuring the elevation of mountains are so constructed

---

28. How is the principle of the barometer explained in fig. 16? Why does the mercury in *a* fall? Why does that in *b* rise? 29. What is the pressure of air on a square inch of surface? How is this shown by the barometer? How is the barometer a weather-glass?

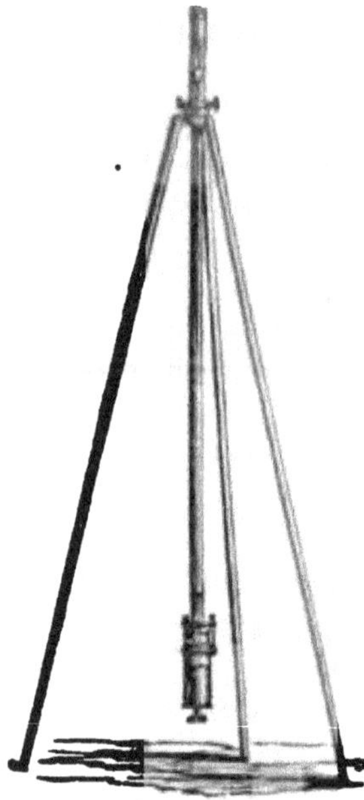
Fig. 17.

as to be easily transported. A good form of the mountain barometer is shown in fig. 17, supported on a tripod, which, with the instrument, can be safely packed in a leather case.

30. *The Aneroid Barometer* is designed to supersede the mercurial instrument in those situations where the oscillating motion of the mercury destroys the value of its indications, as in travelling, in aeronautical excursions, at sea, and on many other occasions when the common barometer is inconvenient. It depends on the variation in form of a thin vase D D (fig. 18) of copper, which being partially exhausted of air changes its dimensions with every variation in atmospheric pressure. These motions are multiplied and transferred by the combination of levers C, K, 1, 2, and 3, &c., in such a manner that the index reads the barometric conditions of the atmosphere on a dial. The index is set by adjusting screws, to correspond with a standard mercurial instrument, and the accuracy of each *aneroid* is tested by the air-pump.

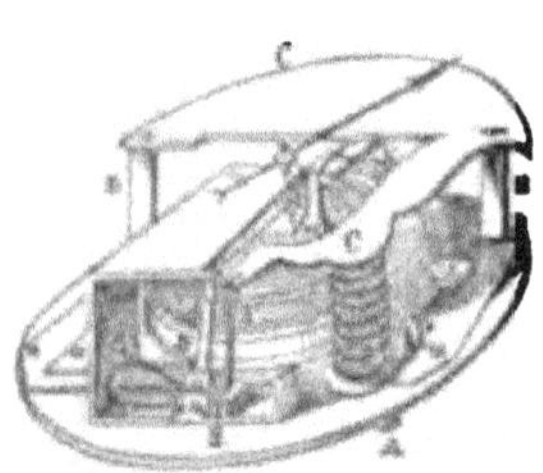
Fig. 18.

31. *Weight of the Atmosphere.*—One hundred cubic inches of atmospheric air at 30 inches of the barometer and 60° Fahr. weigh $30\frac{829}{1000}$ grains, while the same bulk of water would weigh about 25,250 grains. Air of the above condition is assumed as the standard unity for the density of all other aeriform bodies. A man of ordinary size has a surface of about 15 square feet, and he must consequently sustain a pressure on his body of over 15 tons. This prodigious load he bears about with him unconsciously, because the mobility of the particles of air causes it to bear with equal force on every

30. What is the aneroid barometer? 31. What is the weight of air? What weight of air does a man sustain?

part of his body, beneath his feet as well as on his head, and in the inner cavities as well as on the outer surface.

32. *Limits of the Atmosphere.*—A person who has risen in a balloon, or on a mountain, to the height of 2·705 miles, or 14,282 feet, has passed through one-half of the entire weight of the air, and finds his barometer to indicate this by standing at 15 inches.

The air grows more and more rare as we ascend, and the barometer falls in exact proportion. The inconvenience which travellers have experienced in ascending high mountains has, it is said on good authority, been very much exaggerated. The heart continues its action under a diminished external pressure, and no serious consequences, it is believed, ever follow, as the bursting of bloodvessels or lesion of the lungs, as some have asserted. On the summit of Chimborazo, Baron von Humboldt found that his barometer had sunk to 13 inches 11 lines; and the same philosopher descended into the sea in a diving-bell until the mercurial column rose to 45 inches: he consequently has safely experienced a change of 31 inches of pressure in his own person.

The upper limits of the atmosphere cannot be determined very accurately; but, from the refraction of light as observed in the rising and setting of stars, astronomers have inferred that it is probably about forty-five miles high.

Weight and Specific Gravity.

33. *Weight* is the measure of the force of gravity, and is directly proportional to the quantity of matter in a given space. Weight is determined by the balance, an instrument to which the chemist appeals at every step of his investigations. Modern instruments enable us to determine this element of accurate science, to the greatest nicety.

The *specific gravity* of a body is its weight as compared with an equal bulk of some other substance assumed as the unit of comparison. A cubic inch of gold is more than 19 times as heavy as a cubic inch of ice or of water: hence the gold is said to have a *specific* gravity of 19, compared with water.

Pure water has been adopted as the standard of compari-

---

32. What is the height of the atmosphere? 33. What is weight? What is specific gravity? What is the standard of specific gravity?

son for the specific gravity of all solid and liquid substances, taken at 60° Fahrenheit. For gases and vapours, common air, dry and at the temperature of 60° and 30 inches of barometric pressure, is the standard assumed. Regard is had to the conditions of temperature and pressure because the bulk of all bodies varies sensibly with these conditions.

34. The specific gravity of solids is determined by the theorem of the renowned Archimedes, that "when a body is immersed in water, it loses a portion of its weight exactly equal to the weight of the water displaced." He thus detected the fraud of the goldsmith who furnished to King Hiero of Syracuse, as a crown of pure gold, one fashioned of base metal—the specific gravity of the debased alloy was too small for gold. It is plain that a solid displaces, when immersed, exactly its own bulk of water, and loses weight to a corresponding amount. Hence, if we weigh a body first in air and then in water, the loss of weight observed, is equal to the volume of water, corresponding to the bulk of the solid. Fig. 19 shows a group of crystals of quartz suspended from the underside of the scale-pan by a filament of silk. Its weight in air was previously determined. Its diminished weight in the water, subtracted from the weight in air, gives a sum equal to the bulk of water displaced.

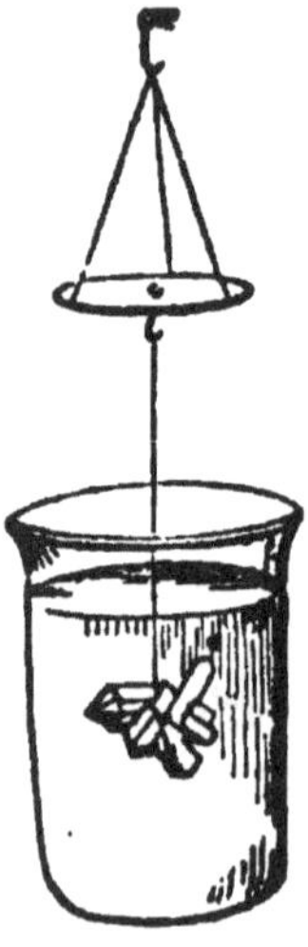

Fig. 19.

From these elements is deduced the rule to find the specific gravity of a solid. "Subtract the weight in water from the weight in air, divide the weight in air by this difference, and the quotient will be the specific gravity." Fig. 20 shows the balance ar-

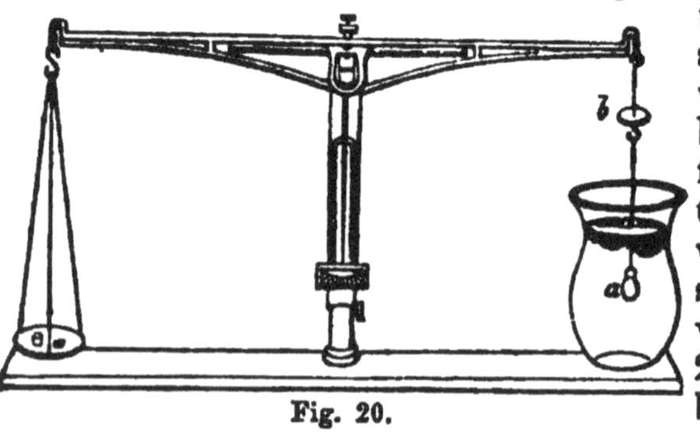

Fig. 20.

How is it determined? What is the theorem of Archimedes? 34. How is this illustrated in fig. 19? Give the rule for specific gravity

ranged for taking the specific gravity of the solid *a* suspended in water from the hook *b*. A single example will serve to illustrate this rule. We find, on trial, that the

Weight of a substance in *air*, is....................	357·95 grs.
Weight of the substance in *water*.................	239·41 "
Difference..	118·54 "

$$\frac{357 \cdot 95}{118 \cdot 54} = 3 \cdot 01 \text{ specific gravity.}$$

35. The specific gravity of substances lighter than water may be determined by attaching them to a mass of lead or brass, of known weight and density. Subtances in small fragments or in powder are placed in a small bottle, fig. 21, holding, for example, a thousand grains of water. Those soluble in water are weighed in a fluid in which they are insoluble and whose density is separately determined. In these cases a simple calculation refers the results to the known density of pure water.

Fig. 21.

36. The specific gravity of liquids may be ascertained in a small bottle holding a known weight of pure water. These bottles usually have a small perforation in the stopper, as seen in the figure 22, through which the excess of fluid gushes out, and may be removed by careful wiping. The weight of the bottle, dry and empty, is counterpoised by a weight kept for that purpose.

Fig. 22.

37. *The Hydrometer* is an instrument of great use in determining the specific gravity of liquids without a balance. It is simply a glass tube, fig. 23, with a bulb blown on one end of it, containing a few shot, to counterbalance the instrument; and a paper scale of equal parts is sealed within the

---

Give an example. 35. How is specific gravity determined on bodies lighter than water? on powders? on solnble substances? 36. On fluids? 37. What is the hydrometer? Describe its use.

stem. This scale indicates the points to which the stem sinks when immersed in fluids of different densities. The fluid, for convenience, is placed in a tube or narrow jar, (fig. 24): the more dense the liquid is, the less quantity will the hydrometer displace, while in a lighter fluid it will sink deeper. The zero point of the scale is always placed where the instrument will rest in pure water, after which the graduation is effected on a variety of arbitrary scales, all of which can, however, be referred to the true specific gravity by calculation, or by reference to a table such as may be found at the close of this volume. Hydrometers are also prepared with the true specific gravities marked upon them, reading even to the third decimal place accurately. The scales of these instruments read either up or down, according as the fluid to be measured is either heavier or lighter than water. In case of alcohol, the graduation of the hydrometer is made to indicate the number of parts of pure alcohol in a hundred parts of a liquid—absolute alcohol being 100, and water 0. The hydrometers of Baumé (French scale) are much used in the arts. These instruments are of the greatest service to the manufacturer, and, when carefully made, are sufficiently accurate for most purposes of the laboratory. They should always be proved by comparison with the balance and thermometer before they are accepted as standards. For many purposes they are made of brass or ivory, as well as of glass.

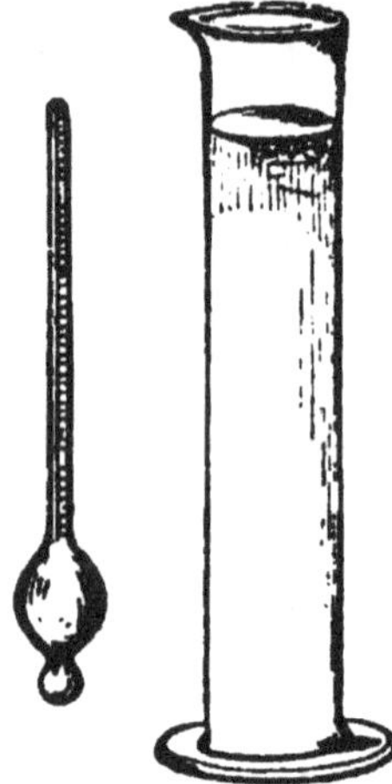
Fig. 23. Fig. 24.

830

Fig. 25.

Little *balloons* or *bulbs* of glass, are frequently employed to find, in a rough way, the density of fluids. When several of them are thrown in a fluid of known density, some will sink, some rise even with the surface, and others will just float. Those which just float are taken, and being marked (as in fig. 25) with the density of the liquid which they represent, are then used to determine the specific gravity of liquids of unknown density. They are called specific gravity bulbs, and are of great service in as-

What scales are used in Hydrometers? What use is made of little bulbs of glass?

certaining the density of gases reduced to a liquid by pressure in glass tubes, when, from the circumstances of the experiment, all the usual modes of ascertaining specific gravity are inapplicable.

38. The water balloon, or "Cartesian devil," is an elegant illustration of the law of specific gravity. In this toy the balloon, or figure, contains a portion of water just sufficient to enable it to float. It is placed in a tall jar of water, over the top of which is tied a cover of India-rubber. Pressure upon this cover forces an additional quantity of water into the balloon by an opening (*v*, fig. 26). The density of the mass is thus increased, and it sinks until the pressure is removed, when, the air in the balloon expanding, forces out the superfluous water, and the glass rises again. Such is the mode provided by nature in the structure of the nautilus and ammonite, by which means those curious animals are able, at will, to rise or sink in the ocean.

Fig. 26.

39. *Specific Gravity of Gases.*—It remains only, under this head, to speak of the modes used for determining the specific gravity of gases and vapors. For this purpose a globe, (fig. 28,) or other conveniently formed glass vessel, holding a known quantity by measure, (usually 100 cubic inches,) is carefully freed from air and moisture, by the air-pump or exhausting syringe. It is then filled with the gas or vapor in question, at 60° Fahrenheit, and 30 inches of the barometer, (33,) and weighed. The weight of the apparatus filled with common air being previously known, the difference enables the experimenter to make a direct comparison. Figure 27 shows an apparatus for this purpose; the globe *b* is provided with a stopcock *e*, and fitted by a screw to the air-jar *a*. The jar is graduated so that the quantity of air or other gas entering may be known from

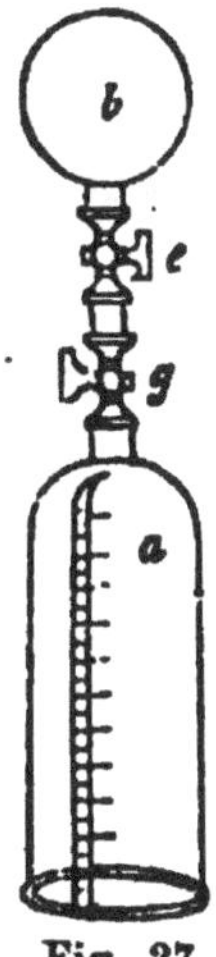

Fig. 27.

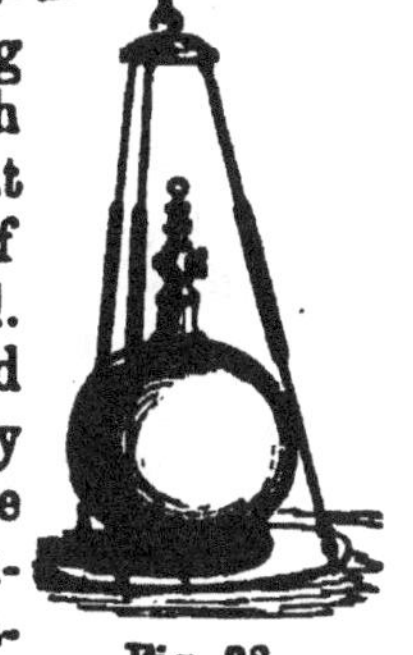

Fig. 28.

38. What is the water balloon. What animal has the same principle? How is air weighed? 39. Describe figures 27 and 28. How do we find the specific gravity of gases?

the rise of the water in *a*. It is thus found that 100 cubic inches of pure dry air weigh 30·829 grains, while the same quantity of hydrogen gas weighs only 2·14 grains, being about fourteen times lighter than air. To dry the air or gas it must be made to pass through a chlorid of calcium tube, or other drying apparatus, before entering the balloon.

CRYSTALLIZATION.

Nature of Crystallization and Forms of Crystals.

40. *Nature of Crystallization.*—The forms of living nature, both animal and vegetable, are determined by the laws of vitality, and are generally bounded by curved lines and surfaces. Inorganic or lifeless matter is fashioned by a different law. Geometrical forms, bounded by straight lines and plane surfaces, take the place in the mineral kingdom which the more complex results of the vital force occupy in the animal and vegetable world. The power which determines the forms of inorganic matter is called crystallization. A crystal is any inorganic solid, bounded by plane surfaces symmetrically arranged and possessing a homogeneous structure.

Crystallization is, then, to the inorganic world, what the power of vitality is to the organic; and viewed in this, its proper light, the science of crystallography rises from being only a branch of solid geometry to occupy an exalted philosophical position.

The cohesive force in solids is only an exertion of crystalline forces, and in this sense no difference can be established between solidification and crystallization. The forms of matter resulting from solidification may not always be regular, but the power which binds together the molecules is that of crystallization.

41. *Circumstances influencing Crystallization.*—Solution is one of the most important conditions necessary to crystallization. Most salts and other bodies are more soluble in hot than in cold water. A saturated hot solution will usually deposit crystals on cooling. Common alum and Glauber's salts are examples of this. Solution by heat, or

---

How much do we thus find the air to weigh? 40. What is crystallization said to be? What is the cohesive force? 41. Name some circumstances which influence crystallization.

fusion, also allows of crystallization, as is seen in the crystalline fracture of zinc and antimony. Sulphur crystallizes beautifully on cooling from fusion, and so do bismuth and some other substances. The slags of iron-furnaces and scoriæ of volcanic districts present numerous examples of minerals finely crystallized by fire. Numerous minerals have been formed by heating together the constituents of which they are composed. Blows and long-continued vibration produce a change of molecular arrangement in masses of solid iron and other bodies, resulting often in the formation of broad crystalline plates. Rail-road axles are thus frequently rendered unsafe. In short, any change which can disturb the equilibrium of the particles, and permits any freedom of motion among them, favours the reaction of the polar or axial forces, (42,) and promotes crystallization.

42. *Polarity of Molecules.*—The laws of crystallization show that the molecules have *polarity*. That is, these molecules have three imaginary axes passing through them, whose terminations, or *poles*, are the centre of the forces by which a series of similar particles are attracted to each other to form a regular solid. These molecules are either spheres (fig. 29) or ellipsoids, (fig. 31,) and the three axes (N S)

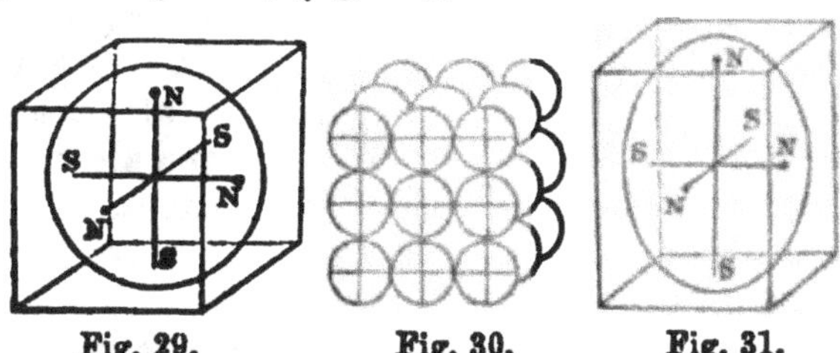

Fig. 29. Fig. 30. Fig. 31.

are, always, either the fundamental axes, or the diameters of these particles. In the sphere (fig. 29) these axes are always of equal length, and at right angles to each other, and the forms which can result from the aggregation of such spherical particles can be only symmetrical solids, such as the *cube* and its allied forms. The cube drawn about the sphere (fig. 29) may be supposed to be made up of a great number of little spheres (fig. 30) whose similar poles unite N and S. In the *ellipsoid* (fig. 31) all the axes may vary in length,

42. What do the laws of crystallization show? What are the *axes* of molecules? What forms have the molecules of bodies? What forms can come from the spherical particles? How may the structure of the cube be shown? How are the axes of the ellipsoid?

giving origin to a vast diversity of forms. Under the influence of heat, the crystallogenic attraction loses its polarity and force, and the body becomes liquid or gaseous, and subject to repulsive force. The return to a solid state can occur again only when the attractions become polar or axial.

43. *Crystalline Forms.*—The mineral kingdom presents us with the most splendid examples of crystals. In the laboratory we can imitate the productions of nature, and in many cases produce beautiful forms from the crystallization of various salts, which have never been observed in nature. The learner who is ignorant of the simple laws of crystallography, sees in a cabinet of crystals an unending variety and complexity of forms, which at first would seem to baffle all attempts at system or simplicity. Numerous as the natural forms of crystals are, however, they may be all reduced to *six classes*, comprising only *thirteen or fourteen* forms. From these all other crystalline solids, however varied, may be formed by certain simple laws.

44. *The first class* of crystalline forms includes the cube, (fig. 32,) the octahedron, (fig. 33,) and the dodecahedron, (fig. 34.) The faces of the cube are equal squares. The eight solid angles are similar, and also the twelve edges. The three

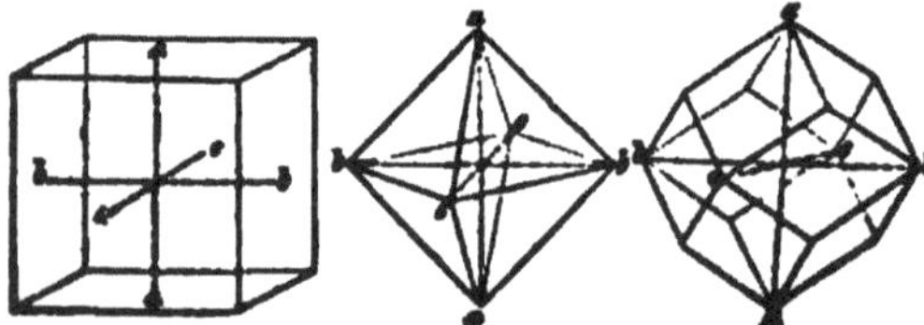

Fig. 32. Fig. 33. Fig. 34.

axes are equal, (*aa*, *bb*, *cc*,) and connect the centres of opposite faces. The *regular octahedron* (fig. 33) consists of two equal four-sided pyramids, placed base to base. The six solid angles are equal, and so also the edges, which, as in the cube, are twelve in number. The plane angles are 60°, and the interfacial 109° 28′ 16″. The *axes* connect the opposite angles; they are equal and intersect at right angles. This class is also called the *monometric*, (*monos*, one, and *metron*, measure,) the axes being equal.

45. *The second class* includes the square prism (fig. 35) and square octahedron (fig. 36.) In the square prism (fig. 35) the eight solid angles are right angles, and similar, as in the cube. The eight basal edges are similar, but differ from

---

43. How are the complex forms of crystals arranged and simplified?
44. Describe the first class of fundamental forms.

the four lateral. The two basal faces are squares, the four lateral are parallelograms. The *axes* connect the centres of opposite faces, and intersect at right angles. Square prisms vary in the length of the vertical axis, (*a*, *a*,) which is hence called the varying axis; the lateral axes (*bb*, *cc*) are equal This class is also called the *dimetric*, (*dis*, twofold, and *metron*, measure.)

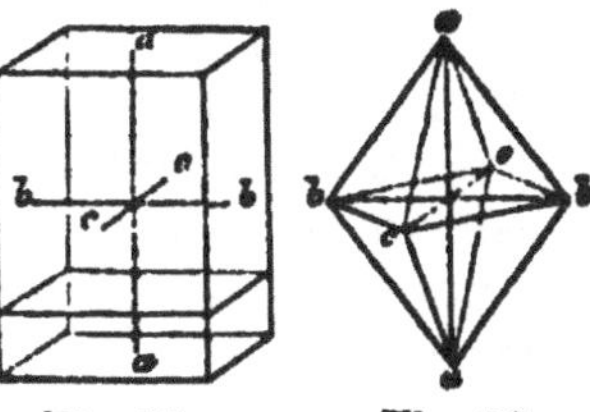
Fig. 35. Fig. 36.

46. *The third class* contains the rhombic prism, (fig. 37,) the rectangular prism, (fig. 38,) and the rhombic octahedron, (fig. 39.) The rhombic prism (fig. 37) has two sorts of edges, two acute and two obtuse. The solid angles are, therefore, of two kinds, four obtuse and four acute. The axes are unequal and cross at right angles. The lateral connect the centres of opposite *edges*, *bb*, *cc*. The basal faces are rhombic. The *rectangular prism* (fig. 38) has all its solid angles similar. There are three kinds or sets of edges, four lateral, four longer basal, and four shorter basal. The axes connect the centres of opposite faces, and intersect at right angles. The three are unequal. The rhombic octahedron (fig. 39) has three unequal axes, connecting opposite solid angles. All the sections in this solid are rhombic. This class is also called the *trimetric*, from *tris*, threefold, and *metron*, measure.

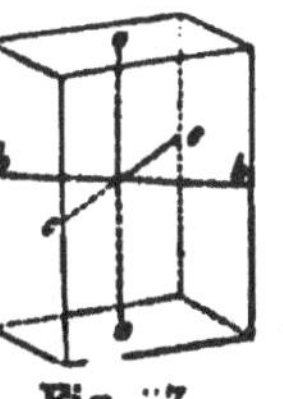
Fig. 37.

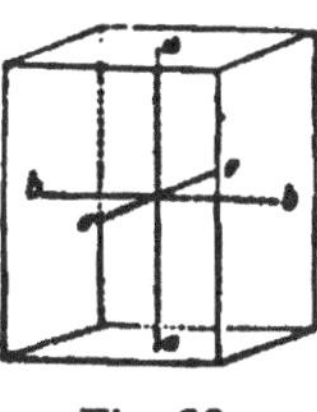
Fig. 38.

Fig. 39.

47. *The fourth class* contains the oblique rhombic prism, (fig. 40,) and the right rhomboidal prism, (fig. 41.) The *oblique rhombic prism* is represented in the figure as inclining away from the observer, the prism being in position when standing on its rhombic base. The upper and lower solid angles in front are dissimilar, one obtuse and the other acute. The four

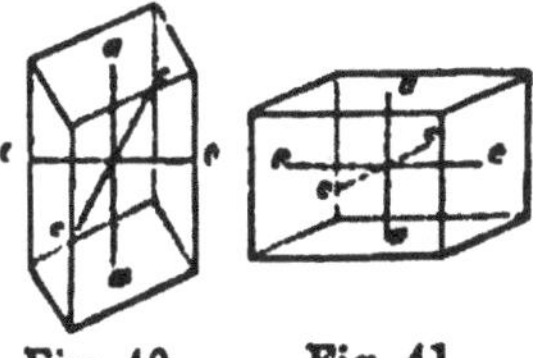
Fig. 40. Fig. 41.

45. What are the forms of the second class? Describe them. 46. What forms make up the third class? Describe them. 47. What forms does the fourth class contain? How do they differ?

lateral solid angles are similar. Two of the lateral edges are acute, and two obtuse; and the same is true of the basal. The lateral axes are unequal; they connect the centres of opposite lateral edges, and intersect at right angles. The vertical axis is oblique to one lateral axis, and perpendicular to the other. The *right rhomboidal prism* (fig. 41) has two obtuse and two acute lateral edges, and four longer and four shorter basal edges. The solid angles are of two kinds, four obtuse and four acute. The axes connect the centres of opposite faces; one is oblique, the others cross at right angles. This is also called the *monoclinate*, (*monos*, one, and *clino*, to incline,) having one inclined axis.

48. *The fifth class includes the oblique rhomboidal prism.* In this solid only those parts diagonally opposite are similar, and consequently it has six kinds of edges. The axes connect the centres of opposite faces. They are unequal, and all their intersections are oblique. This is called the *triclinate* class, from *tris*, three, and *clino*, to incline, the three axes all being obliquely inclined.

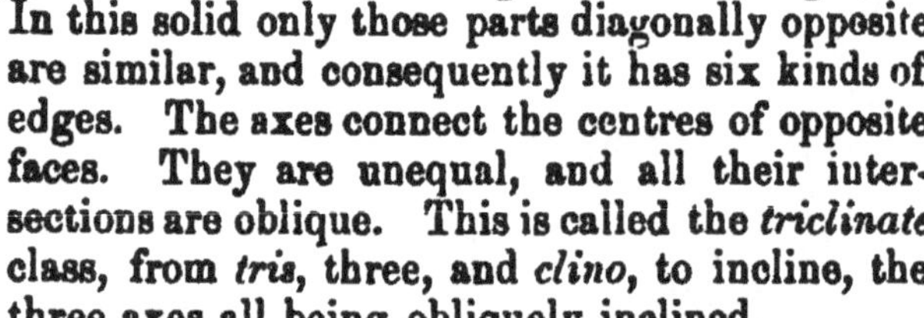

Fig. 42.

49. *The sixth class* includes the hexagonal prism (fig. 43) and the rhombohedron, (figs. 44 and 45.) The *hexagonal prism* has twelve similar angles, and the same number of similar basal edges. The lateral edges are six in number, and similar. The lateral axes are equal, and cross at 60°, connecting the centres of opposite lateral faces or lateral edges.

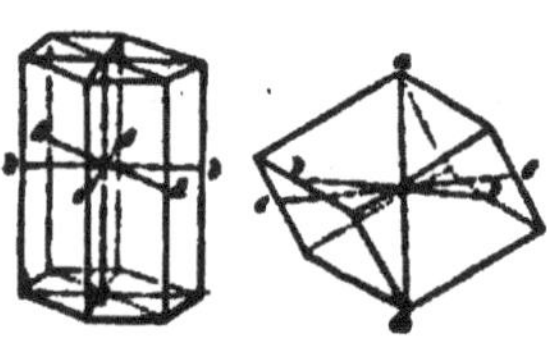

Fig. 43. Fig. 44. Fig. 45.

The *rhombohedron* is a solid whose six faces are all rhombs. The two diagonally opposite solid angles (*a a*) consist of three equal obtuse or equal acute plane angles, and the diagonal connecting these solid angles is called the vertical axis, (*a a*.) When the plane angles forming the vertical solid angles are *obtuse*, the rhombohedron is called an obtuse, (fig. 44,) and if *acute*, it is called an acute rhombohedron, (fig. 45.) The three lateral axes are equal, and

---

What other names have the first, second, and third classes? 48. What solid is included in the fifth class? 49. Name the two solids in the sixth class of fundamental forms. How are the hexagonal prism and rhombohedron related? How are rhombohedrons distinguished?

intersect at angles of 60°: they connect the centres of opposite *lateral* edges. This will be seen on placing a rhombohedron in position and looking down upon it from above. The six lateral edges will be found to be arranged around the vertical axis, like the sides of an hexagonal prism.

50. *The mutual relations* of the forms of crystals are well shown in the foregoing arrangement. Thus, in each of the six classes, the first named solid alone is, properly considered, a fundamental form, the others in each class being frequently found as secondaries to these. The six fundamental forms are the *cube*, *square prism*, *right rectangular prism*, *oblique rhombic prism* or *right rhomboidal prism*, *oblique rhomboidal prism*, and the *hexagonal prism* or *rhombohedron*.

51. The structure of crystals is often seen by lines on their surfaces, or by the ease with which the crystal splits in certain directions. Common mica cleaves in leaves; galena breaks only in cubes, fluor-spar in octahedra, calc-spar only in rhombohedrons. This property is called *cleavage*. It does not exist in all crystals, and is not of equal facility in all directions. Thus, in mica, cleavage is easy in one direction only; while in fluor-spar and calcite it is equally easy in three directions respectively.

Measurement of Crystals.

52. *Common Goniometer.**—The angles of crystals are measured by means of instruments called goniometers. The common goniometer, which is here figured, consists of a light semicircle of brass, (fig. 47,) accurately graduated into degrees, and having a pair of steel arms (fig. 46) moving on a central pivot, and so arranged as to slip in

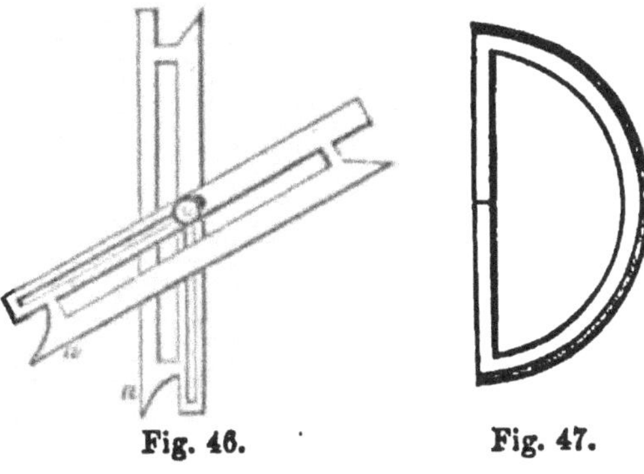

Fig. 46. Fig. 47.

50. What is said of the relations of fundamental forms? What six fundamental forms are named? 51. What is cleavage in minerals? On what does it depend? Give examples. Is it equal in all minerals?

* From the Greek, *gonia*, an angle, and *metron*, measure.

a groove over each other. The points *a a* can thus be made to embrace the faces of a crystal whose angle we wish to measure. The graduated semicircle is applied with its centre at the point of intersection, when the angle is read on the arc. Where the greatest nicety is required, a much more delicate instrument is used.

53. *Wollaston's Reflective Goniometer.*—The principle of this instrument may be understood by reference to fig. 48, which represents a crystal (*o*) whose angle (*a b c*) is required. The eye at P, looking at the face (*b c*) of the crystal, observes a reflected image of M in the direction of P N. The crystal may now be so turned that the same image is seen reflected in the next face, (*b a*,) and in the same direction, (P N.) To effect this, the crystal must be turned until *a b* has the present position of *b c*. The angle *d b c* measures, therefore, the number of degrees through which the crystal must be turned. But *d b c* subtracted from 180° equals the required angle of the crystal *a b c*; consequently, the crystal passes through a number of degrees, which, subtracted from 180°, gives the required angle.

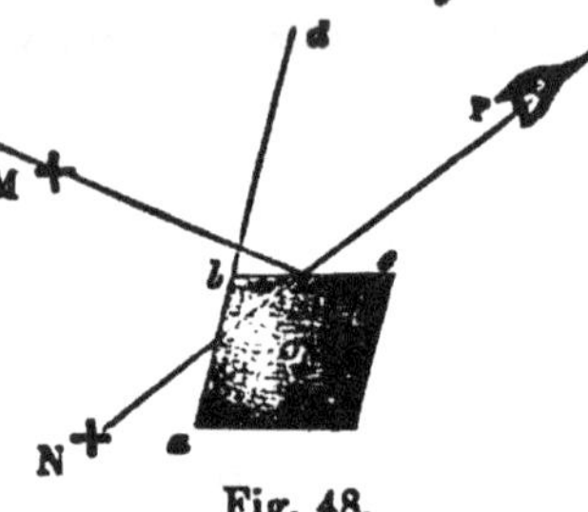

Fig. 48.

When the crystal is attached to a graduated circle, we have the goniometer of Wollaston, which is represented in fig. 49. The crystal to be measured is attached at *f*, and may be adjusted by the milled head *c* and arm *d*, moving independent of the great circle *a*. When adjusted in the manner described above, the wheel is revolved until the image of M is seen in the second face. This movement is practically a subtraction of the angle *a b c*

Fig. 49.

---

52. What is a goniometer? Explain the common one and its use. 53. Explain the principles of Wollaston's goniometer from figure 48. How is this principle used in Wollaston's instrument?

from 180°, and the result is read directly by the vernier *e*. —The subject of crystallography cannot be further illustrated here; but the learner who desires to pursue it, is referred to the highly philosophical treatise on mineralogy by Professor J. D. Dana.

II. LIGHT.

54. The physical phenomena of light properly belong to the science of Optics, a branch of natural philosophy not necessarily connected with chemistry. A knowledge of some of the laws of light is, however, required of the chemical student.

55. *Sources and Nature of Light.*—The sun is the great source of light, although we know many minor and artificial sources. Of the real nature of light we know nothing. Sir Isaac Newton argued that it was a material emanation from the sun and other luminous bodies, consisting of particles so attenuated as to be wholly imponderable to our means of estimating weight, and having the greatest imaginable repulsion to each other. These particles, by his theory, are supposed to be sent forth in straight lines, in all directions, from every luminous body, and, falling on the delicate nerves of the eye, to produce the sense of vision. This is called the Newtonian or corpuscular theory of light. It is not generally adopted by physicists, but the language of optical science is formed mainly in accordance with it. The other view or theory of light, which is now almost universally accepted, is called the wave or undulatory theory. It is known that sound is conveyed through the air by a series of vibrations or waves, pulsating regularly in all directions, from the original source of the sound. In the same manner it is believed that light is conveyed to the eye by a series of unending and inconceivably rapid pulsations or undulations, imparted from the source of light to a very rare or attenuated medium, which is supposed to fill all space. This medium is called the *luminiferous ether.*

Astronomy furnishes evidence of the presence in space of a medium resisting the motion of the heavenly bodies

---

54. What is optics? 55. Name sources of light. What is the Newtonian hypothesis? What is the other theory? What is the medium of light? What evidence does astronomy give of an ether?

Encke's comet is found to lose about two days in each successive period of 1200 days. Biela's comet, with twice that length of period, loses about one day. That is, the successive returns of these bodies is found to be accelerated by this amount. No other cause for this irregularity has been found but the agency of the supposed ether.

56. *Undulations.*—The propagation of force by undulations, pulsations, or waves, is a general fact in physics. A vibrating cord communicates its waves of motion to the surrounding air, and a musical tone results.

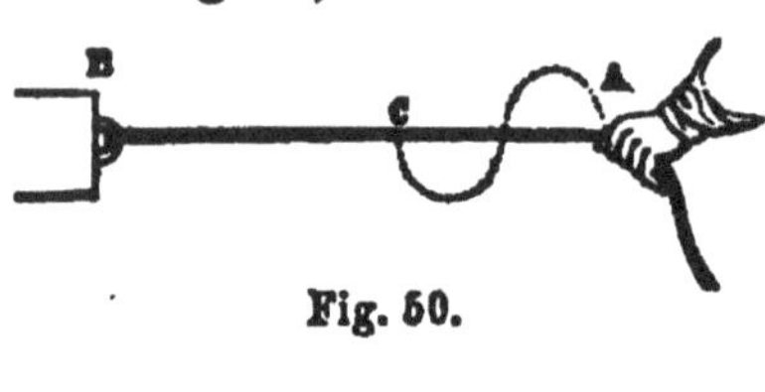

Fig. 50.

Fig. 51.

If a long cord A B, fig. 50, be jerked by the hand, the motion is propagated from the hand A, in the curve A C, and so on successively to B, when the motion is again reflected in the opposite phase to the hand, as in fig. 51, where the continued line shows the primary vibrations, and the dotted one that which is reflected.

Fig. 52.

A pebble dropped on the surface of a quiet pool, produces a series of circular waves receding to the shore, (fig. 52.) The waves produced do not transport any light bodies *a* accidentally floating on the surface of the water. These only rise and fall as each wave passes.

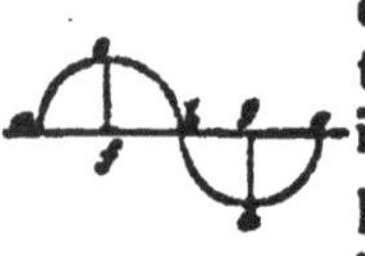
Fig. 53.

57. The measure of the waves on the surface of water is from crest to crest, or from hollow to hollow, and in every complete wave or entire vibration (fig. 53) the following parts are recognised: *a e b d c* is the whole length of the wave; *a e b i* the phase of elevation, and *b d e* the phase of depression. The height of the wave is *e f*, and its depth *g d*. The points in which the phases of elevation and of depression intersect, as in fig. 51, are called nodal points, and are always at rest: so

---

56. How is force propagated? Illustrate by figs. 50 and 51. Describe the progress of waves from fig. 52. 57. Name the parts of a wave in fig. 54. Distinguish the phases of elevation and of depression. What are nodal points?

that light bodies resting on them would remain undisturbed, which placed elsewhere would be immediately thrown off. If two waves of equal altitude and arriving from opposite directions unite, so that the elevations and depressions of the two correspond, then the resulting wave is doubled. But if the two meet at half the distance of their respective elevations and depressions, so that the crest of one correspond to the hollow of the other, then both are obliterated, and the surface becomes quiet; or if one wave was larger than the other, a third wave, corresponding to the difference only of the other two, results.

58. This is equally true whether we speak of waves of sound, of heat, of light, or in fluids. That two waves of sound may meet so as to produce silence, may easily be shown by vibrating a tuning-fork over an open glass A, and holding another similar glass B lip to lip with the first, and at right angles with it, as shown in fig. 54. The vibrations may be increased by sticking a piece of circular card-board on one leg of the fork, and by pouring water into the first glass until the tone is adjusted to a maximum. Or a second fork may be used in place of B, differing half a tone from the other fork, (fig. 55.) In this case a series of swells and cadences will be heard in place of entire silence. In these cases, the waves of sound interfere, as before, in the case of the water. In like manner, two currents of thermo-electricity may meet in such a manner as to freeze a drop of water in one end of the arrangement, the current being excited by heating the opposite end of the system.

Fig. 54.

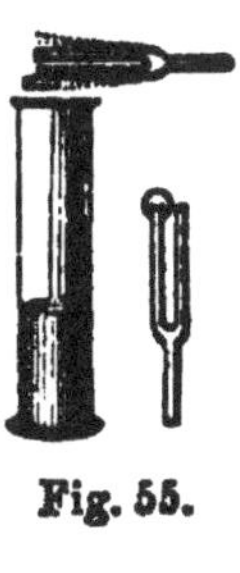

Fig. 55.

59. So two rays of light, A B, C D, fig. 56, meeting at the proper interval, (*a*,) will produce a beam of double intensity; but if they meet at the half interval of vibration, darkness results. This is interference of light. In mother of pearl and many other natural bodies, a beautiful play of colors is seen. The microscope reveals on such sur-

Fig. 56.

When are waves made double, and when set at rest? 58. Illustrate the interference of waves of sound in figs. 54 and 55. What of thermo-electricity? 59. Describe the interference of light from fig. 56.

faces delicate grooves and ridges, and these are at such distances as to produce interference in the light-waves, resulting in partial obscuration and partial decomposition. The same effect is artificially produced in medal-ruling. This irised effect can be transferred by pressure or copied by the electrotype, or even on wax.

60. The transverse vibrations of a ray of light distinguish this from all other modes of undulation or vibration. Dr. Bird illustrates this by fig. 57, which represents a spherical particle of ether alternately extended and depressed at its poles and equator, oscillating, or trembling, rather than undulating. Thus, each particle in turn communicates the impulse which it receives, and yet the centre of each may remain unmoved from its place; as motion in a series of ivory balls causes only the terminal one to swing, the intermediate ones remaining unmoved. In light-waves, the vibration or pendulation of each particle is perpendicular to the path of the ray; and yet the alternate effect of the movements of contiguous particles will produce a progressive vibration. Thus, in fig. 58, A B C D may represent particles of ether in the path of a ray of light, the phases of elevation in A and C and those of depression in B and D being coincident. The fact of the vibrations of light-ether being transverse to the path of the ray was first observed by Fresnel. These vibrations are conceived to occur in any or every transverse plane. Leaving these interesting generalizations, we must briefly recapitulate the well-established

Fig. 57.

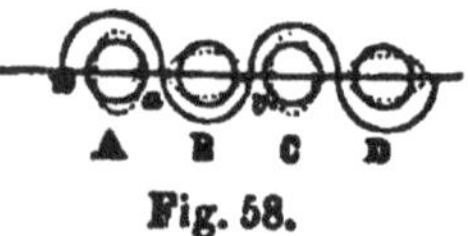

Fig. 58.

61. *Properties of Light.*—1st. Light is sent forth in rays in all directions from all luminous bodies. 2d. Bodies not themselves luminous become visible by the light falling on them from other luminous bodies. 3d. The light which proceeds from all bodies has the color of the body from which it comes, although the sun sends forth only white light. 4th. Light consists of separate parts independent of each other. 5th. Rays of light proceed in straight lines. 6th. Light moves with a wonderful velocity, which has been computed

What instances are named from nature? 60. What are transverse vibrations in light? How is the undulation thus produced? What is said of progressive motion? 61. Enumerate six properties of light.

by astronomical observations to be at least one hundred and ninety-five thousands of miles in a second of time. This velocity is so wonderful as to surpass our comprehension Herschel says of it, that a wink of the eye, or a single motion of the leg of a swift runner, or flap of the wing of the swiftest bird, occupies more time than the passage of a ray of light around the globe. A cannon-ball at its utmost speed would require at least seventeen years to reach the sun, while light comes over the same distance in about eight minutes.

62. When a ray of light falls on the surface of any body, several things may happen. 1st. It may be absorbed and disappear altogether, as is the case when it falls on a black and dull surface. 2d. It may be nearly all reflected, as from some polished surfaces. 3d. It may pass through or be transmitted; and, 4th. It may be partly absorbed, partly reflected, and partly transmitted. All bodies are either luminous, transparent, or opake. Bodies are said to be opake when they intercept all light, and transparent when they permit it to pass through them. But no body is either perfectly opake or entirely transparent, and we see these properties in every possible degree of difference. Metals, which are among the most opake bodies, become partly transparent when made very thin, as may be seen in gold-leaf on glass, which transmits a greenish-purple light, and in quicksilver, which gives by transmitted light a blue color slightly tinged with purple. On the other hand, glass and all other transparent bodies arrest the progress of more or less light.

63. *Reflection.*—Light is reflected according to a very simple law. In fig. 59, if the ray of light fall from P′ to P, it is thrown directly back to P′; for this reason, a person looking into a common mirror sees himself correctly, but his image appears to be as far behind the mirror as he is in front of it. The line P P′ is called the *normal.* If the ray fall from R to P, it will be reflected to R′, and if from *r*, then it will go in the line *r′*, and so for any other point

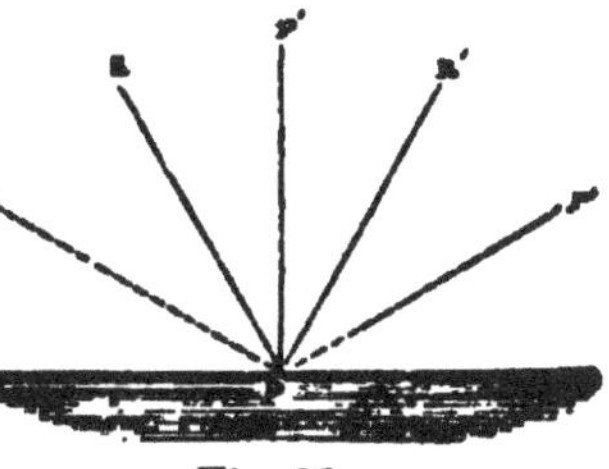

Fig. 59.

Illustrate its velocity. 62. What happens to incident light? How are bodies divided in respect to light? Give illustrations of imperfect opacity. 63. What is the law of reflection? What is the normal?

If we measure the angles R P P′ and P′ P R′, we shall find them equal to each other, and so also the angles r P P′ and P′ P r′. These angles are called respectively the angles of *incidence* and *reflection*. We therefore state that the angle of incidence is equal to the angle of reflection, which is the law of simple reflection. This law is as true of curved surfaces as it is of planes; for a curved surface (as a concave metallic mirror) is considered as made up of an infinite number of small planes.

64. *Simple Refraction.*—If a ray of light falls perpendicularly on any transparent or uncrystallized surface, as glass or water, it is partly reflected, partly scattered in all directions, (which part renders the object visible,) and partly transmitted in the same direction from which it comes. If, however, the light come in any other than a perpendicular or vertical direction, as from R to A, on the surface of a thick slip of glass, as in fig. 60, it will not pass the glass in the line R A B, but will be bent or *refracted* at A, to C. As it leaves the glass at C, it again travels in a direction parallel to R A, its first course. *Refraction, then, is the change of direction which a ray of light suffers on passing from a rarer to a denser medium, and the reverse.* In passing from a rarer to a denser medium, (as from air to glass or water,) the ray is bent or refracted toward a line perpendicular to that point of the surface on which the light falls; and from a denser to a rarer medium the law is reversed.

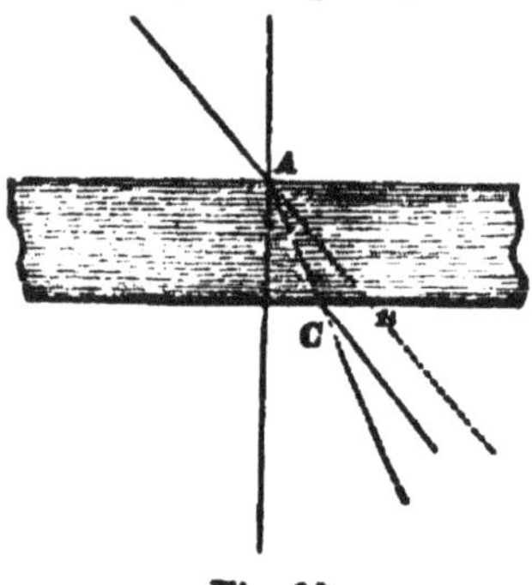

Fig. 60.

A common experiment, in illustration of this law, is to place a coin in the bottom of a bowl, so situated that the observer cannot see the coin until water is poured into the vessel; the coin then becomes visible, because the ray of light passing out of the water from the coin is bent toward

---

What is the angle of incidence? What of reflection? What is true of curved surfaces? 64. What is refraction? Demonstrate the law by fig. 60. Which way is the ray bent? Give a familiar illustration of refraction.

the eye. In the same manner, a straight stick thrust into water appears bent at an angle where it enters the water.

65. *Index of Refraction.*—The obliquity of the ray to the refracting medium determines the amount of refraction. The more obliquely the ray falls on the surface, the greater the amount of refraction. A little modification of the last figure will make this clear. Let R A (fig. 61) be a beam of light falling on a refracting medium : it is bent as before to R′. If we draw a circle about A as a centre, and let fall the line *a a*, from the point *a*, where the circle cuts the ray R, and at right angles to the normal A′ A, the line *a a* is called the *sine of the angle of incidence;* while the line *a′ a′* is called *the sine of the angle of refraction.*

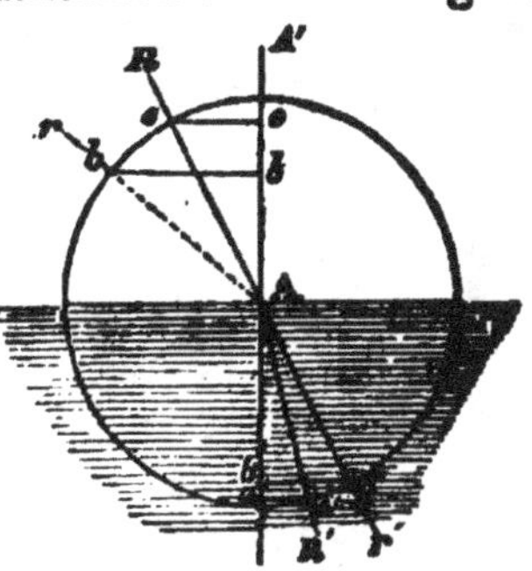

Fig. 61.

If a more oblique ray *r* cuts the circle at *b*, the line *b b* will be longer than the line *a a*, inasmuch as the angle *b* A *a* is greater than the angle *a* A *a*.

The line measuring the obliquity before refraction, when the ray passes into a denser medium, is always greater than that which measures it after. The ratio of these lines expresses the refractive power of the medium. This is called the *index* of refraction.

In rain water the ratio of these lines is as 529 : 396 or 1·31 ; in crown glass it is as 31 : 20 or 1·55; in flint glass 1·616, and in the diamond 2·43.

66. Substances of an inflammable nature, or rich in carbon, and those which are dense, have, as a general thing, a higher refracting power than others. Sir Isaac Newton observed that the diamond and water had both high refracting powers, and he sagaciously foretold the fact, which chemistry has since proved, that both these substances had a combustible base, or were of an inflammable nature.

67. *Prism.*—In the cases of simple refraction just explained, the ray, after leaving the refracting medium, goes on in a course parallel to its original direction, because the

---

65. What is the index of refraction? Demonstrate this from fig. 61.
66. What substances have highest refraction? What was Newton's suggestion about the diamond?

Fig. 62.

two surfaces of the medium are parallel. If, however, the surfaces of the refracting medium are not parallel, the ray, on leaving the second surface, will be permanently diverted from its original path. The common triangular glass prism (fig. 62) illustrates this. As already explained, the ray R is bent toward the normal in media more dense than air. But in the prism the emergent ray R is, by the same law, still farther refracted in the direction R′. By altering the form of the surfaces, we may thus send the ray in almost any direction, as in the common multiplying-glass, which gives as many images as it has surfaces of reflection. In this way it is that concave metallic mirrors concentrate, and convex ones disperse a beam of light. Fig. 63 shows the prism conveniently mounted for use.

Fig. 63.

68. *Analysis of Light.*—By means of the prism, Sir Isaac Newton demonstrated the compound nature of white light, such as reaches us in the ordinary sunbeam. In fig. 64 a pencil of rays from R, falling from a small circular aperture in the shutter of a darkened room on a common triangular prism, is refracted twice, and bent upward toward the white screen R′, placed at some distance from the prism, where it forms an oblong colored image, composed of seven colors. This image is called the *prismatic* or *solar spectrum.* The spectrum has the same width as the aperture admitting the beam of light, but its length is greatly increased beyond its diameter, the ends retaining the rounded form of the opening. This image or spectrum presents the most beautiful series of colors, exquisitely blended, and each possessing a degree of intensity, splendor, and purity far exceedingly the colors of the most brilliant natural bodies. These colors are not separated by distinct lines, but seem to

Fig 64.

---

67. How is light refracted by surfaces not parallel. What is the prism?

melt into one another, so that it is impossible to say where one ends and the next begins.

The light from flames of all kinds, the oxy-hydrogen blowpipe, and the electric spark, or galvanic light, is also compound in its nature, like that of the sun and other celestial bodies.

69. *Prismatic Colors.*—The colors of the solar spectrum are in the following order, reading upward: red, orange, yellow, green, blue, indigo, violet. These colors are of very different refrangibility, and for this reason are presented in a broad and blended surface, the red being the least refracted, and the violet the most. The seven colors of Newton, it is believed, are really composed of the three primitive ones, red, yellow, and blue. This idea is well expressed in the following diagram, (fig. 65.) The three primitive colors each attain their greatest intensity in the spectrum at the points marked at the summit of the curves; while the four other colors, violet, indigo, green, and orange, are the result of a mixture, in the spectrum, of the first three. A portion of proper white light is also found in all parts of the spectrum, which cannot be separated by refraction. We may hence infer that there is a portion of each color in every part of the spectrum, but that each is most intense at the points where it appears strongest. The light is most intense in the yellow portion, and fades toward each end of the spectrum.

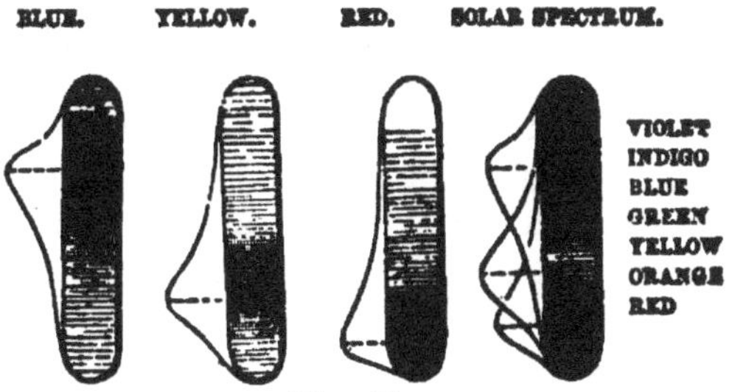

BLUE. YELLOW. RED. SOLAR SPECTRUM.

VIOLET
INDIGO
BLUE
GREEN
YELLOW
ORANGE
RED

Fig. 65.

Sir John Herschel has detected rays of greater refrangibility than the violet of the spectrum and are beyond it, which have a lavender color. They have this color after concentration, and are therefore not merely, as might be supposed, dilute violet rays.

If the spectrum is formed by a beam of light passing through a slit not over $\frac{1}{30}$th of an inch in width, the image

---

68. Describe the analysis of light. What is the image called? What is the form of the spectrum? How are the colors arranged? Describe the blending of the colors from fig. 65. What is lavender light?

will be crossed by a great number of dark lines, which always appear in the same relative position. They are called the *fixed lines* of the spectrum, and are much referred to as boundary lines in optical descriptions.

70. Each of the prismatic colors has some other, which blended with it produces white light, and hence is called its *complementary* color. Let indigo be regarded as a deeper blue, and each of the three primary colors has its secondary colors. Fig. 65 shows the three primary tints blending to form white light at the céntre: at the other parts the complementary colors are opposite to each other, *e. g.* red and green, blue and yellow.

Fig. 65 (*bis.*)

71. *Double refraction* of light is a phenomenon observed in many crystalline transparent bodies, and is due to their peculiar structure. It is also seen in bone, shell, horn, and other similar substances. The beam of light in passing through such bodies is split into two portions, each of which gives its own image of any object seen through the doubly refracting substance. In calcite, carbonate of lime, or Iceland-spar, this phenomenon is beautifully seen.

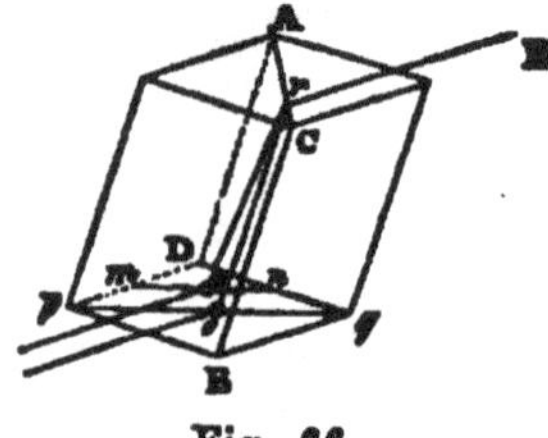

Fig. 66.

A sharp line, like $p\,q$, fig. 66, when seen through a rhomb of calc-spar, in the direction of the ray R r, will seem to be double, a second parallel line $m\ n$, being seen at a short distance from it, and the dot o will have its fellow e. In this case the light is represented as coming from R to r, and, passing through the crystal, it is split and emerges in two beams at e and o. The same effect would be produced if the light fell so as to strike any part of the imaginary plane A C B D, which divides the crystal diagonally and is called its principal section. The axis or line drawn from A to B is contained in this plane. But if we look through the crystal in a direction parallel to this plane (A C B D) there is only simple refraction, and only one line is seen. One of these beams is called the *ordinary* and the other the *extraordinary* ray. In the case of crystallized minerals, this result is due to the naturally unequal

· What lines are seen in the spectrum? 70. What of the colors of natural bodies? 71. What is double refraction? Describe fig. 66. What is the ordinary ray? Which the extraordinary? What relation has this phenomenon to crystallization?

elasticities of the molecules in the crystals—and it is observed only in those minerals whose molecules are ellipsoidal —and is wanting in those, like fluor-spar, &c., which belong to the cube and its derivatives, in which the molecules are spherical. In well annealed glass, by mechanical pressure, a sufficient separation of the two rays may be produced to cause color by interference, though not enough to cause two images

72. *Polarization.*—The light which has passed one crystal of Iceland-spar by extraordinary refraction is no longer affected like common light. If we attempt to pass it through another crystal of the same substance, there will be no further subdivision, and only a greater separation of the two beams. This peculiarity of the extraordinary ray is called *polarization.* This interesting phenomenon was accidentally discovered in 1808 by Malus, while looking through a doubly-refracting prism at the light of the setting sun, reflected from the surface of a glazed door standing at an angle of about 56° 45′, which is the angle at which glass polarizes light by reflection.

It is the peculiarity of light which has been polarized that it will no longer pass through certain substances which are transparent to common light. Many crystalline substances possess the power of polarizing light. The mineral called tourmaline has this property in a remarkable degree. The internal structure of this mineral is such that a ray of light which has passed through a thin plate of it cannot pass through a second, if it is placed in a position at right angles with the first.

For example, in the annexed figure (67) we have two thin plates of tourmaline placed parallel to each other in the same direction. A ray of light passes through both, in the direction of R R′, and apparently suffers no change: if, however, these plates are so placed as to cross each other at right angles, as in fig. 68, the ray of light

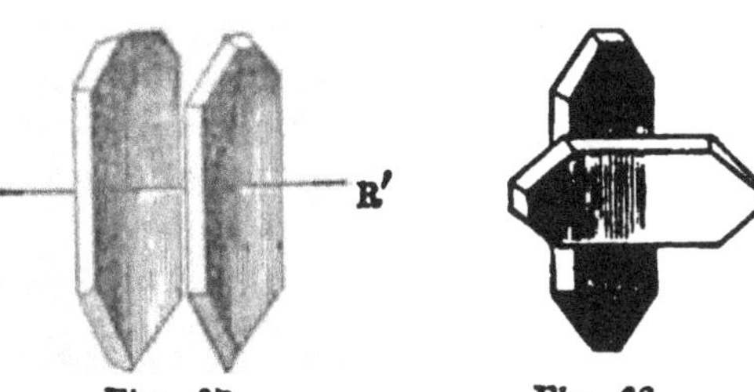

Fig. 67. Fig. 68.

72. What is polarization? Who discovered this phenomenon? What is the peculiarity of polarized light? Illustrate this from the tourmaline.

is totally extinguished; and two such points may be found in revolving one of the plates about the ray as an axis.

73. For illustration, we may suppose the structure of this mineral to be such that a ray of light can pass between the ranges of particles in one direction only, as a flat blade may pass between the wires of a bird-cage, fig. 69, if placed parallel to them; but will be arrested by the bars, if presented at right angles to the wires.

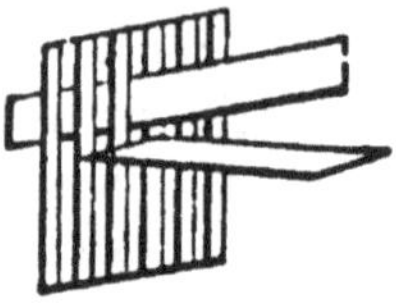

Fig. 69.

Fig. 70.

Light is polarized in many ways, as, for example, by passing through a bundle of plates of thin glass or of mica, as in fig. 70, by reflection from the surface of unsilvered glass, of a polished table and of most polished non-metallic surfaces, and at a particular angle for each. This is *plane* polarized light.

Fig. 71. Fig. 72.

74. The beautiful phenomenon of circular and elliptic polarization is seen in many crystalline bodies. Plates of quartz, a mineral having one axis, show the prismatic colors, when viewed by polarized light, arranged in circles and a cross, as in fig. 71; and by the revolution of the plane of polarization through 90°, the colors are changed, and a light cross (fig. 71) occupies the plane of the dark one. Nitre gives two axes of polarization, which in the revolution of the plane show the changes seen in figures 73 and 74. Uniaxial crystals uniformly give circular, and binaxial ones elliptical figures.

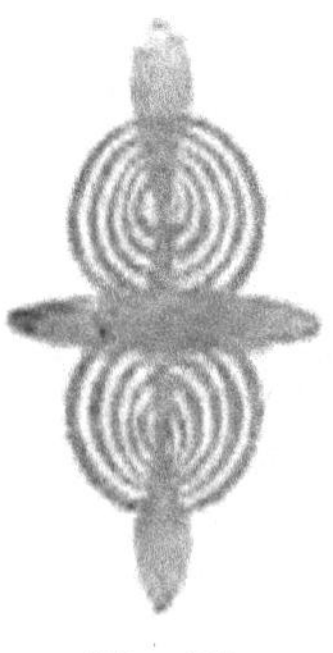

Fig. 73.  Fig. 74.

When is the ray extinguished? 73. How is this phenomenon explained in reference to the structure of the crystal? In what ways is light polarized? 74. What crystalline bodies give circular, and what elliptical polarization? Illustrate this from quartz and nitre.

75. The *chemical power of* the sun's rays is seen in the blackening of chlorid of silver, which Scheele long ago observed to take place much more rapidly in the violet ray than in any other part of the solar spectrum. It was afterward observed by Ritter that this blackening likewise occurred beyond the violet ray, apparently in the dark.

The researches of Neipce, Daguerre, and others, have greatly enlarged the boundaries of our knowledge on this subject, and given to the world the elegant arts of the daguerreotype and photography. The darkening of metallic salts by light is owing to a peculiar class of rays in the spectrum, called by Dr. Herschel the *chemical rays*, which are diffused indeed in all parts of the spectrum, but which are concentrated with more power beyond the violet. This influence has also been variously denominated actinism, energia, and tithonicity.

76. The accompanying diagram (fig. 75) will enable the student to comprehend this subject as at present understood. From A to B we have the solar spectrum, with the colors in the same order as already described. The chemical power is greatest at the violet, and the greatest heat at the red ray. At *b* another red ray is discovered, and at *a* is the lavender light. The luminous effects are shown by the curved line C, the maximum of light being found at the yellow ray. The point of greatest heat is at D, beyond the red ray, and it gradually declines to the violet end, where it is entirely wanting, the other limit of heat being at *c*. The chemical powers are greatest about E, in the limits of the violet, and gradually extend to *d*, where they are lost. They disappear also

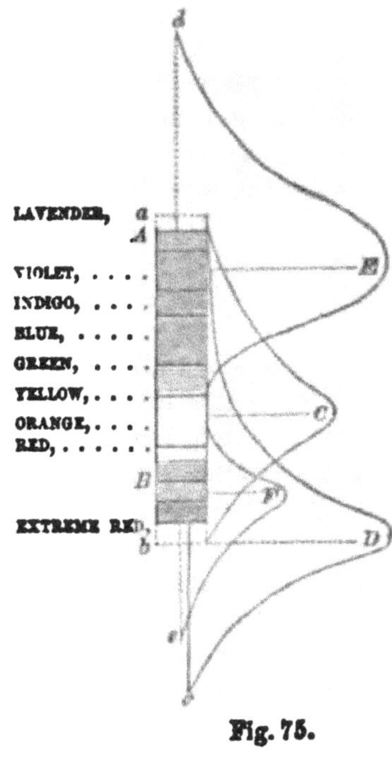

Fig. 75.

75. What is the chemical power of the sunbeam? 76. Illustrate the relations of the chemical and other rays, from fig. 75.

entirely at C; the yellow ray, which is neutral in this respect, attains another point of considerable power at F, in the red ray, which gives its own color to photographic pictures, and disappears entirely at *e*. The points D, C, E, therefore represent respectively the three distinct phenomena of Heat, Light, and Chemical Power. This last is believed to be quite independent of the other powers; for all light may be removed from the spectrum by passing it through blue solutions, and yet the chemical power remains unaltered.

77. It will readily be perceived that these phenomena connected with the sunbeam exert no inconsiderable or unimportant influence in the order of events, whether as connected with the development of life on our planet, or with those great physical changes which depend on the calorific and magnetic agencies that seem inseparably connected with the light and heat of the sun. Plants can decompose carbonic acid and carry on the functions of nutrition only under the power of solar light; and the yellow ray has been shown by Dr. Draper to be the one by whose agency this change is effected in the vegetable kingdom.

78. *Phosphorescence* is a property possessed by some bodies of emitting a feeble light, often at ordinary temperatures. The diamond and some other substances, after being exposed to the rays of the sun, will emit light for some time in the dark. Fluor-spar, feld-spar, and some other minerals, give out a fine light of varied hues, when gently heated or scratched. Oyster-shells which have been calcined with sulphur and exposed to the sunlight, will shine in a dark place for a considerable time afterward, and even an electrical spark will renew this emanation. The glow-worm, the firefly, rotten wood, decaying fish, and various marine animals possess the same power, although in these cases the cause is probably different from that which excites the same phenomenon in crystallized bodies.

---

77. What consequences follow the phenomena described? 78. What is phosphorescence?

III. HEAT.

Sources and Properties of Heat.

79. THE phenomena of Heat, or Caloric, are eminently interesting to the chemical student. They may be discussed under two general divisions: 1. The Physical; and, 2. The Chemical. Under the first head are included the communication of heat, by radiation, by conduction, and convection; the transmission of heat by various substances, and the phenomena of expansion, including thermometers and pyrometers; and lastly, specific heat. Under the second head are placed the changes produced by heat in the states of bodies; for example, liquefaction and latent heat of liquids, vaporization and latent heat of vapors, liquefaction of gases, natural evaporation and congelation, density of vapors, and so forth.

80. The *sources of heat* are chiefly the sun, combustion, and chemical changes; friction, electricity, vitality; and, lastly, terrestrial radiation.

Solar heat, as is well known, accompanies the sun's light, and it unquestionably results from the intensely high temperature of the sun itself. It is believed that the sun's rays do not heat the regions of space, and the earth's atmosphere is heated almost entirely by contact with the surface of the heated earth. A portion of the sun's heat is however taken up by the air before the rays reach the earth.

Combustion and chemical change, including vital heat, are sources of heat, limited by the quantity of matter suffering change, and to the time in which the change takes place. The stores of fossil fuel laid up in the coal formations and the vegetable combustibles now on the earth's surface may be considered as a result of the sun's action through the powers of vegetable life.

Friction causes heat, as a result of mechanical motion. The heat of friction continues as long as the mechanical power required to produce motion is maintained. No change of state or loss of weight is necessarily experienced

---

79. What is said of heat? How is the subject discussed? 80. What are the sources of heat? What of solar heat? What of combustion? What of friction?

in the substances employed. Count Rumford showed that in the boring of cannon under water, the heat evolved was so considerable as to bring the water, in a short time, to the boiling point. The same observer succeeded in warming a large building by the heat evolved from the constant movement of large plates of cast-iron upon each other. Friction-heat may be regarded as the equivalent of the motion producing it. The heat of the electrical spark and of the galvanic current will be considered elsewhere.

81. *Terrestrial radiation* is a constant source of heat, escaping from the interior of the earth, and has doubtless some effect in modifying the climate of our globe. Geologists consider it proved that the earth has cooled to its present condition from a state of intense ignition, and that this state still remains in the interior, at no very considerable distance from the surface. All deep mines and Artesian wells show a constant and progressive increase of temperature in going down, and below the line of atmospheric influence. The Artesian well in the yard of the great Grenelle slaughter-house, in Paris, is 2000 feet deep, and the water rises with a temperature of 85° degrees Fahrenheit. At Neusalzwerke, in Westphalia, is a well 2200 feet deep, and its water has a temperature of 91°. The average increase of temperature from this cause is estimated to be 1°8, for every hundred feet of descent. Assuming this ratio, we shall have at two miles the boiling-point of water; and at about twenty-three miles, or only $\frac{1}{180}$th of the earth's radius, there must be a temperature of near 2200 degrees of Fahrenheit. At this heat, cast-iron melts, and trap, basalt, obsidian, and other rocks are perfectly fluid. The geological importance of these facts is self-evident; and we cannot fail to remark here an efficient cause for all hot-springs.

82. *Properties of Heat.*—Heat is invisible and imponderable. It proceeds, like light, in rays, with great but hitherto undetermined velocity. The intensity of heat-rays varies inversely as the square of the distance from the source of heat. Rays of heat, like those of light, may be concentrated from a metallic mirror, but not from those of glass, as this substance absorbs heat very largely. They are

---

81. What is said of terrestrial radiation? What is determined in deep wells? What is the rate of increase? At what depth would iron melt? 82. What are the properties of heat? How is it like light?

also of various refrangibility, and capable of double refraction and polarization. Therefore, they move in waves or undulations. Heat is self-repellant, as two bodies heated in vacuo repel each other. It is communicated by conduction and by convection as well as by radiation. It is variously absorbed and transmitted by various substances, and produces different degrees of expansion, varying with the nature of matter affected. Lastly, it determines the phenomena of congelation, liquefaction, and vaporization. The physiological sensation of cold and heat experienced in our persons is not to be confounded with the physical and chemical phenomena of heat now to be discussed. This sensation is, within certain limits, entirely relative. For example, if one hand is plunged in a vessel of iced-water and the other into moderately warm water, a strong contrast is evident immediately; but if we suddenly transfer both hands to a third vessel of water, at the common temperature, our sensations are instantly reversed. The third vessel is warm as compared with ice-water, and cold compared with the tepid water.

Communication of Heat.

83. Heat is communicated from a hot body, 1. By radiation, or transmission of rays of heat in all directions; 2. By contact of the atmosphere conveying it away, (convection;) and, 3. By communication to the substance supporting it, (conduction.) By one or all these modes, a body placed in vacuo or in the air, and differing in temperature from surrounding bodies, gradually regains the equilibrium of temperature. If hot, it loses, and surrounding bodies gain; if cold, it gains at the expense of those substances having a higher temperature.

84. *Radiation* takes place from all bodies wherever there is a disturbance of equilibrium, but in very various degrees, according to the nature of the body and of its surface. All bodies have a specific radiating and absorbing power in respect to heat. To these the retaining and reflecting powers are strictly opposed. Radiation takes place in a vacuum more easily than in air, and is, therefore, quite

---

What is said of the sense of heat and cold? Give an illustration. 83. How is heat communicated? 84. How does radiation happen?

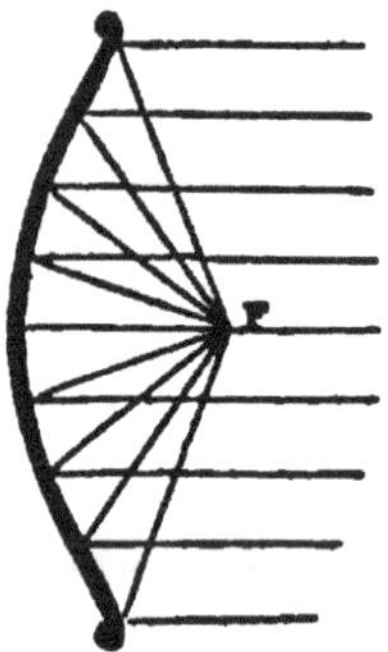

Fig. 76.

independent of any conducting medium. Rays of heat may be concentrated by the parabolic metallic mirror. All rays of heat or light falling on this form of mirror are collected at F, the focus, (fig. 76,) and a hot body placed there will have its rays sent forth in parallel straight lines, as shown in the figure. A second and similar mirror may be so placed as to receive and collect in a focus all the rays proceeding from any body in the focus of the other, where they will become evident by their effect on the thermometer. If the hot body be a red-hot cannon-ball, and the mirrors are carefully adjusted, so as to be exactly opposite each other in the same line, the accumulation of heat in the focus of the second mirror is such as to inflame dry tinder, or gunpowder, even at many feet distance.

85. This striking experiment is shown by the conjugate mirrors, arranged as in fig. 77. Ice placed in the focus of one of the mirrors will depress a thermometer in the other focus,—not because cold is radiated, (as cold is a mere negation,) but because in this case the thermometer is the hot body and parts with its heat to fuse the ice. A thermometer suspended midway between the two mirrors is not affected. A plate of glass held between the mirrors will cut off the calorific rays—thus proving a difference of penetrating power between the rays of heat and of those of light. As soon as the screen is raised the phosphorus in the focus is inflamed.

Fig. 77.

86. *Radiation and Absorption* of heat are exactly equal to each other in a given surface, but, as before stated, the nature of the substance and of the surface have much influence in these respects. All black and dull surfaces absorb heat very rapidly when exposed to its action, and part

---

How does a metallic mirror affect heat? 85. Describe the experiment in fig. 77. 86. What of absorption? How does color affect it?

with it again by secondary radiation. The sun shining on a person dressed in black is felt with much more power than if he were dressed in white. The former color rapidly absorbs heat, while from the latter a considerable part of it is reflected. The color of bodies has, however, nothing to do with their radiating powers, and one colored cloth is as warm in winter as another, as regards the emission of heat. (Bache.)

If the radiating power of a surface covered with lamp-black be assumed as 100, that of a surface covered with Indian ink will be 88, with ice 85, with graphite 75, with dull lead 45, with polished lead 19, with polished iron 15, with polished tin, copper, silver, or gold, 12. (Leslie.) Hence the polished metallic vessel, which is so well adapted to retain the heat of boiling water, is the very worst vessel in which to attempt to boil it. The sooty surface next the fire, however, transmits heat with the greatest rapidity. In the experiment with the mirrors just described, the polished surfaces remain cool, reflecting nearly all the heat which falls upon them. A glass mirror in the same experiment would be useless, as glass absorbs nearly all the heat, of low intensity, which falls upon it.

87. The *formation of dew* is owing to radiation, cooling the surface of the earth so rapidly, that the moisture of the air, which is always abundant in summer, is condensed upon it: as we see it on the outside of a tumbler of iced-water in a hot day. Radiation takes place more rapidly from the surface of grass and vegetation than from dry stones or dusty roads: for this reason, plants receive abundant dew, while the barren sand has none.

88. *Conduction of heat.*—A metallic bar placed by one end in the fire, slowly becomes hot, the heat being transmitted by *conduction* from particle to particle. Each solid has its own peculiar rate of conducting heat, but in all it is a progressive operation, the heat seeming to travel with greater or less rapidity, according to the nature of the solid. If we hold a pipe-stem or glass rod in the flame of a spirit-lamp or candle, we can heat it to redness within an inch of our fingers without inconvenience; but a wire of silver or copper held in the same manner soon be-

---

Give some results of radiation from different substances. 87. How is dew formed? 88. What is conduction? Why does it fall on plants?

comes too hot to hold. This is owing to an inherent difference in these solids, which we call conducting power. The progress of conducted heat in a solid is easily shown, as in fig. 78, representing a rod of copper, to which are stuck by wax several marbles at equal distances; one end is held over a lamp, and the marbles drop off, one by one, as the heat melts the wax; that nearest the lamp falling first, and so on. If the rod is of copper, they all fall off very soon; but if a rod of lead or platinum is used, the heat is conveyed much more slowly.

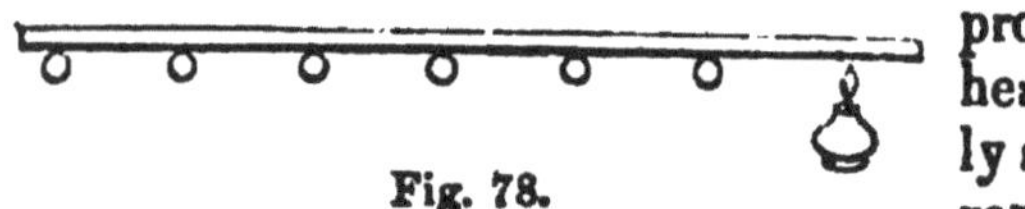

Fig. 78.

Little cones of various metals and other substances may be tipped with wax or bits of phosphorus, as shown in fig. 79, and placed on a hot surface. The wax will melt, or the phosphorus inflame, at different times, according to the conducting power of the various solids. A screen is needed to cut off the radiant heat, which would otherwise inflame the phosphorus prematurely. Accurate experiments have been made, which have enabled us to arrange most solids in a table showing their conducting powers. The metals, as a class, are good conductors, while wood, charcoal, fire-clay, and similar bodies are bad ones. Thus gold is the best conductor, and may be represented by the number 1000; then marble will be 23·5, porcelain 12, and fire-clay 11. Metals, compared with each other, are very different in conducting power. Thus—

Fig. 79.

Gold	1000	Iron	375
Silver	973	Zinc	363
Copper	898	Tin	304
Platinum	381	Lead	180

89. *Vibrations* occur in masses of metals and other substances when conducting heat, which seem to indicate the production of waves or undulations among the particles. Mr. Trevellyan has remarked that if a mass of warm brass is placed on a support of cold lead, the rounded surface of

What is its rate in different substances? 89. How is an undulation proved to exist in heated bodies? Mention Trevellyan and Page's experiments.

the brass resting on the flat surface of the lead, the brass bar is thrown into a series of vibrations, accompanied by a distinct sound and a rocking motion of the brass, until equilibrium is restored. Dr. Page has shown that a current of galvanic electricity passed through a similar apparatus produces the same results. Fig. 80 shows Page's apparatus, in which a feeble current of electricity produces a rocking motion of the metallic masses resting on the bars of brass. The best effects are produced between good and bad conductors of heat, the former being the hot bodies.

Fig. 80.

90. Heat is conducted in crystallized bodies, in curves springing from the sources of heat. In plates of homogeneous substances these curves are circles; in those of a crystalline texture, belonging to the rhombohedral system, the curves are ellipses of very exact form, whose longer axes are in the direction of the major crystalline axis—proving the conducting power of such bodies to be greatest in that direction. The mode of experimenting in such cases is to cover the surface of the crystalline plate with wax, heat very gradually, and watch the lines of fusion on the surface.

91. The *sense of touch* gives us a good idea of the different conducting power of various solids. All the articles in an apartment have nearly the same temperature; but if we lay our hand on a wooden table, the sensation is very different from that which we feel on touching the marble mantel or the metal door-knob. The carpet will give us still a different sensation. The marble feels cold, because it rapidly conducts away the heat from the hand; while the carpet, being a very bad conductor, retains and accumulates the heat, and thus feels warm. Clothing is not itself warm, but, being a bad conductor, retains the heat of the body. A film of confined air, is one of the worst conductors; loose clothes are therefore warmer than those which fit closely. For the same reason, porous bodies, like charcoal, are bad conductors; and a wooden handle enables us to manage hot bodies with ease.

92. The *conducting power of fluids* is very small. A

---

90. How is heat conducted in crystals? 91. What does touch inform us of? 92. What of the conducting power of fluids?

simple and instructive experiment will prove this satisfactorily. A glass, like that in fig. 81, is filled nearly to the brim with water. A thermometer-tube, with a large ball, is so arranged within it that the ball is just covered with the water: the stem passes out at the bottom through a tight cork, and has a little colored fluid, L, in it, which will, of course, move with any change of bulk in the air contained in the ball.

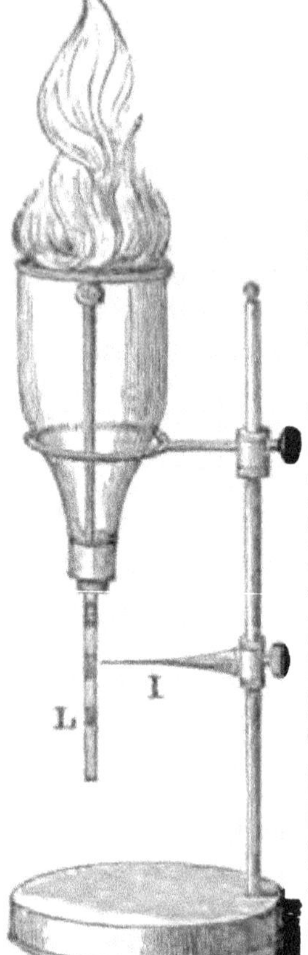

Fig. 81.

Thus arranged, a pointer I marks exactly the position of one of the drops of enclosed fluid, when a little ether is poured on the surface of the water, and set on fire. The flame is intensely hot, and rests on the surface of the water; the column of fluid at I is, however, unmoved, which would not be the case if any sensible quantity of heat had been imparted to the water. The warmth of the hand touching the ball will at once move the fluid at I, by expanding the air within. By heating a vessel of water on the top, then, we should never succeed in creating any thing more than a superficial elevation of temperature: at a small depth the water would remain cold. Liquids do possess a very low conducting power, contrary to the opinion of Count Rumford, and heat appears to be propagated in them by the same law as in solids, when care is taken to avoid the production of currents.

93. The *conducting power of gases* is also very small. Heat travels with extreme slowness through a confined portion of air. This is a very different thing from the convection of heat in gases, which we will presently explain. Double windows and doors, and furring (so called) of plastered walls, afford excellent illustrations of the slow conduction of heat through confined air. We have no proof that heat can be conducted in any degree by gases and va-

---

Explain the experiment, fig. 81. What of the conducting power of gases?

pors. To illustrate the relative conducting powers of solids, fluids, and gases: if we touch a rod of metal heated to 120°, we shall be severely burned; *water* at 150° will not scald, if we keep the hand still, and the heat is gradually raised; while *air* at 300° has been often endured without injury. The oven-girls of Germany, clad in thick socks of woollen, to protect the feet, enter ovens without inconvenience where all kinds of culinary operations are going on, at a temperature above 300°; although the touch of any metallic article while there would severely burn them.

94. *Convection of heat* is its transportation, as in liquids and gases, by the power of currents. Heat applied from beneath to a vessel containing water, warms the layer or film of particles in contact with the vessel. These expand with the heat, and consequently, becoming lighter, rise, and colder particles supply their place, which also rise in turn, and so the whole contents of the vessel come in quick succession into contact with the source of heat, and convey it through the mass. This is well illustrated in fig. 82, which shows how water acts in a vessel of glass, when heated at a point beneath by a spirit-lamp. Each particle in turn comes under the influence of heat, because of the perfect mobility of the fluid. A series of such currents exists in every vessel in which water is boiled, and they are rendered more evident by throwing into it a few grains of some solid (like amber) so nearly of the same gravity of water that it will rise and fall with the currents.

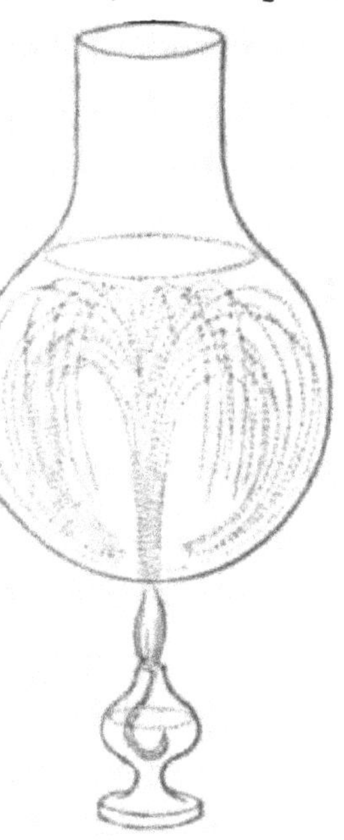

Fig. 82.

95. *In the air*, and in all gases and vapors, the same thing happens. The earth is heated by the sun's rays, and the film of air resting on the heated surface rises, to be replaced by cold air. The rarefied air may be easily seen, on a hot day, rising from the surface of the earth, being made

---

94. What is convection? Illustrate it in water. 95. How is heat distributed in air.

visible by its different refractive power. Hence arise many aerial currents and winds. The currents of the ocean are also influenced by the same cause.

Transmission of Heat.

96. *Light* passes through all transparent bodies alike, from what source soever it may come. The rays of heat from the *sun* also, like the rays of light from the same luminary, pass through transparent substances with little change or loss. Radiant heat, however, from terrestrial sources, whether luminous or not, is in a great measure arrested by many transparent substances. If the sun's rays be concentrated by a metallic mirror, the heat accompanying them is so intense at the focus as to fuse copper and silver with ease. A pane of colorless window-glass interposed between the mirror and the focus, will not stop any considerable part of the heat. If the same mirror is presented to any other source of heat, however, (as, for example, to the red-hot ball, 85,) the glass plate will stop nearly all the heat, although the light is undiminished. We thus distinguish two sorts of calorific rays, which are sometimes called Solar and Culinary Heat; and we discover that substances transparent to light are not, so to speak, transparent to heat in a like degree. This property is distinguished from transparency by the term *Diathermancy*, (meaning the easy transmission of heat.) It appears that many substances are eminently diathermous, which are almost opake to light; like smoky quartz, for example. The temperature of the source of heat has the greatest influence on the number of rays of heat which are transmitted by a given screen; as in the case of the glass plate, which permits nearly all the sun's rays to pass, but arrests over 65 per cent. of the rays from a lamp-flame.

97. Our knowledge on this subject has been derived almost entirely from the researches of M. Melloni, of Naples. This philosopher, by the use of a peculiar apparatus, called the thermo-electric pile, was able to detect differences of temperature altogether inappreciable by common thermometers. This instrument is an arrangement of little bars of the two metals,

---

96. Distinguish transmission of heat from that of light. What is diathermancy? What was Melloni's research?

Fig. 83.

antimony and bismuth, about fifty of which are soldered together by their alternate ends, the whole being, with its case, not more than 2½ inches long, by ½ to ¾ of an inch in diameter. The least difference of heat between the opposite ends of this little battery will produce an electrical current capable of influencing a magnetic needle in an instrument called a *galvanometer*, (§202.) The needle of the galvanometer will move in exact accordance to the intensity of the heat. This is so delicate an instrument, that the radiant heat of the hand held near the battery will cause the needle to move some 10° over its graduated circle. In fig. 84, *a* is the source of heat, (an oil-

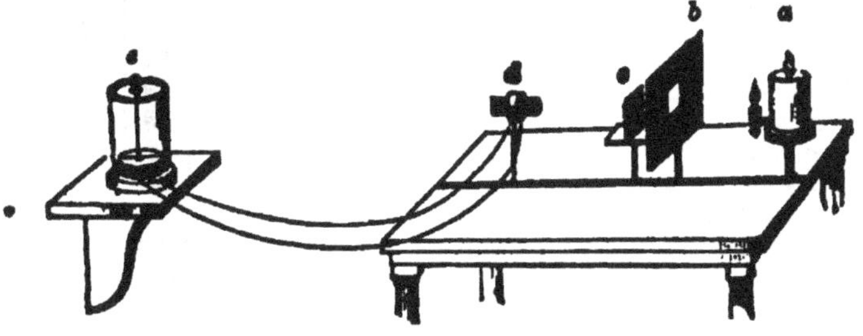

Fig. 84.

lamp in this case,) *b* a screen having a hole to admit the passage of a bundle of rays; *c* is the substance on which the heat is to fall; *d* the thermo-multiplier, or battery, which is to receive the rays after they have passed through the substance *c*. Two wires connect the opposite members of this battery with the galvanometer *e*, which, for steadiness, is placed on a bracket attached to the wall. Thus arranged, and with various delicate aids which we cannot here explain, a vast number of most instructive experiments have been made on radiant heat from different sources, and its effect ascertained on various substances. Four different sources of heat were employed: 1. The naked flame of an oil-lamp; 2. A coil of platinum wire heated to redness by an alcohol-lamp; 3. A surface of blackened copper heated to 734°; and, 4. The same heated to 212° by boiling water. The first two of these are luminous sources of heat, the last two non-luminous.

98. As already stated, the temperature of the source

---

97. What are Melloni's researches? Describe the arrangement in figs. 83 and 84.

greatly influences the number of rays transmitted. That which has passed through one plate of rock-salt has less liability to be arrested by a second, still less by a third, and so on.

The following table will show a few of the principal results:—

Names of interposed substances, common thickness, 0.102 inch.	Transmission of 100 rays of heat from			
	Oil-lamp.	Red-hot platinum.	Copper at 734°.	Copper at 212°.
Rock-salt, transparent and colorless..............	92	92	92	92
Iceland-spar..	36	28	6	0
Plate-glass	39	24	6	0
Rock-crystal..	38	28	6	0
Rock-crystal, brown....................................	37	28	6	0
Alum, transparent......................................	9	2	0	0
Sugar-candy..	8	0	0	0
Ice, pure and transparent............................	6	0	0	0

Thus it appears that rock-salt is the only substance which permits an equal amount of heat from all sources to pass. In other cases, the number of rays passing seem proportioned to the intensity of the source. M. Melloni has called rock-salt the *glass of heat*, as it permits heat to pass with the same ease that glass does light. It is supposed that the difference found by experiment in the diathermancy of bodies is owing to a peculiar relation which the various rays of heat sustain to these bodies, analogous to that difference in the rays of light which we call color. Thus all other bodies, except salt, act on heat as colored glasses act on light, entirely absorbing some of the colors, and allowing others to pass. In this view, rock-salt may be said to be colorless as respects heat, while alum and ice are in the same sense almost back. Opake bodies, like wood and metals, entirely prevent the transmission of heat; but dark-colored quartz crystal is seen, by the table, to differ only 1 from white crystal, and even perfectly black glass does not entirely stop all heat.

99. By cutting rock-salt into prisms and lenses, the heat from radiant bodies may be reflected, refracted, and concen-

---

98. What substance transmits heat most readily? Which least so? What is rock-salt called? 99. How is heat polarized, &c.?

trated, like light, and doubly refracting minerals, like Iceland-spar, will polarize it.

Expansion of Bodies by Heat.

100. ***All bodies expand*** with an increase of heat, and diminish with its loss. The expansion of a *solid* may be shown by a bar of metal which, as in the fig. 85, is provided with a handle, which at ordinary temperatures exactly fits the gauge. On heating this over a spirit-lamp, or by plunging it into hot water, it will be so much expanded in all its dimensions as no longer to enter the gauge. On cooling it with ice, it will again not only enter freely, but with room to spare. The same fact is shown by a ball, to which, when cold, a ring with a handle will exactly fit; but on heating the ball, the ring will no longer encircle it.

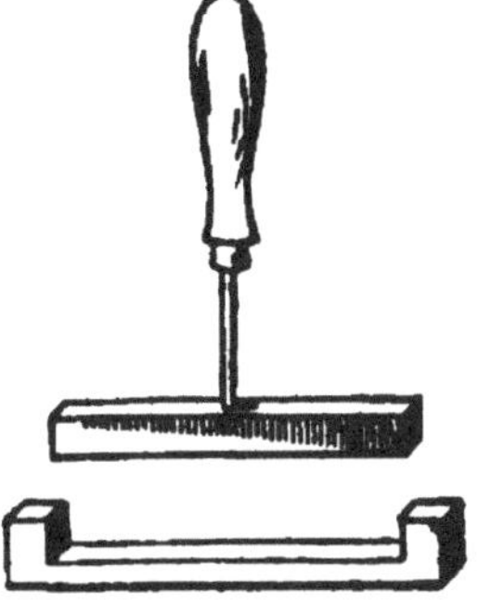

Fig. 85.

The expansion of a *fluid* may be shown by filling the bulb of a large tube (fig. 86) with coloured water to a mark on the stem. On plunging the bulb into hot water, the fluid is seen to rise rapidly in the stem. If it be cooled by a mixture of ice and water, it is seen to sink considerably below the line. A similar bulb (fig. 87) filled with *air*, and having its lower end under water, is arranged as in the figure, to show the expansion of air by heat. The warmth of the hand applied to the naked ball will be sufficient to cause bubbles of air to escape from the open end through the water; and on removing the hand, the contraction of the air in the ball, from the cooling of the surface, will cause a rise of the fluid in the stem, corresponding to the volume of air expelled, as

Fig. 86.  Fig. 87.

---

100. What is expansion? Illustrate it for a solid. For a liquid. For a gas.

shown in the figure. The slightest change of temperature will cause this column of fluid to move, as the air expands or contracts. In fact, it is the old air-thermometer.

101. *Expansion of Solids.*—Expansion by heat varies greatly: 1. According to the nature of the substance; and, 2. Not in degree only, but also in the law which it follows. In solids, between the freezing and boiling of water, the rate of expansion *in the same* solid is equal for each additional degree. In experiments on this subject, rods of equal length are used, composed of the various subjects of experiment, whose expansion in length is accurately measured.

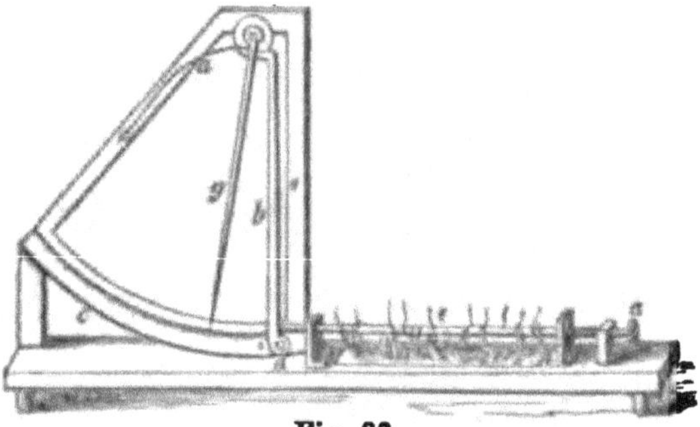

Fig. 88.

In fig. 88, the rod *t* is confined by *a*, so that its free end bears against *b*. Heated by an alcohol lamp, or other source of heat, it expands and carries forward the index *g* over the graduated arc *c*. On cooling, it contracts, and the spring *a* moves the index back again to the starting point. This linear expansion, multiplied by 3, gives the expansion in volume very nearly. Thus, for example, in the following solids, when heated from 32° to 212° Fahrenheit, the expansion is—

In Length.						In Bulk.			
339	parts of	zinc	=	340	or	112	parts	=	113
349	"	lead	=	350	"	116	"	=	117
523	"	silver	=	524	"	174	"	=	175
583	"	copper	=	584	"	194	"	=	195
643	"	gold	=	644	"	217	"	=	218
810	"	iron	=	811	"	270	"	=	271
921	"	antimony	=	922	"	307	"	=	308
1006	"	platinum	=	1007	"	335	"	=	336
1113	"	white glass	=	1114	"	371	"	=	372
2831	"	black marble	=	2832	"	943	"	=	944

102. The expansion of fluids is ether *apparent* or *absolute*, according as the dilatation of the containing vessel is or is not

101. What is the rate of expansion in solids? Describe fig. 88. Give examples from table, in length and bulk.

taken intc account. This fact may be illustrated in the annexed apparatus, (fig. 89,) where a tube of glass is bent twice at right angles, the open ends *a* and *b* uppermost; a larger tube surrounds each, leaving two cells, in which water of different temperatures may be poured. The inner tube is filled, for example, with colored water, of the ordinary temperature, to the level P; hot water is now poured into the outer cell of *b*, when an immediate elevation of level in the colored fluid is seen to *m*. This is on the principle that the heights of columns of liquids in equilibrium are inverse to their densities. In this manner it has been determined that in heating from 33° to 212°, 9 measures of alcohol becomes 10; of water, 23 measures becomes 24; and of mercury, 55 measures becomes 56. Thus it happens that in the common changes of the seasons the bulk of spirits varies about 5 per centum. It has been determined, also, that liquids are progressively more expansible at higher than at lower temperatures. The liquefied gases illustrate this law in a remarkable manner, for fluid carbonic acid, as observed by M. Thilorier, has a dilatation four times greater than is observed in common air at the same temperatures. The law of expansion in liquids is not yet well made out.

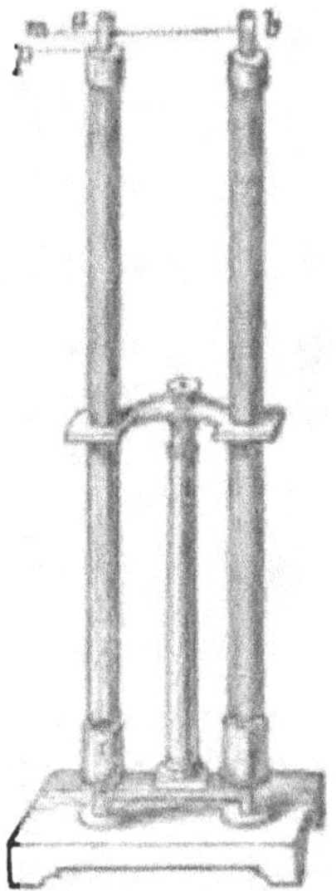

Fig. 89.

103. *Unequal Expansion of Water.*—The general law of expansion for nearly all solids and fluids, especially within the limits of the freezing and boiling points of water, is, that each solid or fluid expands, or contracts, an equal amount for every like increase, and reduction of, temperature, each body having its own rate of dilatation. There are, however, some exceptions to this law, of which water offers a remarkable example. As the comfort, and even habitability of our globe, are in a great degree dependent on this exception to the ordinary laws of nature, it is worthy of special notice.

If we fill a large thermometer-tube or bulbed glass (fig. 90) with water, and place it in a freezing mixture, where we

---

102. Describe the apparatus fig. 89. What is the expansion of water? Of alcohol? 103. What inequality in the expansion of water?

Fig. 90.

can observe the fall of the temperature by the thermometer, we shall see the column descend regularly with the temperature, until it reaches 39·°1 F., when the contrary effect will take place: the water then begins suddenly to rise in the tube, by a regular expansion, until the temperature falls to 32°, when so sudden a dilatation takes place as to throw the water in a jet from the open orifice. If, on the other hand, we heat water in such an apparatus, commencing at 32°, we shall find that, until the temperature rises to 40°, the fluid, in place of expanding as we might expect, will actually contract. Water has, therefore, its greatest density at 39°·5, and its density is the same for equal temperatures above and below this point; thus we shall find it having a similar density at 34° and 45°.

104. *Beneficial Results.*—Let us now observe what useful end this curious irregularity in the expansion of water subserves. When winter approaches, the lakes and rivers, by the contact of the cold air, begin to lose their heat on the surface; the colder water, being more dense, falls to the bottom, and its place is supplied by warmer water rising from below. A system of circulation is thus set in motion, and its tendency, if the mass of water is not too large, is to reduce the whole gradually to the same temperature throughout. When, however, the water has cooled to 39°·5, this circulation is arrested by the operation of the law just explained: below this point the water no longer contracts by cooling, and of course does not sink; but on the contrary expanding, as before explained, it becomes relatively lighter, and remains on the surface: the temperature of this layer or upper stratum gradually falls, until the freezing point is reached, and a film of ice is formed. But as ice is a very bad conductor, the heat now escapes with extreme slowness; all currents tending to convey away the cooler parts of the water are arrested, and the thickness of the ice can increase only by the slow conduction through the film already formed: the consequence is, that our most severe winters fail to make ice of any great thickness. Other causes, also, which we shall

---

What is its maximum density? 104. What beneficial result follows? Why is freezing a slow process? Describe the mode of freezing of lakes and rivers.

presently explain, co-operate at all times to render the freezing of water a very slow process. We cannot fail to be impressed by the wisdom of that Power, which not only frames great general laws for the government of matter, but also makes exceptions to them, when the welfare of His creatures requires them.

105. *The expansion of all gases* and vapours is the same for an equal degree of heat, and equal increments of heat produce equal amounts of expansion. The rate of expansion amounts to $\frac{1}{490}$th part of the volume of the gas at 0° for each degree of Fahrenheit's scale, or between 32° and 212° to 0·366, or more than $\frac{1}{3}$ of the initial volume of the gas.

When gases are near the point of compression at which they become liquid, this law becomes irregular, and is not *strictly* true for all gases; but the departures from the law are so small that we need not mention them here.

106. *Practical application* of the laws of expansion in solids are frequently made with great advantage in the arts. The rivets which hold together the plates of iron in steam-boilers are put in and secured while red-hot, and on cooling draw together the opposite edges of the plates with great power. The wheelwright secures the parts of a carriage-wheel by a red-hot tire, or belt of iron, which being quickly quenched, before it chars the wood, binds the whole fabric together with wonderful firmness. The walls of the Conservatory of Arts, in Paris, after they had bulged badly, were safely drawn into a vertical position, by the alternate contraction and expansion of large rods of iron passed across it, and so secured by screw-nuts and heated by Argand lamps as to draw the walls inward. Towers of churches and other buildings have been thrown down or otherwise injured by the expansion of large iron rods (anchors) built into the masonry with the design of strengthening them. The Bunker Hill monument is daily bent out of a perfect vertical by the heat of the sun expanding the granite of which it is built. The mechanical arts are, in fact, full of beautiful applications of the principles of expansion. Among these we may mention

107. The *Compensation Pendulum*, adapted to regulating the rate of time-pieces. The length of the pendulum is

---

105. What is the law of expansion in gases? How much does air dilate for each degree? 106. Mention some instances of expansion in the arts.

altered by variations of temperature, and of course the rate of the clock is disturbed. A perfect compensation for this error is obtained by the use of a compound pendulum of brass and iron, or other two metals, arranged as is shown in fig. 92, in such a manner that the expansion of one metal downward will exactly counteract that of the other metal upward; thus keeping the ball of the pendulum at a uniform distance from the point of suspension. The shaded bars represent the iron, and the light ones the brass. The same object is accomplished by using mercury, as shown in fig. 91, contained in a glass or steel vessel at the end of the pendulum-rod. The expansion which lengthens the rod also increases the volume of the mercury; this increase of bulk in the mercury raises the centre of gravity to an exactly compensating amount, and the clock remains unaltered in rate. Watches and chronometers are regulated by a like beautiful contrivance. The balance-wheel, (fig. 93,) on whose uniform motion the regularity of the watch or chronometer depends, is liable to a change of dimensions from heat or cold. If made smaller, it will move faster, and if larger, slower. To avoid this error, the outside of the wheel is made of brass, the inside of steel, and cut at two opposite points; one end of each part is screwed to the arm, and the loose ends of the rim, being united by a screw, are drawn in or thrown out by the changes of temperature, in precise proportion to the amount of change; thus perfectly adapting the revolution of the wheel to the force of the spring. The principle of this wheel, it will be seen, is the same as in the compound bars, (107.) A pendulum of pine-wood is sometimes employed for clocks, because it is so little changed by variations of temperature.

Fig. 91. 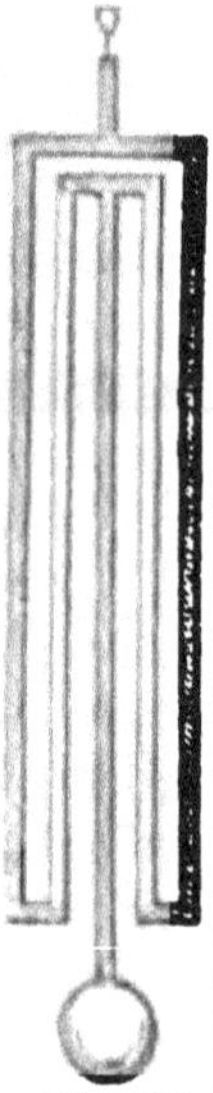 Fig. 92.

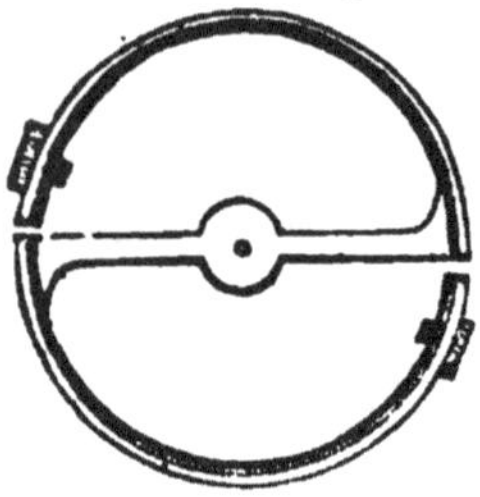

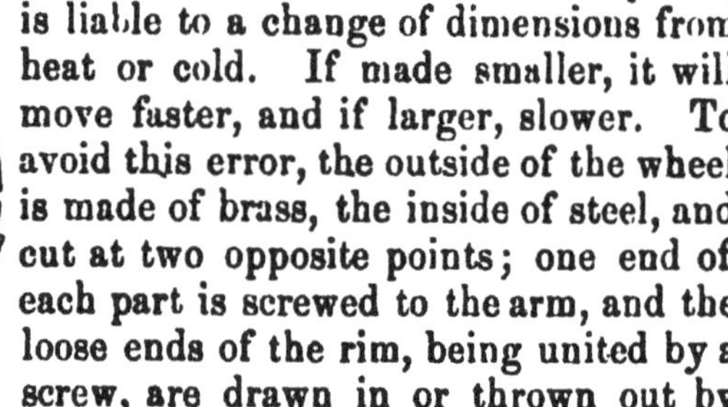

Fig. 93.

108. The *unequal expansion of solids* is well shown by

---

107. What is the compensation pendulum? What the mercurial? What is the compensation balance?

joining firmly, by rivets, two bars, one of iron and one of brass, as in fig. 94. When they are heated, the brass expanding most, will cause the compound bar to bend, as shown in the fig. 95. If they are cooled by ice, the brass contracting most, will bend the united metals in an opposite direction.

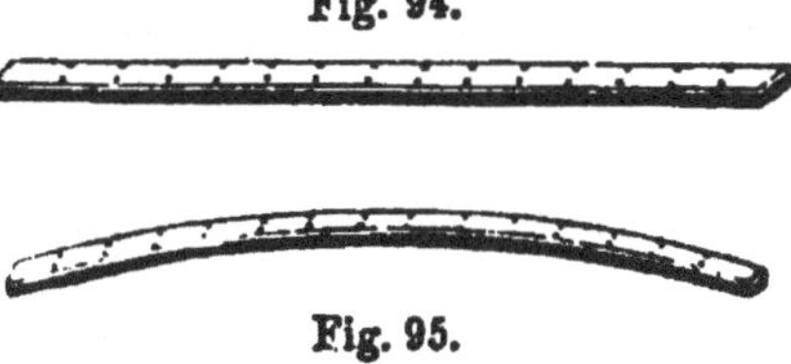

Fig. 94.

Fig. 95.

The Thermometer.

109. The *Thermometer* is an instrument for measuring heat by the expansion of various liquids and solids. This instrument was invented by Sanctorio, an Italian, in A. D. 1590. His was an air-thermometer, such as is figured in the context. A bulb of glass with a long stem is placed with its mouth downward, in a vessel containing a portion of colored water, (fig. 96.) A part of the air being first expelled from the ball by expansion, the fluid rises to a convenient point in the stem, to which is attached a scale of equal parts, with degrees or divisions marked by some arbitrary rule. Thus arranged, the instrument indicates with great delicacy any limited change of temperature in the surrounding air. The portion of air confined in the ball, when heated, expands, and pressing on the column of fluid in the stem, drives it down, according to the amount of expansion or the degree of heat; and the reverse results from a decrease of temperature. The air thermometer has given place to

Fig. 96.

110. *The Common Thermometer.*—This instrument indicates changes of temperature by the expansion of mercury or of alcohol contained in the bulb blown upon the end of a very fine glass tube. Mercury possesses very remarkable properties fitting it for a thermometric fluid: it may easily be obtained pure; its rate of expansion is singularly uniform between its boiling and freezing points, and the range of temperature between these points is greater than in any other fluid, (about 660° Fahr.) For very low temperatures alcohol is preferred, as it has never yet been solidified, even with the intensest

108. Describe figs. 94 and 95. 109. What is the thermometer? Describe Sanctorio's thermometer. 110. Describe the common thermometer.

artificial cold of the carbonic acid bath (§151,) or of the arctic regions. The precautions needed to make a thermometer, such as will meet the demands of modern science, are too numerous to be fully described here. Suffice it to say, that by expanding the air in the empty ball, while the open end of the tube is covered with mercury, a portion of it is carried in by the pressure of the atmosphere, and by boiling this, all air is expelled and the tube entirely filled with mercury. The quantity is so adjusted by trial that it will stand at a convenient height in the tube. Finally, the tube is sealed by the lamp, while the contained mercury is expanded to completely fill it. The empty space in a good thermometer is therefore a torricellian vacuum.

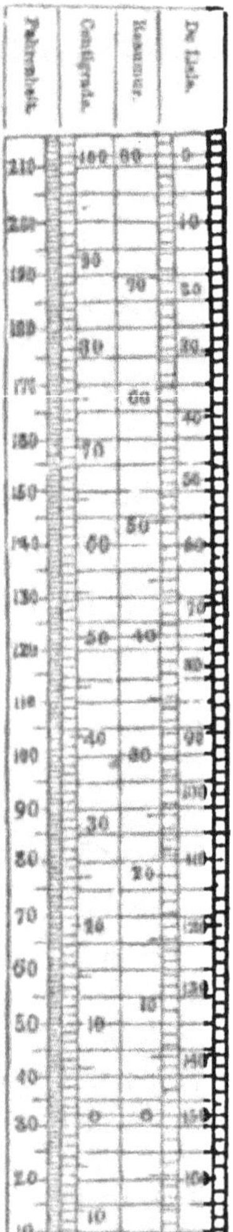

Fig. 97.

111. *Graduation of Thermometers.*—The scales adapted to the thermometer in various countries are divided into arbitrary degrees, and, unfortunately for science, the scales differ widely. There are, however, two *fixed points* in all, which are determined by direct experiment. These are the boiling and freezing points of water, or, more accurately, the melting point of ice. The space between these two points is divided into a certain number of equal parts, according to the scale to be employed. In France, and on the continent of Europe generally, the scale of Celsius, or Centigrade, is employed, which divides this space into 100 degrees. In England and America the scale of Fahrenheit, a Hollander, is adopted. This scale adopts for its zero point the cold produced by a freezing mixture of snow and salt; which its author assumed to be the greatest possible cold. The word *zero* signifies nothing, but we know that as cold is the mere absence of heat, it is hopeless to expect an absolute zero. The scale of Réaumur, adopting the melting of ice as zero, divides the space between that point and the boiling of water into 80 degrees. The

---

111. How are thermometers graduated? What are fixed points?

scale of De Lisle, which is no longer used, read downward from zero at boiling water to 150°, the freezing of the same. Annexed, in fig. 97, we have these four scales compared. It will be seen that zero Centigrade is zero Réaumur and 32° Fahrenheit; while 100° C. = 80° R. = 212° F. In other words, these three scales divide the space between the two fixed points respectively into 100° C., 80° R., and 180° F.; or, reducing to smallest terms, 5° C. = 4° R. = 9° F. To reduce Centigrade to Fahrenheit, we can multiply by 9 and divide by 5, and add 32° to the quotient, and *vice versa*. Suppose we wish to know what 70° C. is on Fahrenheit's scale; we have the proportion 5 : 9 : : 70° : 126°. If we add 32°, which is the difference between zero of F. and C., we have 126° + 32° = 158°, which is the number required, for 70° C. = 158° F. In stating thermometrical degrees, the sign + is used for points above zero, and — for those below. Fahrenheit's scale is the one employed in this work.

112. The *Self-Registering Thermometer* is a form of the instrument contrived for the purpose of ascertaining the extremes of variations which may occur, as, for instance, during the night. It consists of two horizontal thermometers attached to one frame, as in fig. 98; *b* is a mercurial thermometer, and measures the *maximum* temperature, by pushing forward, with the expansion of the column, a short piece of steel wire, of such size as to move easily in the bore of the tube; it is left by the mercury at the remotest point reached by the expansion; *a* is a spirit-of-wine thermometer, and measures the *minimum* temperature. It contains a short cylinder of porcelain, shown in the figure, which retires with the alcohol on the contraction of the column of fluid, but does not advance on its expansion.

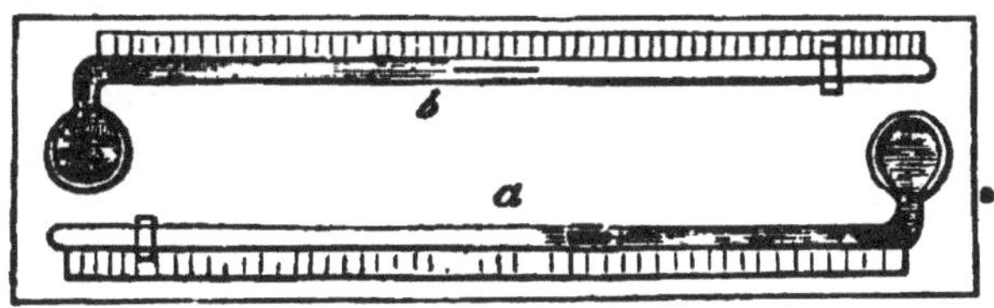

Fig. 98.

Name the three scales. What is boiling water in each? What freezing? Convert Centigrade 70° to Fahrenheit. 112. What is the self-registering thermometer?

113. The *Differential Thermometer* is a form of air-thermometer, so named because it denotes only differences of temperature. It consists of two bulbs on one tube, bent twice at right angles, and supported, as shown in fig. 99. A little sulphuric acid, water, or other fluid partly fills the stem only. When the bulbs of this instrument are heated or cooled alike, no change is seen in the position of the column; but the instant any inequality of temperature exists between them, as from the bringing the hand near one of them, the column of fluid moves rapidly over the scale. A modification of this instrument, of great delicacy, was contrived by Dr. Howard of Baltimore, in which sulphuric ether was the fluid used, the bulbs being vacuous of air.

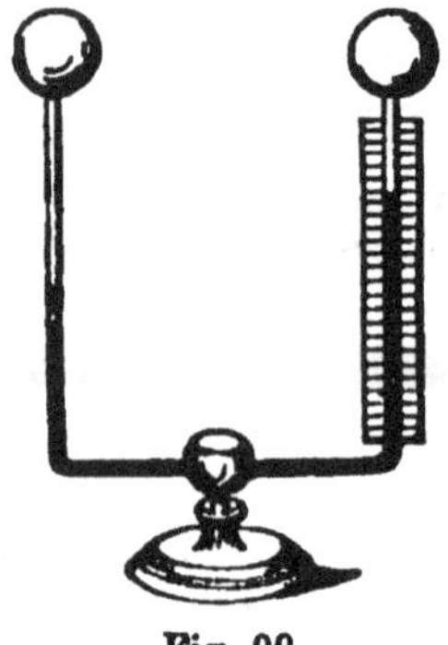
Fig. 99.

114. A *Pyrometer* is an instrument for measuring *high* temperatures. As mercury boils at about 660°, we can estimate the temperature of fused metals, and the like, only by the expansion of solids. The only instrument of this sort which we need mention, as it is the only one susceptible of accuracy, is Daniell's Register Pyrometer. It consists of a hollow case of black-lead, or plumbago, into which is dropped a bar of platinum, secured to its place by a strap of platinum and a wedge of porcelain. The whole is then heated, as, for instance, by placing it in a pot of molten silver, whose temperature we wish to ascertain. The metal bar expands much more than the case of black-lead, and being confined from moving in any but an upward direction, drives forward the arm of a lever, as shown in fig. 100, over a graduated arc, on which we read the degrees of Fahrenheit's scale: (this graduation has been determined beforehand with great care.) This instrument gives very accurate results; by it the melting point of cast iron

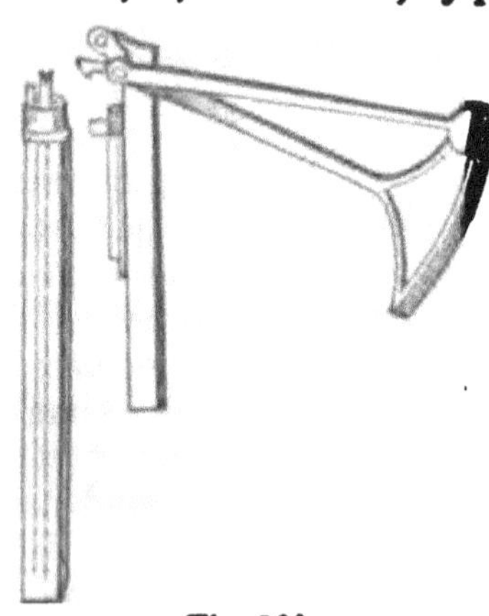
Fig. 100.

---

113. What the differential? 114. What are pyrometers? Describe Daniell's.

has been found to be 2786° F., and of silver 1860° F The highest heat of a good wind-furnace is probably not much above 3300°. Fig. 88 (101) is a pyrometer of ordinary construction.

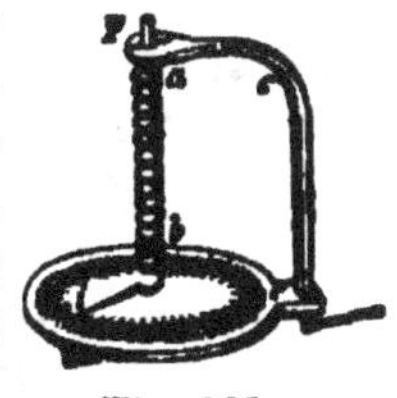
Fig. 101.

115. *Breguet's* thermometer is constructed upon the principle of the unequal expansion of metals, (107.) A compound piece of metal is formed by soldering together two equal masses of silver and platina—two metals whose expansion is very unequal. This is rolled thin and coiled into a spiral as shown in *a b*, (fig. 101.) It is suspended from a fixed point *p*, while its lower end is free and carries an index *i*. Variations of temperature cause this spiral to unwind or wind up, and these motions are indicated by the motion of the pointer. This is a more delicate thermometer than any mercurial or spirit one. A beautiful modification of Breguet's thermometer has been contrived by Mr. Saxton, to measure the temperature of the sea in deep soundings.

116. All thermometers for accurate research are divided on the glass stem by aid of a graduating engine and micrometer; each instrument being, according to the plan of Regnault, graduated by an arbitrary scale.

Capacity for Heat, or Specific Heat.

117. Different bodies have different capacities for heat. If equal measures of mercury and of water, for example, are exposed to the same source of heat, the mercury will reach a given temperature more than twice as soon as the water, and it will cool again in half the time. Mercury is said, therefore, to have only half the *capacity* for heat which water has. We learn by trial that each substance in like manner has its own relations to heat as respects capacity This is called also *specific* heat, a term synonymous with capacity. Water is adopted as the standard of comparison for this property, and the trial is usually made upon equal weights rather than upon equal measures of the substances compared. Specific heat connects itself curiously with the atomic constitution of matter. Several modes may be em-

115. What is the metallic thermometer? 116. How are thermometers accurately graduated? 117. What is capacity for heat? Give examples. What is specific heat?

ployed to determine it; as by mixture, by melting, by warming, or by cooling. The determination of this property is called *calorimetry*, and the modes of experiment most usual are either by mixture or by the fusion of ice.

118. *The Method of Mixtures.*—If a pint measure of water, at 150°, be mixed quickly with an equal measure of the same fluid at 50°, the two measures of fluid will have the temperature of 100°, or the arithmetical mean of the two temperatures before mixture. If, however, we rapidly mingle a measure of water at 150°, and an equal measure of mercury at 50, we shall find that they will have the temperature of 118°. The mercury has gained 68°, and the water lost about half as much, or only 32°. Hence we infer that the same quantity of heat can raise the temperature of mercury through twice as many degrees as that of water, and that the specific heat of water will be to that of mercury as 1 : 0·47, when compared by measure. But if we divide this number (0·47) by the density of mercury (13·5) we obtain the number 0.035, which expresses the specific heat by a comparison of weights. Water has then more than 30 times the capacity for heat which is found in mercury; and in this peculiarity we find an important reason of the singular fitness of this fluid metal for the construction of thermometers.

119. *By the melting of ice* in the calorimeter of Lavoisier, as in fig. 102, the capacity of most substances for heat has been determined. A set of metallic vessels *a b c* are so arranged that when a warm body is placed in *c*, all the heat it gives off in cooling will go to melt the lumps of ice surrounding it. The water of fusion escapes at the cock *s*, and is measured in the graduated glass beneath. To cut off the heat of the surrounding air, the space between *a* and *b* is also filled with ice. The water which melts from this portion is carried away by *r*. In this apparatus the relative capacities of all solid and fluid substances may, with proper precautions, be accurately

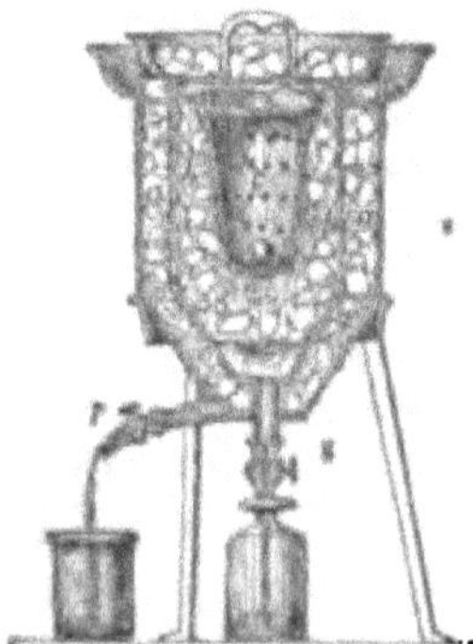

Fig. 102.

What is calorimetry? 118. Describe the method of mixtures. 119. What is Lavoisier's calorimeter?

determined by the respective measures of water which flow from *s* during the experiment, in which each body cools from an agreed temperature, (*e. g.* 212°) to 32°, the constant temperature of *c*. The same result may be reached in some cases more simply by employing a large lump of solid ice *a* (fig. 103) in which a well W has been scooped out, and covered by a lid of ice *b*. Any solid substance, or a fluid contained in a glass flask, may be placed in W, and, when the temperature has fallen to 32°, the water contained in W may be measured as before. To estimate the capacity of heat in gases, atmospheric air is chosen as unity—and the method of melting is adopted by passing a certain volume of gas through a tube refrigerated by ice.

Fig. 103.

120. It is plain, from what has been said, that the capacity of bodies for heat is a phenomenon not indicated by the thermometer. In the foregoing experiments, water and mercury have been each heated to 212°, and yet the result demonstrates that an equal weight of water contains at that temperature about 30 times as much heat as the mercury. The thermometer can indicate only actual intensity of heat, and not its volume or quantity.

In the following table of specific heats, it will be seen that this property has much connection with the physical condition of bodies as respects fluidity or crystalline arrangements, as is evident by comparing the capacity of water and ice, and of the various forms of carbon:—

Water	1000	Sulphur	177	Zinc	95
Ice	513	Sulphur lately fused	184	Brass	94
Turpentine	468	Ether	520	Silver	57
Carbon (charcoal)	241	Alcohol	660	Antimony	51
Anthracite (Pa.)	201	Mercury	33	Gold	32
Graphite	201	Iron	114	Lead	31
Diamond	146	Copper	95	Phosphorus	118
Steel	116			Glass	197

Changes produced by Heat in the State of Bodies.

121. *Fluidity* is a result of temperature, as is seen in the familiar case of water, which is either ice, water, or steam,

What simpler one is described? 120. What does the thermometer fail in indicating? Give examples from table. 121. What is fluidity?

according to the temperature to which it is subjected. Many solids can be melted by an increase of temperature, and the melting point is always the same for a given solid. Some substances pass at once to the fluid state, while others, as wax, assume an intermediate pasty condition, and others, like ice, fuse very slowly indeed. The degree of heat at which bodies melt varies exceedingly. Thus platinum is not melted at 3280°. Iron melts at about 2800°; gold, at 2016°; silver, 1873°; zinc, 773°; lead, 612°; tin, 442°; Newton's alloy, 212°; potassium, 136°; phosphorus, 108°; wax, 142°; tallow, 92°; olive oil, 36°; ice, 32°; milk, 30°; wines, 20°; mercury, —39°; fluid ammonia, —46°; ether, —47°; while pure alcohol is not solid at 175° below Fahrenheit's zero.

122. *Liquefaction* is attended by a remarkable absorption of heat. We have already seen that two equal measures of water at different temperatures assume when mingled the mean of their previous temperatures, (118.) If, however, we take a pound of ice at 32°, and a pound of water at 212°, we shall find, when the ice is melted, that the two pounds of water have the temperature of only 52°; the ice gains only 20°, while the water has lost 160°. There are, then, 140° of heat lost in producing this change. We can take another mode of trial. Let us expose a pound of ice and a pound of water, each at 32°, to a constant source of heat, in two vessels every way alike, and note the changes of temperature by the thermometer. The same quantity of heat is flowing into each vessel. When the ice is all melted, we shall find that the water into which it is converted has still only the temperature of 32°, while the other pound of water has risen from 32° to 172°: here again we see the loss of 140° of heat used in converting the ice into water. We may reverse the last experiment, and take equal weights of ice at 32° and water at 172° and mix them: when the ice is all melted the mixture will still have the temperature of only 32°; so that, in whatever way we may make the trial, we constantly observe the loss of 140° of heat. This is called the *heat of fluidity*, it being necessary to the existence of the water in a fluid state; and it is also designated *latent heat*, because it is lost, absorbed, or con-

---

Name the fluidity-points of several bodies. 122. What phenomenon attends liquefaction? Give an example. How is this reversed? What is latent heat?

cealed, as it were, and no indication of it can be found by the thermometer.

123. This law is equally illustrated by the slow freezing of water. If a vessel filled with water at 52° be placed in an atmosphere of 32°, it will rapidly cool down to 32° by the loss of 20° of temperature. After this, it will, as may be seen by the thermometer, remain at 32°, until it is all converted to solid ice; although we cannot doubt that it is all the while giving out a quantity of heat, which had before been insensible or latent. If the water had been ten minutes in cooling from 52° to 32°, (or in losing 20°,) then it would require one hour and ten minutes, or seven times as long, for it to become completely frozen. If, then, in equal times it lost equal degrees of heat, its latent heat will be $20° \times 7 = 140°$, which is the same result as before.

Thus we arrive at the seeming paradox that freezing is a warming process. By experiment we may show that water may be cooled some 8 or 9 degrees below its freezing point and still remain liquid, if its surface be covered with a thin film of oil, or if it is a thin smooth vessel, kept quite still; but the least disturbance will cause it, when in this situation, to become solid at once, and the temperature will immediately rise from 23° or 24° to 32°. The freezing of a part has therefore given out heat enough to raise the temperature of the whole from 24° to 32°, or through 8°. Our domestic experience in cold climates often supplies examples of this fact. The solidification of a saturated solution of sulphate of soda is also an example of the same nature; the vessel containing the solution becomes sensibly warm. In like manner, it is true that melting is a cooling process. A solid can melt only by absorbing heat from surrounding bodies, which must, of course, become cooler. Hence, in part, the cooling influence of an iceberg, which is often felt for many leagues, or of a large body of snow on a distant mountain; and the chill felt in the air on a bright day in spring, when snow is rapidly melting on the ground.

It is a wise order of nature that makes the freezing and thawing of snow and ice extremely slow and gradual pro-

---

123. Illustrate it by the freezing of water. How may water remain liquid below 32°? How is freezing a warming process? What proof of design is here indicated?

cesses. If water became solid at once on reaching 32°, it would be suddenly frozen to a great depth; and if ice melted as quickly on reaching the same temperature, the most sudden and dreadful floods would accompany these events, and the common changes of the seasons would be calamitous to human comfort and life.

124. *Freezing mixtures* owe their powers to the principles just explained. Ice-cream is frozen by a mixture of snow or pounded ice with common salt. In this case, the two solids are rapidly changed to fluids; the ice is melted by the salt, and the salt is dissolved by the water from the melting ice. Both these operations absorb a large quantity of heat. The surrounding bodies are called on to supply the heat required, and the cream in a thin metallic vessel cools so rapidly as to be soon turned to ice. The thermometer will fall in this operation to 0° F.; and this was the very experiment by which Fahrenheit (111) assumed that he had attained to a true zero of cold.

Nitrate of ammonia dissolved in water at 46° will sink the temperature to zero, and the exterior of the vessel becomes at once thickly covered with hoar-frost. Common saltpetre, (nitrate of potassa,) dissolved in water, lowers its temperature about 15° or 18°, and is therefore much used in the hot regions of Asia, where it abounds, for cooling wine. Mercury may be frozen by using a mixture of three parts of chlorid of calcium and two of dry snow; this mixture will sink the temperature from +32° to —50°. Five parts of finely-powdered sal ammoniac and five of nitre, dissolved in nineteen of water, will reduce the temperature from 50° to 10°; and a little powdered sulphate of soda, drenched with strong hydrochloric acid, will sink the thermometer from 50° to 0°. But the most intense cold is that which results from the volatilization of liquefied carbonic acid and nitrous oxyd gases, by which the enormously low temperatures of —175° and even 220° are reached.

125. Diminution of volume causes a portion of latent heat to become sensible. Air suddenly compressed into a small space, as in the fire-syringe, (fig. 104,) evolves heat enough to fire a portion of dry punk on the end of the piston. Metals rapidly struck, as on an anvil, become hot

---

124 What are freezing mixtures? Give their theory. What is the most intense artificial cold? 125. What ignites tinder in the fire-syringe?

enough to enable the smith to light his fire. Water poured on quicklime combines with it, with the evolution of much heat; the water in this case taking on the solid form. Sulphuric acid and water, when mingled, give out great heat, and the bulk of the mixture is less than that of the two before mixing. Liquefaction is always a cooling process, and solidification or condensation a heating one. A certain quantity of heat may be considered as necessary to preserve each body in its natural condition: if it be condensed, less is required, and it gives out the excess; and if expanded, it absorbs more.

Fig. 104.

Vaporization.—The Boiling Points of Bodies.

126. A continuance of the heat which melted the ice into water, will turn the water into vapor or steam. The phenomena which attend this physical change are not less curious or instructive than the last.

If we place a known quantity of water over a steady source of heat, we shall see the thermometer indicating each moment a higher temperature, until, at 212°, the fluid boils; after which the thermometer indicates no further change, but remains steady at the same point until all the water is boiled away. Let us suppose that, at the commencement of the experiment, the temperature of the water was 62°, and that it boiled in six minutes after it was first exposed to the heat: then the quantity of heat which entered into it each minute was 25°, because 212°, the boiling point, less 62°, leaves 150° of heat accumulated in six minutes, or 25° each minute. Now if the source of heat continue uniform, we shall find that in forty minutes all the water will be boiled away; and hence there must have passed into the water, to convert it into steam, $25° \times 40 = 1000°$. One thousand degrees of heat, therefore, have been absorbed in the process, and this constitutes the *latent heat* of steam. So much heat, indeed, was imparted to the water, that if it had been a fixed solid, it would have been heated to redness; and yet the steam from it, and the fluid itself, had during the whole time a temperature of only 212°.

---

125. Give examples of heat evolved from condensation. 126. What is vaporization? What is the latent heat of water? How is it observed?

127. The capacity of water for heat is greater than that of any other body known; and in vapor it preserves the same distinction. The latent heat of steam has been variously stated by different experimenters at 940°, 956°, 960°, 972°, and 1000°. The latest, and probably the most accurate determination, is that of Brix, viz. 972°. The latent heat of vapors has no relation to their points of boiling. The superiority of vapor of water in respect to latent heat will be seen by a comparison with that of several other bodies, viz. latent heat of vapor of water = 972°, of ammonia 837°, of alcohol 386°, of ether 162°, of oil turpentine 133°. The large amount of latent heat contained in steam becomes again sensible on its condensation to water; thus enabling us to make great use of it as a means of conveying heat. The steam, so to speak, takes up a large quantity of heat, and transports it to the point where we wish it applied. One gallon of water converted into steam, at the ordinary pressure of the atmosphere, will raise five gallons and a half of ice-cold water to the boiling point. In this way we can boil water in wooden tanks, heat large buildings by steam-pipes, and make numberless other useful applications of steam-heat in the arts. It is found in practice that to heat buildings by steam, every 2000 feet of space to be heated to 75° requires one cubic foot of boiler capacity, and that every square foot of radiating surface on the conducting pipes will heat 200 cubic feet of space.

128. The boiling point of each fluid is constant, other things being equal, but is peculiar to itself; thus, ether boils at 96°, ammonia at 140°, alcohol at 173°, water at 212°, nitric acid 250°, oil turpentine 314°, phosphorus 554°, sulphuric acid 620°, whale-oil 630°, and mercury at 662°.

129. *Boiling* is the mechanical agitation of a fluid by its own vapor. This happens whenever the liquid becomes so hot that its vapor can rise in bubbles to the surface, uncondensed by atmospheric pressure or by the temperature of the fluid. The elasticity or tension of the vapor then becomes greater than the united pressure of the fluid and the air. When the boiling is vigorous, a great number of these bubbles of uncondensed vapor rise to the surface at the same

---

127. What capacity has water for heat? Give other latent heats. Why the superiority of water for steam purposes? 128. What of the boiling points of fluids? 129. What is boiling?

instant, and the liquid is thrown into violent agitation. If a vessel containing cold water be heated suddenly, the lower surface receives the most heat; bubbles of vapor are formed, and rise a little way, when, meeting the colder water, the vapor is at once condensed, and the liquid, before sustained by the elastic vapor, falls with a blow on the bottom of the vessel, often destroying it, if of glass.

130. The boiling point is much affected by the nature and condition of the vessel. In a metallic vessel, water boils at 210° and 211°. If a glass vessel be coated inside with shellac, water boils in it at 211°; but if it be thoroughly cleaned with sulphuric acid, water in it may be heated to 221° or more, without the escape of bubbles. A few grains of sand, a little fragment of wire, or a small piece of charcoal will, however, at once equalize these differences, and cause the water to boil steadily at 212°. This simple means will prevent the unpleasant jar from sudden escape of vapor, and frequent fracture of the glass vessel. The boiling point is more remarkably affected by variations in atmospheric pressure than by any other cause, and we shall presently advert more in detail to the phenomena connected with it.

131. *Spheroidal State of Liquids.*—If drops of water are let fall on a metallic plate heated considerably above the boiling point, it is observed that they do not evaporate very rapidly, and that there is no hissing sound, while the globules of water roll about quietly, floating, as it were, over the hot surface. Thus situated, water is said to be in the "spheroidal state," a term employed by M. Boutigny, who has made many curious and instructive experiments on this subject. Water passes into this condition at 340°, and may attain it even at 288°. A grain and a half of water in this state at 392° requires 3·30 minutes to evaporate; at a dull red-heat, the same quantity will last 1·13 minutes, and at a bright red, 0·50, the rate of evaporation increasing with the temperature. The water, in these experiments, does not touch or wet the hot surface, but is kept at a sensible distance from it by the elas-

Fig. 105.

130. What affects the boiling point? 131. What is the spheroidal state? Describe the experiment in fig. 105.

tic force of an atmosphere of its own vapor, as well also as by the repulsive action of hot surfaces. The vapor is a non-conductor, and its formation abstracts the sensible heat from the fluid; so that, notwithstanding the proximity of the red-hot metal, the temperature of the fluid is found to be always lower than its boiling point, being, for water, 205°·7; for alcohol, 168°; for ether, 93°·6; for hydrochloric ether, 50°·9, and for sulphurous acid 13°·1. The temperature is estimated as shown in fig. 105, where the liquid is contained in a metallic capsule in the flame of a good eolipile.

132. If a thick and heavy silver capsule is heated to full whiteness over the eolipile, it may by an adroit movement be filled entirely with water, and set upon a stand, some seconds before the heat declines to the point when contact can occur between the liquid and the metal. When this happens, the water, before quiet, bursts into steam with almost explosive violence, and is projected in all directions, as shown in fig. 106.

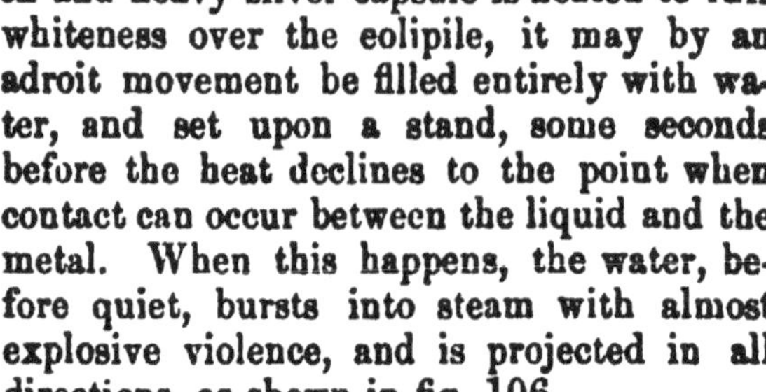

Fig. 106.

On the principle explained, the hand may be bathed in a vase of molten iron, or passed through a stream of melted metal unharmed; and we find here an explanation of the success of some instances of magic.

133. The *pressure of the atmosphere* determines the boiling point of fluids. It follows, therefore, that by a diminution of pressure, water may be made to boil at a much lower temperature than 212°. If we place some warm water in a glass under the air-pump bell (fig. 107) and exhaust the air, the water will boil vigorously, although the temperature, as noted by the thermometer, is observed to fall constantly. So, in ascending high mountains, the boiling point falls with the elevation, from the diminished pressure of the air. On this account, a difficulty is experienced at the hospice of Saint Bernard, on the Swiss Alps, in cooking eggs and other viands in boiling water. This place is 8400 feet above the sea, and water boils there at 196°: on the summit of Mount Blanc, it boils at 184°. We

Fig. 107.

---

132. Describe fig. 106. Why can the hand be safely plunged in fluid iron? 133. What determines the boiling point of fluids? How is it on high mountains?

learn that it is the temperature, and not the boiling which performs the cooking. The Rev. Dr. Wollaston proposed to determine the height of mountains by the boiling point. He found an ascent of 530 feet to be equal to a decrease of 1° in the boiling point; and with a thermometer having large spaces considerable accuracy may be attained. In deep pits (as in mines) the boiling point rises.

134. The *culinary paradox* gives a very good illustration of the phenomena of boiling under diminished pressure. A small quantity of water is boiled in a glass vessel, as in the figure: when the water is actively boiling, a good cork is firmly inserted, and the vessel removed from the heat. It may now be supported in an inverted position, with the mouth under water, as seen in the figure. The boiling will still continue, even more rapidly than before; and if we attempt to check it by affusion of cold water, we shall only cause it to boil more vehemently. A little hot water will, however, at once arrest the ebullition. In this case, the air is driven out of the vessel on the first boiling of the water; and, as we close the orifice while the steam is still issuing, there is only the vapor of water in the cavity. As this condenses from cooling, the pressure on the water diminishes, and it boils more easily from the heat it still contains: the affusion of cold water, by producing a more perfect condensation, occasions a more violent ebullition. Hot water, however, increases the elasticity of the uncondensed vapor, and represses the boiling. These alternations can be produced as long as the water in the vessel is warmer than the cold water poured on it. When cold, the space over the water will be a good vacuum, and if we turn the water from the ball into the neck, it will fall like a solid body, with a smart blow and rattling sound. This is sometimes called the *water-hammer*. The perfection of the vacuum can be tested by withdrawing the cork under water: the pressure of the atmosphere will then drive in a quantity of water equal to the vacuum produced by the first expulsion of the air.

Fig. 108.

134. What is the culinary paradox? Explain the continued boiling.

Fig. 109.

135. The *Pulse Glass* of Dr. Franklin is a very good illustration, also, of boiling under diminished pressure; and the cool sensation felt by the hand at the instant when the fluid boils most violently, is proof of the heat absorbed in converting a part of the fluid into vapor.

Practical application of these facts is made in the arts on a large scale, as in manufacturing sugar. The boiling of the syrup is performed in vacuo, in large pans of copper, holding several hundred gallons, the air and vapor being removed from the vessels by the air pump of a steam-engine: the syrup is thus rapidly boiled down at a temperature of 150° to 180°, without any danger of burning. Vegetable extracts are frequently made, and saline solutions boiled, in the same way. Nothing in the arts shows more clearly the value and beauty of scientific principles.

136. *Elevation of the Boiling Point by Pressure.*—In Papin's digester, (fig. 110,) a strong iron vessel with a safety-valve, water may be heated under the pressure of its own vapor to 400°, or higher. This apparatus may be so arranged with a thermometer and pressure gauge, (fig. 111,) that we can note the relations of pressure and temperature (Marcet's apparatus): the thermometer-ball is in the steam cavity; the gauge descends into some mercury in the bottom. It is supported by a tripod *f* over a lamp *e*, and a stopcock *d* cuts off the external air, when the boiling has commenced.

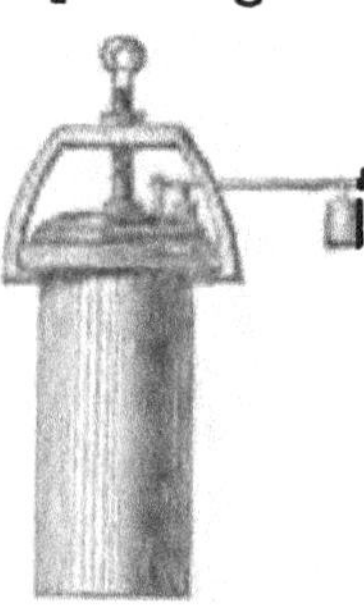
Fig. 110.

As the steam accumulates, it, pressing on the mercury, forces it up the tube, against the imprisoned air in the gauge *b*. When the gauge shows double the pressure of the air, the thermometer will indicate a temperature of 250°·5. 3 atmospheres of pressure raise the temperature to 275°, 4 to 293°·7, 5 to 307°, 10 to 358°, 15 to 392°·5, 20 to 418°·5, 25 to 439°, 30 to 457°, 40 to 486°, and 50 atmospheres raise it to 510°. Perkins heated steam so highly that a jet of it set fire to combustible bodies.

---

135. Explain the pulse-glass. What practical application is made of these principles? 136. What is Papin's digester? What Marcet's? What relation is there between boiling points and pressure?

The *elastic power* of steam in contact with water is limited only by the strength of the containing vessel; but if steam alone be heated without water, then its elastic or expansive power is exactly like that of other gases or vapors. M. de la Tour has shown that many liquids may be entirely converted into vapor in a space but little greater than their own volume.

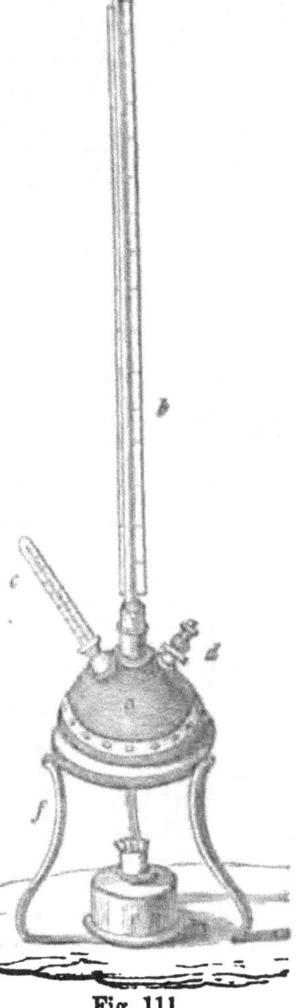

Fig. 111.

137. The *increase of volume* in changing from a liquid to a gaseous state is such, that 1 cubic foot of water becomes nearly 1700 cubic feet of steam; or, in whole numbers, a cubic inch of water becomes nearly a cubic foot of steam; while 1 cubic foot of alcohol and ether yield respectively 493 and 212 cubic feet of vapor. The latent heat of steam diminishes as the sensible heat rises, so that the heating power of steam at 400° is no greater than that of an equal volume at 212°. On the other hand, the latent heat of steam produced at low temperatures, as in a partial vacuum, increases as the sensible heat falls. Hence there is no fuel saved by distilling in vacuo. There is a constant ratio between the latent and sensible heat of steam; the two added together always give the same sum. Thus, steam at 212° has latent heat = 972°; giving the sum 1184°. Subtract the sensible heat of steam at any temperature from the constant number 1184, and we have the latent heat for that temperature, *e. g.* steam at 280° has a latent heat of 904°. So, also, at 100°, steam has 1084° of latent heat.

138. Equal volumes of different vapors contain equal quantities of latent heat. By *weight*, water vapor has about twice

---

What was De la Tour's observation? 137. What is the dilatation of steam? What relation between sensible and latent heat?

and a half more latent heat than alcohol vapor, (972 : 385;) but the specific gravity of alcohol vapor is about 2·5 times greater than that of water-vapor, (1590 : 622.) Consequently, if the same expenditure of heat produces from all vapors the same bulk of vapor having equal quantities of latent heat, there can be no advantage in substituting any other fluid for water as a source of vapor in the steam-engine.

Fig. 112.

139. *The Steam-Engine.*—The principle of this apparatus is simple, and easily illustrated by the little instrument contrived by Dr. Wollaston, (fig. 112.) A glass tube, with a bulb to hold a little water, is fitted with a piston. A hole passes from the under side through the rod, and is closed by a screw at *a*. This screw is loosened to admit the escape of the air, and the water is boiled over a lamp: as soon as the steam issues freely from the open end of the rod, the screw is tightened, and the pressure of the steam then raises the piston to the top of the tube; the experimenter withdraws it from the lamp, the steam is condensed, and the air pressing freely on the top of the piston forces it down again; when the operation may be repeated by again bringing it over the lamp.

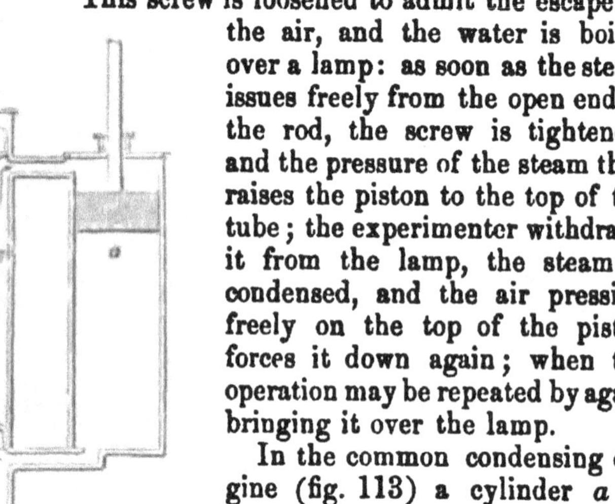

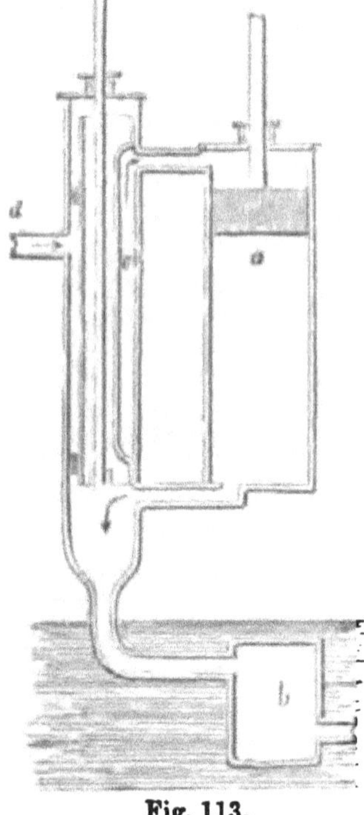

Fig. 113.

In the common condensing engine (fig. 113) a cylinder *a* is fitted with a solid piston, the rod of which moves through a tight packing in the cover, and to it the machinery is attached. A pipe *d* brings the steam from a boiler to the valve arrangement *c* by which the steam is admitted, alternately, to the top and bottom of

138. What of equal volumes of different vapors? Compare alcohol and water. 139. What is Wollaston's toy? Give the principle of the steam-engine in fig. 112.

the cylinder; and also an alternate communication is opened with the condenser *b*. Thus, when the steam enters at the top, (in the direction of the arrow,) that at the bottom of the piston is driven through the lower opening to *b*, where it is condensed. The valves are moved at the proper time by the machinery.

140. *Evaporation* from the surface of liquids takes place at all temperatures. Even snow and ice waste by evaporation, at temperatures much below 32°. Mercury rises in vapor even at the temperature of 60°. Faraday found at that temperature that a slip of gold-leaf suspended in a vacuum over mercury was, in a few hours, whitened by amalgamation with the vapor of that metal. The state of the atmosphere as to dryness and pressure influences natural evaporation, which is greatly increased by heat and a rapid wind. It must be remembered that all the water which falls to the earth in snow and rain has arisen in evaporation. That natural evaporation takes place only from the surface is proved, by its being entirely prevented by a film of oil on the fluid.

141. *Influence of Pressure on Evaporation.*—If we introduce a few drops of water into the vacuum above the mercury in a barometer tube, a part of it will be vaporized, and the level of the mercury will be correspondingly reduced. The tension of the vapor is increased by an elevation of temperature. A larger tube may be placed over the barometer tube, the lower end of which dips under the mercury, and we may then fill the intervening space with hot water, (fig. 114.) The vapor of the confined water will force down the column of mercury in direct proportion to the temperature; and, by means of a thermometer and a scale of inches, we can tell exactly the tension of the vapor of water for every temperature under 212°.

Fig. 114.

142. *Maximum Density of Vapors.*—Into the torricellian vacuum introduce a portion of sulphuric ether: a part of it is instantly converted into vapor, and the mercury depressed thereby to

---

140. What of natural evaporation? 141. What influence has pressure on evaporation?

about 14 inches. If we have a deep cistern, as in fig. 115, in which we can depress the tube by the pressure of the hand, it will be seen that the film of liquid on the surface of the mercury increases as the tube descends, until the vapor of ether is at last entirely converted to the fluid state. On withdrawing the hand, the ether again flashes into vapor. There is then, it is plain, a point of density (or pressure) for the vapor of ether, which cannot be passed without again converting it to a liquid. This is true of all volatile liquids; and this point is called the maximum density of vapors. The weight of 100 cubic inches of water vapor at 212° is 14·962 grains, while, at 32°, the same volume of vapor of water is only 0·136. The point of maximum density of a vapor is lowered by cold as well as by pressure, and when these two effects are united, we can convert many gases, which are quite permanent at the common pressure and temperature of the air, into liquids, and even to solids.

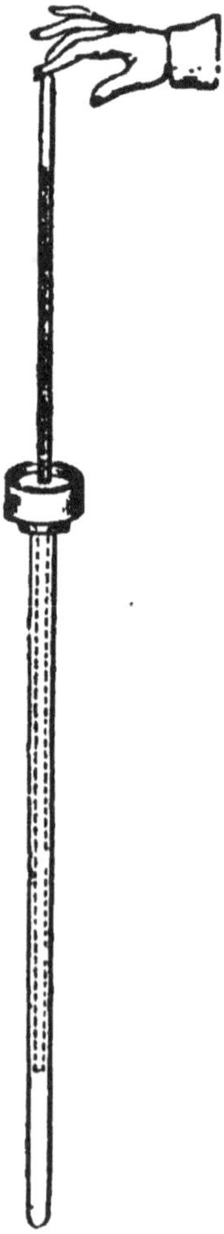

Fig. 115.

143. The *cold produced by evaporation* is owing to the assumption of heat by the newly formed vapor. Availing ourselves of this principle, water may be frozen by the evaporation of ether, even in the open air. Leslie showed that water might be frozen by its own evaporation, as in the experiment figured in the margin, (fig. 116.) Water is contained in a shallow capsule supported by a tripod of wire over a dish containing sulphuric acid, and the whole is covered by a low air-jar. On working the pump, the water evaporates so rapidly in the vacuum as to boil even at 72°: its vapor is instantly absorbed by the sulphuric acid, and in this way both the sensible and latent heat are removed so rapidly that the water is frozen, while still apparently boiling.

Fig. 116.

---

142. What is meant by maximum density of vapors? 143. Whence the cold of evaporation? What is Leslie's experiment?

The *Cryophorus*, or *frost-bearer*, offers another illustration of the same principles. This instrument, invented by Dr. Wollaston, consists of two glass bulbs blown upon the same tube (fig. 117): one of them contains a little water; the space over the water is a vacuum, the tube having been sealed when the water was boiling. On placing the empty bulb in a freezing mixture, the vapor of water is so rapidly condensed as to freeze the fluid in the ball which is remote from the freezing mixture, and which is usually protected by an envelope of muslin.

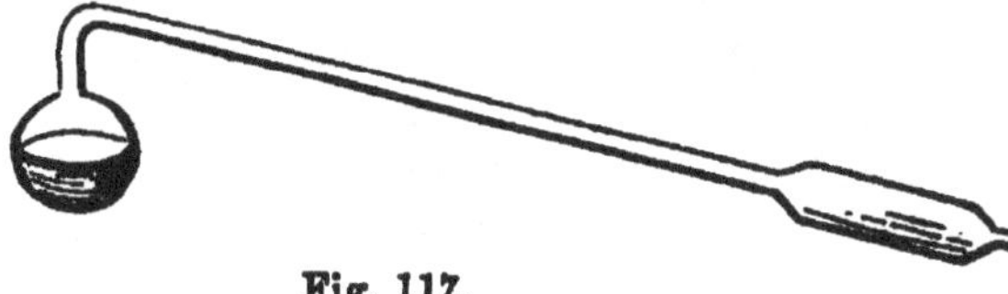
Fig. 117.

144. *Dew-Point.*—If we drop bits of ice into a tumbler of water (one of polished silver is best) having the same temperature with the air, and watch the fall of a thermometer placed in it, we can denote with accuracy the temperature of the water, when it has cooled so far that moisture begins to be deposited on the clean surface of the glass. This temperature is called the *dew-point;* and the number of degrees between it and the temperature of the air is an accurate indication of the actual dryness of the air. In this climate, in summer, this difference amounts often to 40° or more, and in India it has been known to be as much as 61°; that is, with an external temperature of 90°, the dew-point has been seen as low as 29°. The amount of moisture in the air has an influence on the indications of the barometer, and it is always requisite, in making barometrical observations, to make a correction for the tension of the vapor of water in the air.

Several common facts are explained by a reference to these principles. When the air is highly charged with humidity, it deposits dew on any substance colder than itself. A glass of iced water in summer is immediately covered with a coat of condensed vapor; when a warm humid morning succeeds a cool night, we see the pavements and walls of the houses reeking with deposited water, as if they had been drenched with rain. The fall of dew (as has been already explained)

Describe the cryophorus. 144. What is the dew-point? How observed? What common facts are explained by it?

occurs in consequence of the radiation from the earth reducing its temperature below the "dew-point."

145 *Hygrometers* are instruments to determine the amount of moisture in the air. One much used is called the *wet bulb* hygrometer, (fig. 118,) or psychrometer, and consists of two similar delicate mercurial thermometers, the bulb of one of which is covered with muslin and is kept constantly wet by water, led on to it by a string from a tube in the centre. The evaporation of the water from the wet bulb reduces the temperature of that thermometer to which it is attached, in proportion to the dryness of the air, and consequent rapidity of evaporation. The other thermometer indicates the actual temperature; and the difference being noted, a mathematical formula enables us to determine the dew-point.

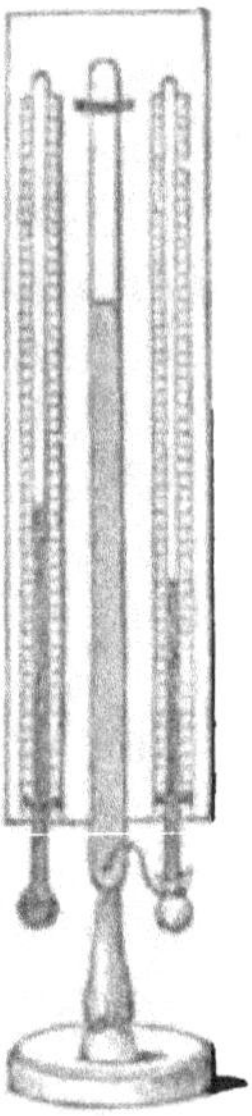

Fig. 118.

146. But a much more delicate instrument for this use is that of Mr. Daniell, which is constructed on the principle of the *cryophorus*, (143.) It is represented in fig. 119. The long limb ends in a bulb, which is made of black glass, that the condensed vapor may be more easily seen on it. It contains a portion of ether, into which dips the ball of a small and delicate thermometer contained in the cavity of the tube. The whole instrument contains only the vapor of ether, air having been removed. The short limb carries an empty bulb, which is covered with muslin. On the support is another thermometer, by which we can observe the temperature of the air. When an observation is to be made by this instrument, a little ether is poured on the muslin: this evaporates rapidly, and of course reduces the temperature of the other ball. As soon as this has fallen to the dew-point, the moisture collects and is easily seen on the black glass. At this instant, the temperature indicated by the two thermometers is noted, and

Fig. 119.

145. What are hygrometers? Describe the wet bulb. 146. Describe Daniell's. What is the principle of Daniell's? Which is the best?

the difference gives us the true dew-point. The latest and most improved form of hygrometer is that of Regnault: it involves the principle of Daniell's, with important means of additional accuracy.

147. *Diffusion and Effusion of Gases and Vapors.*—The vapor of water will rise and fill a confined vessel of air, and have the same tension as if no air were present. It will take a longer time to do it, but as much will ultimately rise as if the space were a vacuum. The air seems to be an impediment only to the rapid rise of the vapor. On the same principle, probably, is explained the curious and important fact, that, when different gases are in contact, they will not remain separate, but will soon mingle uniformly, even against the force of gravity. Our atmosphere, for instance, is composed of two gases, the specific gravities of which are as 976 to 1130, and we might suppose that the heavier would be at the bottom, as would be the case in two such liquids as water and oil. But they are found to be in a state of uniform mixture. If we connect together by a narrow tube two bottles, (fig. 120,) containing, one a light gas, hydrogen, and the other a heavier gas, oxygen, and place the heavy one uppermost, in a few hours we shall find them perfectly commingled; as may be proved by the fact that the mixture will explode violently on touching a match to the open mouth of one of the vessels, which we know a mixture of these two gases will always do.

Fig. 120.

148. If we fill the end of a glass tube (fig. 121) of moderate size with a plug of plaster of Paris, we form what is called Graham's diffusion tube. When the plaster is *dry*, if the tube be filled, for example, with hydrogen gas, and its open end introduced into a vessel of water, this liquid is seen to rise rapidly, owing to the escape of the light gas into the air. At the same time the air enters the tube, and renders the mixture explosive; but nearly four volumes of

Fig. 121.

---

147. What is meant by diffusion of gases? Give an illustration. 148. What is the diffusion tube? In what proportion does the air enter?

hydrogen escape for one of air which enters, and these are called the diffusion volumes of hydrogen and air. Every gas has its own diffusion volume depending on its density, these being inversely as the square root of the densities of the gases. The same law pertains to the rapidity with which gases rush into a vacuum through a minute orifice.

149. The *passage of gases through moist membranes* is connected with this subject, but involves also another condition, viz. the solubility of certain gases in water. For example, a bladder partly full of air, and tied tightly at the neck, is introduced into an air-jar full of carbonic acid; after some hours the bladder is found much distended, and may finally burst, from the passage of the carbonic acid gas into it. This is effected by the solubility of this gas in water: it thus passes the pores of the membrane, and is rapidly diffused again in the air of the bladder. Dr. Mitchell found that the time required to pass the same volume of several gases through the same membrane was 1 minute for ammonia, 2¾ minutes for sulphuretted hydrogen, 3½ for cyanogen, 5½ for carbonic acid, 6½ for nitrous acid, 28 for olefiant gas, 37½ for hydrogen, 113 for oxygen, and 160 for carbonic oxyd. For nitrogen the time was much greater.

150. *Liquefaction and Solidification of Gases.*—In 1823, Faraday first demonstrated the possibility, by united cold and pressure, of reducing several gases to the liquid and even solid state. The apparatus originally employed in these interesting but hazardous experiments, was simply a stout glass tube, bent as in figure 122, containing the materials to evolve the gas, and heated at both ends. If cyanogen is to be liquefied, dry cyanid of mercury is placed in one end of the tube, and heated, while the empty end is cooled in a freezing mixture: the gas, accumulating in a narrow space, is liquefied by the force of its own elasticity. Some hazard attends these experiments, and the operator should be protected by gloves and a mask of wire-gauze. In this way, chlorine, cyanogen,

Fig. 122.

What is the law of diffusion? 149. What of the passage of gases through membranes? Give an example. What are Mitchell's results? 150. Who first liquefied gases? What was the means?

carbonic acid, nitrous oxyd, and several other gases have been reduced to the liquid state, and some to the solid condition. Several of these gases—as ammonia, cyanogen, and sulphurous acid—may be liquefied by cold alone, without additional pressure.

151. *M. Thilorier's apparatus* for liquefaction of carbonic acid involves the same principle. In fig. 123, *g* is the generator of the gas, a strong cast-iron vessel, hung by centres on a frame *f*; in it is put the requisite quantity of carbonate of soda and water, and a tube *a* of copper, holding an equivalent amount of strong sulphuric acid; the cap of red metal is strongly screwed in, the valve closed, and the position of the apparatus inverted, by turning it over on its centres; the acid then runs out among the carbonate of soda, and an enormous pressure is generated by the successive portions of gas evolved. After a time, when the action is complete, the generator is connected by a metallic tube with the receiver *r*; stopcocks, simple screw-plugs having a conical point, confine the gas, and being opened, the liquefied gas collects in *r*, which is cooled by a freezing mixture for the purpose of condensing it. In this way, several successive quarts of the liquid carbonic acid gas are accumulated in *r*. A portion of this liquid may be safely drawn off into a strong glass tube refrigerated. It can then be drawn off by a jet *j* secured to the top, which enters a metallic box *b* with perforated wooden handles. The rapid evaporation of a part of the liquid gas absorbs so much heat from the rest, that a considerable portion is converted to a fine white solid, like dry snow, which fills the box. When once solidified, it wastes away very slowly, and may be handled and moulded with ease. If suffered to rest on the hand, however, it destroys the vitality of the flesh, like a hot iron. It is now in a condition analogous to bodies in the spheroidal

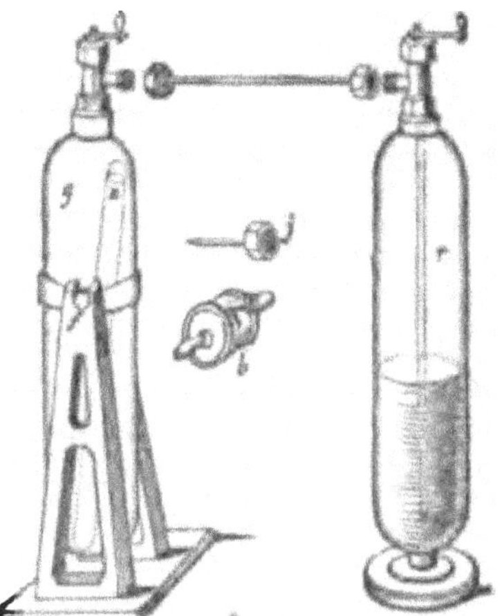

Fig. 123.

What gases have been liquefied? Describe Thilorier's apparatus.

state (131;) being surrounded by an atmosphere of its own vapor, the radiation of heat to it from surrounding bodies is cut off, and it acquires the very low temperature of —140° If it is wet with ether in a capsule containing mercury, the latter is frozen solid, and can then be hammered with a wooden mallet, and drawn out like lead. When moistened with ether in vacuo, with certain precautions, the very low temperature of —166° is produced. Carbonic acid at 0° has a tension of nearly 23 atmospheres; at 32° its tension is 38½ atmospheres; at —34°, 12½; at —75°, 4.60; and at —111°, 1·14 atmospheres. It becomes at —71° a clear transparent solid, sinking in the surrounding fluid.

This apparatus once exploded in Paris, killing the assistant in a frightful manner. It is, however, due to Mr. Chamberlain, of Boston, to say that the author has repeatedly used several of these instruments of his construction with entire safety.

152. By the use of mechanical pressure, and the enormously low temperature of the bath of carbonic acid and ether in vacuo, Faraday has succeeded in reducing several other gases to the liquid or solid state. These facts will be mentioned under the history of the several substances.

The greatest artificial cold hitherto observed is 220° below zero of Fahrenheit, and was obtained by Natterer, with the aid of a bath of liquid nitrous oxyd and sulphuret of carbon in vacuo. The greatest natural cold recorded is —76° below zero.

Several gases have resisted all attempts to reduce them to a liquid state, viz. hydrogen at 27 atmospheres; oxygen at 58½; nitrogen, nitric oxyd, and carbonic oxyd at 50, and coal gas at 32 atmospheres, aided by the greatest artificial cold.

IV. ELECTRICITY.

153. More than 600 years B. C. the ancients observed in amber a remarkable power of excitation by friction. Modern science has conferred on this power the name of electricity, from the Greek word for amber, (*electron*.) This force, or power, has various modes of existence or manifesta-

---

152. How has Faraday reduced other gases? What is the lowest temperature observed? What in nature? What gases have resisted liquefaction? 153. What was the first electrical observation?

tion, which are chiefly, 1. Magnetic electricity; 2. Frictional, or statical electricity; 3. Dynamical, voltaic, or galvanic electricity, (from chemical action;) 4. Thermo-electricity; and, 5. Animal electricity.

Magnetic Electricity, or Magnetism.

154. *Lode-stone.*—A kind of iron-ore has been known from remote antiquity, that has the property of attracting to itself small particles of iron; this is called the *lode-stone.* By contact, it can impart its virtues to iron and steel, and also, to a considerable degree, to cobalt and nickel. As it abounded in *Magnesia*, it was called by Pliny *magnes*, and hence the name *magnet.* This ore mounted in a frame of soft iron *l l*, (fig. 124,) constituted the original magnet: *p p'* are the poles. A bar, or needle of steel, which has received the magnetic influence, when suspended on a point, will be found to have a directive tendency, by which one end turns invariably to the north. The needle, therefore, has polarity, and the end turning north is called the north pole, and the other end the south pole.

Fig. 124.

155. *Polarity.*—If we bring the north end of a magnetic bar near to the similar end of the suspended needle, the latter will move away, as indicated by the arrows, being repelled by the similar power of the bar. If, however, we bring the end N toward the opposite end of the needle S, it will be attracted to the bar, and strive to move as near to it as possible. The reverse is, of course, true of the opposite end of the bar. If, in place of a magnetic bar, we had used a bar of unmagnetic iron, we should have found both ends of the suspended needle equally, but less powerfully, attracted by it. We thus learn (1) that the magnet has *polarity;* and (2) that *poles of the same name repel, and those of opposite names attract each other.*

Fig. 125.

Fig. 126.

156. *Induction of Magnetism.*—The manner in which a magnet, or lode-stone, imparts its own power to surrounding

---

What modes of electricity are named? 154. What is the lode-stone? What is the needle? 155. What is polarity? What is the law of repulsion? 156. What is induction?

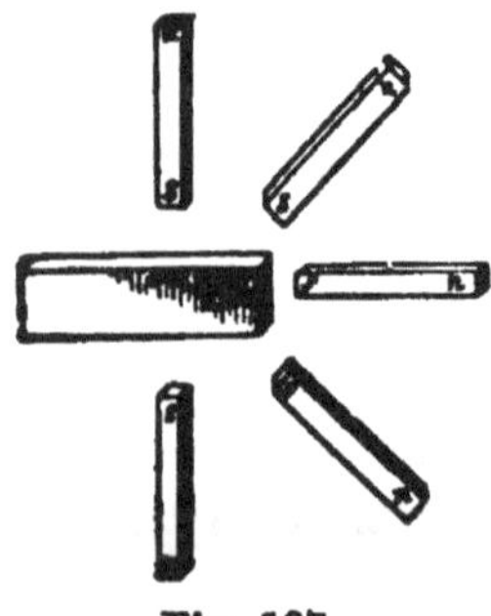
Fig. 127.

substances, is called *induction*, and those bodies capable of manifesting this power are said to be magnetized by the *inductive influence*. Thus, a series of bars of soft iron laid about a magnetic bar, as in the figure, will all become temporarily magnetic by induction; and in obedience to the law just stated, their ends next the N are all S, and their remote ends all N. Every magnet, so to speak, is surrounded by an atmosphere of influence, which has its centre in the poles of the magnet, and diminishes in intensity inversely as the square of the distance. This decrease of force is prettily illustrated by an experiment shown in the annexed cut. The bar magnet holds a large key; this can hold a second smaller than itself; this, a nail; the nail, a tack-nail; and lastly, a few iron-filings are held by the tack-nail; and the whole receive their magnetism by induction from the bar, and each article has its own separate polarity. Induction takes place through a glass-plate, or any similar substance.

Fig. 128.

157. *Permanent magnets* can be made only of hardened steel. Soft iron and steel become magnets only while under the influence of other magnets, and lose their own power as soon as removed from them. Magnetism is imparted by '*touch*,' as it is technically called, from a previously existing magnet. An unmagnetic bar of hardened steel, when properly rubbed by the poles of a magnet, will itself soon acquire polarity and magnetic power. Magnetism is thought to rest mostly on the surface of the metal. Every magnet is regarded as made up of a great number of small magnets, so to speak, each particle of steel having its own polarity. We cannot conceive of one sort of polarity existing without the other. Thus, in figure 129, we see a magnified representation

Fig. 129.

Explain figs. 127 and 128. 157. What are permanent magnets? What is attraction and 'touch'? How are the forces in a magnet distributed?

of this condition. Each little magnet has its own *n* and *s*. Those which occupy the middle of the bar, being acted on alike in all directions, can show no power; but the force accumulates toward each end, until we find the greatest power in the last range of particles, which we term the poles.

If we dip a magnetic bar in iron-filings, we shall find only the ends attracting a tuft of the metallic particles, while the middle is free. If two magnetic bars, however, like the figure, are placed together, (+ and —,) and a sheet of paper laid over them, they will attract iron-filings scattered on the paper, in the way represented in the figure: here a pair of central poles have power to attract the iron, which the middle part of the simple bar had not. The particles of iron arrange themselves in what are called magnetic curves. These curves represent very nearly the lines of *magnetic force* which always environ a magnet, and tend to impart magnetic properties to all bodies—solid, liquid, or gaseous—which come within their range.

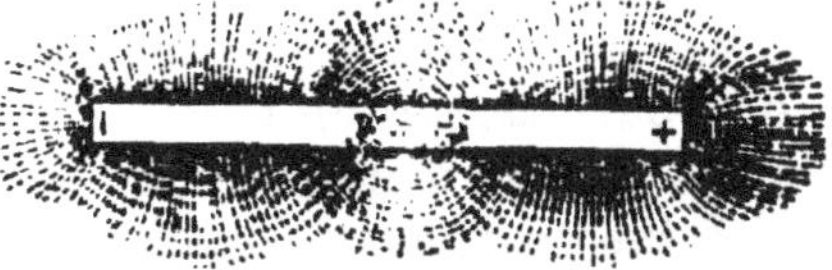

Fig. 130.

158. *Artificial Magnets* are made of all forms, the most common being the so-called horse-shoe magnet, shaped like figure 131. It is found that the power of magnets is much increased by uniting several thin plates of hardened steel, each of which is separately magnetized. A bar of soft iron, called the keeper, is placed across the poles of the horse-shoe magnet, to prevent it from losing power; and if it be made to hold a weight nearly equal to the power of the magnet, it will be found to gain strength daily up to a certain point, and in like manner to lose its magnetism if unemployed. Artificial magnets, weighing one pound, have been made to sustain 28 times their own weight.

U

Fig. 131.

159. *The Earth's Magnetism.*—The earth is regarded as a great magnet. Its power is equal, according to Gauss, to that which would be conferred if every cubic yard of it contained six one-pound magnets. The sum of the force is equal to 8,464,000,000,000,000,000,000 such magnets. The magnetism which we see in bars of steel and the lode-

Illustrate this as in fig. 129. 158. How are magnets formed and preserved? What is terrestrial magnetism? What its force in a cubic yard?

stone is the result of induction from the earth. Magnetism from the earth is induced in all bars of steel or iron which stand long in a vertical position. Tongs and blacksmiths' tools are often found to be magnetized. A bar of iron held in the magnetic meridian, and at the proper inclination, becomes immediately magnetic from the induction of the earth; and the effect may be hastened by striking it on the end with a hammer: the vibration seems to aid in inducing the magnetic force. The tools used in boring and cutting iron are also generally found to be magnets. The magnetic poles of the earth are not in the same points with the poles of revolution or the axis of the earth, and for this reason the magnetic needle does not point to the true north and south, but varies from it more or less, and differs at different times, as the magnetic pole alters its position. This is called the *variation* of the needle.

160. *Dipping Needle.*—The magnetism of the earth is beautifully shown by the *dipping needle*, represented in the annexed figure. The needle *n* is suspended on the horizontal bar *a*, so as to move in a vertical plane, instead of horizontally, as in the compass-needle. The graduated vertical circle *c* is placed in the magnetic meridian, and the needle then assumes, in this latitude, (41° 18′,) the position shown in the figure, dipping at an angle of 73° 27′. Over the magnetic equator it would stand horizontal, being equally attracted in both directions. At either magnetic pole it would be vertical. The horizontal variation of the needle, its dip, and the intensity of the polar attraction, are subject to daily and local changes, from the fluctuations of temperature influencing the magnetic conditions of the atmosphere, as shown by the late results of Faraday.

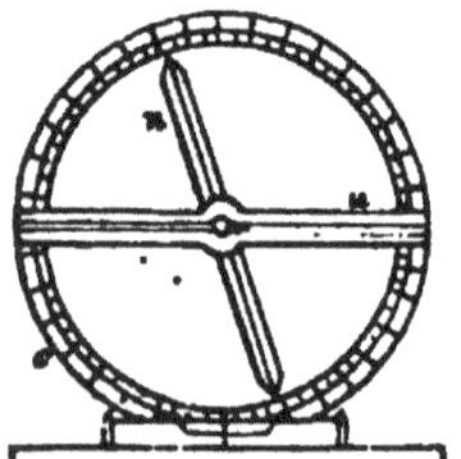
Fig. 132.

161. *Magnetics and Diamagnetics.*—Dr. Faraday, in 1845, made the important discovery that *all* solid and liquid substances, and many gases, were subject to the magnetic influence. According to his results, confirmed by numerous subsequent observers, all bodies may be subdivided into two great classes—the *magnetic* and *diamagnetic*. To the first

---

How are objects affected by it? Where are the magnetic poles? 160. What is the dipping needle? What is said of variations in dip, &c.?

class belong all bodies which act like iron and nickel—that is, which place themselves, when suspended as a needle, *axially* or in the line connecting the poles of a magnet—and which also exhibit the familiar mode of attraction by either pole of a magnet alike. The bodies belonging to this class are either metals or oxyds and salts of metals, (both solid and liquid.) To the second class belong all liquids and solids which do not belong to the magnetic class. Bismuth appears to be the most remarkable substance in diamagnetic energy. A suspended needle of this metal places itself at right angles to that position which iron assumes under the same circumstances. A few bodies of each class are enumerated in the following list, where we observe that iron and bismuth are at the extremes, each standing as the type of its own class, while air and vacuum occupy the zero, or neutral point of quiescent inactivity:—Iron, nickel, cobalt, manganese, palladium, crown-glass, platinum, osmium, —0°, air and vacuum, arsenic, ether, alcohol, gold, water, mercury, flint-glass, tin, heavy glass, antimony, phosphorus, bismuth. It is a curious sight to see a piece of wood, or of beef, or an apple, or a bottle of water, repelled by a magnet; or, taking the leaf of a tree and hanging it up between the poles, to observe it take an equatorial position.

162. The latest results of Faraday show that oxygen gas is to be reckoned as a magnetic, having about $\frac{1}{333}$th part the capacity of iron for magnetic induction. This fact connects itself in the most important manner with the magnetic condition of the atmosphere—the daily variations in dip and intensity—as probably also with the aurora borealis.

Electricity of Friction, or Statical Electricity.

163. *Statical electricity is evolved* by several of the same causes which we have named as sources of heat. Friction excites it abundantly; chemical action still more so. It attends animal life, and is powerfully exhibited in some animals, as in the torpedo and electrical eel: heat evolves it, as in the mineral tourmalin; and we have reason to

---

161. What are magnetics and diamagnetics? Name some of them. 162. What is Faraday's discovery regarding oxygen? 163. What are sources of frictional electricity?

believe that the sun's rays are perpetually exciting electrical currents in the earth. Like heat, it neither adds to nor subtracts from the weight of matter; but, unlike heat, it produces no change in dimensions, and does not affect the power of cohesion in bodies. In powerful discharges, however, it overcomes cohesion by rending or fusion. All matter is subject to its influence, and it can be transferred from an excited body to one previously in a neutral state.

We shall treat this curious and most interesting subject very briefly, as its chemical relations are much more limited than those of galvanism.

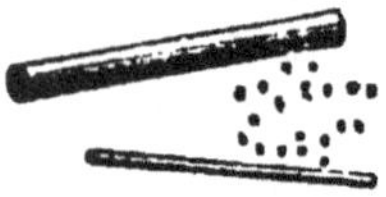

Fig. 133.

164. *Electrical Excitement.*—If we briskly rub a glass tube with warm and dry silk, and bring it near to any light substance, as some pith, on the table, (fig. 133,) a flock of cotton, some shreds of silk, or, as in fig. 134, to two balls of pith suspended on a hook by delicate wire, the light substances will at first be strongly attracted to the tube, but in an instant will fly from it, as if repelled by some unseen force; and any further effort to attract them to the excited glass will only cause their continued removal. Each separate thread of silk and each pith-ball seems to retreat as far as possible from the glass tube and from its fellows. If, in the place of the glass tube, we use a stick of sealing-wax rubbed with dry flannel, and present this to the light substances which have been excited by the glass tube, we shall find a very strong attraction manifested between them: the light substance previously excited by the glass will move to the excited resin much more actively than a substance not previously excited in this way; and two substances separately excited, one by the glass and the other by the resin, will attract each other with equal power. The first of these is called *vitreous*, and the second *resinous* electricity. These simple phenomena form the basis of all electrical science.

Fig. 134.

165. *Electrical Polarity.*—There is a strong analogy between the two sorts of electrical excitement and the opposite powers of the magnet. The vitreous is to the resinous elec-

---

What similarity has it to heat? What differences? 164. How do you excite a glass tube? How does it affect pith-balls, &c.? How if wax is used? 165. What is electrical polarity?

tricity as the north pole of a magnet is to the south. Hence we call the vitreous the *positive* electricity, and the resinous the *negative* electricity. A row of pith-balls, (fig. 135,) when excited by induction, or influence, stand related to each other as shown by the signs plus and minus.

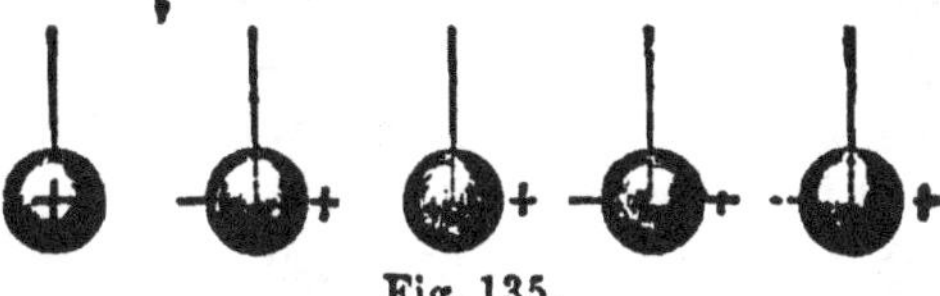

Fig. 135.

166. *Electrical machines* are constructed for the easy excitation of large quantities of electricity. Two forms of this machine—the cylinder and the plate—are in common use. In the plate machine, (fig. 136,) *c k* is a wheel of plate-glass, turned on an axis by a handle *m*. The electricity is excited by the friction of two cushions or rubbers pressing against the plate, and covered with a soft amalgam of mercury, tin, and zinc, which greatly heightens the effect. The rubbers are connected with the earth by a metallic chain. The excited glass delivers its electricity to several sharp points of wire attached to the bright brass arms *i i*, and connected with the great conductors *f g*. The conductors are perfectly insulated by glass supports *h h*.

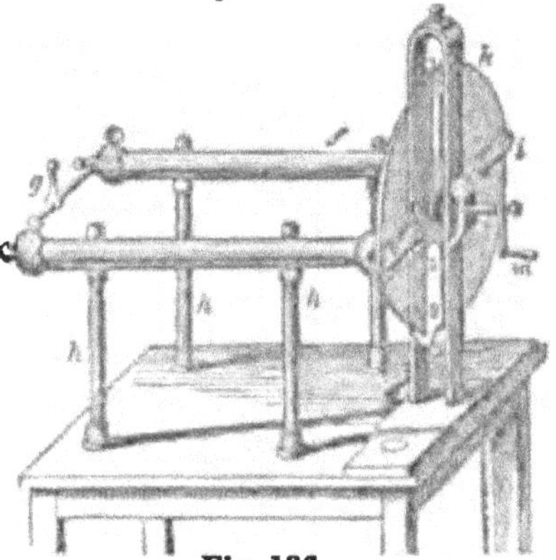

Fig. 136.

In the cylinder machine, (fig. 137,) a hollow cylinder of glass *v* is used, to excite the electricity; *c* is the rubber, and *a r* are the prime conductors. When the winch is turned, bright sparks of a violet color, forming zigzag lines like lightning, dart with a sharp sound to any conducting substance brought near to the

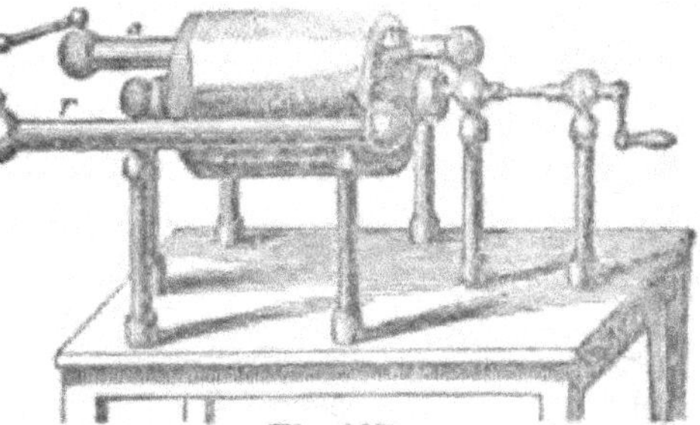

Fig. 137.

How is it like magnetic? 166. What is the plate machine? What the cylinder? Describe figs. 136 and 137.

great conductors. This is *positive* electricity. If negative electricity be wanted, we must insulate the rubbers, and, connecting the opposite conductor with the earth, draw the sparks from the rubber. For this purpose, the construction in fig. 137 is most convenient. Every care must be taken, in the use of an electrical apparatus, to keep it clean and smooth, and particularly free from moisture. Warm flannel or silk is to be used to wipe the surface.

Fig. 138.

167. *Electroscopes, or Electrometers.*—The quadrant electroscope (fig. 138) is usually attached to the prime conductor, to indicate the activity of the machine by the more or less elevated angle assumed by the arm. The pith-balls of fig. 135 answer the same purpose, and may also denote the *kind* of excitement. For example, if they are excited by glass, on approaching them with another excited body, if they are attracted, then we know that the second body has negative excitement—if repelled, positive excitement is found.

Fig. 139.

The gold-leaf electrometer (fig. 139,) is, however, a much more delicate test of electrical excitement. It consists of two leaves of gold, suspended in an air-jar, and communicating by a wire with a small plate of brass; the approach to this plate of a body in any degree excited, will occasion an immediate movement of the gold-leaves, from which we can tell the nature of the excitement, as above described, having previously imparted to the gold-leaves a particular kind of electricity.

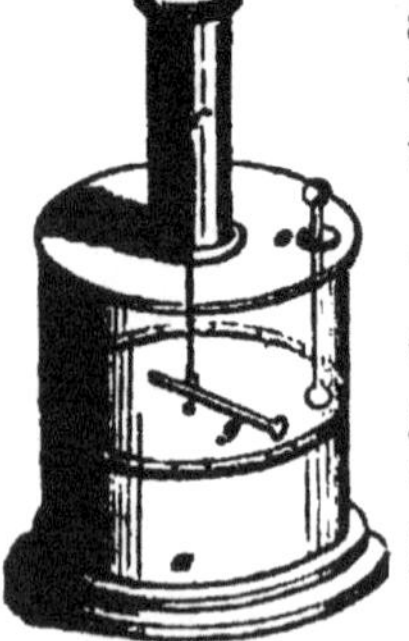

Fig. 140.

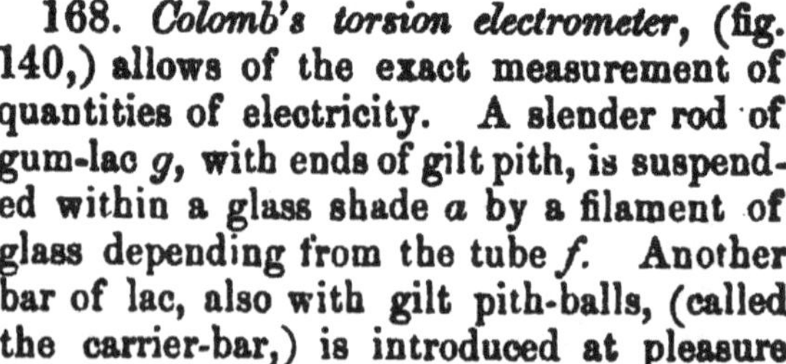

168. *Colomb's torsion electrometer,* (fig. 140,) allows of the exact measurement of quantities of electricity. A slender rod of gum-lac *g,* with ends of gilt pith, is suspended within a glass shade *a* by a filament of glass depending from the tube *f.* Another bar of lac, also with gilt pith-balls, (called the carrier-bar,) is introduced at pleasure

---

What is an electroscope? Describe the gold-leaf. 168. Describe Colomb's electrometer, fig. 140. What does it enable us to do?

by an opening *o* in the cover of the instrument. By a screw *t* at top the needle may be adjusted. When unexcited, the needle and carrier-bar stand in close proximity. To measure electricity by this instrument, the lower ball of the carrier-rod is charged and introduced into the cylinder. It will repel the movable ball in proportion to the intensity of the charge; and by turning the milled head at *m* we may measure the degree of deflection, or torsion, of the thread of glass. This we can also note on the graduated circle upon the cylinder.

169. *Conductors and Insulators of Electricity.*—The pith-balls or glass tubes, which have been electrically excited, return to a natural state very slowly indeed, if left untouched, in dry air. But the hand, or a metallic rod, will at once restore them to the unexcited state, while dry silk, glass, and resin will not remove the excitement. Bodies are, therefore, divided into conductors and non-conductors of electricity, or, more properly, into good and bad conductors. The electrical discharge takes place through good conductors (as the metals) with an inconceivable velocity, which can be compared only to the velocity of light. Among good conductors, in the order of their conducting power, are the metals, charcoal, plumbago, and various fused metallic chlorids, strong acids, water, damp air, vegetable and animal bodies; among bad or imperfect conductors are spermaceti, glass, sulphur, fixed oils, oil of turpentine, resin, ice, diamond, and dry gases. The latter substances are also called *insulators*, because by their aid we can insulate or confine electricity.

170. The *distribution of electricity* in an excited body is upon the surface. In proof of this, if on the insulated stand *b* (fig. 141) we excite a spherical body *c c*, provided with glass handles, we may separate its halves and observe that the inner sphere *a* has no excitement whatever. All the electricity remains on the outer surface. If the body is egg-shaped, the excitement becomes more concentrated in the extremities. A small point at the end of the prime conductor will convey off all the excitement of a power-

Fig. 141.

---

169. What are conductors and insulators? Name some of each. 170. How is electricity distributed? Describe fig. 141. What is true of a point on the prime conductor?

ful machine insensibly, unless in the dark, when a track of light will be seen proceeding from the point.

The excitement of a powerful machine may be withdrawn by pith-balls, or figures of pith arranged as is figure 142, which convey away the electricity as fast as it is produced—being attracted and repelled between the two surfaces.

Fig. 142.

171. *Lightning conductors* were devised by Dr. Franklin, after his memorable experiment with the kite, by which he proved the identity of atmospheric electricity with that of machine excitation. The efficacy of lightning conductors, now so general, depends on the power of a point to draw away insensibly very powerful charges of electricity. It is essential that they should be well insulated, and that the lower end should enter so deep into the earth as always to be in damp ground.

172. *Two theories* have been proposed to explain the ordinary phenomena of electricity. The first is called the *Franklinian hypothesis*, proposed by our distinguished countryman, Dr. Franklin. It supposes that there is a simple, subtle, and highly-elastic fluid, which pervades all matter. This fluid is self-repellent, but attracts all matter, or its ultimate particles. In the natural state of bodies, this fluid is uniformly distributed over them, and its increase or diminution produces electrical excitement. Accordingly, when a glass tube is rubbed with a silk handkerchief, the electrical equilibrium is disturbed, the glass acquires more than its natural quantity, and is over-charged, the silk possesses less, and is under-charged.

The *second hypothesis* is that of Du Fay, who assumes that electrical phenomena are due to two highly elastic, imponderable fluids, the particles of which are self-repellent, but attractive of each other. These two fluids exist in all unexcited bodies in a state of combination and neutralization, when no electrical phenomena are seen. Friction occasions the separation of the fluids, and the electrical excitement in a body continues until an equal amount of opposite electricity to that excited has been restored to it.

How do the dancing figures discharge electricity? 171. How do lightning conductors act? 172. What is the Franklinian hypothesis? What is that of Du Fay?

According to Dr. Franklin's theory, the two states are denominated positive and negative; according to Du Fay, they are distinguished as vitreous and resinous.

Whichever theory we may adopt, we can clearly see how it is impossible ever to develop one electrical condition without at the same time giving rise to the other.

173. The *Leyden jar* was invented by Cunæus, of Leyden, in 1746. By it the experimenter collects and transfers a portion of the electricity evolved by his machine, and applies it to the purposes of experiment. It is simply a glass jar, (fig. 143,) covered inside and out with tin-foil up to the line seen in the figure. A brass ball communicates by a wire and chain with the *interior* coating, the mouth being stopped by a cover of dry wood. On approaching the ball to the conductor of the electrical machine, when in action, a series of vivid sparks will be received by it, and a great accumulation of vitreous electricity takes place in the interior, provided the exterior be not insulated. On forming a connection by a conductor between the interior and exterior surfaces, the equilibrium is at once restored by a rush of the opposing forces, accompanied with a brilliant flash of artificial lightning. If the hand of the operator is the conducting medium, a violent shock is felt, commonly known as the electrical shock. A series of such jars, arranged so as to be charged by one machine, is called an electrical battery, as shown in figure 144, where all the inside coatings unite, and also all the outsides are connected. The battery may also be so constructed as to allow of the jars, after they are charged, being shifted so that the series shall be discharged consecutively, each outer connected with the next inner coating. Great intensity is thus obtained.

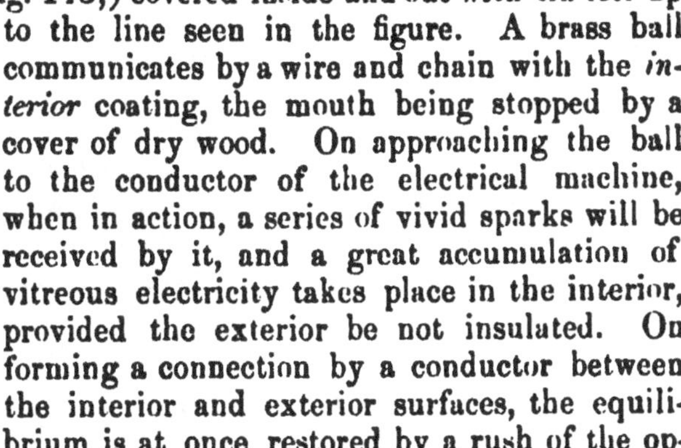

Fig. 143.

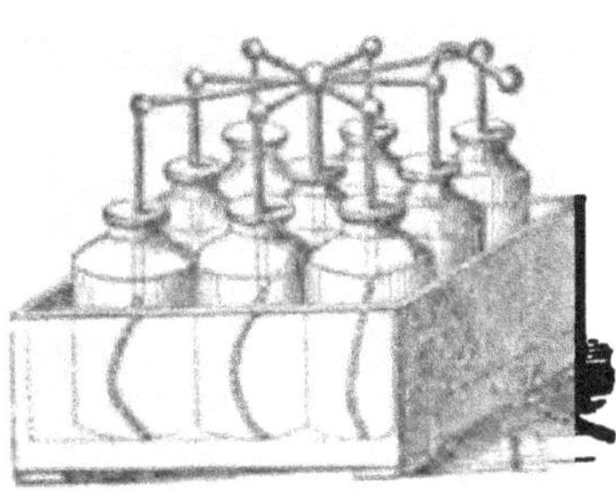

Fig. 144.

What terms describe these conditions? 173. What is the Leyden jar? What its theory? What is an electrical battery?

Fig. 145.

174. By using an insulated jointed rod, (fig. 145,) called a discharging rod, the experimenter avoids receiving the shock.

When the shock of the electrical battery is passed through a card, (fig. 146,) the hole which is pierced is burred on both sides. This fact has been adduced as a proof that there were two fluids, moving in different directions. Otherwise it would seem that the burr should exist only on one side.

Fig. 146.

175. The dissected Leyden jar (fig. 147) is so constructed that we may remove the interior coating from its glass jar *b*, leaving the outer coating alone. This may be done after the jar is charged, when the separate parts will not manifest excitement, as tested by the electroscope. When reunited, however, a spark can still be drawn from it.

Fig. 147.

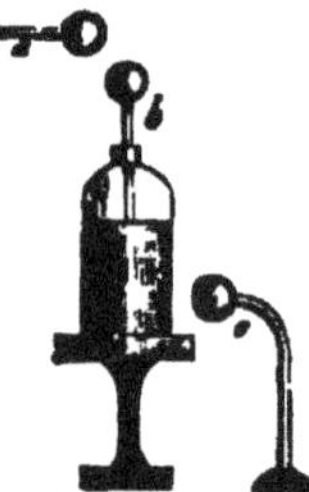
Fig. 148.

If the Leyden jar is placed on an insulating stand *s*, (fig. 148,) it will be found impossible to charge it. The most powerful machine *a* will communicate only one or two sparks to it, *b*. This is because the negative excitement cannot pass off from the outer coating. Accordingly, if the ball of a second jar *c*, uninsulated, be brought near the outer coating, a torrent of sparks flows off, and both jars are quickly charged. Attention to the laws of attraction and repulsion gives us an easy solution of this problem, which involves the whole theory of the Leyden jar. It is also obvious that glass is not an impediment to the *induction* of electrical excitement, however perfect it may be as a *non-conductor*.

176. Dr. Faraday has shown that the inductive action of ordinary electricity takes place in curves which are analogous to the lines of force surrounding a magnet—forming its atmosphere of influence, so to speak.

---

174. What is a discharging rod? What does the card experiment show? 175. What is the dissected jar? Describe the experiment in fig. 148. 176. How does electrical induction occur? Name the inductive power of glass, lac, sulphur, &c.

Substances also differ in their specific power of inductive capacity: thus, air being unity, the inductive capacity of glass is 1·76, of lac 2, and of sulphur 2·25. All gases also have the same inductive capacity, however they may differ in density or other respects.

177. The *Electrophorus* is a convenient mode of obtaining an electrical spark, when no electrical machine is to be had, and consists of a shallow tray of tin, the size of a dining plate, partly filled with melted shellac *a*, or some other resinous preparation, made as smooth as possible. A disc of brass *b*, with a glass handle, is provided, and the bed of resin is rubbed with a dry flannel or cat-skin: this excites negative electricity, and the metal disc is then laid on the excited surface, and touched with the finger, which receives a negative spark. A coating of positive electricity is induced on *b*, which may be raised, and discharged by a conductor, giving a vivid spark, sufficient to explode gases. The resinous electricity not being conducted away from the shellac, the spark may be repeated as long as the excitement lasts. It is plain that the electricity in this case is induced by the excited lac.

Fig. 149.

If a mixture of red-lead and flowers of sulphur, previously well mixed in a mortar, be blown from a tube over the excited surface of the electrophorus, the two substances are immediately separated, because of their opposite electrical relations, and are arranged in curious figures on opposite sides of the excited disc.

178. A *jet of high steam*, issuing from a locomotive or other insulated steam-boiler, will, with certain precautions, give a stream of electrical sparks more powerful than any electrical machine. This has been called hydro-electricity, and is produced by the friction of the hot steam on the edges of the orifice from which the steam issues.

---

177. What is the electrophorus? What is its theory? How does red-lead, &c. behave on it? 178. What is hydro-electricity?

Galvanism, Voltaism, or Electricity of Chemical Action.

179. *History.*—Galvani, of Bologna, in the year 1790, accidentally observed that the freshly denuded legs of a frog, suspended on a metallic conductor, were powerfully convulsed when brought near to an active electrical machine. From this trivial observation has sprung one of the most wonderful departments of human knowledge. The same fact had been previously noticed, and Swammerdam had exhibited it before the Grand Duke of Tuscany, but no result of value was deduced from it. It was suggested that there was a peculiar sensitiveness to electrical excitement in animal substances, due to some remaining vital energy. This explanation failed to satisfy Galvani, who observed similar convulsions in the frog's limbs when hanging from a copper wire *b* (fig. 150) on an iron rail. He found that the effects were produced whenever the muscles touched the iron while the nerves touched the copper, but that contact with the copper alone did not produce them. The crural nerves are easily exposed by separating the large muscles with the fingers at *a a*. From his observations, Galvani inferred that there was a peculiar variety of electricity in animals, which he called *animal electricity*—that this was developed whenever connection was made between the muscle and naked nerve by means of two metals. This theory fascinated the physiologists, and for ten years Galvani's experiments were repeated with great zeal in all civilized countries.

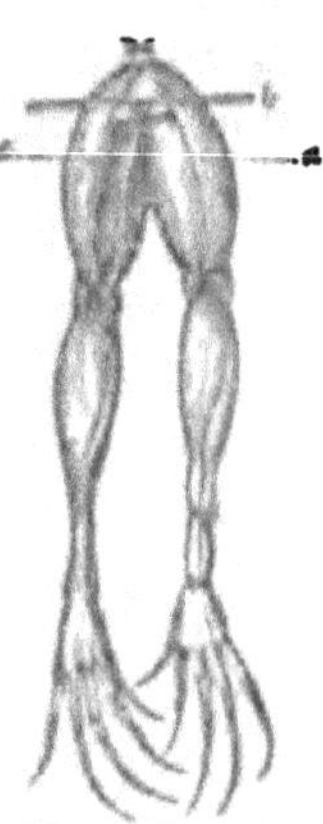

Fig. 150.

180. Volta, of Pavia, maintained that it was the contact of two metals which generated the electricity, of which the frog's legs were only a delicate electroscope. This experiment can never fail to excite wonder, however often we may perform it. We suspend from a metallic conductor a pair of frog's legs recently skinned, and with a part of the spine attached. With two metallic slips, one of zinc and one of copper, we touch at the same time the naked nerve and the

179. What was Galvani's observation? What was the suggestion? What did Galvani infer? How was his animal electricity excited 180. What did Volta maintain? What was his observation with the frog's legs?

muscle, as shown in fig. 151. Convulsions immediately throw the limbs into the position indicated by the dotted lines; and we may repeat the trial until, after a time, this power gradually dies out. In proof of his views, Volta invented and brought forward his memorable *pile*, of which a more particular mention will be made presently.

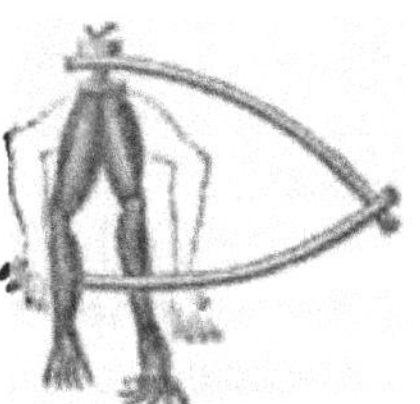

Fig. 151.

181. This is not the place to record in detail the history of science, but this discovery is one of the few grand achievements of the human mind which must ever mark the moment of a new era in experimental philosophy. It is both wonderful and instructive to reflect that so simple an observation as the twitching of a frog's legs should have led immediately to a revelation of the metallic basis of the entire crust of our planet—to the adoption of a new classification of elements and of their compounds—to almost miraculous performances in metallurgy—and to the instantaneous communication of thought, by the annihilation of time and space!

182. *Voltaic Pile.*—Volta sagaciously reasoned that the effects observed by Galvani could be produced with simple metals and a fluid, or substances saturated with a fluid. The truth of this conjecture is easily verified by placing on the tongue a silver coin, and beneath it a slip of zinc or a copper coin. On touching the edges of the two metals so situated, we perceive a mild flash of light and a sharp prickling sensation or twinge, giving notice of the production of a voltaic current. This simple experiment was made long before the discoveries of Galvani and Volta, and is to be regarded as the first recorded observation in the remarkable science of galvanism. Volta accordingly arranged a series of copper and silver coins in a pile, with cloths wet in a saline or acid fluid between them. The arrangement is seen in fig. 152. The copper *c* and zinc *z* alternate with the wet cloth between. The pile begins with *z* and ends with *c*, and care

Fig. 152.

What did he invent? 181. What reflection is here made? 182. What was Volta's reasoning? What is the simplest form of battery?

must be taken that the order be strictly maintained, viz. copper—cloth—zinc. On establishing a metallic communication between these extremes (poles) by a wire, a current of electricity flows in the direction of the arrow on the wire. If one hand be placed on each end of the pile, a shock will be experienced, similar in some respects to that from the electrical machine, and yet very unlike it. If the pile has many members, on touching the wires communicating between the extremes the shock is very intense, and a vivid spark will be produced, which is increased if points of prepared charcoal are attached to the ends of the wires. The conducting wires held together will grow hot, and if a short piece of small platina wire is interposed, it will be heated to bright redness. Such is an outline of the remarkable discovery of Volta, whose pile was made known to the world in 1800. The principle involved in this arrangement is unaltered, although more manageable and efficient forms of apparatus have supplied the place of the original pile.

183. *Simple Voltaic Circle.*—A voltaic current is established whenever we bring two dissimilar metals (as copper, silver, or platina, with zinc or iron) into contact in an acid or saline fluid. Thus, if we place a slip of copper in a glass of acid water, and beside it in the same vessel a slip of amalgamated zinc, (fig. 153,) as long as the two metals do not touch there will be no action, but on bringing together the upper ends of the two slips of metal, a vigorous action will commence, bubbles of gas will be rapidly given off from the copper, while the zinc will be gradually dissolved in the acid water. This action will be arrested at any moment, on separating the two metals. If this separation is made in the dark, a minute spark will also be seen. The action here is entirely electrical. The end of the zinc in the acid is +, or positive, and that in the air —, or negative; the copper has the reverse signs. These relations are expressed in the figures by the signs + and —, and by the direction of the arrows showing the + electricity of the zinc passing to the — of the copper in the acid; while the bubbles of gas (hydrogen) set free at the + end of the zinc

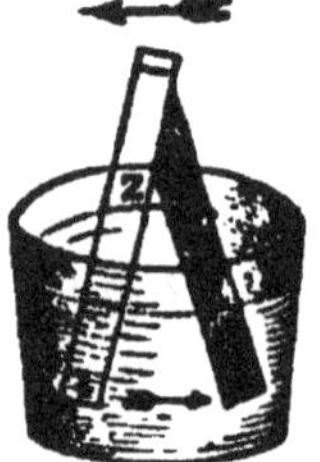
Fig. 153.

Describe the pile, fig. 152. 183. What are the conditions of a voltaic circuit? How is its action suspended? What are the electrical states of the immersed metals? Illustrate by figs. 153, 154.

are delivered at the — of the copper. Fig. 154 shows how the current may be established by wires, without the direct contact of the slips. In this case the wires (as in the pile) carry the influence in the direction of the arrows, and the existence of the current and its positive and negative characters may be shown by the effect produced by it on a small magnetic needle, which will be influenced by the wires carrying the current, just as by the magnet—being attracted or repelled according as it is above or below the wire, and in either case endeavoring to place itself at right angles to the conducting wire, (201.) The *direction* of the voltaic current (and of course the + or — qualities of the metals from which it is evolved) depends entirely on the nature of the chemical action produced. Thus, if, in the arrangement just described, strong ammonia were used in place of the dilute acid, all the relations of the metals and the fluid would be reversed, since the action would then be upon the copper.

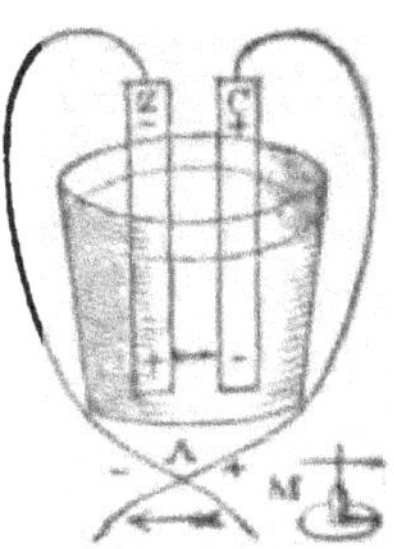
Fig. 154.

184. Thus is electricity the result of chemical action; and conversely we see that, under the arrangement described, chemical action is controlled by the electrical condition of the metals. This is electricity in motion, or dynamic electricity; and frictional electricity may be regarded as stagnant or *statical* electricity. Let us attend somewhat further to the theory of the voltaic circle.

185. In the compound voltaic circuit, composed of two or more members, connection is formed, not between members of the same cell, but between those of opposite names in contiguous cells. This is seen by inspecting the arrows and signs + and — in figure 155. The electricity always flows, both in simple and compound circles, from the zinc to the copper, in the

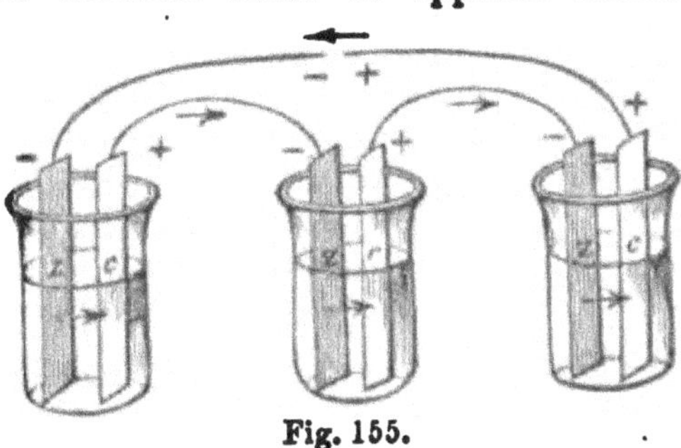
Fig. 155.

184. How is this mode of electricity regarded? 185. What are the conditions of a compound voltaic series? Describe it in fig. 155.

fluid of the battery; and from the copper to the zinc, out of the battery. This is important to be remembered, since the zinc is called the electro-positive element of the voltaic series, although out of the fluid it is negative; and consequently, in voltaic decomposition, that element which goes to the zinc-pole is called the *electro-positive* element, being attracted by its opposite force; while the element going to the copper is called, for the same reason, the *electro-negative*. The compound circle, reduced to the simplest form of expression, would be—

Copper—zinc—fluid—copper—zinc.

Here the copper end is negative and the zinc positive, but the two terminal plates are in no way concerned in the effect; so that, throwing them out of the question, we bring it to the state of the simple circle, which is simply—

Zinc—fluid—copper;

and here we find the zinc end negative, and the copper end positive.

186. A certain resistance to the passage of a voltaic circuit is offered by every element used in its construction. New properties are thus acquired by the compound circuit, which are never seen in the single couple, while the latter possesses certain attributes not seen so well in the compound series. For example, no single pair of plates, however large, will afford a current capable of decomposing water or of affording an electrical shock, although a maximum of magnetic effect may thus be produced. These differences were formerly ascribed, rather vaguely, to what has been called *quantity* and *intensity*. Thus, in the compound circuit, supposing each + and — in the circuit to neutralize each other, then only the final quantities + and — remain as expressed in the poles; and it was argued that the *quantity* of electricity was no greater than would be afforded by a single couple, while its *intensity*, owing to the resistance overcome in each cell, was greatly increased. This matter has been placed on the basis of mathematical demonstration by

187. *Ohm's Law*—Ohm, of Berlin, in 1827 first demonstrated that, as the voltaic apparatus itself is composed

---

186. What effect is due to each element? What new properties does the current thus acquire? What was meant by quantity and intensity?
187. What law expresses the conditions of a voltaic circuit?

solely of conductors, the electric current must proceed, not only along the connecting wire, from pole to pole, but also through the whole apparatus; that the resistance offered to the passage of the current consisted therefore of two parts, one exterior to, and one within, the apparatus. This explanation cleared up at once the difficulties which had previously beset this subject when regarded only in view of the exterior resistance.

Let the ring *a b c* in fig. 156 represent a homogeneous conductor, and let a source of electricity exist at A. From this source the electricity will diffuse itself over both halves of the ring, the positive passing in the direction *a*, the negative in *b*, and both fluids meeting at *c*. Now it follows, if the ring is homogeneous, that equal quantities of electricity pass through all cross sections of the ring in the same time. Assuming that the passage of the fluid from one cross section of the ring to another is due to the difference of electrical tension at these points, and that the quantity which passes is proportional to this difference of tension, the consequence is that the two fluids proceeding from A must decrease in tension the farther they recede from the starting point.

Fig. 156.

188. This decreasing tension may be represented by a diagram. Suppose the ring in fig. 156 to be stretched out to the line A A′. Let the ordinate A B represent the tension of positive electricity at A, and A′ B′ that of the negative fluid; then the line B B′ will express the tension for all parts of the circuit, by the varying lengths of A B, A′ B′ at every point of A *c* or *c* A′. Hence Ohm's celebrated formula, $F = \frac{E}{R}$, where F represents the strength of the current, E the electro-motive force of the battery, and R the resistance. Therefore the greater the length of the circuit, the less will be the amount of electricity which passes through any cross section in a given time. In exact terms, this law states that *the strength*

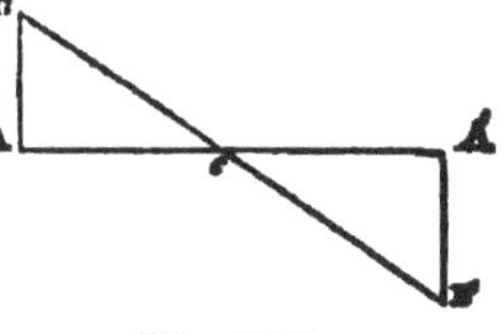

Fig. 157.

Demonstrate fig. 156. 188. How do you express the decreasing tension? What is Ohm's formula? Give the meaning of each expression. What is the law as stated?

of the current is inversely proportional to the resistance of the circuit, and directly as the electro-motive force.

189. But in the simplest voltaic circuit we have not a homogeneous conductor, but several of various powers in this respect. To illustrate this, let the conductor A A′ (fig. 158) consist of two portions having different cross sections. For example, let the cross section of A d be n times that of d A′; then if equal quantities pass through all sections in equal times, if through a given length of the thicker wire no more fluid passes than through the thinner wire, the difference of tension at both ends of this unit of length of the thicker wire must be only $\frac{1}{n}$th of what it is in the latter. Thus, "the electric fall," as Ohm calls it, will be less in the case of the thick wire than of the thinner, as shown by the line B a in the figure. The result is expressed in the law that the "*electric fall*" *is directly as the specific resistances of the conductors, and inversely as their cross sections.* Hence, the greater the resistance offered by the conductor, the greater the fall. The very simplest circuit must therefore present a series of gradients expressive of the tension of its various points—as one for the connecting wire, one for the zinc, one for the fluid, and one for the copper. The electro-motive force of a voltaic couple ("E" of Ohm's formula) may be experimentally determined, and it is proportional to the electric tension at the ends of the newly broken circuit.

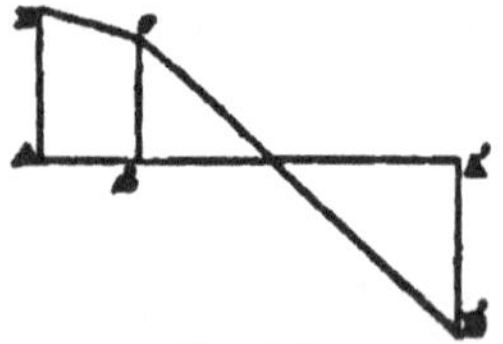

Fig. 158.

190. *Galvanic Batteries* are constructed of various forms, according to the purpose for which they are to be used. One of the earliest forms contrived was the Cruickshank's trough, (fig. 159,) in which the plates of copper and zinc soldered together are secured in grooves by cement, water-tight, all the zincs facing in one direction. The acid was poured into the

Fig. 159.

---

189. How does it apply to conductors not homogeneous? What is the electric fall? Give the law. Describe the course of the current in and out of the fluid. What is the simplest expression of the compound circle? 190. What was Cruickshank's battery?

trough until the cells were filled. To avoid the inconvenience arising from loss of power, (which in this form of instrument is greatest at the first moment of contact between the plates and the acid,) Dr. Hare contrived his revolving *deflagrators*. These were so constructed, that by a quarter revolution of the trough, the acid could at pleasure, and without disturbing the arrangements of the operator, be thrown off or on the plates, and the maximum effects of this kind of the battery be obtained. But recent improvements in the construction of the battery have supplied us with several superior forms of the instrument, suited to various purposes, and possessing the valuable quality of constancy of action.

191. *Amalgamation.*—In the original form of the galvanic battery, made of copper and of unamalgamated zinc, there is a great amount of local action in each cell, arising from the impurity of the zinc. When the surface of the zinc is amalgamated with mercury, the local action ceases; and the amalgamated surface, being reduced to one uniform electrical condition, will remain for any length of time in the acid fluid unacted on, until connected with the electro-negative element. All improved batteries are therefore now constructed with amalgamated zinc. It should be remarked that the *local* action in a battery cell, arising from the cause named, not only consumes the power of that member, but reduces the energy of the whole series. In order to have a constant voltaic circuit of equal power, not only the evils arising from local action must be avoided, but also, as far as possible, the exhaustion of the fluid of excitation. Batteries so constructed as to meet these difficulties are called sustaining batteries, or constant batteries. Some of the more important of these we will briefly describe.

192. *Smee's Battery* is formed of zinc and silver, and needs but one cell, and one fluid to excite it. The silver plate (S, fig. 160) is prepared by coating its surface with platinum, thrown down on it by a voltaic current, in the state of fine division, which is known as platinum-black. The object of this is to prevent the adhesion of the liberated hydrogen to the polished silver. Any polished smooth surface of metal will hold bubbles of gas with great obstinacy,

---

What was Hare's improvement? 191. What is amalgamation? What its use? What is said of local action? 192. What is Smee's battery?

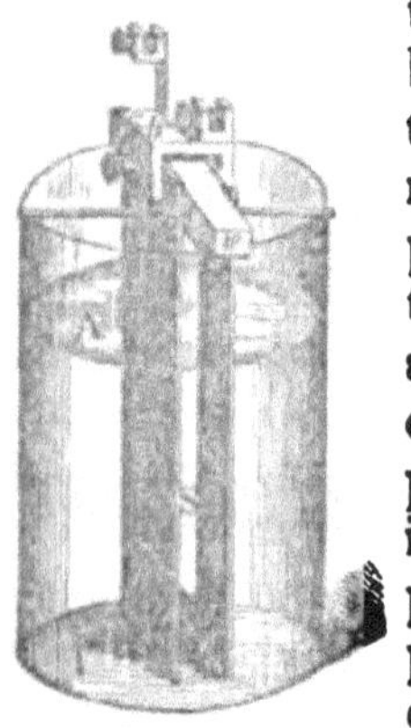

Fig. 160.

thus preventing in a measure the contact between the fluid and the plate by the interposition of a film of air-bubbles. The roughened surface produced from the deposit of platinum-black entirely prevents this. The zinc plates *z z* in this battery are well amalgamated, and face both sides of the silver. The three plates are held in position by a clamp at top *b*, and the interposition of a bar of dry wood *w* prevents the passage of a current from plate to plate. Water, acidulated with one-seventh its bulk of oil of vitriol, or, for less activity, with one-sixteenth, is the exciting fluid. The quantity of electricity excited in this battery is very great, but the intensity is not so great as in those compound batteries to be described. This battery is perfectly constant, does not act until the poles are joined, and, without any attention, will maintain a uniform flow of power for days together. A plate of lead, well silvered, and then coated with platinum-black, will answer equally as well, and indeed better than a thin plate of pure silver This battery is recommended over every other for the stu-

Fig. 161.

dent, as comprising the great requisites of cheapness, ease of management, and constancy. A form of it, well calculated for the student's laboratory, is shown in fig. 161, which is a porcelain trough with six cells. This battery is the one universally employed in electro-metallurgy.

193. *Daniell's Constant Battery.*—This truly philosophical instrument (fig. 162) is made up of an exterior circular

---

What are the advantages of Smee's battery?

cell of copper C, three and a half inches in diameter, which serves both as a containing vessel and as a negative element; a porous cylindrical cup of earthenware P (or the gullet of an ox tied into a bag) is placed within the copper cell, and a solid cylinder of amalgamated zinc Z within the porous cup. The outer cell C is charged by a mixture of eight parts of water and one of oil of vitriol, saturated with blue vitriol, (sulphate of copper.) Some of the solid sulphate is also suspended on a perforated shelf, or in a gauze bag, to keep up the saturation. The inner cell is filled with the same acid water, but without the copper salt. Any number of cells so arranged are easily connected together by binding screws, the C of one pair to the Z of the next, and so on. This instrument, when arranged and charged as here described, will give out no gas. The hydrogen from the decomposed water is not given off in bubbles on the copper side, as in all forms of the simple circuit of zinc and copper; because the sulphate of copper there present is decomposed by the circuit, atom for atom, with the decomposed water, and the hydrogen takes the atom of oxyd of copper, appropriating its oxygen to form water again, and metallic copper is deposited on the outer cell. No action of any sort results in this battery, when properly arranged, until the poles are joined. Ten or twelve such cells form a very active, constant, and economical battery.

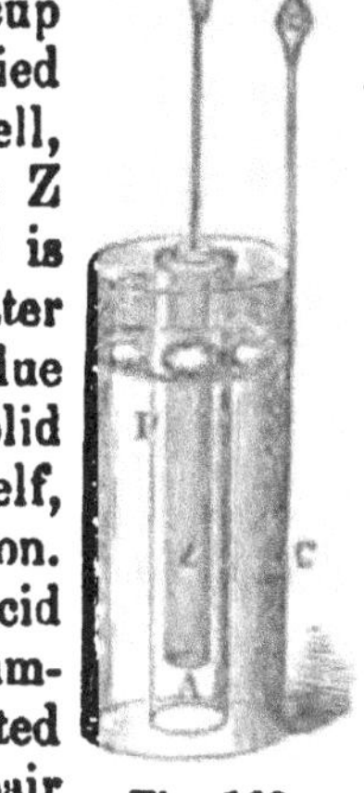

Fig. 162.

194. In the common sulphate of copper battery (fig. 163) only the acid solution of sulphate of copper is used. The surface of zinc becomes soon encumbered by the metallic copper in a state of fine division thrown down upon its surface. It is a very useful battery for electro-magnetic purposes.

Fig. 163.

195. *Grove's Battery.*—Mr. Grove, of London, has contrived a compound sustaining battery, of great power and most remarkable intensity of action. The metals used are platinum and amalgamated

---

193. What is Daniell's battery? 194. What is the sulphate of copper battery? What is Grove's battery?

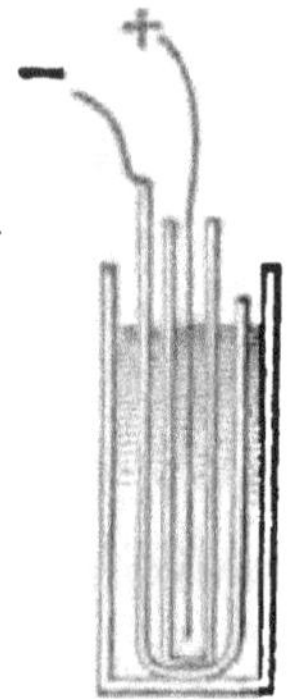
Fig. 164.

zinc. A vertical section of this battery is shown in fig. 164. The platinum + is placed in a porous cell of earthenware, containing strong nitric acid. This is surrounded by the amalgamated zinc — in an outer vessel of dilute sulphuric acid, (six to ten parts water to one of acid, by measure.) The platinum, being the most costly metal, is here surrounded by the zinc, in order to economize its surface as much as possible. In this battery the hydrogen of the decomposed water on the zinc side enters the nitric acid cell, decomposes an equivalent of the acid, forming water with one equivalent of its oxygen, while the deutoxyd of nitrogen is given out as a gas, and, coming in contact with the air, is converted into hyponitric acid fumes. No other form of battery can be compared with this for intensity of action. A series of four cells (the platinum foil being only three inches long and half an inch wide) will decompose water with great rapidity; and twenty such cells will evolve a very splendid arch of light from points of prepared charcoal, and deflagrate all the metals very powerfully. It is rather costly, and troublesome to manage, as are all batteries with double cells and porous cups.

196. *Bunsen's carbon battery* is a valuable addition to our resources in this department. It employs a cylinder of carbon for the negative element, in place of the platinum in Grove's battery. The carbon is that of the gas-works, pulverized and moulded with flour, and afterward baked like pottery into compact cylinders. This battery (fig. 165) has the advantage of large members and great cheapness of construction. Fifty large-sized members, 10 inches high, the outer cups 5 inches in diameter, cost about fifty-five dollars in Paris, made by Deleuil, Rue du Pont-de-Lodi, No. 8. The author has found this, on the whole, the most efficient and economical of all batteries suited to show the more splendid and intense effects of voltaic electricity.

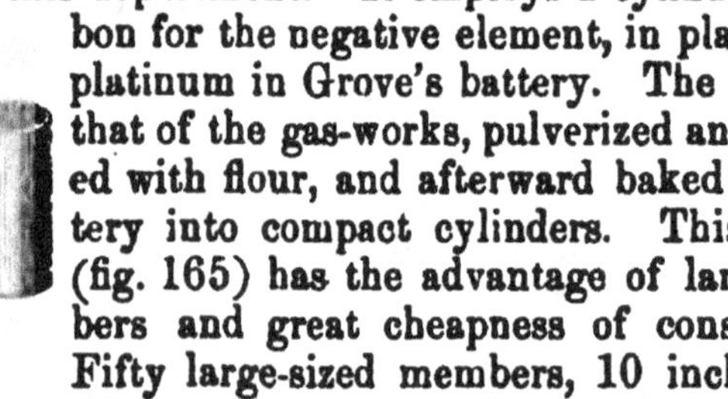
Fig. 165.

---

196. What is Bunsen's battery? What is the reaction in these compound batteries?

197. The *effects of voltaic electricity* are, 1. Physical; 2. Chemical; and, 3. Physiological. Under the first head are included the electrical, luminous, calorific, and electro-magnetic phenomena of the circuit.

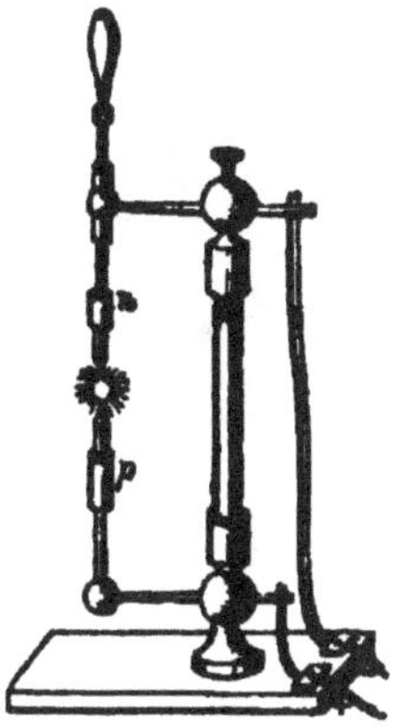

Fig. 166.

198. *Deflagration.*—When the current from a series of 20 or 50 pairs of Grove's or Bunsen's battery is passed through points of prepared charcoal, as in the discharger, (fig. 166), a most brilliant light and intense heat are produced. No effect is seen until contact is made between the poles *p* and *n*, when, on withdrawing them, the arch of light elongates, and connects the separated poles, in the manner shown in fig. 167. This arch is in a powerful pile some inches in length. It is accompanied with an elongation of the pole on the — or carbon side of the battery, and a depression or hollowing out of the + or zinc side. This flame is a conductor of electricity, and is attracted and repelled by the magnet, as shown in fig. 168. By holding a magnet in a certain position the flame may be made to revolve, accompanied at the same time with a loud sound. In the small capsule of carbon S, (fig. 169,) gold, platinum, steel, mercury, and other substances are speedily fused and deflagrated, with various colored lights and volatilization. The easy fusion of platinum by the pile is a proof of the intensity of the heat, as this effect can be produced by no other source of heat known, except that of the oxyhydrogen blowpipe. By the union of the currents from several hundred carbon cells, M. Despretz has lately volatilized the diamond. The ingenuity of the teacher will vary the experiments, always so surprising and instructive.

Fig. 167.

Fig. 168.

Fig. 169.

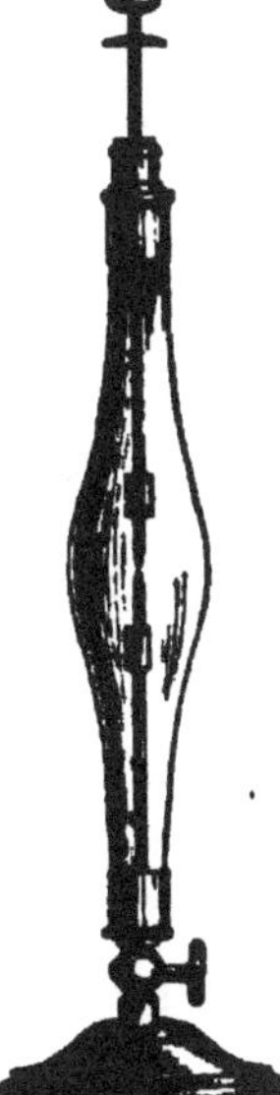

Fig. 170.

197. Classify the effects of voltaic electricity. 198. Describe the effects of deflagration. Which pole elongates?

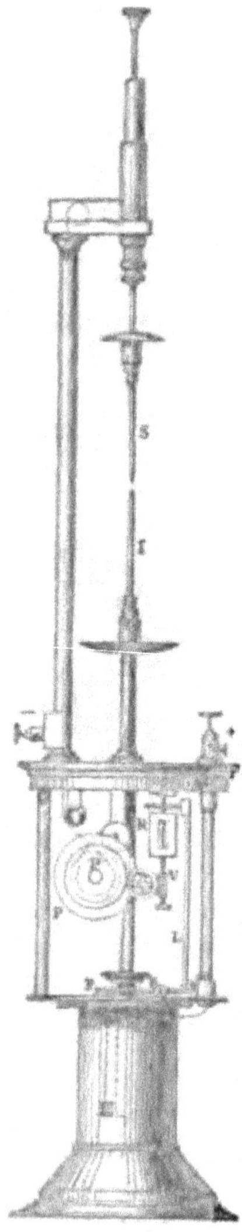

Fig. 171.

199. The electrical light of the voltaic circuit is in no degree dependent on combustion, as may be proved by establishing connection between the poles in a *vacuum* in a glass vessel exhausted by the air-pump, and containing the poles conveniently arranged, as in fig. 170. No less brilliancy is perceived in this case than in the air.

200. A *constant* light is produced from the battery of Grove or Bunsen, by an ingenious mechanical arrangement of the poles. Fig. 171 shows that of M. Duboscq, of Paris. The poles S and I are preserved at the same distance by the action of an electro-magnet in the foot E, upon a soft-iron bar F F in connection with an endless screw V, moving the pullies P P′, which are connected by cords with the poles S and I. The contact of S and I induces magnetism in the electro-magnet E, while the springs R L regulate the motion of the machinery. The apparatus is simple and portable, and its effect is to make the electrical light so steady and constant that it may be used for all optical experiments. The author has also shown that good daguerreotypes may be taken with it in a few seconds. For this purpose the light is concentrated by a large parabolic mirror, so placed that the poles meet in its focus. The positive pole consumes much more rapidly than the negative, both from a more intense action upon it and because its particles are carried over and deposited on the negative pole, elongating the point of the latter. To provide for this difference, the pulley P′ is variable, and carries the pole I up proportionably faster, so that the focal position of the light remains unchanged.

How does a magnet affect the arc of flame? 199. How does a vacuum affect the electrical light? Describe fig. 170. 200. What is the arrangement for rendering the light constant? Describe fig. 171.

Electro-Magnetism.

201. Prof. Œrsted, of Copenhagen, in 1819 first made known the law of electro-magnetic attraction and repulsion. If a wire conveying a voltaic current is brought above and parallel to a magnetic needle, (as shown in fig 172,) the latter is invariably affected, as if influenced by the poles of another magnet. If the current is flowing, as indicated by the arrow on the wire, say to the north, then the north pole of the needle will turn to the east; if the current is flowing south, it will turn to the west. If the wire carrying the current is placed *beneath* the needle, the same effect is produced as if the current had been reversed; the needle turns in the opposite way to what it does when the wire is above. The effort of the needle is to place itself at right angles to the wire, as if influenced by a *tangential* force. That the wire conveying a voltaic current is itself magnetic, is proved by this experiment. If the wire is bent in a rectangle, as in fig. 173, and wound with silk or cotton, to prevent metallic contact, and the *lateral* passage of the power from wire to wire, then it is evident that a current flowing over the wire will have to pass many times completely around the needle, and the effect which is produced will be nearly in proportion to the number of turns made by the wire. In this way we can make a very feeble current give decided indications. Such an arrangement is called a galvanoscope or galvanometer.

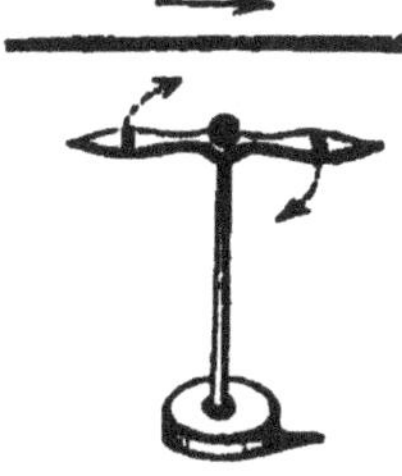

Fig. 172.

Fig. 173.

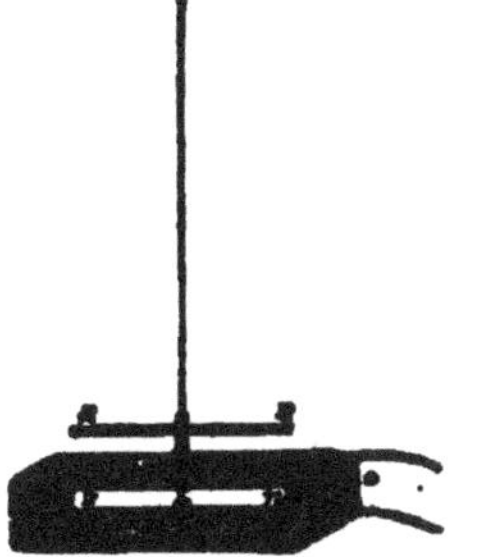

Fig. 174.

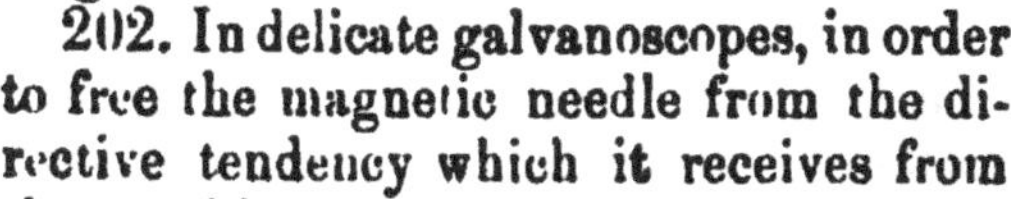

202. In delicate galvanoscopes, in order to free the magnetic needle from the directive tendency which it receives from the earth's magnetism, two needles are used, with their unlike poles placed opposite to each other, (fig. 174,) one

---

201. Who discovered electro-magnetism? What effect has a current on a wire? What is meant by a tangential force? What is a galvanometer?

within and the other above the coil. They will then hang suspended by the silk fibre which supports them, with no tendency to swing in any direction, since they are wholly occupied with their own attractions and repulsions, and their directive power is neutralized. Consequently, they are free to move with the slightest influence of any current passing through the coil. Such an arrangement is called an *astatic* needle. To give it greater delicacy, and prevent the currents of air from moving it, a glass shade (fig. 175) is placed over it, and the movements of the needle are read on the graduated circle. By means of a screw provided for that purpose, the coil is revolved until it is parallel with the needle, as the point of greatest sensitiveness. The tendency of the galvanometer needle, it will be remembered, is always to place itself at right angles to the direction of the electrical current, that position being the *equator* of the attracting and repelling powers, and consequently a point of equilibrium.

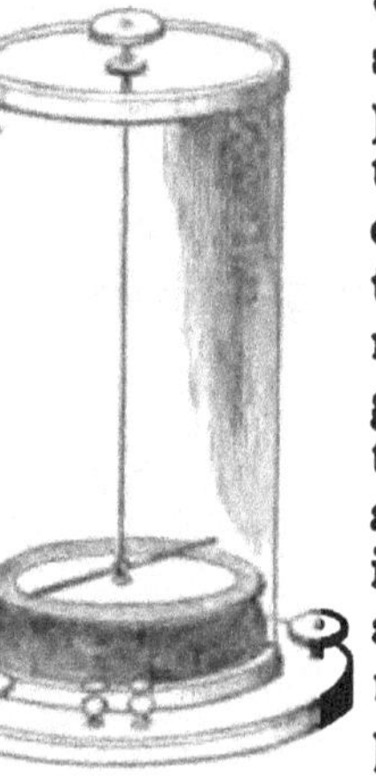

Fig. 175.

203. *Ampère's Theory.*—In 1820, while the original discovery of Œrsted was attracting the greatest attention, M. Ampère, of Paris, proposed to account for the phenomena of terrestrial magnetism by supposing a series of electrical currents circulating about the earth from east to west, in spirals nearly at right angles to its magnetic axis. The sun's rays impinging on the surface of the earth, encircle it, so to speak, with an unending series of spiral lines, producing, by thermo-electricity, the phenomena of magnetic induction. Arago found, in accordance with these views, that if iron-filings were brought near a connecting wire while a voltaic current was passing, that they adhered to it in concentric rings. These fell off the moment the circuit was broken. Hence it was inferred that if a voltaic current was made to pass in a spiral about any conductor, it would become magnetic. This inference was verified by the

---

202. What is an astatic needle? How is it freed from the influence of terrestrial magnetism? 203. What was Ampère's theory? What demonstration did M. Arago devise?

204. *Helix.*—A wire coiled as in fig. 176, made the medium of communication for a voltaic current, becomes capable of manifesting very strong magnetic influence on any conductor placed in its axis. A delicate steel needle, laid in the helix, will be drawn to the centre and held suspended there, without material support, like Mahomet's fabled coffin. If the needle is of steel, the magnetism it thus receives will be retained by it; but if it be of soft iron, it is a magnet only while the current is passing. Brass, lead, copper, or any other metallic conductor, can by galvanism be made to manifest temporary magnetic power. The polarity of the needle in the helix will depend on the direction in which the current is carried; if from right to left, the south pole will be at the zinc end; if from left to right, this polarity is reversed. If the spiral is reversed in the middle, then a pair of poles will be found at the point of reversal, and this as often as the reversal may happen. A steel needle placed in such a helix receives the same reversals. Such an arrangement is shown in fig. 177.

Fig. 176.

Fig. 177.

205. The polarity of the helix is well shown by the arrangement represented in fig. 178, called De la Rive's ring. A small wire helix, whose ends are attached to the little battery of zinc and copper contained in a glass tube, floats on the surface of a basin of water, by means of a large cork, through which the glass tube is thrust. On exciting this small battery by a little dilute acid, poured into the tube, and placing the apparatus on the water, it will at once assume a polar direction, as if it were a compass-needle, the axis of the helix being in the magnetic meridian; and it will then obey the influence of any other magnet brought near it, manifesting the ordinary attractions and repulsions

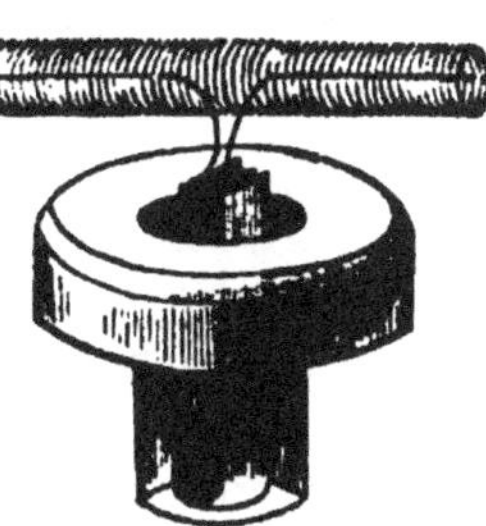
Fig. 178.

---

204. What is the helix? How is a needle in it affected? What polarity has it? What does fig. 177 illustrate? Why are the poles reversed at N? 205. What shows the polarity of the wire itself? Describe fig. 178.

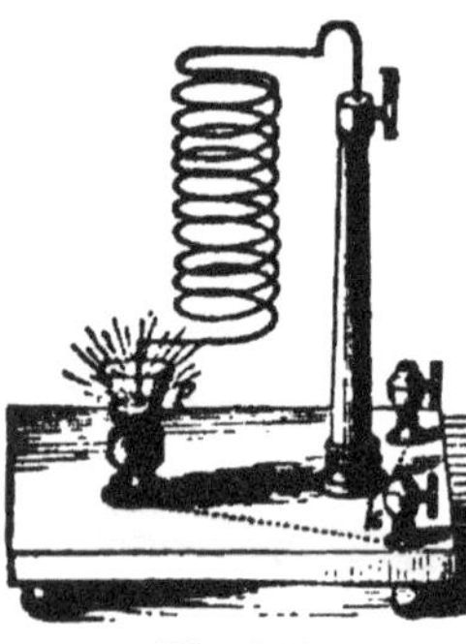
Fig. 179.

206. The helix is placed as in figure 179, its lower end dipping into a cup of mercury *p*, in connection with one pole *k*, while it is held by its upper end *n* in connection with the other pole. In this situation, when the current passes, the separate turns of the helix attract each other, thus shortening the spiral and raising the point out of the mercury, with a vivid spark. This breaks the connection—the unmagnetized helix falls—the point again touches the mercury, when a fresh contraction happens. These effects are made very striking by holding one end of an iron rod, or of a bar magnet, within the spiral. If a magnetic bar is used, the vibrations obey the ordinary law of polarity, ceasing entirely when a pole of like name is introduced.

207. *Electro-Magnets.*—The induction of magnetism in soft iron by the voltaic current, furnishes us the means of producing magnets of astonishing power. Let *a b* (fig. 180) be a cylinder of soft iron, fitting the opening of a helix. If the current from several Grove's batteries be passed through the wires *m n*, sufficient magnetic power will be developed to sustain *a b*, oscillating in a vertical line, even should it weigh eight or ten pounds. This is one of the most surprising of all experimental demonstrations.

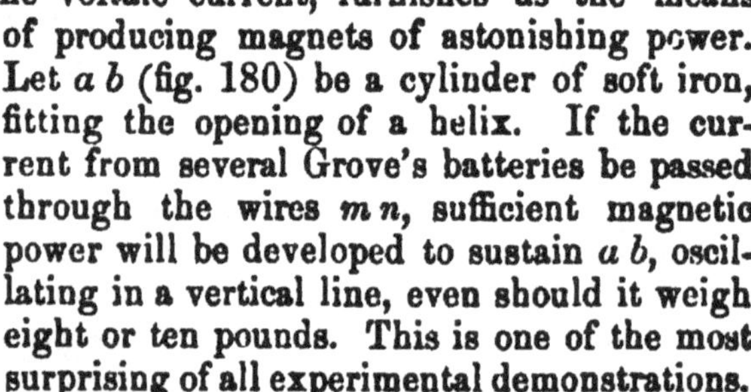
Fig. 180.

By the use of this arrangement on a large scale, and with a battery of 100 members of platina, a foot square, Dr. Page sustained a mass of soft iron 600 pounds in weight, with a vertical movement of eighteen inches. On this principle he has propelled a magnetic engine on a railway at considerable speed, and sought to apply the power to other mechanical uses.

208. Professor Henry first demonstrated the fact that the power of an electro-magnet with a given voltaic current was greatly increased when the helix wire was divided into

---

206. Explain the action of the helix in fig. 179. 207. What is an electro-magnet? What remarkable result is mentioned? 208. What did Professor Henry first show?

coils of limited length. Availing himself of this principle, he constructed electro-magnets lifting over two thousand pounds, with a single cylinder battery of small size. All the corresponding ends of the helices are carried to their appropriate poles.

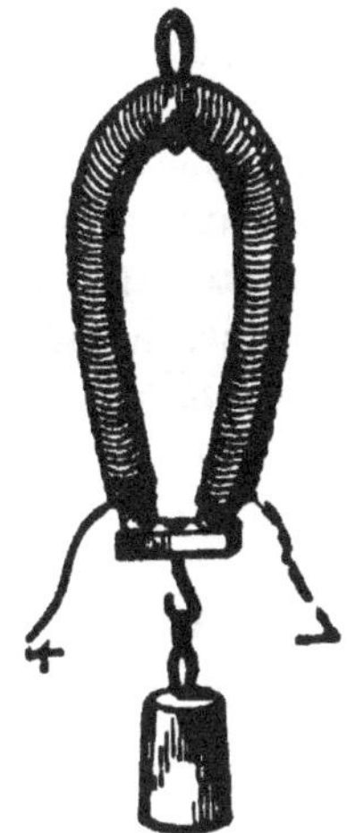

Fig. 181.

209. The *ring* helix (fig. 182) is a striking mode of exhibiting the inducing effect of a voltaic current. Here two semicircles of soft iron, fitted with handles, are magnetized by the current passing in R, the ends *a b* being in connection with a battery. The rings of iron and of wire are quite separate, and, when the current passes, the iron (about ¾ inch diameter) becomes so strongly magnetic as to sustain, easily, 50 pounds. Small electro-magnets have been made to sustain 420 times their own weight.

210. *Electro-magnetic Motions.*—Faraday first produced motion by the mutual action of magnets and conductors, and Prof. Henry, in this country, about the same time. By various combinations of the principles already explained, a great number of ingenious pieces of electro-magnetic apparatus have been contrived for showing motion; by wires attracting and repelling—by circles and rectangles of wires revolving the one within the other—by armatures revolving before the poles of permanent or electro-magnets, and these adapted to carry various forms of machinery. But as these illustrate no new principles, we refer the student to the excellent manual of magnetism by Daniel Davis, Boston, where the whole subject will be found very ably discussed.

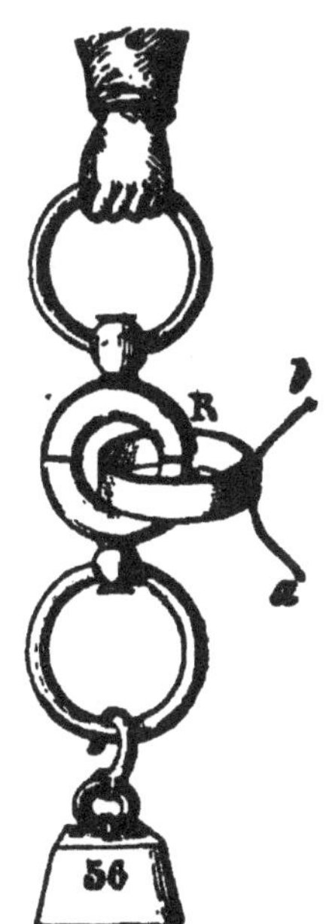

Fig. 182.

211. The *Electro-magnetic Telegraph* is a contrivance which very happily illustrates the application of abstract

---

209. What does fig. 182 show? 210. Who first observed electro-magnetic motions?

scientific principles and discovery to the wants of society. The inconceivably rapid passage of an electrical current over a metallic conductor was discovered by Watson in 1747, and this discovery gave the first hint of the possibility of using electricity as a means of telegraphic communication. Numerous attempts were made, very early after this discovery, to construct a telegraph to be worked by ordinary electricity; but from difficulties inherent in the mode, these attempts were attended with only very partial success. The discovery of electro-magnetism by Œrsted, in 1820, supplied the necessary means of successful construction. Superior to all other contrivances in the essential conditions of simplicity, in construction and notation, is the beautiful contrivance patented by Professor Morse in 1837. In the accompanying figure (183)

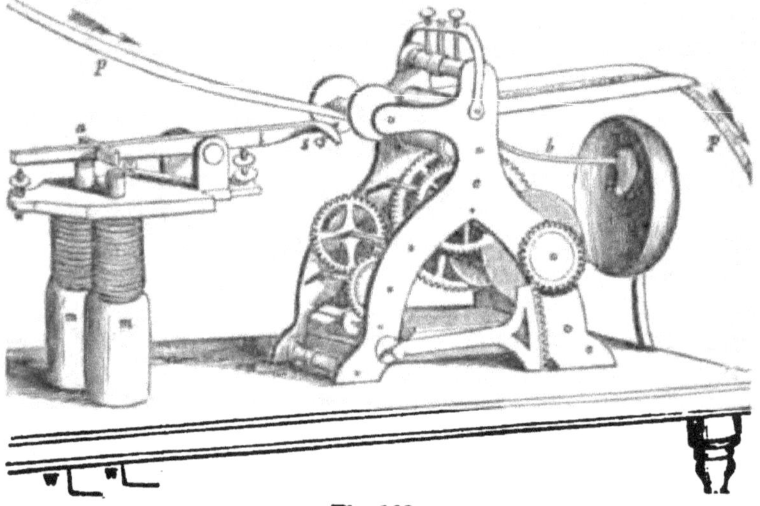

Fig. 183.

we have a view of the most essential parts of Morse's telegraphic register. A simple electro-magnet *m m*, with its poles upward, receives its induced magnetism from a current of electricity conducted by the wires W W from the distant station. As soon as the circuit is completed, *m m* becomes a magnet, and draws to its poles an armature or bar of soft iron *a* on the lever *l*. The motion of this lever starts a spring which sets in motion the clock arrangement *c*. This clock machinery, in consequence of the weight attached to

---

211. Explain the principles of the electro-magnetic telegraph and its operations.

it, will, when once set in motion, continue to move. The immediate object of the clock machinery is to draw forward a narrow ribbon of paper *p p* in the direction of the arrows, and to cause it to advance with a regular motion. The paper ribbon passes by the end of the pen-lever *l*, in which is a steel point *s*, that indents the paper whenever this end of the lever is thrown upward by the attraction of the armature *a* to the magnet *m*. If *m m* were constantly magnetized, the mark made by the point *s* would be a continuous line. But we can make and discharge an electro-magnet as often and as fast as we please; the instant, therefore, the circuit W W is broken, *m m* ceases to be a magnet, and lets go the iron armature *a*, when the point *s* of the lever falls, so as no longer to mark the paper. The circuit being renewed, the point marks again; and this may be repeated as often as the operator pleases. The length of time that the circuit is closed will be exactly registered in the corresponding length of the mark made by *s*. The completing of the circuit is performed by touching a spring on the operator's table, which establishes a metallic communication between the poles of the battery. A touch will produce a dot, a continued pressure a long line, and intermitting repeated touches a series of dots and short lines. These easily form an alphabet. To complete the arrangement, each operator must have his own battery in connection with the register at the distant station. In practice, only one wire is used with each register, the circuit being completed by connecting the other pole of the battery with the moist earth by means of a buried metallic plate and a wire. The remarkable observation that the earth could be used in this manner as a part of the circuit, was made by Steinheil, in Germany, in 1837. Such is a brief account of one of the most remarkable discoveries of modern times. In Bain's telegraph, the circuit decomposes a salt of iron, staining a paper with the marks of the conductor, and no magnet is employed.

212. The telegraph has become an important auxiliary in astronomical observations, by furnishing an exact means of determining longitudes. For this purpose the principal astronomical observatories in the United States are connected by telegraphic wires, and such is the velocity of the electrical wave that any communication made from one station will be

---

212. How is the telegraph auxiliary to astronomy?

received at all the others at almost the same instant. The velocity of the wave has been determined by the experiments of the Coast Survey to be about 15,000 miles in a minute. Wheatstone asserts that the wave of electricity moves as rapidly at least as that of light. Other very ingenious and important applications have been made of the telegraph for regulating time-pieces and for signalizing fires. The city of Boston is provided with such a system, a detailed description of which may be found in the American Journal of Science for January, 1852.

One curious fact connected with the operation of the telegraph is the induction of atmospheric electricity upon the wires to such an extent as often to cause the machines at the several stations to record the approach of a thunder-storm. This induction occasions a serious inconvenience in working the telegraph, not unattended with danger to the operators.

213. Professor Henry observed that when the current from a single pair of plates was passed through a long conducting wire, a vivid spark appeared at the instant of breaking contact between the conductor and the battery; accompanied, also, by a feeble shock. A long conductor, then, supplies the place of an increased number of plates in a voltaic series, and to some degree imparts the quality of intensity to a current of quantity. A flat spiral of copper ribbon, one hundred feet long, wound with cotton, and varnished, shows these effects well. The magnetic needle indicates the direction of the current, (fig. 184.) The opposite sides of the spiral of course produce opposite effects on the needle. The magnetism produced is, however, to be distinguished from the new effects excited by the passage of the feeble current through the coiled conductor, on breaking contact, *i. e.* the vivid spark and the shock. The latter is feeble with 100 feet of copper ribbon, and becomes more intense if the length of the conductor be increased, the battery remaining the same; but the sparks are diminished by lengthening

Fig. 184.

What other facts are mentioned regarding the telegraph? 213. What was Henry's observation on the spiral?

the conductor beyond a certain point. The increase of intensity in the shock is also limited by the increased resistance or diminished conduction of the wire, which finally counteracts the influence of the increasing length of the current. On the other hand, if the battery power be increased, the coil remaining the same, these actions diminish.

214. These effects Prof. Henry ascribed to the generation of a *secondary* current at the moment of breaking contact. This secondary current moves in a direction opposite to that of the battery current. If a long coil of fine, insulated wire be brought within a small distance of the flat spiral, this new current will be detected in the second coil. The arrangement used by Prof. Henry is seen in the annexed figure. A small battery L is connected with the flat spiral of copper ribbon A by wires from the battery cups Z and C. This communication is broken at will, by drawing the end of one of the battery wires Z over the rasp. When the coil of fine wire W is in the position indicated in fig. 185, and the hands

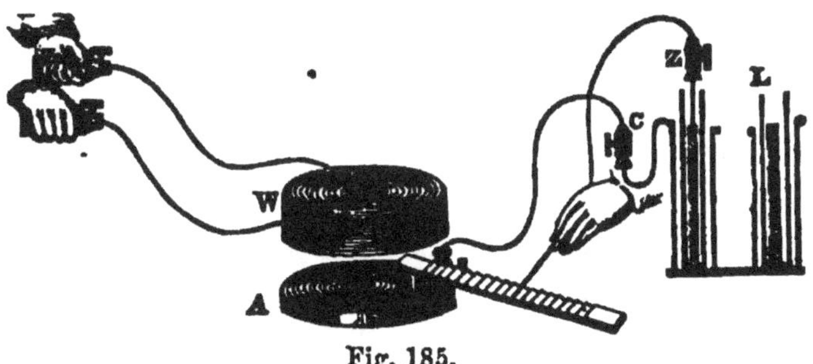

Fig. 185.

grasp the conductors, a violent shock is felt as often as the circuit is broken by the passage of the wire over the rasp. When the coil W contains several thousand feet of wire, and is brought near A, the shocks are too intense to be borne. As this induction takes place through a distance of many inches, we can, by placing the spiral A against a division wall, or the door of a room, give shocks to a person in another room, who grasps the conductors of the wire coil W, and brings it near to the wall on the side opposite to A. A screen or disc of metal introduced between the two coils will cut off this inductive influence. But if it be slit by a cut

---

214. What were these currents called? How do they move? What of the spark and shock?

from the centre to the circumference, as *a b* in fig. 186, the induction of an intense current in W is the same as if no screen were present.

Fig. 186.

Discs or screens of wood, glass, paper, or other non-conductors, offer no impediment to this induction.

215. *Induced Currents of the third, fourth, and fifth order.*—If the wires from W be connected with another flat spiral, and it with a second coil of fine wire, and so on, (fig. 187,) a series of currents will be induced in each alternation of coils. The secondary intense current in B will induce a quantity current in the second flat spiral C; and a second fine wire coil W will induce a tertiary intense current, and so on. These currents have been carried to the ninth order,

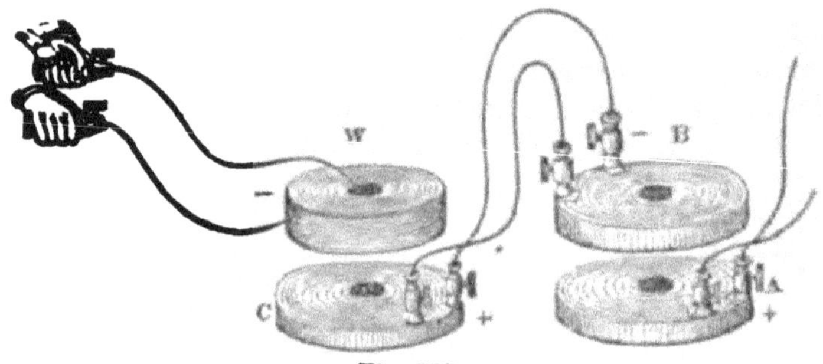

Fig. 187.

decreasing each time in energy by every removal from the original battery current. The polarity, or direction of these secondary currents, alternates, commencing with the secondary. Thus the current of the battery is +; and the secondary current is +; the current of the third order is —; the current of the fourth order is +; and the current of the fifth order is —. These alternations are marked in the figure above, and were also determined by Prof. Henry.

216. *Compound Electro-magnetic Machine.*—By combining the results just briefly enumerated, a great number of ingenious electro-magnetic machines have been produced, adapted to medical use, and illustrative of the induction of magnetism and secondary currents. One of these, contrived by Dr. Page, is seen in fig. 188. In this little machine, a short coil of stout insulated copper wire forms a helix, within which some straight soft-iron wires M are placed. The

---

215. To what degree have they been carried?

battery current is made to pass through this stout wire, by which means magnetism is induced in the soft iron. The conducting wires are so arranged beneath the board that the glass cup C containing some mercury is in connection with the battery. The bent wire W dips into this mercury, and also by a branch into B, and when in the position shown in the figure, the current from the battery will flow uninterruptedly. As soon, however, as the battery connection is completed, M becomes strongly magnetic, and draws to itself a small ball of iron on the end of P; this moves the whole wire P W and raises the point out of the mercury C; as the wire leaves the mercury, a brilliant spark is seen on its surface, the contact being thus broken with the battery, M ceases to receive induced magnetism, and the ball P being consequently no longer attracted to M, the wire W falls by its gravity to the position in the figure. This again establishes the battery connection, and the same effects just described recur; thus the bent wire W receives a vibratory motion, and at each vibration a brilliant spark is seen at C, and M becomes magnetic. It remains only to mention that the short quantity wire is surrounded by a fine intensity wire, 2000 to 3000 feet long, having no metallic connection with the battery or quantity wire, with its ends terminating in two binding screws on the left of the board. The fine wire receives a secondary induced current like the coil W, (185,) which, if touched, produces the most intense shocks at each vibration of the wire. These shocks are graduated by withdrawing part or all of the soft-iron wires M.

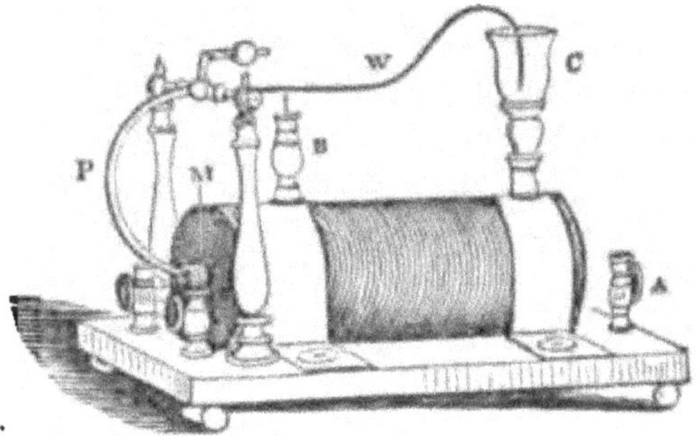

Fig. 188.

217. *Magneto-Electricity.*—As we have seen effects produced from galvanism which exactly resemble those of ordinary machine electricity and the magnetic influence, so, conversely, we might expect the production of electrical effects from the magnet. The electrical current from a single

---

216. Explain the apparatus, fig. 188.

galvanic pair, we have seen, produces magnetism in a spiral wire at right angles with its own course; so the induction of magnetism in soft iron from a permanent magnet, in like manner, produces an electrical current at right angles to itself in the wire coiled on the armature. This class of phenomena was discovered by Faraday in 1831, and our countryman, Mr. J. Saxton, soon contrived a machine very similar to the one in fig. 189, called a magneto-electrical

Fig. 189.

machine. This consists of a powerful magnet S, secured to a board, with its poles so situated that an armature, formed of two large bundles of insulated copper wire W, wound on *soft-iron* axes, may be revolved on an axis before its poles, by the multiplying wheel M. A current of electricity is thus induced in W, just as in the flat coils, the permanent magnet here taking the place of the flat spiral. The current excited in W is led off by conductors to the binding screws *p* and *n*, the continuity of the current being broken (in imitation of the rasp in 185) by a contrivance at *b* on the axis, called a break-piece, (fig. 190,) which is made by alternate ribs of metal *c* and ivory *i*, the current is broken by the ivory and renewed by the metal, and at every break, the person whose hands grasp the conductors, secured to *p* and *n*, feels a sharp shock, which may be graduated at will by the rapidity of the revolutions of M, and by the adjustment of the break *b*. A long and fine wire--say

Fig. 190.

217. What is magneto-electricity? Explain fig. 189.

3000 feet of wire $\frac{1}{98}$ of an inch in diameter—is required to produce shocks and chemical decompositions. A shorter and stouter wire, as 250 feet of wire $\frac{1}{10}$ or $\frac{1}{20}$ inch in diameter will produce no shock, but will deflagrate the metals powerfully, and produce a secondary current of induction in soft iron. We thus imitate in magnetism the effects produced from a voltaic current, the short and stout wire of the armature is the simple circuit of large plates; the long and fine wire is like the compound circuit of smaller plates.

Thermo-Electricity, or the Electrical Current excited by Heat.

218. If two metals unlike in crystalline structure and conducting power are united by solder, and the point of their union is heated or cooled, an electrical current will be excited, which will flow from the heated point to the metal which is the poorer conductor. Bismuth and antimony are such metals, being bad conductors, and unlike in crystalline structure. If two bars of these metals are united, as in fig. 191, and the point *c* is warmed by a lamp, a current will be set in motion, which will flow from *b* to *a*, as in the figure.

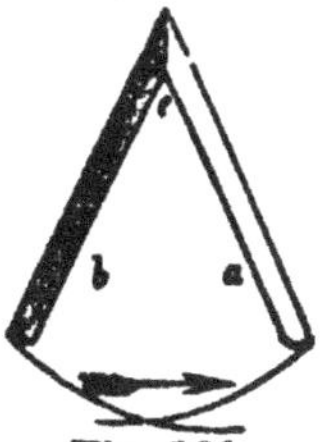

Fig. 191.

The compass-needle may be thus affected, as by the voltaic current. For this purpose two bars may be mounted as in fig. 192, and their junction being heated by a lamp, the needle will swing, in consequence of the electrical current excited by the heat.

Fig. 192.

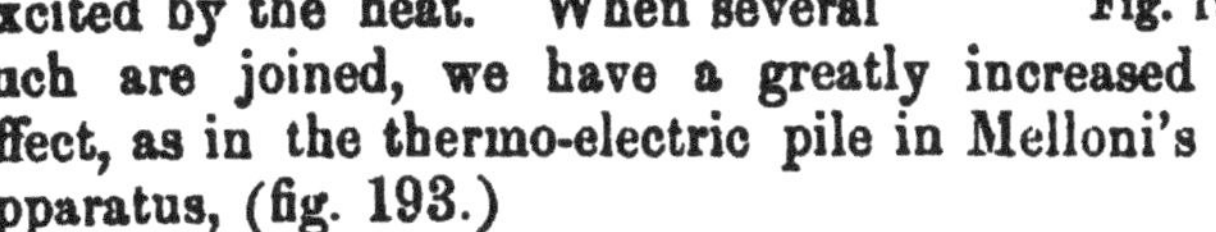

When several such are joined, we have a greatly increased effect, as in the thermo-electric pile in Melloni's apparatus, (fig. 193.)

Fig. 193.

219. Thermo-electric effects are not confined to metals, for they may be produced from other solids, and even from fluids; and a single metal, as an iron wire, which has been twisted or bent abruptly, will originate a thermo-electric current when the distorted part is greatly

218. What is thermo-electricity? How does the current move?

heated. The rank of the principal metals in the thermo-electric series is as follows, beginning with the positive:—Bismuth, mercury, platinum, tin, lead, gold, silver, zinc, iron, antimony. When the junction of any pair of these is heated, the current passes from that which is highest to that which is lowest in the list, the extremes affording the most powerful combination.

If we pass a feeble current of electricity through a pair of antimony and bismuth, the temperature of the system rises, if the current passes from the former to the latter; but if from the bismuth to the antimony, cold is produced in the compound bar. If the reduction of temperature is slightly aided artificially, water contained in a cavity in one of the bars may be frozen. Thus we see that as change of temperature disturbs the electrical equilibrium, so conversely the disturbance of the latter produces the former.

Animal Electricity.

220. The existence of free electricity in the animal body is proved by the results of Aldini and Matteucci. In some animals we see a special apparatus for the purpose of exciting at will intense currents of electricity. There are also such currents in all animals. For example, when the lumbar nerves of a frog, held in the manner shown in fig. 194, are touched to the tongue of an ox lately killed, and at the same instant the operator grasps with the other hand, well wetted in salt water, an ear of the ox, a convulsion of the frog's legs indicates the passage of an electric current.

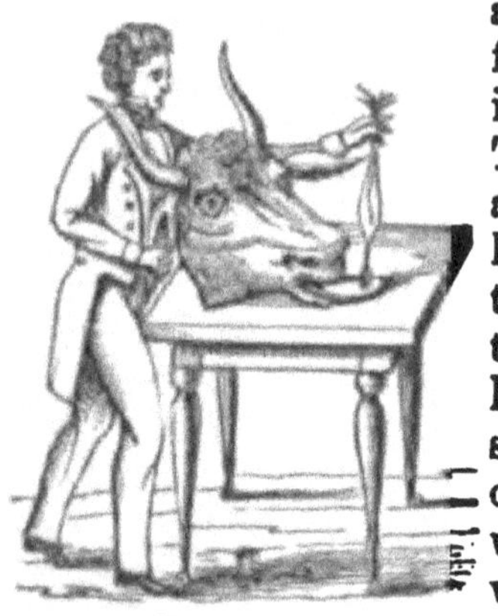

Fig. 194.

221. The same delicate electroscope also shows similar excitement when its pendulous ischiatic nerves touch the human tongue, the toe of the frog being held between the

---

219. What range have these effects? How is a fall of temperature observed in a compound bar of antimony and bismuth? 220. What is animal electricity? Explain the experiment in fig. 194. 221. How else is the same fact shown? How does the current circulate?

moistened thumb and finger of the experimenter. This is what Donné calls the musculo-cutaneous current; passing from the external, or cutaneous, to the internal, or mucous, covering of the body. This current may be detected, as was shown by Aldini, in the frog's legs above. For this purpose he prepared the lower extremities of a vigorous frog, (fig. 195,) and, by bending up the leg, brought the muscles of the thigh in contact with the lumbar nerves: contractions immediately ensued. Thus it appears from experiments made by Matteucci, that a current of positive electricity is always circulating from the interior to the exterior of a muscle, and that although the quantity is exceedingly small, yet by arranging a series of muscles, having their exterior and interior surfaces alternately connected, he produced sufficient electricity to cause decided effects. By a series of half thighs of frogs, arranged as in fig. 196, he decomposed the iodid of potassium, deflected a galvanometer needle to 90°, and by a condenser caused the gold-leaves of an electroscope to diverge. The irritable muscles of the frog's legs form an electroscope 56,000 times more delicate than the most delicate gold-leaf electrometer. Professor Matteucci's frog-galvanoscope (fig. 197) is therefore far the most sensitive test of electricity that can be employed. When the pendulous nerve is touched simultaneously in the places where electrical excitement is suspected, the muscles in the tube are instantly convulsed.

Fig. 195.

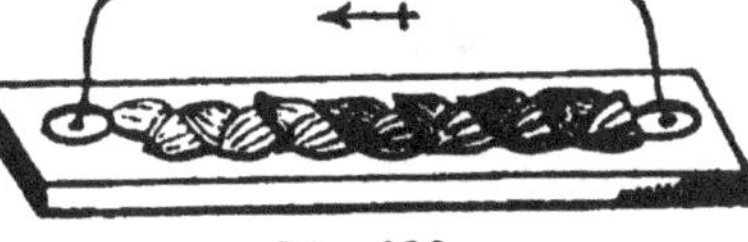

Fig. 196.

222. The electrical eel of South America mentioned by Humboldt, and the torpedo—a flat fish found on our own coast—are remarkable examples of those animals having a special electrical apparatus of nervous matter and cellular tissue arranged in the manner of the pile. The student is referred to the lectures of Pro-

Fig. 197.

What has Donné called it? How is it shown in the legs of the frog alone? How does this current circulate? How does fig. 196 prove it? What is the delicacy of the frog-galvanoscope? 222. What animals have a special electric apparatus?

fessor Matteucci on living beings for further details on this very interesting subject. We can only add, that the shock from these animals is sufficient to charge a Leyden jar, to produce chemical decompositions, and to paralyze vigorous animals.

The legs of the common grasshopper are, it is said, equally sensitive electroscopes as those of the frog.

Electro-Chemical Decomposition.

223. By far the most interesting chemical result of Volta's pile was the new power it placed in the hands of chemists, of unfolding the secrets of combination, and of assigning their relative positions to the several elements. Indeed, the electro-chemical theory has been carried so far by some chemists, that every chemical decomposition has been referred to the play of electrical forces.

224. The *decomposition of water* is the finest possible illustration of this power. Water is a compound of oxygen and hydrogen gases, in the proportions of one measure of the former to two of the latter. When two gold or platinum wires are connected with the opposite ends of the battery, and held a short distance asunder in a cup of water, a train of gas-bubbles will be seen rising from each and escaping at the surface. With two glass tubes placed over the platinum poles, (fig. 198,) we can collect these bubbles as they rise, and shall soon find that the gas given off from the — plate is twice the volume of that obtained from the + plate. When the tubes are of the same size, this difference of volume becomes at once evident to the eye. By examining these gases, we shall find them, respectively, pure hydrogen and pure oxygen, in the exact proportion of two volumes of the former to one of the latter. The rapidity of the decomposition is greater when the water is made a better conductor, by adding a few drops of sulphuric acid.

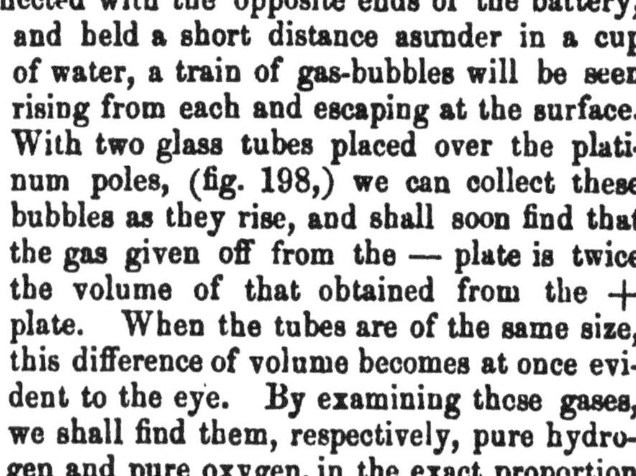

Fig. 198.

223. What was the most interesting result of Volta's pile? 224. How is water decomposed by it? Describe fig. 198.

If we employ a decomposing cell with only one tube over the conductors, it will be found that the gaseous contents will explode by the electric spark or by a lighted taper; and if this is done over water the perfection of the vacuum resulting from the explosion will be seen by the height of the column which rises in the tube, (fig. 199.)

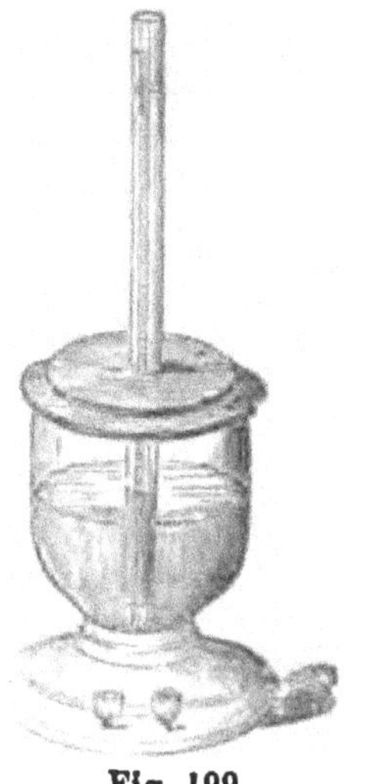

Fig. 199.

225. We learn from this most instructive experiment, that the voltaic current has power to decompose chemical compounds, that this decomposition takes place in definite proportions of the constituents—and that these constituents appear invariably at opposite poles of the battery.

226. A decomposing cell interposed in the circuit will give us an exact account of the amount of electricity flowing. Such an instrument has been called by Faraday a *voltameter*, (fig. 200.) It differs from the common decomposing cell, in having a ground-glass tube at top bent twice, so as to deliver the accumulating gases into a graduated air-vessel, in which their volume is measured. A more simple form of the apparatus is easily constructed, as in figure 201, (page 144,) of two glass tubes, two corks, and the conductors *p p*.

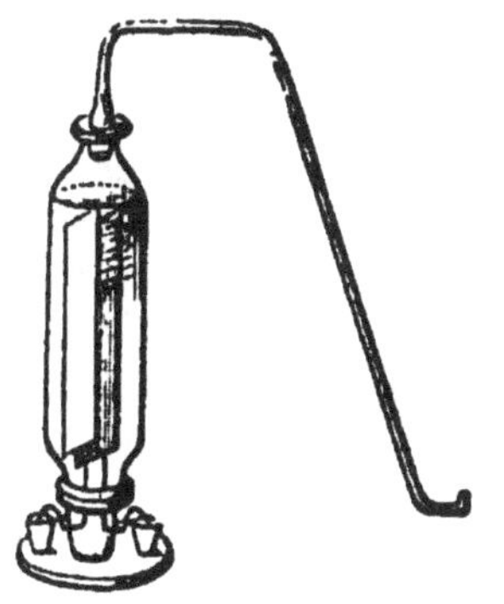

Fig. 200.

227. *The experimental researches in electricity by Dr. Faraday*, which are the basis of modern science on this subject, required the introduction of certain new terms, some of which require explanation. The terminal wires or conductors of a battery are often termed the *poles*, as if they possessed some attractive power by which they draw bodies to themselves, as a magnet attracts iron. Faraday has shown that this notion is a mistake, and that the terminal wires act merely as a path or door

---

225. What does this experiment teach? 226. What other cells are named? 227. What is said of Faraday's researches? What did they require? What does he call the poles, and why?

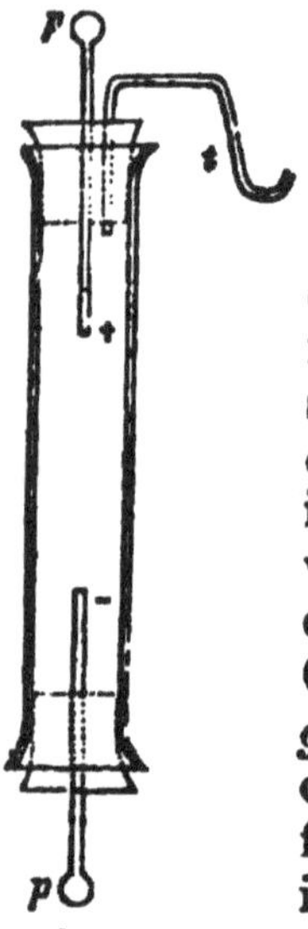

Fig. 201.

to the currents, and he therefore calls them *electrodes*, from *electron* and *odos*, a way. The *electrodes* are any surfaces which convey an electric current into and out of a decomposable liquid. The term *electrolysis*, from *electron*, and the Greek verb *luo*, to unloose, is used to express decomposition; and the substances suffering decomposition are termed *electrolytes*. Thus, the experiment mentioned in the last section is a case of *electrolysis*, in which water is the *electrolyte*. The elements of an electrolyte are called *ions*, from the Greek particle *ion*, going, since the elements *go* to the + or — electrode. The electrodes are distinguished as the *anode* and the *cathode*, from *ana*, upward, and *odos*, way, or the way in which the sun rises; and *kata*, downward, and *odos*, or the way in which the sun sets; the anode is +, and the cathode —. We will now briefly consider the

228. *Conditions of Electro-Chemical Decomposition.*—(1.) All compounds are not electrolytes, that is, they are not directly decomposable by the voltaic current. Many bodies, however, not themselves electrolytes, are decomposed by a secondary action. Thus, nitric acid is decomposed in the electrical circuit by the secondary action of the nascent hydrogen, which, uniting with one equivalent of the oxygen, again forms water and nitrous acid. Sulphuric acid is not an electrolyte, while hydrochloric acid is; and the nascent chlorine from the latter attacks the + electrode, if it be of gold. (2.) Electrolysis cannot happen unless the fluid be a conductor of electricity; and no solid body, however good a conductor, has ever been thus decomposed. A plate of ice, however thin, interposed between the electrodes, will entirely prevent the passage of the power; but the electrolysis will proceed as soon as the least hole melts in the ice, through which the power can pass. Fluidity is therefore a very essential condition of electrolysis. The fluidity may be that of heat, or of solution; thus, the

---

Explain the terms electrode, electrolysis, and electrolyte. What are ions? 228. Are all compounds electrolytes? Give examples. What is the second condition of electrolysis? Give examples.

chlorids of lead, silver, and tin are not electrolysed in a solid state, but when fused they are decomposed with ease. (3.) The ease of electro-chemical decomposition seems in a good degree proportioned to the conducting power of the fluid. Thus, pure water is by no means a good conductor, and its electrolysis is difficult; but the addition to it of a few drops of sulphuric acid, or of some other soluble conductor, greatly promotes the ease with which it is decomposed. (4.) The amount of electrolysis is directly proportioned to the quantity of electricity which passes the electrodes. (5.) The binary compounds of the elements, as a class, are the best electrolytes. Water and iodid of potassium are instances; while sulphuric acid, which has three equivalents of base to one of acid, is not an electrolyte. No two elements seem capable of forming more than one electrolyte. (6.) Most of the salts are resolvable into acid and base. Thus, sulphate of soda is resolved into sulphuric acid, which appears at the + electrode, and will there redden a vegetable blue; and the soda which appears at the — electrode will restore the previously reddened blue; so that by reversing the direction of the current, these striking effects are also reversed.

229. (7.) *A single ion*, as bromine, for instance, has no disposition to pass to either of the electrodes, and the current has no effect upon it. There can be no electrolysis except when a separation of ions takes place, and the separated elements go one to each electrode. (8.) There is no such thing, in fact, (as has been often supposed,) as an actual transfer of ions from one part of the fluid to either electrode. In the case of water, for example, oxygen is given out on one side, and hydrogen on the other. In order that this may be the case, there must be water between the electrodes. We cannot believe that the separation of the elements takes place at the electrode where one element is evolved, and that the other travels over unseen to the opposite electrode. We may,

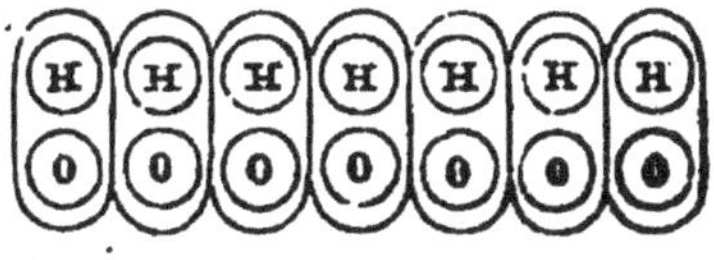

Fig. 202.

(3.) To what is the ease of the electrolysis proportioned? (4.) To what is its *amount* owing? (5.) What class of compounds are the best electrolytes? Give examples. (6.) What of salts? Give examples. 229. (7.) What is said of a single *ion*? (8.) What of the transfer of ions? Give the explanation offered of the decomposition of water.

however, conceive of water in its quiet state, as represented by the diagram, (fig. 202,) each molecule being firmly united by *polar attractions* (218) to every other, and that the electrolytic force of the electric current has power to disturb this polar equilibrium, each molecule being similarly affected. In this case the electrolysis will proceed from particle to particle through the whole chain of affinities, decomposing and recomposing, until the ultimate particle on each side, having no polar force to neutralize it, escapes at that electrode which has a polarity opposite to itself. This explanation may be better understood, perhaps, by inspecting the second diagram, (fig. 203,) which represents a series of compound molecules of water undergoing electrolysis, the H and O being eliminated at the opposite extremities. The same explanation will be found to serve for all other cases of electrolysis, both simple and secondary.

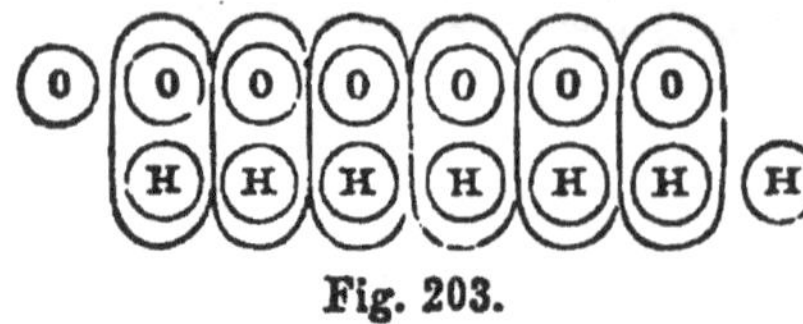

Fig. 203.

230. (9.) A *surface of water, and even of air,* has been shown capable of acting as an electrode, proving that the contact of a metallic conductor with the decomposing fluid is not essential. The discharge from a powerful electrical machine was made to pass from a sharp point through air to a pointed piece of litmus paper moistened with sulphate of soda, and then to a second piece of turmeric paper similarly moistened. This discharge had power to effect a true electrolysis; the blue litmus was reddened by the sulphuric acid set free from the sulphate of soda, while the yellow turmeric was turned brown by the alkaline soda from the same salt.

231. (10.) *Electrolysis takes place in a series of compounds in the precise order of their equivalents.* Thus, if wine-glasses are arranged in a series, and in one is placed sulphate of soda, in another acidulated water, in another iodid of potassium, and in another hydrochloric acid, and if the whole series be connected together by siphon tubes, or moistened lampwick, passing from glass to glass, and a

---

230. (9.) What is said of electrolysis without metallic conductors? Explain the experiment of the electrolysis of sulphate of soda by the electrical machine. 231. How does electrolysis occur in a series of compounds?

powerful galvanic current be then passed through them, electrolysis will occur in all, but unequally.

It has been proved by accurate experiment, that the decomposition which ensues is in exact proportion to the equivalents of each substance. In other words, we may say it requires one equivalent of electricity to decompose one equivalent of an electrolyte formed from the union of an equivalent of acid and another of base. Conversely, from the fact that an equivalent of electricity is required to decompose any compound, it is proved that the opposite elements of this compound, in uniting, will disengage the same equivalent of electricity.

232. (11.) *The passage of a current within the cells of a voltaic battery* depends also upon the decomposition in each cell, equally with that between the platinum electrodes. The same phenomena which we notice in the decomposing cell (224) take place also in each battery cell. Water is decomposed, and the hydrogen is given off from the positive plate, while the oxygen combines with the zinc, and thus escapes detection. Therefore, no fluid not an electrolyte is suitable to excite a battery. Acid water acts, for this purpose, only by the decomposition of the water and oxydation of the zinc. The presence of the acid is useful only so far as it combines with the oxyd of zinc constantly accumulating on the zinc plate, which must be removed as fast as formed, in order to keep up a steady flow of electricity.

233. The *theories* which have been proposed to account for electro-chemical decomposition and the action of the voltaic circuit, we cannot discuss here, any further than to say that the *chemical theory* first proposed by Dr. Wollaston is now generally accepted. Volta argued that the contact of different metals was essential to the production of a current. The researches of Faraday, however, in confirming the chemical view of Wollaston, have completely disproved the contact theory. A very simple experiment by Faraday illustrates this statement. A slip of amalgamated sheet zinc bent at a right angle is hung in a glass of dilute acid; on it is laid a folded piece of bibulous paper moistened with

---

In other words, what do we say? Conversely, what? 232. How does a current pass in the cells of a battery? What happens in each cell? What is requisite in the fluid used to excite a battery? How does acid water act in the battery? 233. What two theories have been proposed to account for the electrical phenomena of electrolysis? What simple experiment disproves the contact theory?

Fig. 204.

iodid of potassum. A platinum plate, with an attached wire of the same metal, is now placed in the acid water, but not in contact with the zinc; the sharpened end of the wire is bent, so as to touch the moistened paper, and very soon it is discolored by a brown spot made by the free iodine, liberated from the electro-chemical decomposition of the iodid of potassium, with which the paper is moistened. There is no contact of metals, and the current is excited only from the decomposition of the iodid out of the cell, and of the water in it. A very strong argument in favor of the chemical theory has been before mentioned, that the direction of the current is always determined by the *nature of the chemical* action—the metals most acted on being always positive.

234. The *electrotype*, or deposition of metals from their solution by the voltaic current, seems to have been suggested by Daniell's battery. It has been remarked, that the copper of the sulphate of copper in the outer cell of that battery is deposited in a metallic state. The procuring of a pure metal in a perfectly malleable state, by means of a current of electricity, is a most important fact, and has given rise to a new and valuable art, which has become wonderfully extended in its applications. We thus accomplish, in fact, a cold casting of copper, silver, gold, zinc, and many other metals; and a new field of great extent has been thus opened for the application of metallurgic processes. The tinting of metals of various hues by metallic oxyds, and the coloring of their surfaces by palladium, are among the most surprising of its effects. The very simple apparatus required to show these results experimentally, is represented in the figure, (205.) It is nothing, in fact, but a single cell of Daniell's battery. A glass tumbler S, a common lamp-chimney P, with a bladder-skin tied over the lower end and filled with dilute acid, is all the apparatus required. A strong solution of sulphate of copper is put in the tumbler, and a zinc rod Z in P,

Fig. 205.

234. What is the electrotype? Explain its uses.

the moulds, or casts, *m m* are seen suspended by wires attached to the binding screw of Z. Thus arranged, the copper solution is slowly decomposed, and the metal is evenly and firmly deposited on *m*, *m*. A perfect reverse copy of *m* is thus obtained in solid, malleable copper. The back of *m* is protected by varnish, to prevent the adhesion of the metallic copper to it. In this manner the most elaborate and costly medals are easily multiplied, and in the most accurate manner. In practice, casts are made in fusible metal of the object to be copied, and the operation is conducted in a separate cell, containing only the sulphate of copper, one of Smee's batteries supplying the power. The art is also now extensively applied to plating in gold and silver from their solutions; the metals thus deposited adhering perfectly to the metallic surface on which they are deposited, provided these be quite clean and bright

All the copper-plates of the charts of the Coast Survey are reproduced by the electrotype—the originals are never used in the press, but only the copies, and any required number of these may be produced at small expense.

PART II.—CHEMICAL PHILOSOPHY.

ELEMENTS AND THEIR LAWS OF COMBINATION.

235. The number of elements, (or simple substances,) as now recognized, is sixty-two, forty-nine of which are metals The elements are usually divided into metals and metalloids, or non-metallic substances. This convenient distinction is not strictly accurate, since there are several elements, as tellurium, carbon, arsenic, silicium, and others, which seem to possess an intermediate character. The term metalloid is therefore preferable. Only fourteen of the elementary bodies are of common occurrence, and of these the atmo sphere, water, and the great bulk of the planet are composed. The remainder are comparatively rare, and are known only to the chemist. Of these, twenty-one, marked in the table with an asterisk (*), will not be discussed in this work, or will be very briefly considered, because of their great rarity, and the difficulty of procuring the substances containing them.

236. At common temperatures, and when set free from combination, nearly all the elements are solids. Two, mercury and bromine, are fluids, and five are gases, namely, chlorine, fluorine, hydrogen, oxygen, and nitrogen. A few only of the elements are found naturally in a free or uncombined state, among which we may name oxygen, nitrogen, carbon, sulphur, and nine or ten metals. All the rest exist in combination with each other, and so completely disguised as to manifest none of their properties.

237. The names of the elements are arbitrary or conventional, while the nomenclature of their compounds is subject to the strictest laws. Some of the elementary bodies have been known from the remotest antiquity, and were in common use long before the science of chemistry was heard of. Thus several metals, as Copper, (*Cuprum*,) Gold, (*Aurum*,) Iron, (*Ferrum*,) Mercury, (*Hydrargyrum*,) Sil-

---

235. What is the number of elements? How divided? What occupy an intermediate position? 236. What is the physical condition of the elements? Which are fluid? Which gaseous? Which found uncombined? 237. What of the names of elements? Which have been long known?

ver, (*Argentum*,) Lead, (*Plumbum*,) Tin, (*Stannum*,) have long been known either by the names we now give them, or by those Latin terms of which our English names are translations. The alchemists named the metals after the various planets. Thus, Gold was called *Sol*, the Sun; Silver, *Luna*, the Moon; Iron, *Mars*; Lead, *Saturn*; Tin, *Jupiter*; Quicksilver, *Mercury*; and Copper, *Venus*. Hence, formerly the astronomical signs or symbols of these planets were employed to represent the names of these metals, and they are still in use in some countries.

Several of the elements have been named from some prominent or distinguishing physical property of color, taste, or smell, which they possess: thus, Bromine is so called from the Greek word *bromos*, fetor; Chlorine, from *chloros*, green, in allusion to its greenish color; Chromium, from *chroma*, color, because it makes highly-colored compounds, as *chrome-yellow*; Glucinum, from *glukus*, sweet, from the sweet taste of its salts; Iodine, from *ion*, a violet, and *eidos*, in the likeness of. Another class of names has been contrived from what was supposed to be the characteristic attribute of the body in combination. Thus, Oxygen was so named because many of its compounds are acids, from the Greek, *oxus*, acid, and *gennao*, I produce. Hydrogen is from *hudor*, water, and *gennao*, I produce.

238. It has been discovered that the elements, in combining among themselves, unite always in certain weights, invariable in each case, and supposed to have an immediate relation to the atomic constitution of the substance. These weights represent respectively the quantities in which the elements unite with each other, and they are called equivalent atomic weights or combining numbers. In the following table, the equivalent or combining numbers of all the elementary bodies are given in accordance with the latest and best authorities. Because hydrogen enters into combination with other bodies in a smaller weight than any other known element, it has generally been used in Great Britain and in this country as the basis of the scale of equivalent numbers. It is supposed also, by some good chemists, that the numbers expressing the combining weights of all bodies

---

What of astronomical signs? Whence such names as bromine, Hydrogen? Iodine, &c.? 238. How do the elements unite? What do the weights represent? What are they called? Why is hydrogen unity?

would be found, on more accurate research, to be simple multiples of the unit of hydrogen. If this view were correct, it would give us the great convenience of avoiding fractional numbers. The latest investigations have so far confirmed this idea, that in the present edition of this work a largely increased number of elements stand with simple numbers. Berzelius determined more atomic numbers than any other chemist, and his labors have in most cases stood the severest review, and deserve the everlasting gratitude of chemists. Most chemists of continental Europe assume oxygen as 100; therefore, to convert the numbers of the following table to the oxygen scale, multiply them by 12·5.

TABLE OF ELEMENTARY SUBSTANCES, WITH THEIR SYMBOLS AND ATOMIC WEIGHTS OR EQUIVALENTS.

Name.	Symbol.	H = 1.	Name.	Symbol.	H = 1.
Aluminum	Al	13·7	Nickel	Ni	29·6
Antimony (Stibium)	Sb	129·	Molybdenum	Mo	46·
Arsenic	As	75·	*Niobium	Nb	
Barium	Ba	68·50	Nitrogen	N	14·
*Beryllium (Glucinum)	Be	4·7	*Norium	No	
Bismuth	Bi	208·	*Osmium	Os	99·6
Boron	B	10·9	Oxygen	O	8·
Bromine	Br	80·	*Palladium	Pd	53·3
Cadmium	Cd	56·	*Pelopium	Pe	
Calcium	Ca	20·	Phosphorus	P	32·
Carbon	C	6·	Platinum	Pt	98·7
*Cerium	Ce	47·	Potassium (Kalium)	K	39·2
Chlorine	Cl	35.50	*Rhodium	R	52·2
Chromium	Cr	26·7	*Ruthenium	Ru	52·2
Cobalt	Co	29·5	Selenium	Se	40·
*Columbium (Tantalum)	Cm,Ta	184·	Silicium	Si	21·3
Copper	Cu	31·7	Silver (Argentum)	Ag	108·
*Didymium	D		Sodium (Natrium)	Na	23·
*Erbium	E		Strontium	Sr	44·
Fluorine	Fl	19·	Sulphur	S	16·
Gold (Aurum)	Au	197·	Tellurium	Te	64·
Hydrogen	H	1·	*Terbium	Tb	
Iodine	I	127·	*Thorium	Th	59·6
*Iridium	Ir	99·	Tin (Stannum)	Sn	59·
Iron	Fe	28·	*Titanium	Ti	25·
*Lantanium	La	36·	*Tungsten (Wolframium)	W	95·
Lead (Plumbum)	Pb	103·5	Uranium	U	60·
Lithium	Li	6·5	*Vanadium	V	68·6
Magnesium	Mg	12·2	*Yttrium	Y	32·2
Manganese	Mn	27·6	Zinc	Zn	32·5
Mercury	Hg	100·	*Zirconium	Zr	22·4

Combination by Weight.

239. The laws by which the elements unite to form compounds, are included in the four following propositions:—

What of its multiple relations? Who determined most atomic weights?

1st The law of *definite* proportions, or, a compound of two or more elements, is always formed by the union of certain definite and unalterable proportions of its constituent elements.

2d. The law of *multiple* proportions, which requires that when two bodies unite in more proportions than one, these proportions bear some simple relation to each other.

3d. The law of *equivalent* proportions, according to which when a body (A) unites with other bodies, (B, C, D, &c.,) the proportions in which B, C, and D unite with A shall represent in numbers the proportions in which they will unite among themselves, in case such union takes place.

4th. The law of the *combining numbers* of compounds, by which the combining proportion of a compound body is the sum of the combining weights of its several elements.

240. These general laws of combination are subject to some modifications, which will be explained as they arise. The first of the laws above given is the result of chemical analysis, and is proved by synthesis. Thus, from nine grains of water we obtain eight grains of oxygen and one of hydrogen, and by the union of the like weights of these two substances we obtain nine grains of water. Constancy of composition is the essential feature of chemical compounds.

By the law of *multiple proportions* we learn that if a body (A) unites with a body (B) in more proportions than one, these proportions bear a simple relation to each other. Thus, we may have the series of compounds $A + B : A + 2B : A + 3B : A + 4B : A + 5B$, as in the case of nitrogen and oxygen, between which this very series occurs, forming five distinct compounds, in which one, two, three, four, and five, parts by weight (atoms) of oxygen unite with one of nitrogen. (2.) In place of this simple ratio we may have one intermediate: thus, the expressions $2A + 3B : 2A + 5B : 2A + 7B$ represent a series of compounds which are equal to the fractional ratios $1 : 1\frac{1}{2}$, $1 : 2\frac{1}{2}$, $1 : 3\frac{1}{2}$.

241. As by chemical analysis the law of definite proportions is established, so by the same direct experimental method do we prove the law of equivalent proportions. Oxygen is an element forming at least one definite compound with every

---

239. What is the 1st law of combination? The 2d? The 3d? The 4th? 240. Whence is law 1st derived? Give an example? What of the law of multiple proportions? Give examples of the 2d modification? 241. How is the law of equivalent proportions demonstrated? What is said of oxygen?

other element known except fluorine. These compounds are termed oxyds, (246.) By analysis we find that water always contains in 100 parts 11·11 parts of hydrogen and 88·89 parts of oxygen. If we ask how much oxygen is proportional, or equivalent to a unit of hydrogen, we state the simple proportion 11·11 : 100 : : 88·89 : x in which $x = 8$, which is therefore the equivalent of oxygen. In like manner, we might go on making analyses of all the compounds of oxygen until we had completed the whole list, when we should have a table of equivalents for all the elements, hydrogen being unity. Thus,

8 parts of oxygen unite with {
16 parts of sulphur,
6 parts of carbon,
1 part of hydrogen,
35·5 parts of chlorine,
100 parts of mercury,
28 parts of iron,
14 parts of nitrogen.

Of course, 16, 6, 1, 35.5, 100, 28, and 14, are respectively the *equivalents* of sulphur, carbon, hydrogen, chlorine, mercury, iron, and nitrogen. Chemical equivalent and atomic weight have the same meaning in this work.

242. If any of those bodies unite to form compounds, the union will always happen in quantities by weight exactly proportional to those numbers. Thus, hydrogen (1) unites with chlorine (35·5) to form chlorohydric or muriatic acid. In 36·5 pounds, therefore, of this acid, there will be 1 pound of hydrogen and 35·5 pounds of chlorine. If sulphur combines with mercury, it will require 16 parts of sulphur and 100 parts of mercury, and there will be 116 parts of sulphuret formed; or it may require 32 parts of sulphur to 100 parts of mercury, when we should have a bisulphuret. If oxygen is assumed as the standard of comparison for atomic weights, then, calling it 100, hydrogen will be 12·5, and all the other elements will have numbers just twelve and a half times as large as their equivalents on the hydrogen scale.

It follows, as a necessary result of this law of equivalent proportions, that the combining numbers of a compound should be the sum of the equivalents of its constituents.

Give the mode of determining atomic weights? Give some examples? What is the meaning of chemical equivalent? Of atomic weight? 242. What is the relation among elements in combination? How is it in chlorohydric acid? In sulphuret of mercury? What of the combining numbers of compounds?

Chemical Nomenclature and Symbols.

243. It would have been a hopeless task for the strongest memory to retain all the names of chemical compounds, if they had—like the names of the elements—been bestowed by the caprice of those who first discovered, or described them. A committee of the French Academy, with Lavoisier at their head, in 1787, settled the principles of chemical nomenclature, which endure to this day, although the actual state of the science requires great changes in them. All chemical compounds are made to derive their names from one or more of their constituents. Before stating the rules of nomenclature, we must define certain general terms of common occurrence.

244. Bodies are divided into *acids*, *bases*, and *salts*. Salts result from the union of acids with bases. By the voltaic pile salts are decomposed (228 [6]) into acids and bases—the acids go to the positive pole, the bases to the negative. We therefore call the acid, in reference to electrical law, the *electro-negative* constituent, and the base the *electro-positive*. This is equally true of those compounds which render up their *elements* in electrolysis as of salts which are simply separated into acids and bases: *e. g.* common salt by electrolysis yields chlorine, an electro-negative element, and sodium, an electro-positive one. The former is an acid, the latter a base.

Acids and bases are further distinguished, in that *acids* redden the blue vegetable infusions, while *bases* restore the colors which the acids have reddened. Some vegetable colors, like syrup of violets, or tincture of dahlia or of purple cabbage, are made *green* by alkalies, and are reddened by acids. If no change of this sort is indicated, the body is said to be neutral.

245. When *two* elements unite, the product is called a *binary* compound, from *bis*, twice; thus water, sulphuric acid, oxyd of silver, and oxyd of iron, are binary compounds. Compounds of binary combinations with each other, as of

---

243. What of the names of compounds? Who settled the principles of nomenclature? How are the names divided? 244. How are bodies divided? How are salts formed? What of the pile? What does electro-positive mean? What electro-negative? How of common salt? How are acids and bases further distinguished? What is neutrality? 245 What is a binary compound?

sulphuric acid with soda, forming sulphate of soda, or Glauber's salts, are called *ternary* compounds, (from *ter*, thrice.) Compounds of salts with each other, (as in the case of alum, which is a compound of sulphate of potash and sulphate of alumina,) are named *quaternary* compounds, from *quatuor*, four.

246. The compounds of oxygen are called either *oxyds* or *acids:* thus, water is an *oxyd* of hydrogen; and one of the oxygen compounds of sulphur is called sulphuric *acid.* The *binary* compounds of chlorine, bromine, iodine, fluorine, and some other elements, which resemble oxygen in their mode of combination, are also distinguished by the same termination *id* or *ide.* Thus, chlorine forms chlorids; bromine, bromids; iodine, iodids; and fluorine, fluorids.

The binary compounds of sulphur, selenium, phosphorus, arsenic, and some others, receive usually the termination *uret.* Thus we say sulphuret, seleniuret, phosphuret, &c., although sulphid, selenid, phosphid, &c., are more in obedience to the rules of the nomenclature.

247. In all cases, the name of the *electro-negative* constituent of a compound rules the name of the genus of the compound. Thus, chlorid of potassium, sulphuret of iron, and sulphate of soda, all imply that the chlorine, sulphur, or sulphuric acid, are the electro-negative constituents, and that potassium, iron, and soda are the electro-positive elements in those compounds. The same rule holds in all the salts also, however complex.

248. When the same element unites with oxygen in more than one proportion, forming two or more oxyds, then these are distinguished as *protoxyd*, *deutoxyd*, *tritoxyd*, from the Greek *protos*, first; *deuteros*, second; and *tritos*, third; corresponding to the first, second, and third degree of oxydation. The word *bi* (double) *binoxyd* is also used in place of deutoxyd. The oxyd which contains the largest proportion of oxygen with which the body is known to unite, is also called the *peroxyd*, from the Latin, *per*, which is a particle of intensity in that language. Thus, there are two oxyds of hydrogen, the *protoxyd* (water) and the *peroxyd*. There

---

A ternary? A quaternary? 246. What of the oxygen compounds? How of the compounds of chlorine, &c.? How of sulphur, &c.? 247. What of the electro-negative constituent? Give examples. 248. How are the first, second, third, &c., oxyds distinguished? What are binoxyds?

are three oxyds of manganese: 1. The *protoxyd*; 2. The *deutoxyd*; 3. The *peroxyd* of manganese. Some oxyds are formed in the proportion of 2 to 3, or once and a half. Such oxyds are distinguished by the term *sesquioxyds*, from the numeral *sesqui*, (once and a half) Certain inferior oxyds are called *suboxyds*, as suboxyd of copper, Cu_2O.

249. The *acid* compounds of oxygen derive their names by adding the terminations *ous* or *ic* with the word *acid* to the electro-negative constituent. Thus, for the two acids of sulphur we have sulphurous acid and sulphuric acid: the first signifies the lowest, the second the highest oxygen compounds of the substance known at the time when the rules of the nomenclature were framed. As the progress of science has made known other and intermediate compounds, in order to bring them into the system, it was necessary to employ the terms *hypo* and *hyper*, from hupo, *under*, and huper, *above*. Thus, we have hyposulphurous and hyper-sulphurous, for two acids of sulphur respectively under and above sulphurous in their quantities of oxygen. The prefix *per* has been added to signify a degree of oxydation higher than that implied by *ic*. Thus, chloric acid was for a long time the highest known degree of oxydation of chlorine; but now we have *perchloric* acid also. Peroxyd means the highest oxyd known.

250. Sulphur, selenium, tellurium, arsenic, &c., and chlorine, bromine, iodine, and fluorine, also form acid compounds with hydrogen. These are named after the electro-negative compounds, sulphydric, selenhydric, chlorohydric, bromohydric, &c. Sulphuretted hydrogen, arseniuretted hydrogen, &c., are also used, as well as hydrochloric, hydrobromic, &c.; but the first named are more in accordance with the principles of the nomenclature.

251. The salts (ternary compounds) are named in an equally simple manner. The acid supplies the *generic*, the base the *specific* name. Sulphate of soda, nitrate of potassa, sulphite of soda, and nitrite of potassa, are respectively salts of sulphuric, nitric, sulphurous, and nitrous acids. Thus,

---

What sesquioxyds? Suboxyds? 249. How are the acid compounds of oxygen named? What of hypo and hyper? What of the prefix *per*? Give examples. 250. How are acid compounds of sulphur, &c., with hydrogen named? 251. How are salts named? What gives generic, and what specific names? How do the acids change the terminations *ous* and *ic*?

in forming salts, the acids change the terminations *ous* and *ic*, into *ite* and *ate*.

When there are more oxyds of a base than one entering into combination, the resulting salts are distinguished, for example, as sulphate of the protoxyd of iron or sulphate of the peroxyd.

252. Chemistry enjoys the peculiar advantages of possessing a descriptive and defining nomenclature. Permanganate of potassa is not a trivial name, but supposing that we now saw it for the first time, we learn from its simple inspection that the compound contains permanganic acid, and the base potash; and further, that the acid in question is the highest oxygen compound of manganese known.

Convenient as the nomenclature of chemistry is, the progress of the science has made known so many and such complex compounds, that it long since became necessary to devise some simple mode of notation by which they might be expressed, briefly and with certainty. Berzelius supplied this requisite in the system of *chemical symbols*, by which all chemical compounds may be described with mathematical precision.

253. In the table of elementary bodies, (238,) the "symbols" of the several elements will be found opposite to their names. The symbols are merely the first letter of each name, or the first two. By a happy thought, Berzelius made each symbol represent not merely the *substance* for which it stands, but *one equivalent* of each substance. Thus, O stands not for oxygen in general, but for one *equivalent* of that element; or, hydrogen being unity, for the number 8. O and 8 are therefore interchangeable expressions, while O^2, O^3, &c. represent 2×8 and 3×8, or 16 and 24.

Compounds are represented by using merely the symbols, and sometimes uniting them by the sign of addition, (+.) Thus, water will be represented by HO, or one equivalent of each element, $1 + 8 = 9$, the combining number for water. Protoxyd of lead is thus written PbO; and PbO^2 is the peroxyd.

The co-efficient attached to a symbol signifies how many

When there are more oxyds than one, how is it? Give examples. 252. What advantage of nomenclature has chemistry? Give an example. What inconvenience was found? Who supplied the want? 253. What are symbols? What do they express? Give an instance. What of co-efficients?

atoms of the element are concerned: thus, O, O^2, O^3, O^4, O^5, &c., are respectively 1, 2, 3, 4, and 5 atoms of oxygen, which may also be written O_2, O_3, &c., or 2O, 3O, 4O, &c. *Formulæ* are expressions by which we recognize the constitution of compounds; thus, sulphuric acid has the formula SO_3, oxyd of iron is FeO, and sulphate of protoxyd of iron is $FeO+SO_3$, or *one* equivalent of that compound. *Two* equivalents would be written $2(FeO+SO^3)$. If we write $2FeO+SO_3$, it means two atoms of protoxyd of iron, plus one of sulphuric acid. In chemical formulæ, the electro-negative element is placed last, the electro-positive is written first. Thus HO is water, not OH. When the sign plus is used in a chemical expression, it usually signifies a union less close than if a comma or no sign at all had been used. Thus SO_3 HO + 2HO signifies a hydrate of sulphuric acid in which *two* atoms of water are loosely retained, while one is in more close combination.

Water unites with *bases* to form hydrates, as the common hydrate of potash or hydrate of lime, and also with *acids* to form compounds analogous to salts. Thus, with sulphuric acid, forming what in strictness should be called a sulphate of water; but such cases are usually known as *hydrated acids*. As 1, 2, or 3 atoms of water may unite with an acid, so we have monohydrated, bihydrated, and terhydrated sulphuric or phosphoric acids.

254. Since chemical analysis only makes known to us the number of constituents found in a compound, and the mode in which these are arranged is undetermined, except by theoretical considerations, it is becoming more the habit of chemists to write formulæ expressing only the results of analysis. Thus, acetic acid is written C_4 H_4 O_4, since this is the result of an analysis of this substance. In accordance with some views it is written C_4 H_3 O_3+HO. Sulphuric acid, usually written SO_3 HO, is written, perhaps more unexceptionably, SO_4 H. These two modes of expression are denominated *rational* and *empyrical* formulæ.

255. Professor Graham suggests what he calls antithetic or polar formulæ, which shall place all the electro-positive elements of a compound in one line, and all the electro-

---

What are formulæ? Give an example. Which constituent is placed first? What of sign +? Give an example. What of hydrates and acids? 254. What two modes of stating analytic results are here mentioned? 255. What are antithetic or polar formulæ?

negative in a line above them, like the numerators and denominators of fractions. Thus, water will be $\frac{O}{H}$, sulphuric acid $\frac{O_3}{S}$, sulphate of soda $\frac{O}{Na}\,\frac{O_3}{S}$ or $\frac{O_4}{NaS}$.

256. The symbols are sometimes abbreviated still further, to simplify the expression of very complex combinations. This is done by expressing one equivalent of oxygen by a dot, two, by two dots, &c. Thus, $\dddot{S}$ signifies the same as SO_3, (dry sulphuric acid.) Common crystallized alum is written in full, thus,

$$Al_2O_3,3SO_3+KO,SO_3+24HO.$$

We can conveniently condense this long expression; thus

$$\underline{\dddot{Al}}\,\dddot{S}_3+\dot{K}\dddot{S}+24\dot{H}.$$

The short line under the $\underline{\dddot{Al}}$ signifies two equivalents of the base. Sulphur is in like manner signified by a comma; thus, bisulphuret of iron, Fe,S_2, may be more shortly written $\overset{\prime\prime}{Fe}$. Symbolic formulæ have contributed very much to the progress of the science, and are invaluable as a ready means of comparing as well as expressing the composition of compound bodies.

257. There is an interesting relation between the atomic weights, the specific gravities, and the combining measures or volumes of those elements which exist in the gaseous state, or are capable of assuming it. One grain of hydrogen occupies 46·7 cubic inches, but the same *bulk* or volume of chlorine weighs 35·5 grains, of nitrogen 14 grains, of iodine 127·1 grains, of bromine 80 grains, and of oxygen 16 grains. These weights respectively represent the density of the several gases compared with hydrogen as unity; but they are also identical with the atomic weights of the several elements, except oxygen, which is double. We have before seen (224) that two volumes of hydrogen and one volume of oxygen are evolved in the electrolysis of water. The volumes in which gaseous elements unite are therefore as 1 : 1 or as 1 : 2, or some simple ratio. Sulphur has $\frac{1}{3}$ the volume of oxygen and mercury four times. The combin-

---

256. How are symbols abbreviated? Illustrate by alum. 257. What relation is named between bodies in the gaseous state? Give illustrations of this. How do elements unite by volume?

ing measure of oxygen being one volume, the combining volume of hydrogen, nitrogen, chlorine, bromine, iodine, and mercury, will be two volumes.

258. In the following table, hydrogen is taken as the unit of combining measures, and we observe that where the numbers in the second column are the same as the equivalents, then a volume represents an equivalent; otherwise some simple multiple of it. As with sulphur (16×6 =96) and oxygen, (2×8=16.)

Gases and Vapors.	Specific Gravities.		Chemical Equivalents.	
	Air=1.	Hydrogen=1.	By volume.	By weight.
Hydrogen..........	0·069	1·	100 or 1	1·
Nitrogen............	0·972	14.	100 or 1	14·
Oxygen.............	1·105	16·	50 or ½	8·
Chlorine............	2·421	35·50	100 or 1	35·50
Iodine vapor........	8·716	127·1	100 or 1	
Bromine vapor.....	5·544	80·	100 or 1	80·
Mercury vapor.....	6·976	100·	200 or 2	100·
Sulphur vapor.....	6·617	96·	16	16·

259. The combining measure of *compound* gases is variable, but they bear a simple and constant ratio to each other; and hence the density of a compound gas may often be more accurately calculated from the known density of its constituents, and its change of volume in combination, than it can by direct experiment. A single example will illustrate this. Water consists of 1 atom of each of its constituents, represented by 1 volume of O and 2 volumes of H. These *three* volumes weigh 1105·6+69·3 +69·3=1244·2=two volumes of *steam*, one of which= half this sum, or 622, the density of steam, air being unity. From a comparison of the experimental results obtained by chemists, it appears that there exists a very simple relation between the combining measures of bodies in the gaseous state, compound as well as simple. Of a few bodies the combining measure is like that of oxygen, *one volume;* of a large number double that of oxygen, or two volumes; of a still larger number four times that of oxygen, or four volumes; while combining measures of *three* and *six*, or of fractional portions of a volume, as *one-third*, are compara-

258. Illustrate this further from the table. 259. How in compound gases? What is the case with water? What relations are established?

tively rare. These results in regard to combining measures were first obtained by Humboldt and Gay-Lussac, and have afforded the most remarkable confirmation of the atomic theory of Dalton.

260. *Atomic volumes* are those numbers which are obtained by dividing the atomic weights of bodies by their densities, and this whether we speak of simple or compound bodies. In mineralogy, as shown by Dana, this relation is often of great importance in determining the relations of species.

Specific Heat of Atoms.

261. *Specific heat* has already been explained, (117.) If in place of comparing equal weights of different bodies together, we take them in atomic proportions, we shall find the numbers representing the specific heat of lead, tin, zinc, copper, nickel, iron, platinum, sulphur, and mercury, to be identical; while tellurium, arsenic, silver, and gold, although equal to each other, will be twice that of the nine previous bodies, and iodine and phosphorus will be four times as much. The general conclusion drawn from these and other similar facts is, that the atoms of all simple substances have the same capacity for heat. The specific heat of a body would thus afford the means of fixing its *atomic weight.* There can be no doubt of the truth of this in numerous cases, but experiments are still wanting to show it to be universally true. Compound atoms have in some cases been shown to have the same relations to heat as the simple. This is true of many of the carbonates, and some sulphates.

Isomorphism and Dimorphism.

262. *Isomorphism* is identity of crystalline form, with a difference of chemical constitution. Identity of crystalline form was formerly supposed to indicate an identity of chemical composition. We now know that certain substances may replace each other in the constitution of compounds, without changing their crystalline form. This property is called *isomorphism*, and those basis which admit of mutual substitution are termed *isomorphous.* Chemistry

---

Who first observed these relations? 260. What are atomic volumes? 261. What of specific heat of atoms? 262. What is isomorphism? Give examples.

furnishes us many examples of these isomorphous bodies. Thus, alumina and peroxyd of iron replace each other indefinitely. The carbonate of iron and carbonates of lime, magnesia, and manganese, are also examples, as the common sparry iron, (*spathic iron,*) which is a carbonate of iron, in which a large portion of carbonate of lime sometimes exists without producing any change of form in the mineral. Oxyd of zinc and of magnesia, oxyd of copper, and protoxyd of iron, also take the place each of the other in compounds, without any alteration of crystalline form. When those bodies unite with acids to form salts, the resulting compounds have the same crystalline form, and, if they have the same color, are not to be distinguished from each other by the eye.

In double salts, like common alum, these relations are also found. Sulphate of iron may take the place of sulphate of alumina in common alum, and no change of form will occur; and soda may, in like manner, replace the potash. In fact, all the similar compounds of isomorphous bodies have a great resemblance to each other in general appearance and chemical properties. The two bases in a double salt are, however, never taken from the same group of isomorphous bodies.

263 A knowledge of this law is of great importance to the chemist, and often enables him to explain, in a satisfactory manner, apparent contradictions and anomalies, and to decide many doubtful points. It is supposed that the elements whose compounds are isomorphous, are themselves isomorphous.

The following group of isomorphous bodies is given by Professor Graham in his "Elements." 1st family: Chlorine, Iodine, Bromine, Fluorine. 2d family: Sulphur, Selenium, Tellurium. 3d family: Phosphorus, Arsenic, Antimony. 4th family: Barium, Strontium, Lead. 5th family: Silver, Sodium, Potassium, Ammonium. 6th family: Magnesium, Manganese, Iron, Cobalt, Nickel, Zinc, Copper, Cadmium, Aluminum, Chromium, Calcium, Hydrogen.

264. *Dimorphism and Polymorphism.*—Some substances have two forms, under both of which they are found. Thus,

---

In what double salts is it found? 263. What does this law explain? What groups are given? 264. What are dimorphism and polymorphism?

common calc-spar (carbonate of lime) generally occurs in rhombohedrons, (49, fig. 13,) but in arragonite (which is only pure carbonate of lime) it is seen as a rhombic prism, (46, fig. 37.)

Bin-iodid of mercury is another example of the same kind; and in both these cases the change of form is effected by heat. Polymorphism is where more than two forms of the same substance are known; as in titanic acid, of which rutile, anatase, and brookite are three distinct crystallographic species.

Chemical Affinity.

265. Chemical affinity, or the capability of chemical union between bodies, is not possessed alike by all. Oyxgen is the only element capable of forming chemical compounds with all other elements. Carbon can unite with oxygen, sulphur, hydrogen, and some other bodies, but no compound has been formed between it and gold, silver, fluorine, aluminum, iodine, and bromine. It is, therefore, said to have no affinity for those bodies, or no capability of union with them. The power of union among bodies, or affinity, is exceedingly different in degree, and is much affected by many circumstances. Thus A may unite with B, forming AB; but if C had been present, A might have so much more affinity for C than it has for B, as to unite with it, forming AC, while B would remain unaffected. For example, sulphuric acid and soda unite to form Glauber's salts, or sulphate of soda; but if soda and baryta had both been present, and sulphuric acid were added, only the sulphate of baryta would be formed, and the soda would remain disengaged, unless there was sulphuric acid enough to satisfy both. This is what is sometimes called elective affinity, as if the acid selected the baryta rather than the soda.

266. The *more unlike*, as a general thing, any two bodies are in chemical properties, the stronger is their disposition to unite. The metals, as a class, have very little disposition to unite with each other. But they unite with oxygen, chlorine, and sulphur, forming fixed and determinate compounds. The alkalies, potash and soda, form no proper

---

265. What of chemical affinity? What of oxygen? What of carbon? What determines the union of A and B? How if C were present? What is this sort of affinity called? 266. What of the similarity of bodies? Illustrate by an example.

compound with each other, and their alkaline properties are not altered by such union. Sulphuric and nitric acid may be mingled in any proportion, but no new compound is formed, and the mixture is still acid. But if the potash and soda respectively be added to nitric and sulphuric acid, the result will be saltpetre, or nitrate of potash, and Glauber's salts, or sulphate of soda, two salts having neither alkaline nor acid properties.

267. *Solution* is the result of a feeble affinity, but one in which the properties of the dissolved body are unaltered: thus, sugar is dissolved in all proportions in water or weak alcohol. Camphor is soluble in alcohol, but the addition of water to the solution will, by engaging the alcohol, cause the camphor to be thrown down. Gum is soluble in water, but not in alcohol. We have already seen that the solution of various salts in water would produce cold (124) from the change of state in the body dissolved.

268. The *circumstances* which modify the action of affinity are numerous, some of which we may briefly notice. We have said (8) that chemical affinity existed only among unlike particles, and at insensible distances. Intimate contact among particles is, therefore, in the highest degree necessary to promote chemical union. Any circumstance which favors such contact will increase the activity of, or disposition to, chemical combination. Solution brings particles near together, and leaves them free to move among each other: substances in a state of solution have, therefore, an opportunity to unite, which they do not possess when solid. Hence the old maxim, "Corpora non agunt nisi sint soluta." Carbonate of soda and tartaric acid, for example, both in a dry state, remain unchanged; but the addition of water will at once, by dissolving them, bring about a union. Heat being, in fact, a most powerful means of solution; will often cause union to take place. Sand or silica will not unite with soda or potash by contact or aqueous solution, but if the mixture in proper proportions is strongly heated, union takes place and glass is formed. Sulphur will not unite with cold iron, but if the iron be heated to rednesss, or the sulphur melted, a vigorous union takes place, and a sulphuret of iron results. Cohesion is destroyed by heat and solution, and substances in fine

---

267. What of solution? 268. Name circumstances affecting affinity.

powder unite more readily than in masses of large size. Dry sal-ammoniac and dry lime, in fine powder, mingled together, evolve ammonia. This is an interesting example of chemical action, by mere contact of dry substances.

269. *Bodies in the nascent** state (as it is called) will often unite, when under ordinary circumstances no affinity is seen between them. Thus hydrogen and nitrogen gases, under ordinary circumstances, do not unite if mingled in the same vessel; but when these two gases are set free at the same time, from the decomposition of some organic matter, they readily unite, forming ammonia. The same is true of carbon under the same circumstances, which will then unite in a great variety of proportions with hydrogen and nitrogen, although no such union can be effected among these bodies under ordinary circumstances.

270. The *quantity of matter*, as well as the order and condition in which substances may be presented to each other, often exerts an important influence on the power of affinity. Thus, vapor of water, when passed through a gun-barrel heated to redness, will be decomposed, the oxygen uniting with the iron, while the hydrogen escapes at the other end of the tube. On the contrary, if dry hydrogen is passed over oxyd of iron in a tube heated to redness, the hydrogen unites with the oxygen of the oxyd of iron, leaving metallic iron, while vapor of water escapes at the open end of the tube. Other examples of this sort are observed, where the play of affinities seems to be determined by the preponderance of one sort of matter over another, or by the peculiar condition of the resulting compounds, as regards insolubility, or the power of vaporization.

271. The *presence of a third body* often causes a union, or the exertion of the force of affinity, when this third body takes no part in the changes which happen. Thus, oxygen and hydrogen gases may be mingled without any combination taking place between them, although a strong affinity exists. If, however, a portion of platinum in a state of very fine division (spongy platinum) be introduced into the mixture, union takes place, sometimes slowly, but more

---

269. What of the nascent state? Give an example. 270. What of quantity of matter? What is catalysis? Give examples.

---

* From *nascens*, being born, or in the moment of formation.

often with an explosion, the platinum being at the same time heated to redness from the rapid condensation of the gases which takes place in its pores. Advantage is taken of this fact in constructing the common instrument for lighting tapers by a stream of hydrogen falling on spongy platinum. No change is suffered in this case by the platinum, which seems to act by its presence only. Berzelius has proposed the term *catalysis*, from the Greek *kata*, by, and *luo*, to loosen, to express the peculiar power which some bodies possess of aiding chemical changes by their presence merely.

PART III.—INORGANIC CHEMISTRY.

CLASSIFICATION OF ELEMENTS.

272. It is usual to divide elementary bodies into two great groups, the non-metallic and metallic elements. This convenient arrangement is founded on characters which in a general and popular sense are correct and easily distinguished, but which fail in several cases to afford any accurate distinction. No one can doubt to which class, for example, gold and sulphur should be respectively referred; but it is impossible to say why carbon and silicon are not as well entitled to be classed in the same group with the metals as tellurium and arsenic, if we except the single character of lustre.

We will discuss the first division of elementary bodies in six classes, in the following order:—

Class	Elements	Characters
CLASS I.	1. Oxygen......	The only element which forms compounds with all others, and the type of electro-negative bodies.
CLASS II.	2. Chlorine..... 3. Bromine..... 4. Iodine....... 5. Fluorine.....	Four elements very similar in all their sensible properties, forming similar compounds with the metals, whose acid compounds with oxygen are also similar, and have the constitution expressed by RO, RO_4, RO_5, RO_7.
CLASS III.	6. Sulphur...... 7. Selenium.... 8. Tellurium...	These stand in close relation with each other, while their compounds with the metals are more similar to the oxyds of those metals than are the analogous compounds of the second class. Their oxygen acids have the formula RO_2, RO_3.
CLASS IV.	9. Nitrogen..... 10. Phosphorus.	This group properly includes also arsenic and antimony, which are, however, from convenience, discussed elsewhere. The four form similar compounds with oxygen, RO, RO_3, RO_5, and peculiar gaseous compounds with hydrogen, RH_3.
CLASS V.	11. Carbon....... 12. Silicon....... 13. Boron........	These three bodies are similar, non-volatile, combustible bases, and alike in forming feeble acids with oxygen. The formula RO_3 is adopted by some chemists.
CLASS VI.	14. Hydrogen.	This highly electro-positive body is unlike any of the preceding, and has analogies with the succeeding group of metals.

---

272. How are the elements divided? What of the accuracy of this division? How many classes are named for 1st division? Name the 1st class, the 2d, the 3d, the 4th. What other elements belong to this group? What is the formula of the hydrogen compounds of this group? What is class 5? Class 6?

273 We will consider these several classes separately. The compounds which each element forms with those before it, wi'l be taken up in order; and we shall then be better able to understand the relation of each element to its associates in the same group. The several classes, too, will then be better understood in the analogies which unite, and the differences which separate them.

CLASS I.

OXYGEN.

Equivalent, 8. *Symbol*, O. *Density*, 1·106.

274. Dr. Priestley discovered oxygen in 1774. It was also rediscovered by Scheele, of Sweden, immediately after, and without a knowledge of Priestley's discovery. Before this time, all gaseous bodies were considered to be only modes of common air, and oxygen was first called *vital air*, and, in allusion to the then existing theories, *dephlogisticated air*. It was the illustrious Lavoisier, author of the present nomenclature of chemistry, who proposed the name *oxygen*, (from *oxus*, acid, and *gennao*, I form.) Lavoisier had also rediscovered oxygen in 1775. At that time it was supposed that all acids contained oxygen.

Oxygen is the most widely diffused and important of the elements. It forms over one-fifth part of the atmosphere by weight, eight-ninths of the waters of the globe, and probably one-third part of its solid crust. It has also the widest range of affinities of all known substances, and by its immediate agency combustion and life are alone sustained.

275. *Preparation.*—Oxygen gas is procured by heating the oxyds of lead, mercury, or of manganese, or the salts, nitrate of potassa, chlorate of potassa, or nitrate of soda. Chlorate of potassa is, however, the salt generally employed, as yielding a large volume of pure oxygen with a gentle heat. This salt contains six equivalents of oxygen, and parts with them all at a moderate heat, leaving a residue of chlorid of potassium. Thus $ClO_5,KO = ClK + 6O$. One ounce of chlorate of potassa yields 543 cubic inches of pure oxygen, or over a gallon and a half. The arrangement of

---

273. In what order are they discussed? 274. Who discovered oxygen, and when? How were gases formerly considered? Who named oxygen? Whence the name? What of the importance and diffusion of oxygen? 275. How is it prepared?

apparatus for this purpose is shown in fig. 206. A convenient portion of chlorate of potassa is pulverized and mixed with its own weight of manganese, or better with the black oxyd of copper. The dry mixture is placed in the flask *a* of hard glass, where it is heated by the lamp below. A bent tube fitted to *a* by a cork, conveys the gas to the air-bell *b*, previously filled with water and inverted in the water-trough. The heat of the lamp decomposes the salt, and pure oxygen is freely given off, displacing the water in the air-jar. By aid of the oxyds of manganese or copper the decomposition of the chlorate of potassa is rendered gradual and safe. Without this precaution the operation proceeds with almost ungovernable energy; the whole volume of gas being given off almost at the same instant, when the point of decomposition is reached. The metallic oxyd seems to act by distributing the heat, and by the mechanical distribution of the salt: clean sand may be used with nearly equal success. The glass may be protected from fusion by a thin metallic cup *c* employed as a sand-bath.

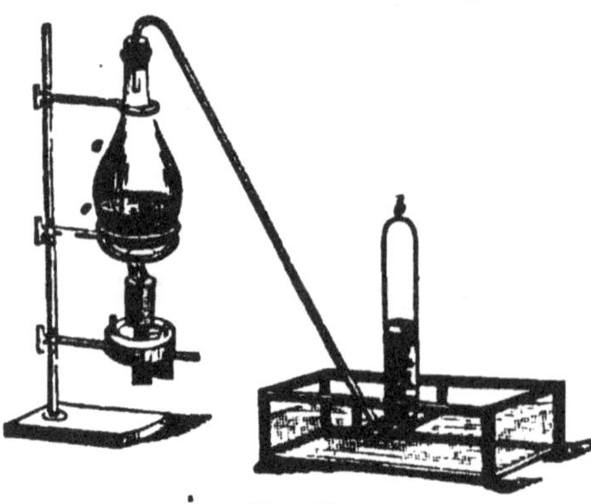

Fig. 206.

276. When large volumes of oxygen gas are required, a more economical plan is to heat the peroxyd of manganese strongly in an iron retort arranged in a reverberatory furnace, (fig. 207.) One pound of good oxyd of manganese will

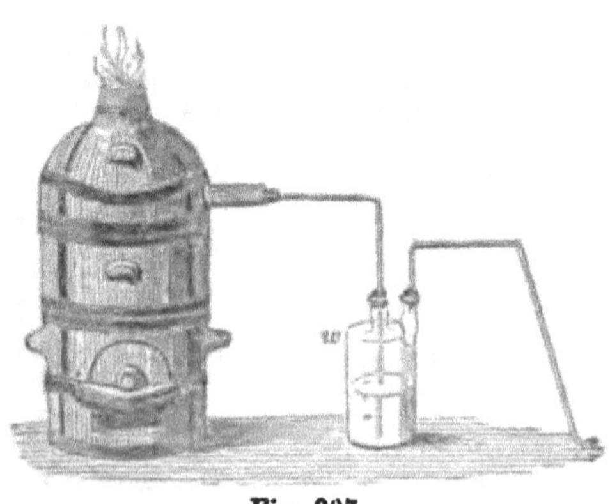

Fig. 207.

Give the way by chlorate of potassium. Why is oxyd of manganese used? How does it act? 276. What is the process by fig. 207?

yield seven gallons of oxygen, with some carbonic acid. This last is removed by passing the gas through the wash-bottle *w* containing solution of potash, which absorbs carbonic acid. In this process MnO_2 becomes $MnO + O$; about twelve per cent. of the weight of oxyd employed being obtained as oxygen. Oxygen gas may also be procured from oxyd of manganese by aid of strong sulphuric acid and a moderate heat. The mixture is placed in a balloon *d*, (fig. 208,) and heat applied. Sulphate of manganese is formed, and half the quantity of oxygen in the original oxyd, or one equivalent, is given off. Carbonic acid is removed by the potash solution in *w*. Bichromate of potash may be substituted for the oxyd of manganese in this case with good results. Both should be in fine powder.

Fig. 208.

277. *Properties and Experiments.*—Oxygen, when pure, is a transparent, colorless gas, which no degree of cold or pressure has ever reduced to a liquid state. It is a little heavier than the atmosphere, its density being, compared to air, as 1·1057 : 1·000. One hundred cubic inches of the dry gas weigh 34·19 grains. It is without taste or smell. It is very slightly dissolved in water, one hundred volumes of water dissolving only about four and a half of the gas. Its most remarkable property is the energy with which it supports combustion. Any body which will burn in common air, burns with greatly increased splendor in oxygen gas. A newly extinguished candle or taper, (fig. 209,) which has the least fire on the wick, will instantly be rekindled in oxygen, and burn in it with great beauty. A quart

Fig. 209

How is gas of this source purified? What is the reaction of heat on manganese? How is O procured by sulphuric acid as in fig. 208? 277. What are the properties of O? How does it act on combustibles?

Fig. 210.

of this gas in a narrow-mouthed bottle, will easily relight a candle fifty times. A bit of charcoal bark (fig. 210) with only a spark of ignition on it, attached to a wire and lowered into a jar of this gas, will burn with intense brilliancy, producing carbonic acid. A steel watch-spring dipped in melted sulphur and ignited, when lowered into a jar of pure oxygen gas, bursts into the most magnificent combustion, (fig. 211.) The oxyd of iron which is formed falls down in burning globules, like glowing meteors, which fuse themselves into the glazed surface of an earthen plate, although covered with an inch of water. If, as often happens, a motion of the spring throws a globule of this fused oxyd against the side of the glass vessel, it melts itself into the substance of the glass, or, if that is thin, goes through it. This is one of the most brilliant and instructive experiments in chemistry. If the orifice at top is closed air-tight, and water is poured into the plate, we shall find, as the experiment proceeds, that the water will rise in the jar as the gas is consumed. If we could collect and weigh the globules of oxyd of iron, we should find in them an increase of weight equal to the weight of the oxygen consumed.

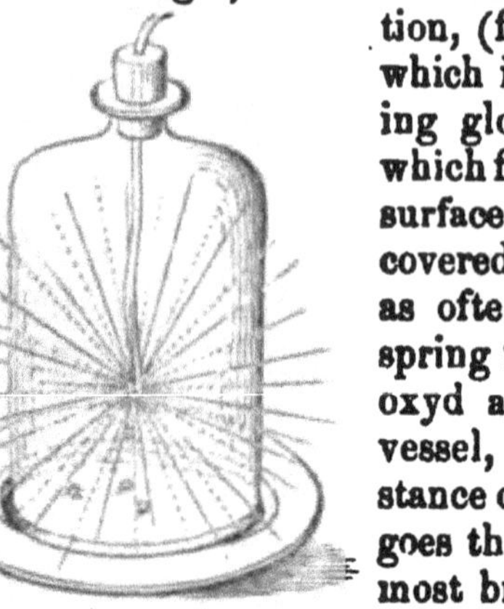

Fig. 211.

If the watch-spring or wire is coiled into a helix, as in fig. 212, then the combustion proceeds in a most beautiful series of revolutions, greatly heightening the splendor of the experiment. These experiments should be conducted in a dark room to have the full effect of their brilliancy.

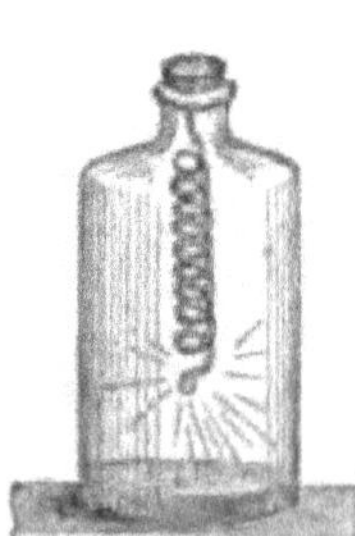

Fig. 212.

If the flame of a lamp, (Fig. 213,) is supplied by a jet of oxygen, the temperature of combustion is so much elevated

---

Explain the experiments in figs. 210, 211, and 212.

that a platina wire may be fused in it. We thus imitate the oxyhydrogen blow-pipe to be described further on, (385.)

Fig. 213.

278. Oxygen, when inhaled, affects life by quickening the circulation of the blood, and causing an excitement, which, if continued, would result in general inflammatory symptoms and death. In an atmosphere of pure oxygen we would live too fast, exactly as combustion is too rapid in an atmosphere of this gas. It exerts, however, no specific poisonous influence, being, when used in moderation, altogether salutary, and often resorted to, to inflate the lungs of drowned persons, and not unfrequently with the most beneficial results. The blood is constantly brought into contact with the air in the lungs, and it is the oxygen in the air which is the active agent in rendering it fit to sustain life. Pure oxygen is constantly supplied to the atmosphere by the processes of vegetable life.

279. *Ozone*, the allotropic or double condition of oxygen. When a stream of electrical sparks is passed through a tube in which a current of dry pure oxygen is flowing, the gas assumes new properties. The same result is obtained also where water is electrolysed, (224,) when phosphorus slowly consumes in a globe of moist air, or when a Leyden battery is discharged. In all these cases there is a peculiar odor, perceived also after a powerful discharge of electricity from the clouds. Hence the name *ozone*, from *ozumi*, to smell. However this result may be obtained, it is observed that oxygen in this condition, or air containing it, presents much more powerful oxydizing powers than ordinary oxygen. It will turn strips of white paper dipped in protosulphate of manganese to brown from the production of peroxyd of manganese. It will decolorize solution of indigo as promptly as nitric acid, and it bleaches even more powerfully than chlorine. This body, Schönbein, its discoverer, regards now as an allotropic condition of oxygen, (as suggested by Berzelius.) Its presence in the air is shown by the discoloration of papers dipped in iodid of starch solution. It has been argued, but on insufficient grounds, that this body in the

---

278. How is the lamp flame affected? How does it act on life? How on the blood? **279.** What of ozone? How obtained? What its characters?

air was a miasmatic agent. A few words will be in place here, upon the

Management of Gases.

280. *Pneumatic Troughs.*—Gases not absorbed by water, are always collected in a vessel of water, called a pneumatic trough. Figure 214 shows a small neat one, made of glass, proper for the lecture-table ; but, for general purposes, they are usually made, like the one below, (fig. 215,) of japanned copper, of tin plate, or of wood, to hold several gallons of water. The essential parts are the well W, in which the air-jars are filled, and a shelf S, covered with about an inch of water. A groove or channel *d* is made in the shelf, to allow the end of the gas-pipe to dip under the air-jar. If nothing better is at hand, a common wooden tub or water-pail, with a perforated shelf and inverted funnel, will answer for small operations. Learners are sometimes puzzled to tell why the water stands in an air-jar above the level of the cistern. A moment's thought, however, on the principles of atmospheric pressure (27) already explained, will make this clear. We must remember, too, that gases are only light fluids, and must be poured upward in water, by the same laws which require fluids heavier than air to be poured downward.

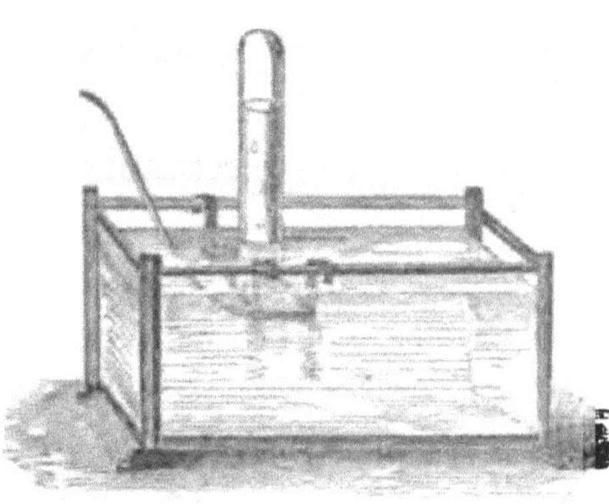

Fig. 214.

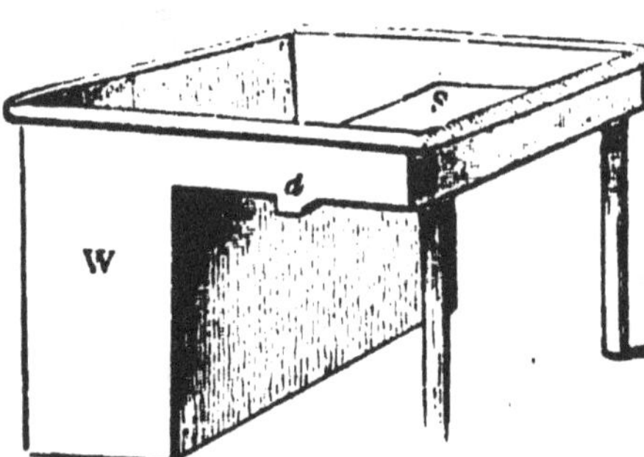

Fig. 215.

281. *To store large quantities of gases*, capacious vessels

---

280. What is a pneumatic trough? How are gases managed? How poured? 281. How are they stored?

of copper or tinned iron are used, which are called gas-holders. These vessels are made frequently to hold 30 to 50 gallons. The simplest form is that of a large air-jar, provided with stopcocks at the top for the entrance and escape of the gas, and contained in an exterior cylindrical vessel of water. A more convenient gas-holder for some purposes is that contrived by Mr. Pepys, a view and section of which are shown in the annexed figures, (216 and 217.) It is a tight cylinder of copper or tin *g*, with a shallow pan of the same metal, supported above it by several props, two of which are tubes with stopcocks, *a b*. Near the bottom is a large orifice *o*, for receiving the gas. To use this instrument, it is first filled with water by closing the lower orifice *o* with a large cork, and opening all the upper ones *a b s*. Water is then poured into the shallow pan *p*, until it runs out at *s*, which is then closed; the remainder of the air escapes through *b*; when it is full, the cocks *a b* are shut, and the lower orifice being then opened, the water, sustained by the pressure of the air, cannot escape except as it is driven out by the entrance of the gas at *o*, from which it runs as fast as the gas enters. When used, arrangements must be made to provide for the water driven out by the gas entering at *o*. The gas is obtained for use by drawing it off from the orifice *s* or *b* at the same time that the shallow pan *p* is full of water, and the cock *a* open. The tube to which this cock is attached goes nearly to the bottom of the vessel. An air-jar is easily filled with gas from the holder by placing it full of water in the upper

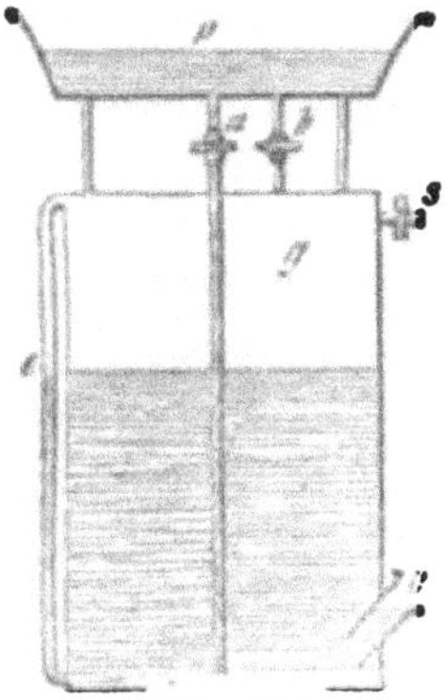

Fig. 216.

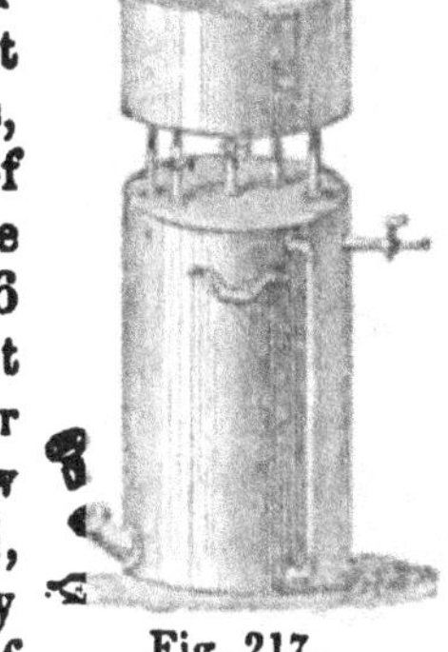

Fig. 217.

Fig. 218.

Explain figures 216 and 217. How is gas drawn from the gas holder? Explain figure 218.

pan, (see fig. 218,) over the orifice b; on turning the twc stopcocks a b, the gas issues from b and fills the jar, while the water of the jar runs down the pipe a to supply the place of the gas.

In collecting gas, the precaution should never be neglected of first allowing all the atmospheric air to escape from the vessels, before any of the gas is saved for use.

Bags of vulcanized India-rubber cloth are prepared by the instrument-makers as gas-holders, which can be used without the inconvenience of employing water. They are

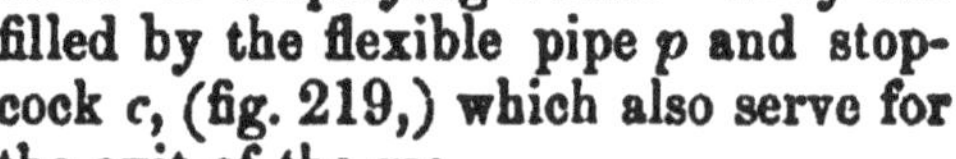

filled by the flexible pipe p and stopcock c, (fig. 219,) which also serve for the exit of the gas.

Fig. 219.

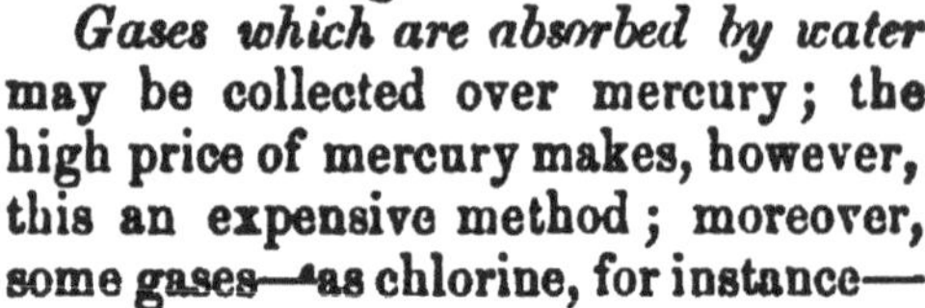

Gases which are absorbed by water may be collected over mercury; the high price of mercury makes, however, this an expensive method; moreover, some gases—as chlorine, for instance—act chemically on the mercury. We may better collect the absorbable gases in clean dry vessels, by displacement of air, as is explained in the next section.

CLASS II.

CHLORINE.

Equivalent, 35·50. *Symbol*, Cl. *Density*, 2·44.

282. *History and Preparation.*—This very remarkable element was first noticed by Scheele, in 1774, while examining the action of chlorohydric acid on peroxyd of manganese. For a long time it was believed to be a compound body. It was called chlorine by Davy, who established its elementary character.

It is easily obtained from chlorohydric acid HCl, by its action upon pulverized oxyd of manganese, in an apparatus similar to figure 220. The acid is poured in at pleasure by the safety tube s, after the manganese has been made into a paste with the first portions. The heat of a lamp or a pan of coals evolves the gas freely. It is rapidly absorbed by cold water; but if the vessels are filled with water of

---

What of India-rubber bags? What of absorbable gases? 282. When and by whom was chlorine discovered? How is it obtained? How is it collected?

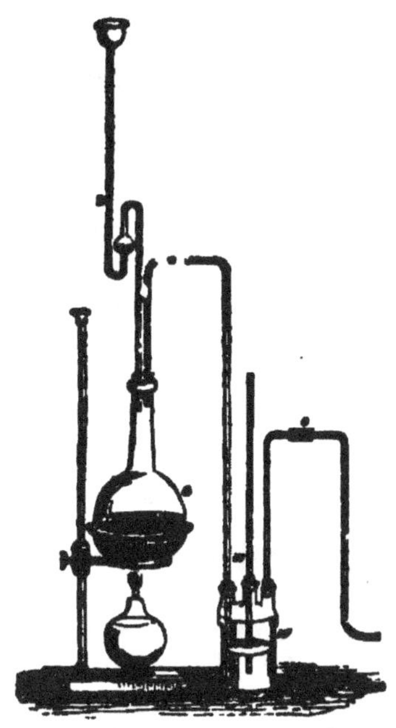

Fig. 220.

Fig. 221.

100° to 150° temperature, it is collected with little loss. Any acid vapors are washed out in *w*. A strong solution of common salt (brine) does not absorb chlorine, and may be usefully employed in some cases to collect this gas in a small porcelain or other trough. Owing to its great weight, it may also be very conveniently collected by displacement of air in dry vessels, using an apparatus like figure 221. The fluctuations of the air are prevented by a bit of card-board with a slit on one side, and the greenish color of the gas enables the operator to see when the vessel is full. The vessels must have glass stoppers or covers of glass ground tight; in such, the gas may be preserved at pleasure. The operation should be performed in a well-ventilated apartment, to avoid injury from the corrosive and irritating gas.

283. In this process the affinities are between the manganese, for one equivalent of the chlorine in the acid, forming chlorid of manganese, and between the oxygen of the manganese and the hydrogen of the acid, forming water The following symbols will render this more clear: we take

MnO_2 and 2HCl, and obtain MnCl, 2HO, and Cl.

How by figure 221? What precaution is advised? 283. What are the affinities in this process? Give the equation.

The last equivalent of chlorine, having nothing to detain it, is given off.

Pure chlorine is also easily obtained by acting on one part of powdered bichromate of potash, in a small retort, with six parts of strong hydrochloric acid. A gentle lamp-heat is required to begin the process, which then goes on without further application of heat, yielding abundance of gas.

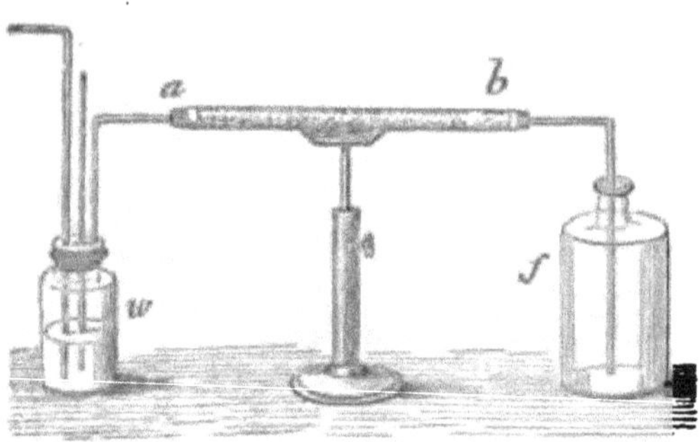

Fig. 222.

Dry chlorine is obtained by using an apparatus, figure 222, attached to the evolution flask fig. 220 by *o*; any acid vapors are washed out in the bottle *w*, and all moisture is removed by the chlorid of calcium tube *a b*, the dry gas being collected by displacement in *f*.

284. *Properties.*—Chlorine is a greenish-yellow gas, (whence its name, from *chloros*, green,) with a powerful and suffocating odor. It is wholly irrespirable and poisonous. Even when much diluted with air, it produces the most annoying irritation of the throat, with stricture of the chest, and a severe cough, which continues for hours, with the discharge of much thick mucus. The attempt to breathe the undiluted gas would be fatal; yet, in a very small quantity, and dissolved in water, it is used with benefit by patients suffering under pulmonary consumption. For this purpose an inhalation apparatus is used, like fig. 223. The mouth is applied at *o*, the air enters at *a*, and, passing through the dilute solution, becomes more or less charged with chlorine. Cold water recently boiled absorbs about twice its bulk of chlorine gas, acquiring its color and characteristic properties. This solution is much used in the laboratory in

Fig. 223.

How is it obtained dry? 284. What are its properties? How does it affect respiration? How is it safely inhaled?

preference to the gas. It should be preserved in a blue bottle, or in one covered by black paper, to avoid decomposition, (228.) The moist gas exposed to a cold of 32° yields beautiful yellow crystals, which are a definite compound of one equivalent of chlorine and ten of water, (Cl,10HO.) If these crystals are hermetically sealed up in a glass tube, (fig. 224,) they will, on melting, exert a pressure of five atmospheres, so as to liquefy a portion of the gas, which is distinctly seen as a yellow fluid, of density 1·33, not miscible with the water which is present. It does not solidify at zero. Chlorine is one of the heaviest of the gases, its density being 2·44, and 100 cubic inches weighing 76·5 grains.

Fig. 224.

285. Chlorine solution readily dissolves gold-leaf, forming chlorid of gold: silver solution produces in it a dense precipitate of chlorid of silver, which ammonia redissolves. A rod *a*, (fig. 225,) moistened in ammonia water, and held over chlorine solution, produces a dense cloud of chlorid of ammonium. A crystal of green vitriol dropped into a test-tube containing chlorine water, gives a dark solution at bottom of perchlorid of iron.

Fig. 225.

286. The *bleaching* power of chlorine is one of its most remarkable and valuable properties. The solution of chlorine immediately discharges the color of calico rags or of writing-ink. The moist gas does the same, but the dry gas does not bleach. Chlorine is evolved in the arts from a mixture of salt, sulphuric acid, and manganese, for the bleaching of paper and rags, and of all manner of cotton or linen stuffs. It does not bleach woollens, nor printers' ink, probably because of its indifference to carbon, which forms the basis of printers' ink. The bleaching power is probably due to its affinity for hydrogen.

287. *Chlorine* spontaneously inflames phosphorus, and powdered metallic arsenic, or antimony, forming chlorids of those substances. A rag or bit of paper, wet with oil of turpentine and held in a bottle of chlorine, is inflamed, and

---

What of its solution? How crystallized? How liquefied? How dense? 285. What are tests for chlorine? 286. What valuable property of Cl is named? How if dry gas is used? How is it evolved in the arts? What exceptions to its bleaching? Whence this property? 287. How does Cl act on phosphorus, &c.? How on oils?

the interior of the vessel is coated with a brilliant black varnish of carbon, derived from the oil. A candle lowered into a vessel of chlorine, (fig. 226,) is slowly extinguished, with the escape of a dense volume of smoke. In these cases, the action is between the chlorine and the hydrogen of the organic substances. The disinfection of offensive apartments, sewers, and other like places, is rapidly accomplished by chlorine and the "bleaching powders."

Fig. 226.

288. *Double Condition, or Allotropism of Chlorine.*—Chlorine exists both in an active and a passive state. The first is its condition as ordinarily known, when prepared in daylight. If an aqueous solution of chlorine be prepared as before mentioned, in recently boiled water, and a part of it be exposed in an inverted bulb to the direct rays of the sun, or a strong daylight, while another portion, as soon as prepared, without exposure to light, is set aside in a dark closet, and in a similar vessel, we shall find them very differently affected. That which was in the dark will have undergone no change, while that in the sunlight will have suffered decomposition; a notable quantity of nearly pure oxygen will have collected in the bulb, as shown in fig. 227, and chlorohydric acid will have been formed in the fluid, from the union of the chlorine and the hydrogen of the water, whose oxygen is set free. The rapidity of this decomposition of water by the chlorine, depends on the intensity of the sun's rays, and the temperature, and being once begun, it continues afterward even in the dark. The indigo rays (76) are chiefly instrumental in producing this effect. (Draper.)

Fig. 227.

Compounds of Chlorine with Oxygen.

289. Chlorine and oxygen have no disposition to unite, under any circumstances, directly; but numerous compounds of these two elements are produced indirectly, of which we tabulate five, as follows:—

How on a candle? Whence this peculiarity? What of disinfection? 288. How does light affect chlorine? Illustrate by fig. 227. What ray effects this?

	Symbol.
Hypochlorous acid	ClO
Chlorous acid	ClO_3
Hypochloric acid, (peroxyd of chlorine,)	ClO_4
Chloric acid	ClO_5
Hyperchloric acid	ClO_7

As the most simple method, we commence with—

290. *Chloric Acid*, (ClO_5).—This most important compound of chlorine and oxygen is formed when a current of chlorine is passed through a solution of potash, to saturation. On evaporating this solution, flat tabular crystals of a white salt are gradually formed, which are chlorate of potassa, while chlorid of potassium remains in the solution. The reaction is between 6 equivalents of chlorine and 6 of potassa, forming 5 of chlorid of potassium and 1 of chlorate of potassa; thus, $6Cl+6KO=5KCl+KO,ClO_5$. Chloric acid is obtained separate with some difficulty, by decomposing a solution of chlorate of baryta by the requisite amount of sulphuric acid, and gradually evaporating the filtered liquid to a syrup. In this state its affinity for all combustible matter is so great, that it cannot be kept in contact with any substance containing carbon or hydrogen. Paper moistened by it takes fire as it is dried. The chlorates are recognized by their powerful action on combustible matter, by yielding pure oxygen when heated, and by giving out the yellow chlorous acid when treated with sulphuric acid.

291. *Hypochlorous Acid*, (ClO.)—This acid gas is obtained when a current of chlorine traverses a *weak* solution of potassa, when, if cold, no chlorate of potassa is formed, but a solution having most remarkable bleaching powers. It contains both chlorid of potassium and hypochlorite of potassa; thus, $2KO+2Cl=KO,ClO+KCl$. It is obtained also by the agitation of chlorine with red oxyd of mercury, or better by passing dry chlorine over red oxyd of mercury, contained, as in fig. 228, in a horizontal tube *b*, (shown only in part,) and condensing the evolved gas ClO in

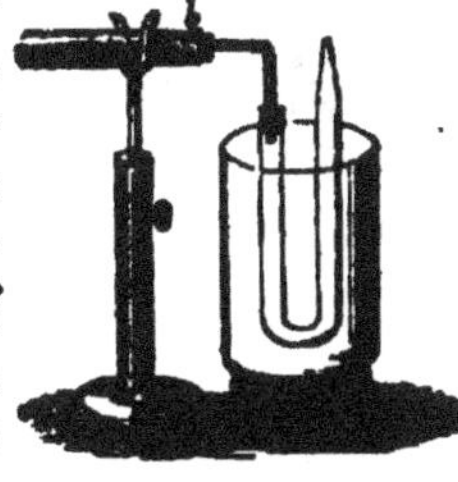

Fig. 228.

289. Name the compounds of Cl and O. What are their formulas? 290. What is chloric acid? How formed? What the reaction? What character has chloric acid? What of its salts? 291. What is hypochlorous acid? How obtained? Give the reaction. Explain its production by fig. 227.

the U tube, refrigerated by means of ice and salt in the outer vessel. Chlorid of mercury is formed, and oxyd of chlorine ClO. Hypochlorous acid is a light-yellow gas, much resembling chlorine; condensed, it is a reddish-yellow corrosive liquid, boiling at 68°, and sparingly soluble in water. The vapor detonates with a hot iron: water absorbs 200 times its volume of it, and gains a beautiful yellow color and powerful bleaching properties. Its aqueous solution is very unstable, being decomposed by light, and even by agitation with irregular bodies, as broken glass. Hypochlorous acid is one of the most powerful oxydizing agents known, raising sulphur and phosphorus to their highest state of oxydation—a result which only strong nitric acid can accomplish. It is formed from two volumes of chlorine and one of oxygen condensed into two volumes. Thus,

2 volumes of chlorine weigh.....................	4·880
1 " oxygen "	1·105
	5·985 ÷ 2 = 2·992

while experiment gives us 2·977 for the density of this substance. The *euchlorine* of Davy is a mixture of chlorine and chloro-chlorous acid, and not a protoxyd of chlorine, as was supposed. It is obtained when chlorohydric acid acts on chlorate of potassa, is a greenish-yellow gas, darker than chlorine, of a very pungent and persistent odor. It explodes with a hot iron.

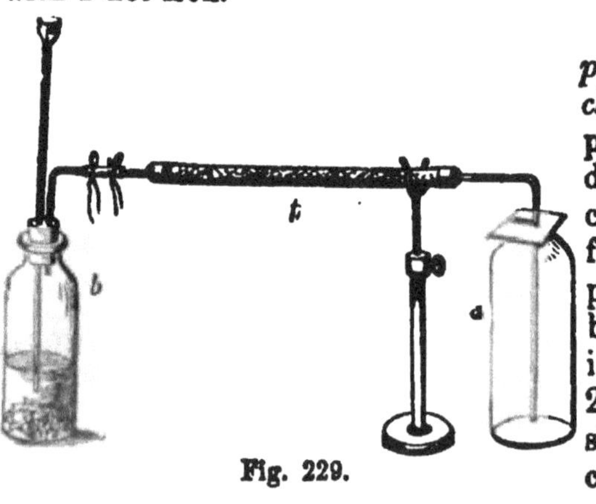

Fig. 229.

292. *Chlorous, hypochloric,* and *perchloric acids* are all procured from the decomposition of chloric acid. When fused chlorate of potassa is acted on by sulphuric acid, in the vessel *b*, (fig. 229,) a very explosive, yellow gas collects in *a*. This

What are its characters? What is its volume, constitution, and density? What is euchlorine? What of chlorous and hyperchlorous acids?

experiment demands great precautions to avoid accident. The vessel *b* may be secured by setting it into an outer vessel of warm water. The gas explodes by a warm iron, by pressure, and sometimes without any apparent cause.

293. If strong sulphuric acid is poured upon a small quantity of crystals of chlorate of potash in a wine glass, a violent crackling is heard, and the glass is soon filled with the heavy yellow vapors of the chlorous acid gas, which at once inflame a rag held over it wet with turpentine, with a smart explosion. If chlorate of potash is mixed with sugar, (both separately pulverized and mingled with caution,) a drop of sulphuric acid will inflame the mixture with a brilliant combustion. Phosphorus burns spontaneously in chlorous acid gas: if some small fragments of phosphorus are added to a glass of water at the bottom of which a few crystals of chlorate of potash have been placed, (fig. 230,) and sulphuric acid is introduced by means of a long-tubed funnel to the bottom of the vessel, the salt is decomposed, and the phosphorus flashes under water in the chlorous acid which is set at liberty.

Fig. 230.

BROMINE.

Equivalent, 80. *Symbol*, Br. *Density, in vapor*, 5·39.

294. *History.*—This element was discovered in 1826, by M. Balard, in the mother-liquor, or residue of the evaporation of sea-water, and by him named from its offensive odor, (*bromos*, bad odor.) It is widely diffused in nature, existing in minute quantities in combination with various bases in the salt-water of the ocean, of the Dead Sea, and of nearly all salt-springs. It is also found in a few minerals. The salines of our Western States are many of them rich in bromids. It has been largely prepared at Freeport, Pennsylvania, on the Ohio, för use in pharmacy.

295. Bromine is a dense red fluid, exhaling at common temperatures a deep reddish-brown vapor. It is one of the heaviest non-metallic fluids known, its density being from 2·97 to 3·187. Sulphuric acid floats on its surface, and is

---

What precaution is given? 293. What of sulphuric acid on chlorate of potassa? What is the action on phosphorus? 294. Give the history of bromine. Where is it found? 295. Give its characters.

used to prevent its evaporation. At zero it freezes into a brittle solid. It boils at 116·5°. A few drops in a large flask will fill the whole vessel, when slightly warmed, with blood-red vapors, which have a density of 5·39. It is a non-conductor of electricity, and suffers no change of properties from heat or electricity. It dissolves slightly in water, forming a bleaching solution; and at 32°, if left in contact with water, it forms a crystalline hydrate with it, of a red bronze color, analogous to the hydrate of chlorine. It is a corrosive and deadly poison, disorganizing organic structures with great energy. One drop on the beak of a bird produced instant death. It has even been used for suicide. Its odor resembles chlorine, but is more offensive and persistent. It has bleaching properties. In a word, bromine in all its properties and combinations, has the greatest analogy to chlorine, but is less energetic in its affinities, being displaced by chlorine from its combinations.

Bromine acts with explosive violence on phosphorus, potassium, antimony, and other similar substances, forming bromids.

296. Bromine is used in photography, and its compounds also in medicine. It is detected in the mother-liquor of salt-water by chlorine gas, or solution of chlorine, which sets it free, when it is recognized by its peculiar color. Ether added to this solution takes up the liberated bromine on agitation, and floats on the surface in a reddish-brown stratum. It is prepared in the arts by distilling a mixture of bromid of sodium, manganese, and dilute sulphuric acid, and collecting the product in a cold receiver.

Bromic acid BrO_5 is similar in all its reactions to chloric acid, and forms salts with alkaline bases, called bromates.

The chloride of bromine $BrCl_5$ is soluble in water and decomposed by alkalies.

IODINE.

Equivalent, 127. *Symbol*, I. *Density in vapor*, 8·7.

297. *History.*—Like chlorine and bromine, this substance has its origin in the sea, being secreted by nearly all seaweeds from the waters of the ocean. It was discovered in

---

What smell has it? How does it act on combustibles? 296. How used? How detected? What compounds does it form? 297. What is the history of iodine?

1811, by M. Courtois, of Paris, in the *kelp*, or ashes of sea-weeds. The common bladder sea-weed, (*fucus vesiculosus*,) and many other sea-weeds of our own coasts, abound in salts of iodine. It has been found in mineral springs associated with bromine, but less abundantly, and also in one or two minerals. In the arts its chief uses are for the photographic pictures, and in the process of dyeing. In medicine it is of great value, in glandular and other diseases.

298. *Preparation.*—Kelp is treated with water, which washes out all the soluble salts, and the filtered solution is evaporated until nearly all the carbonate of soda and other saline matters have crystallized out. The remaining liquor, which contains the iodine, as iodid of magnesium, &c., is mixed with successive portions of sulphuric acid in a leaden retort, and after standing some days to allow the sulphuretted hydrogen, &c., to escape, peroxyd of manganese is added, and the whole gently heated. Iodine distils over in a purple vapor, and is condensed in a receiver, or in a series of two-necked globes.

299. *Properties.*—Iodine crystallizes in brilliant blue-black scales of a metallic lustre, somewhat resembling plumbago. When slowly cooled from a state of dense vapor in a glass-tube hermetically sealed, it crystallizes in acute octahedrons with a rhombic base, (46.) The density of iodine is 4·95, it melts at 235°, and boils at 247°, forming a superb violet vapor of unequalled beauty; (hence its name, *iodes*, like a violet.) For this purpose a few grains of it may be volatilized in a bolt-head, or from a hot surface under a bell, as in fig. 231, when on cooling it is deposited in brilliant crystals lining the glass. It assumes the sphreoidal state in a red-hot crucible, forming a splendid experiment, (131.) It is almost insoluble, one part dissolving in 7000 parts of water. Alcohol dissolves it largely, forming *tincture* of iodine. Sal-ammoniac, nitrate of ammonia, and soluble iodids also dissolve it. It temporarily stains the skin deep brown, and its odor reminds us somewhat of chlorine.

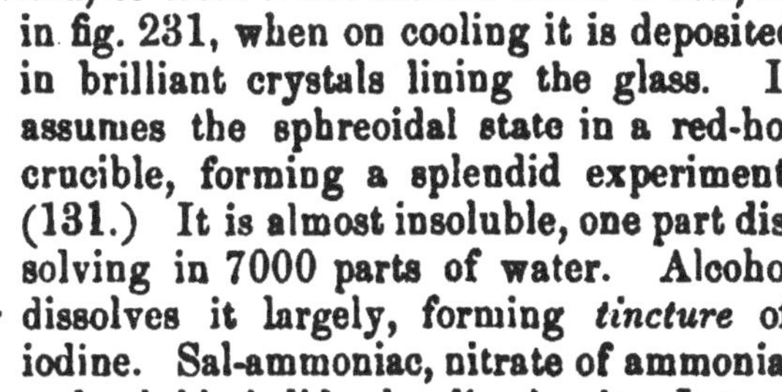

Fig. 231.

300. Chlorine and bromine both decompose the com-

In what is it found? How prepared? 299. What are its characters? What of its vapor? How soluble? What dissolves it?

pounds of iodine. Iodine is an energetic poison. Iodine forms a beautiful deep-blue compound with a cold solution of common starch. By this test a millionth part of iodine can be detected. In combination it is detected by the same agent, if a little nitric acid or chlorine water is previously added to the fluid supposed to contain an iodid, whereby the iodine is set free. Acetate of lead added to solutions of salts of iodine produces a yellow crystalline precipitate. The iodid of potassium is the salt most familiarly known of all the iodine compounds, and is the usual form in which this substance is administered medicinally.

Compounds of Iodine with Oxygen.

301. *Iodine unites with oxygen,* forming *hypoiodic, iodic,* and *hyperiodic acids.* Their constitution is seen in the following formulæ:

Hypoiodic acid	IO_4
Iodic acid	IO_5
Hyperiodic acid	IO_7

These acids are analogous to the hypochloric, chloric, and perchloric acids. Iodic acid is formed by the action of strong nitric acid on iodine, and subsequent evaporation, to expel the free nitric acid remaining. It is a very soluble substance, and crystallizes in six-sided tables. Chlorine unites with iodine, forming two, and possibly three distinct chlorids, (ICl, ICl_3, and ICl_5.) These are formed by the direct action of chlorine on dry iodine. There are also bromids of iodine of uncertain composition.

FLUORINE.

Equivalent, 19. *Symbol,* F. *Density,* (hypothetical,) 1·292

302. This element is known entirely by its compounds Its remarkable energy of combination with other elements, and especially with silicon, which is a constituent of all glass, has rendered its isolation very difficult. It is a yellowish-brown gas, having the smell and bleaching properties of chlorine. It does not act on glass, (as its compound with hydrogen does,) but unites directly with gold. Its specific gravity is 1·292.

Fluorine forms no compound with oxygen, and probably

---

300. Give tests for iodine. Give its oxygen compounds? 302. What of fluorine? Why is it difficult to isolate?

holds a place intermediate between oxygen and chlorine. Its most remarkable compound, fluohydric acid, we shall mention in the section on hydrogen. Its power of etching glass was known long before fluorine was suspected to exist.

303. When a mixture of fluor-spar with peroxyd of manganese and sulphuric acid is heated, a reaction takes place, by which fluorine in an impure form is disengaged. If the gas thus produced is passed through water having iodine suspended in it, combination takes place, and a fluorid of iodine is formed, which crystallizes in yellow scales. A fluorid of bromine is formed by a similar process, which has been used in the photographic art with success. It is not crystallizable. The precise composition of these bodies is not known

The atomic weight of fluorine is very nearly an aliquot part of the equivalents of chlorine, bromine, and iodine, and these four bodies form a well-marked natural family, closely related by many similar properties.

CLASS III.

SULPHUR.

Equivalent, 16·0. *Symbol*, S. *Density in vapor*, 6·654.

304. *History.*—Sulphur is one of those elements which, occurring abundantly in nature, have been known from the remotest antiquity. It is found in many volcanic regions, as in the Island of Sicily, the vicinity of Naples, in Cuba, and many islands of the Pacific. Recent volcanic regions producing sulphur are called *solfataras*. It is also found in beds of gypsum, as a rock, near Cadiz in Spain, and at Cracow in Poland. Sulphurets of iron, copper, and other metals are widely diffused in the earth; and in combination as sulphuric acid, sulphur forms nearly half of the weight of common gypsum, or plaster of Paris.

305. *Properties.*—It is a straw-yellow, brittle solid at common temperatures, having a gravity of 1·98. It is tasteless, and without odor until rubbed. By warmth and friction it acquires its well-known brimstone odor. It is a non-conductor of heat and electricity. By friction it gives

---

How is fluorine disengaged? What of its atomic weight? 304. What is the history of sulphur? 305. What are its equivalent and characters?

negative electricity abundantly. It is very volatile, subliming in "flowers of sulphur"—minute crystals—even below the melting point, or 226°. By this means it is freed from earthy and other impurities. When fused below 280° it is an amber-colored mobile fluid, lighter than solid sulphur, which sinks in it. It is cast in moulds, giving *roll* sulphur. On cooling, it shrinks so as to fall from the mould, (fig. 232.) The roll sulphur held for a moment in the hand gives a peculiar crackling sound, from the disturbance of its particles by heat, and it often breaks when so held. It is insoluble in water, and nearly so in alcohol and ether. In oil of turpentine and some other oils, it is partly soluble, and largely so in bisulphid of carbon. Vapor of alcohol also dissolves sulphur vapor.

Fig. 232.

Sulphur is very combustible, burning with a blue flame and the familiar odor of a match, due to the production of *sulphurous acid.* It combines energetically with metals, forming sulphurets or sulphids, supporting combustion like oxygen. Thus, a bundle of iron wires, as shown by Dr. Hare,

Fig. 233.

Fig. 234.

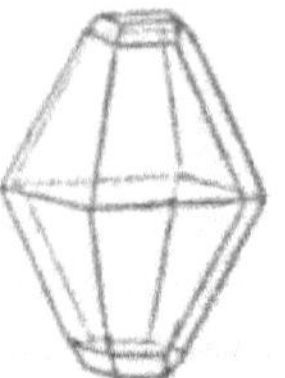

Fig. 235.

(fig. 233,) is rapidly burned with scintillations, when held in the jet of sulphur vapor issuing from a gun-barrel, the end of which has been heated to redness, bits of roll sulphur thrown in, and the muzzle stopped with a cork.

306. Sulphur occurs in two distinct crystalline forms, one of which is the right rhombic octohedron and the other is the oblique rhombic prism. Figures 234 and 235 give its usual form as found in nature or as crystallizing from solution. When slowly cooled from fusion, as in a crucible, if the crust formed on the surface be pierced while the interior is

How is it purified? How does heat affect it? What solubility has it How does it act on combustibles? What is Hare's experiment? 306 What of the form of sulphur?

still fluid, and the liquid part turned out, the interior will present, as in fig. 236, long, slender, compressed prisms. These belong to the second form of sulphur. This was one of the first instances of *dimorphism* noticed by Mitscherlich.

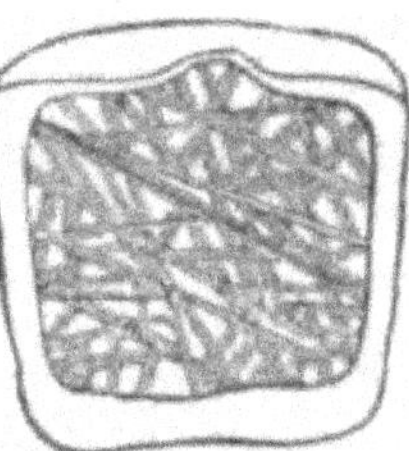
Fig. 236.

307. The fusion of sulphur at different temperatures presents remarkable facts. At 226°–280° it is a clear, straw-yellow fluid; before reaching 280° it begins to grow darker; from that point to 300° it assumes a deep yellow color; at 374° it has an orange tint and becomes somewhat viscid; at 500° it becomes dull-brown, and at this high temperature its viscidity is such that the vessel containing it may be turned over without the sulphur falling out. Above this last temperature it begins to grow more fluid. If at this moment it is thrown into cold water, it remains pasty, transparent, preserves its brown color, and may be drawn out into long threads which have almost the elasticity of caoutchouc. It regains its original brittleness only after many hours. In this pasty state, sulphur may be moulded by the hands, and is used to copy medallions and other works of art. At 600° it is volatilized in a deep red-brown vapor, resembling the vapor of bromine. The density of its vapor is 6·654.

308. In its *chemical relations*, sulphur much resembles oxygen. It forms sulphurets with most of the elements that form oxyds, and these sulphurets often unite to form bodies analogous to salts, as the oxyds do. Berzelius insists, very properly, that its binary combinations, from their analogy to the oxyds, should be called *sulphids*, and not sulphurets.

Its *uses* are well known. It is one of the essential ingredients of gunpowder, and is the basis of matches of all kinds. Nearly all the sulphuric acid used in the arts is made from it. The gas arising from its combustion is employed in bleaching straw and woollen goods; and in medicine it has a specific power in certain obstinate cutaneous diseases.

The flowers of sulphur of commerce nearly always have an acid reaction, due to the sulphurous acid formed in sublima-

---

How is it obtained crystallized? 307. Give the facts observed in its fusion. What of its vapor? 308. What are the relations of sulphur? What its uses?

tion. All the sulphur of commerce is obtained from its ores by sublimation in large chambers,—or, when cast in blocks, by distillation and fusion in earthenware pots.

Compounds of Sulphur with Oxygen.

309. The compounds of sulphur and oxygen are numerous, but only two of them will engage our attention at present, namely:

Sulphurous acid.. SO_2
Sulphuric acid.. SO_3

The other compounds of sulphur and oxygen are expressed by the formulæ S_2O_2, S_2O_5, S_3O_5, S_4O_5, S_5O_5.

310. *Sulphurous Acid*, SO_2.—*Preparation.*—This is the sole product of the combustion of sulphur in oxygen, as in the experiment figured in fig. 237, where burning sulphur

Fig. 237.

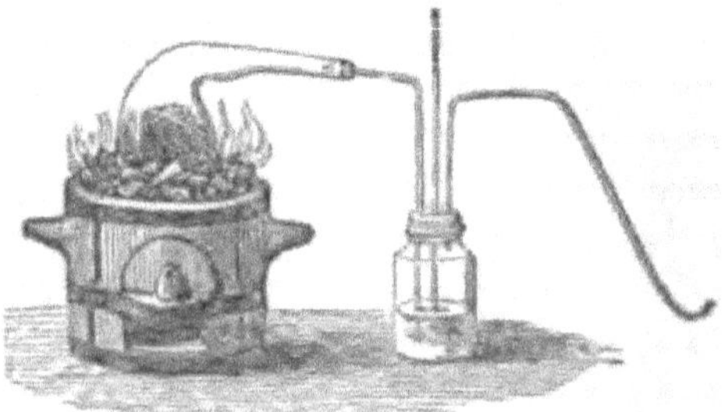

Fig. 238.

in a spoon is lowered into a jar of oxygen gas. Other methods are used however in the laboratory to procure this gas. One of the best is to heat in a retort or flask (fig. 238) an intimate mixture of six parts of peroxyd of manganese and 1 of flowers of sulphur, in fine powder. The sulphur is burned at the expense of one portion of the oxygen of the peroxyd of manganese. The sulphurous acid gas is given off abundantly, and may be freed of a little volatilized sulphur, by a wash-bottle. Mercury and copper also decompose sulphuric acid, yielding sulphurous acid, by aid of heat; but the first method is much preferable on every account. It must be collected in dry vessels or over mercury.

309. What are its oxygen compounds? 310. What is SO_2? How prepared in fig. 237? How collected?

311. *Properties.*—Sulphurous acid is a colorless acid gas, with a pungent, suffocating odor, recognized as that of a burning match. It extinguishes flame. A lighted candle lowered into a jar containing it is extinguished, and the edges of the flame, as it expires, are tinged with green.

A solution of blue litmus or purple cabbage turned into a jar of the gas is at first reddened by the acid, and then bleached. Articles bleached by it, after a time regain their previous color. Water at 60° absorbs nearly fifty times its volume of sulphurous acid, forming a strongly acid fluid. Hence the necessity for collecting this gas over mercury, or by displacement of air in dry vessels. Its avidity for moisture is so great that it forms an acid fog with the water in the atmosphere, and a bit of ice slipped under a jar of it on the mercurial cistern is instantly melted; the water absorbs the gas, and the mercury rises to fill the jar.

312. *Sulphurous acid* is easily liquefied under ordinary pressures at 14° and below, using a tube with a bulb E, like fig. 239, placed in a refrigerating vessel F. The gas is first dried by chlorid of calcium before passing into E. The liquid gas is easily preserved by turning it into a tube drawn out like A B, (fig. 240,) and previously refrigerated. The part A serves for a funnel. The blowpipe flame seals it hermetically at *a*, and it may be then preserved for future use. Under a pressure of two atmospheres, this gas is condensed at a temperature of 59°. It is a colorless mobile fluid of a density of 1·42. Its evaporation produces intense cold. If the ball of a mercury thermometer is enveloped in cotton and moistened by liquid sulphurous acid, the mercury is frozen, and a spirit of wine thermometer indicates a temperature as low as — 60°. By its evaporation water is frozen in a red-hot crucible. It is a crystalline solid, transparent and colorless, at 105°, sinking in the liquid gas.

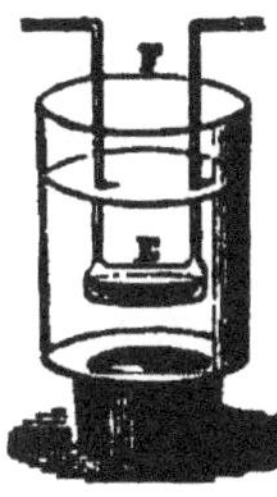

Fig. 239.

Fig. 240.

313. The *volume* of sulphurous acid is the same as that of the oxygen employed in producing it. In other words, sul-

---

311. Give its properties. What of its bleaching? Of its avidity for moisture? 312. How and at what temperature liquefied? How collected and preserved? What of its sudden evaporation? What temperature? 313. What of the volume of SO_2? Give the calculation.

phurous acid contains 1 volume of oxygen and ⅙ volume of sulphur vapor (258) condensed into 1 volume. Thus,

One volume of sulphurous acid density	2·247
Substract the weight of 1 volume of oxygen	1·106
Leaving	1·141
Which represents very nearly ⅙th volume of sulphur vapor $= \frac{6·654}{6}$	1·109

By weight, sulphurous acid contains sulphur 50·87, oxygen 49·13 = 100. One hundred cubic inches of it weigh 68·70 grains.

314. Besides its use in bleaching straw and woollen goods, sulphurous acid is employed as a bath for diseases of the skin, and is a powerful disinfectant, even arresting putrefaction and fermentation.

Sulphites are salts containing sulphurous acid. Their solutions are gradually changed to sulphates by absorbing oxygen.

315. *Sulphuric acid*, $SO_3.HO$.—This acid is one of the most important compounds known; its affinities are very powerful, and no class of bodies is better understood by chemists than the sulphates. In the arts great use is made of sulphuric acid, many millions of pounds of it being annually consumed in manufacturing nitric and muriatic acids, the sulphates of copper and alum, in the process of dyeing, and more than all, in the manufacture of carbonate of soda from sea-salt.

It is not formed by the direct union of its elements, since we have seen that only sulphurous acid can result from the combustion of sulphur in oxygen. Sulphurous acid must be oxydized to form sulphuric acid.

316. This may be done by passing a mixture of sulphurous acid with common air over spongy platinum, heated to redness in a tube, when there will issue from the open end of the tube a mixture of sulphuric acid in vapor, with nitrogen from the air. In the arts, however, this process cannot be used; but sulphuric acid is made on a large scale by bringing together sulphurous acid SO_2, hyponitric acid NO_4, and water HO, all in a state of vapor, in a large chamber, or series of chambers, lined with lead, when sul-

---

What of its density? 314. What of the uses of sulphurous acid? 315. What of SO_3? What its use? 316. How is SO_3 formed?

phurous acid SO_2 passes to a higher state of oxydation SO_3 at the expense of one-half the oxygen of the hyponitric acid NO_4, which thus becomes reduced to the state of the deutoxyd of nitrogen, (NO_2.) The arrangement employed is represented in fig. 241. A A is a chamber, fifty feet or more long, lined on all sides with sheet-lead. A very large leaden tube B, opening into one end of the chamber, communicates with a furnace. Its lower end rests in a gutter *o o* of dilute acid, to prevent the effects of too much heat and the escape of the vapors. The sulphur is introduced by a door *c* to an iron pan; and a fire built beneath, *n*. The heat melts the sulphur, which burns in a current of air passing over it, and the sulphurous acid thus formed enters the chamber, in company with air, and the vapors of nitric and hyponitric acids set free from small iron pans standing over the sulphur, and containing the materials to evolve nitric acid, (sulphuric acid and saltpetre.) A small steam-boiler *e* furnishes a jet of steam *x* as required, and a quantity of water covers the floor, which is inclined so as to be deepest at *h*. A chimney with a valve or damper *p* allows the escape of spent and useless gases. Things being thus arranged, the chamber receives a constant supply of sulphurous acid, common air, nitric acid vapor, and steam.

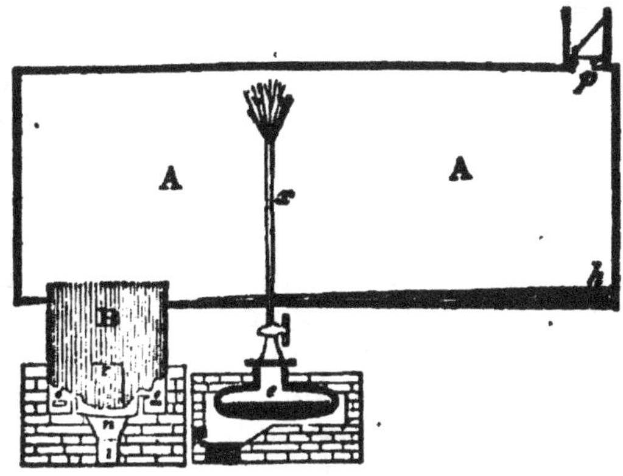

Fig. 241.

317. These compounds react with each other in such a manner that the oxygen of the air is constantly transferred to the sulphurous acid, to form sulphuric acid. Deutoxyd of nitrogen NO_2 in contact with air becomes hyponitric acid NO_4, and this last in presence of a large quantity of water is transformed into nitric acid NO_5 and deutoxyd of nitrogen. Thus, $6NO_4+nHO=4NO_5+nHO+2NO_2$. Now, sulphurous acid, in presence of hydrated nitric acid (NO_5+nHO)

Explain the fig. 241. 317. Whence the oxygen to form SO_3? Give the reactions by the formulæ.

is changed into sulphuric acid, and transforms the nitric acid into hyponitric acid, thus renewing the reaction continually. Thus, $SO_2+NO_5+nHO=SO_3+nHO+NO_4$. In this way a small quantity of nitric acid can be made to oxydize an indefinite amount of sulphurous acid; serving the purpose, as it were, of a carrier of oxygen from the atmospheric air to the sulphurous acid. Meanwhile the water on the floor of the chamber grows rapidly acid; and when it has attained a specific gravity of about 1·5, it is drawn off and concentrated by boiling, first in open pans of lead until it becomes strong enough to corrode the lead, and afterward in stills of platinum until it has a density of about 1·8, in which state it is sold in carboys, or large bottles, packed in boxes.

318. The *process of forming sulphuric acid* is easily illustrated in the class-room by an arrangement of apparatus like that shown in fig. 242. Two flasks *b e* are so connected

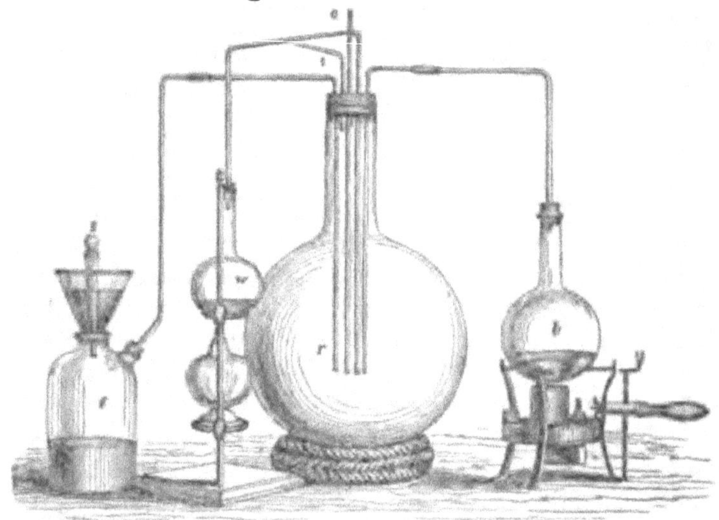

Fig. 242.

by bent tubes with a large balloon, that from one *b* sulphurous acid, and from the other *e* deutoxyd of nitrogen are supplied to the large balloon *r*. A third flask *w* furnishes steam as it is wanted. Fresh air must be occasionally blown in at the open tube *t*, the effete products escaping at *o*. Thus arranged, the reactions above described take place. If but little vapor of water is present, the sides of the globe are soon covered

---

What is the density of SO_3 in the chambers? 318. Explain the figure and process 242.

with a white crystalline solid, which appears to be a compound of sulphurous and of nitrous acids (SO_2,NO_4.) This substance is decomposed by a larger quantity of water into sulphuric acid and hyponitric acid, and as it is known to be formed in the leaden chambers in large quantities, it is supposed to have an important influence in the production of sulphuric acid.

319. This process by the leaden chambers is known in the arts as the English process for sulphuric acid. Formerly sulphuric acid was procured by distilling dry sulphate of iron (green vitriol) in earthenware retorts, at a high temperature. The oily fluid thus obtained was hence vulgarly called *oil of vitriol*. This old process is still in use at Nordhausen, in the Hartz Mountains, producing an acid which is commonly known as Nordhausen acid. It is the most concentrated form possible for fluid sulphuric acid. Sulphuric acid unites with water in four proportions, forming definite compounds, namely:

Nordhausen acid, sp. gr.		1·9	$2(SO_3)HO$
Oil of vitriol,	"	1·83...............	SO_3,HO
Acid of	"	1·78...............	$SO_3,HO+HO$
Acid of	"	1·63...............	$SO_3,HO+2H$

320. Nordhausen acid is a dark-brown, oily fluid, fuming when exposed to air, and hissing like a hot iron when water is let fall into it drop by drop. To mingle the two rapidly in any quantity is unsafe. Cautiously heated in a retort protected by a hood of earthenware A, as in fig. 243,

Fig. 243.

319. What is this process called? What was the old one? Whence the vulgar name? What is the most concentrated SO_3? What hydrates of SO_3? What of Nordhausen SO_3?

a white, crystalline, silky product distils over and is collected in the cool receiver. This is anhydrous sulphuric acid SO_3. It does not possess acid properties by itself, but by contact with water or moisture it is changed to common sulphuric acid. It must be preserved in tubes hermetically sealed. It has therefore been inferred that sulphuric acid cannot exist without water, or that water is essential to the acid property. In this case it is supposed that the oxygen of the water joins that already with the sulphur, (forming SO_4,) while the new compound thus produced unites with hydrogen, forming SO_4H.

321. When exposed to a temperature of — 29°, sulphuric acid freezes; and acid of 1·78 exposed to a temperature of 32° freezes in large crystals. One hundred parts of concentrated sulphuric acid contain 81·64 real acid, 18·36 water, SO_3HO. At 620° it boils, giving off a dense, white, and very suffocating vapor. It is intensely acid to the taste, and deadly, if by any accident it is swallowed, corroding and burning the organs with intense heat. It blackens nearly all inorganic matters, charring or burning them like fire. Its strong disposition for water enables us to employ it in desiccation, and in the absorption of aqueous vapor; using for this purpose a shallow pan (fig. 243) containing SO_3HO, while the substance to be dried is placed above it, and the whole then covered with a low bell-jar or a tight-fitting plate.

Fig. 244.

322. Great heat is generated from the mixture of 4 parts by weight of strong sulphuric acid and 1 of water, and a diminution of bulk attends the mixing. The temperature rises as high as 200°. So that water in a test tube *b* (fig. 245) may be made to boil when placed in the mixture contained in the beaker-glass *a*. If common sulphuric acid is used for this purpose, it becomes milky when water is added to it, from the precipitation of sulphate of lead, derived from the boilers in which it was made. This salt is soluble in strong sulphuric acid, but is precipitated by addition of water.

Fig. 245.

How is crystalline SO_3 obtained? What formula is given? 321. When does SO_3 freeze? What of sp. gr. 1·78? Give other traits of SO_3. 322. What if water and SO_3 are mingled? Why is the mixture milky?

323. Sulphuric acid forms sulphates, a class of salts most minutely known to chemists, and many of which are familiarly known in common life.

Chloride of barium, added to sulphuric acid, or to a soluble sulphate, throws down an abundant precipitate of sulphate of baryta, a salt insoluble in all menstrua. The same test gives a precipitate also with sulphurous acid, (sulphite of baryta,) but the latter is soluble in chlorohydric acid.

324. There are several *chlorids* of sulphur. The apparatus figured in fig. 245 shows the manner of preparing one of

Fig. 246.

them ClS_2. Sulphur is placed in the small retort P and fused by the lamp beneath, while a current of chlorine liberated from the ballon *c*, and dried over the chloride of calcium tube *a*, is delivered gently by the descending tube almost in contact with the fused sulphur in P. Combination ensues, chloride of sulphur distils over and is condensed in the receiver *r*, kept cool by water from the fountain. This chlorid of sulphur is a reddish-yellow fluid, of a disagreeable odor. It boils at 280°, giving a vapor of density 4·668. The density of the liquid is 1·68. Water decomposes it, forming sulphur and chlorohydric acid. One volume of this substance in vapor is formed of

1 vol. chlorine	2·440
⅓ " sulphur $\frac{6·654}{3}$	2·218
Giving the theoretical density	4·658
While experiment gives	4·668

323. What salts does SO_3 form? What tests for SO_3? 324. How is ClS_2 formed? Describe fig. 245. What are its characters? Give its volume and density.

The bromids and iodids of sulphur possess very little interest.

SELENIUM.

Equivalent, 40. *Symbol*, Se. *Density*, 4·3.

325. *History and Properties.*—This element was discovered by Berzelius, in 1818, and named by him from *selene*, the moon. It is associated in nature with sulphur in some kinds of iron pyrites, and in a lead ore from Saxony, and also at the Lipari Islands combined with sulphur and accompanied by other volcanic products.

It closely resembles sulphur in most of its properties, as well as in its natural associations. At common temperatures it is a brittle solid, opake, and having a metallic lustre like lead, but in powder it is of a deep red color. Its specific gravity is 4·28 for the vitreous, and 4·80 for the granular variety from slow cooling. It softens at 212°, and may then be drawn out into red-colored threads; at a little higher temperature it melts completely, and boils at 650°, giving a deep yellow vapor without odor. It passes through the same changes of state by heat as sulphur. It is insoluble. When heated in the air, it combines with oxygen, and gives out a disagreeable and strong odor, like putrid horse-radish. Before the blowpipe, on charcoal, it burns with a pale blue flame, and $\frac{1}{50}$ of a grain, so heated, will fill a large apartment with its odor. It is a non-conductor of heat and of electricity, and excites resinous electricity.

326. The *compounds of selenium with oxygen* are three, two of which are acids, analogous to sulphurous and sulphuric acids. They are—

Oxyd of selenium	SeO
Selenious acid	SeO_2
Selenic acid	SeO_3

Oxyd of selenium is formed when selenium is heated in the air. It is a colorless gas, and possesses the strong odor before mentioned.

327. *Selenious acid* is formed when selenium is burned

---

325. What of selenium? Give its characters. Its equivalent. 326. What compounds of O has it?

in a current of oxygen gas, as in the tube *a*, (fig. 247.) A small portion of selenium is placed at *b*, and fused by a lamp; at this temperature, oxygen flowing, from a reservoir, in at *a*, combines with the selenium, forming SeO_2, which is a white crystalline body, very soluble in water, and sublimed by heat unchanged. *Selenic acid* is formed when selenium is burned by nitrate of potash, forming selenate of potash. It resembles sulphuric acid in its properties. Both selenious and selenic acids form salts with the alkalies and bases, every way similar to the sulphites and sulphates. *Selenid of sulphur* is found native among volcanic products

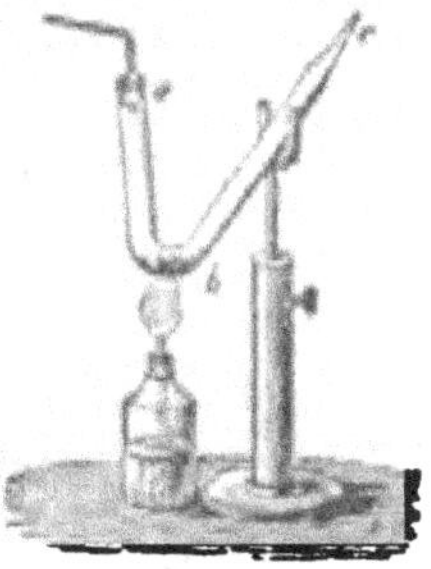

Fig. 247.

TELLURIUM.

Equivalent, 64. *Symbol*, Te.

328. This rare substance is related to selenium and sulphur. It forms compounds with gold and bismuth, found native as minerals. Pure tellurium is a tin-white, brittle substance, with a metallic lustre, and density of 6·26. It melts at low redness, and takes fire in the air, forming tellurous acid, TeO_2. With hydrogen it forms a compound, analogous to arseniuretted hydrogen, and sulphuretted hydrogen.

CLASS IV.

NITROGEN, OR AZOTE.

Equivalent, 14. *Symbol*, N. *Density*, ·972.

329. *Preparation and History.*—This gas forms four-fifths of the air, and is an essential constituent of most organic substances. It was first described by Rutherford, in 1772. It is only mingled mechanically with oxygen in our atmosphere, which is not a chemical compound.

It is most easily procured for purposes of experiment from the atmosphere, by withdrawing the oxygen of the air

---

327. What of selenious acid? 328. What of tellurium? 329. Give the history of nitrogen.

Fig. 248.

by phosphorus. This is easily done by burning some phosphorus in a floating capsule, under an air-jar, upon the pneumatic cistern, (fig. 248.) The strong affinity of phosphorus for oxygen enables it to withdraw every trace of this element, leaving behind nitrogen nearly pure, containing about $\frac{1}{40}$th of phosphorus. The water soon absorbs the snow-white phosphoric acid. The first combustion of the phosphorus expels a portion of the air by expansion; but as the combustion proceeds, the water rises in the jar, until it occupies about $\frac{1}{5}$th of its space. When this experiment is performed over mercury, the white phosphoric acid remains unchanged. Nitrogen may be procured pure by passing a current of air over copper turnings in a tube of hard glass heated to redness: the oxygen is all retained by the copper, while nitrogen is given off. Nitrogen can also be obtained, by decomposing strong water of ammonia, by chlorine gas: the ammonia yields its hydrogen to the chlorine, and the nitrogen is given off. The apparatus (fig. 249) may be used for this purpose, in which *p* is an evolution-flask for chlorine, and the strong ammonia water is in *w*. Great care should be taken to prevent all the ammonia becoming saturated, as in that case a

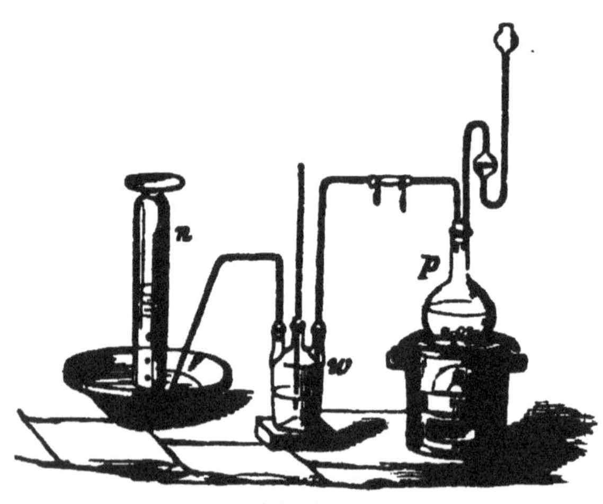

Fig. 249.

How prepared? How from ammonia? What precaution is noted? What is the reaction?

very dangerous compound (chloride of nitrogen) will be formed by the action of the chlorine, on the chlorid of ammonia produced in the process. The nitrogen collects in *n*. $3Cl + NH_3 = 3HCL + N$.

330. The *properties* of nitrogen are mostly negative. It is a colorless, tasteless, odorless, permanent gas. It has not been liquefied. It combines directly with no element, but indirectly it enters into most powerful combinations. In the atmosphere it appears to act chiefly as a diluent of oxygen. Its density is 0·972, or a little less than air. A taper immersed in it (fig. 250) is extinguished immediately. An animal placed in nitrogen dies from want of oxygen, and not because of any poisonous character in the gas, as might be inferred from its abundance in our atmosphere. Hence its name *azote*, from *a* privative, and the Greek *zoe*, life, to deprive of life. Nitrogen is derived from Latin *nitrium*, nitre, and *gennao*, I form. One hundred volumes of water dissolve about two and a half volumes of nitrogen.

Fig. 250.

The Atmosphere.

331. The mechanical properties of the atmosphere have already been considered, (20.) The number and proportion of the constituents of the atmosphere are constant, although their union is only mechanical. Repeated analyses have shown that atmospheric air is always formed of nitrogen, oxygen, watery vapor, a little carbonic acid, traces of carburetted hydrogen, and a small quantity of ammonia. The air on Mount Blanc, or that taken in a balloon by Gay-Lussac from 21,735 feet above the earth, had the same chemical composition as that on the surface, or at the bottom of the deepest mines. The carbonic acid, being liable to changes in quantity from local causes, is found to vary slightly.

To the constituents already named, we may add the aroma of flowers and other volatile odors, and those unknown, mysterious agencies, which affect health, and are called miasmata. From the results of numerous analyses, we state the composition of the atmosphere in 100 parts, to be—

---

330. What its properties? What its function in air? How affects life? Hence, what name has it? Define the word *nitrogen*. 331. What of air? How are its constituents? What of its purity? What are its constituents?

	By weight.	By measure.
Nitrogen	76·90	79·10
Oxygen	23·10	20·90
	100·00	100·00

To this we must add from 3 to 5 measures of carbonic acid in 10,000 of air, about the same quantity of carburetted hydrogen, a variable quantity of aqueous vapor, and a trace of ammonia. Nitric acid is also sometimes found in small quantity in rain-water, formed in the air by the electrical discharges of thunder-clouds, and washed out by the rains. 100 cubic inches of dry air weigh 31·011 grains. In 10,000 volumes the constitution of the air will be, therefore—

Nitrogen	7901
Oxygen	2091
Carbonic acid	4
Carburetted hydrogen	4
Ammonia	trace
	10,000

332. The analysis of air is accomplished by any substance which will remove the oxygen. But the accurate performance of this process requires numerous minute precautions, any notice of which is out of place here. *Eudiometry* is the term applied to the common method of analysis for air. This term is derived from Greek words signifying a good condition of the air, and was employed because it was formerly thought that an analysis of the air would show if it was in a salutary condition. One of the simplest means of analyzing the atmosphere, consists in removing the oxygen by the slow combustion of phosphorus. For this purpose a stick of phosphorus is sustained on a platinum wire (fig. 251) in a confined portion of air, contained in a graduated glass tube, whose open end is beneath water. A gradual absorption takes place, and in about twenty-four hours the water ceases to rise in the tube, by which we know that the phosphorus has removed all

Fig. 251.

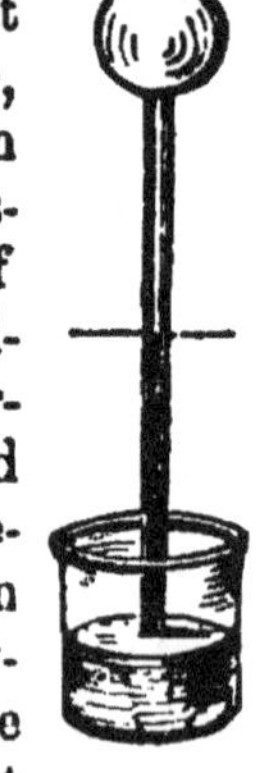

Fig. 252.

Give analyses of air? What is its composition in 10,000 volumes? 332. How analyzed? What is eudiometry?

the oxygen. The water absorbs the resulting phosphorous acid, and we may read off, by the graduation on the tube, the amount of oxygen removed. A narrow-necked bolt-head shows this result in a more striking manner in the class-room, the large volume of air in the ball causing a very appreciable rise of water in the stem during the course of a lecture, (fig. 252.) When speaking of hydrogen, we will mention another method of eudiometry. The agency of the air in combustion and respiration will also be explained under the appropriate heads. The air dissolved in water, and on which water-breathing animals live, is found to be decidedly more rich in oxygen than the atmospheric air. This is owing to the fact that oxygen is much more abundantly absorbed by water than nitrogen, in the proportion of ·046 to ·025. These numbers express, respectively, the ratio of solubility of the two gases in water. The air in water has the constitution—

	By analysis.	By theory.
Oxygen	32	31·5
Nitrogen	68	68·5
	100	100·0

Compounds of Oxygen and Nitrogen.

333. *Nitrogen unites with oxygen,* forming five compounds, three of which are acids. Their names and constitution are thus expressed:—

	Symbol.
Protoxyd of nitrogen (nitrous oxyd)	NO
Deutoxyd of nitrogen (nitric oxyd)	NO_2
Nitrous acid	NO_3
Hyponitric acid	NO_4
Nitric acid	NO_5

As nitric acid is the source whence all the other compounds of nitrogen are obtained, we will commence with the history of that compound:—

This important compound was known in the earliest days of alchemy, but it was Cavendish who, in 1785, first made known its constitution. He formed it by direct union of its elements over a solution of potash, by aid of a series of electrical sparks continually passed through a mixture of the two gases N and O, for several successive days,

What of air dissolved in water? 333. What are the oxygen compounds of nitrogen? Give the series. What is the source of other nitrogen compounds?

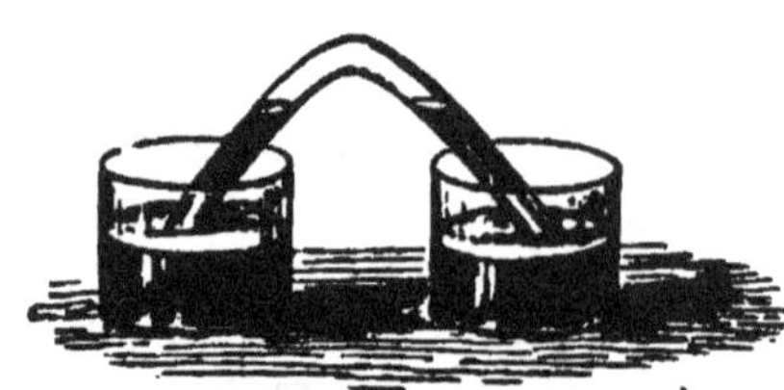
Fig. 253.

in a close tube, (fig 253) The ends of the tube, containing the gases and pot ash solution, dipped into and contained mercury as a conducting medium for the electricity. Nitre was, subsequently, found in the solution, thus giving the strongest evidence of a union of the two gases.

334. *Nitric Acid*, "*Aqua Fortis*," NO_5HO.—This powerful acid is obtained by heating saltpetre (nitrate of potassa) or nitrate of soda with strong sulphuric acid. The nitric acid is displaced by the sulphuric, and distils over, being much more volatile than the sulphuric acid.

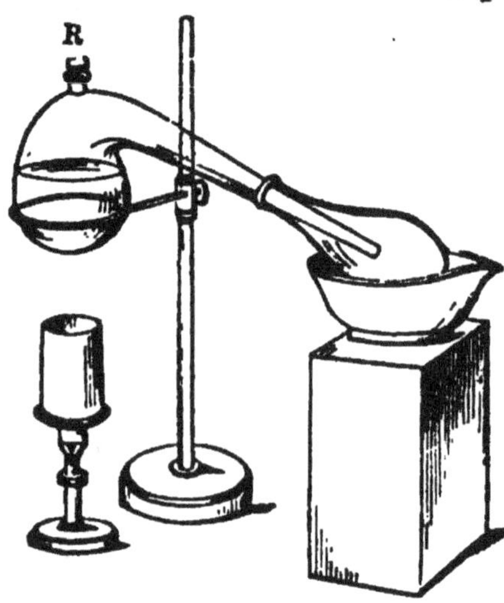

Fig. 254.

335. The arrangement of apparatus required is seen in figure 254. The retort R contains the nitre in small crystals, and should be supported in a sand-bath; or, if the quantity of nitre does not exceed a pound or two, a naked fire answers very well. An equal weight of sulphuric acid is then added, with care not to soil the interior neck of the retort. Heat is gradually applied, and the receiver kept cold by a constant stream of water distributed over its surface by a piece of filtering paper. No corks or luting of any kind can be used about the apparatus, as the vapors of concentrated nitric acid attack all organic substances with energy, as also the alumina and other bases of clay-lute. In the first moments of the operation the vessels are filled with deep-red vapors of hyponitrous acid, due to the decomposition of the first formed portions of nitric acid by the great

---

334. What is the history of NO_5? What was the experiment of Cavendish? What is the process, fig. 254? What precautions are given?

excess of sulphuric acid. As the distillation proceeds, the vessels become colorless and the distillate very nearly so. The red vapors appear again at the close of the operation, and furnish a signal when to arrest the process and change the recipient. This is because the temperature rises toward the close, to the decomposing point of nitric acid. The bisulphate of potash in the retort remains some time after the heat is withdrawn in a state of quiet fusion, having a temperature of about 600°. When reduced to about 250°, hot water may be added in small portions at a time, and with care the retort may be saved, although it is often sacrificed from the crystallization of the sulphate of potassa. In the arts this process is conducted in large vessels of iron set in brick furnaces.

336. *Properties.*—Nitric acid is a mobile fluid, nearly colorless, fuming, intensely acid, staining the skin instantly yellow, and acting with great energy on most metals and organic substances. It has usually a reddish color, due to the presence of hyponitric acid. When most concentrated it has a density of 1·51–1·52, and contains 86 parts in 100, real acid. It boils at 187°. It is decomposed by light, evolving red fumes of hyponitric acid and free oxygen, which sometimes forcibly expels the stopper. It should, therefore, be kept in a dark place, or in black bottles. Poured on pulverized charcoal which has recently been ignited, it deflagrates it with energy; warm oil of turpentine is immediately fired by it; and its action on phosphorus is too violent to be a safe experiment, without great precaution. The concentrated acid freezes at —40°; but if diluted with half its weight of water, it freezes at about 1½°. The green hydrous acid (343) freezes to a bluish-white solid. The dilute acid yields by distillation a product, at first more concentrated, but when it has a boiling point of 250° the product is of uniform strength, and contains 40 parts real acid in 100. Like sulphuric acid, it forms several definite hydrates, of which the highest is the strong acid described above. Anhydrous nitric acid NO_5 has been lately obtained by decomposing dry nitrate of silver by perfectly dry chlorine. Anhydrous ntric acid crystallizes in colorless rhombs, which fuse at 30°; and it boils at 50° with decom-

---

336. What are the properties of NO_5? How does it act on combustibles? What of its hydrates? Of anhydrous NO_5?

position. It is soluble in water, evolving much heat, and yielding colorless, hydrous nitric acid

337. Nitric acid is a powerful solvent of the metals, and carries them to their highest state of oxydation. This action is always attended with the production of binoxyd of nitrogen NO_2 and hyponitric acid. The nitrates are all soluble in water. When fused with carbon they are decomposed with brilliant deflagration of the charcoal. Nitric acid decolorizes a solution of sulphate of indigo, and with a few drops of chlorohydric acid it dissolves gold-leaf.

Passed in vapor through a porcelain tube heated white-hot it is decomposed, yielding nitrogen and oxygen.

338. *Protoxyd of Nitrogen* NO, *Nitrous Oxyd*, or *Laughing Gas.*—This gaseous compound of nitrogen is prepared by heating nitrate of ammonia $NH_4O.NO_5$ in a glass flask, (fig. 255,) by the aid of a spirit-lamp. The gas is given off at about 400° to 500°, and is delivered by the bent tube to an air-jar on the pneumatic trough. The nitrate of ammonia, which is a crystalline white salt formed by neutralizing dilute nitric acid by carbonate of ammonia, is so constituted as to be resolved by heat alone into nitrous oxyd and water; thus, $NH_4O.NO_5$ become by heat $4HO + 2NO$ Consequently, the equivalents of these elements show us, that 80 grains of nitrate of ammonia, will yield 44 grains of nitrous oxyd, and 36 grains of water.

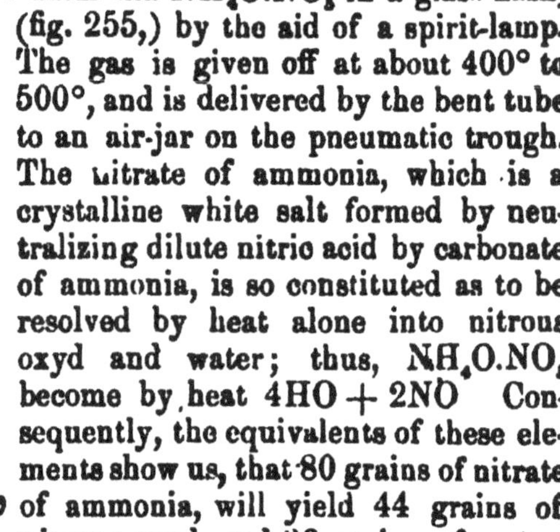

Fig. 255.

Care must be taken not to heat this salt too highly, as it then yields nitric oxyd and hyponitric acid. If a red cloud is seen during any part of the operation, the heat must be abated.

339. *Properties.*—Protoxyd of nitrogen is a colorless gas, with a faint, agreeable odor, and a sweetish taste. With a pressure of fifty atmospheres at 45° F. it becomes a clear liquid, and at about 150° degrees below zero freezes into a beautiful clear crystalline solid. By the evaporation of this solid, a degree of cold may be produced far below that of the carbonic acid bath (151) in vacuo, (or lower than — 174°

337. How does it affect metals? What of nitrates? 338. How is NO prepared? Give the reaction? What precaution is noted? 339. What are its properties? What of its liquid? What temperature?

F.) It evaporates slowly, and does not freeze, like carbonic acid, by its own evaporation. The specific gravity of nitrous oxyd is 1·527; 100 cubic inches of it weigh 47·29 grains. Cold water absorbs about its own volume of this gas. It cannot, therefore, be long kept over water, but may be collected over the water-trough in vessels filled with warm water. It supports the combustion of a candle, (fig. 256,) and sometimes relights its red wick with almost the same promptness as pure oxygen. Phosphorus burns in it with great splendor. With an equal bulk of hydrogen, it forms a mixture that explodes with violence by the electric spark or a match: the residue is pure nitrogen, the oxygen forming water with the hydrogen. Passed through a red-hot porcelain tube it is resolved into its constituent gases. One volume of protoxyd of nitrogen contains

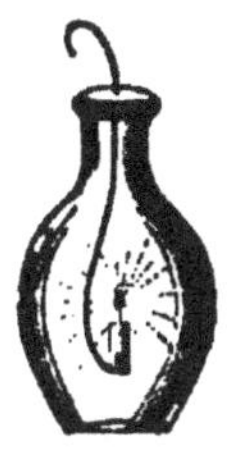

Fig. 256.

1 volume of nitrogen	0·972
½ volume of oxygen	0·552
Theoretical density	1·524

340. It may be breathed without injury, but it produces a remarkable excitement in the system, amounting to intoxication, and, if carried far, even to insensibility. To produce these effects without injury, it should be quite pure, and especially free from chlorine, and inhaled through a wide tube, from a gas-holder or bag. The presence of chlorid of ammonium in the nitrate employed should be especially avoided, as producing chlorine. There is a sweetish taste, and a sensation of giddiness, followed by joyous or boisterous exhilaration. This is shown by a disposition to laughter, a flow of vivid ideas and poetic imagery, and often by a strong disposition to muscular exertion. These sensations are usually quite transient, and pass away without any resulting languor or depression. In a few cases, dangerous consequences have followed its use, and it should always be employed with great caution. In at least one case, in the laboratory of Yale College, it produced a joyous exhilaration of spirits, which continued for months, and permanent restoration of health. Its effects, however, on different individuals, are various.

How does it act on combustibles? What is its volume? 340. What its effect if breathed?

341 *Deutoxyd or Binoxyd of Nitrogen, Nitric Oxyd.*—This gas is easily prepared by adding strong nitric acid to clippings of sheet-copper, contained in a bottle arranged with two tubes, (fig. 257.) A little water is first put with the copper cuttings, and the nitric acid poured in at the tall funnel-tube until brisk effervescence comes on. In this case the copper is oxydized by a part of the oxygen of the acid, and the oxyd thus formed is dissolved by another portion of acid. The nitrogen, in union with the two equivalents of oxygen, is given off as nitric oxyd, which, not being absorbed by water, may be collected over the pneumatic-trough. Many other metals have the same action with nitric acid. The action is renewed by continued additions of nitric acid. It is also obtained very pure by heating nitrate of potash $KO.NO_5$ with a solution of protochlorid of iron FeCl, in an excess of chlorohydric acid.

Fig. 257.

342. *Properties.*—Nitric oxyd is a transparent, colorless gas, tasteless and inodorous, but excites a violent spasm in the throat when an attempt is made to breathe it. It has never been condensed into a liquid. Its specific gravity is 1·039, and 100 cubic inches weigh 32·22 grains. It contains equal measures of oxygen and nitrogen uncondensed.

A lighted taper is usually extinguished when immersed in it, but phosphorus previously well inflamed will burn in it with great splendor. When this gas comes into contact with the air, deep-red fumes are produced, by its union with the oxygen of the air to form hyponitric acid. If to a tall jar, nearly filled with nitric oxyd, standing over the well of the cistern, pure oxygen gas be turned up, deep blood-red fumes instantly fill the vessel, much heat is generated, and a rapid absorption results from the solution of the red nitrous acid vapors in the water of the cistern.

343. Nitric oxyd is rapidly absorbed by solution of green sulphate of iron, forming a deep-brown solution of sulphate of peroxyd of iron. Colorless nitric acid also absorbs nitric

---

341. What of NO_2? How evolved? 342. Give its properties. Why irrespirable? How affects combustibles? In contact with air produces what? Give an illustration. 343. What absorbs it?

oxyd, and acquires first a yellow, then an orange-red, and finally a lively green color. This operation is best conducted in an apparatus of bottles arranged as in fig. 258, and called Woulf's apparatus. The gas generated in *a* passes

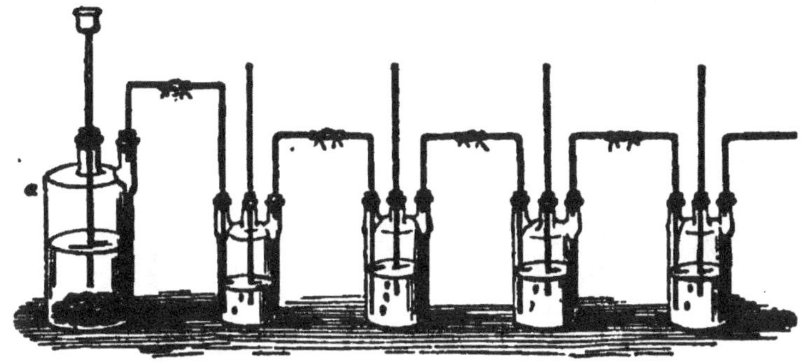

Fig. 258.

in succession into the fluid of each vessel. The central tubes serve as safety-tubes. The colors named above are beautifully seen in the several bottles, the first becoming green before the last has gained an orange tint. By carefully heating the green acid, the hyponitric acid contained in it may be expelled. The deutoxyd of nitrogen decomposes the nitric acid, forming hyponitric acid, (345.)

344. *Nitrous Acid*, NO_3.—This is a thin, mobile liquid, formed from the mixture of four measures of deutoxyd of nitrogen with one measure of oxygen, both perfectly dry, and exposed after mixture to a temperature below zero of Fahrenheit. It has an orange-red vapor: the liquid at common temperatures is green, but at zero is colorless. Water decomposes it, forming nitric acid and deutoxyd of nitrogen. It forms salts, called *nitrites*.

345. *Hyponitric Acid*, NO_4.—When the green nitric acid obtained in the process just described (fig. 258) is cautiously distilled, hyponitric acid in notable quantity is collected in the refrigerated receiver. The apparatus is arranged as in fig. 259. The green acid is heated in the retort *r*, by means of a water-bath *w*, over the lamp *e*, and the product is collected in the U tube *t*, placed in a refrigerant mixture. This acid is also procured by decomposing nitrate of lead in a porcelain retort by heat. Oxygen and hyponitric

How does it affect NO_2? Explain the apparatus, fig. 257. 344. What of NO ? What are its salts? 345. How is NO_4 obtained?

acid are obtained, and the latter is collected as above. This is an orange-colored fluid, density 1·42, becoming red when

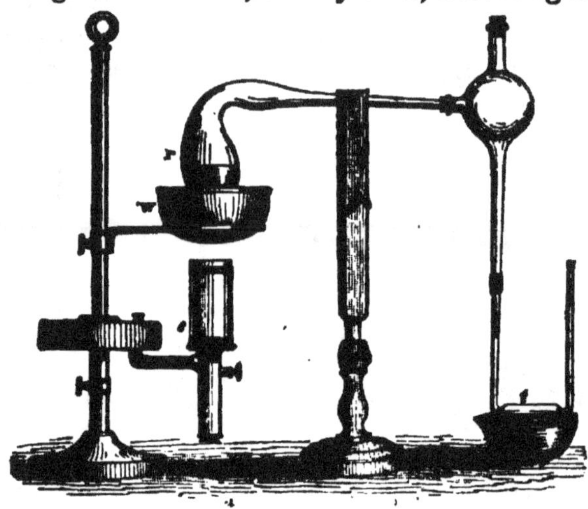

Fig. 259.

heated. It boils at 82°, and solidifies at 8°. Its vapor is intensely red, and has the density 1·73. This compound is hardly entitled to be considered as an acid, it does not form salts, but in contact with a base is decomposed, producing a nitrate and a nitrite.

PHOSPHORUS.

Equivalent, 32. *Symbol*, P. *Density*, 1·863.

346. *History.*—Phosphorus is an element nowhere seen free in nature, but it exists largely in the animal kingdom, combined with lime, forming bones, and is found also in other parts of the body. In the mineral kingdom it exists widely diffused in several well-known forms, particularly in the mineral called apatite, which is a phosphate of lime. It is introduced into the animal system by the plants used as food, whose ashes contain a notable quantity of phosphate of lime. It was discovered in 1669, by Brandt, an alchemist of Hamburg, while engaged in seeking for the philosopher's stone, in human urine. Its name implies its most remarkable property, (*phos*, light, and *phero*, I carry.)

347. *Preparation.*—Phosphorus is procured in immense

How as in fig. 258? What are its properties? 346. Give the history of phosphorus. Whence its name?

quantities from burnt bones, for the manufacture of friction matches. The bones are calcined until they are quite white; they are then ground to a fine powder, and fifteen parts of this are treated with thirty parts of water and ten of sulphuric acid: this mixture is allowed to stand a day or two, and is then filtered, to free it from the insoluble sulphate of lime, formed by the action of the oil of vitriol on the bones. The clear liquid (which is a soluble salt of lime and phosphoric acid) is then evaporated to a syrup, and a quantity of powdered charcoal added. The whole is then completely dried in an iron vessel and gently ignited. After this, it is introduced into a stoneware or iron retort, to which a wide tube of copper is fitted, communicating with a bottle in which is a little water, that just covers the open end of the tube, (fig. 260:) a small tube carries the gases given out to a chimney or vent. The retort being very gradually heated, the charcoal decomposes the phosphoric acid, carbonic acid and carbonic oxyd gases are evolved, and free phosphorus flows down the tube into the bottle, where it is condensed. The operation is a critical one. Splendid flashes of light are constantly given out during the operation, from the escape of phosphuretted hydrogen. The crude phosphorus thus obtained is purified by melting under water, and it is then cast into glass tubes, forming the sticks in which it is sold.

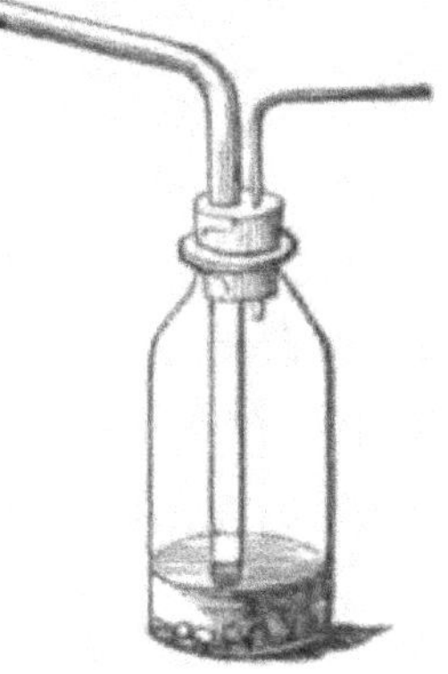
Fig. 260.

348. *Properties.*—Phosphorus is an almost colorless, semi-transparent solid, which at ordinary temperatures, cuts with the consistency and lustre of wax. At 32° it is brittle, and breaks with a crystalline fracture. Exposed to light, it soon becomes yellow and finally red. Its density by the late determinations, is 1·826–1·840, and liquid 1·88. It is insoluble in water; but dissolves readily in bisulphuret of carbon; in ether, alcohol, and various oils, it is partially soluble. It is obtained in fine dodecahedral crystals, from its solution in bisulphuret of carbon. It melts at 111° to

---

347. How prepared? How is the crude PO_5 decomposed? 348. What are its characters? How crystallized? How soluble?

a limpid liquid: when fused beneath water, it is safely re-cast in small sticks, by drawing it into narrow glass tubes. It boils at 554°, forming a colorless vapor with the density 4·226. Owing to its great inflammability, it is a very unsafe substance to handle, producing severe burns, very difficult to heal. Any impurity, such as the presence of partly oxydized phosphorus, as from the nitrogen experiment, (fig. 248) renders it much more liable to inflammation. The heat of the hand, or the least friction, suffices to set fire to it. It must be kept under water, to which alcohol enough may be added to prevent its freezing in winter. If exposed to the air, it wastes slowly away, forming phosphorous acid. When in the dark, it is seen to be luminous. The vapor which comes from it has a strong garlic odor, which does not belong, either to the pure phosphorus, or its acid compounds. By this action the ozone of Schönbein is formed, (279.) A little olefiant gas, the vapor of ether, or any essential oil, will entirely arrest the slow oxydation of phosphorus in air. The presence of nitrogen or hydrogen seems to be essential to this operation, as, in pure oxygen, phosphorus does not form phosphorous acid at common temperatures. It burns in pure oxygen gas with great splendor, forming one of the most brilliant experiments in chemistry, (354.) Phosphorus is a violent poison.

349. *Red*, or *amorphous phosphorus*, is a peculiar isomeric modification of common phosphorus, produced by heating it for a long time near its point of vaporization, in an atmosphere of hydrogen, or of carbonic acid. This effect takes place also when phosphorus is long exposed to the light: the exterior of the sticks becomes encrusted with a red powder, formerly supposed to be oxyd of phosphorus. Red phosphorus presents properties strikingly different from common phosphorus: the latter fuses, as we have seen, at 111°; the former remains solid even at 482°, and at 500° returns to the condition of ordinary phosphorus. Red phosphorus can be preserved without change in air, has no sensible odor, and may even be heated to 392° without becoming luminous. Its specific gravity is 1·964. It does not combine with sulphur at the fusion point of that body, while

---

What renders it more inflammable? How is it kept? If exposed to air, what happens? How is its combustion in O managed in fig. 264? 349. What is red phosphorus? How produced? Give its characters. How is it recognised as the same body?

common phosphorus unites with sulphur with a terrible explosion. It is only from the identity of the compounds from these two modifications of phosphorus that it is shown that they are indeed one and the same body. The red phosphorus is preferred, from its greater safety, in the manufacture of matches, and in medicine.

Compounds of Phosphorus with Oxygen.

350. The *compounds of phosphorus with oxygen* are four in number, namely:

Oxyd of phosphorus	P_2O
Hypophosphorous acid	PO
Phosphorous acid	PO_3
Phosphoric acid	PO_5

351. *Oxyd of phosphorus* is formed when a stream of oxygen gas is allowed to flow from a tube upon phosphorus, melted under warm water, as seen in fig. 261. The phosphorus burns under water and forms a brick-red powder, which is the oxyd in question, mingled with much unburnt phosphorus. The presence of oxyd of phosphorus with unburnt phosphorus renders the latter much more inflammable. The water over the oxyd of phosphorus in this experiment becomes a solution of phosphorous and phosphoric acids.

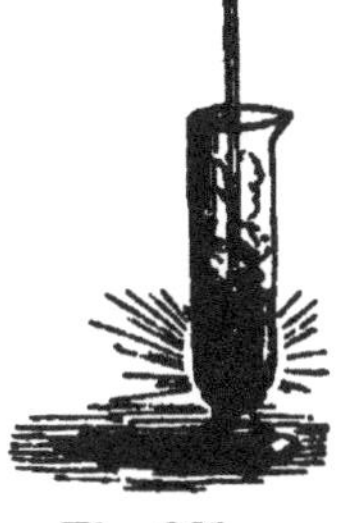
Fig. 261.

352. *Hypophosphorous acid* is a powerful deoxydizing agent, decomposing the oxyds of mercury and copper, and even sulphuric acid, with precipitation of sulphur and liberation of sulphurous acid: by these reactions it becomes exalted to phosphorus or phosphoric acid. It is prepared by decomposing the hypophosphite of baryta.

353. *Phosphorous acid* PO_3 is formed by the slow combustion of phosphorus in the air: a stick of phosphorus exposed to air is immediately surrounded by a white cloud of this acid. Sticks of phosphorus, cast in small glass tubes, may be arranged as in fig. 262, in a funnel. Each stick is placed in a glass tube *a b*, slightly larger than itself, and drawn to a point, fig. 263; and these are arranged in a funnel and

350. What are the O compounds of P? 351. How is P_2O formed? 352. What of PO? 353. How is PO_3 formed?

Fig. 262.

covered with an open bell, to keep out dust and the fluctuations of air. The action then proceeds gradually, and a considerable quantity of the product is collected in the bottle beneath. When formed by combustion of phosphorus in a limited quantity of air, phosphorous acid is a dry white powder. Contact of humid air converts it into the above form, which always contains some phosphoric acid. It is one of the less powerful acids. By heat it decomposes the oxyds of mercury and silver. It forms salts called phosphites.

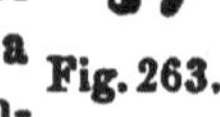

Fig. 263.

354. *Phosphoric Acid*, PO_5.—This acid is formed by the action of strong nitric acid on phosphorus, as well as from bones, by the action of sulphuric acid, as in the process for obtaining phosphorus, (347.) When phosphorus is burned in a full supply of oxygen gas, this acid is the product. For this purpose, an arrangement like fig. 264 is adopted.

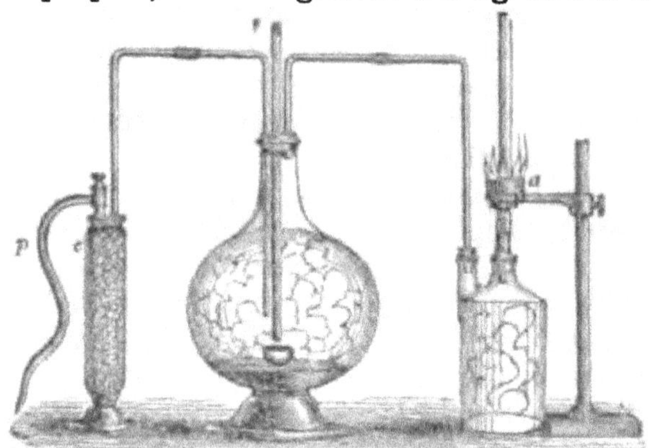

Fig. 264.

The large globe is filled by displacement with oxygen, dried by the chlorid of calcium vessel *c*. The phosphorus is burned in a capsule, supported at the bottom of the globe on a bed of dry gypsum, and is dropped in at pleasure by the porcelain tube *t*, whose orifice is closed by a cork. The

Describe the arrangement, fig. 262. What are its properties? 354. How is PO_5 formed?

bottle with two necks receives the vapors of phosphoric acid, a draft being kept up by the porcelain tube *p*, which is made to act as a chimney, by the alcohol flame from the cup *a*. In this way the combustion is kept up at pleasure, as fresh oxygen is supplied by the hose *p*. In a dark room this experiment forms a most magnificent display of mellow light. Such is its avidity for water, that phosphoric acid hisses like a hot iron when added to it. It makes an intensely acid solution, which, evaporated to dryness and ignited, yields on cooling a transparent glassy solid, called *glacial phosphoric acid*.

355. Phosphoric acid forms three distinct hydrates with water, and three classes of salts. These salts give a beautiful example of the substitution of a metal for hydrogen in the production of salts. Let M represent a metal in the following formulæ, and we have

	Acids.			Salts.
Monobasic or metaphosphoric acid..........	$HO.PO_5$,	giving	metaphosphate	$MO.PO_5$
Bibasic or pyrophosphoric acid...............	$2HO.PO_5$,	"	pyrophosphate	$2MO.PO_5$
Tribasic or common phosphoric acid........	$3HO.PO_5$,	"	phosphate.......	$3MO.PO_5$

For a full account of these interesting modifications of phosphoric acid, the student is referred to Dr. Graham's excellent Elements of Chemistry.

The compounds of phosphorus, especially the phosphates of lime and of magnesia, are very widely distributed in nature, and enjoy an important function in the economy of life. The tribasic phosphates produce with nitrate of silver a yellow precipitate; with solutions of magnesia and ammonia a fine granular one, (ammonio-phosphate of magnesia;) and the molybdate of ammonia detects the smallest trace of this acid even in the fluids of the body.

356. *Chlorids of Phosphorus.*—Of these there are two, the perchlorid PCl_5, and the terchlorid PCl_3. The first is formed when phosphorus is introduced into a jar of dry chlorine. It inflames and lines the sides of the vessel with a white matter, which is the perchlorid of phosphorus. This compound is very unstable, and when put in water both it and the water suffer decomposition, and hydrochloric and phosphoric acids result. To form the other, PCl_3, the apparatus used for the chlorid of sulphur may be employed, substituting phosphorus for sulphur in the retort P, (fig. 245.)

How from bones? What are its properties? What is glacial PO_5? 355. What of its hydrates? What tests for PO_5? 356. What chlorids of phosphorus are there? How is PCl_3 formed?

The bromids, iodids, and sulphurets of phosphorus have the same constitution as the chlorids, and are formed by contact of the elements. They are unimportant, and the sulphuret is a very violent and dangerous compound to form.

CLASS V. THE CARBON GROUP.

CARBON.

Equivalent, 6. *Symbol*, C. *Specific gravity in vapor*, 0·829.

357. *History.*—Carbon is an element found in all three kingdoms of nature. Charcoal and mineral coal, which are the two common forms of carbon, have been known from the remotest times of history. Its great importance in the daily wants of society makes it one of the most interesting of the elementary bodies, and our interest in it is not diminished from the fact that the charcoal and mineral coal which we use as fuel and the black-lead of our pencils are, essentially, the same thing with that rare and costly gem, the diamond. The three distinct and very dissimilar forms of existence which this element assumes, give us one of the best examples known of the allotropism of bodies. We will very briefly mention the principal characters of the three forms of carbon: 1. The diamond; 2. Graphite or plumbago; 3. Mineral coal and charcoal.

358. The *diamond is pure carbon crystallized.* It takes the forms of the regular system, or first crystalline class, (44,) of which the annexed figures are some of the common modifications. Its crystalline faces are often curved, as in fig. 266. The diamond is the hardest of all known substances, and can be scratched or cut only by its own dust.

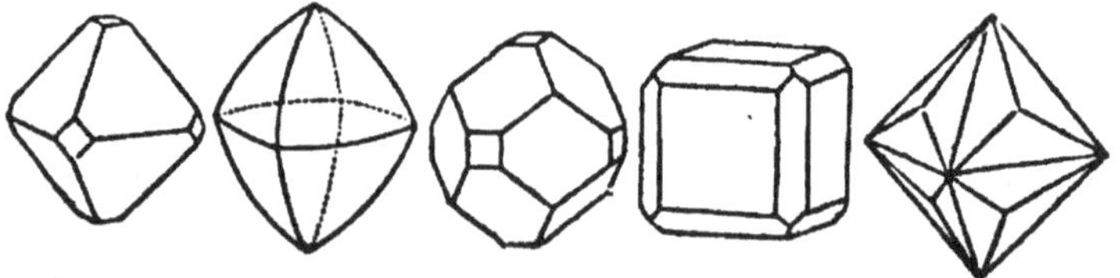

Fig. 265. Fig. 266. Fig. 267. Fig. 268. Fig. 269.

The solid angles of this mineral, formed by the union of curved planes, are much used, when properly set, for cutting glass,

---

What of the bromids and sulphurets? 357. Give the history of carbon. What is its equivalent? What of its allotropism? 358. What of the diamond?

which it does with great ease and precision. It has a specific gravity of 3·52, and the highest value of any kind of treasure. The most esteemed diamonds are colorless, and of an indescribable brilliancy, described as the "adamantine lustre." They are often slightly colored, of a yellowish, rose, blue, or green, and even black tint. The largest known diamond formerly belonged to the Great Mogul, and when found weighed 2769·3 grains, or nearly six ounces: it had the form of half a hen's-egg. The Pitt,or Regent diamond, was sold to the Duke of Orleans for £130,000. It weighs less than an ounce. This was the gem which Napoleon mounted in the hilt of his sword of state. The Koh-i-noor, or mountain of light, (the Great Mogul diamond,) which now belongs to Queen Victoria, was valued to the British government at two million pounds sterling, but its commercial value is about three millions of dollars, or £622,000. It weighed before its recent cutting, 1108 grains, or 277 carats. This gem was found at Golconda. The diamond is usually found in the loose sands of rivers, and is generally accompanied by gold and platinum. Its native rock is supposed to be a peculiar flexible kind of sandstone, called itacolumite; and it is sometimes found loosely imbedded in a ferruginous conglomerate in Brazil. A few diamonds have been found in the United States; chiefly in North Carolina.

359. From its *high refractive power* the diamond is sup posed to be of vegetable origin. The sun's light seems to be absorbed by the diamond, since it phosphoresces beautifully for some time in a dark place, after it has been exposed to the sun. It is a non-conductor of heat and electricity, and is very unalterable by chemical means. It is infusible, and not attacked by acids or alkalies. But heated to redness in the air, it is totally consumed, and the sole product of its combustion is carbonic acid gas.

360. (2.) *Graphite or Plumbago.*—This form of carbon is sometimes improperly called "*black-lead*," but it does not contain a trace of lead in its composition, and bears no resemblance to it, except that both have been used to mark upon paper.

This peculiar mineral is found in the most ancient rocks,

Give its form and characters. What is its lustre? What are some of the highly valued diamonds? What of Koh-i-noor? Where is the diamond found? 359. What of its supposed origin? 360. What is plumbago?

as well as with those of a more modern era. It is also frequently found in company with coal, and is sometimes formed artificially, as in the fusion of cast-iron. It almost always contains a trace, and sometimes several per cent. of iron, which is, however, foreign to it; otherwise it is pure carbon. It is very much used for making pencils, and the coarser sorts are manufactured into very useful and refractory melting pots. The most valued plumbago for the finest drawing pencils has been brought chiefly from the Borrowdale mine, in Cumberland, England; but it is a common mineral in this country, as, for instance, at Sturbridge in Massachusetts, St. John in New Brunswick, and many other places. It is found crystallized in flat, six-sided prisms, a form altogether incompatible with that of the diamond. It is soft, flexible, and easily cut; its density is 2·20; feels greasy, and marks paper. It is quite incombustible by all ordinary means, but burns in oxygen gas, forming only carbonic acid gas, and leaving a red ash of oxyd of iron.

361. (3.) *Coal.*—The vast beds of mineral carbon, known as anthracite, bituminous coal, brown coal, and lignite, are all of them nearly pure carbon. Of the first two of these, no country has such abundant and excellent supplies as the United States. These accumulations of fuel are the remains of the ancient vegetation of the planet, which, long anterior to the creation of man, a bountiful Providence laid away in the bowels of the earth for his future use. Bituminous coal differs from anthracite only in having a quantity of volatile hydrocarbon united with it, which is wanting in the anthracite. This opake combustible mineral is entirely a non-conductor of electricity, and some of its varieties excite resinous electricity.

362. *Charcoal* from wood is the carbonized skeleton of the woody fibre which is found in all plants. The best charcoal is made by heating sticks of wood in tight iron vessels, without contact of air, until all gases and vapors cease to be given off. A great quantity of acetic acid, tar, and oily matters, with water, are given out, and a jetty black, brittle, hard charcoal is left behind, which is a perfect copy of the form of the original wood. It is a non-conductor of heat, but conducts electricity almost as well as a metal. It is a very unchangeable substance, insoluble in

---

Where found? What its character? 361. What of coal? What its origin? What difference between anthracite and bituminous? What of its electrical character? 362. What is charcoal? What its characters?

water, acids, or alkalies, suffers little change from long exposure to air and moisture, and does not yield to the most intense heat to which it can be subjected, if air is excluded.

363. Charcoal has *the property of absorbing gases* to a most remarkable degree, at common temperatures. A fragment of recently heated charcoal, of a convenient size to be introduced under a small air jar over the mercurial cistern, will soon take up many times its own volume of air, as will appear by the rise of the mercury in the air-jar. In this case it absorbs more oxygen than nitrogen, the residual air having only eight per cent. of oxygen in it. On heating, it again parts with the gas it has absorbed. The power of absorption seems to depend entirely on the natural elasticity of the gas, and not at all on its affinity for carbon. Those gases that are most easily reduced to a fluid condition by cold and pressure, are most abundantly absorbed by charcoal. Charcoal from hard wood with fine pores has this property in the highest degree. Thus, charcoal from boxwood freshly prepared, will absorb of ammoniacal gas 90 times its own volume; of muriatic-acid gas, 85 times; of sulphuretted hydrogen, 81 times; of nitrous oxyd, 40 times; of carbonic acid, 32 times; of oxygen, 9·25 times; of nitrogen, 1·5 times; and of hydrogen, 1·75 times its own volume.

364. Charcoal also *has the power of absorbing the bad odors* and coloring principles of most animal and vegetable substances. Tainted meat is made sweet by burying it in powdered charcoal, and foul water is purified by being strained through it. The highly colored sugar-syrups are completely decolorized by being passed through sacks of animal charcoal, (bone-black,) prepared by igniting bones. It also precipitates bitter principles, resins, and astringent substances from solution. Common ale or porter becomes not only colorless, but also in a good degree deprived of its bitter principles, by being heated with and filtered through animal charcoal. This property is lost by use, and regained by heating it afresh. Its power of absorption seems similar to that possessed by spongy platinum, (251.) Hydrogen, in small quantity, is very obstinately retained in the pores of charcoal, and water is consequently always produced from

---

363. What of its absorbing power? What regulates its power with various gases? 364. What of its disinfecting and decolorizing powers?

the combustion of carbon in pure oxygen gas. Carbon has a greater affinity for oxygen at high temperatures than any other known substance, and for this reason it is useful in reducing the oxyds of iron and other oxyds to the metallic state. Lamp-black is a pulverulent variety of carbon, produced from the imperfect combustion of oils and resins.

Compounds of Carbon with Oxygen.

365. The compounds of carbon, oxygen, and hydrogen embrace a majority of the bodies described in the organic chemistry; which is therefore not improperly termed the chemistry of the carbon series. We will consider at present, however, only carbonic acid and carbonic oxyd.

366. *Carbonic Acid*, CO_2.—*History.*—This is the sole product of the combustion of the diamond or any *pure* carbon in the air, or in oxygen gas. It was first recognized and described by Dr. Black, in 1757, under the name of *fixed air.* This philosopher proved that limestone and magnesian rocks contained a large quantity of this gas in a state of solid combination with the earths, and also that it was freely given out in the processes of fermentation, respiration, and combustion.

367. *Preparation.*—Carbonic acid is easily procured by treating any carbonate with a dilute acid. Carbonate of lime, in the form of marble powder, is usually employed for this purpose: it is put with a little water into a two-mouthed bottle A, (fig. 270;) dilute chlorohydric acid is turned in at the tube-funnel *b*, when the gas is

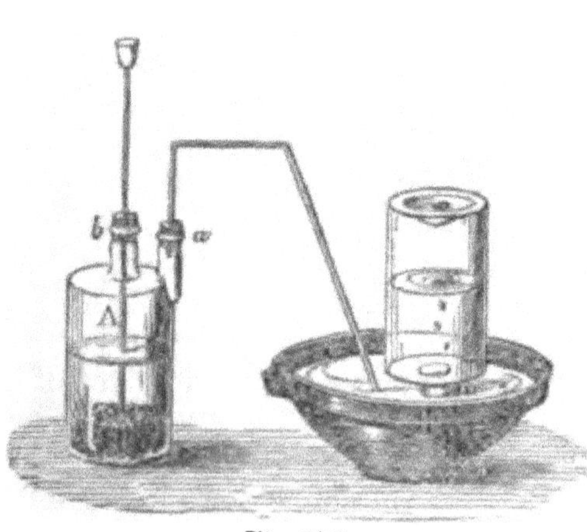

Fig. 270.

What is lamp-black? 365. What of the compounds of C with hydrogen, &c.? 366. What is CO_2? What was Black's discovery? 367. How is CO_2 prepared?

set free with effervescence, and escapes through the bent tube at *a*. Its weight enables us to collect it in dry bottles, by displacement of air, as in the case of chlorine. It may also be collected over water. No heat is required, and the acid is added in small successive portions, the gas being freely evolved at each addition. When obtained by the action of monohydrated nitric acid on bicarbonate of ammonia, the carbonic acid evolved retains a cloudy appearance, even after passing through water, which renders it visible—a point of some importance in experiments with this gas.

368. *Properties.*—At the common temperature and pressure, carbonic acid is a colorless, transparent gas, with a pungent and rather pleasant taste and odor. At a temperature of 32°, and a pressure of 30 to 36 atmospheres, it is condensed into a clear limpid liquid, not as heavy as water, which freezes by its own evaporation into a white, snow-like substance. We have already described (151) the apparatus and process by which this interesting experiment is performed. Carbonic acid is about once and a half as heavy as common air, having a specific gravity of 1·529; and 100 cubic inches therefore weigh 47·26 grains. Owing to its weight, it may be poured from one vessel to another, (fig. 271.) Carbonic acid instantly extinguishes a burning taper lowered into it, even when mingled with twice or three times its bulk of air. Burning sulphur and phosphorus are also immediately extinguished in this gas. Potassium, however, quite clean, may be burned in a Florence flask filled with dried carbonic acid; the potassium is ignited by application of heat, and the carbon is then deposited on the glass vessel. Fresh lime-water agitated with this gas, rapidly absorbs it, becoming at the same time milky, from the production of the insoluble carbonate of lime; soluble, however, in excess of carbonic acid. In this way the pre-

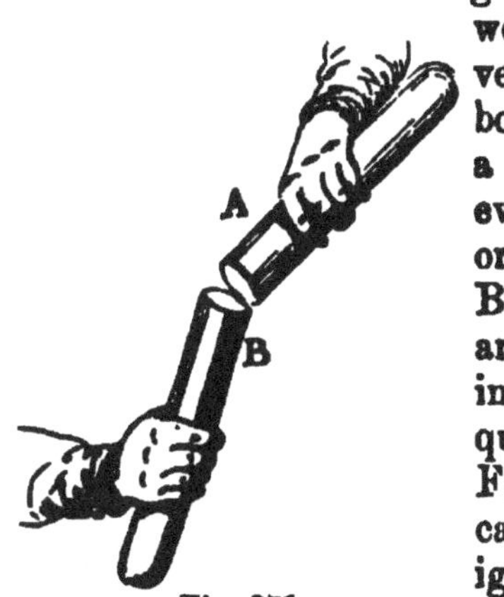

Fig. 271.

368. What its properties? What its density? How does it affect combustion? How is it decomposed?

sence of carbonic acid in the atmosphere is easily detected, and this gas is distinguished from nitrogen by the same test.

369. Cold water recently boiled absorbs rather more than its own volume of carbonic acid gas, but with pressure more will be taken up, in quantity exactly proportioned to the pressure exerted. The solution has a pleasant acid taste, and temporarily reddens blue litmus paper. The "soda water," so much used as a beverage, is usually only water strongly impregnated with carbonic acid, the soda being generally omitted in its preparation. The effervescence of this, as well as of small beer and sparkling wines, is due to the escape of this gas. Natural waters have usually more or less of this gas dissolved in them; and some mineral springs, like the Saratoga and Ballston springs, and the Seltzer water, are highly charged with carbonic acid.

370. *Death follows the inspiration of carbonic acid,* even when largely diluted with air. It kills by a specific poisonous influence on the system, resembling some narcotics, and is unlike nitrogen in this particular, which kills only by exclusion of air. Instances of death from sleeping in a close room where a charcoal fire is burning, and from descending into wells which contain carbonic acid, are lamentably frequent. The latter accident may be avoided by taking the obvious precaution to lower a burning candle into the well before going into it, when if the candle burns with undiminished flame, all may be considered safe, but its being extinguished is certain evidence that the well is unsafe. Wells containing carbonic acid may often be freed from it by lowering a pan of recently-heated charcoal into the well, which will soon absorb thirty-five times its bulk of this gas, (363,) thus removing the evil. Even so small a quantity of carbonic acid as 1 or 2 per cent. produces, after some time, grave effects on respiration. Small animals thrown into a vessel full of this gas, may be recovered by immersion in cold water. The so-called Black Hole of Calcutta is a noted instance of the fatal effects of respiring an atmosphere overcharged with carbonic acid.

---

369. What of its solution in water? 370. What is its effect on life? Where do accidents often happen? How prevented? What quantity is injurious?

371. Numerous *natural sources* evolve large quantities of carbonic acid, particularly in volcanic districts. The Grotto del Cane, in Italy, (dog's grotto,) is a well-known example of the natural occurrence of this gas. But the quantity evolved there is trifling compared to that, which escapes constantly from Lake Solfatara, near Tivoli, whose surface is violently agitated with the gases boiling through it.

It is always present in the air, being given off by the respiration of all animals; and, besides the other sources already named, is an invariable product of all common cases of combustion.

All the carbon which plants secrete in the process of their development, is derived either from the carbonic acid of the atmosphere, which they decompose by the aid of sunlight and their green leaves, retaining the carbon and returning the pure oxygen to the air; or it is absorbed by their rootlets, and then decomposed by the sun's light at the surface of the leaf.

372. *Carbonic acid is formed of equal volumes* of its two constituent gases, condensed into one. For this reason the air suffers no change of bulk from the enormous quantities of this gas which are hourly formed and decomposed on the earth. This acid unites with alkaline bases, forming an important class of salts, (the carbonates,) which are decomposed by even the vegetable acids, with the escape of carbonic acid.

373. *Carbonic Oxyd*, CO.—*Preparation.*—This gas is most easily obtained from oxalic acid. This acid, when treated with five or six times its volume of sulphuric acid, in the flask *a*, (fig. 272), is decomposed, yielding equal volumes of car-

Fig. 272.

371. What sources are named for it? How in the air? Whence the carbon of plants? 372. What is its constitution? What are its salts called? 373. How is CO prepared? What of oxalic acid?

bonic acid and carbonic oxyd. Thus, $C_2O_3 + HO = CO_2 + CO$, the water remaining with the sulphuric acid. The carbonic acid is easily removed by a solution of caustic potash in the wash-bottle *o*. Dry, finely-powdered, yellow prussiate of potash, when decomposed by ten times its weight of sulphuric acid, in a very capacious vessel, yields an abundant volume of pure oxyd of carbon.

374. *Properties.*—This is a colorless, almost inodorous gas, burning with a beautiful pale-blue flame, such as is often seen on a freshly-fed anthracite fire. Its specific gravity is a little less than that of air, or ·967; and 100 cubic inches of it weigh 30·20 grains. Water absorbs about $\frac{1}{18}$ of its volume of it; it does not render lime-water milky, and explodes feebly with oxygen. It is not respirable, but is even more poisonous than carbonic acid, producing a state of the system resembling profound apoplexy. This gas is very largely produced in the process of reducing iron from its ores in the high furnace.

Carbonic oxyd is formed of half a volume of oxygen, and one volume of carbon, or two volumes of carbon and one of oxygen, condensed into two volumes.

375. *Chloro-carbonic oxyd* is formed of equal volumes of chlorine and oxyd of carbon. This union with chlorine is produced by the influence of light, and hence the product was called *phosgene gas.* This is a pungent, highly odorous, suffocating body, possessing acid properties, and decomposed by water. Its formula is CO.Cl, or carbonic acid in which chlorine occupies the place of an atom of oxygen. Its density is 3·407.

Compounds of Carbon with the Chlorine Group.

The chlorids of carbon will be described in the organic chemistry.

376. *Bisulphuret of Carbon,* $C.S_2$.—This remarkable product is formed by the direct union of its elements. In a retort of fire-clay C, (fig. 273,) fragments of charcoal are placed. A porcelain tube *b* descends nearly to the bottom of the retort, being luted with clay at *a.* When the retort is red hot, small bits of roll sulphur are from

---

374. What are the properties of CO? 375. What is chloro-carbonic oxyd? 376. How is bisulphuret of carbon prepared in fig. 273?

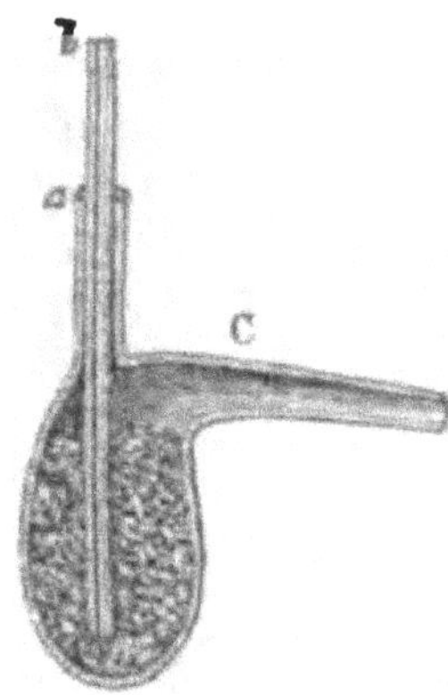

Fig. 273.

time to time dropped in at b, and this orifice immediately closed by a cork. The vapor of sulphur rising among the ignited carbon combines with it, and bisulphuret of carbon distills, is condensed by a refrigerating tube, (fig. 274,) and collected in the bottle surrounded by cold water, o. The first product is yellow, from free sulphur, and is purified by a second distillation. When pure, bisulphuret of carbon is a colorless, very mobile and volatile fluid, with a disgusting odor, altogether peculiar. Its density at 32° is 1·293; at 60°, 1·271. It boils at 110°, and its vapor has a density of 2·68. Its power of refracting light is very remarkable. It dissolves sulphur, phosphorus, and iodine, these bodies being deposited again in beautiful crystals by the evaporation of the sulphuret of carbon. Gutta percha and India-rubber are also soluble in it. It burns in the air at about 600°, with a pale blue flame, producing carbonic and sulphurous acids. It forms an explosive mixture with oxygen, and a combustible one with binoxyd of nitrogen. It dissolves easily in alcohol and ether, and is precipitated again by water.

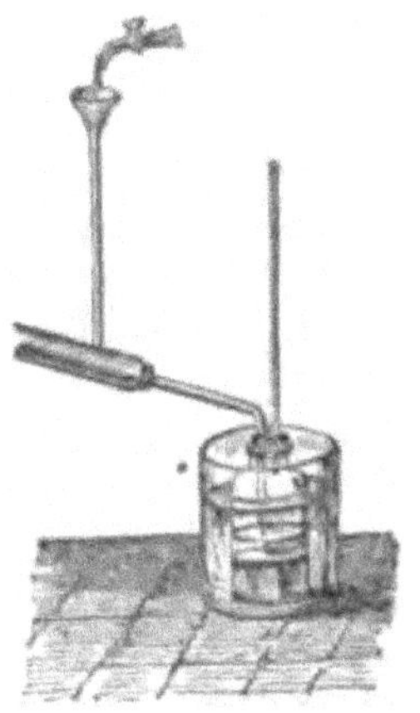
Fig. 274.

Carbon with Nitrogen.

377. *Cyanogen*, C_2N or Cy.—This important and interesting compound of carbon and nitrogen belongs appropriately to the organic chemistry; but it deports itself so much like an elementary substance and its compound with hydrogen, (cyanhydric or prussic acid,) and its metallic compounds also, are of so much general interest, that it is proper to mention this compound-radical here.

What are its properties? What its solvent powers? 377. What of cyanogen? Give its formula.

Carbon and nitrogen combine only indirectly. If carbonate of potassa and carbon are heated together in a porcelain tube, while nitrogen is passing over them, oxyd of carbon escapes, and cyanid of potassium in considerable quantity remains in the tube, and may be dissolved out by water. Cyanogen is usually prepared in the laboratory, by decomposing cyanid of mercury (CyHg) in a small retort by heat, and collecting the gas over mercury. It is more economically and abundantly prepared, however, by heating a mixture of 6 parts of dried ferrocyanid of potassium, and 9 parts of bichlorid of mercury in a flask of hard glass. The cyanid of mercury formed is decomposed immediately into mercury and cyanogen.

378. *Properties.*—Cyanogen is a colorless gas, of a strong and remarkable odor, resembling peach-pits. Its density is 1·86. At a temperature of —4°, it is liquefied, and at common temperatures, with a pressure of 4 or 5 atmospheres. Liquid cyanogen is a colorless, very mobile fluid, whose density is about 0·9. By keeping a short time, it undergoes a change, becomes brown, and deposits a brown powder in the glass. This is paracyanogen, an isomeric form of cyanogen, a portion of which is always seen as a residue in the retort after decomposing cyanid of mercury.

Cyanogen burns with a magnificent and characteristic purple flame, giving carbonic acid and free nitrogen. For this purpose a large vessel may be filled with the gas, by displacement. Water dissolves 4 or 5 times its volume of cyanogen, and alcohol 24 or 25 times its volume. Cyanogen forms *cyanids*—compounds almost exactly analogous to the chlorids of the same metals, and in which cyanogen comports itself like an element.

Cyanogen is formed from 1 volume of carbon vapor, weighing		0·8290
and 1 volume of nitrogen	"	0·9713
		1·8003

which is a close approximation to 1·86, the result of experiment.

How do C and N unite? How is Cy usually prepared? How from bichlorid of mercury and ferrocyanid of potassium? 378. What are its properties? How liquefied? How does the liquid change? How does Cy burn? What compounds does it form? Analogous to what? What is its volume composition?

SILICON.

Equivalent, 21·3. *Symbol*, Si. *Density in vapor, (hypothetical,)* 15·29.

379. Silicon combined with oxygen, forming silica, is abundantly distributed throughout the earth. It is said to form ⅙th part of the crust of the globe.

Silicon is prepared by decomposing the double fluorid of silicon and potassium by metallic potassium. The potassium, in small pieces, is mingled with ⅛th its weight of the dry white powder of the double fluorid, in a test-tube, (fig. 275,) which is then heated. Reaction occurs as soon as the bottom of the tube is red, and spreads through the whole mass. The cool residue is treated with water, which dissolves the fluorid of potassium, and leaves silicon. Thus,

Fig. 275.

$$3KF.2SiF_3+6K=9KF+2Si.$$

380. *Properties.*—Silicon is a nut-brown powder, and a non-conductor of electricity. Heated in air or oxygen it burns, forming silica. If heated in a close vessel, it shrinks, and becomes more dense. Before ignition it is soluble in hydrofluoric acid, but after this it is insoluble, and is incombustible in the air or oxygen gas. It seems then to resemble the graphite variety of carbon. These two diverse conditions of silicon are probably connected with the two states in which silica occurs.

381. *Silicic acid*, or *silica*, SiO_3, is far the most important of all the compounds of silicon. It exists abundantly in nature, in the form of rock crystal, agate, common uncrystallized quartz, silicious sand, &c.; it also enters largely into combination with other substances to form the rock masses of the globe. It is a very hard substance, easily scratching glass, and is difficult to reduce to a powder; its specific gravity is 2·66. Its usual crystalline form (fig. 276) is a six-sided prism, with two similar pyramids. It is infusible

---

379. What of silicon? Give its equivalent. How is it prepared? Give the reaction. 380. What are its properties? What two States? 381. What is silica?

Fig. 276.

alone, except by the power of the compound blowpipe. It dissolves with effervescence in fluohydric acid and in fused carbonate of soda or potash. No acid, except the hydrofluoric, has any effect on silica. When in its finest state of division it is still harsh and gritty to the touch or between the teeth.

382. When silica is fused in 4 or 6 times its weight of carbonate of soda or potassa, and this mass is treated with a large volume of dilute chlorohydric acid until it manifests a decidedly acid reaction, the silica after some time separates as a transparent, tremulous jelly. This is soluble hydrated silica. If dried, it again becomes gritty and insoluble as before. Most natural waters contain some small portion of soluble silica; it has often been seen in this state in mines; and on breaking open silicious pebbles, the central parts are sometimes semifluid and gelatinous. The hot waters of the great geysers in Iceland, and of other hot springs, also dissolve large quantities of silica, probably aided by alkaline matter. Agates, chalcedony, carnelian, onyx, and similar modifications of silica have been deposited from the soluble state. It is in this condition, no doubt, that silica enters the substance of many vegetables, as, for instance, the reeds and grasses, which have often a thick crust of silica on their bark. It is in this form also that silica acts as the agent of petrifaction.

383. The acid powers of silica are seen only at high temperatures, when it saturates the most powerful alkalies and displaces other acids, forming *silicates*. Hence its great use in the art of glass-making, as it is the basis of all vitreous fabrics, including porcelain and potters' ware, which are all silicates. Soluble glass is formed when an excess of alkali is employed; and liquor of flints is an old term applied to a solution of silicate of potassa or soda.

384. Chlorine, bromine, fluorine, and sulphur, all form compounds with silicon, having the formula SiR_3, or exactly the formula for silica. The chlorid of silicon is formed by passing dry chlorine over a mixture of fine silicious sand and charcoal in a porcelain tube heated to redness. It is a colorless, mobile liquid, having a density of 1·52, and boiling at 138°. It is decomposed by water into silica and

---

What its forms in nature? 382. When fused with alkali, how is it separated? How does it exist in water and plants? 383. What of its acid powers? 384. What does S form with class II? What of its chlorid?

chlorohydric acid. Bromid of silicon is formed in a similar manner.

385. *Fluorid of Silicon,* (*fluo-silicic acid,*) may be prepared by heating sulphuric acid with fluor-spar in powder, to which is added twice its own weight of fine silica or powdered glass. The apparatus should be quite dry:

Fluor-spar.	Silica.	Sul. Acid.		Sul. Lime.	Water.	Fluorid Silicon.
$3CaF +$	$SiO_3 +$	$3(SO_3.HO)$	$=$	$3(CaO.SO_3) +$	$3HO +$	SiF_3.

Fluorid of silicon is a colorless gas, irrespirable, and decomposed by water. Its density is 3·57. It forms dense white vapors in contact with the moisture of the air. Passed into water it is immediately decomposed, gelatinous silica is precipitated, and the water becomes a solution of hydro-fluosilicic acid. The reaction is

$$3SiF_3 + 3HO = 3HF.2SiF_3 + SiO_3.$$

The fluorid of silicon should not pass directly into the water from the gas tube, but into some mercury on which the water rests, as in fig. 277. If this precaution be neglected the open end of the gas tube will become plugged with deposited silica. The silica obtained in this operation, when well washed, is quite pure. The hydro-fluosilicic acid forms an insoluble salt with potassium $3KF.2SiF_3$.

Fig. 277.

BORON.

Equivalent, 10·90. *Symbol,* B. *Density in vapor,* (*hypothetical,*) ·751.

386. Boron is known chiefly by its compounds, borax and boracic acid. Boracic acid is found in nature, either free or combined with various bases; but it is rather a rare substance. Boron is prepared by heating the double fluorid of

---

385. What is its fluorid? Give the reaction by which it is produced? What its characters? How does water affect it? What is hydro-fluosilicic acid? Explain its production as in fig. 277. 386. What is boron? How distributed in nature? What its equivalent?

boron and potassium in an iron vessel, with potassium, as in case of silicon. Boron is a dark olive-green powder. Heated to 600° in air it burns brilliantly, forming boracic acid. It does not conduct electricity, and is insoluble in water. Heated out of contact of air it suffers no change.

387. *Boracic Acid*, BO_3, is exhaled from volcanic vents, as in Vulcano, one of the Lipari Islands, and also more abundantly in the *Tuscan maremma*, not far from Leghorn. There it issues, accompanied by jets of steam, from the soil. These jets have been carried into lagoons of water constructed around them, where the boracic acid is taken up by the water. The heat of the earth affords the means of evaporating the water. Figure 278 shows one of these masonry basins, O, built around the jets, (*suffoni*.) A series of these, four or five in number, are arranged one above the other: the least concentrated solutions occupy the upper basin, and are in turn, once in twenty-four hours, drawn off to the lower, and finally to the evaporating pans E F, also heated by the escaping steam from the earth. In this manner the solution is brought to crystallize, and is purified by repeated crystallization. The production of boracic acid from this source equals two millions and a half pounds per year.

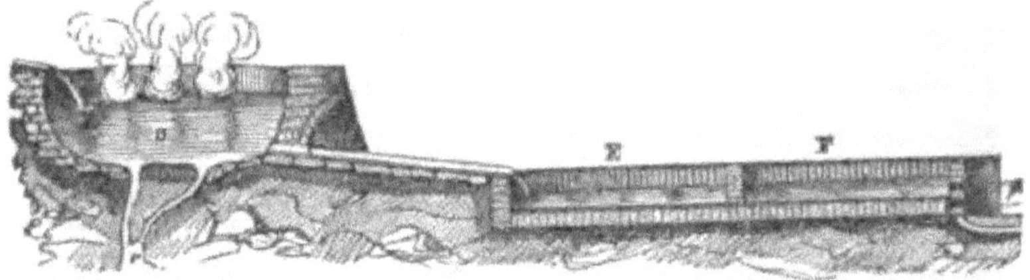

Fig. 278.

388. In the laboratory, boracic acid is obtained by decomposing borax of commerce. For this purpose, one part of borax is dissolved in two and a half parts of boiling water, and chlorohydric acid added until the liquid is strongly acid. On cooling, the boracic acid crystallizes in elegant tufts of scaly crystals, and is purified by a second crystallization. Boracic acid is a white pearly substance in thin scales: these have a feeling like spermaceti, are feebly acid to the taste, and soluble in twelve parts of boiling and in fifty parts of

387. How is BO_3 found? Describe the Tuscany lagoons. How are they heated? Whence the BO_3? 388. How is BO_3 prepared in the laboratory? What are its properties?

cold water. A boiling saturated solution deposits ⅘ths of its acid on cooling. The crystals contain 43 per cent. of water. By heat it fuses in its crystallization-water, which is finally expelled, and the acid, when heated to redness, fuses to a clear glass, which may be drawn out in fine threads. This glassy acid loses its transparency by keeping for some time. Boracic acid is a feeble acid in solution, but it expels sulphuric acid from the sulphates at a red heat and forms glass with oxyds of lead and bismuth, of very high refractive powers. Alcohol dissolves boracic acid, and the solution, when set on fire, burns with a peculiar green flame, characteristic of boracic acid. Hydrous boracic acid is volatile by vapor of water, but the glassy acid is quite fixed at the highest temperatures. Boracic acid and the borates are much used as fluxes, to promote the fusion of other bodies.

389. *Chlorid of Boron*, BCl_3, is formed in the same manner as chlorid of silicon. It is a colorless gas of a specific gravity of 4·09, decomposed by water into chlorohydric and boracic acids.

390. *Fluorid of Boron*, BF_3.—This gas is obtained when we heat together 2 parts of fluor-spar and 1 part of fused boracic acid in a vessel of porcelain at redness. $7BO_3+3CaF=3(CaO2BO_3)+BF_3$. It is a colorless, suffocating gas, strongly acid, very soluble in water, and exceedingly greedy of it, so that it even carbonizes organic substances to obtain it, in the manner of sulphuric acid. Water dissolves 700 or 800 times its volume of this gas.

If fluor-spar, boracic acid, and concentrated sulphuric acid are heated together in a glass retort, a gas of a brownish color, very acid, and breaking on the air in white fumes, is obtained: this is hydro-fluoboracic acid. It must be collected over mercury.

CLASS VI.

HYDROGEN.

Equivalent, 1. *Symbol*, H. *Density*, 0·0692.

391. *History.*—Hydrogen was first described as a distinct substance by the English chemist Cavendish, in 1766, and was called by him *inflammable air*. It had previously

---

What dissolves it? What is characteristic of BO_3? How does heat affect it? 389. What of BCl_3? 390. What of fluorid of boron? What of its properties? 391. What is the history of hydrogen? Its equivalent?

been confounded with other combustible gases, several of which had been long known. Hydrogen exists abundantly in nature as a constituent of water, and also of nearly all animal and vegetable substances, in such proportions as to form water when these bodies are burned. It is named from the Greek *hudor*, water, and *gennao*, I form.

392. *Preparation.*—This gas is generally prepared by the action of dilute sulphuric acid on zinc or iron. Zinc is usually preferred. The acid is diluted with four or five times its bulk of water, and the operation may be conducted

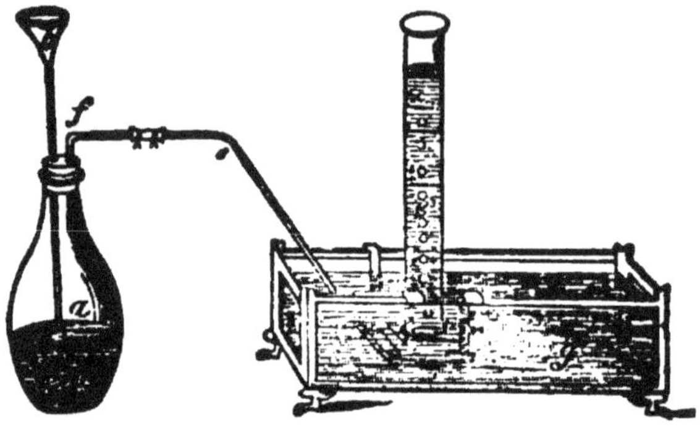

Fig. 279.

in a glass retort, or more conveniently by using a gas-bottle *a*, (fig. 279,) containing the zinc in small fragments, to which the dilute acid is turned through the tube-funnel *b*. The shorter tube *f*, with a flexible joint, conveys the gas to the air-jar standing in the cistern *g*. No heat is required in this operation. An ounce of zinc yields 615 cubic inches of hydrogen gas. Zinc is readily granulated, by being turned, when melted, into cold water. When hydrogen is required in large quantity, a leaden pot or stone jar, properly fitted, and holding a gallon or more, is used to contain the requisite charge of materials, and the gas is stored for use in a gas-holder, or India-rubber bag, (fig. 280,) (281.)

Fig. 280.

393. The reaction in this case is between the zinc and

How does it exist? 392. How is it prepared and stored? 393. What is the reaction?

the sulphuric acid, the hydrogen of the latter being replaced by the zinc, thus: $SO_3.HO+Zn=SO_3.ZnO+H$.
If chlorohydric acid had been used, the reaction is still more simple, thus: $HCl+Zn=ZnCl+H$.

Water is essential to the rapidity of the action, by dissolving the sulphate of zinc, which is insoluble in strong sulphuric acid, and unless removed, immediately arrests the process.

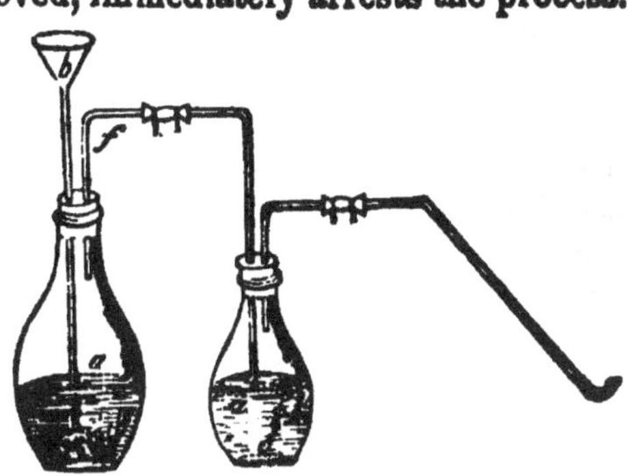

Fig. 281.

394. Hydrogen gas, when obtained from iron, has a peculiar and offensive odor, due to the presence of a volatile oil formed from the carbon always present in iron. That procured from zinc is also somewhat impure. Traces of sulphuretted hydrogen and carbonic acid are usually found in hydrogen, from impurity in the metals employed; and also a trace of both iron and zinc is raised in vapor, and gives color to the flame of common hydrogen. Most of these impurities are removed by passing the gas through a second bottle *d*, (fig. 281,) containing an alcoholic solution of caustic potash. Water only, in *d*, removes the vapor of acid found usually in the gas.

395. *Properties.*—Hydrogen is a colorless, inflammable gas: it has never been liquefied. It refracts light very powerfully, and has the highest capacity for heat of any known gas. It is, when quite pure, inodorous and tasteless, and may be breathed without inconvenience when mingled with a large quantity of common air. The voice of a person who has breathed it acquires for a time a peculiar shrill squeak. It cannot, however, support respiration alone, and an animal plunged in it soon dies from want of oxygen. Water absorbs only about one and a half per cent. of its bulk of pure hydrogen gas. Sounds are propagated in hydrogen with but little more power than in a vacuum.

Hydrogen is the lightest of all known forms of matter,

How is water necessary to it? 394. What renders it impure? How is it purified? 395. What are the properties of hydrogen? How as respects respiration?

being sixteen times lighter than oxygen, and fourteen times and a half lighter than common air. 100 cubic inches of it weigh only 2·14 grains. Soap-bubbles blown with it rise rapidly in the air; and it is often employed to fill balloons in absence of the cheaper coal gas. A turkey's crop, well cleansed, makes a good balloon on a small scale, for the class-room, and very beautiful small balloons (from 1½ to 5 feet diameter) are prepared in Paris of gold-beaters' skin.

396. Hydrogen is the *most attenuated* as well as the lightest form of matter with which we are acquainted. We have reason to suppose the molecules of this body to be smaller than those of any other now known to us. Dr. Faraday, in his attempts to liquefy hydrogen, found that it would leak freely with a pressure of 27 or 28 atmospheres, through stopcocks that were perfectly tight with nitrogen at 50 or 60 atmospheres. This extreme tenuity, together with the remarkable law of diffusion of gases already explained, (147,) renders it unsafe to keep this gas in any but perfectly tight vessels. A small crack in a bell-jar, quite too narrow to leak with water, will soon render the hydrogen with which it may be filled explosive. The superiority in diffusive power which hydrogen has over common air, is well seen in what is called Mr. Graham's diffusion tube, of which a figure is annexed. A glass tube, 11 or 12 inches long, (fig. 282,) and of convenient size, has a tight plug of dry plaster of Paris at the upper end, and being filled with dry hydrogen by displacement of air, and its lower end put into a glass of water, the hydrogen escapes so rapidly through the plaster plug, that the water is seen to rise in the tube, so as in a few moments to replace a considerable portion of the hydrogen, and the remaining portion of gas is found to be explosive. Hydrogen also enters into combination in a smaller proportionate weight than any known body, (238,) and consequently has been chosen as the unit of the scale of equivalents.

Fig. 282.

What of its density? What the weight of 100 cubic inches? What use is made of its levity? 396. What is the tenuity of hydrogen? Give illustrations from Faraday? What is Graham's diffusion tube? What of the atomic weight of hydrogen? Why has it been adopted as unity?

397. Hydrogen is a most eminently combustible gas, taking fire from a lighted taper, which is instantly extinguished by being plunged into the gas. It burns with a bluish-white flame and a very faint light. A dry bottle with its mouth downward (fig. 283) is well suited to collect this gas by displacement of air, as the heavier gases are collected by the reverse position. When lighted, the gas burns quietly at the mouth of the bottle; and the extinguished taper may be relighted by the flame at the mouth. If the bottle is suddenly reversed after the gas has burned awhile, the remaining gas, being mixed with common air, will burn rapidly with a slight explosion. Three of the most remarkable properties of hydrogen are thus shown by one experiment, viz. its extreme levity, its combustibility, and its explosive union with oxygen. If this gas is incautiously mingled with common air, or much more, with pure oxygen, a severe explosion results when the mixture is fired. The eyes or limbs of inexperienced operators have thus too often paid the forfeit of carelessness by the explosion of glass vessels. Particular caution is required not to employ any gas until all the common air is expelled, as well from the generator, as from the receiving-vessel or gas-holder.

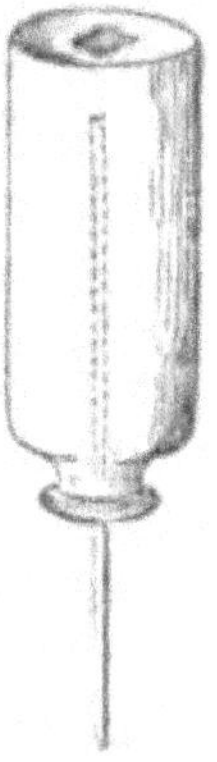

Fig. 283.

398. Water is the sole product of the combustion of hydrogen. The production of water from this combustion, and certain musical tones, are neatly shown by an arrangement like fig. 284. The gas is generated in the bottle *a*, and a perforated cork at the mouth has a small glass tube, from the narrow end of which the stream of hydrogen is lighted. An open glass tube *b*, about two feet long, held over this flame, is at once bedewed by the water produced in the combustion, and a musical tone is also generally heard. This arises from the interruption which the flame suffers from the rapid current of air ascending

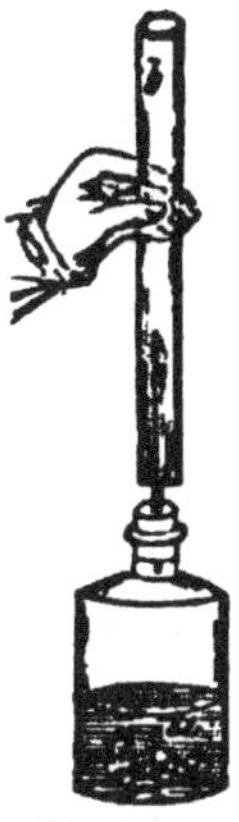

Fig. 284.

Fig. 285.

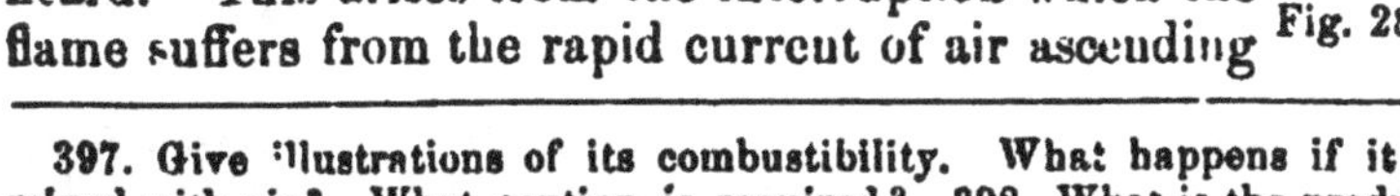

397. Give illustrations of its combustibility. What happens if it is mixed with air? What caution is required? 398. What is the product of its combustion? What happens if it is burned from a jet in a tube?

through the tube, causing it to flicker, and being momentarily extinguished, there occur a series of little explosions, so rapid as to give a tone. The pitch of the note produced, depends on the length and size of the glass chimney (fig. 285) and the size of the jet of hydrogen, which should be small. If the jet is fitted to the gas-holder, we can modulate the tone by regulating the supply of gas with the stopcock. The little gas bottle (fig. 284) is often called the "philosopher's lamp."

Compounds of Hydrogen with Oxygen.

399. There are two known compounds of hydrogen with oxygen, viz.:

Water (the oxyd of hydrogen) .... HO
Binoxyd of hydrogen .... HO_2

The first of these is the most remarkable compound known, whether we contemplate it in its purely chemical relations, or in reference to the wants of man and the present condition of the globe.

400. *Water.*—The student has already become familiar with the composition of water, as formed by the union of two volumes of hydrogen and one of oxygen. In examining the compounds of hydrogen and oxygen, as in all other chemical investigations, we can pursue the subject either analytically or synthetically; that is, we can either form the compounds by the direct union of the elements, or we can decompose these compounds, and thus gain a knowledge of their constitution.

The simplest case of the decomposition of water is that where metallic potassium, or sodium, is employed. The potassium, from its great affinity for oxygen, takes it from the water, (fig. 286,) and the hydrogen escaping, is burned. If sodium is introduced into an inverted test-tube under water, the hydrogen is collected. The reaction is $K + HO = KO + H$.

Fig. 286.

401. The voltaic decomposition of water (224) is, however, by far the most satisfactory experiment to this point which

How is this explained? 399. What compounds does hydrogen form with oxygen? 400. What of the constitution of water? What is the simplest case of its decomposition? How does potassium effect this?

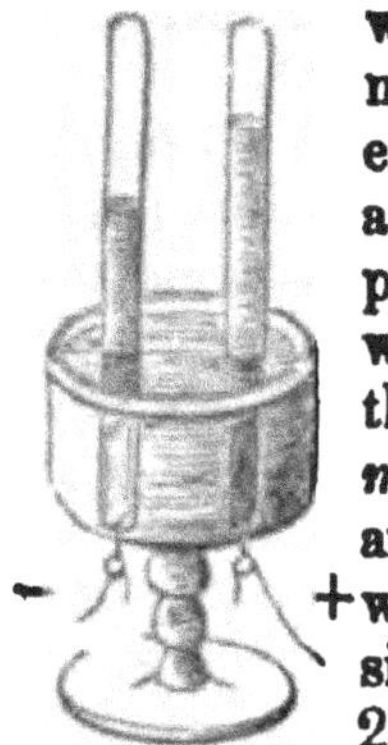

Fig. 287.

we possess, since both elements of the water are evolved in a pure form and in exact atomic proportions by volume and weight, (fig. 287.) In fact, this is a complete *experimentum crucis*, being both analysis and synthesis; for we may so arrange the single tube apparatus (fig. 288) that the mixed gases from the electrolysis of water may be fired by an electric spark, as soon as a sufficient volume of the mixture has been collected. A complete absorption follows the explosion, and the gases again go on collecting. Platinum, heated very hot, decomposes water, and both gases are evolved: this happens when vapor of water is passed through a tube of platinum heated to intense whiteness.

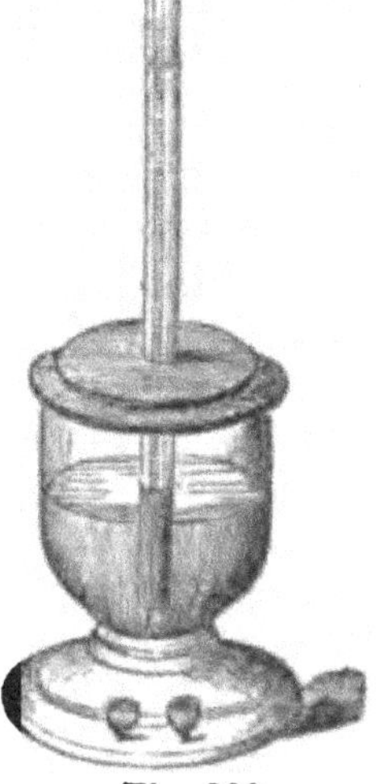
Fig. 288.

402. What potassium and sodium accomplish at ordinary temperatures, is accomplished by iron, only at a red heat. The experiment figured in fig. 289 was devised by Lavoisier: an iron tube, (as a gun-barrel,) or better a tube of porcelain, protected by an exterior tube of iron, heated in a furnace to full redness. The tube contains clean turnings of iron, or better a bundle of clean iron wire of known weight. A small retort *a*, holding a little water, is boiled by a spirit-lamp at the moment when the tube is at a full red-heat: the vapor of the water coming into contact with the heated iron is decomposed, the oxygen is retained by the iron, forming oxyd of iron, and the hydrogen is given off from the tube *f*, which may be made to conduct it to the pneumatic trough. For every eight

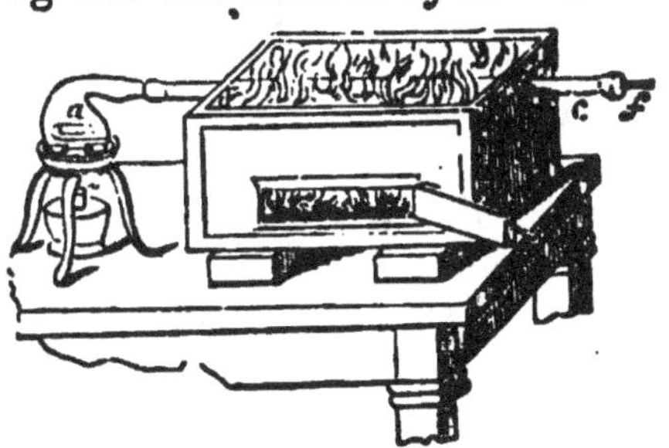

Fig. 289.

401. What of the voltaic decomposition of water? How does platinum decompose water? 402. Describe Lavoisier's experiment, fig. 289. What becomes of the oxygen?

grains of weight acquired by the iron, 46 cubic inches of hydrogen, weighing one grain, have been evolved.

403. *The iron in this case* is evidently substituted for the hydrogen, taking its place with the oxygen to form the oxyd of iron, while the hydrogen is set free. The oxyd of iron resulting from this action, is the same black oxyd which the smith strikes off in scales under the hammer, being a mixture of protoxyd and peroxyd. This case of affinity is an interesting one, because it is seemingly reversed when, under the same circumstances, we pass a stream of hydrogen over oxyd of iron. The iron is then reduced to the metallic state, and water is produced. It will be remembered that we cited this instance (270) while speaking of the influence of quantity of matter in determining the nature of the chemical changes which might take place among bodies.

Referring to the case (393) of sulphuric or chlorohydric acids and zinc, we cannot fail to observe the similarity of the two cases of decomposition. That water, or the oxydation of a base, is not essential to the evolution of hydrogen is conclusively shown in the case of *dry* chlorohydric acid (HCl) and zinc, which evolve hydrogen, when no compound containing oxygen is present: $HCl + Zn = ZnCl + H$.

404. Zinc and iron do decompose water even without the aid of an acid, but only with great slowness, and the action ceases as soon as the metal is covered by the coating of the oxyd thus formed, which protects it from further corrosion. A dilute acid removes this coating of oxyd, and also aids, no doubt, in establishing such electrical relations as to make the zinc highly electro-positive. That this is the fact seems quite probable, because *pure* zinc is hardly affected by dilute acids, and we have already noticed the effects of amalgamation (191) in rendering the zinc incapable of decomposing water.

Much mystery formerly hung over this case of chemical action, which is quite cleared away by the view now presented. It was formerly said that the presence of an acid in water with zinc *disposed* the zinc to decompose the water. This is what was meant by "disposing affinity." But there can be no oxyd of zinc to exert this influence on the acid,

---

403. What is the theory of the process? Why is this an interesting case of affinity? What similarity is noticed with a previous case? 404. What of the slow decomposition of water by zinc? What view was held formerly? What of disposing affinity?

until the water is decomposed; so that the idea that the acid disposed the zinc to decompose the water is quite futile.

405. The *real nature of hydrogen* was for a long time not well understood. It was associated with oxygen and chlorine, because it was supposed to bear the same relations to chlorohydric acid, that oxygen bears to sulphuric and chloric acids. It is now known that hydrogen is most closely allied to the metals, particularly to zinc and copper; that the chlorids, iodids, and fluorids of hydrogen, although they possess the characters which we assign to acids, resemble in many respects the chlorids, iodids, &c., of the same metals; that in fact, hydrogen is a metal exceedingly volatile, probably standing in that respect in the same relation to mercury, that mercury does to platinum, but still possessed of all truly chemical peculiarities of the metallic state, and no more deprived of the commonplace qualities of lustre, hardness, or brilliancy, than is the mercurial atmosphere which fills the apparently empty space in the barometer tube. (Dr. Kane.) The vapor of mercury, and of other volatile metals, is, like hydrogen, a non-conductor of heat and electricity; but we cannot on this account deny their metallic character. We must not forget, moreover, that hydrogen may yet, by sufficient cold and pressure, be made fluid or solid, when doubtless we shall see its resemblance in physical, as well as we now do in chemical characters, to the metals. The propriety of assigning to hydrogen the place in our classification which it occupies, will thus be more apparent to those who have usually seen it placed next to oxygen.

406. A mixture of oxygen and hydrogen gases will never unite under ordinary circumstances of temperature and pressure; but the passage of an electric spark through them, or the application of red-hot flame, or an intensely heated wire, will produce an explosive union, destructive to the containing vessel, unless the gas is in extremely small quantities. The re-composition or synthesis of water, was proved in the experiment in the-single cell decomposing apparatus, (fig. 288.) If that explosion had taken place in a dry vessel over mercury, the interior would have been bedewed with moisture from the regenerated water. This may be done, as in fig.

---

405. What is said of the real nature of hydrogen? What reasons exist for supposing it a metal? 406. How is the union of hydrogen and oxygen affected?

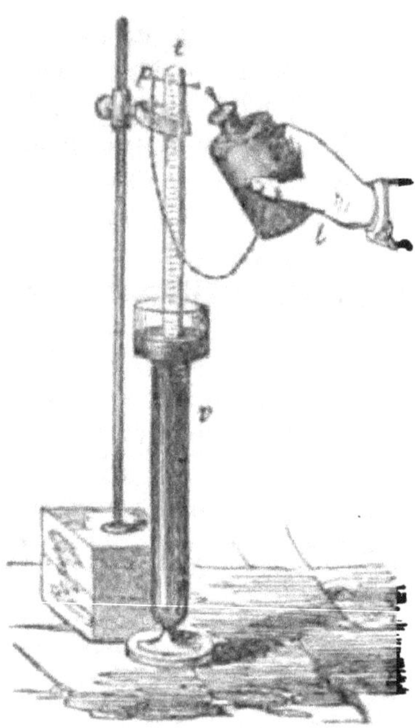
Fig. 290.

290, where a strong glass tube *t* is divided into equal parts, for convenience of measuring, and supported firmly in the mercury vase *v*. An electrical spark from the Leyden vial *l* is made to pass through the gaseous mixture by means of the platinum wires *p* soldered into the walls of the upper part of the tube. Such an arrangement is an eudiometer, some allusion to which was made in 332. Hydrogen furnishes us the most convenient means of analysis of gases containing oxygen, by combining with it to form water. In eudiometrical analysis it is always from the *volume* that the result of the analysis is deduced, and not, as in case of solids, from the weight. A very good form of eudiometrical tube is that of Dr. Ure, (fig. 291.) It is a graduated tube, closed as before at one end, and bent on itself. When used, it is filled with dry mercury, by placing it horizontally in the mercury trough. A portion of the gaseous mixture to be detonated is then introduced, the thumb placed over the open end, and all the mixture adroitly transferred to the closed limb. The mercury is made to stand at the same level in both limbs, by forcing out a portion with a glass rod thrust in at the full side. These adjustments being made, the whole bulk of the mixture is read on the graduation, and while the thumb is firmly held over the open end of the tube, an electrical spark is made to explode the gases. The air between the thumb and

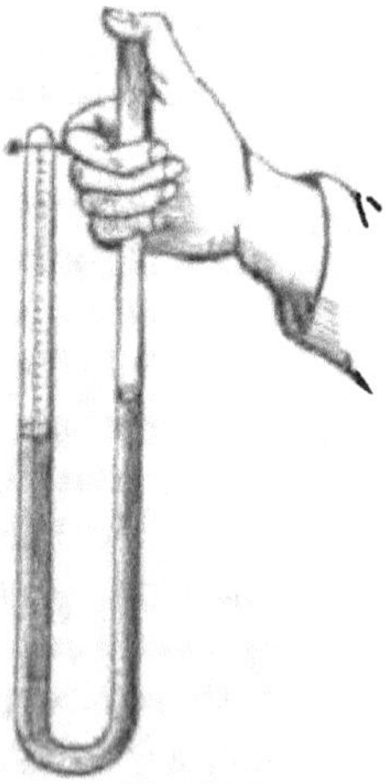

Fig. 291.

Describe fig. 290. How is hydrogen useful in gas analysis? What is Ure's eudiometer? How is it used?

the mercury acts like a spring to break the force of the explosion; and afterward, on removing the thumb, the weight of the atmosphere forces the mercury into the shorter leg, to supply the partial vacuum occasioned by the union of the gases. Proper allowances being made for temperature and pressure, the quantity of residual gas is read on the graduation, and a calculation can then be made of the amount of oxygen present. If the gas contains carbon, carbonic acid would be formed, and must be absorbed by potash solution.

407. *Volta's* eudiometer, represented in fig. 292, is a very complete instrument for gas analyses over the pneumatic-trough. In this instrument the explosion is made in a thick glass tube A B, into which the electrical spark is passed by *t*. The graduated measure *p* screws into the funnel D, and is used to measure the portion of gas to be detonated, which is poured in by the funnel C at bottom. Before use, the tube P is removed, the cocks R and S are both opened, and the whole instrument sunk in the cistern until it is entirely full of water. The cock R is then shut, the portion of gas measured in P and introduced by C, the cock S closed, and explosion made. If any residue remains, its quantity is measured by opening R, when it rises into P, previously filled with water, and its quantity is read off on the graduation. The metallic strap *p* serves as a communication for the electric circuit, and also as a scale of equal parts for ruder measurements of gas. This instrument is well adapted for rapid class illustration, in the lecture room, and is applicable in all eudiometrical experiments in which gaseous analysis is to be performed by oxygen and hydrogen. For accurate research, the beautiful eudiometer of Regnault is the most reliable instrument.

Fig. 292.

408. The explosion of oxygen and hydrogen gases, when mingled in atomic proportions, is very severe, and can be performed safely only on very small volumes of the gases, or in strong vessels of metal. The ingenuity of the demonstrator will devise many instructive and amusing experi-

How is the carbonic acid removed? 407. What is Volta's eudiometer? How is it used? 408. What illustrations are given of the severity of the explosion of oxygen and hydrogen?

ments depending on the explosion of this mixture. The gas-pistol, and hydrogen-gun, (fig. 293,) a bladder filled and fired from a pin-hole or by an electric spark, soap-bubbles, and other familiar illustrations, all give evidence of the energy of the action by which water is formed from the union of its elements. The explosion is probably due to the rush of air consequent on the sudden expansion and immediate condensation of a volume of steam formed at the most intense heat which can be produced by art.

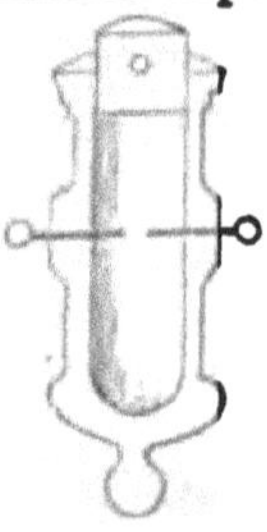

Fig. 293.

The union of oxygen and hydrogen can, however, be effected slowly and quietly, without any explosion or visible combustion. This is accomplished by passing the mixed gases through a tube heated below redness; and at a still lower temperature, if the tube contains coarsely powdered glass or sand. We see in this case an instance of that remarkable phenomenon called "surface action," (251) before alluded to.

409. Professor Döbereiner, of Jena, observed, in 1824, that platinum in the state of fine division, known as spongy platinum, would cause an immediate union of these gases. A drop of strong chlorid of platinum evaporated on writing paper, and the paper burned, gives platinum in that state, and such a pellet of paper may be prepared in an instant and used to fire hydrogen. The common instrument employed for lighting tapers is made by taking advantage of this principle. A little spongy platinum is formed into a ball, and mounted on a ring of wire (fig. 294) which slips within the cup *d* on the top of gas-holder *a* (fig. 295.) The gas is generated by the action of dilute acid in the outer vessel *a* on a lump of zinc *z* hanging in the inner vessel *f*, and is let out at pleasure by the cock *c*, issuing in a stream on the spongy platinum. The latter is at once heated to redness by the stream of hydrogen, which is condensed within its pores to such a degree that it combines with a portion of oxygen, always present in the sponge by atmospheric absorption. The union of these gases is attended by intense heat, and, as a consequence, the platinum at once glows with redness, and the hydrogen is inflamed. After

Fig. 294.

How is this union effected slowly? 409. What was the observation of Döbereiner? Describe the hydrogen lamp?

some time the sponge loses this property to a certain extent, but it is again restored by being well ignited. When the spongy platinum is mixed with clay and sal-ammoniac made into balls and baked, its effects are less intense, and such balls are often used in analysis to cause the gradual combination of gases. Faraday has shown that clean slips of platinum foil, and even of gold and palladium, can effect the silent union of hydrogen and oxygen. For this purpose the platinum is cleaned in hot sulphuric acid, washed thoroughly with pure water, and hung in a jar of the mixed gases. Combination then takes place so rapidly as to cause at every instant a sensible elevation of the water in the jar. If the metal is very thin, it sometimes becomes hot enough during the process of combination to glow, and even to explode the gases.

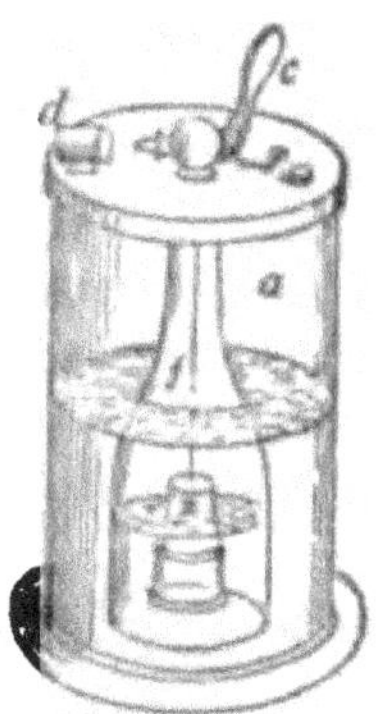

Fig. 295.

410. The same effect of platinum in causing combination is seen in other bodies besides oxygen and hydrogen. Several mixtures of carbon gases will act with platinum in the same way; and the vapors of alcohol or ether may be oxydized by a coil of platinum wire hung from a card in a wineglass (fig. 296) containing a few drops of either of these fluids. The coil of wire is heated to redness in a lamp, and, while still hot, is hung in the glass; it then, if air has free access, retains its red-hot condition as long as any vapor of ether or alcohol remains. In this case, only the hydrogen of the ether, or alcohol, is oxydized, and the carbon is unaffected; a peculiar irritating acid vapor is given off, which affects the nose and eyes unpleasantly. Little balls of platinum sponge suspended over the wick of an alcohol lamp will, in like manner, glow for hours after the lamp is extinguished. A spirit-lamp fed with alcoholic ether will cause the coil of platinum wire (fig. 297) to glow for hours in the same way, constituting what has been called the aphlogistic lamp.

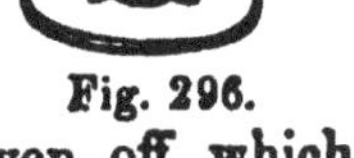

Fig. 296.

Fig. 297.

What has Faraday shown on this point? 410. How does platinum act on vapors? What is the aphlogistic lamp?

411. The *oxyhydrogen blowpipe of Hare* enables the chemist to use safely the intense heat produced by the combustion of oxygen and hydrogen. In Dr. Hare's instrument the two gases were brought from separate gas-holders and mingled only in the moment of contact. The flame of the oxyhydrogen blowpipe differs from the flame of a lamp or candle by being, so to speak, a cond of aerial matter entirely ignited in every part, while the flame of a candle is ignited only on the outside, (460.) The structure of the jet contrived by Professor Daniell illustrates this, where the oxygen tube *o* is seen (figure 298) to pass through that carrying the hydrogen, H. Thus the combustible gas is in contact with the oxygen to burn it both from the air and from the instrument. The jet may be provided with a cock (fig. 299) and connected with the gas-holders by two flexible pipes attached at O and H. The

Fig. 298.

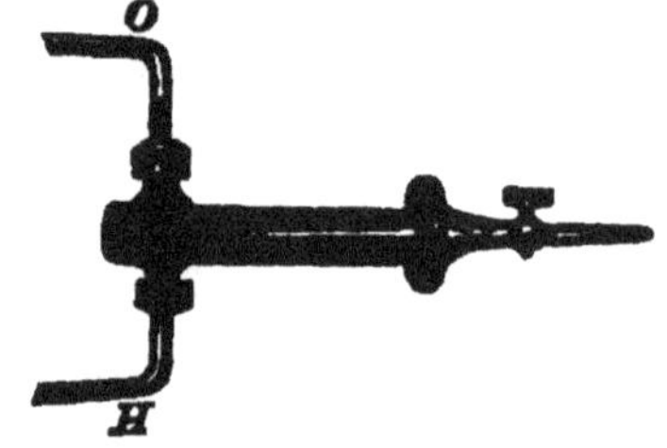

Fig. 299.

Fig. 300.

gas-holders may conveniently be made of impervious caoutchouc cloth, arranged with pressure boards, and weights as in fig. 300, an arrangement which admits of convenient transportation and dispenses with the use of water. The gas is admitted and expelled by the flexible pipes *p* and controlled by the cocks *c*. The effects of the compound blowpipe may also be safely produced by passing a stream of oxygen from a gas-holder (fig. 301) through the

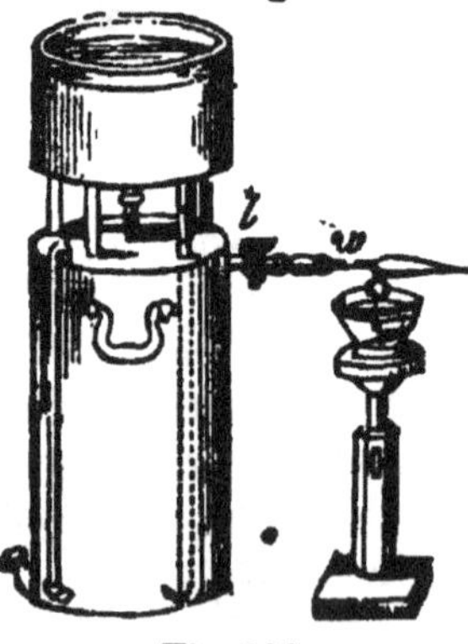

Fig. 301.

---

411. What is Hare's blowpipe? How does its flame differ from common flames? How is the jet fig. 298 constructed? How are the gases disposed?

flame of a spirit-lamp *w*. The jet is regulated by the cock *l*, while the lamp-flame supplies the hydrogen.

412. The mixed gases, in atomic proportions, are sometimes forced by a condensing syringe into a very strong metallic box, from which they issue by their own elasticity. To prevent the danger of explosion, a contrivance is employed called "Hemming's safety tube." This is a brass tube, six or eight inches long, filled with fine brass wire, closely packed, and having a conical rod of brass forcibly driven into their centre, by which the wires are very closely crowded together. This forms in fact a great number of small metallic tubes, through which the gas must pass. It is a property of such small tubes entirely to arrest the progress of flame as we shall presently see. (Safety lamp of Davy, 464.) The jet is screwed to one end of this tube, and the other end is connected with the holder of the mixed gases. Several severe explosions, it is said, have occurred, even with all these precautions; so that if the mixed gases are used at all, it should only be in a bag or bladder, the bursting of which can be attended with no danger.

Fig. 302.

413. The effects of the compound blowpipe are very remarkable. In the heat of its focus the most refractory metals and earths are fused, or dissipated in vapor. Platinum, which does not melt in the most intense furnace of the arts, here fuses with the rapidity of wax, and is even volatilized. Even those metallic oxyds, as lime, magnesia, and alumina, which are entirely infusible in any other artificial heat, yield to this focus. By the adroit management of the keys, which a little practice soon teaches, we can either reduce metallic oxyds, or oxydize substances still more highly. The flame of the mixed gases falling on a cylinder of prepared lime, adjusted to the focus of a parabolic mirror, produces the most intense artificial light known. This is what is called the Drummond light. It is extensively employed in distant night-signals, and can be seen farther at sea than any

---

412. How are the mixed gases burned safely? What is Hemming's safety jet? 413. What are the effects of the compound blowpipe? What is the Drummond light?

other light. It is also used as a substitute for the sun's light in optical experiments. The galvanic focus alone, among artificial sources of light, surpasses it, (200.)*

History of Water.

414. Water, when pure, is a colorless, inodorous, tasteless fluid, which conducts heat and electricity very imperfectly, refracts light powerfully, and is almost incapable of compression. We have already made so much use of water, in illustration of the laws of heat and of chemical combination, in the former part of this volume, that the student must already be familiar with many of its attributes. Its greatest density, it will be remembered, (103,) is found to be at 39°·5, or, more exactly, 39°·83. It is the standard of comparison (33), for all densities of solids and liquids. In the form of ice, its density is 0·94, and at 32° it freezes. One imperial gallon of water weighs 70,000 grains, or just ten pounds. The American standard gallon holds, at 39°·83 Fahr., 58,372 American troy grains of pure distilled water. One cubic inch, at 60° and 30 inches barometer, weighs $252\frac{458}{1000}$ grains, which is 815 times as much as a like bulk of atmospheric air. One hundred cubic inches of aqueous vapor, at 212° and 30 inches barometer, weigh 14·96 grains, and its specific gravity is 0·622. Water boils under ordinary circumstances at 212°; but we have seen that its boiling point was very much affected by the nature of the vessel. It evaporates at all temperatures.

415. The conversion of water into ice is attended with the exercise of crystallogenic attractions, although the resulting forms are rarely visible. But in snow we often see beautifully grouped compound crystals, resulting from the union of forms derived from the hexagonal prism. Figure 303 gives some of the more simple of

Fig. 303.

414. What are the properties of water? What the temperature of its greatest density? What the density of ice? What that of a cubic inch? of a gallon? of its vapor? 415. What is said of the crystallization of water?

* Mr. E. N. Kent, of New York, furnishes a very efficient and cheap form of compound blowpipe, with gas-bags and Drummond light apparatus.

these forms. The laws of congelation of water have already been fully explained, 123.

416. Pure water is never found on the surface of the earth; for the purest natural waters, evaporated to dryness, leave always a visible residue, containing small quantities of earthy or saline matters which have been dissolved from the rocks and soil. Moreover, all good water—that which is fit for the use of man—has a considerable quantity of carbonic acid and atmospheric air dissolved in it, (332,) and without which it would be flat and unpalatable. A jar of spring water placed under a bell on the air-pump (fig. 304) will appear to boil as the exhaustion proceeds from escape of the dissolved air. It is upon this air that the fish and other water-breathing animals depend for life; and consequently, when a vessel containing fish is placed on the air-pump and the air exhausted, the fish are seen soon to give signs of discomfort, (fig. 305,) and will die if the operation is continued.

Fig. 304.

Many mineral springs, besides the saline matters they hold in solution, are highly charged with sulphuretted hydrogen, carbonic acid, and other gases derived from chemical changes going on in the beds from which they flow.

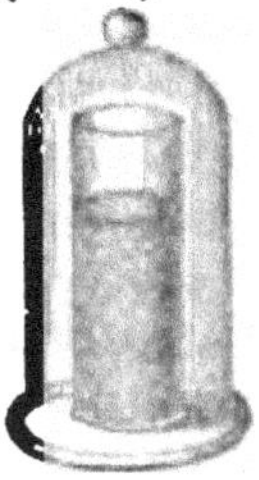

Fig. 305.

Pure water can be procured only by distillation, and it is a substance of such indispensable importance to the chemist, that every well-furnished laboratory is provided with means for its abundant preparation. A copper still, well tinned, and connected with a pure block-tin worm or condenser, answers very well to produce the common supply. But very accurate operations require it to be again distilled in clean vessels of hard glass.

417. *The solvent powers of water far exceed* those of any other known fluid. Nearly all saline bodies are, to a greater or less extent, dissolved by water, and heat generally aids this result. In the case of common salt, however, and a few other bodies, cold water dissolves as much as hot.

What depends on the presence of air in the water? What other gases are found in it? How is pure water obtained? 416. What foreign substances are found in water? How is the air in water shown? Why important to animal life? 417. What are the solvent powers of water?

The solvent powers of pure water are generally greater than those of common water.

Gases are nearly all absorbed or dissolved in cold water, and some of them to a very great extent, while others, as hydrogen and common air, very slightly. Hot water dissolves many bodies which are quite insoluble in cold, especially when aided by small portions of alkaline matter. The waters of the hot springs in Iceland and Arkansas deposit much silicious matter before held in solution; and Dr. Turner found that common glass was dissolved in the chamber of a steam-boiler at 300°, and stalactites of silica were formed from the wire basket in which the glass was suspended.

418. Water always absorbs the same volume of a given gas, whatever may be its density: thus, of carbonic acid, of ordinary tension, it dissolves its own volume; it would do no more if the gas were reduced to half its first density; and it dissolves the same volume when the pressure is at 30 atmospheres. Hence water which has absorbed gases under pressure, parts with them in effervescence when that pressure is removed. Again, if a mixture of gases is present at a given tension, water absorbs of each the same volume as it would take up if only that one was present. Such, it will be remembered, is the fact with regard to the gases of the atmosphere, (332.) Gases dissolved in water are all expelled by boiling. If, therefore, we would know what volume of a given gas was dissolved in water, the fact is accurately determined by boiling a measured quantity in a flask quite full, as in figure 306, and conveying the escaping gas by a bent tube (also previously filled with water) to a graduated jar on the

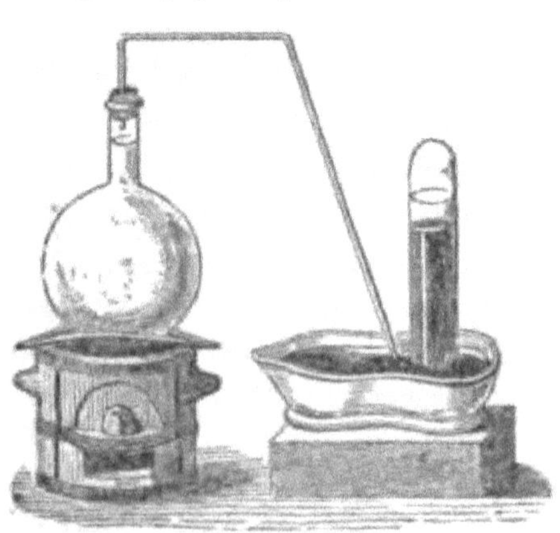

Fig. 306.

What of the action of hot water? 418. What volume of gases does water absorb? How does pressure affect this? How of mixed gases? How is the volume of gases contained in water determined? Describe fig. 306.

mercurial cistern. We then measure the volume of gas expelled directly.

419. *The powers of water as a chemical agent* are very various and important. From its neutral, mild, and salutary character, we are accustomed to regard it only as a negative substance, possessed of little energy, while it is in fact one of the most important chemical agents in our possession. Besides its solvent powers, we know that it combines with many substances, forming a large class of hydrates: hydrate of lime and potash are examples. It is also, as we have seen, (320,) essential to the acid properties of common sulphuric, phosphoric, and nitric acids, acting here the part of a much more energetic base than in the hydrates. It forms an essential part in the composition of many neutral salts, and can be replaced in composition by other neutral saline bodies; while as *water of crystallization* it discharges still another important and distinct function, the crystalline forms of many salts being quite dependent on its presence in atomic proportions. Of organic structures, both animal and vegetable, it forms by far the most considerable constituent. Its vapor at high temperatures displaces some of the most powerful acids, as Tilghmann has shown, in his patent process for procuring the alkaline bases by decomposing their sulphates, chlorids, and even, to some extent, silicates, by vapor of water at a high temperature. Sulphate of lime, for example, so treated, has all its sulphuric acid driven off as SO_2, and caustic lime is left behind. The geological importance of these facts can hardly be overestimated.

420. *Peroxyd or Binoxyd of Hydrogen.*—This curious compound was discovered in 1818, by M. Thenard. It is obtained in decomposing the peroxyd of barium by as much very cold solution of hydrofluoric acid (fluosilicic or phosphoric acid may be used as well) as will exactly saturate the base, the whole being precipitated as fluorid of barium. The reaction may be expressed thus:

Peroxyd of barium.		Fluohydric acid.		Fluorid of barium.		Peroxyd of hydrogen.
BaO_2	+	HF	=	BaF	+	HO_2.

The peroxyd of hydrogen remains dissolved in the water, which is freed from the insoluble fluorid of barium by filtra-

419. What are the chemical powers of water? What is crystallization-water? What are Tilghmann's experiments? 420. What is the peroxyd of hydrogen? How procured? Give the reaction.

tion, and then evaporated in the vacuum of an air-pump by the aid of the absorbing power of sulphuric acid.

421. *Properties.*—The properties of this body are very remarkable. When as free from water as possible, it is a syrupy liquid, colorless, almost inodorous, transparent, and possessed of a very nauseous, astringent, and disgusting taste. Its specific gravity is 1·453, and no degree of cold has ever reduced it to the solid form. Heat decomposes it with effervescence and the escape of oxygen gas. It can be preserved only at a temperature below 50°. The contact of carbon and many metallic oxyds decomposes it, often explosively, and with evolution of light. No change is suffered by many bodies which decompose it; but several oxyds, as those of iron, tin, manganese, and others, pass to a higher state of oxydation. Oxyd of silver, and generally those oxyds which lose their oxygen at a high temperature, are reduced to a metallic state by this decomposition. When diluted, and especially when acidulated, the peroxyd of hydrogen is more stable. It is dissolved by water in all proportions, bleaches litmus paper, and whitens the skin. None of its compounds are known, nor does it seem to have any tendency to combine with other bodies.

Compounds of Hydrogen with the II. *and* III. *Classes.*

422. *The eminently electro-positive character of hydrogen* causes it to form well-characterized and analogous compounds with all the members of the oxygen group. These binary compounds have frequently been called the *hydracids*, in distinction from those acid bodies already considered, which, in parity of language, have been called the *oxacids*.

It is, however, more in accordance with facts and the principles of a philosophic classification, to look upon these bodies as having in reality the same essential characters as the chlorids, bromids, iodids, &c., of other electro-positive bases. The principles of our nomenclature require these compounds to be called after their electro-negative elements, *i. e. chlorohydric acid*, *bromohydric acid*. Their general formula is HR. The compounds of hydrogen to be considered under this head are—

---

421. What are its properties? 422. What are the hydracids? What view is taken of their constitution? What compounds are enumerated under this head? What is their general formula?

Chlorohydric acid	HCl	Sulphydric acid	HS
Bromohydric acid	HBr	Selenhydric acid	HSe
Iodohydric acid	HI	Tellurhydric acid	HTe
Fluohydric acid	HF		

423. *Hydrogen and chlorine*, mingled in the gaseous state, combine with explosion by the touch of a match, forming chlorohydric acid. The rays of the sun effect the same result instantaneously, while in diffuse light combination follows in a gradual manner and quietly. In the dark, no union occurs, showing that light in this case plays the part of heat, and impresses, as we shall see, a peculiar condition on chlorine. If two vessels of equal capacity (fig. 307) are filled, the one, A, with dry hydrogen, the other, B, with dry chlorine, by displacement, and are then united, as seen in the figure, on exposing them with precaution to the sun's direct rays, an immediate explosion follows. Dr. Draper has shown that chlorine gas which had been exposed alone and dry to the sun's light acquired the power of forming this explosive union with hydrogen, even in the dark, and retained it for some time; while, on the other hand, chlorine prepared in the dark manifests no avidity for hydrogen unless exposed to the light. This fact was before mentioned (288) when speaking of the active and passive conditions of chlorine. In its *passive* state, (as prepared in the dark,) it actually replaces hydrogen in the constitution of many organic bodies, or, in other words, assumes an electro-positive condition. The effect of the sun's light is to confer a new state upon it, probably by a new arrangement of its molecules, by which its character is completely changed. It then apparently becomes highly electro-negative.

Fig. 307.

The decomposition of water by chlorine (288) evinces its strong affinity for hydrogen. Chlorine thus becomes one of the most powerful oxydizing agents known, since the nascent oxygen given off during the decomposition of water attacks with energy any third body which may be present that is capable of combining with it.

424. *Chlorohydric Acid*, HCl.—If the experiment (fig.

---

423. How do chlorine and hydrogen act when mingled? Describe fig. 307. What has Draper shown? What is the passive state of chlorine? What relation has it in this state to organic bodies? On what does the decomposition of water by chlorine depend?

307) is placed in diffuse light, the green color of the gas is seen gradually to diminish and finally to disappear altogether; and, on opening the junction beneath mercury, no absorption occurs, and the vessels are found to be filled with chlorohydric acid gas. It appears therefore that this acid is formed by the union of equal volumes of the constituent gases without condensation Its density is consequently equal to half the sum of the united densities of chlorine and hydrogen, *i.e.* $2{\cdot}44 + {\cdot}069 = 2{\cdot}509 \div 2 = 1{\cdot}254$, theoretical density of chlorohydric acid gas. Experiment gives 1·2474.

425. *Chlorohydric acid* is a colorless, acid, irrespirable gas. It forms copious clouds of acid vapor with the moisture of the air, very suffocating, and irritating the eyes. It extinguishes a lighted candle, and is not decomposed by electricity. It is very soluble in water, which at 32° takes up about 500 times its volume and acquires a density of 1·21. At a higher temperature it absorbs less. This gas is therefore collected over mercury. A bit of ice passed up to a jar of it on the mercury cistern, is fused immediately by its avidity for water, a dilute solution of chlorohydric acid results, and the mercury rises to fill the jar. With a pressure of over 26 atmospheres it becomes a colorless liquid, which has never been frozen.

426. *Preparation.*—For experimental purposes in the laboratory it is sufficient to warm the strong commercial liquid acid, which parts with a large portion of gas at a gentle heat. This may be dried by passing it through a chlorid of calcium tube. The apparatus thus arranged is shown in figure 308. The concentrated acid is placed in *c* and its moisture is removed by the chlorid of calcium apparatus *a*. The weight of the gas enables us to collect it by displacement of air in dry vessels *b*. For this purpose it is not usually requisite to dry it.

Fig. 308.

In the arts it is always obtained from the decomposition

424. What is the constitution of chlorohydric acid? What is its theoretical composition and density? Its experimental? 425. What are its properties? How soluble in water? How collected? 426. How is it prepared for experiment in the laboratory? Describe fig. 308.

of common salt, (chlorid of sodium, $NaCl$,) by sulphuric acid. The reaction is sufficiently simple: $NaCl + SO_3 . HO = (NaO.SO_3) + HCl$. The apparatus employed in this process is shown in fig. 309. Common salt is placed in the flask *a*, provided with a safety tube *f* and an eduction tube *b*. The sulphuric acid for decomposing the salt is introduced at pleasure through *f*. The action is aided by a gentle heat from the furnace below. The chlorohydric acid is rapidly evolved and passes into *c*, where it is washed by a little warm water and thence by *e* to the last bottle *d*, where it is absorbed by the ice-cold water which it contains. In the middle bottle is a tube *g*, of large size and open at both ends,

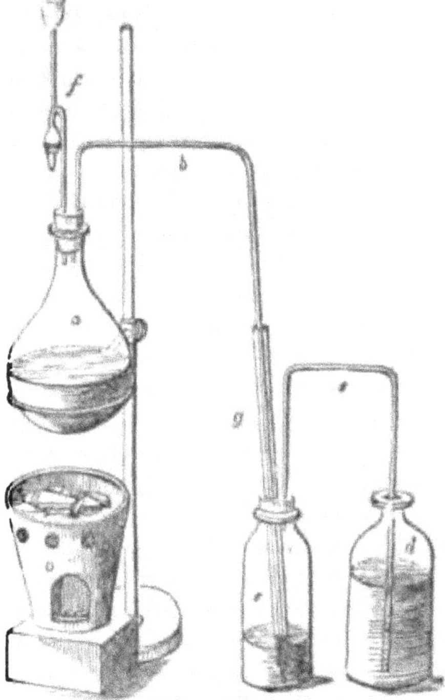

Fig. 309.

its lower extremity dips into the wash-water. This contrivance prevents the accident which is otherwise likely to happen should a partial vacuum occur in *a*, from a cessation of the action; when the pressure of the air on the fluid in *d* would carry it back into *c*, and finally into *a*. The safety tube (fig. 310) attached to the flask *a* also serves to prevent this accident as well as to introduce the acid. When a liquid is poured in at the funnel-top, it must rise as high as the turn, before it can pass down into the flask, and a portion of the fluid is therefore always left behind in the bend, which serves as a valve against the entrance of air, and also effectually prevents an explosion of the flask in case the tube of delivery should become stopped. This simple con-

Fig. 310.

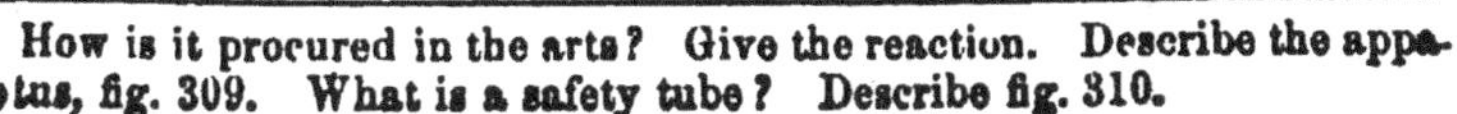

How is it procured in the arts? Give the reaction. Describe the apparatus, fig. 309. What is a safety tube? Describe fig. 310.

trivance we have often employed but have not before explained its action. This same apparatus may be employed in making solutions of all the absorbable gases, and is so simple as to be within the means of the humblest laboratory; the essential parts being only wide-mouthed bottles, glass tubes, a gas bottle or flask, and corks.

427. Pure chlorohydric acid is procured by distilling the commercial acid. The distilling apparatus employed for this purpose is seen in fig. 311. The heat is applied by a sand-bath beneath the retort. The gas given off is absorbed by a little water placed in the last bottle, which is connected by a bent tube with the two-necked receiver. If the com-

Fig. 311.

mercial acid is diluted by water until it has the specific gravity 1·11, it no longer evolves acid fumes when heated, and the fluid distilled has the same density as that in the retort, retaining 16 equivalents of water.

428. *Properties.*—Liquid chlorohydric acid is a colorless, highly acid, fuming liquid, having when saturated a specific gravity of 1·247: it then contains 42 parts in a hundred of real acid. Its purity is tested by its leaving no residue on evaporating a drop or two on clean platinum, and by its giving no milkiness when a solution of chlorid of barium is added to it, (due to sulphuric acid.) Neutralized by ammonia, it ought not to become black when hydrosul-

---

427. How obtained pure? Describe fig. 311. At what density does it distill unchanged? 428. What are the properties of the liquid acid? What are tests of its purity?

phuret of ammonium is added, (due to iron.) This acid is an electrolyte, and is also decomposed by ordinary electricity. A mixture of muriatic acid gas with oxygen, passed through a red-hot tube, produces water and chlorine. The commercial acid is always impure, and colored yellow by free chlorine, iron, and organic matters.

Tests.—A solution of nitrate of silver detects the presence of a soluble chlorid, or of chlorohydric acid, by forming with it a white curdy precipitate of chlorid of silver, which is soluble in ammonia, but insoluble in acids or water. A rod *a*, if dipped in ammonia and held over a glass containing chlorohydric acid, gives off a dense white cloud of chlorid of ammonium.

Fig. 312.

429. The uses of chlorohydic acid are very numerous. Its decomposition by oxyd of manganese affords the easiest mode of procuring chlorine, (282.) It dissolves a great number of metals and oxyds, forming chlorids, from which these metals may be obtained in their lowest state of oxydation. In chemical analysis and the daily operations of the laboratory it is of indispensable use.

Chlorohydric acid is made in the arts in immense quantities, especially in England, where the carbonate of soda is largely made from common salt (chlorid of sodium) by the action of sulphuric acid. Mingled with half its own volume of strong nitric acid, it makes the deeply colored, fuming, and corrosive *aqua-regia.* This mixed acid evolves much free chlorine, which in its nascent state has power to dissolve gold, platinum, &c., forming chlorids of those metals, and not nitromuriates as was formerly supposed. As soon as all the chlorine is evolved, this peculiar power of the aqua-regia is lost.

430. *Bromohydric Acid*, HBr, *Bromid of Hydrogen.*—Hydrogen and bromine do not act upon each other in the gaseous state, even by the aid of the sun's light; but a red heat or the electric spark causes union—only among those particles, however, which are in immediate contact with the heat, the action not being general. Bromohydric acid may be prepared by the reaction of moist phosphorus on bromine in a glass tube (fig. 313.) The gas given off must be collected

---

What tests are named? 429. What are its uses? What is aqua-regia? 430. What is bromohydric acid? How prepared?

over mercury. It is composed, like chlorohydric acid, of equal volumes of its elements not condensed. Its specific gravity is 2·731, and it is condensed by cold and pressure into a liquid. In its sensible properties it bears a close resemblance to chlorohydric acid. With the nitrates of silver, lead, and mercury, it gives white precipitates similar to the chlorids. It has a strong avidity for water, and dissolves largely in it, giving out much heat during the absorption. The saturated aqueous solution has the same reactions as the dry acid, and fumes with a white cloud in contact with air. It dissolves a large quantity of free bromine, acquiring thereby a red tint.

431. *Iodohydric Acid.*—This body may be formed by the direct union of its elements at a red-heat, but is more easily prepared by acting on iodine and water with phosphorus, by which means the gas is formed in large quantities. The action of phosphorus and iodine is violent and dangerous, but may be regulated and made safe by putting a little powdered glass between each layer of phosphorus and iodine, (fig. 313.) Phosphoric acid is formed and remains in solution, while the iodohydric acid gas is given out, and may be collected over mercury, or dissolved in water. The dry gas has a great avidity for water. Its specific gravity is 4·443, being formed, like the last two compounds, of one volume of each element uncondensed. Cold and pressure reduce it to a clear liquid, which, at —60° Fahr., freezes into a colorless solid, having fissures running through it like ice. It forms a very acid fluid by solution in water, which has, when saturated, a specific gravity of 1·7, and emits white fumes. The aqueous solution is also prepared by transmitting a current of hydrosulphuric acid through water in which free iodine is suspended. The gas is decomposed, sulphur set free, and hydriodic acid produced, which is purified from free hydrosulphuric acid by boiling, and from sulphur by filtration.

Fig. 313.

432. *Properties.*—The aqueous iodohydric acid is easily

---

431. How is iodohydric acid prepared? What are its properties? How is its aqueous solution prepared?

decomposed by exposure to the air, iodine being set free. It forms characteristic, highly colored precipitates with most of the metals, particularly with lead, silver, and mercury. Bromine decomposes it, and chlorine decomposes both hydrobromic and hydriodic acids, thus showing the relative affinities of these bodies for hydrogen. This acid is a valuable reagent; its presence in solution is easily detected by a cold solution of starch, which, with a few drops of strong nitric or sulphuric acid, instantly gives the fine characteristic blue of the iodid of starch.

433. *Fluohydric acid* is obtained from the decomposition of fluor-spar by strong sulphuric acid. The operation must be performed in a retort of pure lead, silver, or platinum, and requires a gentle heat. Fig. 314 shows the form of retort used for this purpose, the junction of the head and body is made tight by a lute of gypsum and water, as any lute containing silica will be attacked by the fluohydric acid. The sulphate of lime resulting from the action forms a solid insoluble mass in the body of the retort: hence the necessity of so large an opening. The fluohydric acid resulting is condensed in a large tube of lead, bent as in fig. 315, so as to enter a refrigerant apparatus: at one end it is luted to the beak of the retort, at the other is narrowed to a small aperture. The reaction is expressed as follows:

Fig. 314.

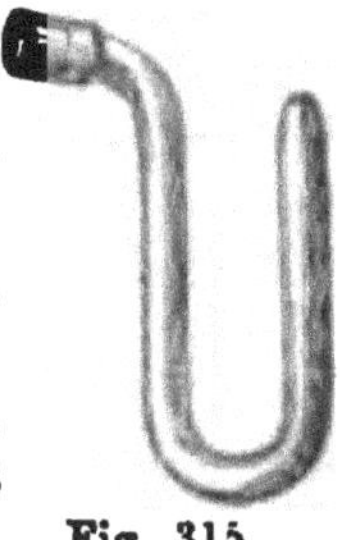

Fig. 315.

Fluorid of calcium.		Sul. acid.		Sul. lime.		Fluorid of hydrogen.
CaF	+	$SO_3.HO$	=	$SO_3.CaO$	+	HF

The fluor-spar employed should be quite free from silica and sulphur.

434. *Properties.*—Concentrated fluohydric acid is a gas which at 32° is condensed into a colorless fluid, with a density of 1·069. Its avidity for water is extreme, and when brought in contact with it, the acid hisses like red-hot iron. Its aqueous solution, as well as the vapor of the acid, attack glass and all compounds containing silica very powerfully. It

---

432. What are its characters? 433. How is fluohydric acid prepared? Describe the apparatus, fig. 314. What is the reaction? 434. What are its properties?

is often used in the laboratory for marking test-bottles or graduated measures, or biting in designs traced in wax on the surface of glass plates. It is a powerful acid, with a very sour taste, neutralizes alkalies, and permanently reddens blue litmus. On some of the metals its action is very powerful; it unites explosively with potassium, evolving heat and light. It attacks and dissolves, with the evolution of hydrogen, certain bodies which no other acid can affect, such as silicon, zirconium, and columbium. Silicic, titanic, columbic, and molybdic acids are also dissolved by it.

Fluohydric acid, in its most concentrated form, is a most dangerous substance. It attacks all forms of animal matter with wonderful energy. The smallest drop of the concentrated acid produces ulceration and death, when applied to the tongue of a dog. Its vapor floating in the air is very corrosive, and should be carefully avoided. If it falls, even in small spray, on the skin, it produces an ulcer, which it is very difficult to cure. For this reason it is quite inexpedient for unexperienced persons to attempt its preparation. By using a weaker sulphuric acid, however, or by having water in the condenser, no risk is incurred. As before remarked, it attacks silica more powerfully than any other body. This fact puts us in possession of an admirable mode of analyzing silicious minerals, when we do not wish to fuse them with an alkali.

435. *Sulphydric Acid, Sulphuretted Hydrogen.*—When the protosulphuret of iron or the sulphuret of antimony is treated with a dilute acid, effervescence occurs, and a gas is given out having a most disgusting, fetid odor, which at once reminds us of the nauseous smell of bad eggs. This process is performed in the evolution-bottle A, (fig.

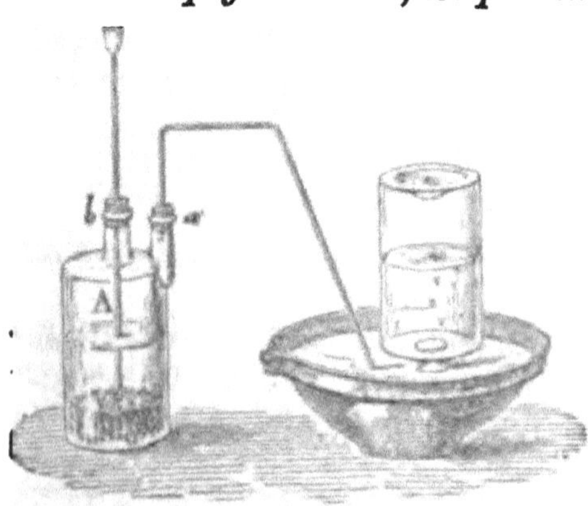

Fig. 316.

What its uses? What of its safety? How does it act on the organs? What is its great affinity? 435. What is hydro-sulphuric acid? What is its common name?

316) in which a portion of sulphuret of iron is acted on by dilute sulphuric acid turned in at the funnel-tube *b*. The escaping gas is led by *a* to the inverted bottle. This operation should be performed in a well-drawing flue or in the open air. The reaction is $FeS+SO_3+HO=FeO.SO_3+HS$.

If sulphuret of antimony is used, heat is needed; and we must employ the apparatus fig. 317, and chlorohydric in-

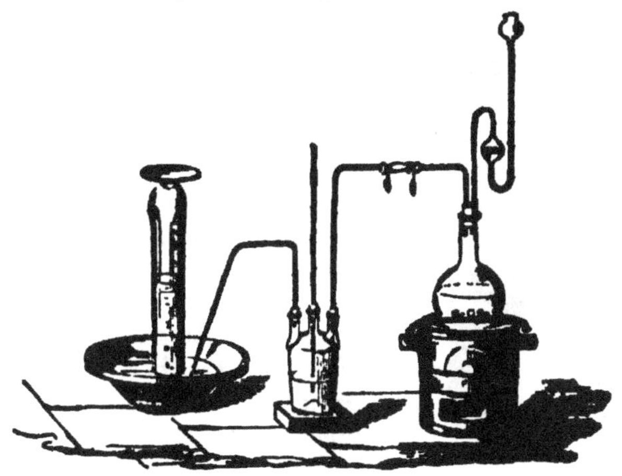

Fig. 317.

stead of sulphuric acid. This mode evolves no free hydrogen, which is present in small quantities when protosulphuret of iron is used. This is sulphuretted hydrogen gas, one of the most useful reagents to the chemist, especially in relation to the metallic bodies.

436. *Properties.*—Sulphydric acid is a colorless gas, of a disgusting odor, like that of putrid eggs. Its density is 1·191, or a little heavier than air. It is liquefied at 50° by a pressure of 15 or 16 atmospheres, and at —122° Fahrenheit it freezes into a white confused crystalline solid, not transparent, and which is much heavier than the fluid, sinking in it readily. Heat partially decomposes it. It burns with a blue flame, depositing sulphur on the interior of the bottle. Sulphurous acid and water are its products of combustion. Mingled with 1½ volumes of oxygen the combustion is complete, no sulphur is deposited, and there

---

How prepared? Give the reaction. Why is sulphuret of antimony sometimes preferred? 436. What are its properties? Is it combustible? How is it decomposed? How much oxygen burns it? What are the products of combustion?

is a shrill explosion. Strong nitric acid also inflames and burns it. Chlorine, bromine, and iodine also decompose it. Mingled with a considerable volume of air in contact with organic matter, it slowly forms sulphuric acid. It is a true but feeble acid.

Water, if cold, and recently boiled, dissolves 2½ or 3 times its volume of sulphydric acid. Woulf's apparatus (fig. 321) is best adapted for this purpose. The solution has the characteristic smell and taste of the gas and all its properties. If boiled it loses all its gas, and if kept a short time it becomes troubled from precipitation of sulphur: this is due to oxygen dissolved in the water. The solution of sulphydric acid should therefore be kept in well-stopped bottles, quite full. This solution is much used in the laboratory. Added to solutions of metallic salts it throws down characteristic precipitates, offering to the chemist an easy mode of distinguishing substances or of separating them from one another. The gas passed directly into solutions of metals as in fig. 318, answers the same purpose. Such an apparatus is conveniently kept for use, and should be always at hand.

Fig. 318.

437. *It occurs in nature* in many mineral springs, giving the water highly valuable medicinal characters. Many such springs in this country are much resorted to, as at Sharon and Avon, N. Y., and the sulphur springs of Virginia. At Lake Solfatara, near Rome, this gas is given off copiously with carbonic acid. The disgust at first felt at drinking these nauseous waters is soon overcome, and those patients who take them in large quantity soon observe the gas to penetrate their whole system and exude in their perspiration. Silver coin, and other silver articles in the pockets of such persons, are soon completely blackened by the coating of sulphuret of silver formed on their surface.

Although salutary when taken into the stomach, it is, even when present in the air in only a small quantity, a deadly poison to the more delicate animals. Numerous deaths are also recorded of those who have attempted to work in vaults and sewers where it abounds.

How soluble is it? Will the solution remain unchanged? Why not?
437. What is its natural history? How does it affect life?

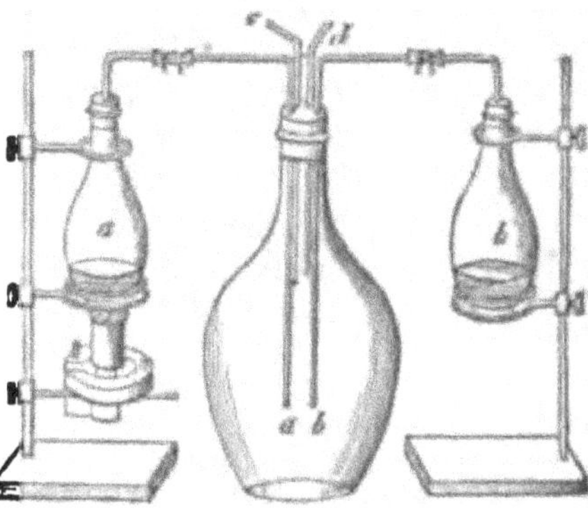

Fig. 319.

438. When sulphurous acid and sulphuretted hydrogen gas are brought together in a common receiving vessel, mutual decomposition ensues, and the sulphur of both is thrown down, which attaches itself to the sides of the vessel in a thick yellow pellicle. The sulphurous acid is evolved in *a*, (fig. 319,) (310,) and sulphydric acic in *b*, and both are carried to the bottom of the middle bottle at *a b*.

Sulphydric acid is formed from 1 volume of hydrogen =	0·0692
And ⅙ volume of sulphuric vapor $\frac{6.6540}{6}$ = ...	1·1090
Giving for the theoretical density of the gas................	1·1782
While experiment gives......................................	1·1912

There is a bisulphydric acid, HS_2, but no further mention will be made of it.

439. Selenhydric and tellurhydric acids are exactly analogous to the last-named compound, and their general interest is so small that we pass them without further notice.

Compounds of Hydrogen with Class III.

440. The compounds which hydrogen forms with the nitrogen group are strongly contrasted in chemical and physical characters with the remarkable natural family which has just engaged our attention. The latter are all acid, and generally in an eminent degree. The compounds of hydrogen with the nitrogen group are, on the contrary, either neutral or strongly basic, forming a series of salts or peculiar compounds with the hydracids before named.

The compounds named under this head are—

Ammonia..	NH_3
Phosphuretted hydrogen......................................	PH_3

We might add in the same connection the hydrogen compounds of arsenic and antimony, AsH_3 and SbH_3, sub-

438. What is the experiment in fig. 319? What is the composition of this gas? What its theoretical and experimental density? 439. What compounds are used in this section? Give the formulæ. What other similar compounds are named?

stances quite similar to PH_3 in many of their attributes, but convenience refers these to the metallic bodies.

441. *Origin of Ammonia.*—Hydrogen and nitrogen do not unite in mixture, nor by the aid of heat. A series of electrical sparks, as in the case of nitrogen and oxygen, (333,) passed through a mixture of hydrogen and nitrogen, will produce a limited quantity of ammonia. But it is only when these gases come together at the moment of their evolution from previous combination, (nascent state, 269,) and while, so to speak, they still have the impression of change upon them, that they unite with freedom. Ammonia is therefore a constant product in the decomposition of those organic substances which contain nitrogen. It is in fact from the destructive distillation of horns, hoofs, and other highly nitrogenized forms of animal matter, that the ammonia of commerce is in great measure derived.

This nascent union also occurs without the aid of the products of life. A fragment of metallic iron in moist air soon contracts a film of oxyd of iron, which, like other porous bodies, absorbs the atmospheric gases, while the electrical influence of the oxyd of iron with water and metallic iron, forming in fact a voltaic circuit, effects a slow decomposition of water, whose hydrogen unites in its nascent state with atmospheric nitrogen to form ammonia. Thus we reach an explanation of the well-known fact, that oxyd of iron often contains a notable proportion of ammonia.

442. Again: Hydrogen is evolved, as all know, by the action of dilute sulphuric acid on zinc. Nitric acid effects the same end, if of a certain concentration. But if nitric acid be added drop by drop to dilute sulphuric acid, while hydrogen is being evolved by its action on zinc, the effervescence from escaping hydrogen is checked, and, if the addition of nitric acid is cautiously made, a point is reached when the evolution of hydrogen ceases entirely. The zinc is still dissolving, but the hydrogen is immediately seized as fast as it is evolved, by the nitrogen from the decomposed nitric acid, ammonia is formed, and the fluid is found to contain a notable quantity of nitrate and sulphate of ammonia.

---

441. What is the origin of ammonia? How do the two gases unite? How does this happen from the dung of animal matters? How without their aid? 442. How is ammonia formed by the solution of zinc? Describe the process.

443. Ammonia was known to the ancients, and bears proof of its antiquity in its very name. They obtained *sal-ammoniac* by burning the dried dung of camels in the desert, whence the name, ammonia, from *ammos*, sand, in allusion to the desert, which was also called Ammon, one of the names of Jupiter. The sal-ammoniac, sulphate of ammonia, and ammonia-alum, are found among the products of volcanos. Free ammonia is exhaled from the foliage and found in the juices of certain plants, in the perspiration of animals, in iron rust, and absorbent earths. Rain water also contains a small quantity of ammoniacal salts, washed out of the atmosphere; and the guano so much valued as a manure, is rich in various ammoniacal compounds.

444. *Preparation.*—Ammonia is prepared by decomposing sal-ammoniac, by dry lime and heat. For this purpose equal parts of dry powdered sal-ammoniac and freshly slaked dry lime are well mingled and heated in a glass, or, if the quantity is considerable, in an iron vessel. The lime takes the chlorohydric acid, forming chlorid of calcium, and ammonia is given out as a gas. Fig. 320 shows the arrangement for the purpose. The ammonia is collected over mercury. In the laboratory it is more convenient to employ in the flask *e* strong solution of ammonia, which yields a large volume of gas at a gentle heat. If it is required to dry the gas, it cannot be done by chlorid of calcium, which absorbs it largely in the cold, but dry caustic lime or potassa must be used.

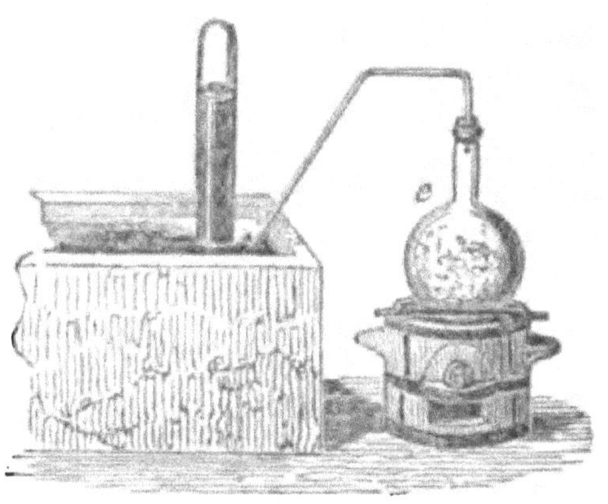

Fig. 320.

445. *Properties.*—The dry gas is colorless, having the very pungent smell so well known as that of "*hartshorn*," (because it was procured formerly from the horns of the hart.)

---

443. What of the antiquity of ammonia? What natural sources are named for it? 444. How is it prepared? Describe the process, fig. 320. 445. What are its properties?

It is, when undiluted, quite irrespirable, and attacks the eyes, mouth, and nose powerfully. It is strongly alkaline, and is often called the *volatile alkali*. It restores the blue of reddened litmus, turns green the blue of cabbage and dahlia, and neutralizes the most powerful acids. Its density is about half that of air, or 0·597. It does not support combustion, but the flame of a candle as it expires in the gas is slightly enlarged, and surrounded with a yellowish fringe. A small jet of ammoniacal gas may also be burned in an atmosphere of oxygen. With its own volume of oxygen it explodes by the electric spark, and produces water and free nitrogen. Passed through a tube filled with iron wire, and heated to redness, dry ammonia is entirely decomposed; yielding for every 200 measures of ammonia, 300 measures of hydrogen, and 100 of nitrogen. The metal in the tube acts to decompose the ammonia solely by its *presence*, (271.) At a temperature of 50° it is liquefied with a pressure of 6½ atmospheres, and with the ordinary pressure it is liquid at —40°, producing a white, translucent, crystalline solid, heavier than the liquid.

446. Ammonia is instantly absorbed by water. A fragment of ice slipped under the lip of an air-jar filled with dry ammonia over the mercury cistern is melted at once, and the mercury rapidly rises to supply the place of the absorbed gas. This forms a weak solution of ammonia, as may be shown by its action with reddened litmus. Cold water dissolves 500 times its volume of ammonia, all of which is

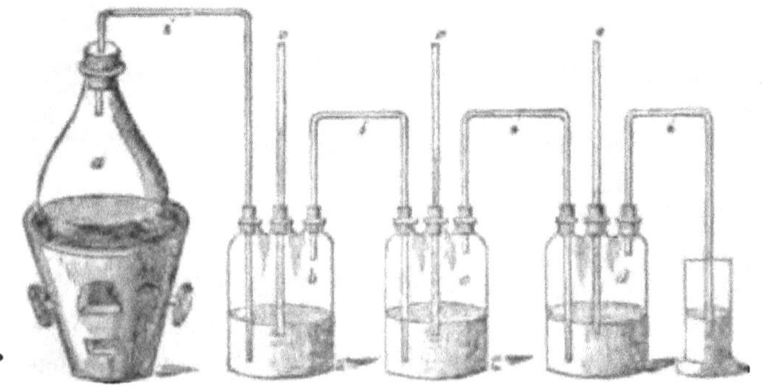

Fig. 321.

How does it act with other bodies? How is it classed? What its density? How as respects combustion? How is it decomposed? What is the product? 446. How absorbable is it?

expelled by heat. This solution is called *aqua ammoniæ.* It is prepared in a Woulf's apparatus *b, c, d,* (fig. 321,) and is evolved from dry lime and sal-ammoniac in *a*. The tubes *i* dip to the bottom of the water in each bottle, and slight pressure may be made by causing the last *i* to dip into mercury. The fluid is seen to mount in *o, o, o,* indicating the pressure, which of course is greatest in *b*.

447. Solution of ammonia, if saturated in the cold, is lighter than water, being sp. gr. 0·870, containing 32½ parts in 100 of real ammonia. Its odor is overpowering, causing suffusion of the eyes and a strong alkaline taste. It boils at 130°, and freezes only at —40°. It saturates acids, and forms definite salts. Ammonia is always recognized by its odor and its restoring the blue of reddened litmus, carrying other vegetable blues to green, and browning yellow turmeric. Its salts are decomposed by dry lime or caustic potassa, evolving the characteristic ammoniacal odor. A rod moistened in chlorohydric acid brought near a vessel evolving ammonia causes an immediate cloud of chlorid of ammonium, (fig. 322.) It must be preserved in well-stopped bottles in a cool place, as the heat of summer or of a warm room causes gas enough to be evolved to blow out the stopper of the bottle.

Fig. 322.

448. *Hydrogen and Phosphorus.—Phosphuretted Hydrogen*—This gaseous body is conveniently prepared by employing quicklime recently slacked, water, and a few sticks of phosphorus, in a small retort, (fig. 323,) the ball of which

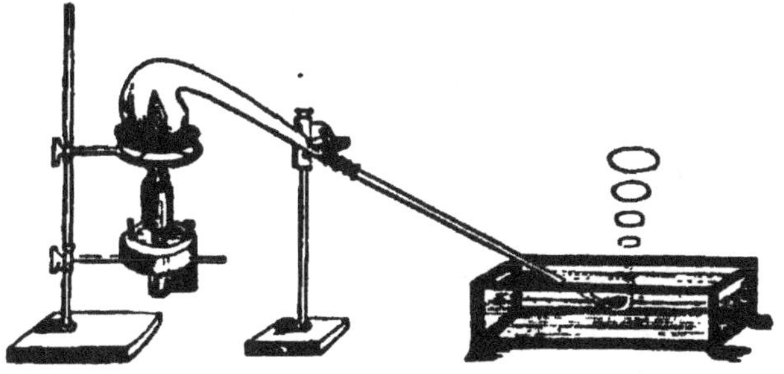

Fig. 323.

is nearly filled with the mixture. A gentle heat generates

How is aqua ammoniæ formed? Describe Woulf's apparatus. 447. What are the properties of the solution? How are its salts decomposed? 448. How is phosphuretted hydrogen obtained?

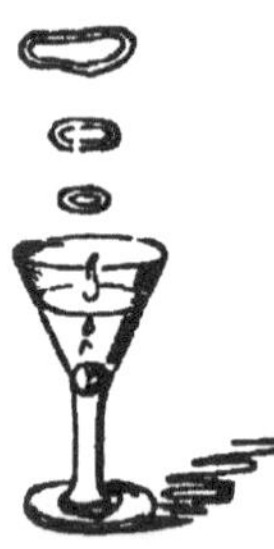
Fig. 324.

the gas, which breaks from the surface of the water (beneath which the beak of the retort dips very slightly) in bubbles, that inflame spontaneously as they reach the air, rising in beautiful wreaths of smoke, which float in concentric, expanding rings. Phosphuret of calcium thrown into a glass of water (fig. 324) is instantly decomposed, and evolves the spontaneously inflammable gas. Chlorohydric acid evolves from this compound the variety of this gas which is not spontaneously inflammable.

449. *Properties.*—This gas has a digusting, heavy odor, like putrid fish, which is far more annoying than that of sulphuretted hydrogen. It is transparent and colorless, has a bitter taste, and, if dry, may be kept unchanged either in the light or dark. It loses its spontaneous inflammability by standing a time over water, a body being deposited which is probably phosphorus, in its red modification. It is deadly when breathed. It acts very violently with oxygen gas. If bubbles of it are allowed to enter a jar of oxygen, each bubble burns with a most brilliant light and a sharp explosion. The mixture of even a very small quantity with oxygen would be quite hazardous, destroying the vessels. Its property of spontaneous inflammability is undoubtedly owing to a portion of free vapor of phosphorus. In its chemical relations phosphuretted hydrogen is nearly neutral, but is in some respects a base, as it forms crystalline salts with bromohydric and iodohydric acids, which are decomposed again by water.

There are three phosphurets of hydrogen, P_2H, PH_2, and PH_3. The second of these is a liquid, the third is the substance described above.

Compounds of Hydrogen with the Carbon Group.

450. *Carbon and Hydrogen* form a vast number of compounds in the organic kingdom, many of which will come under our consideration in the organic chemistry.

---

449. What are its properties? What is its most remarkable property? What its constitution? 450. What compounds of hydrogen and carbon are named?

There are two gases, marsh gas and olefiant gas, or the light and heavy carburetted hydrogens, which are found in the inorganic kingdom, although they are derived from the destruction of organic bodies. These two compounds we will now consider. They are—

Light carburetted hydrogen gas....................	CH_2	or	C_2H_4
Olefiant, or heavy carburetted hydrogen gas...	C_2H_2	"	C_4H_4

451. *Light Carburetted Hydrogen Gas; Marsh Gas; Fire Damp.*—This gas occurs abundantly in nature, being formed nearly pure by the decomposition of vegetable matter under water, (marsh gas.) The bubbles which rise when the leaves and mud of a stagnant pool or lake are stirred, are light carburetted hydrogen, with some nitrogen and carbonic acid. It may be collected in such situations by means of an inverted funnel and bottle, as in figure 325. In coal mines it is copiously evolved in company with heavy carburetted hydrogen and carbonic acid, (fire damp.) In the salt region of Kanawha, it flows so abundantly from the artesian wells with the salt water, as to furnish heat enough by its combustion for evaporating the salt water. The village of Fredonia, in New York, has for many years been illuminated with this gas, derived from the saliferous deposits.

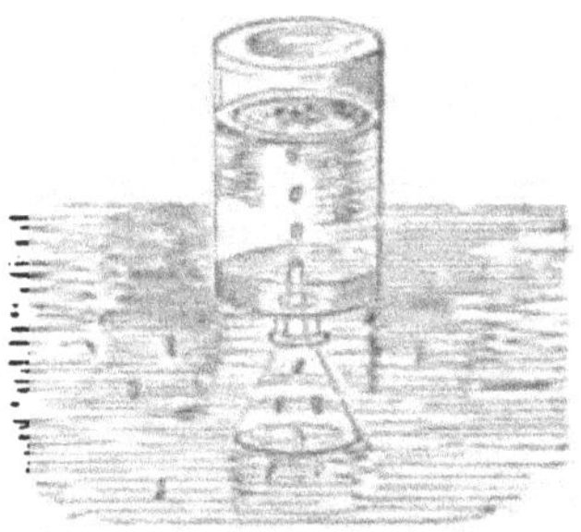

Fig. 325.

452. *Preparation.*—Marsh gas is prepared by treating equal parts of acetate of soda and solid hydrate of potash with one and a half parts of quicklime. The materials are ground separately, well mingled, and strongly heated in a retort of hard glass protected by a thin sand-bath of sheet-iron. The acetic acid $C_4H_4O_4$ of the acetate is decomposed by the potash, which removes from it 2 equivalents of carbonic acid, and marsh gas is evolved, thus:

Acetic acid......	$C_4H_4O_4$ =	Carbonic acid, 2 equivalents	C_2	O_4
		Marsh gas........................	C_2H_4	
	$C_4H_4O_4$		C_4H_4	O_4

Give their composition. 451. What is marsh gas? How may it be collected? What other natural sources are named? 452. How is it prepared? Give the reaction.

The lime preserves the glass of the retort from the action of the potash.

453. *Properties.*—Marsh gas is colorless, inodorous, slightly absorbed by water, and is respirable when mingled with common air. Its weight is about half that of air, or ·559, and 100 cubic inches weigh 17·41 grains. It burns with a yellow flame, giving as the products of combustion water and carbonic acid. Mingled with common air, it forms an explosive mixture, which collects in large quantities in the upper part of the galleries of coal-mines, giving origin to fearful explosions and the destruction of many lives of miners. Twice its volume of oxygen burns it completely. It has never been liquefied. In a tube of porcelain, at full redness, it is decomposed, carbon is deposited, and hydrogen evolved. With moist chlorine in the sunlight, it forms carbonic and chlorohydric acids, but is not affected by it in the dark. It is composed in 100 parts, of hydrogen 25, vapor of carbon 75; or by volume, of

2 volumes of hydrogen..........................	= 0·696 × 2 = 0·1392
and ½ volume of carbon vapor......................	= ·829 ÷ 2 = 0·4145
Theoretical density of marsh gas...............................	0·5537

454. *Olefiant Gas, or heavy Carburetted Hydrogen Gas.*—This gas was discovered in 1796, by an association of Dutch chemists, who gave it the name of olefiant, because it forms a peculiar oil-like body with chlorine. It is prepared by mixing strong alcohol with five or six times its weight of oil of vitriol in a capacious retort, and applying heat to the mixture. The action is complicated, and cannot be well explained at this time. The gaseous products are olefiant gas, carbonic acid, and sulphurous acid. The alcohol is

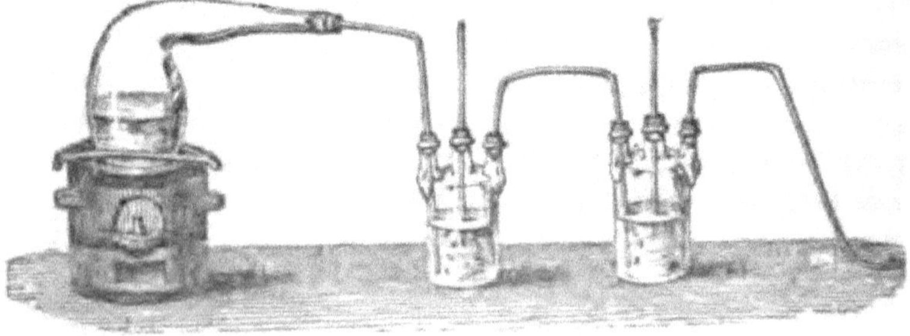

Fig. 326.

453. What are its properties? What danger arises from it in coal-mines? How is it composed by volume? 454. How is it prepared?

charred, and at the end of the operation froths up very much. The gas can be purified by passing it first through a wash-bottle containing a solution of potash, and then through oil of vitriol; the potash removes the acid vapors, and the oil of vitriol retains the ether, (fig. 326.)

455. *Properties.*—Olefiant gas is a neutral, colorless, tasteless gas, nearly inodorous, and having a density of 0·9784; 100 cubic inches of it weighing 30 57 grains. It burns with a most brilliant white light and evolves much free carbon. With three volumes of oxygen gas it burns completely, with a tremendous detonation, which is too severe even for very strong glass vessels. Bubbles of the mixture may be exploded by a burning paper, as they rise from beneath the surface of water. Water and carbonic acid are the sole products of this combustion. It is partially decomposed by passing through tubes heated to redness, and much carbon is deposited. This effect happens in the iron retorts of city gas-works, in which crusts of pure carbon, sometimes of great thickness, accumulate from the decomposition of the gas. 100 parts of olefiant gas contain 200 hydrogen and 100 vapor of carbon. Thus,

2 volumes of hydrogen weigh	0·1392	14·29
1 volume of carbon vapor	0·8290	85·71
	0·9672	100·00

Its formula is thence C_4H_4, and the experimental density (0·9784) is a near approach to the theoretical.

456. The chlorine compound will be described in the organic kingdom. It burns with chlorine, forming chlorohydric acid, and depositing its carbon in a dense cloud. Illuminating gas is formed of a union of marsh gas and of olefiant with some free hydrogen. The power of illumination is derived from the olefiant gas. Ammonia, its sulphuret, carbonic acid, tar, and resinous pyrogenic compounds require to be removed from coal gas before it is fit for use; and this is accomplished by passing it through water, cooling it in condensers, and transmitting it through dry lime purifiers, and through dilute solution of sulphate of iron to remove HS and CO_2.

The other compounds of hydrogen with boron, &c., are too little known to require description now.

---

455. What its properties? How much oxygen burns it? What are the products? How decomposed? What is its composition? 456. Whence its name? What is illuminating gas?

Combustion, and the Structure of Flame.

457. *Combustion.*—This familiar phenomenon is the disengagement of light and heat which accompanies some cases of chemical union. Nearly all our operations being performed in the atmosphere, the term combustion has come to be restricted, in a popular sense, to the union of bodies with oxygen, with development of light and heat. Thus, carbon, sulphur, phosphorus, &c., are familiar examples of elementary combustibles, while oil, tar, coal, wood, &c., are compound ones. The products of the combustion of organic bodies are all gases or vapors, and are no longer combustible; while the products of the combustion of iron, phosphorus, potassium &c., are oxyds, bases, or acids, and generally are incapable of further change from similar action. Thus, iron burns brilliantly in oxygen gas, (277,) forming a compound, capable of no further change in oxygen. Iron also burns in vapor of sulphur, (fig. 232,) but the protosulphuret of iron so formed is still capable of burning in oxygen. For such reasons as these, bodies were for a long time divided by chemists into two classes, of *combustibles* and *supporters of combustion.* This mode of arrangement is now for the most part abandoned. It was radically defective as a philosophical classification of elements, since it seized on a single phenomenon accompanying chemical union, and disregarded all those natural analogies which group the elements into distinct classes.

458. In all cases of combustion the action is reciprocal. Hydrogen burns in common air; but if a stream of oxygen is thrown into a jar of hydrogen, through a small aperture at the top, when the latter is burning, the flame is carried down into the body of the jar, and the oxygen will continue to burn in the hydrogen, as it issues from the jet. In this case the oxygen may be said to be the combustible, and the hydrogen the supporter. The simple statement in both cases is, that oxygen and hydrogen combine, and combustion—that is, the disengagement of light and heat—is the consequence. (Daniell.) The diamond burns in oxygen gas, but the latter is as much altered by the union as the former;

---

457. What is combustion? How is the term restricted? What division of elements was founded on this phenomenon? 458. What of the reciprocal nature of combustion? What of light and heat evolved?

and we cannot therefore say whether the oxygen or the carbon is the most burnt. Heat and light attend this union: but the carbon of the human body is as truly burnt in the lungs by the atmospheric oxygen, as is the fuel on our fires. The product of this combustion, the carbonic acid, thrown out by the lungs at every exhalation, is the same thing as the carbonic acid which is discharged at the mouth of a furnace. In the case of the animal body, the combustion is so slow that no light is evolved, and only that degree of heat (98° to 100°) which is essential to vitality. The term combustion must have, then, a chemical sense vastly more comprehensive than its popular meaning. The rust which slowly corrodes and destroys our strongest fixtures of iron, and the gradual process of decay which reduces all structures of wood to a black mould, are to the chemist as truly cases of combustion as those more rapid combinations with oxygen which are accompanied by the splendid evolution of light and heat.

The heat produced by combustion has received no satisfactory explanation. We know that any change of state in a body is accompanied by an alteration of temperature. When two liquids become solid, we can better understand why heat should be produced, (124.) But why the union of carbon and oxygen, or of oxygen with hydrogen, to form a gas, should evolve such intense heat as to fuse the most refractory bodies, is as yet unexplained.

459. Bodies become visible in the dark at about 1000° of heat. This fact has been lately confirmed by the researches of Draper, on the shining by heat of a strip of platinum in the dark, when heated by a current of voltaic electricity. It is true of all bodies capable of being heated, whether solids, or fluids, as melted metals. It is impossible by any means to render a gaseous body visibly red. A coil of platinum wire suspended in the current of air escaping from an argand-lamp chimney is at once heated to redness, while, as every one knows, the hot air itself is entirely invisible. Combustible gases heated to a certain point in the air, take fire and burn, as when we apply to our gas-burner the flame of a match. The color of red-hot bodies depends on the temperature. Yellow light begins to be evolved

---

What chemical extension is given to the term? Whence the heat evolved in combustion? 459. At what temperature do bodies become visible in the dark?

at about 1325°, and at 2130° all the colors of the spectrum were observed by Draper in the light viewed by a prism as it came from incandescent platinum. A full white heat, seen by day-light, is supposed to be at least 3000°. The increase of brilliancy in the light from hot bodies is at a much higher ratio than the temperature. Thus, the same observer found the brilliancy of light at 2590° more than thirty-six times as great as it was at 1900°.

Of Flame.

460. The structure and nature of flame deserve particular notice. If we look attentively at the flame of a candle, (fig. 327,) we see that it is formed of several distinct parts, wrapped, so to speak, conically about each other. 1st. There is the interior cone *a a'*, formed entirely of combustible gases, and giving no light. 2d. The cone *e f g*, which is very brilliant, and where the gaseous contents of the first portion become mingled with atmospheric oxygen; the hydrogen is burned, and the carbon, precipitated in minute particles, reflects light powerfully. And 3d. We see the thin outer envelope *c d b*, where the combustion is completed, but where there is much less brilliancy of illumination than in *e f g*. In the flame of a gas jet A, (fig. 328,) the same parts are recognized, similarly lettered, simplified by the absence of the candle-wick, whose place is occupied by the ascending stream of gas. A section of the candle-flame midway between *a a'* would give us three distinct rings, each marked by its own chemical condition. In the centre is the olefiant gas of the decomposed fat H, (fig. 329.) The hydrogen of this burns first, forming water, and the carbon is raised by the heat of the burning hydrogen to whiteness, and fills the space *c*; while, exterior it, the thin film *o* is formed from the union of the carbon with oxygen to form carbonic acid. Flame may therefore be considered as a hollow cone of ignited combustible gas, covering as with a shell

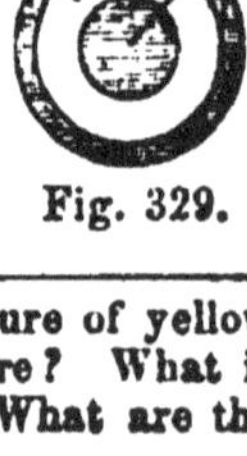

Fig. 327.

Fig. 328.

Fig. 329.

What was Draper's experiment? What is the temperature of yellow light? What the brilliancy as compared with temperature? What is noticed in the structure of flame? Describe fig. 327. What are the parts of the flame? Define flame.

an interior unignited mass of inflammable gas. This is easily demonstrated by introducing a small tube of glass *b*, fig. 330, into the cone H, by which a portion of the inflammable gas is led out and may be burnt at the open end of the tube. In like manner, by bringing a sheet of platinum foil over the flame of a large spirit-lamp, it will be heated to redness in a ring on the outer circle, while the centre remains black, showing that the interior is comparatively cold. Phosphorus fully ignited in a metallic spoon is at once extinguished by immersion in the interior of a voluminous flame, like that from alcohol, burning in a small capsule. The air is shut out by the screen of flame: the phosphorus, finding no oxygen, goes out, but may be seen fused in the spoon: bringing it again to the air, it is rekindled, and so on.

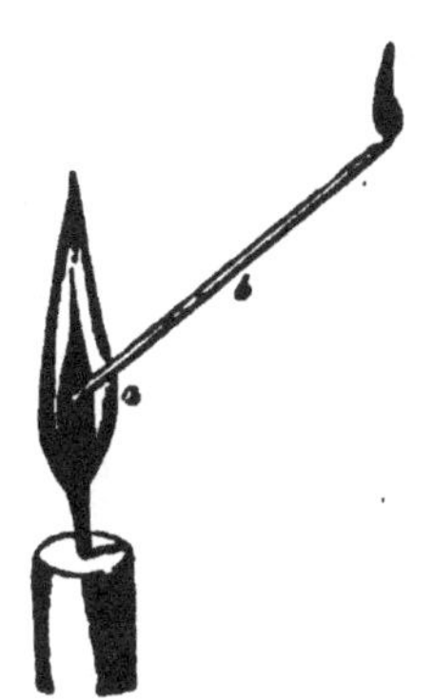

Fig. 330.

461. A high temperature, it will be easily seen, is an indispensable condition for a perfect and brilliant combustion, as the light reflected from the ignited carbon is vastly greater at 3000° than at 2500°, (459.) A plentiful supply of oxygen is of course the antecedent of a perfect combustion. The candle or lamp becomes smoky whenever these conditions are imperfectly fulfilled—as when the wick of a candle becomes too long and reduces the temperature of the flame below the point of brilliant combustion, supplying at the same time a superabundance of material. The candle must then be snuffed; or it may be provided with a flat plaited wick, as in fig. 331, which bends outward as it burns, and coming in contact with the air, consumes as fast as it protrudes. In all flames like that of the candle, when the air has contact only on one side, combustion is very imperfect. A more rapid and abundant supply of oxygen is the object in the construction of the argand and solar lamps and all similar contrivances.

Fig. 331.

462. This is accomplished in the argand burner by

How is it demonstrated by fig. 330? What other experiments are given? 461. What are the conditions of perfect combustion? Why is a candle an imperfect illumination? What is the principle of the argand burners?

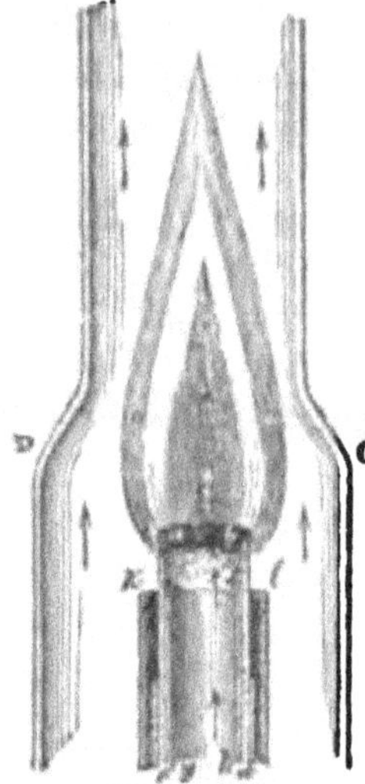

Fig. 332.

employing a circular wick *a b c d* (fig. 332) arranged between the metallic tubes through the centre of which *g h* a draft of air rises, as shown by the central arrows. The draft is made more powerful by using a glass chimney, contracted at D C so as to deflect the ascending outer current of air strongly against the flame. Thus, at the same instant, fresh supplies of oxygen are brought in contact with the inner and outer surfaces of flame, which still retains the same relation of parts as before. The heat of combustion is enormously increased by these means; and with the same amount of fuel, a much more brilliant light is produced. In the common double-current spirit-lamp, employed in the laboratory for high heats, the construction is similar, a metallic chimney replacing the glass. A section of this lamp is seen in fig. 333. Dr. C. T. Jackson has described a modification of the double-current spirit-lamp, in which a blast of air from a bellows is introduced within the inner tube. The arrangement is such that the blast issues in a narrow ring, concentric with the wick and in close contact with it. Properly managed, this lamp forms the most powerful lamp-furnace in use. The invention in fact applies the principle of the mouth blowpipe to the argand lamp.

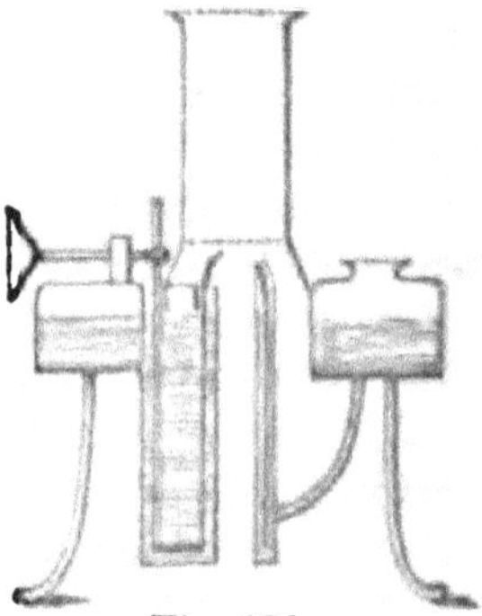

Fig. 333.

Fig. 334.

In places where gas is used, the gas-lamp, (fig. 334,) fed by a flexible pipe and supplied with a metallic or mica chimney, leaves nothing to be desired for a powerful and economical

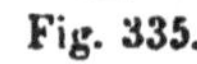

Fig. 335.

Describe fig. 332. Why is the heat increased? What is Jackson's lamp? What the gas-lamps?

heat. A small glass spirit-lamp, with a close cover, (fig. 335,) to prevent evaporation, is an indispensable convenience in even the humblest laboratory.

463. *The Mouth Blowpipe* (fig. 336) converts the flame of a common lamp or candle into a powerful furnace. By the blast from the jet of the blowpipe, the operator turns the

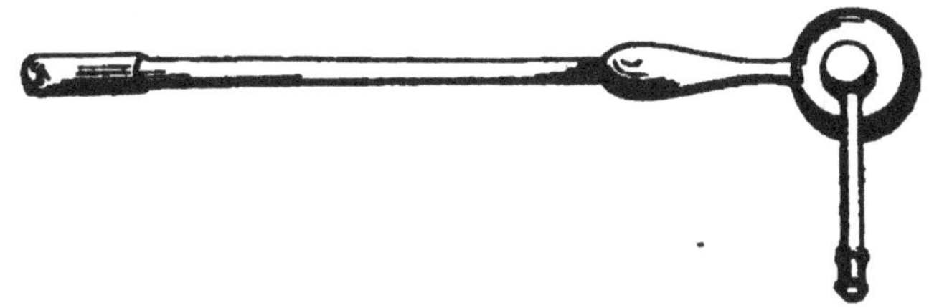

Fig. 336.

flame in a horizontal direction upon the object of experiment, at the same time that he supplies to the interior cone of combustible matter a further quantity of oxygen. The flame suffers a remarkable change of appearance as soon as the blast strikes it, and the inner blue point *b* has very different chemical effects from the exterior or yellow point *c*, (fig. 337.) Immediately before the exterior flame is a stream of intensely heated air, which is capable of powerfully oxydizing a body held in it, and this point is therefore called the *oxydizing flame*. The inner or blue point *b a* is called the reducing flame, and in it all metallic oxyds capable of reduction are easily brought to the metallic state or to a lower degree of oxydation. Between the outer and inner flames is a point of most intense heat, where refractory bodies are easily melted. Charcoal is generally employed to support bodies before the blowpipe flame, when we would heat them in contact with carbon. Forceps of platinum are used to hold the substance when it is to be heated alone.

Fig. 337.

If the substance is to be submitted to the action of borax,

---

463. What is the principle of the mouth blow pipe? What parts are noted in the flame before the jet, fig. 337? What is the reducing and what the oxydizing flame?

Fig. 338.

or of carbonate of soda, or any similar reagent, a small platinum wire, bent into a loop at one end, is used to hold the fused globule, as seen in fig. 338. Then, by varying its position in the flame as above described, we may submit it successively to the reducing agency of carbon vapor, and oxyd of carbon at *b*, to the intense heat of burning carbon at *c*, or to the powerful oxydizing influence of the current of hot air immediately in front of the point *c*. The art of blowing an unintermitting stream is soon acquired, by breathing at the same time through the mouth and nostrils; and an experienced operator will blow a long time without fatigue. No instrument is more useful to the chemist and mineralogist than the mouth blowpipe. By its means we may in a few moments submit a body to all the changes of heat, or the action of reagents, which can be accomplished with a powerful furnace.

Safety Lamp.

464. The temperature of flame may be so reduced by bringing cold metallic bodies near it as to be extinguished. Davy also observed that a mixture of explosive gases, could not be fired through a long narrow orifice like a small tube. On these simple facts rests the power of the "safety lamp" of Sir Humphry Davy to protect the life of the miner. If a narrow coil of copper wire, (fig. 339,) be brought over a candle or lamp so as to encircle it, the flame will be extinguished; but if the wire be previously heated to redness, the flame continues to burn. The same effect will be produced by a small metallic tube. A wire held in the flame is seen to be surrounded with a ring of non-luminous matter. If many wires, in the form of a gauze, are brought near the flame of a candle, it will be cut off and extinguished above; only a current of heated air and smoke will be seen ascending, (fig. 340,) while the flame continues to burn beneath, and heats the wire gauze red-hot in a ring, marking the limits of the flame. The flame may be relighted

Fig. 339.

---

464. What is the effect of a cold body on flame? What was Davy's observation?

above the gauze, and will then burn as usual, as seen in fig. 341. Sir Humphry Davy found that a wire gauze would in all cases arrest the progress of flame, and that a mixture of explosive gases could not be fired through it. A wire gauze is only a series of very short square tubes, and their power to arrest flame comes from the fact that they cool the gases below their point of ignition. Happily, the heat required to ignite the carbon gases is much higher than that which causes the union of oxygen and hydrogen.

Fig. 340. Fig. 341.

465. The *fire damp* or explosive atmosphere of coal-mines, is a mixture of light and heavy carburetted hydrogen, with many times their volume of common air. These gases, being lighter than the air, are found especially in the upper part of the galleries of mines, and when the naked flame of the miner's lamp meets such an atmosphere, a terrible explosion often follows. These explosions in coal-mines have destroyed thousands of those whose duties required them to submit to the exposure. To avoid these lamentable accidents, Davy invented the safety lamp. This is only a common lamp surrounded by a cage of wire gauze, completely enclosing the flame, (fig. 342.) When this lamp is placed in an explosive atmosphere, the gas enters the cage, enlarges the flame on the wick, and burns quietly, the gauze effectually preventing the passage of the flame outward. We thus enter the camp of the enemy, disarm him, and make him labor for us. The miner is not only protected by this instrument, but is rendered conscious of the danger by the enlargement of the flame. As long as the lamp can burn, it is safe to stay, as an irrespirable atmosphere would extinguish the flame. The powerful blast of wind which sometimes sweeps

Fig. 342.

Explain figs. 340 and 341. What is the application? What peculiarity is noticed of the carbohydrogen gases? 465. What is the fire damp? Where does it chiefly collect? How was Davy's lamp constructed? What is its action?

through the mines may render the lamp unsafe, by forcing the flame against the gauze, until it is heated so hot as to inflame the external atmosphere. This accident is prevented by the addition of a glass to cover the sides, the air being admitted from below through flat gauze discs.

II. METALLIC ELEMENTS.

General Properties of Metals.

466. The number of the metals is forty-eight, of which about half are entirely unknown, except in the laboratory, and as the rarest minerals in our cabinets. Of the other half, only fourteen or fifteen are familiarly known, or possess in a remarkable degree those qualities of ductility, lustre, and malleability, which are inseparable from our common notions of the metallic character.

A metal is an opaque body, of a peculiar brilliancy, described as the metallic lustre. It conducts heat and electricity, and in electrolysis it goes to the negative pole of the voltaic battery, and is therefore an electro-positive body. These are the chief characters peculiar to the class.

Metallic Veins.

467. In nature, the metals exist commonly in union with sulphur, oxygen, and arsenic. A few, as gold, copper, platinum, and mercury, are found *native*, or uncombined, or are occasionally alloyed with each other, as native gold nearly always contains a portion of silver. When the metals are combined with sulphur, or other mineralizing agents, by which their proper metallic characters are masked or concealed, they are called *ores*. The native metals, gold, copper, platinum, &c., are not properly denominated ores, being obtained in a metallic state from the sands. The discovery and extraction of the ores of the metals constitutes the art of *mining*. The separation of the metals from their ores, by heat or other means, is a separate branch of chemical art, known as *metallurgy*. Mining demands a minute knowledge of the mineralogical character of the ores of metals and of

---

466. What is the number of metals? How many are commonly known? What is a metal? 467. How do the metals exist in nature? What are ores? What is mining? What is metallurgy? What does mining require?

the earthy minerals with which these are associated; as well as the mode of occurrence of mineral veins and ore beds, and the mechanical methods adopted for the raising of the ores from the earth, their separation from foreign substances, and their preparation for market.

468. The ores of metals are seldom scattered through the rocks in a diffused manner, but are usually collected in veins or *lodes*, accompanied by quartz, carbonate of lime, and various other minerals, called the *vein-stone*, or *gangue*. The metal-bearing veins occur more frequently in regions where primitive rocks abound, as in granite and its associates. Often, however, they extend from these rocks to those which rest above them, and are stratified; showing that the veins fill fissures in the earth, occasioned by the cooling of its heated mass, and into which the minerals now filling them came by injection or infiltration. These fissures usually occur together, in a degree of order, the veins being more or less parallel, as seen in *c*, *c*, *c*, &c., (fig. 343,) which is an ideal section of a metallic deposit, (the veins are here seen to reach from the granite *c* to the stratified rocks *a*, *a*.) Cross veins, or courses, often intersect in a different direction, as *d*, *e*, &c, and these have usually a mineral character entirely distinct, and showing a different age and origin. At the intersection of veins there is usually an enlargement of the lode, and often a more abundant deposit of the metallic ore. It is very rare, if ever, that the metallic ore fills the vein entirely. It usually forms small threads running through the vein-stone, now expanding, and again contracting, as seen in the vertical section of a vein in fig. 344, where *a*, *b*, *c* show the rocky gangue surrounding

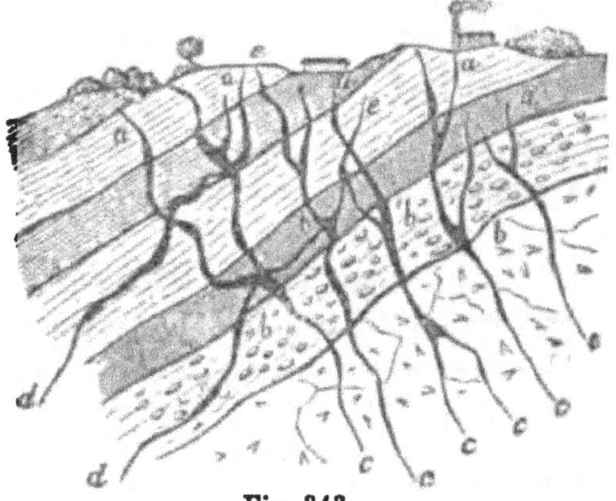

Fig. 343.

---

468. How are ores found? What is a vein-stone or gangue? Where do veins most frequently occur? Describe fig. 343. Where are veins enlarged? How is the ore usually distributed in mineral veins?

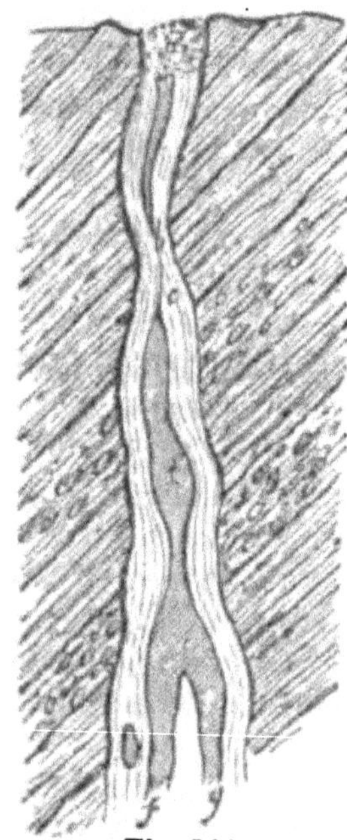

Fig. 344.

the metallic ore *d*, *e*, *f*, *g*. Often the ore dies out entirely, as at *b*, *c*, and is again renewed farther on. A few minerals only are found in beds regularly stratified between layers of other rocks. Some of the ores of iron are so found, as well as coal and rock-salt. But the mode of origin of these last is quite distinct from that of the ores of the metals. Fig. 345 shows the mode of occurrence

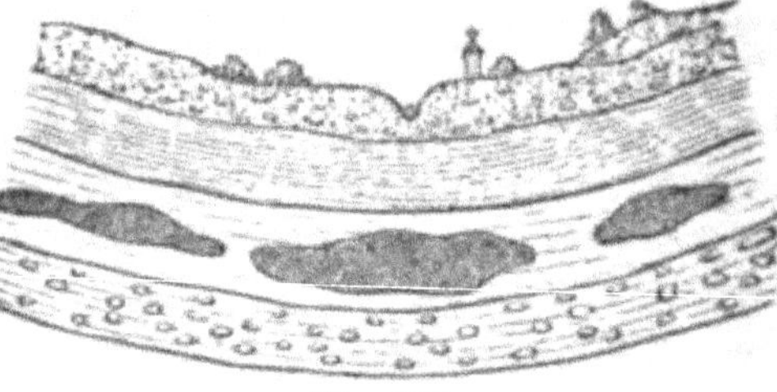

Fig. 345.

of rock-salt in masses, filling cavities formed probably by the solution of minerals previously existing there.

Physical Properties of Metals.

469. The physical properties of the metals include their density, lustre, color, opacity, malleability, ductility, laminability, tenacity, crystallization, fusibility, and conducting power. In *density*, metals present every variety, from potassium (·865) and sodium, (·972,) floating on water, to gold (19·26) and platina, (21·5,) the heaviest bodies known. In *lustre* they range from the splendor of gold and of burnished silver, to the dulness of manganese and of chromium. This property often depends on the mechanical condition of the metal; thus, gold and platinum, as thrown down from solution in fine powder, are dull yellowish-brown, and black powders, which show the lustre and color appropriate to the metals only under the burnisher. The *color* of most of the metals is dull white or gray. Silver is nearly pure white; gold, yel-

---

Describe fig. 344. What substances are found in beds? What is shown in fig. 345? 469. What are the physical properties of metals? What of density? What of lustre? How do mechanical conditions affect lustre?

low; and copper and titanium are red. Copper is the basis of all colored alloys; being fused with tin and zinc to form bell and gun metal and yellow brass. To determine the color of a polished metal accurately, the light must be reflected many times from its surface, as may be done by placing two polished surfaces of the same metal opposite each other, and examining with a prism the light reflected at an angle of 90° from them. In this way it is found that the proper color of copper is orange-red; of gold, after ten reflections, a beautiful red; of silver, a reddish-white; of zinc, a delicate indigo-blue; of bronze, an intense red; of steel, a feeble violet, &c. In looking into a deep vase of polished metal, or into a highly polished bronze cannon, or the bore of a new steel rifle, these tints of color by reflection are seen. *Opacity* is not absolute in metals, as is proved in the case of gold-leaf on glass, through which a beautiful violet-green light is seen. This light is found by optical experiments to be truly transmitted light, and not a color caused by the minute fissures of the gold-leaf. It is worthy of remark that this greenish color is complementary to the red, which is the reflected color of the gold.

470. *Malleability*, or the capability of being beaten by blows into thin leaves, is found in the highest perfection in gold, and in a good degree in many other metals. Some metals are perfectly malleable when cold, as silver, gold, lead, and tin; others are malleable when hot, as iron, platinum, &c., and are not without this property, though in a much less degree, even when cold. Some, like zinc, are laminable at a moderate heat, but brittle above and below it; others, like antimony, are brittle at all temperatures short of fusion. Gold leaf has been beaten so thin as to require 250,000 leaves to equal one inch in thickness, or 1,365 such leaves would about equal in thickness one leaf of this book. Ductility and laminability are properties closely allied to malleability. Iron, for instance, unless heated, can not be beaten like gold, but it may be drawn into fine wire, (ductility,) and plated by rollers into thin sheets, (laminability).

What of color? Enumerate colored metals and alloys? How are metallic colors accurately determined? What are thus found to be the colors of gold, of copper, of silver, zinc, and bronze? Is opacity absolute? Why not? What is proved of the green color of gold? To what is it complementary? 470. What of malleability, ductility &c.?

Metals are rolled in a machine composed of two equal cylinders of iron or steel, seen in section in fig. 346. These move in the direction shown by the arrows. During this process, the metal becomes more hard and elastic, owing to a rearrangement of its particles. Heated to a redness and slowly cooled, it is again softened, and is then said to be *annealed*. Copper is annealed by plunging the red-hot metal into water, while the same treatment renders steel intensely hard.

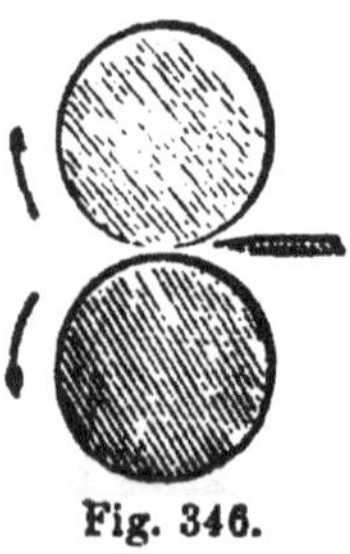

Fig. 346.

471. *The tenacity of metals* is compared by using wires of the same size of different metals, and ascertaining how much weight they will sustain. Iron is the most tenacious, and lead the least. The tenacity of wires $\frac{7}{100}$ of an inch in diameter is equal,

For Iron, to	444 pounds.	For Zinc, to	100 pounds.
" Copper	300 "	" Nickel	97 "
" Platinum	275 "	" Tin	32 "
" Silver	171 "	" Lead	24 "
" Gold	137 "		

Wires are drawn through smooth conical holes in a steel plate, (fig. 347,) each succeeding hole being a little less than its predecessor. In this way, wires of extreme fineness may be drawn from several of the ductile metals. Dr. Wollaston succeeded, by a peculiar method, in making a gold wire so small that 530 feet of it weighed only one grain; it was only $\frac{1}{5000}$ of an inch in diameter; and a platinum wire was made by the same philosopher, of not more than $\frac{1}{30000}$ of an inch. Metals passed repeatedly through a wire plate, also become stiff and brittle, as in the rolling mill.

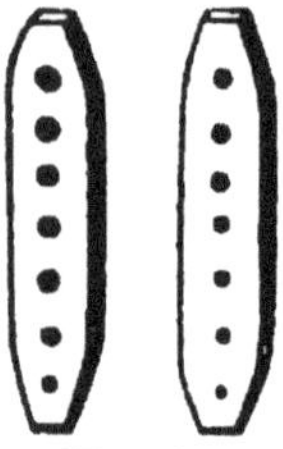

Fig. 347.

472. Many metals crystallize beautifully, from fusion, when slowly cooled, as described for sulphur, (306;) bismuth offers the most remarkable example of this: others solidify without crystallization, or the traces of crystalline structure are seen only feebly marked by lines on the surface. Copper, gold,

---

How are metals rolled? What is annealing? 471. How is tenacity shown? Give examples. How is air formed? 472. What of crystallization?

silver, platina, and some other metals are found crystallized in nature. We can also imitate nature in this respect by the voltaic battery, which enables us to procure many metals in perfect crystals. Iron, brass, and other metals often take on a crystalline structure by vibration materially influencing their tenacity. The fusion points of several metals were given in § 121.

Many metals are volatile, of which mercury, arsenic, tellurium, cadmium, zinc, potassium, and sodium are examples, being volatile below a red-heat. Even gold, silver, and platinum are raised in vapor by the heat of the voltaic focus, (198)

Some metals assume a semi-fluid or pasty condition before melting, such as platinum and iron, both of which can be welded or made to unite without solder, when in this soft state; lead, potassium, and sodium can be welded in the cold, as also can mercury, when it is frozen. The conducting power of some of the principal metals was given in § 88, and their capacity for heat in § 120.

473. The metals unite with each other to form *alloys*, many of which are familiarly known, as ⅔ copper and ⅓ zinc to form brass. Tin and copper form very various alloys, according to the proportions employed: 90 copper and 10 tin form speculum metal, which is as brittle as glass and almost white. The alloys of mercury with other metals are called *amalgams.* The fusibility of alloys is often greater than that of the constituent metals. Newton's fusible metal, an alloy of 5 parts lead, 3 of tin, and 8 of bismuth, is an example of this fact. Lead fuses at 617°, bismuth at 509°, and tin at 442°, while Newton's alloy fuses at 203°.

Chemical Relations of the Metals.

474. The metals, as already stated, are positive electrics. Their affinity for oxygen is universal, but various in degree. Sodium, potassium, magnesium, and generally the metallic bases of the alkalies and earths, have such an avidity for oxygen, that they pass at once to the condition of oxyds on contact with air. Iron, zinc, copper, &c., are very slowly

---

How produced by art? What metals are volatile? What is welding? 473. What are alloys? What are amalgams? What of Newton's metal? 474. What are the chemical relations of the metals?

oxydized, and are soon covered by a coat of oxyd, which protects the metal from further action. Gold, platinum, and silver, on the contrary, resist the action of oxygen perfectly, and are called, from their unalterable nature, noble metals.

The metallic oxyds may be divided into three classes:—

1. *Basic oxyds*, which include the protoxyds generally, as potash, soda, lime, and protoxyd of iron. Basic oxyds unite readily with acids to form crystallizable salts. Their formula is RO.

2 *Acid oxyds*, which themselves form salts with powerful bases, and rarely, if ever, combine with other acids. Chromic acid CrO_3, manganic acid MnO_3, and other metallic acids are examples. Their usual formula is RO_2 or RO_3.

3. *Neutral* or *indifferent oxyds*, which, like alumina Al_2O_3, may form salts with either powerful acids, or energetic bases. Their formula is R_2O_3.

475. Besides these there are oxyds which unite neither with acids nor bases without change, and others which seem themselves to be true salts. Of the first the common peroxyd of manganese is an example, MnO_2. Heated with sulphuric acid it is decomposed, oxygen is evolved, (276,) and sulphate of protoxyd of manganese is formed, $MnO.SO_3$. Suboxyd of lead Pb_2O in contact with acids is also transformed into metallic lead and protoxyd of lead.

Of the saline oxyds we have examples in the oxyds of manganese, iron, and chromium, whose general formula is R_3O_4. In these compounds two oxyds of the same metal form, as it were, respectively, acid and base, and we may write their formulæ $RO.R_2O_3$. Magnetic iron is an instance.

Certain metals form a great number of compounds with oxygen, as iron, manganese, and chromium, whose oxyds may be represented by the general formulæ—

$R\ O$ the protoxyd, forming a powerful base.
R_2O_3 (sesquioxyd,) a feeble base, or neutral, but acting not as an acid.
$R\ O_2$ the binoxyd, neither base nor acid, but decomposed by acids.
R_3O_4 a saline compound, whose true constitution is $RO.R_2O_3$.
$R\ O_3$ a metallic acid; and also
R_2O_7 a hyper-acid.

What their affinity for oxygen? How are the oxyds divided? What are basic? What acid? What neutral? Give their general formulas. What other two classes are named? Give an example of the first. 475. Give examples of saline oxyds. Give the general formulæ for the oxyds of iron, manganese, and chromium.

Other metals, as arsenic and antimony, have no protoxyds and form only strong acids with oxygen, by which feature they strongly resemble some of the metalloids.

476. The chlorids, bromids, iodids, sulphurets, &c. of the metals bear a very striking analogy in composition to the oxyds of the same metals. So true is this, that knowing what oxyds a given metal forms, we can almost certainly tell what the composition of its sulphurets, chlorids, &c. will be. Thus the oxyds of iron being FeO and FeO_2O_3, we find that the sulphurets of the same metal are FeS and Fe_2S_3, and the chlorids $FeCl$ and Fe_2Cl_3. It might be inferred from this statement that where these metallic bodies unite with acids to form salts, there would be the same conformity among *them* that is found among their bases, and such we find to be the fact.

Salts.

477. A salt, as usually understood, is a compound formed by the union of two binary compounds, which stand to each other as electro-positive and electro-negative, or as base and acid. The bases result always from the union of a metal with a metalloid; the acids usually are derived from the union of two metalloids. For example, sulphate of soda contains for base, soda (NaO,) formed from the metal sodium and the metalloid oxygen, while the sulphuric acid results from the union of the two metalloids, oxygen and sulphur. The salts of metallic acids, as just explained, (475,) constitute an exception, as the metal is present alike in acid and base.

478. Salts are formed only between members of the same class, that is oxygen acids unite with oxygen bases, chlorine acids with chlorine bases, sulphids with sulphids, &c., as sulphuric acid with oxyd of iron to form sulphate of protoxyd of iron.

On the other hand, compounds belonging to different series, either do not unite at all, or they mutually decompose each other. Thus, sulphuric acid cannot unite with sulphuret of potassium, a sulphur base, but mutual decomposition occurs, sulphydric acid escapes, and sulphid of potassium is formed.

What metals have no protoxyds? To what are these affined? 476. What analogy have the chlorids, bromids, &c. of the metals? 477 What is a salt? How are bases formed? How the acids? Give an example. What are exceptions? 478. Between what are salts formed? How do compounds of different classes act together? Give examples.

Or if chlorohydric acid and oxyd of potassium are brought together, chlorid of potassium and water result; thus, $KO + HCl = HO + KCl$.

479. Neutral salts are formed, when there are as many equivalents of acid engaged, as there are of oxygen in the base itself. Thus, potash KO has one equivalent of oxygen and demands, to form neutral sulphate of potash ($KO.SO_3$) one equivalent of sulphuric acid. But one equivalent of SO_3 contains three times as much oxygen as there is in the base, and this is true of all the neutral sulphates. The nitrate of potash contains five atoms of oxygen in the acid to one in the base, and so on.

The same is true also of those acids which contain no oxygen, as the chlorohydric, provided the metallic oxyd dissolves in chlorohydric acid without the evolution of chlorine. For example, peroxyd of iron dissolved in chlorohydric acid produces water and a perchlorid of iron: 3HCl and Fe_2O_3 giving rise to 3HO and Fe_2Cl_3.

480. The binary compounds of chlorine, iodine, &c., with many of the metals, particularly those of the alkaline class, have in an eminent degree the properties of salts. Among them we recognize particularly, the chlorid of sodium, or common salt, which is, so to speak, the parent of all salts. If the definition of a salt, just given, (477,) be rigidly enforced, these bodies cannot be called salts, since, according to that view, a salt is a compound of two binary compounds, forming a quaternary compound, (245.) To avoid this difficulty, two classes of salts have been instituted, the first of which includes all those binary compounds which, like common salt, have a metallic base in direct union with a *salt-radical;* and the second includes those salts which, like sulphate of soda, are supposed to be constituted of the oxyd of the metal and of an oxygen acid. The first have been called the *haloid* salts,* and the second the *oxy-salts.*

---

479. How are neutral salts formed? What of sulphate of potash? What is the oxygen ratio in the sulphates? How in case of chlorohydric acid? 480. What is said of binary compounds of chlorine, &c., with metals? What of common salt? What two classes of salts are named? What is meant by salt-radical? What by haloid salts?

---

* From *hals,* sea-salt, and *eidos,* in the likeness of.

The term salt-radical includes all the members of the oxygen group except oxygen itself, and also those compound bodies which, like cyanogen, act the part of elements.

481. In stating the constitution of sulphuric acid, (320,) it will be remembered that the expression SO_4+H was stated, in the view of some chemists, to be equivalent to the common formula SO_3+HO. It is claimed that all the hydrated acids are in reality compounds of hydrogen with a similar radical, and accordingly nitric acid will be NO_6+H, or corresponding to chlorohydric acid ClH. One principal objection to this view is, that these hypothetical radicals have in general never been isolated. It is, however, true that those acids which are capable of existing dry and in a separate state, as sulphuric, (SO_3,) phosphoric, (PO_5,) nitric, (NO_5,) and carbonic, (CO_2,) *are not acids* as long as they remain dry; and although they form compounds with dry ammonia, that these compounds are not salts. Sir Humphry Davy long ago suggested that hydrogen was the real acidifying principle in all acids.

482. If the salt-radical theory is finally adopted, all acids must be considered as hydrogen acids, and all salts as haloid salts. For example, let us take two common saline bodies and present them according to these two views.

	Old view.	New view.
Sulphate of zinc	$ZnO + SO_3$	$Zn + SO_4$
Nitrate of soda	$NaO + NO_5$	$Na + NO_6$

According to the new view, when an acid dissolves a metal, there is no necessity for supposing water to be decomposed. The metal takes the place of the hydrogen, and the latter is given off in a gaseous form; or if the oxyd of the metal is used, the oxygen and hydrogen unite to form water, and no effervescence ensues.

The apparent simplicity of this view renders it attractive, and it has been most warmly supported by Profs. Graham and Liebig, while in this country it has found an able opponent in Dr. Hare.

---

481. What is said of the formula of SO_3? What view of acids is suggested? What objection is urged? What is true of dry SO_3 &c. Who formerly proposed this view? 482. What will be the constitution of salts in the new view? How does a metal then enter into a salt? Who support and who opposes this view?

The nomenclature of the salts has already been explained, (251 :) we shall consider the more interesting salts under each metal.

The order in which the metallic bodies are discussed in the following pages, is not very different from that usually adopted in elementary works.

CLASS I. METALS OF THE ALKALIES.

POTASSIUM.

Equivalent, 39·2. *Symbol*, K (*Kalium.*) *Density*, ·865.

483. *History.*—Potassium was discovered by Sir Humphry Davy in 1807; at the same time with its congeners, sodium, barium, strontium, and calcium. Before that time, the alkalies and alkaline earths were looked upon as simple elementary bodies, and were so treated in all chemical works. Davy found, on passing the electric current from a powerful voltaic battery through a cake of moistened potash, (oxyd of potassium,) both electrodes being of platinum, that violent action followed; oxygen was evolved with effervescence at the positive pole, and bright metallic globules, like mercury, appeared at the negative pole, accompanied by hydrogen gas. Some of these globules flashed and burned with a violet light as they reached the air, while others remained, and were soon covered with a white film that formed on their surfaces. These globules were the metal potassium, whose discovery constitutes one of the most interesting chapters in chemical history.

Potassium in combination, chiefly as silicate of potash, is widely diffused over the globe. It forms a part of all fertile soils. The chief source from which it is procured is the ashes of hard-wooded forest-trees, which take it up from soils on which they grow. It is also present in sea-water, as chlorid of potassium, and is consequently found in the ashes of sea-plants.

484. *Preparation.*—The expensive and troublesome method of procuring this metal by galvanism, has been

---

What is the nomenclature of the salts? 483. What is the symbol and equivalent of potassium? When, and by whom, and how was it discovered? How is this metal distributed in nature? 484. How is potassium prepared?

replaced by a much more convenient and productive furnace operation, founded on the decomposition of potash at a white heat by charcoal. For this purpose carbonate of potash is mingled with charcoal. This mixture is best prepared by ignited cream of tartar in a covered crucible; a black mass is then obtained commonly known as *black flux*, consisting of carbonate of potassa in intimate mixture with charcoal derived from the burning of the organic acid. This mass is finely powdered, and $\frac{1}{10}$ of charcoal in small fragments is added. The mixture is then placed in an iron bottle V (fig. 348) laid horizontally in the furnace M G C.

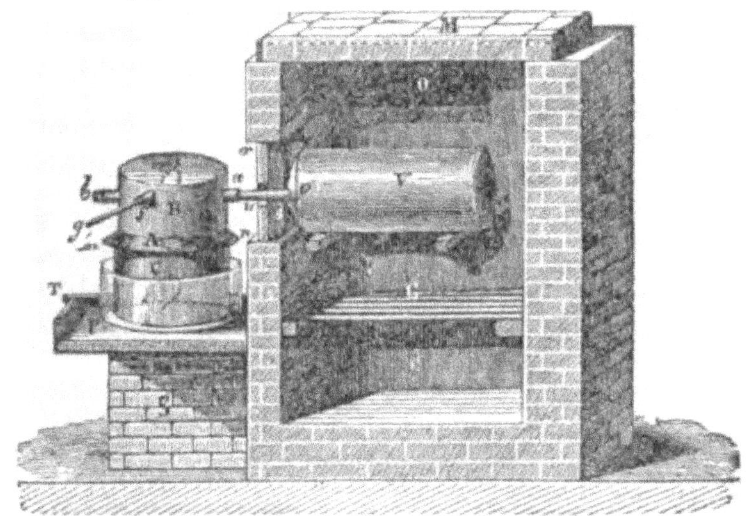

Fig. 348.

The bottle should be about ⅔ full, and well protected with a refractory lute of 5 parts fine sand and one part fire-clay, laid on moist, and well dried in the sun. The cover of the furnace M admits the fuel, the draft O is regulated by a damper, and a temporary front *r n* closes the side-opening. A short iron tube *a o* connects the retort with a copper condensing chamber A B C containing naphtha, and supported on T P S. The heat is gradually raised to the most intense whiteness. Decomposition of the carbonate of potash ensues, the free carbon takes the oxygen of the carbonate, carbonic oxyd (CO) is evolved, and the potassium distils

---

Describe fig. 348. What is the reaction? Where does the potassium collect?

over in metallic globules, which condense in the receiver A. This copper vessel is constructed of two parts B C, as seen in fig. 349. The upper B enters C, in which the naphtha is placed. A vertical partition *c d* divides B into two chambers, and two openings *a b* opposite each other correspond to the iron tube *a o*, (fig. 348:) the partition is also pierced in the same line. The outer opening *b* is closed by a cork, and a glass tube *g* is adapted to the opening *f*, (fig. 348,) by which the oxyd of carbon escapes. This condenser is kept cold by a constant stream of cold water directed on its surface, and the collar *m n* prevents this from entering the lower vase *c*.

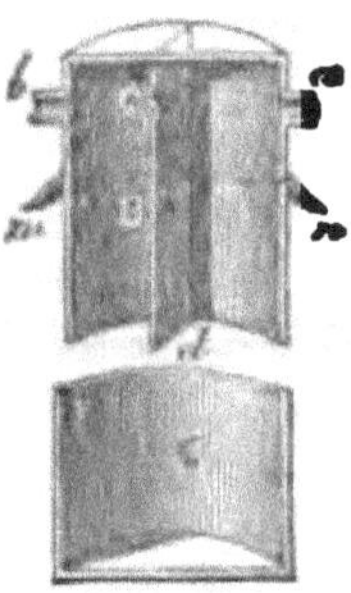

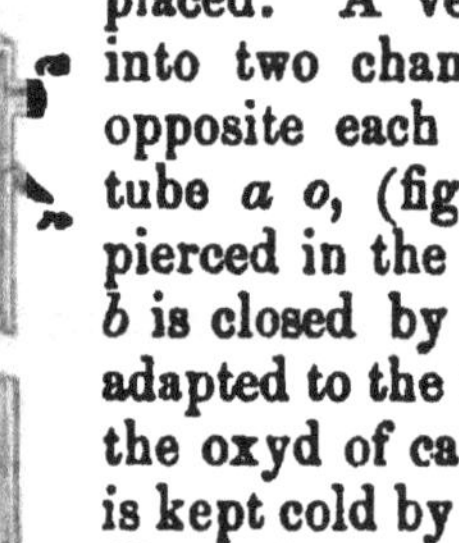

Fig. 349.

The tube *a o* is very likely to become stopped in the process by carbon, and, to avoid this accident, the iron rod, (fig. 350,) moistened in naphtha, is introduced at *b* from time to time to clear it. The potassium collects in irregular masses in C, contaminated with carbon and other impurities, from which it is freed by a second distillation in an iron retort with a little naphtha, by which means it is obtained quite pure.

Fig. 350.

Naphtha is employed in this process because it contains no oxygen, and does not suffer any change from the action of the potassium, which is always preserved beneath its surface and out of contact of air.

485. *Properties.*—Potassium, when unoxydized, is a white metal with a bluish shade and eminently brilliant. The dull masses found in commerce show these metallic characters on the fresh-cut surface; but the proper color and brilliancy disappear in the air, which instantly tarnishes it. Exposed to the air it is gradually converted into a white, brittle mass, (potash.) Fused under naphtha, its metallic lustre and color are beautifully seen; and a small quantity may thus be forced between two test tubes, fitting closely the one within the other, so as to exhibit an extended white or bluish-white metallic surface, that may be preserved indefinitely under naphtha. At 32° it is brittle and crystalline, at 60° soft and yielding to the fingers, between which it may be moulded and welded.

Describe fig. 349. What precautions are required? Why is naphtha used? 485. What are its properties? How is its metallic lustre seen?

Heated in air it takes fire and burns with a violet-colored flame. At 151° it melts, and below redness it may be distilled unchanged in vessels free from oxygen.

Its density is only ·865, being the lightest metal known. Consequently it floats on water, which it instantly decomposes; appropriating its oxygen to form oxyd of potassium, while the liberated hydrogen burns, with a portion of the volatilized metal, with a beautiful violet-colored flame. If this experiment is conducted on a vase of water reddened by a vegetable color, (fig. 351,) the alkali produced changes this color to blue or green. The heat produced in this experiment is sufficient to fuse the potassium, which assumes immediately a spherical form and brilliant lustre, and is rapidly driven over the surface of the water by the steam and vapors produced about it, forming altogether one of the most pleasing and instructive of chemical experiments. If the quantity of potassium exceeds a few grains, the heat produced by its action with the water causes an explosion, projecting the burning metal in all directions. An irritating cloud fills the air, which is a portion of the alkali (potash) volatilized by the heat.

Fig. 351.

486. The *uses* of potassium are confined to the laboratory, where, from its energetic affinity for oxygen, it is a powerful means of research. By its means we are able to decompose the oxyds of aluminum, glucinum, yttrium, thorium, magnesium, and zirconium, and to obtain the metallic bases of these compounds. By it also, as before stated, (379,) we obtain boron and silicon from boracic and silicic acids.

Compounds of Potassium.

Potassium unites with all the members of the first three classes, forming compounds, several of which are of great importance in the arts and in pharmacy: of these we can describe only a few of the most important.

487. There are two *oxyds of potassium*, the protoxyd KO and the peroxyd KO_3. When potassium is heated in a current of dry oxygen it takes fire, burns, and leaves a yellowish residue, which is the *peroxyd of potassium*. This substance

---

What is its density? How does it act on water? What causes the motion? 486. What are its uses? 487. Name the oxyds of potassium.

dissolves in water, with the escape of two equivalents of oxygen, and forms hydrate of potash-solution, KO.HO. Heated with twice its own weight of potassium in an atmosphere of dry nitrogen, it forms dry oxyd of potassium, thus $KO_3+2K=3KO$. This important compound demands our attention.

488. The *oxyd of potassium* KO is a powerful base, and forms a large class of salts. With water it forms two distinct hydrates, KO.HO and KO.5HO, true salts, of which *caustic* potash KO.HO, the monohydrate, is the one chiefly interesting. This substance is procured usually by decomposing pure carbonate of potash, dissolved in 10 parts of water, in a clean iron vessel, with half its weight of good quicklime, previously slaked and mingled with so much water as to form a thin paste, called milk of lime. This is added in small portions to the potash solution, while the latter is boiling, a short interval allowed between each addition; all the lime being added, the whole is boiled for a few minutes, and then is removed from the fire and covered up. The lime displaces the carbonic acid, forming carbonate of lime and caustic potash. Care is needed to keep the solution dilute, to prevent the caustic potash formed from decomposing the resulting carbonate of lime. The success of the operation is determined by testing a small portion of the clear fluid with chlorohydric acid, which should occasion no, or only a feeble, effervescence.

The clear dilute solution is drawn off by a siphon, boiled away rapidly, (to prevent absorption of CO_2 from the air,) to an oily consistency in a clean iron or silver vessel, and finally carried to low redness. The carbonate of potash, if any remains, then floats as a scum, being less fusible than the caustic, and may be skimmed off. The fused caustic, turned out on a plate of copper or iron, hardens into a white crystalline cake, which is at once broken up and put in close bottles. To insure its purity from sulphates and chlorids, (often present in the original carbonate,) it is dissolved in absolute alcohol, which leaves the other salts undissolved. The alcoholic solution is decanted, distilled in a retort, and evaporated in a silver capsule, fused and cast as before. No degree of heat will expel the equivalent of water which

---

How are they obtained? 488. What of KO? What is KO.HO? How procured? What the reaction? How freed from sulphates, &c.?

this hydrate retains. Pure caustic potassa is also obtained by decomposing sulphate of potash solution by exactly as much oxyd of barium as is required to saturate it. The reaction is $KO.SO_3+BaO.HO=BaO.SO_3+KO.HO$.

489. The hydrate of potash is a white solid, with a crystalline fracture. It has a great avidity for moisture and is soluble in half its weight of water. Exposed, it forms a solution in the moisture of the atmosphere. It is a most powerful base, decomposing by fusion the silicates of nearly all metallic oxyds. Cast in cylinders, it forms the caustic potassa of surgeons, for which use the mixture of caustic and carbonate of lime with potassa is commonly employed in pharmacy, under the name of *potassa cum calce;* and the crude potash of commerce, cast in cylinders of a brown color, are sold under the name of *lapis infernalis.*

The *solution of caustic potash* is intensely alkaline, saturates the most powerful acids, restores the colors of reddened vegetable blues, and turns many of them green. It has an acrid and most disgusting taste, peculiar to alkalies, and, when strong, attacks all organic matters, dissolving and disorganizing them, feeling for this reason soapy to the fingers on first contact with the solution. With the fats it forms soaps, true salts, produced between the fatty acids and the alkaline base. It dissolves silica in its soluble form, (382,) and even attacks, when concentrated, the glass vessels in which it is kept. It absorbs carbonic acid completely, and is employed for that purpose in organic analysis. The moderately concentrated solution, (sp. gravity 1·2,) as procured in the process, (488,) is sufficient for laboratory use. Potash is a fatal corrosive poison.

490. The *tests* for the presence of potash or its salts are chlorid of platinum, an alcoholic solution of which produces a yellow crystalline double salt of potassium and platinum in concentrated solutions: perchloric, tartaric, and hydrofluosilicic acids also form sparingly soluble salts with potassium and its salts.

491. The *chlorid of potassium* KCl, is a soluble compound, crystallizing in cubes. It is formed when potassium is heated in chlorine, and when potash or its carbonate is

---

489. What are its properties? What are potassa cum calce, and lapis infernalis? What of potash solution? What does it absorb? 490. What are its tests? 491. What is chlorid of potassium?

dissolved in chlorohydric acid. It has a saline bitter taste, is deliquescent, and does not possess the antiseptic properties of its congener, the chlorid of sodium.

The *bromid* of potassium KBr is also a soluble cubical salt, possessing the medical properties of bromine. It is produced in the mother liquor of the salines, (294,) and has been sold fraudulently for the iodid of potassium, which it much resembles, but does not replace in medical use. Chlorine and the stronger acids decompose it with evolution of bromine.

The *iodid of potassium* KI, often called the *hydriodate of potash*, is a compound of great importance in medical practice and in photography. It occurs in cubical crystals, which are soluble in ¾ parts of water and in 6 parts of alcohol of .85. It is obtained when iodine is dissolved in potash solution to saturation, and also at the same time iodate of potash, ($KO.IO_5$.) The iodid is separated by repeated crystallization, or if the whole saline mass is ignited, oxygen is expelled and only iodid of potassium is left. Its solution dissolves iodine largely and acquires thereby a dark color. Starch paste, as before stated, is the appropriate test for it. The *fluorid* of potassium KF, is also a soluble cubical salt, exactly analogous to the foregoing compounds.

The *cyanid of potassium* is described in the organic chemistry.

492. The *sulphurets of potassium* are numerous, five of which are described, viz. KS, KS_2, KS_3, KS_4, KS_5. The protosulphuret KS is found in an impure state, when an intimate mixture of 2 parts of sulphate of potash and 1 part of lamp-black are fused together in a crucible. Owing to the minute division of its particles with the excess of carbon, it forms a very inflammable mass, which takes fire on exposure to air. This has been called a *pyrophorus*, or bearer of fire. The protosulphuret of potassium is also formed by saturating a solution of potassa with sulphydric acid, which, evaporated, leaves a white crystalline mass. From this salt all the other sulphurets of potassium may be formed.

How different from chlorid of sodium? What of bromid? What fraud has it served? What sources has it? What is iodid of potassium? How obtained? What importance has it? 492. What sulphurets of potassium are named? How is the protosulphuret formed? What is the pyrophorus?

The *pentasulphuret* KS_5 is produced most readily by heating a strong solution of potassa with an excess of sulphur. A large part of the sulphur is dissolved, forming a deep yellow liquid which contains pentasulphuret of potassium, and hyposulphite of potassa. The pentasulphuret of potassium in the solid state has the old name of *liver of sulphur*, and its solution is used in diseases of the skin and as a depilatory.

493. When potassium is heated in dry ammonia, an olive-green compound is formed, ($K.NH_2$,) which when heated evolves ammonia and leaves a dark gray powder resembling graphite, which is a compound of nitrogen and potassium, having the formula K_3N. The other compounds of potassium, with phosphorus, carbon, boron, &c., are comparatively unimportant.

Salts of Potash.

494. The *salts of potash* are numerous and important. We shall, however, mention now only the carbonates, sulphates, nitrate, and chlorate. As it will be altogether impossible to give even the names of all the salts of the metals, we must content ourselves with a selection of the most important and interesting.

495. *Carbonates of Potash.*—There are three carbonates of potash, the neutral carbonate $KO.CO_2$, the sesquicarbonate $KO.\frac{3}{2}CO_2$, and the bicarbonate $KO.2CO_2$.

The *neutral carbonate* $KO.CO_2$ is procured from the ashes of plants, and in an impure form is made on a great scale in America, under the names of *pot* and *pearl ashes*, which are the alkali as obtained from the lixiviation and combustion of the ashes of forest-trees.

The crude carbonate of potash of commerce is contaminated by silica, sulphate of potash, and chlorids of potassium and sodium. The latter impurity is frequently added in the process of manufacture, either through ignorance or from fraudulent motives. The best potash is made by using hot water to lixiviate the ashes, in small leach-tubs. The brown mass left by evaporating the lixivium to dryness in iron

---

How is pentasulphuret of potassium formed? What uses has it? 493. What is the action of dry ammonia with K? 494. What salts of potash are formed? 495. What carbonates? How is the neutral carbonate obtained? What are pot and pearl ashes? What impurities has the crude article? How does "*pearlash*" differ from "*potash?*"

kettles is the *potash* of commerce. This is moderately calcined to burn off the coloring matter, when a spongy mass of a fine light blue color is left, which is the *pearlash*.

Several samples of American potash examined by Dr. L. C. Beck, yielded 73·6, 74·6, 75 and 76·9 per cent. of carbonate and hydrate of potash; from 6 to 15 per cent. of chlorids of potassium and sodium; with from 1 to 15 per cent. of insoluble matter, consisting of silica and the oxyds of iron and manganese, with lime, alumina, &c., being the ingredients derived from the inorganic parts of the plant.

496. The pure carbonate is obtained by calcining the cream of tartar, (acid tartrate of potash,) and dissolving out the carbonate from the coaly mass by water. The filtered solution is evaporated to dryness in a silver capsule, and the salt obtained pure.

The carbonate of potash has a strong alkaline taste, turns blue cabbage or dahlia-paper green, and is somewhat caustic; it dissolves in about twice its weight of water, forming a solution, which is much used in the laboratory. It crystallizes with difficulty, and takes up two equivalents (20 per cent.) of water in so doing. It is quite insoluble in alcohol. It is a very deliquescent salt, and must be kept in well-stopped bottles. Its solution acts as a poison if taken in a concentrated form. It usually retains a trace of silica, which is soluble in the concentrated solution.

Bicarbonate of Potash $KO.2CO_2$ is formed by passing a stream of carbonic acid gas through a cold solution of carbonate of potash. It crystallizes in large and beautiful crystals, referable to the right rhombic system. These crystals contain 9 per cent. of water and have the formula $KO.2CO_2+HO$. Four parts of water dissolve it; the solution has an alkaline taste and reaction, but is not caustic; by heat it is converted to the simple carbonate, and it loses a portion of carbonic acid by solution in hot water.

497. *Alkalimetry.*—The value of commercial samples of the carbonates of potassa and soda is determined by the process of *alkalimetry*, which consists in ascertaining how much dilute sulphuric acid of a standard strength is required to neutralize, exactly, a known weight of the sample exa-

---

What is the composition of commercial potash? 496. How is pure carbonate obtained? What are its characters? How is the bicarbonate obtained? What its form and character? 497. What is alkalimetry?

mined. The strength of the acid is such that 100 parts of it by measure will exactly saturate 10 parts by weight of the pure alkaline carbonate. It is foreign to our present purpose to give the full details of this process.

498. *Sulphate of Potash*, $KO.SO_3$.—This salt is prepared by neutralizing a concentrated solution of potash by strong sulphuric acid, added drop by drop. It is also a result of many processes in the arts. It fuses at a red heat without change. It is an anhydrous, crystallized salt, which decrepitates with heat, and has a density of 2·4. This salt requires 100 parts of water to dissolve 8·36 parts at 32°, and 0·096 parts more of the salt dissolve for every degree above that. It is one of the hardest of the saline bodies. It is wholly insoluble in alcohol.

Bisulphate of Potash $KO.SO_3+HO.SO_3$ is a result of the nitric acid process (334) when a double equivalent of sulphuric acid is used. It is properly a double sulphate of potassa and water. It is formed also when sulphate of potassa is added to its own weight of SO_3. It fuses at 392° without change and without loss of water. A higher heat expels one equivalent of sulphuric acid. It is decomposed by absolute alcohol, leaving $KO.SO_3$. It is dimorphous, one of its forms being identical with crystallized sulphur. The solution is strongly acid, and acts on bases nearly as powerfully as if potash were not present. When this salt is exposed to air, beautiful silky crystals, resembling asbestus, effloresce upon its surface. These are *sesquisulphate of potash* $2KO.SO_3+HO.SO_3$.

499. *Nitrate of Potassa; Saltpetre; Nitre;* $KO.NO_5$. This important salt is a natural product in the hot and dry regions of India and South America, being formed by the gradual decomposition of animal matters in the soil. It is also formed artificially by heaping together beds of old mortar and earth with dung and other animal matters, and occasionally wetting the mass with fermenting urine. In the Mammoth Cave in Kentucky, and other caverns, the soil on the floors becomes strongly impregnated with nitrate of lime, which is decomposed by wood ashes, and yields

---

Give the principle of the process. 498. What is sulphate of KO? Give its properties, &c. Give the formula for bisulphate of potash. What is its proper name? Give its properties. What is sesquisulphate of KO? How produced? 499. What is $KO.NO_5$? How formed and found? How formed artificially? What the origin of the NO_5?

nitrate of potassa. In all these cases, the nitre is obtained by lixiviating the nitrous earth with water, evaporating and crystallizing the solution, redissolving and crystallizing a second time, until the salt is obtained pure. Nitre also crystallizes from the juices of some plants.

It appears that the nitre of caverns must come from the union of the elements of the atmosphere, under the influence of carbonate and nitrate of ammonia, always found to some extent in the air. Rain water usually contains a trace of nitrate of ammonia, produced, as is supposed, by the union of the elements of the air by natural electricity, (§ 331 and fig. 252.)

500. *Properties.*—Nitre crystallizes in long, six-sided prisms, with dihedral summits, derived from the right rhombic prism. Its density is 1·94. It is anhydrous, and fusible at about 660°: at a higher temperature it is decomposed, yielding oxygen and nitrite of potassa. It is unaltered in the air and insoluble in alcohol, but dissolves in about 3 parts of water at 60°. In hot water it is much more soluble, 100 parts of water at 206·6° dissolving 236 parts of the salt. Its solution has a cooling taste, and is slightly bitter. It is an antiseptic, and is used in the brine for preserving meats, to give a fine red color to the flesh.

Nitrate of potassa (as well as nitrate of soda) has been much esteemed as a manure. It is employed also to procure oxygen, (275,) and the best nitric acid is made from it, (334.)

501. The great quantity of oxygen contained in nitre, and the ease with which it parts with it, render it a powerful means of oxydation. Fused on a coal it deflagrates brilliantly. It is the chief constituent of gunpowder, imparting oxygen to the carbon and sulphur in that mixture, to form with explosive energy those gases which are generated by the combustion of the materials. It is also much used in all pyrotechnic mixtures, as well as to deflagrate and scorify metals The surface of silver-ware is often scorified by nitre, which burns out the alloyed copper, and leaves a surface of pure silver. Good gunpowder is composed very nearly of 1 equivalent of nitre, 3 of carbon, and 1 of sulphur. Thus

---

How is it procured from the nitrate of lime? 500. What are the properties of nitre? 501. What renders nitre a valuable reagent? What is an antiseptic? Of what is nitre the chief constituent?

the powder used in war has the following composition in different countries :—

	Theoretical mixture.	French.	Prussian.	English and Austrian.	Swedish.	Chinese.
Sulphur	11·9	12·5	11·5	10	9	9·9
Charcoal	13·5	12·5	13·5	15	16	14·4
Nitre	74·6	75·	75·	75	75	75·7

Much of the explosive energy of gunpowder depends on its granulation; a fine dust, of the same composition with powerful powder, burns with a rapid deflagration, but without explosion. The constitution of gunpowder is varied according to the use for which it is intended. Thus, 20 sulphur, 18 charcoal, and 62 nitre, are used for blasting-powder in mines, and its combustion may be rendered still slower by mixing it with several times its bulk of sawdust. The effect then is more powerful in moving large masses of rocks.

The gases formed in the combustion of gunpowder are carbonic acid and nitrogen, while sulphuret of potassium remains as a solid residue. The combustion of a squib, or moist gunpowder, gives a much more complicated result; nitric oxyd, sulphuretted hydrogen, carbonic acid, carbonic oxyd, nitrogen, and other products being formed.

502. *Chlorate of Potash*, $KO.ClO_5$.—This salt is the salt already named (275) as the best source of pure oxygen gas. It is formed by passing chlorine gas through a strong solution of carbonate of potash, chlorate of potash and chlorid of potassium being formed, the chlorate being easily crystallized out by its less solubility. The carbonic acid escapes. The reaction is between $6KO.CO_2 + 6Cl = 5KCl + KO.ClO_5 + 6CO_2$.

503. *Properties.*—Chlorate of potash crystallizes in flat, pearly tables, referable to the oblique rhombic prism. Water at 32° dissolves only 3·3 parts in 100; at 60° only 6 parts, while boiling water dissolves nearly 60 parts; it is therefore much more soluble in hot than in cold water. It is insoluble in alcohol. Its taste is cooling and disagreeable, resembling nitre. It fuses at 750°; above that heat, oxygen is given off, and chlorid of potassium left behind. It is a most

---

What is the constitution of gunpowder in different countries? On what does its explosive energy depend? What are the products of its combustion? If wet, what are they? How is blasting-powder made more efficient? 502. What is chlorate of potassa, and how formed? 503. What are its properties?

energetic oxydizing agent. It forms explosive mixtures with nearly all combustible bodies.

504. With sulphur and charcoal it forms a compound that explodes by friction, or by a drop of sulphuric acid, and was formerly much used in the preparation of friction matches. With sulphur alone, it detonates powerfully when wrapped in a paper and struck by a hammer. With phosphorus its reaction is extremely violent; a deafening explosion follows the slightest compression of the ingredients, and burning phosphorus is projected in all directions. Its large consumption in the preparation of matches has rendered it a cheap salt.

All attempts to form a gunpowder of chlorate of potash have failed, the action of the mixture being so violent as to rend asunder the arms employed. A mixture of sugar and chlorate of potash is instantly inflamed by a drop of sulphuric acid, and burns with the violet color which belongs to all the salts of potassium.

The characters of the salts of potash are the same with reagents as those of potassa before given, (490.) The salts of the alkalies are distinguished from all other metallic salts by yielding no precipitate to an alkaline carbonate. All the potash salts form with sulphate of alumina a crystalline double sulphate of potassa and alumina—common alum—crystallizing in octahedrons.

SODIUM.

Equivalent, 23. *Symbol*, Na. *Density*, ·972.

505. *Sodium was discovered by Davy* soon after the discovery of potassium, and in the same way. It is now prepared by a process quite similar to that already described (484) for potassium; the carbonate of soda being used in place of the carbonate of potassa.

This metal forms more than 40 parts in 100 of common salt, and is also frequent in various combinations in the mineral kingdom. The ashes of sea-plants afford crude

---

What its solubility? What is its reaction with combustibles? 504. Why not fit for gunpowder? What color does it burn with? What are the characters of potash salts? What compound do they form with alumina? 505. Give the history and distribution of sodium. How procured?

carbonate of soda, in place of the carbonate of potash procured from land-plants.

506. Sodium is a *white metal*, with a silvery brilliancy, and much resembles potassium in its general properties. Its color is much whiter than that of potassium, and its disposition to tarnish less. Its density is ·972, and it melts at 194°. At common temperatures it is harder than potassium, but is easily moulded in the fingers. It does not inflame on cold water, unless in masses of considerable size, but moves about rapidly, fused into a brilliant sphere, until it is all consumed. It may be alloyed with potassium by simple pressure, and is then inflamed on water, or alone on hot water, burning with a bright yellow light, characteristic of sodium, and strongly contrasted with the violet color of the potassium flame. The same color is seen when a piece of soda-glass, or any mineral containing soda, is held in the flame of the blowpipe; the flame is instantly tinged yellow. Exposed to the air, sodium soon falls to a white powder of oxyd of sodium.

The compounds of sodium are so similar to those of potassium that we can pass them with a brief notice.

The oxyds of sodium and their hydrates are the same in composition as those of potassa.

507. The *hydrate of soda*, or *caustic soda*, NaO.HO, is procured by decomposing the carbonate by quicklime, in the same manner as has already been described for caustic potash, (488.) It is a powerful alkaline base, very soluble in water, and deliquescent in moist air. It forms a white crystalline cake, resembling potassa. It is a corrosive and energetic poison. All its salts are soluble, which renders it somewhat difficult to detect its presence in solution.

508. *Chlorid of Sodium, or Common Salt*, NaCl.—This familiar and abundant substance is too well known to need much description. It is formed when sodium burns in chlorine gas, as well as when soda, or its carbonate, is neutralized by chlorohydric acid. In Poland, Austria, Spain, Sicily, and Switzerland, extensive beds of pure rock-salt are found, which are regularly mined. Common salt forms about 27 of every 1000 parts of sea-water, and in warm

---

506. What its properties? What is the color of its flame? What of its compounds? 507. What is NaO.HO? How procured? Give its properties. What of its salts? 508. What is NaCl? How artificially formed? How found in nature?

climates, especially in the West Indies, sea-water is evaporated in large quantities by the sun's heat, to obtain salt. Numerous saline springs are found in New York, Ohio, Kentucky, and other places in this country, which afford vast quantities of salt by evaporation. The brine springs in Onondaga county, New York, are among the most valuable, and have been worked since 1789. Their water contains one-seventh part of dry salt. The water of the Great Salt Lake, in Deseret, contains 200 parts of salt in 1000, or over $\frac{1}{5}$th of its weight. This salt is nearly pure. The Dead Sea has a still greater concentration, (§ 544.)

Common salt crystallizes in cubes, which are anhydrous, and crackle, or decrepitate, when heated, owing to water mechanically entangled in them. Salt forms singular hopper-shaped crystals, (fig. 352.) These are produced on the surface of the evaporating brine, and grow by increase of the outer edges, as gravity sinks them constantly, a trifle below the surface of the fluid, each additional row of particles being built upon the upper and outer edge of the last. It requires 2·7 parts of water for its solution, and it is equally soluble in hot and cold water. In pure alcohol it is scarcely at all soluble. Its density is 2·557. It fuses at redness, and sublimes in vapor at a higher temperature. It is employed for this reason to glaze earthenware, since its vapor is decomposed by the oxyd of iron of the clay, chlorid of iron being driven off, while soda unites with the silica of the clay to form the glaze.

Fig. 352.

The *bromid*, *iodid*, and *sulphurets* of sodium resemble the corresponding compounds of potassium, and the two former likewise crystallize in cubes.

509. *Neutral Sulphate of Soda, Glauber's Salt*, $NaO.SO_3+(10HO)$.—This familiar salt is found abundantly in commerce in large crystals, which contain more than half their weight of crystallization water, viz :

1 eq.	anhydrous sulphate of soda	71	44·10
10 "	water	90	55·90
1 "	crystallized sulphate of soda	161	100·00

How much in sea water ? in salines ? in the Great Salt Lake ? What of its crystallization ? How are the hoppers formed ? How soluble ? Its density ? Why used to glaze pottery ? 509. Give the formula for Glauber's salt. What is its composition ?

It fuses at a moderate temperature in its own water and leaves, on heating, anhydrous sulphate of soda. Exposed to air, the crystals of Glauber's salt effloresce, and fall to powder, from loss of water. If its solution is heated above 93°, anhydrous sulphate of soda is thrown down. The solubility of sulphate of soda presents very remarkable anomalies. Below 32° it is slightly soluble. At 32°, 12 parts dissolve in 100 parts of water: the quantity dissolved increases very rapidly with the temperature up to 93°, which presents the maximum of solubility of the salt, being 322 parts in 100 of water. Above that point the solubility diminishes rapidly with each increment of temperature, until at 218° it has diminished to 210 parts in 100 of water. The line A B C on the diagram (fig. 353) illustrates the relations of solubility and temperature in this salt at a glance. The vertical divisions O to O′ register the range of temperature from 32° to 218°; the horizontal ones O O″ indicate the degree of solubility, which reaches 322 parts at 93°. The curve of solubility then descends from B to C, when 210 parts are dissolved at 218°. The cause of this sudden diminution of solubility, is the decomposition of the hydrous salt in solution at that heat, and the precipitation of a portion of anhydrous sulphate of soda. A solution of Glauber's salts saturated at boiling heat in a vessel capable of being corked while boiling, and suffered to cool, will often crystallize completely on withdrawing the cork, a change from the fluid to the solid state occasioned by the concussion of the air. The same thing happens if a small crystal is dropped into a saturated solution of the salt, (41.)

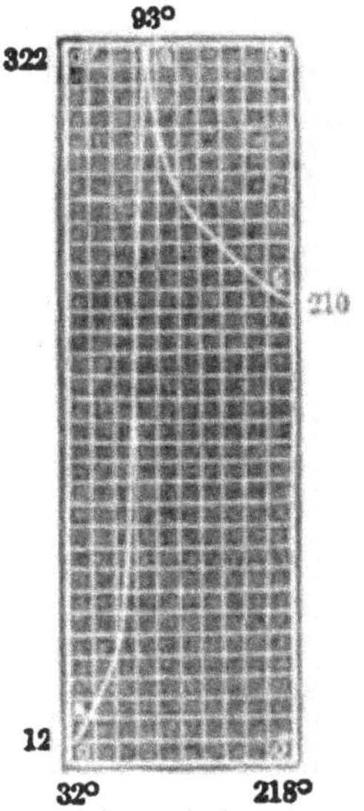

Fig. 353.

Sulphate of soda is a familiar aperient. In the arts, its chief use is in the preparation of carbonate of soda, as will be presently described. It is a result, on a large scale, of

---

How does it fuse? How if exposed? How does it dissolve in water at different temperatures? What is its curve of solubility? Describe the diagram 353. How is its solution in vacuo crystallized? What is its use in the arts?

the preparation of chlorohydric acid, (426.) The other sulphates of soda require no mention at present. The solution of sulphate of soda (12 parts) in strong chlorohydric acid (10 parts) produces cold enough to freeze a considerable quantity of water in summer.

510. *Carbonate of Soda*, $NaO.CO_2$.—Soda replaces in the ashes of sea-plants the potash found in those of land-plants. Hence, formerly, the carbonate of soda of commerce was procured, almost exclusively, from the ashes of sea-weeds. This salt is now obtained entirely from common salt by the process of Leblanc, which will be briefly described. This process depends on the fact that when sulphate of soda, carbonate of lime, and carbon are heated together, carbonate of soda, oxysulphate of lime, and oxyd of carbon are the products. The reaction is between 2 eq. of sulphate of soda, 3 of carbonate of lime, and 9 of carbon; thus, $2(NaO.SO_3) + 3(CaO.CO_2) + 9C = 2(NaO.CO_2) + (2CaS.CaO) + 10CO$. The oxysulphuret of calcium is wholly insoluble in water, which takes out from the pulverized mass only carbonate of soda. This operation is prepared in a reverberatory furnace constructed like the section seen in fig. 354. The parts A and B receive the mingled

Fig. 354.

materials, (1000 parts of anhydrous sulphate of soda, 1040 of chalk, and 530 of charcoal powder.) The fire on the grate F plays upon the charge on the sole of A, and completes the chemical reaction which was begun in B, where the charge is first placed: a bridge-wall separates the two. The workman judges, by the appearance and consistency of a

---

What freezing mixture does it form? 510. Give the formula for carbonate of soda. How was it procured formerly? Describe Leblanc's process? What is the reaction? Describe fig. 354. What gas is formed? How is the progress of the operation determined?

portion withdrawn from time to time, of the progress of the operation. The oxyd of carbon forms a blue flame over the surface, which disappears when the reaction is over. The heat following the arrow, next plays upon solution of carbonate of soda in the boiler C, the lixivium of a previous charge, and evaporates it to dryness, while at the same time the more dilute solution of carbonate is heated in D, to be drawn from time to time into C. The steam and products of combustion escape by the chimney O.

Carbonate of soda crystallizes in great crystals of an oblique form and containing 10 atoms of water, viz. $NaO.CO_2+10HO$, equal to 63 parts water in 100 of the salt. It fuses in its own water of crystallization. The anhydrous carbonate, as it comes from the furnace, is called *soda-ash.*

Bicarbonate of soda is procured by exposing soda-ash to carbonic acid from fermenting grain, as in distilleries, or by passing this acid into solution of carbonate. It is, so to speak, a carbonate of soda plus a carbonate of water, or $NaO.CO_2+HO.CO_2$. It is not a very solute salt: 100 parts of water take up 8 of bicarbonate. Boiling water expels one of the equivalents of carbonic acid. This is the salt used in preparing effervescent draughts.

The *sesquicarbonate of soda, Trona,* $2NaO.3CO_2+4HO$ is found native in certain lakes in Africa and South America. It crystallizes in right rhomboidal prisms, unchanged in air, and little soluble in water.

511. *Nitrate of Soda, Soda Saltpetre,* $NaO.NO_5$.—This salt is found in India and South America, where extensive plains are covered by it, as at Tarapaca in Chili, and Iquique in Peru. It resembles nitrate of potassa, but cannot be used to replace that salt in gunpowder, on account of its strong disposition to attract water from the air. It is much employed, however, in procuring nitric acid, and also as a fertilizer in agriculture. It is a white salt, crystallizing in rhombs, specific gravity 2·09, very soluable, with a cooling taste, and deflagrates on burning coals with a strong yellow light. By carbonate of potassa in solution it is immediately transformed into nitrate of potassa and carbonate of soda.

How is the solution evaporated? How does the salt crystallize? How much water has it? How is the bicarbonate formed? How soluble? What is the sesquicarbonate. 511. What is the history of nitrate of soda? What does it resemble? What its use? How does it act with combustibles?

512. The *phosphates of soda* correspond to the three conditions of phosphoric acid (355) before noticed: they are—

1. *Phosphate of Soda* (*tribasic*) $HO.2NaO.PO_5+24HO$.—The common phosphate of soda of pharmacy is prepared by precipitating the acid phosphate of lime (347) with a slight excess of carbonate of soda. It crystallizes in oblique rhombic prisms, which are efflorescent. The crystals dissolve in four parts of cold water, and undergo the aqueous fusion when heated. The salt has a pleasant saline taste, and is purgative; its solution is alkaline to test-paper. When evaporated above 90° it crystallizes in another form, with 14 instead of 24 atoms of water.

2. *Subphosphate of soda* $3NaO.PO_5+24HO$ is obtained by adding solution of caustic soda to the preceding salt. The crystals are slender six-sided prisms, soluble in 5 parts of cold water. It is decomposed by acids, even the carbonic, but suffers no change by heat, except the loss of its water of crystallization. Its solution is strongly alkaline. The study of these salts by Prof. Graham has greatly enlarged our views of chemical philosophy.

3. *Biphosphate of Soda*, or *Superphosphate*, $2HO.NaO.PO_5+HO$.—This salt may be obtained by adding phosphoric acid to the ordinary phosphate, until it ceases to precipitate chlorid of barium, and exposing the concentrated solution to cold. The crystals are prismatic, very soluble, and have an acid reaction. When strongly heated, the salt becomes changed into monobasic phosphate of soda.

513. *Microcosmic salt*, or *phosphate of soda and ammonia*, ($HO.NH_4O.NaO.PO_5+8HO$,) is much used in blowpipe operations as a flux. It is formed by dissolving with a gentle heat, 1 part of chlorid of ammonium and 6 or 7 parts of phosphate of soda, in 2 of water. Chlorid of sodium is formed, and the microcosmic salt crystallizes out in rhombic prisms, which lose 8HO by heat. Its fanciful name was derived from its supposed virtues in promoting fertility in the impotent.

514. *Bibasic Phosphate of Soda, Pyrophosphate of Soda*, $2NaO.PO_5+10HO$.—Prepared by strongly heating com-

---

512. What phosphates are named? What is the formula of the tribasic? Give its properties. What is the subphosphate? What the superphosphate? What of Graham's researches? What is the biphosphate of soda? 513. What is microcosmic salt? How formed? 514. What is bibasic phosphate? Give its formula.

mon phosphate of soda, dissolving the residue in water, and recrystallizing. The crystals are very brilliant, permanent in the air, and less soluble than the original phosphate: their solution is alkaline. A bibasic phosphate, containing an equivalent of basic water, has been obtained; it does not, however, crystallize.

515. *Monobasic Phosphate of Soda, Metaphosphate of Soda*, $NaO.PO_5$.—Obtained by heating either the acid tribasic phosphate, or microcosmic salt. It is a transparent, glassy substance, fusible at a dull red-heat, deliquescent, and very soluble in water. It refuses to crystallize, and dries up in a gum-like mass.

The tribasic phosphates give a bright yellow precipitate with a solution of nitrate of silver, and with molybdate of ammonia: the bibasic and monobasic phosphates afford white precipitates with the same substances. The salts of the two latter classes, fused with excess of carbonate of soda, yield the tribasic modification of the acid.

516. *Borax; Biborate of Soda; Tincal;* $NaO.2BO_3+10HO$.—Borax crystallizes in right rhomboidal prisms, which are soluble in 15 or 16 parts of water: the solution has an alkaline reaction and sweetish alkaline taste. It loses its water by heat, and being very fusible, is much used as a flux in metallurgic processes and as a blowpipe reagent. It is entirely procured from natural sources of boracic acid already mentioned, and from the waters of several lakes in Thibet, in which it is dissolved.

LITHIUM.

Equivalent, 6·5. *Symbol*, L.

517. This very rare metal is a constituent of several minerals, as spodumene, petalite, lithia-mica: hence its name, from *lithos*, a stone. The electrolysis of the hydrate afforded Davy a white oxydizable metal analogous to sodium. Its small atomic weight is remarkable.

The oxyd LO is an alkali, but much less soluble than

---

515. What is the monobasic phosphate? What are the tests for tribasic phosphates? Of the bibasic? How are the bibasic, &c., converted to the tribasic form? 516. What is borax? What its source and uses? 517. What is lithium? What of LO? What use for its salts?

potash and soda. Its sulphate is a beautiful salt, and gives a rosy flame to alcohol. The lithia compounds all give this tint to the outer flame of the blowpipe. Some of its salts have been used internally with advantage in cases of uric acid calculus.

AMMONIUM.

Equivalent, 18. *Symbol*, NH_4, (*hypothetical.*)

518. *Ammonium*, NH_4.—The compound metallic radical of ammonia has never been isolated, although we have reason to believe in its existence. When a solution of ammonia, or of sal-ammoniac, is electrolyzed, nitrogen escapes at the + side and hydrogen at the — side, fig. 355; but if the latter pole is made by using a portion of mercury in the bend of the tube *b*, no hydrogen is evolved, but the mercury swells up, loses its fluidity, becomes like soft butter, and gradually attains many times its original bulk, having the lustre and general character of an *amalgam*. A more simple mode of forming this amalgam, consists in making a little potassium or sodium combine by heat with about 100 times its weight of metallic mercury. This alloy, when placed in a strong solution of sal-ammoniac, begins at once to increase in volume by the formation of the ammoniacal amalgam, until it has attained very many times its original bulk, and has a pasty, butter-like consistence.

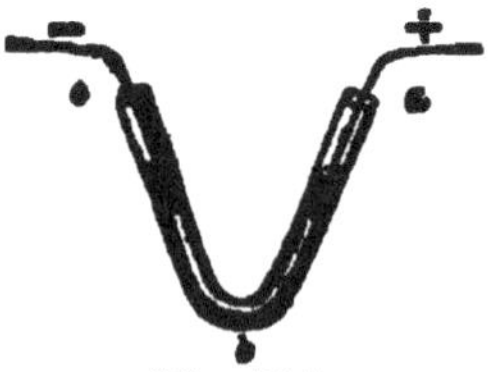

Fig. 355.

When the alloy of potassium is placed in hydrochloric acid, the alkaline metal decomposes the acid, forming chlorid of potassium and evolving hydrogen. If we subsitute for the acid (chlorid of hydrogen) a solution of chlorid of zinc ZnCl, a like decomposition ensues; but the zinc, instead of being set free like the hydrogen, combines with mercury to form an amalgam. The present reaction is precisely similar; chlorid of ammonium NH_4Cl being substituted for the

---

518. What is ammonium? Give its history. How obtained more simply than by electrolysis? What is the appearance of the amalgam? What illustration is given from the alloy in HCl and in ZnCl? What is the reaction in the present case?

chlorid of zinc: the ammonium which is liberated combines with the mercury and forms the light pasty amalgam. It crystallizes in cubes at 32°, whereas pure mercury is fluid even at a temperature of —39° F. It is evident that it has combined with something which has given it new properties. This is supposed to be the metallic radical *ammonium*. The spongy mass, as soon as the electric action ceases, rapidly suffers decomposition. Ammonia and hydrogen are set free in the proportion of 1 to 2, and the mercury regains its original state, unaltered. Berzelius and other able chemists explain this reaction, on the ground that the ammonia, by gaining an additional equivalent of hydrogen, assumes the peculiar character of a metal, and unites with mercury, forming an amalgam. This hypothetical metal can replace potassium and sodium perfectly in combination, and is therefore isomorphous with them. All the salts of ammonia are, on this view, derived from this radical, and its union with the second class gives us a series of bodies analogous to the chlorids, bromids, &c., of the other electro-positive bases.

Compounds of Ammonium.

519. *Chlorid of Ammonium; Sal-Ammoniac*, NH_4Cl.— This salt occurs in nature, sometimes quite pure, as at Deception Island, and in volcanic districts generally. It was originally prepared, in Egypt, (443,) by sublimation from the soot of the burnt camel's dung. This is done in large flasks of glass, (fig. 356,) the sal-ammoniac collects in the upper part, and the cake is removed by breaking the bottle. It is always contaminated by organic matters. It is also obtained largely from the ammoniacal waters of the gas-works. It is purified by evaporating the crude solutions to dryness, after treating them with a slight excess of chlorohydric acid to neutralize the free ammonia, and subliming the dry mass in iron vessels.

Fig. 356.

What is the product of its decomposition? What is the explanation of Berzelius? How are the ammoniacal salts viewed? 519. What is sal-ammoniac? How prepared?

It has a sharp saline taste, corrodes metals powerfully, is soluble in three parts of cold water, and crystallizes from its solution in octahedrons. The sublimed salt has a fibrous texture, and is very tough and difficult to pulverize.

The formation of this compound is easily shown by using the apparatus already figured, (438,) with hydrochloric acid in one flask and strong ammonia water in other; the commingling of the dry gases, driven over by heat to the central bottle, fills it with a white cloud of sal-ammoniac, $HCl + NH_3 = NH_4Cl$. The preparation and properties of ammonia have already been explained, (444.)

520. *Sulphydret of Ammonium, (Hydrosulphuret of Ammonia,)* $NH_4S + HS$.—This very useful reagent is formed by passing a long-continued, slow current of sulphuretted hydrogen from the gas-bottle *a*, (fig. 357,) through the bottles *d*, *e*, *f*, *g*, filled with strong water of ammonia. This arrangement is a simple form of Woulfe's apparatus, (fig. 257.) A single bottle of ammonia (as *d*) is sufficient for all common purposes. It should be kept cold. The ammonia absorbs an enormous quantity of the gas, and the resulting sulphuret, which has the strong odor of the gas, is colorless at first, but gradually assumes a yellow color. It forms numerous salts with electro-negative sulphurets, being itself a powerful sulphur base. It is an invaluable reagent as a precipitant of the metals, and is also used in medicine.

Fig. 357.

There are several simple sulphurets of ammonium, but they are of no particular interest.

521. *Sulphate of Ammonia, or Sulphate of Oxyd of*

What its properties? How formed artificially? 520. What is sulphydret of ammonium? Describe fig. 357. What is the chemical character of this body? What its uses?

Ammonium, $NH_4O.SO_3+HO$.—This salt, which is a powerful fertilizer, is procured in the large way by neutralizing the ammoniacal liquor of the gas-works by sulphuric acid: or it may be easily obtained pure by neutralizing dilute sulphuric acid with carbonate of ammonia.

522. There are several *carbonates of ammonia*. The common *sal-volatile* of the shops, with a pungent smell and alkaline reaction, is nearly a sesquicarbonate $2NH_4O.3CO_2$. Exposed to the air, this salt becomes a white inodorous powder, which is the bicarbonate. The sesquicarbonate is a very valuable salt to the chemist. It forms the basis of the smelling-bottles so much in use. The dry white powder formed by the contact of dry carbonic acid and ammonia in an apparatus like figure 319, is a neutral anhydrous carbonate $NH_3.CO_2$, very pungent and volatile, dissolving readily in water.

523. *Nitrate of Ammonia, or Nitrate of Oxyd of Ammonium*, $NH_4O.NO_5+HO$.—This salt has already been noticed (338) under the description of nitrous oxyd. Its crystals resemble nitre, deliquesce in moist air, and dissolve in 2 parts of cold water, the solution sinking the thermometer to zero, (124.) It deflagrates on burning coals like nitre, and hence received the old name of *nitrum flammens*.

524. All the ammoniacal salts are volatilized by a high temperature, and yield the ammoniacal odor by trituration with caustic potassa or lime, or by boiling with solutions of potash. They are all soluble, and give a sparingly soluble, yellow, crystalline precipitate with chlorid of platinum.

---

521. What is sulphate of ammonia? 522. What carbonates are named? What one is formed from the union of the gases? 523. What is nitrate of ammonia? Give its formula. How decomposed by heat? What is its frigorific power? What name had it? 524. What are tests for ammoniacal salts?

CLASS II. METALS OF THE ALKALINE EARTHS.

525. This class includes barium, strontium, calcium, and magnesium, the bases of the alkaline earths, baryta, strontia, lime, and magnesia: these are all soluble to some extent in water, with an alkaline reaction, but differ very much in the solubility and other properties of their various salts.

BARIUM.

Equivalent 68·5. *Symbol*, Ba.

526. Barium is a silver-white malleable metal, easily oxydized, and melts at a red heat. It was procured by Davy by a process similar to that which yielded potassium, &c. It is better obtained by passing vapor of potassium over baryta (oxyd of barium) heated to redness in an iron tube. Mercury dissolves out the reduced metal, and the amalgam is then distilled. It is named, from the striking weight of its salts, from *barus*, heavy.

527. *Baryta, or Protoxyd of Barium*, BaO.—Baryta is best obtained by decomposing the nitrate at a red heat. It is a dry, gray powder, which combines with water to form a hydrate, slaking with the evolution of great heat and even light. Its density is 5·45. The hydrate dissolves in two parts of hot water, or twenty of cold, and crystallizes in flat tables. The aqueous solution is a valuable test for carbonic acid.

Sulphate of baryta, or heavy spar, is found abundantly, as an associate of other minerals, in veins; and from it, or the native carbonate of baryta, all the artificial compounds of barium are formed.

528. The *peroxyd of barium* BaO_2 is formed by passing pure oxygen gas over the oxyd heated to dull redness in a porcelain tube. It is chiefly interesting as being the means of procuring the peroxyd of hydrogen, (420.)

---

525. What are the metals of the alkaline earths? 526. What is the equivalent of barium? Give its properties. Whence its name? 527. What is baryta? How does it act with water? What its density? 528. How is peroxyd of barium formed, and for what used?

Chlorid of Barium, $BaCl + 2HO$.—This salt occurs in white tabular crystals, containing two equivalents of water, which are expelled by heat. It dissolves in a little more than twice its weight of cold water, and the solution is a valuable reagent for detecting the presence of sulphuric acid.

529. The *nitrate of baryta* $BaO.NO_5 + HO$ is also a soluble white salt, which crystallizes in anhydrous octahedrons, and dissolves in eight parts of cold or three parts of hot water. Both it and the chlorid are prepared by dissolving the native or artificial carbonate in the proper acid.

Sulphate of baryta, heavy spar, $BaO.SO_3$, is a mineral found abundantly in many places in this country, as at Cheshire, Connecticut. It crystallizes in tabular modifications of the rhombic prism, often very beautiful. It is also found massive at Pillar Point, New York. Its specific gravity (4·3 to 4·7) gives it the name of *heavy spar*. It is quite insoluble in water or acids, and not easily decomposed. When strongly heated with charcoal powder, however, it suffers decomposition, $BaO.SO_3 + 4C = BaS + 4CO$; carbonic oxyd is given off, and the soluble sulphuret of barium may be dissolved out from the coaly mass.

Sulphate of baryta is extensively ground up for a pigment, being mixed with white-lead as an adulteration.

530. *Carbonate of Baryta*, $BaO.CO_2$, or the *witherite* of mineralogists, is a mineral of some interest, and useful as the chief source of the various compounds of baryta. All the soluble baryta salts are poisonous, and their presence may always be detected by sulphuric acid, or a soluble sulphate, with which they form the insoluble sulphate of baryta.

The compounds of barium give a peculiar yellow color to the flame of the blowpipe, different from the yellow flame of soda.

STRONTIUM.

Equivalent, 44. *Symbol*, Sr.

531. *Strontium* is obtained from its oxyd in the same manner as barium, and, like it, is a white metal, oxydized

---

Give the characters of the chlorid of barium. For what is it a test? 529. How is the nitrate of baryta characterized? How is heavy spar found in nature? Give its formula and properties. 530. What is carbonate of baryta? What character have the soluble salts of baryta? How is their presence detected? 531. How is strontium obtained, and how characterized?

easily in the air, and decomposing water at common temperatures. There are two oxyds, the protoxyd and the peroxyd of strontium, similar in properties to the like oxyds of barium. The sulphate of strontia (*celestine*) is a rather abundant mineral, and the carbonate (*strontianite*) is much esteemed by mineralogists. They are very similar in properties to the sulphate and carbonate of baryta.

532. The *chlorid of strontium* $SrCl + 9HO$ is a deliquescent salt, soluble in two parts of cold water. It loses its water of crystallization by heat. Both it and the nitrate of strontia $SrO.NO_5$ are much employed by pyrotechnists in forming the *red fire* of theatres and fireworks. All the compounds of strontium give a peculiar red tint to the flame of the blowpipe, while the barytic salts do not. The salts of strontia are not poisonous.

CALCIUM.

Equivalent, 20. *Symbol*, Ca.

533. *Calcium* is a yellowish-white metal, obtained like barium, and has so strong a disposition to combine with oxygen that it is difficult to observe its properties.

534. *Protoxyd of Calcium, Lime*, CaO.—This most valuable substance, so well known as *quicklime*, is procured in a state of great purity by heating the stalactites from caverns, or the purest statuary marble, for some hours to full redness in an open crucible. The carbonic acid and organic coloring matter are driven off, and oxyd of calcium (lime) nearly pure remains. Pure lime is a white, very infusible, and rather hard body, having a density of 3·18. It has a great affinity for carbonic acid, taking it from the air and falling to powder, (air-slaking.) It also combines with water to form a hydrate, evolving great heat, (slaking.) When this operation is performed under a glass bell, (fig. 358,) the vapor of water at first condensed on the walls of the jar soon forms a transparent atmosphere of steam, which, when the bell is raised,

Fig. 358.

What familiar salts of this metal are found native? 532. Describe the chlorid of strontium. What is it used for? 533. What is calcium, and how is it obtained? Give its equivalent? 534. What is lime? How procured? What its density? What is air-slaking? What slaking by water?

breaks on the air in a dense cloud of vapor. The heat is greatest when the water is about half the weight of lime employed. Is sufficiently high often to inflame gunpowder. The hydrate CaO.HO is a dry, bulky powder, soluble in 1000 parts of water, to form *lime-water*. With water it forms a milk of lime; a corrosive paste used to remove hair from hides. Lime-water is a valuable reagent and antacid; it has a disagreeable alkaline taste; blues reddened litmus, and absorbs carbonic acid from the air, by which it becomes milky from precipitation of carbonate of lime soluble in excess of carbonic acid.

535. Common lime is prepared by heating limestone (carbonate of lime) in large stone furnaces, filled from the top with the limestone and fuel; the fire is kept up constantly, by renewed charges of the materials at top, while the prepared caustic lime is drawn out at the bottom. The carbonic acid is much more rapidly expelled when the vapor of water and other products of combustion come in contact with the heated limestone. Indeed, it is hardly possible by heat alone in close vessels to expel the CO_2, since carbonate of lime is fusible under those circumstances without decomposition.

Mortar acts as a cement by the slow formation of carbonate of lime, which binds together the grains of sand that make up the greater part of the mixture. The smaller the portion of lime used, and the sharper the silicious sand employed, the more firm will be the cement at last; but it is then so much more difficult to work, that an excess of lime is usually employed. The presence of oxyd of iron and manganese, of alumina, magnesia, silica, and other like substances in a limestone, gives the lime prepared from it the property of hardening under water, when it is called *hydraulic lime*.

Lime is much used in improved agriculture, as a manure. It acts to decompose vegetable matters, to neutralize acids, dissolve silica, and retain carbonic acid. It is always present naturally in every fertile soil, and is a constant ingredient in the ashes of most plants.

536. *Chlorid of Calcium*, CaCl.—The solution of lime,

What heat is given out in this operation? Where greatest? How soluble is the hydrate? 535. How is common lime prepared? Why is vapor of water useful in the process? How does mortar act as a cement? What is hydraulic lime? 536. What is the chlorid of calcium?

or of its carbonate, in hydrochloric acid to saturation, gives us this chlorid. It is when fused a white crystalline solid, with a great avidity for moisture, and for this reason it is used in the desiccation of gases, &c. It is soluble in alcohol, with which it forms a definite crystallizable compound. It forms a powerful freezing mixture with ice, (124.)

The sulphurets and phosphurets of calcium have little interest. The phosphuret being decomposed by water, is an available source of the spontaneously inflammable phosphuretted hydrogen, (fig. 326.)

537. *Sulphate of Lime—Gypsum—Selenite*, $CaO.SO_3$.—This salt, in the form of hydrate $CaO.SO_3+2HO$, is abundant in nature, and is much used in agriculture as a manure, being ground to powder; and, after expelling the water by heat, as a material for stucco and plaster casts. It is then commonly known as "plaster of Paris." The variegated and fine white varieties are called *alabaster*. When crystallized in transparent flexible plates, it is called *selenite*. These crystals are sometimes compound in such a manner as to present an arrow-head form, like fig. 359. Such crystals are called *hemitropes*. *Anhydrous gypsum* $CaO.SO_3$ also is found native, and is known by the mineralogical name of *anhydrite*.

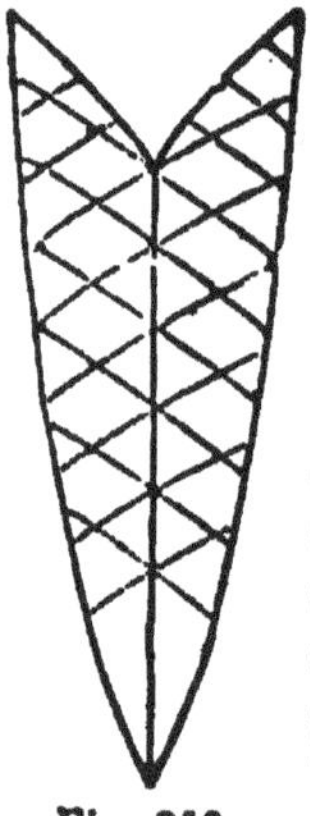

Fig. 359.

Gypsum is frequently associated with rock-salt. It is soluble in about 500 parts of water, and is present in most natural waters. By a heat of 250° to 270° it loses its water of composition: when the anhydrous powder is moistened, the lost water is regained, and it becomes solid; but if heated, even to 330°, it no longer regains its water of composition. It fuses at a red heat to a crystalline anhydrous mass. This power of resolidification, when mixed with water, gives gypsum its value in copying works of art, and in forming stucco ornaments. By using solution of common alum in place of water, gypsum becomes very hard, and is thus treated for producing pavements.

For what is it used? What is the phosphuret of calcium used for? 537. Give the common names of sulphate of lime. For what is it used? Give its properties. What is fig. 359? How is gypsum hardened? On what does its use in stucco depend? What is anhydrite?

538. *Fluorid of Calcium, Fluor-spar*, CaF.—This is a rather abundant mineral, being found beautifully crystallized, of various colors, in the cube and its modifications. It is the principal source from which we obtain the fluohydric acid (433) by decomposition with sulphuric acid. It often phosphoresces very beautifully with heat, emitting a green, yellow, or purple light, at a temperature below redness.

539. *Phosphates of Lime.*—There are several phosphates of lime corresponding to the several phosphoric acids, (355.) The earth of bones is a tribasic phosphate of lime, and the mineral known as apatite is also a phosphate of lime. The phosphates of lime are insoluble in water, but dissolve in dilute acids. All cereal grains, and many other vegetables, contain phosphate of lime in their ashes, and this salt is therefore an indispensable ingredient of all fertile soils, and the form in which phosphorus is introduced into the animal structure.

540. *Carbonate of Lime—Marble—Calcareous Spar*, $CaO.CO_2$.—This is one of the most abundant minerals of the earth, forming in limestone vast mountains and wide-spread geological deposites. It occurs most superbly crystallized in rhombohedral forms, which constitute brilliant ornaments in mineralogical collections. The transparent double refracting Iceland spar, (fig. 360,) and the dimorphous form, *arragonite*, are examples of this salt. It is soluble in dilute acids, with escape of carbonic acid, and is also decomposed by heat, leaving quicklime.

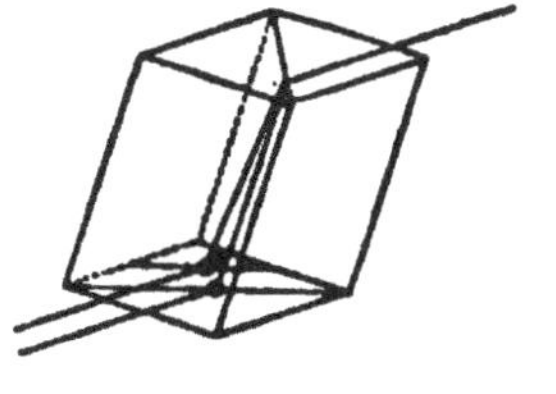

Fig. 360.

Water aided by carbonic acid, and perhaps by the organic acids of the soil also, dissolves carbonate of lime, and again deposits it in *stalactites* and *stalagmites*, on exposure to the air. These phenomena are beautifully seen in Mammoth Cave, Schoharie Cave, and many similar situations. The stalactites depend from the roof, growing by the deposit of freshly precipitated portions of carbonate of lime on their

538. What is fluor-spar? How is it found? For what used? What beautiful property has it? 539. What phosphates of lime are known? In what do we find phosphate of lime? How does phosphorus enter the system? 540. What is the formula of carbonate of lime? What other names has it? What is formed from it? What optical property has it? How does water dissolve it? What are stalactites and stalagmites?

surfaces, which are kept moist by the trickling of water containing the salt in solution. The water which falls to the floor from the point of each stalactite slowly builds up a conical mass called a *stalagmite*, and when these meet they form a column. All these stages are well shown in fig. 361,

Fig. 361.

from Regnault. Before these fairy-like creations of nature's architecture are darkened by torches, their beauty is enchanting.

541. *Hypochlorite of Lime*, CaO.ClO, *Bleaching-Powder.*—This valuable compound is formed when chlorine gas is gradually admitted to hydrate of lime slightly moist and kept cool. The chlorine is absorbed largely, and the *bleaching-powder* of the arts is formed. Bleaching-powders contain a mixture of hypochlorite of lime, chlorid of calcium, and hydrate of lime. It is a soft white powder, easily soluble in about 10 parts of water, giving a highly alkaline solution, which bleaches feebly. It is employed by dipping the goods in the weak solution, and then in very dilute acid water. The chlorine is thus evolved and does its work. Several repetitions are needed to complete the process, and the acid is washed out with care. This compound emits a strong smell, which is similar to chlorine, but is due to

---

Describe their formation as in fig. 361. What is bleaching-powder? How formed? How employed?

hypochlorous acid; it is very useful for disinfecting offensive apartments, and its energy is increased by the addition of a little acid water. The disinfecting liquid of Labarraque is a compound of chlorine with soda, similar in composition to solution of bleaching-powder.

The best bleaching-powders contain 39 parts of available chlorine, and 2 parts, in combination, as chlorid of calcium. If one equivalent of each ingredient were present they would be in the proportion of 48·57 chlorine and 51·43 parts hydrate of lime. Ordinary bleaching-powders contain only about 30 per cent. of chlorine. The mode of determining the amount of chlorine present is called *chlorimetry*, and is based on the quantity of sulphate of indigo which is decolorized by a standard solution of chlorine. The salts of lime are not precipitated by ammonia, but form an entirely insoluble oxalate, with oxalic acid or oxalate of ammonia.

MAGNESIUM.

Equivalent, 12·2. *Symbol*, Mg.

542. *Magnesium is obtained* by decomposing the chlorid of that metal heated to redness in a glass tube, by passing over it the vapor of potassium or sodium. Chlorid of potassium or sodium is formed, and the metallic magnesium is separated by dissolving out the soluble chlorid.

It is a white metal, malleable and brilliant. It fuses with a red heat, and if heated to redness in the air, burns with a brilliant light, producing oxyd of magnesium. It does not tarnish in dry air, and does not decompose water even at 212°, but dissolves in acids with escape of hydrogen.

543. *Oxyd of Magnesium, Calcined Magnesia*, MgO. This substance is left when the carbonate of magnesia is heated to redness. It is a white, very light, earthy powder, insoluble in water, but readily soluble in weak acids. It occurs in nature crystallized in regular octahedrons, forming the mineral *periclase*. It is much used in medicine as a mild and efficient aperient. The hydrate of magnesia

---

What is Labarraque's liquor? What is the composition of bleaching-powder? What is chlorimetry? What precipitates the salts of lime? 542. Give the equivalent and preparation of magnesium. What are its properties? 543. What is the oxyd of magnesium? How is it used? How found in nature?

MgO.HO is formed when magnesia is precipitated from its solutions by an alkali. Heat expels the equivalent of water, leaving *calcined magnesia.* The hydrate is found beautifully crystallized in thin pearly plates at Hoboken, New Jersey.

544. *Chlorid of Magnesium,* MgCl.—This chlorid is best prepared by neutralizing equal portions of chlorohydric acid, one with magnesia and the other with ammonia, mixing the two portions and evaporating to dryness. The dry mass is heated in a covered crucible as long as sal-ammoniac is given off, when pure chlorid of magnesium is left. It is a very deliquescent salt, and supplies the means of procuring metallic magnesium. When magnesia is dissolved in hydrochloric acid, a hydrated chlorid of magnesium results. By heat the water is expelled, carrying with it chlorohydric acid, and leaving pure magnesia behind. The *bittern* of salt springs is chlorid of magnesium; it exists in sea-water, and is the largest ingredient in the waters of the Dead Sea. The iodid and bromid of magnesium are also soluble salts, but the fluorid is insoluble.

545. *Sulphate of Magnesia, Epsom Salts,* $MgO.SO_3+7HO$.—This well-known salt is easily formed by dissolving magnesia, or its carbonate, in sulphuric acid. It is also found native at Corydon, Illinois. In the waters of Epsom Spa, in England, and in numerous mineral waters, it is a large constituent. It is made on a large scale by dissolving serpentine rock in strong sulphuric acid. It is very soluble, and, like all the soluble salts of magnesia, has a peculiar bitter taste.

546. The *carbonate of magnesia, magnesite,* $MgO.CO_2$, is found native in magnesian rocks, and is formed artificially by decomposing any of the soluble salts of magnesia by an alkaline carbonate, giving the *magnesia alba* of pharmacy. It is insoluble in water; but a solution of carbonic acid dissolves it, and forms the celebrated *Murray's solution of magnesia.* It is decomposed by contact of air, carbonic acid escapes, and carbonate of magnesia is thrown down. The double carbonate of magnesia and lime is found as an ex-

---

What is calcined magnesia? 544. How is the chlorid of magnesium prepared? Describe it. When magnesia is dissolved in chlorohydric acid, what happens? 545. What is the composition of sulphate of magnesia? How is it made in the large way? In what waters is it found? 546. What is carbonate of magnesia? What is Murray's solution?

tensive rock formation, called *dolomite*, and when crystal lized, *pearl spar*.

Phosphate of soda with ammonia throws down a crys talline insoluble salt from magnesian solutions, which is the double phosphate of magnesia and ammonia. This is the most ready mode of testing for the presence of magnesia.

547. Magnesia occurs abundantly in nature as a constituent of many minerals, as well as in the form of hydrate and carbonate. The silicates of magnesia form a very important class of minerals, of which talc, soap-stone, pyroxene, hornblende, serpentine, &c., are examples. Magnesia is also found in the ashes of most plants, in union with phosphoric acid.

CLASS III.—METALS OF THE EARTHS.

ALUMINUM. Al.=13·69.

548. *Aluminum* is best obtained, like magnesium, by the action of sodium or potassium on its chlorid. It is a gray powder, not easily melted, has a metallic lustre, and burns, when heated in the air, with a bright light, forming alumina.

549. *Alumina; Sesquioxyd of Aluminum; Corundum*, Al_2O_3.—Pure alumina is found crystallized in those precious gems, the oriental ruby and sapphire, which are next in hardness and value to the diamond. Emery (cornudum) is also nearly pure alumina. Alumina is an abundant ingredient in many other minerals, and forms a large part of many slaty rocks, from whose decomposition clays are produced.

Pure alumina is a fine white powder, not rough and gritty like silica. Its density is 4·154. It is infusible except under the oxyhydrogen blowpipe. After ignition it is almost or entirely insoluble.

Hydrate of alumina Al_2O_3+3HO exists in the minerals *diaspore* and *gibbsite*. Alumina is precipitated as a hydrate from solution, by either potash, soda, or ammonia, and their carbonates; an excess of the first two will redissolve the precipitate. The hydrate is very bulky, and shrinks very

---

What test have we for magnesia? 547. How does magnesia occur in nature? Mention some of its silicates. 548. How is aluminum obtained? What are its properties and density? 549. What is the formula of alumina? In what is it found pure? How are the hydrous and anhydrous alumina distinguished? What precipitates and what redissolves it?

much on drying. Hydrosulphuret of ammonium throws down alumina. The anhydrous alumina is almost insoluble in acids, while the hydrate is readily dissolved, forming salts of a peculiar astringent taste, familiarly known in common alum.

The chlorid of aluminum has no particular interest except as a means of procuring the metal.

Aluminate of potassa $KO.Al_2O_3$ is formed when a solution of alumina in potassa is gently evaporated: it appears in crystalline grains. Baryta and magnesia afford similar examples. *Spinel*, a mineral species, is an aluminate of magnesia $MgO.Al_2O_3$. These are instances of the double function which alumina possesses of acting the part both of acid and base, (474, 3.)

550. *Sulphate of Alumina*, $Al_2O_3.3SO_3+18HO$.—This salt is prepared by saturating dilute sulphuric acid with alumina: it has a sweetish astringent taste, is soluble in 2 parts of water, and crystallizes in thin plates.

Alums.—Sulphate of alumina forms, with potash, soda, and ammonia, double salts of much interest, called *alums*. They are all soluble salts, with a sweetish astringent taste, and crystallize in the regular system, or first class, (44,) usually as modified octahedrons, which have uniformly 24 equivalents of water of crystallization. Common potash-alum has the formula $Al_2O_3.3SO_3+KO.SO_3+24HO$, (256;) it dissolves in 18 parts of cold water, and the solution has an acid reaction. The water of crystallization of the alums is expelled by heat: the salt first suffers watery fusion, and then swells up into a light porous mass, many times the volume of the salt employed, and protruding beyond the vessel employed, as in fig. 362. This is called *burnt-alum*. All the basic sesquioxyds isomorphous with alumina may replace it in the constitution of an alum.

Fig. 362.

Alum and acetate of alumina are largely employed in the arts of dyeing and tanning. Alumina combines with coloring matters, and seems to form a bond of union between the fibre of the cloth

---

What salts does it form? What is aluminate of potassa? What is spinel? Give the formula of alum. 550. What is burnt alum? What is the use of alums?

and the color. In this it is said to act the part of a *mordant.* When alum is added to the solution of a coloring matter, and the alumina is then precipitated with an alkali, all the coloring matter is thrown down with it, and forms what is called *lake.* The common lake used in water-coloring is derived from madder treated in this way. Carmine is a lake made from cochineal.

551. *Silicates of Alumina.*—This is the most extensive and important class of the aluminous salts, and comprises a great number of interesting minerals. *Feldspar,* $Al_2O_3.3SiO_3+KO.SiO_3$, which is one of the chief components of granite and granitic rocks, is of this class, and has the composition of an anhydrous alum, the sulphuric acid being replaced by the silicic. *Albite* is a salt having soda in place of the potash in feldspar, while *spodumene* and *petalite* are similar compounds, with a portion of the soda replaced by *lithia. Kyanite* and *andalusite* are simple basic silicates of alumina. Many other similarly constituted compounds are found among minerals, some of which are hydrous and others anhydrous, and varied by frequent substitution of peroxyd of iron, manganese, or other isomorphous bases, for the alumina.

Plants do not take up alumina, and it is not yet proved that their ashes ever contain it. Its value in the soil seems to be in retaining moisture, ammonia, and carbonic acid, and in giving firmness to the other incoherent components of the soil. The decomposition of these silicates gives origin to clay, whose peculiar qualities derived from the alumina fit it for the purpose of the potter.

This is the place to say a few words upon the two important arts of glass-blowing and pottery.

Manufacture of Glass.

552. *Silicates of Soda.*—Both soda and potash unite by fusion with silicic acid to form silicates of variable composition. If 3 parts of the alkali are used to 1 of the silica, the glass is soluble in water, but whatever may be the pro-

---

What is a mordant? What a lake? 551. What is the most important class of alumina compounds? What is the formula of feldspar? What silicates are named? What is the function of alumina in soils? What are clays? 552. How do the alkalies unite with silica. What is the character of the compounds so obtained?

portions used, the resulting silicate is always an uncrystalline, homogeneous, transparent mass. The "*soluble glass*" formed by fusing together 8 parts of carbonate of soda (or 10 of carbonate of potash) with 15 parts of pure sand and 1 of charcoal, is insoluble in cold, but dissolves in 4 or 5 parts of hot water, forming a sort of varnish, which may be applied to wood or manufactured stuffs, which are to a good degree protected from it by the action of fire.

553. *Glass* is a variable compound of the silicates of potash, soda, lime, and alumina, with oxyds of lead and iron, fused together by a very high and long-continued heat, in proportions suited to the object for which the glass is to be used. The relation between the oxygen in the base and that in the silica determines the degree of fusibility of the glass: thus, the greater the proportion of silica the less the fusibility of glass. The principal varieties of glass are these, viz:

Window glass, a silicate of soda and lime, which requires an intense heat for its fusion, and forms a very hard and brilliant glass. *Plate glass*, such as is used for mirrors, crown glass employed for glazing, and the beautiful *Bohemian glass*, are all silicates of potash and lime.

Crystal glass is formed by fusing together 120 parts of fine sand, 40 of purified potash, 36 of litharge or minium, (oxyd of lead,) and 12 of nitre. This forms a very fusible glass easily worked, and so soft as to be cut and polished with comparative ease. The oxyd of lead greatly increases its brilliancy.

Green bottle-glass is usually a silicate of lime and alumina, with oxyds of iron and manganese, and potash or soda. It is formed of the cheapest refuse of the soap-boiler's waste, and lime which has been used to make caustic potash or soda.

554. The processes of the glass-house are all exceedingly interesting and instructive—the tools few and simple—the results dependent on the adroit manipulations of the workman. The materials are fused in clay pots, of which several are heated in one circular reverberatory furnace, their

---

What is soluble glass? 553. What is glass? What determines the fusibility of glass? What sorts are named? What is the composition of window and plate? What of crystal? What of green bottle-glass? 554. How are the materials fused?

mouths outward. Fig. 363 shows a section of one of them. After two days and nights, the *metal*, or fused glass, is brought to a homogeneous condition and the consistence of honey. The chief instrument of the glass-blower is his *punta* rod, which is simply an iron tube *a b*, fig 364, open at both ends and covered by a wooden collar *c d* to protect the hands from the heat. This rod is thrust into the pot of molten glass while it is turned in the hand, a portion of the fluid glass adheres to it, the rod is withdrawn, and if enough has not adhered to meet the wants of the workman, he takes up a second portion. This he first fashions into a cylindrical form upon a slab of iron, rolling the rod over and over in his hand, (fig. 365.) Suppose it is required to make a glass tube, such as is so much used in the laboratory. He applies his mouth to the end of the punta-rod and blows. The cylinder of glass is inflated, and assumes a pear shape, as in fig. 366. An assistant now applies his tube, containing also a small portion of hot glass, to the opposite extremity of the first mass, (fig. 367,) and drawing against the other, the ellipti-

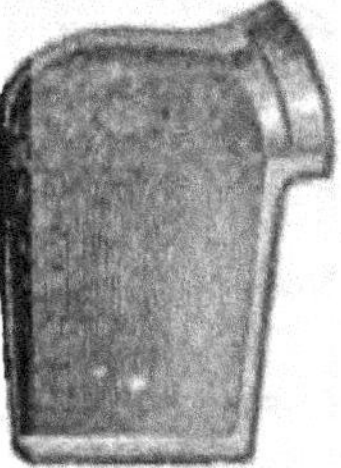

Fig. 363.

Fig. 364.

Fig. 365.

Fig. 366.

Fig. 367.

Fig. 368.

cal mass is elongated and assumes the form seen in fig. 368. The two workmen now walk rapidly away from each other in opposite directions, drawing their tubes in the same line, giving the ductile glass the form of a tube, as seen in fig. 369. A few inches from each punta-tube the glass becomes

Fig. 369.

of a uniform size, the small cavity originally blown in the

What are the instruments used? How is a glass tube formed? Illustrate the process from figs. 363–369. What is pressed glass?

mass (fig. 366) is elongated to a smooth cylindrical bore, and however small the glass tube may be drawn out, this bore always remains circular and entire through its whole length. To fashion a bottle, the operation is commenced in the same manner, but the adroitness of the workman enables him to elongate it by centrifugal force, wheeling the molten mass over his head while he inflates it; and the bottom is drawn in by revolving the rod rapidly on a crotch while he applies the surface of an iron instrument to the revolving flexible glass to fashion it at his will. Most of the cheap glass vessels now manufactured are formed by blowing the glass in a metallic mould opening in two parts. This is called *pressed glass.* In the laboratory a flat lamp, like fig. 370, fed with tallow, is employed to fashion tubes into the various forms required for the construction of the apparatus. The flame is driven by a bellows under the table worked by the foot. With a little practice, the operator soon acquires sufficient skill to make from plain tubes such forms of glass apparatus as are figured in this work.

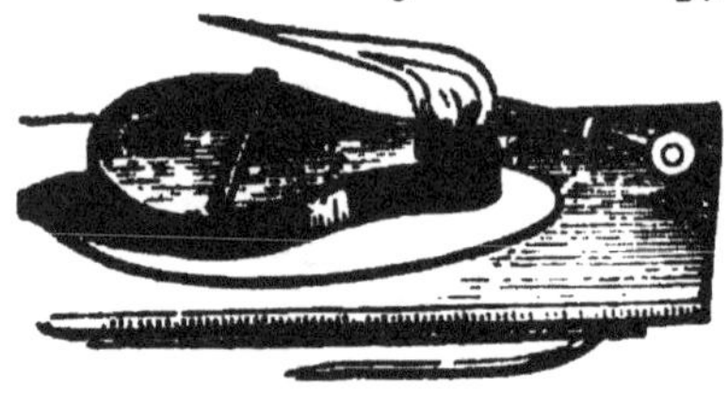

Fig. 370.

All glass must be carefully annealed after it is made, by slow cooling, or it will break in pieces with the least scratch or jar. Slow cooling of heated glass for many hours, or even days, is required for heavy articles. Prince Rupert's drops (fig. 371) are little tears of glass dropped into water when fused. The outer surface becoming solid while the inner parts are still flexible, there comes to be an enormous strain on the exterior, due to the contraction at the centre. If the little end of this tear is broken, the whole suddenly and with an explosion flies into dust. Unannealed glass is to a certain degree under the same conditions of unequal tension. Hence the necessity of annealing or slow cooling to give time for the particles to rearrange themselves without strain. Glass is colored red by the oxyds of copper and gold, blue by oxyds of cobalt, white by tin,

Fig. 371.

How is glass worked in the laboratory? What is annealing? How is this illustrated by Prince Rupert's drops? Explain the illustration. How is glass colored?

arsenic and antimony, yellow by uranium, purple and violet by manganese, and green by chromium, iron, nickel, &c. By the skilful use of these oxyds, with a heavy and highly refracting glass, the various gems are very beautifully imitated. Such imitations are called pastes.

Pottery.

555. One of the oldest of human inventions is the fashioning of vessels of use and ornament out of clay. The bricks of Babylon and Nineveh, covered with arrow-head inscriptions, are among the most ancient memorials of history.

The decomposition of feldspar and other aluminous minerals and rocks gives origin to the clays which are so important in the art of pottery. Decomposed feldspar forms porcelain clay, commonly called kaolin. The undecomposed mineral is often ground up to mix with the materials for porcelain. The difference between porcelain and earthenware consists in the partial fusion of the materials of the former by the heat of the furnace, which gives it the semi-transparency and great beauty for which it is so highly prized. Common earthenware is often glazed with oxyd of lead, an unsafe mode for culinary vessels: common salt (508) is also used, being raised in vapor by the heat of the kiln. The soda unites with silica, while the chlorine escapes as chlorid of iron. The glaze in porcelain is formed of a more fusible mixture of the same materials, put over the articles as a wash, after they have been once through the furnace, (in which state they are called biscuit ware;) they are then baked again at a heat which fuses the glaze, but which does not soften the body of the ware. All porcelain is twice fired and sometimes thrice. If painted, the design is laid upon the surface in colors formed from metallic oxyds, which develop their appropriate tints only after fusion with the ingredients of the glaze. Metallic gold is put on in the form of an oxyd, and the steel lustre is produced by metallic platinum. This beautiful art is carried to a wonderful

---

How made refractive? 555. What is one of the most ancient arts? Whence is potter's clay derived? What is kaolin? What is the difference between porcelain and earthenware? How is pottery glazed? How porcelain? How painted?

perfection in the royal establishments of France and Prussia, where the first talent is employed in modelling and painting. Any further detail of these interesting branches of applied chemistry would be out of place here, and the student is referred to larger works for a fuller description.

556. There are six other metals belonging to this class, which are so rare and comparatively unimportant that we pass them with the most cursory enumeration: *Glucinum* is the base of a sesquioxyd G_2O_3, (glucina,) which is the characteristic earth of the emerald, beryl, and chrysoberyl It is very like alumina, and is named in allusion to the sweet taste of its salts. *Yttrium* is the metal of the earth yttria YO, found in the minerals yttrocerite, &c. *Zirconium* is found as a sesquioxyd of zirconia Zr_2O_3 in *zircon*. *Thoria* was found by Berzelius in the rarest of all minerals, the *thorite*, of Sweden. Thorium has the highest specific gravity (9) of any earth. *Cerium* and *lantanium* are invariably associated, and with them another rare metal, *didymium*. The minerals *cerite*, *allanite*, and *monazite* contain them.

CLASS IV. HEAVY METALS, WHOSE OXYDS FORM POWERFUL BASES.

MANGANESE.

Equivalent, 27·6. *Symbol*, Mn. *Density*, 8.

557. *Manganese* is never found as a metal in nature, but may be produced from its black oxyd by a high heat with charcoal. Metallic manganese is a gray, brittle metal, not magnetic, and resembles some varieties of cast-iron. It dissolves rapidly in sulphuric acid with escape of hydrogen.

Manganese, in the form of the black oxyd, is an important and pretty common metal. Its great use is for producing chlorine (282) and in the manufacture of glass, where it acts by its oxygen to decolorize the compound.

558. We enumerate five compounds of manganese, viz. protoxyd MnO; sesquioxyd (or braunite) Mn_2O_3; peroxyd, or deutoxyd, (pyrolusite,) MnO_2; manganic acid MnO_3; hypermanganic acid Mn_2O_7.

---

556. Enumerate the other earthy metals named in this section. 557. What are the equivalent and properties of manganese? What form of it is most common? For what is it used? 558. How many and what oxyds of manganese are named?

The *protoxyd* is a green-colored powder, formed from heating the carbonate of manganese in an atmosphere of hydrogen. It is a powerful base, attracts oxygen from the air, and is the base of the beautiful rose-colored salts of manganese.

The sesquioxyd or *braunite* occurs crystallized in octahedrons and forms belonging to the dimetric system.

The *hydrated sesquioxyd* Mn_2O_3+HO (manganite) is a finely crystallized mineral, in long black prisms, found in superb specimens at Ilfeld, in the Hartz. In powder the sesquioxyd is brown; it is decomposed by chlorohydric acid with the evolution of chlorine, but sulphuric acid combines with it to form a sesquisulphate, which yields a purple double salt with sulphate of potash, (manganese alum,) isomorphous with the corresponding salt of alumina.

559. The *peroxyd* MnO_2 is the most common and most valuable ore of manganese. From it we obtain oxygen, and, by the decomposition of chlorohydric acid, chlorine. It is found abundantly at Bennington, Vermont, and other places in this country. When crystallized it is called *pyrolusite*. Beautiful specimens of this mineral have been observed at Salisbury and Kent, Connecticut, among the iron ores.

560. *Mangánic acid* is known only in combination, especially as manganate of potash. This is best formed by mixing equal parts of finely powdered black oxyd of manganese and chlorate of potash with rather more than one part of hydrate of potash dissolved in a very little water. This mixture, when evaporated, is heated to a point short of redness, and a dark green mass is formed which contains manganate of potash. In this case the manganese obtains oxygen from the chlorate of potash, and the manganic acid thus formed combines with potash, giving a salt in green crystals. This salt, dissolved in water, gives a brilliant emerald-green solution, which almost immediately changes color, being in quick succession green, blue, purple, and finally crimson-red, and has thence been called *chameleon mineral*. This last color is due to the presence of *permanganic acid*, which, however, cannot be separated from its combinations, but

---

Which is the base of the rose-colored salts? What is the sesquioxyd? Give the formula of the hydrated sesquioxyd? What is said of the sulphate of the sesquioxyd? 559. Which is the most common ore of manganese? Where and how is it found? 560. Describe manganic acid and the salt it forms with potash. What is the changeable compound called

forms a salt with potash in beautiful purple crystals. The compounds of permanganic acid are more stable than the manganates. The salts of these acids are respectively isomorphous with sulphates and perchlorates SO_3 and Cl_2O_7.

561. The *chlorids of manganese* MnCl and Mn_2Cl_3 correspond to the protoxyd and sesquioxyd. The *chlorid* is formed abundantly in acting on black oxyd of manganese (282) with hydrochloric acid. The mixed solution of chlorids of iron and manganese is evaporated to dryness, and then heated to dull redness. The chlorid of manganese is then dissolved out from the dry mass, leaving the insoluble protoxyd of iron behind. It has a beautiful pink tint, and deposits tabular rose-colored crystals on evaporation. It is soluble in alcohol, and fusible by heat.

562. The *salts of manganese* are numerous, and in a chemical view quite important. Sulphate of manganese $MnO.SO_3 + 7HO$ is a very beautiful rose-colored salt, isomorphous with sulphate of magnesia. It is used to give a fine brown dye to cloth, being decomposed by a solution of bleaching-powder, which forms the brown peroxyd in the fibre of the stuffs. It is also used in medicine.

Potassa and soda throw down the oxyd of manganese as a white powder, which immediately turns brown from the formation of a higher oxyd. The carbonates of the alkalies throw down carbonate of manganese from their soluble salts. Any compound of manganese fused upon a slip of platina with carbonate of soda, gives a powerfully characteristic green salt, the permanganate of soda.

IRON.

Equivalent, 28. *Symbol*, Fe. *Density*, 7·8.

563. *Iron is found malleable*, and alloyed with nickel, in large masses of meteoric origin. One of these, discovered in Texas, weighs 1635 pounds, and is now in Yale College cabinet. It is not certain that malleable iron of terrestrial origin has yet been discovered in nature. Iron is the most abundant and most useful metal known to man. Its ores

---

What is said of the salts of manganic and permanganic acid? 561. Describe the chlorids of manganese? 562. What is said in general of the salts of manganese? What tests are named for manganese and its salts? 563. What is the equivalent of iron? How is malleable iron found? What is said of its abundance and value?

are found everywhere, and often in immediate connection with the coal and limestone necessary to reduce them to the metallic state. There is no soil, and scarcely any mineral, which does not contain some proportion of the oxyd of iron. We know iron as malleable iron, steel, and cast iron.

564. To obtain pure iron is not easy, and the best iron of commerce is always contaminated with carbon and silicon. Small quantities of iron are prepared absolutely pure, in the laboratory, by reducing the pure oxyd of iron in a bulb of hard

Fig. 372.

glass *a b* (fig. 372) by a current of dry hydrogen. The bulb A is heated by the flame of a spirit-lamp. This apparatus serves for numerous reductions of metallic oxyds, as, for example, the oxyds of cobalt, nickel, zinc, &c. The bulbed tube *a b* is drawn down at *c* (fig. 373) to a narrow neck, so that while the tube is yet full of hydrogen it may be sealed by the blowpipe both at *c* and *b*: otherwise the pulverulent

Fig. 373.

metallic iron, from its strong affinity for oxygen, will take fire on contact of air, and be carried back again to its original condition of oxyd. If this operation is conducted in a porcelain tube at a high heat, the iron formed assumes a metallic lustre, and does not oxydize; and if protochlorid of iron is used in place of the oxyd, the metal rises in vapor, lining the tube with a brilliant crystalline crust.

565. When quite pure, it is nearly white, quite soft, perfectly malleable, and the most tenacious of all metals, (471.) Its density is 7 8, which may be a little increased by ham-

564. How is pure iron obtained? Describe fig. 372. What happens if the iron so obtained is exposed to air? How is it obtained more dense? 565. What are its properties?

mering. It crystallizes in forms of the first class, as is beautifully shown in the crystalline structure of the meteoric iron, and sometimes in the crust produced in the reduction of the protochlorid. It fuses with extreme difficulty, first becoming soft or pasty, in which state it is *welded*. When intensely heated in air or oxygen gas it combines with oxygen, burning with brilliant light and numerous scintillations, and is converted into oxyd of iron, (fig. 374.) Iron also attracts oxygen from the air at common temperatures, forming rust. This does not happen in dry air, but the presence of moisture, and particularly of a little acid vapor, very much promotes its formation. Iron decomposes water very rapidly at a red-heat, hydrogen being evolved. Its magnetic relations have already been fully explained. Cobalt and nickel are the only other magnetic metals.

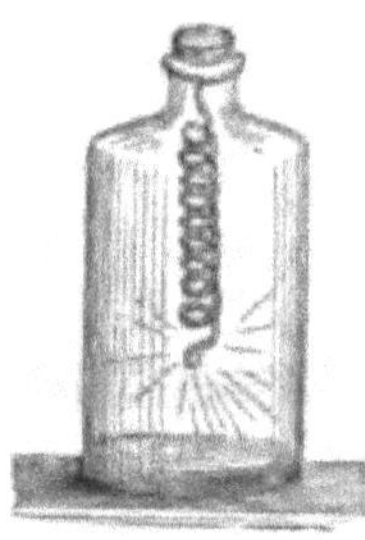
Fig. 374.

566. The *oxyds of iron* are three, viz: 1. Protoxyd, FeO; 2. Sesquioxyd, commonly called peroxyd, Fe_2O_3; 3. Ferric acid, FeO_3. The *magnetic oxyd* Fe_3O_4 is regarded as a compound of protoxyd and sesquioxyd $FeO.Fe_2O_3$, in which the sesquioxyd plays the part of a base, (475.)

1. The *protoxyd of iron* FeO is a powerful base which is unknown in nature except in combination. It saturates acids completely and is isomorphous with a large class of bodies, of which zinc and magnesia are examples, (263.) This oxyd is thrown down from its solutions by potash, as a whitish bulky hydrate, that soon gains another portion of oxygen from the air, becoming brown, and finally red. Its salts, when soluble, have a styptic taste like ink, and a greenish color, of which the most familiar example is *green vitriol*, or sulphate of protoxyd of iron.

2. The *peroxyd of iron* Fe_2O_3 is found native in the beautiful *specular iron* of Elba, and also in the red and brown *hematites*. *Limonite* $2(Fe_2O_3)+3HO$ is a hydrous sesquioxyd. It is slightly acted on by the magnet, and after ignition is almost insoluble in strong acids. It is isomorphous with alumina, and is generally associated with it in soils and many minerals. It is often of a brilliant red,

---

What is welding? 566. What oxyds are named? Give their formulas. Describe the protoxyd and its salts. How is the peroxyd known?

and, as *ochre* of various tints, is much used as a pigment. Ammonia, potassa, or soda precipitates it from its solutions as a bulky red hydrate, which, in its moist condition, is esteemed an antidote to poisoning by arsenic. *Colcothar*, or *rouge*, is this oxyd prepared by calcining the sulphate: it is much used in polishing metals.

Magnetic oxyd of iron Fe_3O_4 is familiarly known in the common magnetic iron ore and native lode-stone. It crystallizes in octahedrons. It forms no salts, and, as has already been remarked, is regarded as a salt of $FeO+Fe_2O_3$. The finery cinders or scales thrown off under the smith's hammer are this oxyd.

3. *Ferric Acid*, FeO_3.—This compound, discovered by M. Fremy, corresponds to manganic acid. Ferrate of potash is formed when one part of peroxyd of iron and four parts of nitre are heated to full redness in a covered crucible for an hour. The ferrate of potash is dissolved out of the porous mass by ice-cold water. The solution has a deep amethystine color, and is easily decomposed by heat. A soluble salt of baryta precipitates ferric acid as a beautiful red ferrate of baryta, which is permanent.

567. The *chlorids of iron* FeCl and Fe_2Cl_3 correspond to the protoxyd and sesquioxyd of the same base. The perchlorid is often used in medicine, and may be formed by saturating hydrochloric acid with freshly prepared peroxyd of iron. The *protiodid* of iron is also a valuable medicine.

The *sulphurets of iron* are found in nature, and are known under the mineralogical names of *pyrites* and *marcasite* FeS_2, and *magnetic pyrites* Fe_7S_8. The protosulphuret FeS is easily formed artificially, by fusing sulphur with iron filings: they ignite with a vivid combustion, and protosulphuret of iron is formed, which is much used in preparing sulphuretted hydrogen. Yellow iron pyrites and white iron pyrites (*marcasite*) are dimorphous forms of the bisulphuret FeS_2: the first is one of the most common of crystallized minerals.

568. Of the *salts of iron*, green vitriol, or *copperas*, a pro-

---

What is colcothar? Give the formula of the black oxyd. How is it found in nature? What is ferric acid? 567. What chlorids of iron are named? What oxyds do they correspond to? What are the sulphurets of iron? For what is the protosulphuret used? What is the name of the ordinary sulphuret? What two forms of it are found in nature?

tosulphate $FeO.SO_3+7HO$, is the most important. It is made in immense quantities, as at Stafford, Vt., from the fermentation of iron pyrites, which furnishes both the acid and the base. This salt crystallizes beautifully, and is much used as the basis of all black dyes and of ink, and in the manufacture of prussian blue. Persulphate of iron is a sulphate of the peroxyd $Fe_2O_3+3SO_3$. *Carbonate of iron* occurs in nature as *spathic iron ore*, which is isomorphous with carbonate of lime. A variety of steel is made directly from this ore without cementation, (570.) It is formed artificially by precipitating a solution of protosulphate by an alkaline carbonate. It is used in medicine.

Water containing carbonic acid dissolves protoxyd of iron and acquires the well-known flavor of chalybeate waters: exposure to air permits the escape of the carbonic acid, when the iron falls as red peroxyd.

Phosphate of iron $FeO.PO_5+8HO$ is formed as a greenish-white gelatinous precipitate when solution of tribasic phosphate of soda is added to solution of protosulphate of iron. It is an article of the materia medica. Vivianite is a mineral having the same formula, found both massive and crystallized, of a beautiful indigo-blue color.

The cyanogen compounds of iron will be described in the organic chemistry.

The presence of a salt of iron is easily detected by the fine blue (prussian blue) formed on adding prussiate of potash to the solution: an infusion of galls gives a black color (ink) to solutions of iron salts.

569. The chief ores of iron are, 1. The *specular iron* or *peroxyd*, including red and brown hematite; 2. *Limonite*, or *hydrous peroxyd*, from which the best iron is made—(bog iron also comes under this head;) 3. *Clay iron-stone*, which is an impure carbonate of iron, or carbonate of iron with carbonate of lime and magnesia—this is the nodular ore and *band* ore of the coal formations; 4. *Black* or *magnetic oxyd of iron*, which is the ore of the iron mountains of Missouri and of Sweden.

The *reduction of the ores of iron* to the metallic state is usually performed in large furnaces called *high* or *blast fur-*

---

568. Which of the salts of iron is of great importance? How and where is it made in this country? What is the carbonate and for what used? What of the phosphate? What tests are named for iron? 569. What ores of iron are enumerated? How is the reduction of iron effected?

naces. These are built of stone, in a conical form, 30 to 50 feet high, and lined internally with the most refractory fire-bricks. The furnace is divided into the throat, the fire-room *b*, the boshes *e*, (that portion sloping inward,) the crucible *f*, and the hearth *h*. The blast of air—supplied from very large blowing cylinders—is introduced by two or three *tuyere* pipes *a a*, near the bottom. In the most improved furnaces, the air-blast is heated by causing it to pass through a series of pipes in the upper portion of the furnace, so as to have a temperature of 500° or more when it enters the furnace. When the furnace is brought into action, it is first heated with coal only, for about 24 hours, to raise it to the proper temperature; and then is charged alternately with proper proportions of coal, roasted ore, and lime for flux, until it is quite full. When once brought into action, the blast is kept up for months or even years, until the furnace requires repairing. The ore is reduced on the boshes, and in the upper part of the crucible, where the oxyd of carbon is found almost pure in presence of an excess of white-hot carbon and ore previously dried and in part reduced in the higher parts of the furnace. The melted metal collects on the hearth, where it rests, covered by the molten flux, which is a glass, formed by the fusion of the lime used, with the earthy parts of the ore. From time to time, the iron is drawn off by an opening level with the hearth, previously stopped with clay, and run into rude open moulds in sand. This is *cast iron*, and is of various qualities, according to the various character of the ore and the working of the furnace. If malleable bar iron is wanted, the cast iron is again melted, in what is called the *puddling furnace*, where it is stirred

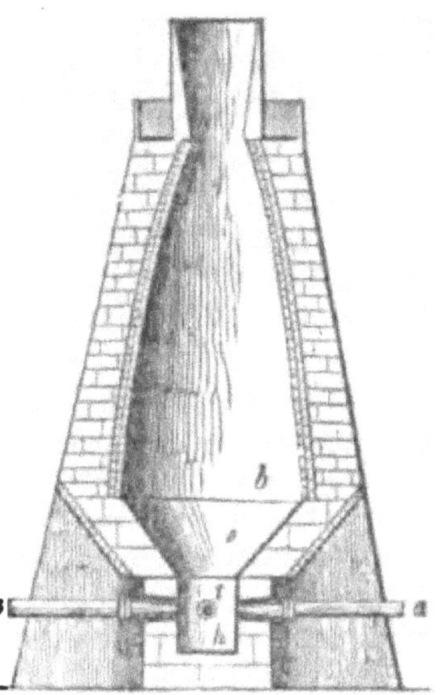

Fig. 375.

Describe the high furnace. What is the hot blast? What is the operation of the furnace? What is cast iron? How is malleable iron made from cast iron?

about by an iron rod, in contact with oxyd of iron, and a current of heated carbonic oxyd from burning wood or coal. It gradually becomes stiff and pasty from the burning out of the carbon, and from some molecular change not well understood. This pasty condition increases until the iron is finally raised in a rude ball and placed under the blows of a huge tilt-hammer, when the scoria is pressed out and the particles made to cohere. It grows tenacious by a repetition of this process, being cut up and *piled* or *faggoted* and reheated several times, until it is finally rolled in the rolling-mill into tough and fibrous metal.

570. *Steel is formed from refined iron* by heating it for days in succession in contact with charcoal in close vessels, (called cementation.) It gains from one to two per cent of carbon, becomes fusible, and can be *tempered* according to the use for which it is designed.

The Catalan forge is a furnace formed like a smith's forge on a large scale, and in which the circumstances of the high and puddling furnace are combined, so that malleable iron is produced from the ore—the cast iron being brought to the ductile state in the same fire where it is reduced from the ore—charcoal is the fuel of the Catalan forge. The best iron is always produced when charcoal is the fuel, being free from sulphur and phosphorus, the two worst enemies of good iron.

CHROMIUM.

Equivalent, 26·4. *Symbol*, Cr. *Density*, 6.

571. *Chromium in combination with iron* is rather an abundant substance, particularly in this country, being found as chromic iron at Barehills, near Baltimore; Lancaster Co., Pa., and in several other places. The beautiful red chromate of lead is also a natural product in Siberia. The metal, from its great affinity for oxygen, is very difficult to procure. It is a hard, almost infusible substance, resembling cast iron, nearly insoluble in acids, and does not decompose water. It may be oxydized by fusion with nitre, but does not change in the air.

---

570. What is steel? What is the Catalan forge? What fuel makes the best iron? 571. What are the symbol and properties of chromium? How distributed in nature?

572. The oxyds of chromium are exactly the same as those of manganese. Chromium bears the strongest analogy in its chemical character to manganese and iron. The parallelism of constitution in the oxyds of these three metals is shown in the following tabular arrangement:—

	Protoxyd.		Sesquioxyd.		Black oxyd.		Peroxyd.	Acids.	
Manganese forms..	MnO	...	Mn_2O_3	...	Mn_3O_4	...	MnO_2	MnO_3	Mn_2O_7
Iron forms............	FeO	...	Fe_2O_3	...	Fe_3O_4	...		FeO_3	
Chromium forms...	CrO	...	Cr_2O_3	...	Cr_3O_4	...	CrO_2	CrO_3	Cr_2O_7

The *protoxyd of chromium* is a strong base, acting in combination like the protoxyd of iron, with which it is isomorphous.

573. *Sesquioxyd of chromium* Cr_2O_3 may be obtained in little rhombohedral crystals by passing the vapor of chlorochromic acid through a heated tube, $2CrO_2Cl = Cr_2O_3 + 2Cl + O$. The crystals are deposited on the walls of the tube in a brilliant deep-green crust. They are as hard as ruby. Their density is 5·21.

The *hydrated sesquioxyd of chromium* $Cr_2O_3 + HO$ is easily prepared by treating a boiling and rather dilute solution of bichromate of potash with an excess of chlorohydric acid, and then with successive portions of alcohol or sugar until it assumes a fine emerald tint. Ammonia throws down a bulky, pale-green precipitate, soluble in acids and shrinking very much in drying—this is the hydrate. On ignition it undergoes vivid incandescence and becomes deep green. The sesquioxyd of chromium is a feeble base like those of iron and alumina, and may replace them in combination, as in the formation of chrome alum with sulphate of potash. Sesquioxyd of chromium forms an alum also with the sulphates of soda and ammonia. All the salts of this oxyd are either emerald green or bluish purple. It imparts a rich tint of green to glass and porcelain, and is the cause of the color of the emerald. Chrome iron is composed of this oxyd and protoxyd of iron $FeO.Cr_2O_3$, isomorphous with magnetic iron $FeO.Fe_2O_3$, and with spinel $MgO.Al_2O_3$. The chrome iron of Pennsylvania contains a little nickel.

574. *Chromic acid* CrO_3 is readily formed by treating

572. What strong analogies has it? Give the parallel oxyds of Mn, Fe, and Cr. 573. How is sesquioxyd of Cr obtained? How is its hydrate? What are its properties? What salts does it form? What is chrome iron? 574. How is chromic acid formed?

a cold and concentrated solution of bichromate of potash with one and a half parts of sulphuric acid. The mixture, when cold, deposits brilliant ruby-red prisms of chromic acid. The sulphate of potash in solution above, may be turned off, and the chromic acid dried on a porous brick, being carefully covered with a glass to prevent access of organic matters, which at once decompose it. If a little of this acid be thrown into alcohol or ether, the violence of the action is such as to set fire to the mixture. Chromic acid forms numerous salts, which are highly colored.

The *protochlorid of chromium* $CrCl$ is obtained as a white and very soluble substance by the action of dry hydrogen gas on the sesquichlorid. The *sesquichlorid* Cr_2Cl_3 is prepared by passing chlorine gas over an ignited mixture of the sesquioxyd and charcoal. It forms a crystalline sublimate of a peach-blossom color, which is insoluble in water. The sesquioxyd dissolves in chlorohydric acid, but the hydrated chlorid thus obtained is decomposed by heat.

Chlorochromic acid CrO_2Cl is a deep-red volatile liquid, much resembling bromine in its appearance. It is formed when 10 parts of common salt and 17 of bichromate of potash are intimately mixed, and heated in a retort with 30 parts of concentrated sulphuric acid. The chlorochromic acid distils over, filling the receiver with a superb ruby-red vapor. Its density is 1·71, and it boils at 248°. Water decomposes it, forming chromic and hydrochloric acids. It may be preserved in tubes hermetically sealed.

575. The *chromate* and the *bichromate of potash* are both familiar compounds of chromic acid. The first, $KO.CrO_3$, is formed on a very large scale, by decomposing the native chromic iron with nitrate of potash, by aid of heat. Chromate of potash is dissolved out from the ignited mass, and crystallizes in anhydrous yellow crystals. It is isomorphous with sulphate of potash, dissolves in two parts of cold water, and is the source of all the preparations of chromium.

Bichromate of potash $KO.2CrO_3$ is formed by adding sulphuric acid to a solution of the yellow chromate, when half the potash is removed, and the bichromate crystallizes

---

Give its properties. Describe the chlorids of chromium. Describe chlorochromic acid. 575. How is chromate of potash formed? How is bichromate of potash formed?

by slow evaporation in brilliant red crystals of a rhombic form, which are soluble in ten parts of cold water.

576. *Chromate of Lead—Chrome Yellow*—($PbO.CrO_3$) is the well-known pigment prepared by precipitating the nitrate or acetate of lead by a solution of chromate or bichromate of potash. *Chrome Green* is the oxyd of chrome, prepared in a particular way.

NICKEL.

Equivalent, 29·6. *Symbol*, Ni.

577. Nickel is rather a rare metal. It is prepared from the *speiss* or crude nickel of commerce. It is white and malleable, having a density of 8 to 8·8, and fuses above 3000°. Reduced from its oxyd by hydrogen (fig. 373) at a low temperature, it takes fire in the air. The compact metal is not easily oxydized. It is the only metal beside iron and cobalt which is magnetic. This property it loses when heated to 700°. Meteoric iron almost invariably contains nickel, sometimes as much as 10 per cent. Its chief ores are *copper-nickel* and *speiss-cobalt.*

Arseniuret of nickel and cobalt is found at Chatham, Conn., and oxyd of cobalt and manganese in Mine-la-Motte, Mo. The *emerald nickel*, a beautiful green hydrous carbonate described by the author, is found in Lancaster Co., Pa. Its formula is $3(NiO)CO_2+6HO$.

578. There are *two oxyds of nickel.* The protoxyd NiO is prepared by precipitating a solution of nickel by caustic potash: this is soluble in ammonia. It gives a grass-green hydrated oxyd, which, by heat, loses its water and becomes gray. The oxyd of nickel is isomorphous with magnesia, and has been obtained crystallized in regular octahedrons. The salts of this oxyd have a fine green color, which they impart to their solutions.

The peroxyd of nickel NiO_2 is a dull black powder, of no particular interest.

579. The *sulphate of nickel* $NiO.SO_3+7HO$ is a finely crystallized salt, occurring in green prisms, which lose their

---

576. What is chrome yellow? What chrome green? 577. In what state does nickel occur in nature? Describe its properties. What of its magnetic property? 578. What are oxyds? In what form does the protoxyd crystallize? 579. Describe the sulphate and oxalate of nickel.

water of crystallization by heat. It forms beautiful, well crystallized double salts, with the sulphates of potash and ammonia. Oxalic acid precipitates an insoluble oxalate of nickel from the solution of the sulphate, and the metallic nickel is easily obtained from the oxalate by heat.

Nickel is chiefly employed in making German silver, a white malleable alloy, composed of copper 100, zinc 60, and nickel 40 parts.

COBALT.

Equivalent, 29·5. *Symbol*, Co.

580. *Cobalt* is a metal almost always associated with nickel, and closely resembling it in many of its reactions. When pure it is a brittle, reddish-white metal, with a density of 8·53, and melts only at very high temperatures. It is nearly as magnetic as iron. It dissolves with difficulty in strong sulphuric acid, and is not oxydized in air. *It forms two oxyds* every way analogous to those of nickel. Its protoxyd is a grayish-pink powder, very soluble in chlorohydric acid. It forms pink salts. This oxyd occurs native.

The *chlorid of cobalt* CoCl is formed by dissolving the oxyd in hydrochloric acid. The solution is pink, and when very dilute may be used as a *blue sympathetic ink*, which may be made green by mixing a little chlorid of nickel. Writing made with this on paper is colorless when cold, but becomes of a fine blue or green when gently warmed, and loses its color again on cooling.

The salts of cobalt and nickel are isomorphous with those of magnesia. They are not thrown down by sulphuretted hydrogen, but give blue or green precipitates with potash, soda, and their carbonates. The same precipitates with ammonia are soluble in excess of that reagent. Oxyd of cobalt imparts a splendid blue to glass, and the pulverized glass of this color is called *smalt* and *powder blue*. *Zaffre* is an impure oxyd of cobalt, used to give the blue color to common earthenware.

What is the composition of German silver? 580. What are the characters of cobalt? What interesting experiment is mentioned with the chlorid? With what oxyd are the oxyd of cobalt and its salts isomorphous? What use is made of the oxyd of cobalt?

ZINC.

Equivalent, 32·5. *Symbol*, Zn. *Density*, 6·86 to 7·20.

581. *Zinc* is an important and rather common metal. It is not found native, but a peculiar red oxyd of zinc abounds at Sterling, New Jersey, and calamine or carbonate of zinc is found abundantly in many places. The ores of zinc are reduced by heat and charcoal, in large crucibles closed at top, but having a clay tube *a b* descending from near the top, as in fig. 376, through the crucible and its support B, to a vessel of water C. The cover is luted on and the heat raised. The metal, being volatile, rises in vapor, which descending through the tube, is condensed in the water below. This is called distillation *per descensum*.

Fig. 376.

582. Zinc is a bluish-white metal, easily oxydized in the air, and crystallizes in broad foliated laminæ, well seen in the fracture of an ingot of the commercial metal. It is called *spelter* in the arts, and is largely used to alloy copper in forming brass, to form sheet zinc, and also for the protection of iron in what is called galvanized iron. Zinc is not a malleable metal at ordinary temperatures, but at a temperature of between 250° and 300° it becomes quite malleable, and is then rolled into sheet zinc. At about 390° it is again quite brittle, and may be granulated by blows of the hammer: at 773° it melts, and if air has access to it, it takes fire, and burns rapidly with a brilliant whitish-green flame, giving off flakes of white oxyd of zinc, anciently called *lana philosophica* and *pompholix*. It is completely volatile at a red heat. We constantly employ zinc in the laboratory to procure hydrogen, and granulate it by turning it slowly into cold water from some height. It dissolves in solutions of soda and of potassa, with evolution of hydrogen and formation of *zincate* of the alkali employed.

583. The *oxyd of zinc* ZnO is formed when zinc burns

---

581. How is zinc reduced from its ores? How distilled? 582. What are its properties? At what temperature is it malleable?

in air. Only one oxyd is known. It is, when pure, a white powder, yellowish while hot. It contains zinc 80·26, oxygen 19·74. It is insoluble in water, but forms a hydrate with it. The anhydrous oxyd mingled with drying oils forms a valuable paint, now coming into use in place of white-lead. It has the advantage of not changing by sulphuretted hydrogen and of not being deleterious to the health of the workmen. It is now largely manufactured from the red zinc of New Jersey, and from the franklinite of the same region, which contains a large quantity of zinc.

Calamine is a native carbonate of zinc $ZnO.CO_2$, and is its most valuable ore. *Electric calamine* is a silicate $3(ZnO)SiO_3+1\frac{1}{2}HO$.

Chlorid of zinc ZnCl is a valuable escarotic, and has been much used in dilute solution to preserve anatomical subjects for dissection.

Sulphuret of zinc, Blende, ZnS, is one of the most common of the ores of zinc. It occurs in beautiful brilliant crystals, modifications of the first system, called by the miners *black-jack.*

Sulphate of Zinc, or White Vitriol, $ZnO.SO_3+7HO$.—This salt has the same form as the sulphate of magnesia, and looks extremely like it. It dissolves in 2½ parts of cold water, at 60°, but at 212° is indefinitely soluble, as it then fuses in its own crystallization water. It forms double salts with the sulphates of ammonia and potash. It is a powerful and very rapid emetic.

Sulphuret of ammonia throws down a characteristic white precipitate of sulphuretted zinc from its neutral solutions

CADMIUM.

Equivalent, 56. *Symbol*, Cd. *Density*, 8·7.

584. *Cadmium* is generally found associated with zinc. It is quite malleable, white, and harder than tin. It fuses at 442°, and volatilizes completely at a temperature a little above this. It is not easily oxydized, and is but slightly soluble in chlorohydric or sulphuric acid. Nitric acid dissolves it with ease, forming a salt from which sulphuretted hydrogen throws down a very characteristic orange-yellow sulphuret. This compound is also found native and crystallized, (*greenockite.*)

---

583. Describe the oxyd ZnO. What large use is being made of it? What is calamine? Blende? Sulphate of zinc? What of its solubility? 584. What are the properties of cadmium?

Its *oxyd* CdO is a bronze powder, formed by igniting the nitrate or carbonate, and rises in a brown vapor when cadmium is placed in the focus of the oxyhydrogen blowpipe.

LEAD.

Equivalent, 103·5. *Symbol*, Pb. *Density*, 11·45.

585. This useful and familiar metal occurs in boundless profusion in this country. Its chief ore is *galena*, or sulphuret of lead, from which the metal is easily obtained by smelting with a limited amount of fuel at a low heat. The carbonate, phosphate, chromate, and arseniate are also natural salts of lead, much prized by the mineralogist.

Lead is a bluish-gray metal, very soft and ductile, but not very tenacious, (471;) it oxydizes in the air quite rapidly, forming a coat of oxyd, or carbonate, which usually protects it from further corrosion. Its destiny is 11·45, and it fuses at about 630°; when melted it combines rapidly with oxygen from the air, forming either protoxyd, or red oxyd, according to the degree of heat employed. It is somewhat volatile above a red heat.

Lead is acted upon by distilled water and by rain water. Water, by reason of its affinity for the oxyd of lead, acts like an acid upon metallic lead. A bright slip of pure lead is tarnished almost immediately in pure water, and after a short time becomes covered with a pellicle of carbonate of lead; while the water yields a dark cloud to sulphuretted hydrogen, showing the presence of oxyd of lead dissolved in it. It is, therefore, unsafe to use water-pipes of lead, unless it has been proved by experiment that the particular water in question does not act on this metal. The carbonate, which is the salt generally produced under these circumstances, is an energetic poison. The presence of a very small quantity of foreign matter in water, and especially of the sulphate of lime, usually arrests this action, and renders the use of lead-pipes in a majority of cases not hazardous.

Lead does not easily dissolve in strong acids, except in nitric, with which it forms a soluble salt: strong sulphuric acid dissolves it only when heated, forming nearly insoluble sulphate of lead.

---

585. What is the chief ore of lead? What are the properties of lead? Its density and fusion point? Is it volatile? What acts on lead? What salt of lead is most poisonous? What arrests the action of water on lead?

There are three oxyds of lead, viz. suboxyd Pb_2O, protoxyd PbO, and peroxyd, or plumbic oxyd PbO_2.

586. *Protoxyd of Lead, Litharge, Massicot*, PbO.—This oxyd is a yellow powder, formed by slowly oxydizing lead with heat. It is slightly soluble in water, and the solution is alkaline: in solution of sugar it is largely soluble. It fuses easily, and dissolves silica with great rapidity; hence its use in glazing pottery (555) and in the manufacture of glass, (553.) It forms a large class of definite salts, which have often a sweet taste, as is seen in the acetate, or sugar of lead.

The *peroxyd* PbO_2 is prepared by acting on the *red-lead* with dilute cold nitric acid: it is a puce-colored body, which plays the part of an acid, forming salts with bases. The oxyd of lead forms insoluble salts with the fatty acids, of which the well-known *diachylum plaster* is an example. There are several intermediate oxyds of lead, called *miniums* which are of variable composition, according to the temperature at which they are prepared. *Red-lead* is a familiar example of these. Its formula is Pb_3O_4 or $2PbO.PbO_2$. It has a fine orange-red color when well prepared, and is sometimes found crystallized in the fissures of the furnaces. It is prepared by exposing lead to a constant temperature of about 700°. Acted on by hydrochloric acid, it evolves chlorine, and, with sulphuric acid, oxygen is given off. It is preferred to litharge for glass-making.

The chlorid and iodid of lead possess no particular interest; the latter crystallizes in beautiful yellow scales from its solution in hot water. The chlorid, iodid, and sulphate are all very insoluble compounds. Sulphuretted hydrogen throws down a black sulphuret from all soluble salts of lead, being the best test of its presence.

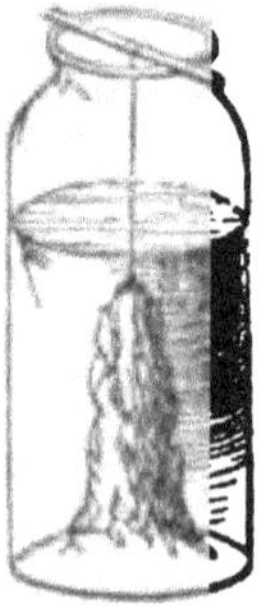

Fig. 377.

587. Zinc precipitates it from its solutions by voltaic action, in beautiful crystalline plates of metallic lead, which assume a branching form, often an inch or two in length, and hence called the lead-tree, or *arbor saturni*, from the alchemistic name of this metal. The acetate is usually employed: an ounce of the salt is dissolved in two quarts of

---

What oxyds of lead are there? 586. What names has PbO? Give its properties. What is PbO_2? What is diachylon plaster? What are the miniums? What use is made of minium? What test is named for lead salts? 587. How is metallic lead precipitated from its solution?

distilled water, and a piece of clean zinc suspended in it by a thread: the precipitation is gradual, and occupies one or two days. The arrangement is seen in the fig. 377.

588. *Carbonate of Lead, White-lead, Ceruse,* $PbO.CO_2$.—This salt is found beautifully crystallized in nature, but is prepared artificially in very large quantities, for the purposes of a paint. This pigment is obtained by casting lead in very thin sheets, which are then rolled up into a loose scroll Z (fig. 378) and placed in a pot over a small quantity of vinegar *u*, supported on the ledge *b b*, so as not to project above the pot, nor touch the vinegar. The vinegar is obtained from the fermentation of potatos. Many thousands of these pots are arranged in successive layers over each other, with covers *n' m* between, and the interstices filled with spent tan, or fermenting stable-dung, which gives a gentle heat to the acid. After a time the lead is completely converted into an opake white crust of carbonate. The theory of this process will be explained when we describe the acetates of lead, (Organic Chemistry.) White-lead is now largely adulterated by sulphate of baryta, but the fraud may be easily detected by dissolving the carbonate in an acid, when the sulphate of baryta will be left behind. Carbonate of lead is highly poisonous.

Fig. 378.

589. URANIUM,(equivalent 60.)—This rare metal is found only in a few very rare minerals, of which the best known are *pitch blende*, an impure oxyd of uranium, and *uranite*, one of the most beautiful of mineral species, which is a phosphate of uranium. The metal is of a silver color, a little malleable, and has so great an affinity for oxygen as to burn in the air. It forms two oxyds, UO and U_2O_3. The salts of uranium possess considerable chemical interest.

COPPER.

Equivalent, 31·7. *Symbol*, Cu. *Density*, 8·87.

590. *Copper* has been in familiar use since the times of Tubal Cain, and is one of the most important metals to the

---

588. How is the carbonate prepared, and for what is it used? 589. In what minerals is uranium found? What oxyd does it form? 590. What is the history of copper?

wants of society. It is often found in the metallic state. The metallic copper of Lake Superior is found in irregular veins, filling fissures, from which it is cut by chisels, and by drills in huge blocks of great purity. Small masses of silver are also often found adherent to the copper. One mass from this region, now at Washington, weighs over 3000 pounds, and such masses are frequent. The most usual ores of copper are the *red oxyd of copper*, *copper pyrites*, and *copper glance*, a pure sulphuret, or sulphuret of copper and iron.

The blue and green malachites, or carbonates of copper, phosphate and arseniate of copper, and many other salts of this metal, are also found in the mineral kingdom. Copper is very malleable, and is the only red metal except titanium. It fuses at 1996°, and has a density of 8·78, which may be increased to 8·96 by hammering. It does not change in dry air, but in moist air becomes covered with a green coat of carbonate, known as verdigris, (corruption of the French *vert de gris.*) It is stiffened by hammering or rolling, and softened again by heating and quenching in water. It may be drawn into very fine wire of good tenacity, which is an excellent conductor of heat and electricity, and is much used in electro-magnetism and for the telegraphic conductors.

Nitric acid is the proper solvent of copper, sulphuric and hydrochloric acids scarcely acting upon it.

591. There are four oxyds of copper, suboxyd Cu_2O, protoxyd CuO, binoxyd CuO_2, and an acid oxyd whose composition is unknown.

The protoxyd, or black oxyd of copper, CuO, is the base of all the blue and green salts of copper. It is formed by decomposing the nitrate with heat. It is black and very dense, quite soluble in acids, and forms many important salts which are isomorphous with those of magnesia. It yields all its oxygen to organic matters at a red heat, and for this purpose is much used in their analysis.

The suboxyd, or red oxyd of copper, Cu_2O, is found native in beautiful octahedral crystals, and is also formed when copper is oxydized by heat. This oxyd communicates

---

How found at Lake Superior? What copper ores are named? Give its equivalent and characters. What is the solvent of copper? 591. What oxyds of copper are known? What relative to the black oxyd of copper? Describe the suboxyd.

to glass a magnificent ruby-red color. The chlorids and iodids of copper are of no great importance.

592. *Sulphate of copper, blue vitriol*, $CuO.SO_3+5HO$, is an important salt, crystallizing in large, beautiful blue rhombs, which are soluble in four parts of cold and two parts of hot water. It loses its water by a gentle heat and falls to a white powder. It is much used in dyeing and for exciting galvanic batteries. With ammonia it forms a dark-blue crystallizable compound.

593. *Nitrate of copper* $CuO.NO_5+3HO$ is formed by dissolving copper in nitric acid to saturation, and is a deep-blue, crystallizable, deliquescent salt, very corrosive, and easily decomposed: a paper moistened with a strong solution of this salt cannot be rapidly dried without taking fire, from the decomposition of nitric acid. The residues of operations for obtaining deutoxyd of nitrogen (341) afford an abundant supply of this salt in the laboratory.

Ammonia detects the smallest traces of this metal in solution, by the deep violet-blue of the ammoniacal salt of copper which is formed. Iron precipitates it from its acid solution as a brilliant red coating. Copper is a metal most readily obtained in a metallic form from its solutions by voltaic decomposition. The sulphate is usually employed for this purpose in the electrotype, the arrangement being made like fig. 379, the operation of which has been already explained in section 234. The alloys of copper are much prized for their various useful applications in the arts. Brass is zinc ⅓, copper ⅔. Dutch metal, of which thin leaves are made, contains 10 to 14 of zinc.

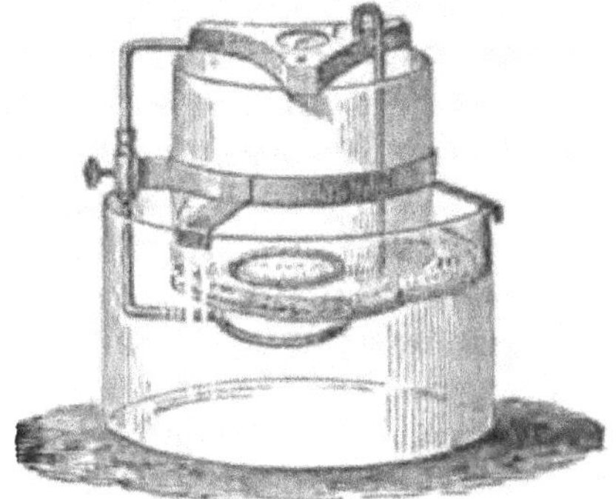

Fig. 379.

592. Describe the sulphate of copper. 593. What is the nitrate? How does it affect organic matter? How is copper detected? Why is copper used in electrotyping? What of its alloys?

CLASS V. METALS WHOSE OXYDS ARE WEAK BASES OR ACIDS.

594. The five first metals in this class are so rare that we may pass them with a very brief mention. They are VANADIUM, TUNGSTEN, COLUMBIUM, TITANIUM, and MOLYBDENUM.

Vanadium appears to be closely allied to chromium. The vanadic acid VO_3 forms salts with lead and copper, found native as *vanadinite*, and *volborthite* $CuO.VO_3$.

Tungsten, so named from its great weight, (12·11,) exists as tungstic acid WO_3 in *wolfram* and *scheeletine* $CaO.WO_3$ or tungstate of lime. Native tungstic acid has been observed in Monroe, Conn.: it is a yellow powder, soluble in ammonia, but insoluble in acids.

Columbium, or *tantalum*, is the metal of a mineral called *columbite*, (in allusion to its American origin, by Hatchett, its discoverer,) or *tantalite*, a salt of iron in which this metal is the acid. It forms two oxyds, TaO_2 and TaO_3, both acids. It is with the columbite of Haddam that the two new metals, *pelopium* and *niobium*, are found, as described by Rose.

Titanium is a copper-red metal, crystallizing in cubes. It forms with oxygen *titanic acid* TiO_2, a substance found pure in three distinct minerals, viz. *rutile*, *anatase*, and *Brookite*, an interesting case of trimorphism. This acid is soluble in strong chlorohydric acid, but precipitates, on dilution and boiling, a white, insoluble powder, much resembling silica. It is used to give a yellowish tint to porcelain in preparing artificial teeth.

Molybdenum is a white, slightly malleable, infusible metal, density 8·6. The *sulphuret* is a common mineral distributed in primitive rocks: it resembles graphite. It forms with oxygen oxyd of molybdenum MoO, binoxyd MoO_2, and molybdic acid MoO_3, which is its most important compound. Molybdic acid forms soluble salts with the alkalies, of which the molybdate of ammonia is the most valuable, being the

---

594. What is vanadium? What is tungsten? In what minerals found? What is columbium? In what mineral found? What new metals have been found with it? What is titanium? What is titanic acid? What natural forms has it? How is molybdenum found in nature? What important salt does it form?

most delicate test known for phosphoric acid. Molybdate of lead is a beautiful native salt of this acid. Heat converts the sulphuret into the impure acid, and it is also oxydized directly by monohydrated nitric acid.

TIN.

Equivalent, 59. *Symbol*, Sn, (*Stnanum.*) *Density*, 7·29.

595. *Tin* is one of those metals which have been known from the most remote antiquity. The mines of Cornwall have been worked for the oxyd of tin since the times of the Phœnicians and Greeks. It has been found in this country only at Jackson, N. H., in small quantities. Tin is a white metal with a brilliant lustre, not easily tarnished, and resisting the action of acids to a remarkable degree. It is soft, very ductile, laminable, malleable, but of feeble tenacity. *Tin foil* is made of one-thousandth of an inch in thickness, or even much thinner. A bar of tin when bent gives a peculiar crackling sound, familiarly called the *cry of tin*, due to the disturbance of its crystalline structure. It is one of the best conductors of heat and electricity.

596. Tin has a density of 7·29, and fuses at 442°. Its alloys are very valuable; gun-metal (copper 90, tin 10) is one of the strongest alloys known, of a reddish-yellow; bell-metal (copper 78, tin 22) is a very sonorous and brittle alloy, of a pale yellow; and speculum-metal (copper 70 to 75, and tin 25 to 30) is a hard, brilliant, almost white, and excessively brittle alloy. Pewter is a mixture of tin and antimony or lead. *Tin-plate* is only sheet-iron coated with tin.

Chlorohydric acid dissolves tin with escape of hydrogen, forming SnCl.

Strong nitric acid does not dissolve tin, but the addition of a little water to the acid causes a violent action, and the tin is speedily converted to stannic acid SnO_2.

597. There are two oxyds of tin: 1. The protoxyd SnO; and 2. The peroxyd SnO_2. There are numerous intermediate oxyds formed of these two. 1. This is obtained by precipitating a solution of protochlorid of tin with an alkaline

595. What history is given of tin? What are its equivalent and general properties? 596. Give its density and fusibility? What is said of its alloys with copper? What is tin-plate and pewter? How does nitric acid affect it? 597. What oxyds of tin are there? What is the protoxyd.

carbonate, which yields a bulky hydrate of the protoxyd. It is a very unstable compound, passing into the peroxyd at a very moderate heat. 2. The *peroxyd* is found native in the beautiful crystallized tin stone. It may be obtained in a soluble and an insoluble condition. When the perchlorid is precipitated by an alkali, the bulky white precipitate of hydrated peroxyd which appears is easily soluble in acids; but if tin is acted on by an excess of moderately strong nitric acid, a white insoluble powder is formed, which is not acted on by the strongest acids. Heat converts both into a lemon-yellow powder, which dissolves in alkalies, but not in acids, and which is known as *stannic acid:* it reddens test-paper, and forms salts. The *putty* used to polish stone and glass is the peroxyd of tin

598. *Protochlorid of tin* SnCl which is prepared by dissolving tin in hot chlorohydric acid, is a powerful deoxydizing agent, and reduces the salts of silver, mercury, platinum, &c., to the metallic state. The anhydrous protochlorid is formed by heating protochlorid of mercury with powdered tin.

599. *Perchlorid of tin* $SnCl_2$ is a dense fuming liquid, long known as the *fuming liquor of Labavius.* It is formed by distilling a mixture of 1 part of powdered tin and 5 of corrosive sublimate. The *tin mordant* used by the dyers is formed by dissolving tin in chlorohydric acid, with a little nitric acid, at a low temperature, or by passing chlorine gas through the protochlorid.

The sulphurets of tin correspond to the chlorids. The bisulphuret (*aurum musivum*) is used as a bronze color for imitating gold in ornamental painting and printing, and also to excite electricity in the electrical machine, (166.)

The alchemistic name for this metal was *Jove*, and the medicinal preparations of tin are still called *jovial* preparations.

BISMUTH.

Equivalent, 208. *Symbol*, Bi. *Density*, 9·8.

600. *Bismuth* is found native, and also in combination with

Describe the peroxyd. What two modifications of it are named? How does heat affect them? What is "putty?" 598. How is protochlorid of tin employed as a reagent? 599. What is perchlorid of tin, and how prepared? What is the *tin mordant?* What sulphurets of tin are there? What was its alchemistic name?

other substances. Native bismuth is found in the United States, at Monroe, Conn. It is a brittle, highly crystalline metal, of a reddish-white color, with a density of 9 8, and fuses at 507°. It is obtained in large and beautiful obtuse rhombic crystals, by fusing several pounds of bismuth in an earthen pot, purifying by successive portions of nitre, and leaving it to cool until a crust is formed on its surface, which is pierced by a hot coal and the still fluid interior turned out. The vessel will be lined with a multitude of brilliant crystals.

It dissolves in nitric acid, but, like other metals of this class, does not decompose water under any circumstances.

601. Two oxyds of bismuth are known. The protoxyd BiO_3 is formed by gently igniting the subnitrate. It is a yellowish powder, easily soluble in acids, and is the base of all the salts of bismuth. It is, however, a very feeble base, since even water decomposes its salts. The peroxyd BiO_5 is not of much interest.

602. The *nitrate of bismuth* $BiO_3.NO_5+3HO$ is the most interesting of its salts. It may be obtained from a strong solution in large transparent crystals, which are decomposed by water. The solution of the nitrate of bismuth turned into a large quantity of water is immediately decomposed, with the production of a copious white precipitate of subnitrate of bismuth. This is owing to the superior basic power of the water, which takes a part of the nitric acid. The white precipitate is a basic nitrate $BiO_3.NO_5+3BiO_3HO$. This white oxyd has been much used as a cosmetic. It blackens by sulphuretted hydrogen.

603. The alloy of bismuth, known as Newton's fusible metal, is formed of 8 parts bismuth, 5 parts lead, and 3 parts tin, and melts at about 208°, (473.) It is much used in taking casts of medals. An alloy of 1 lead, 1 tin, and 2 bismuth, fuses at 200°·75. The expansion of bismuth in cooling renders it a valuable constituent of alloys where sharpness of impression in casting is important.

---

600. What is the color and fusibility of bismuth? Describe its crystals, and the mode of obtaining them. 601. How many oxyds has this metal? 602. What is the most interesting property of the nitrate? What use is made of the subnirate? 603. What its the composition of Newton's fusible metal? What more fusible alloy is named?

ANTIMONY.

Equivalent, 129. *Symbol*, Sb, (*Stibium.*) *Density*, 6·7.

604. This metal is derived chiefly from its native sulphuret, which is a rather abundant mineral. The metal is obtained by fusing the sulphuret with iron-filings, or carbonate of potash, which combine with the sulphur and set free the metal. It is a white, brilliant metal with a blue tint, forming broad rhomboidal crystalline plates in the commercial article, but fine granular if purified from foreign metals, which cause it to assume a coarse crystallization. It is very brittle, and, like bismuth, may be reduced to a fine powder. It fuses at about 842°, and lower if quite pure: a high fusion point is a sign of its impurity. It is, in a current of hydrogen, entirely volatile, but alone and covered very slightly so. It dissolves in hot chlorohydric acid, but nitric acid converts it into the insoluble white antimonic acid.

Its alloy with lead is type-metal, which, like the alloys of bismuth, gives very sharp casts, by reason of the expansion it undergoes at the moment of solidification, which forces the metal into all the fine lines of the mould. It is remarkable that both of the constituent metals shrink when cast separately. Finely powdered antimony is inflamed in chlorine gas, forming the perchlorid.

605. Two *oxyds of antimony* are known, viz:

1. *Antimonic Oxyd*, SbO_3.—This oxyd may be obtained by digesting the precipitate from chlorid of antimony by water, with carbonate of potash or soda, or by burning antimony in a red-hot crucible; and also by subliming it from the surface of fused antimony in a current of air. It is a fawn-colored insoluble powder, anhydrous, and volatile when highly heated in a close vessel. Boiled with cream of tartar, (acid tartrate of potash,) it forms the well-known *tartar emetic*, which may be obtained in crystals from the solution.

The *glass of antimony* is an impure fused oxyd, pre-

---

604. How is antimony obtained? What are its properties? What of its grain? Its fusion? Its alloys? 605. How many compounds does antimony form with oxygen? What important salt does the oxyd form with potash?

pared for the purpose of making tartar emetic. Heated in air, this oxyd gains another equivalent of oxygen, and forms—

2. *Antimonic acid* SbO_5 is formed, as already stated, when antimony is digested in an excess of strong nitric acid, or better in aqua-regia with nitric acid in excess. It dissolves in alkalies, with which it forms definite salts, that are again decomposed by acids, hydrate of antimonic acid being thrown down. The hydrate loses its water below a red heat, becoming a crystalline fawn-colored powder; and by a higher heat one equivalent of oxygen is expelled, antimonious acid being formed.

606. There are *chlorids* and *sulphurets of antimony* corresponding to the oxyd and to antimonic acid.

The *terchlorid, butter of antimony*, $SbCl_3$, is made by distilling the residue of the solution of sulphuret of antimony in strong hydrochloric acid, (fig. 317.) When a drop of the distilled liquid forms a copious white precipitate on falling into water, the receiver is changed, and the pure chlorid is collected. It is a highly corrosive fuming fluid, and by cooling forms a crystalline deliquescent solid. It is used in medicine as a caustic. Water decomposes it, but it dissolves in hydrochloric acid unchanged: water poured into the solution throws down a bulky precipitate, which is a mixture of oxyd and chlorid of antimony, and has long been known by the name of *powder of algaroth*, $SbCl_3.2SbO_3$.

The bromid of antimony is a crystalline volatile compound.

607. The *tersulphuret of antimony* SbS_3 constitutes the common commercial sulphuret, and the beautiful crystallized native mineral, *antimony glance.*

The *pentasulphuret of antimony* SbS_5 is formed by boiling the tersulphuret with potash and sulphur, and throwing down the compound in question by an acid, as a golden yellow sulphuret, known by the name of *sulphur auratum*, or *golden sulphur of antimony*. More generally, however, the decomposition on adding an acid, as above, gives us the oxysulphuret of antimony SbS_3+SbO_3, which is a

---

What is antimonic acid? 606. Describe the terchlorid? How dedecomposed? 607. What is said of the sulphurets? What are the golden sulphuret and *kermes mineral?*

characteristic reddish-orange precipitate. This is the substance known as *kermes mineral*, and is an article of the older medical practice. The solution of sulphuret of antimony in caustic potash and sulphur is a case in which sulphuret of potassium is a sulphur base, and sulphuret of antimony a sulphur acid.

The formation of *tartar emetic* with tartaric acid, and the production of the characteristic reddish-yellow sulphuret of antimony with sulphydric acid are the most signal tests of antimony. The sulphydrate of ammonia produces the same colored precipitate, but this is soluble in excess of the precipitant, as the former also is in the solution of alkalies. The blowpipe also furnishes good evidence: when a bit of metallic antimony is fused under the oxyhydrogen blowpipe it volatilizes and burns, and if it be thrown on the floor or an inclined board, it scatters in numerous burning globules, whose path is marked by a white stain of oxyd of antimony. We will, under arsenic, mention how antimony is to be distinguished in cases of poisoning.

ARSENIC.

Equivalent, 75. *Symbol*, As. *Density*, 5·8.

608. *Metallic arsenic* is found native in thick crusts, called testaceous arsenic, evidently deposited by sublimation. It is, however, more usually obtained in the form of arsenious acid AsO_3, from roasting the ores of cobalt, nickel, and iron, with which metals it is often combined. Mispickel, a double sulphuret of iron and arsenic, is a great source for this metal. The vapors of arsenious acid given out in the roasting are condensed in a long horizontal chimney, or in a dome constructed for the purpose; the first product being purified by a second sublimation. Arsenic is a brilliant crystalline steel-gray metal, brittle, and easily pulverized. In vessels free from air it may be sublimed unchanged at a temperature of dull redness. Its vapor is colorless, very dense, (10·37,) and has a remarkable odor, resembling garlic. The garlic odor is well perceived on subliming a fragment of

---

What is the nature of this salt? What are the best tests of antimony? How does it act under the blowpipe? 608. How is arsenic found, and in what minerals? What are its properties? How is it sublimed unchanged? What is the density and odor of its vapor?

arsenic or of arsenious acid from a live coal. It sublimes without fusion. It may, however, be fused in tight vessels under pressure of its own vapor. Metallic arsenic soon tarnishes in air and assumes a dull cast-iron look. It is sold by druggists under the absurd names of *fly-powder*, *cobalt*, and *mercury*—names intended to deceive and likely to mislead, involving obvious danger. Metallic arsenic is easily obtained in distinct crystals by subliming the commercial metal, or arsenious acid, mingled with charcoal and carbonate of soda, or *black flux*, (484,) in a tube of hard glass, or, if a larger quantity is required, in a small retort. The mixture is put in *a b*, (fig. 380,) and heated to redness while the air is shut out. The metal rises and is deposited in a black metallic mirror in the cool part of the tube just above. Metallic arsenic is an active poison. It burns in the air with a blue flame, and it is also inflamed in chlorine gas.

Fig. 380.

609. The oxyds of arsenic are, 1. *Arsenious acid* AsO_3, and 2. *Arsenic acid* AsO_5.

1. *Arsenious Acid—White Arsenic—Rat's-bane*, AsO_3;—This well-known and fearful poison is formed, as just stated, when metallic arsenic is sublimed in air, or when any of the ores of arsenic are roasted. This oxyd is what is usually meant when the term *arsenic* is used in commerce. When newly sublimed, it is a hard transparent glass, brittle, and with a density of 3·7. It slowly changes to a white opake enamel, resembling porcelain. This change is gradual, the vitreous portions being still found in the centre of the opake masses. As sold in commerce, it is usually reduced to a white powder, rarely found without adulteration. It sublimes at 380°, without change, and crystallizes in brilliant octahedrons, as may be well seen by slowly subliming a small quantity in a glass tube. Its vapor is inodorous, but if sublimed from charcoal it gives the peculiar garlic odor of metallic arsenic, being reduced to that state. It is soluble in about 10 parts of hot water, and is almost tasteless, with a faint sweetish flavor, which renders it the more

---

How may it be fused? How does air affect it? What names has it? How obtained crystallized? 609. What oxyds does it form? Give formulas. What is arsenious acid? What are its common names? What are its characters? What change does it suffer? How does it crystallize? How soluble? What of its taste?

dangerous poison, since no warning is given to the victim who takes it, as in case of most other metallic poisons. The vitreous acid is three times as soluble as the opake. The solution in water is acid to test-paper, and deposits nearly all its arsenic in crystals on cooling, retaining 1 part to 30 of water. Chlorohydric acid dissolves arsenic, and if a solution of 4 parts AsO_3 in 6 of HCl and 2 of water is slowly cooled from boiling, the AsO_3 is deposited in transparent octahedrons, and if in the dark, the formation of each crystal is accompanied by a spark, and sometimes the light produced is such as to illuminate a dark room. The alkalies dissolve arsenic, but do not form crystallizable salts with it. Arsenious acid contains As 75·75, O 24·25.

610. *Arsenic Acid*, AsO_5.—This acid is formed by adding nitric acid to the solution of white arsenic in hydrochloric acid, as long as any red vapors of nitrous acid show themselves, and then carefully evaporating the solution to entire dryness: a white porous subcrystalline mass remains, which is slowly soluble in water. Its solution is a powerful acid, quite similar in chemical characters to phosphoric acid. The analogy is so great that there is a complete similarity in constitution, and even in external appearance, between all the salts of these two acids. For every tribasic phosphate we have an arseniate, not only similar in constitution, but isomorphous, and so resembling it in all its external properties as not to be distinguished by the eye. Thus the tribasic phosphate of soda (512) and the tribasic arseniate of soda, are—

Phosphate of soda............................$HO2NaO.PO_5+24Aq.$
Arseniate of soda............................$HO2NaO.AsO_5+24Aq.$

These, and many other facts, lead to the opinion that the elements are themselves isomorphous; and in fact arsenic has no claim to the metallic character but its lustre, being in chemical properties and natural affinities associated with phosphorus.

611. The *chlorid of arsenic* $AsCl_3$ is a fuming volatile liquid, decomposed by water, and very poisonous. The bromid and iodid are both crystallizable solids, also decomposed by water.

What is said of its chlorohydric solution? 610. How is AsO_5 formed? What are its properties? What analogy has it with PO_5? To what opinion do these facts lead? 611. What of chlorid of arsenic?

The *sulphurets of arsenic* are natural compounds, used as pigments, and also in pyrotechny. The first, AsS_2, is a red transparent body, called *realgar*, and AsS_3 is the golden-yellow *orpiment*. Both these substances are found native, and are usually associated. They are brought from Koordistan in Persia, and from China. The Mohammedans use the yellow orpiment as a depilatory in their ceremonial purifications. Two higher sulphurets may be formed, which are AsO_8 and AsO_9: the former is the product thrown down by sulphuretted hydrogen in a solution of arsenic. The sulphurets are soluble in alkalies and in sulphydrate of ammonia.

612. *Arseniuretted Hydrogen*, AsH_3.—This is a gas produced by the action of dilute sulphuric acid on an alloy of zinc and arsenic, or by the evolution of hydrogen in presence of arsenic or arsenious acid. Figure 381 shows the ordinary gas evolution bottle A, in which are the materials for producing hydrogen. An arsenical solution poured in at *n m*, immediately changes the color of the flame at *b*; before colorless, it now becomes of a peculiar blue, and evolves a cloud of arsenious acid, or deposits metallic arsenic on a cold surface. Marsh's test for arsenic depends on the generation of this gas. It is a virulent poison of the most active description. This gas is readily absorbed by a solution of sulphate of copper, and precipitates an arseniuret of that metal. Its density is 2·69: it has a peculiar disgusting odor, and is decomposed by heat alone with deposition of metallic arsenic. It is liquid at —22°F.: water dissolves it slightly, and chlorine completely decomposes it with flame.

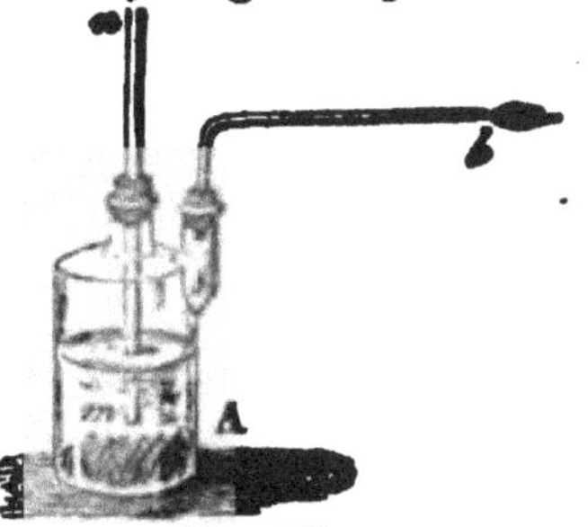

Fig. 381.

Detection of Arsenic in Poisoning.

613. The too frequent use of arsenic as a means of destroying human life renders it of the greatest moment to know certain processes for its detection. Arsenic is almost always

---

What are the sulphurets? 612. What is arseniuretted hydrogen? How produced? What of its flame? What are its properties? 613. What of arsenical poisoning?

fatal when it has time to become absorbed by the circulation in sufficient quantity. The most reliable antidotes which have been proposed are the moist hydrates of sesquioxyd of iron and of caustic magnesia. With both these arsenic forms insoluble salts. The alkalies, being solvents of arsenic, only increase the danger by favoring absorption.

We enumerate a few of the *tests* for arsenious and arsenic acids:

1. *Sulphydric acid* produces in acid or neutral solutions of AsO_3 and AsO_5 a rich orange-yellow precipitate, (orpiment,) soluble in ammonia and alkalies, and in sulphydrate of ammonia, but precipitated again by acids.

2. *Nitrate of silver and ammonia-nitrate of silver* produce in solutions of arsenious acid a lemon-yellow precipitate, (arsenite of silver,) soluble in nitric acid. In solutions of *arsenic* acid they produce a brick-red precipitate.

3. *Ammonio-sulphate of copper* gives a brilliant green precipitate (*Scheele's* green) in alkaline or neutral solutions of arsenious acid, which precipitate (arsenite of copper) is soluble in excess of ammonia.

4. *A slip of bright metallic* copper, placed in a boiling solution of arsenic or arsenious acid made acid by chlorohydric acid, is soon coated with a gray deposit of metallic arsenic. This is called *Reinsch's* test, and is applicable even in presence of organic matters which vitiate, partially or wholly, the previous tests.

5. *Reduction* of the metal from the oxyds or sulphurets is justly esteemed in judicial investigations as the most reliable of all tests. This is accomplished by several modes. The oxyds or sulphurets are mingled with finely-powdered charcoal and carbonate of soda or cyanid of potassium and placed in a small tube *a d* (fig. 382) of hard glass. The part *a b* is heated red hot, when, if arsenic is present, it is sublimed in a black metallic mirror at *c*. A small tube is used, because in many cases very minute portions are opo-

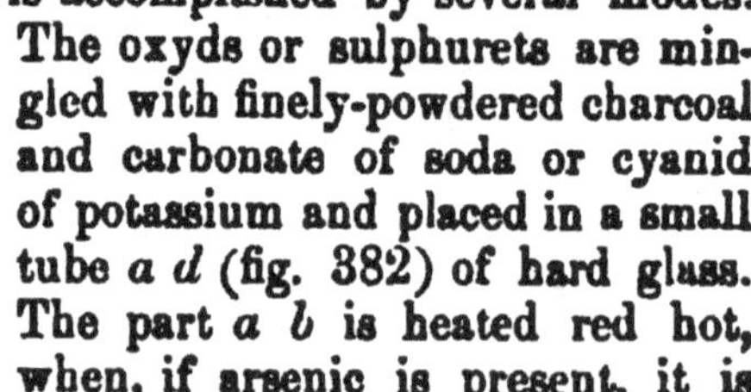

Fig. 382.

What are antidotes, and why? How does sulphydric acid act as a test of arsenic? How nitrate of silver and ammonia? How ammonia-sulphate of copper? What is Reinsch's test? What of the reduction preferred? Describe from fig. 382.

rated on. In order to prove the character of this ring, the tube is broken off at *b*, (fig. 383,) and the flame of a spirit-lamp applied cautiously while the tube is gently inclined. A current of air passing over the ring of metal converts it to arsenious acid, which lines the cooler parts of the tube with small brilliant octahedrons of a size visible by a magnifier. If further proof were required, a current of sulphydric acid will convert the white crust into yellow orpiment, wholly soluble in ammonia, precipitated by chlorohydric acid, and insoluble in that menstruum.

Fig. 383.

6. *Marsh's test*, by means of arseniuretted hydrogen, gives unequivocal testimony when arsenic is present. Fig. 384 shows a convenient form of the apparatus used for this purpose, which is more simply arranged as in fig. 381. This apparatus has the convenience of a cock to regulate the escape of the gas. The zinc is in the lower bulb—the acid water and suspected substance are introduced by the upper bulb. The zinc and all the materials employed must be scrupulously examined as to freedom from arsenic. For this purpose the flame of hydrogen must not give the least spot upon clean porcelain. On adding the arsenical solution, however, the flame becomes livid, larger, gives off white vapors, and deposits a *tache* or spot, in the form of brown-black mirror, on the surface of porcelain, as in fig. 385. Antimony gives a similar spot, which is liable to be confounded with that from arsenic. It is, however, more sooty-black. Exposed to vapor of iodine in a small capsule, antimony spots turn reddish orange, while arsenic spots appear orange yellow, and soon vanish entirely. Exposed for a moment to vapor of chlorine given off from bleaching-powders in a capsule, the spots being on the underside of the cover of the same, the spots disappear. If a drop of nitrate of silver be then let fall on the flat surface, if arsenic was

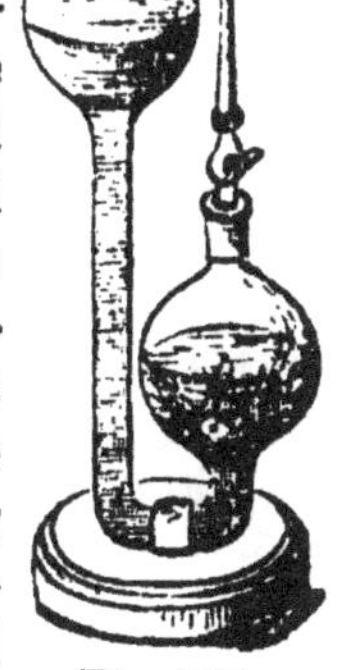
Fig. 384.

How is it oxydized in fig. 383? What further proof may be had? What is Marsh's test? Describe fig. 384. What care is required? What effect is seen on introducing an arsenic solution? What gives a similar spot? How are the spots distinguished? How by chlorine and nitrate of silver?

present there will be a brick-red stain visible, amounting to a precipitate if much of the metal existed—while antimony does no such thing. These distinctions are conclusive.

The arrangement of Marsh's apparatus recommended by the commission of the Paris Academy, in cases of judicial investigation, is shown in fig. 385. The evolution bottle A

Fig. 385.

is provided with a bulb-tube *a b*, to retain moisture, which is more effectually removed by the chlorid of calcium tube *c d*. The gas is conducted through the horizontal tube *f g*, terminating in a jet-point, where the *tache* of the flame can be received upon a clean porcelain surface C. As heat decomposes the arseniuretted hydrogen, means are provided to heat the tube while the gas is passing, the radiant heat being cut off by a screen *c*. In this case the metallic arsenic appears in a ring at *f*, while the flame loses its peculiar character, and no *tache* is seen at *g*. The ring so obtained may be subsequently tested as before indicated, as well also as the tache. The cause of the tache will appear on a moment's attention. Calling to mind what was said on the structure of flame, (460,) it is obvious, by reference to fig. 386, showing a larger view of the jet *g*, (fig. 385,) that the part *a' c'* must contain the reduced arsenic in hot hydrogen gas, surrounded by the burning envelope *a e b*. Now the porcelain surface is held in the line

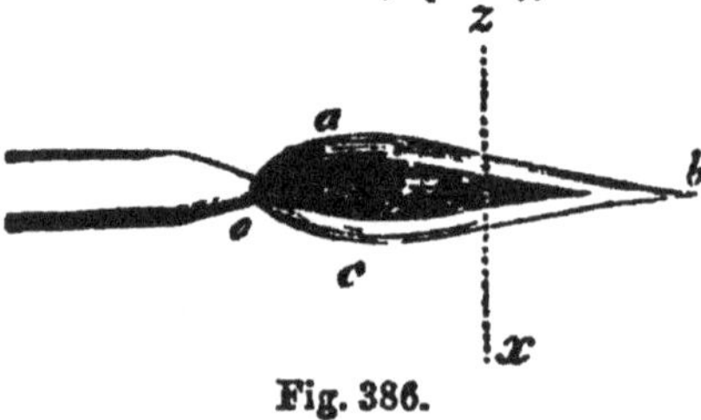

Fig. 386.

Describe fig. 385. What does the heat accomplish? How is the tache obtained in fig. 385?

z x, and must receive the metallic mirror, if any arsenic is present.

614. In most cases of arsenical poisoning it is required to search for proof in the mass of organic matters ejected by the patient, or in the tissues of the body itself; and either case requires all organic matters to be destroyed before tests can be applied. This may be done in a great majority of cases by oxydizing and charring the whole mass to be treated, cut small, in a porcelain capsule, with a mixture of strong nitric acid and oil of vitriol. These are added in small quantity, and gentle heat applied until the coaly mass is nearly dry. Water is then added, and the whole thrown upon a filter and washed: the filtrate contains all the arsenic and other metals. Marsh's, Reinsch's, or any of the other tests just enumerated may then be applied. Such is a very brief account of the most valuable modes of examination in cases of poisoning by arsenic. Further details would be out of place here.

CLASS IV. NOBLE METALS: WHOSE OXYDS ARE REDUCED BY HEAT ALONE.

MERCURY.

Equivalent, 100. *Symbol*, Hg, (*Hydrargyrum.*) *Density*, 13·596.

615. This is the only metal which is fluid at ordinary temperatures. It is found as native, or running mercury, in Spain and Carniola, and also as cinnabar, or sulphuret of mercury. In Upper California a very large deposite of cinnabar has lately been opened. It is also found both in Mexico and Peru. The alchemists supposed it to be silver enchanted, (*quicksilver*,) and made many efforts to obtain from it the solid silver it was supposed to contain.

Pure mercury is a silver-white, fluid metal, unchanged by air, and very brilliant. Cooled below —39·44°, as by carbonic acid, (150,) it solidifies, and is then as malleable as lead. It crystallizes in cubes. It boils at 662°, and forms a colorless vapor, of the density 6·976. Even at 32°, a

---

614. How is proof obtained in case of organic matters being present? What agent of oxydation is used? How is the testing carried on? What are noble metals? 615. What of mercury? How found? Why called quicksilver? What are its properties?

very rare vapor rises from it, as is evident from the effect on daguerrian plates. If heated in the air at or above 600°, it slowly passes to the condition of red oxyd of mercury, which is its highest combination with oxygen. By this experiment Lavoisier proved the composition of air, and performed the first recorded chemical analysis.

616. The uses of mercury are numerous and important in the arts, and also in medicine. It forms alloys (amalgams) with many other metals; with tin it constitutes the brilliant coating of glass mirrors, (called silvering,) and it is of indispensable importance in procuring gold and silver from their ores, and in gilding by the old process. Its use in filling thermometers and barometers has already been noticed. It expands by each degree of Fahr. $\frac{1}{2910}$ of its bulk, in heating from 32° to 212°, and at nearly the same ratio for the whole scale of 662°.

617. The purity of mercury is roughly judged of by its forming no film on glass, and by its breaking into small globules, which should preserve their spherical form, when they run from an inclined surface. If they form a queue, or drag a tail, as the workmen express it, it is owing to the presence of lead or some other similar impurity.

It may be purified from all non-volatile ingredients by

Fig. 387.

distillation in an iron bottle A, (fig. 387,) formed of one of the iron flasks in which quicksilver is imported. This is

---

What of its volatility? 616. What are its uses? What fits it specially for thermometers? What is its rate of expansion? 617. How is its purity judged of? How is it purified? Describe fig. 387.

completely enclosed in the furnace, and the tube *b c* connects with a bag of leather or caoutchouc, reaching to a basin of water, and kept cool by a stream of water from the cock *r*. The tension of its vapor is very small, so that it quickly returns to the fluid state, thus producing a great commotion in the process of boiling. The distilled mercury is only partly purified, and the process must be completed by the action of dilute nitric acid at a gentle heat, which unites to form nitrate of mercury with a part of the mercury. This salt reacts with the other portion of the mercury to form nitrates of all other metals which may be present. After a day or two, with frequent agitation, the action is complete, the water is evaporated at a gentle heat, and the crust of nitrate of mercury removed. The remaining mercury, now quite pure, is washed with much water and dried.

Mercury may be so finely divided by agitation and other mechanical means, as to lose its metallic appearance entirely, as in blue pill, mercurialized chalk, (*creta cum hydrargyro*,) and mercurial ointment, which do not, as has sometimes been stated, contain the suboxyd of mercury, but only mercury in a state of very minute mechanical division.

Nitric acid dissolves mercury very rapidly even in the cold: hydrochloric acid scarcely acts on it, and sulphuric only by the aid of heat, when it forms an insoluble sulphate of mercury, evolving sulphurous acid. The equivalent of mercury is often stated at 200, on the supposition that the gray oxyd is the protoxyd; but this seems to be more properly considered as a suboxyd, and the real protoxyd as the red oxyd. On this view the equivalent is stated at 100.

618. The *gray*, or *suboxyd of mercury*, Hg_2O, is formed by digesting calomel in caustic potash, or by adding the same reagent to a solution of the nitrate of the suboxyd of mercury. It is an insoluble, dark gray powder, which is easily decomposed into metallic mercury and the red oxyd, $Hg_2O = HgO + Hg$.

The *red oxyd*, or *protoxyd*, *red precipitate*, HgO, is prepared in the large way by heating the nitrate very cautiously until it is quite decomposed, and a brilliant red

---

How is the purification completed? How does mechanical action affect it? Give examples. What dissolves it? How does SO_3 affect it? What of its equivalent? 618. How is suboxyd formed? How decomposed? How is the red oxyd formed? What is precipitate *per se*?

crystalline powder produced. It may also be formed by heating metallic mercury for a long time in a glass vessel nearly closed, and in this form is the preparation to which the old name of *red precipitate per se* was applied. Heat decomposes this oxyd, into oxygen and metallic mercury. It is, like the oxyd of lead, slightly soluble in water, and gives to it an alkaline reaction. It is a poison, and is used externally as an irritant and escharotic.

619. The *chlorids of mercury* correspond to the oxyds, and are both very important compounds.

1. *Subchlorid of Mercury, (Calomel,)* Hg_2Cl.—This well-known medicine is formed by precipitating a solution of sub-nitrate of mercury with common salt. A white, insoluble, tasteless powder falls, which is the calomel. Even strong acids, when cold, do not affect it; but it is instantly decomposed by alkalies, and the suboxyd produced. Heat sublimes it unchanged. Its complete insolubility at once distinguishes this safe and mild substance from the highly poisonous corrosive sublimate. It should be in very fine powder for medical use, as then the presence of corrosive sublimate is easily detected in it by imparting its taste to water. Its freedom from adulteration may be determined by heating it on the surface of a clean spatula, when it should volatilise unchanged without leaving any residue. It is obtained by slow sublimation, in beautiful transparent crystals—square prisms with octahedral summits. Its density is 6·5, and in vapor 8·2. Vapor of calomel is composed of

1 volume of mercury vapor	6·976
½ volume of chlorine	1·220
1 volume of calomel vapor.. Hg_2Cl	8·196

Calomel is decomposed by nitric acid, forming corrosive sublimate and nitrate of protoxyd of mercury. Ammonia turns it to a gray powder, which is an amid and chlorid of mercury $Hg_2Cl.HgNH_2$.

2. *Corrosive Sublimate, or Chlorid of Mercury*, HgCl.—This salt is most economically prepared by the decomposition of sulphate of mercury, by common salt, whose

How does heat affect it? How is it used? 619. What of the chlorids? What is the name of the subchlorid? How formed? What are its properties? What of its state and purity? Its density? What is the constitution of its vapor? What decomposes it? What is corrosive sublimate?

simple interchange gives corrosive sublimate and sulphate of soda, $HgO.SO_3 + NaCl = HgCl + NaO.SO_3$. The chlorid is also formed by dissolving the red precipitate in hot chlorohydric acid. Corrosive sublimate is a very heavy crystalline body, soluble in about 16 parts of cold water, and in two or three parts of hot, giving a solution which possesses the most distressing and nauseous metallic taste, and is a deadly poison. It is soluble in alcohol and ether. It melts at 509° and sublimes at about 563°. Its vapor has a density of 9·42, and contains

1 volume of vapor of mercury	6·967
1 volume of chlorine	2·440
1 volume HgCl	9·407

Albumen completely precipitates it, and the whites of eggs or milk are therefore antidotes for this poison. For the same reason it is, doubtless, that timber and animal substances are preserved from decay, as in the *kyanizing* process, by steeping in solution of corrosive sublimate. The albuminous portions of wood suffer decay sooner than the vegetable fibre, and these are rendered completely indestructible in the process of Mr. Kyan, which is now in use in our national shipyards.

Ammonia produces in solution of corrosive sublimate (and also in those of other salts of protoxyd of mercury) a white bulky precipitate of uncertain composition, and long known as *white precipitate*. It is regarded as a double amid and chlorid of mercury $Hg_2Cl.NH_2$.

620. There are two iodids of mercury, Hg_2I and HgI. —The second is a brilliant scarlet-red precipitate, formed by adding solution of iodid of potassium or hydriodic acid to a solution of corrosive sublimate. The iodid is at first yellow, but soon passes by molecular change into the splendid scarlet crystalline powder before noticed. It cannot be used as a pigment on account of its instability.

Two sulphurets of mercury exist Hg_2S and HgS, the first of which is a black powder, formed when sulphuretted hydrogen is passed through a solution of subnitrate of mercury. The sulphuret HgS, or cinnabar, is formed when the *nitrate*

How procured? Give the formula. Give its properties. What is the density of its vapor? What is an antidote for it? What is kyanizing? What is white precipitate? 620. What iodids of mercury are there? What sulphurets?

of mercury (nitrate of the red oxyd) is treated with sulphuretted hydrogen. It is a black precipitate, but turns red when sublimed, and forms the familiar pigment, *vermillion.* This is the common ore of the quicksilver mines.

Salts of Mercury.

621. The salts of protoxyd of mercury HgO are colorless, but the basic salts are yellow.

The Nitrates of Mercury.—The action of nitric acid on mercury varies with the temperature and the strength of the acid. In the cold, dilute nitric acid dissolves mercury, forming a neutral nitrate of the suboxyd; but if the mercury is in excess, a salt is deposited in large and transparent white crystals, which is a nitrate with excess of base. If hot and strong, the *nitrate of the red oxyd* is formed, which is a very soluble salt, not crystallizable. A basic salt of this oxyd may also be formed, which is decomposed by water.

Sulphate of mercury $HgO.SO_3$ results as an insoluble white subcrystalline powder, by the action of the strong acid on metallic mercury, sulphurous acid being evolved. Boiling water decomposes this salt, removing a part of its acid, by which a yellow basic sulphate is formed, known as *turpeth mineral.* Its composition is $3HgO.SO_3$. The sulphate of the gray oxyd $Hg_2O.SO_3$ is formed as a crystalline white powder, by treating a solution of subnitrate of mercury with sulphuric acid. It is slightly soluble in water. Fulminating mercury and other cyanids are described in the organic chemistry.

All the compounds of mercury are volatile at a red heat; and those which are soluble whiten a slip of clean copper, by depositing metallic mercury on its surface.

SILVER.

Equivalent, 108. *Symbol,* Ag. (*Argentum.*) *Density,* 10·5.

622. The mines of Mexico and of the Southern Andes furnish most of the silver of commerce, although many mines of this metal are found in Spain, Saxony, and the Hartz Mountains. Galena, or the native sulphuret of lead, is also

---

What is vermilion? 621. How are the nitrates of mercury obtained? What is the nature of the nitrate of the red oxyd? How is the sulphate formed? What are the characteristics of mercurial compounds? 622. From what sources is silver obtained?

a constant source of silver, as it is never quite free from this precious metal. Silver is often found native. It is more usually in combination with sulphur and antimony.

The brilliant lustre and white color of this valuable metal are familiar to all. It is perfectly ductile and malleable, and in hardness stands between gold and copper. For the purposes of economy and in coinage it is essential to alloy it with about $\frac{1}{10}$ part of copper, to render it sufficiently stiff and hard. It is one of the best conductors of heat and electricity, and its surface reflects light and heat more perfectly than any other metal. It is used for this reason in reflectors; and hot fluids longer retain their heat in vessels of silver than in any other. It remains untarnished in air free from sulphur gases; from these it gains a brown-black surface of sulphuret of silver. It does not combine with oxygen when heated in it; but fused silver absorbs even twenty times its volume of oxygen, parting with it again on cooling. It is slightly volatile even in the furnace, but in the carbon crucible of the galvanic focus (fig. 169) it volatilizes completely. It crystallizes in cubes often very beautifully modified. It fuses at 1873°; and, owing to its absorption of oxygen and disposition to contract in the mould, it is a difficult metal to cast. Nitric acid dissolves silver in the cold with great rapidity, and if it contains any gold, this is left undissolved as a brown powder. Solution of coin alloy appears green, from the copper it contains. Hydrochloric acid scarcely acts on silver, and sulphuric acid only when hot, forming the sparingly soluble sulphate.

Silver is obtained pure from its solution in nitric acid by precipitation with metallic copper, as a finely-divided crystalline powder; also by decomposing its chlorid by fusion with two parts of dry carbonate of potash.

623. Silver is parted from alloys of copper and from argentiferous lead by the process of *cupellation*. This depends on the oxydation of the base metal in a current of heated air, and the absorption of these oxyds by the cupel. This is made of bone-ashes, and compacted in a mould into the form of fig 388; seen in

Fig. 388.

What are the properties of silver? What does fused silver absorb? How volatile? What of coin? What dissolves it? What separates metallic silver from its solution? 623. What is cupellation? Describe the cupel.

section in fig. 389. The bone-ash does not fuse at the most intense heat of the cupellation furnace. The cupels are of various sizes, according to the weight of the assay. In metallurgic art they are employed in the final purification of silver-lead, of immense size, constructed on a hearth of bricks. Those here figured are small, and are heated in a muffle, or low oven-shaped vessel, (fig. 390,) set in the cupellation furnace, as shown in section A, (fig. 392.) Several cupels are accommodated on its hearth, while the air entering its mouth D, partly closed by E, draws over the surface of the fused assay, and out at the lateral slits A in the muffle, thus oxydizing the

Fig. 389.

Fig. 390.

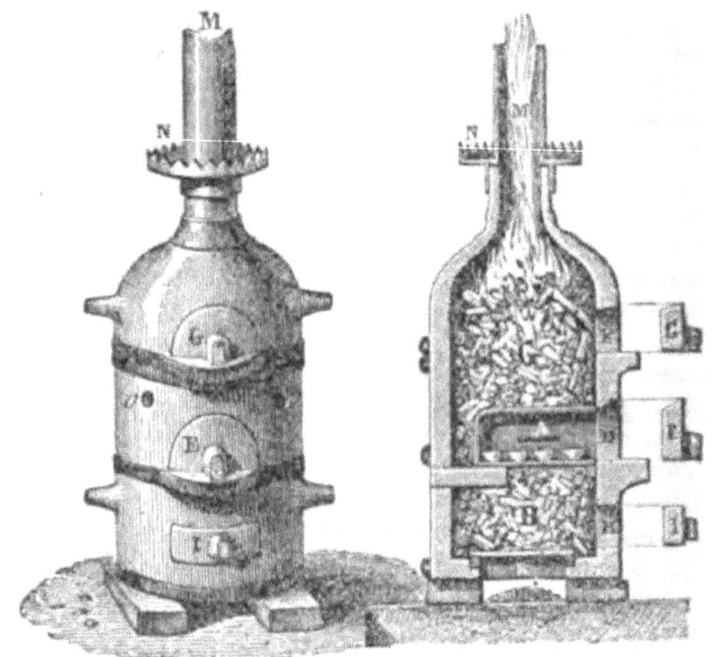

Fig. 391. Fig. 392.

lead. Fig. 391 is a general view of the cupellation furnace, which is formed of three parts, united where the bands are shown. The sectional drawing (fig. 392) indicates more clearly the relations of the parts. Small charcoal is fed to the fire G at F, and the ignited coal finds its way to B, where it rests on the hearth R. To aid this descent, an iron rod

What is the muffle? Describe the process and figs. 391 and 392.

is introduced from time to time at *o o*, (fig. 391.) The opening I H regulates the draft, which is suspended by opening F G. The muffle is thus heated very intensely, and the condition of the assay is observed from time to time by removing E. M is the draft-pipe, and N a sheet-iron shelf to receive the hot cupels. Pure metallic lead is usually added to the alloy to be cupelled, to several times its weight. The oxyd of lead is absorbed as fast as it is formed, carrying with it oxyd of copper and other impurities into the porous bone-ash. Finally, at the close of the process, the globule of silver flashes into a perfectly polished sphere or button of a white color. This is one of the most ancient and valuable of metallurgical operations, and is equally applicable to gold and its alloys as to silver. By this process all the currency of the world is regulated,—in connection with the process of solution in nitric acid, and precipitation by a standard solution of salt, which is known as Gay-Lussac's *wet assay* in distinction from cupellation, which is called the *dry method.*

624. Much of the lead of commerce contains too little silver to allow an economical use of the process of cupellation. The silver is then separated by Pattinson's process, as it is called, founded on the fact that the alloy of silver and lead is more fusible than pure lead; and the latter, on cooling, separates in small crystals, which can be skimmed out of the richer lead by an iron cullender. This process enables the metallurgist to remove with profit even so small a proportion as six ounces of silver from a ton of lead. The small portion of rich lead is then cupelled.

625. Three oxyds of silver are known by chemists: the suboxyd Ag_2O; the protoxyd AgO; and the peroxyd AgO_2. We will now notice only the protoxyd. This is formed when the solution of silver in nitric acid is saturated with caustic potash, or when the chlorid of silver, recently precipitated, is digested in a solution of caustic potash of density 1·3. It is a dark-brown or black powder, if prepared by the first mode, or quite black and dense by the second process. It is a base, forming well-defined salts. Ammonia

---

How does the button appear at the consummation of the process? What is the *wet* and what the *dry* assay? 624. What is Pattinson's process? 625. What oxyds of silver are there? How is AgO formed? What are its properties?

dissolves it readily, and it is also somewhat soluble in water, to which it gives an alkaline reaction. The solution of oxyd of silver in cyanid of potassium forms the silver-plating solution in this branch of electro-plating. The oxyd is easily reduced by heat alone, and by the contact of organic matter.

626. *Chlorid of silver* AgCl is formed when any soluble salt of silver is treated with a soluble chlorid or with chlorohydric acid. This substance fuses at a moderate red heat into a transparent pale-yellow fluid, which is horny and tough when solid, and hence called *horn silver*, a form in which this metal is sometimes found in mines. It is very sensitive to light, turning dark and finally black, especially in contact with organic matter in sunlight. It is easily reduced to the metallic state by the nascent hydrogen generated when zinc is acted on by dilute sulphuric acid in contact with the chlorid. Pure silver and chlorid of zinc result; or it may be reduced by fusion with twice its weight of carbonate of soda or potash, (622.)

The iodid and bromid of silver are, like the chlorid, insoluble in water, and very sensitive to light. The daguerreotype and calotype are both dependent on the sensitiveness of these compounds to light, for the accuracy and beauty of their results.

The sulphurets of silver are found native, and the tarnish which blackens silver articles on long exposure, is formed by sulphuretted hydrogen in the air.

627. The *nitrate of silver* $AgO.NO_5$ is a salt which crystallizes in beautiful flattened tables of an hexagonal form, soluble in half their weight of hot water. By heat it fuses, and, when cast in cylindrical moulds, forms the slender sticks called *lunar caustic*, so much used by the surgeon. Its solution has a disgusting metallic taste, even when very dilute. It is a most delicate test of the presence of chlorine or of any of its compounds. It blackens rapidly in contact with organic matter when exposed to the light, and forms an indelible ink, which is much used in marking linen. Solution of cyanid of potassium will remove the stain produced by nitrate of silver Metallic copper at once throws down metallic silver from the nitrate, and solution of nitrate

---

626. Describe the chlorid. How can it be reduced? What are the relations of the silver compounds to light? What is the action of sulphuretted hydrogen on silver? 627. Describe the nitrate. What is lunar caustic? What are its reactions?

of copper is formed. Mercury precipitates metallic silver from a dilute solution, in beautiful tree-like forms, called *arbor Dianæ*. Ammonia, by acting on precipitated oxyd of silver, forms a fulminating compound. It is extremely hazardous to deal with, as it explodes even when wet.

The fulminating silver produced by the reaction of alcohol, nitric acid, and silver, will be described in the Organic Chemistry.

GOLD.

Equivalent, 98·7. *Symbol*, Au. *Density*, 19·26.

628. This valuable metal is found only in the metallic or native state, being very widely diffused in small quantities in the older rocks. From these, by the action of various causes, it finds its way into the sand of rivers, and is distributed in small quantities, in many widespread deposits of coarse gravel or shingle, as in Alta California, Australia, on the eastern flanks of the Ural mountains, and over a wide belt of country in Virginia, the Carolinas, Georgia, and Alabama. These diluvial deposits furnish nearly all the gold of commerce, by the process of washing and amalgamation with mercury. Large masses of gold sometimes occur, as one of twenty-eight pounds in North Carolina. In Siberia a mass was found, now in the Imperial Cabinet of St. Petersburg, weighing nearly eighty English pounds. Several of still greater size, mingled with quartz, have been found in California. Generally, however, it occurs only in minute rounded and flattened grains or scales. It is also found in veins of quartz, in compact limestone, and distributed in iron pyrites. Native gold is usually alloyed with from 5 to 15 per cent. of silver. Since the discovery of gold in California, in March 1847, it is estimated that at least fifty millions of dollars have been annually obtained there, chiefly from the auriferous sands of those regions.

629. Gold is distinguished by its splendid yellow color, its brilliancy, and freedom from oxidation, by its extreme malleability and ductility, by its high specific gravity, (19·26 to 19·5,) and by its indifference to nearly all reagents. It

---

What is the *arbor Dianæ?* 628. How does gold occur in nature? How is it obtained? What of California? 629. Describe this metal?

fuses at 2016° F., and is dissolved only by aqua regia, (420,) chlorine, nascent cyanogen, and by selenic acid. The first is the solvent commonly known, and yields perchlorid of gold.

630. Gold forms two very unstable oxyds, Au_2O and Au_2O_3, which are decomposed even by light. Two corresponding chlorids exist. The *perchlorid* is a very deliquescent salt, forming a red crystalline mass, soluble in ether, alcohol, and water. Metallic gold is deposited in elegant crystalline crusts from the ethereal solution of the chlorid. Ammonia throws down from solutions of gold an olive-brown powder, fulminating gold, which, when dry, explodes with heat, or by percussion.

631. The solution of protosulphate of iron throws down gold from its solutions in a very fine brown powder, which, when diffused in water, is green, as seen by transmitted light. The protochlorid of tin forms a characteristic purple precipitate in gold solution, called the *purple of Cassius*, which is used in porcelain-painting, and is probably a compound of the oxyds of tin and gold. Gilding of ornamental work is usually performed by gold-leaf; but other metals are gilded, either by applying it as an amalgam with mercury, the mercury being afterward expelled by heat, or preferably by the new process of galvanic gilding from a solution of the double cyanid of gold and potassium. *Gold wash*, as it is called, is applied by a mixture of carbonate of soda or potash in excess, with oxyd of gold, in which small articles cleansed in nitric acid are boiled, and thus become perfectly covered with a very thin film of gold.

632. PALLADIUM, Pd.—This very rare metal is usually associated with gold, being found in a native alloy of gold and silver from Brazil. It is a white metal, more brilliant than platinum, very infusible, malleable, and ductile. It is, however, fused by the compound blowpipe. It gains a blue tarnish, like steel, by heating in the air, which it loses by a white heat. In hardness it is equal to fine steel, and it does not lose its elasticity and stiffness by a red heat. Its density varies from 10·5 to 11·8. It suffers no change by exposure

---

What is its usual solvent? 630. How many oxyds of gold are there? Describe the perchlorid. 631. What tests distinguish gold? How is gilding effected? 632. What of palladium? What peculiar properties has it?

in the air. It gives a peculiar and beautiful color to the surface of brass when applied in the electro-metallurgical process. Its equivalent is 53·3. Its qualities would render it a very valuable metal if it could be obtained in a sufficient quantity. Nitric acid dissolves it slowly, but aqua regia more rapidly. It forms two oxyds and two corresponding chlorids.

PLATINUM.

Equivalent, 98·7. *Symbol*, Pl. *Density*, 19·70 to 21·23.

633. Platinum is a very remarkable metal, and, if abundant, would be extensively useful in domestic economy. It is found native in the gold-workings in South America, and in Siberia on the eastern slope of the Urals. No ore of platinum is known except its alloy with gold, and those with iridium, osmium, and rhodium.

Platinum is a white metal, between tin and steel in color, but harder than gold or silver, and, unless quite pure, is, when unannealed, nearly as hard as palladium. A very little rhodium or iridium renders it more gray in color and much harder. If pure it is very malleable, especially when hot, and can then be imperfectly welded. Its ductility and tenacity are remarkable; but its most valuable property is its infusibility, which is so great that the thinnest platinum foil may be safely exposed to the most intense heat of a wind furnace. It is soluble only by aqua regia. It alloys readily with lead, iron, and other base metals, so that great care is needed in using platinum vessels, not to heat them in contact with any metal or metallic oxyd with which they combine. Caustic potash, and phosphoric acid, in contact with carbon, will also act upon platinum at a red heat. This is a most useful metal to the chemist, and vessels of platinum are quite indispensable in the operations of analysis. Large retorts or boilers are made of it for the use of manufacturers of sulphuric acid, holding sometimes sixty or more gallons. In Russia it has been employed in coinage, for which by its great density and hardness it is well suited. When recently fused by the compound blowpipe or the gal-

---

633. What is the history of platinum? Describe its characters and uses? What of its density?

vanic focus, its density is about 19·9, which is increased to 21·5 by pressure and heat.

634. *Platinum* is obtained pure by digesting crude platinum in aqua regia, and adding to the deep-brown liquid a solution of chlorid of ammonium: this throws down an orange-colored precipitate, which is a double chlorid of platinum and ammonium. This precipitate is reduced by heat to the metallic state,—a porous dull-brown mass, commonly known as platinum sponge. All the platinum of commerce is treated in this way. The sponge is condensed in steel moulds, like fig. 393, by heat and pressure, and when compact enough to bear the blows of the hammer, is heated and forged until it is perfectly tough and homogeneous. The follower K is driven down by the hammer upon the platinum sponge confined in the steel seat *c b*.

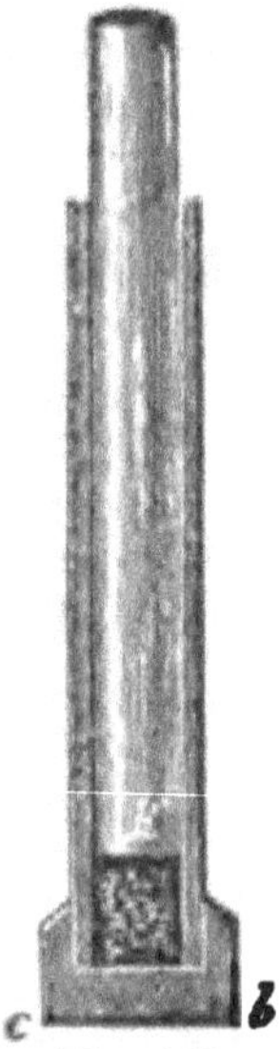

Fig. 393.

Spongy platinum is a very remarkable substance, having, as already noticed, (409,) power to cause the combination of hydrogen and oxygen, and to effect other chemical changes without being itself altered.

Platinum black is a still more curious form of this metal. It is formed by electrolyzing a weak solution of chlorid of platinum, when the black powder appears on the negative electrode. The silver plates in Smee's battery (192) are prepared in this way. It is also prepared by adding an excess of carbonate of soda, with sugar, to a solution of chlorid of platinum, and gradually heating the mixture to near 212°, stirring it meanwhile. The black powder which falls is afterward collected and dried. This powder has the property of causing union among gaseous bodies—as, for example, the elements of water—to a greater degree than the spongy platinum.

635. Platinum forms two oxyds, and two chlorids, viz. PlO; PlO_2 and $PlCl$; $PlCl_2$. The oxyds are prepared from the chlorids by precipitation with alkalies, and are very

---

634. How is it obtained from its ores? How is it condensed? What is platinum black, and what are its properties? 635. How is the bi-chlorid prepared?

unstable. The protochlorid is prepared by heating the bichlorid to 460°, when chlorine is evolved and PlCl is left as a greenish-gray insoluble powder.

The bichlorid of platinum is the usual soluble form of platinum, and is always formed when platinum is digested in aqua regia. It is prepared pure by dissolving spongy platinum in this menstruum, and cautiously expelling the acid by evaporation, at the temperature of a water-bath. It gives a rich orange colored solution both in alcohol and water; and forms insoluble salts of much interest, with many metallic chlorids. Those with the alkaline metals are the most important. The double chlorid of platinum and potassium is a very sparingly soluble salt, ($PlCl_2KCl$,) which falls as a yellow, highly-crystalline precipitate, when chlorid of platinum is added to a solution of chlorid of potassium. The double chlorid of sodium and platinum ($PlCl_2NaCl+6HO$) is, on the other hand, very soluble, and forms large beautiful yellowish-red crystals in a dense solution. Potash and soda are most easily separated, by the different solubility of their double platino-chlorids. The double chlorid of ammonium and platinum ($PlCl_2NH_4Cl$) is the orange precipitate before named, and is the best test to determine the presence of platinum in a solution.

Associated with platinum are iridium, osmium, rhodium, and ruthenium—metals whose rarity permits us to pass them with a very brief mention.

636. Iridium (Eq. 99) is found alloyed with osmium, forming the mineral *iridosmine*, $IrOs_3$, in flat scales, malleable with difficulty. It is the hardest alloy known, being as hard as quartz. It is very infusible. It is true tin-white, crystallizes in hexagonal forms, and its density is from 19·3 to 21·12 being the densest body known. This mineral is much used to point gold pens. It is unacted on by aqua regia. It forms four oxyds.

Osmium (Eq. 99·6) has a density of 10, of a bluish-white color, is neither fusible nor volatile, and forms, by its combustion in air, the very volatile and poisonous osmic acid Os_4. It forms five oxyds, OsO, Os_2O_3, Os_2O, Os_3O, and Os_4O. Fused with nitre, osmium forms osmiate of potassa.

Describe the double chlorids of platinum and the alkalies, their prepation and characteristics. What metals are associated with platinum? 636. What of iridium? What use has iridosmine? What is the density of iridium? What of osmium? Its oxyds?

RHODIUM (Eq. 52·2) is so named from the rose color of its salts. It is a reddish-white metal, density about 10·5, and resembles iridium in hardness, fusibility, and malleability, as well as in resisting the action of acids. It forms two oxyds, RhO and Rh_2O_3.

RUTHENIUM (Eq. 52·2) is another metal observed lately, to the extent of 5 or 6 per cent., in the iridosmine. Its density is about 8·6. It is very like iridium in all its characters, and has until lately been confounded with it.

What of rhodium? Its color and density? Its oxyds? What of ruthenium? Where found? What relations has it?

PART IV.—ORGANIC CHEMISTRY.

[The last edition of this work was written about five years since, and having been desired to prepare this portion of the book for a new edition, it was thought proper to re-write it almost entirely. The views of chemical theory here adopted, have been in part advanced in the pages of the "American Journal of Science" during the last four years. I have there attempted to point out what I conceive to be true in the respective systems of Giessen and Montpellier; and have laid down certain principles, which, in the present work, have been applied to the elucidation of a variety of questions. I have refrained from here developing at full length my own theoretical views, as being from their novelty unsuited to the character of an elementary treatise.

It has been my plan to select from the great amount of matter which the chemistry of the carbon series now embraces, those subjects whose history is well known and best fitted to illustrate the theory of the science, and at the same time to include the matters most interesting, in a practical view, to the medical and general student. Both these classes will, however, find it necessary to resort to more extended works for the history of many series of compounds, which have been omitted or very briefly noticed in these pages; while, on the other hand, it is hoped that the more advanced student will not find the work unworthy of a perusal.

I have not thought it necessary in an elementary treatise to cite authorities; but I may remark that I have availed myself of the works of Liebig, Gerhardt, and Gregory, and of the various chemical memoirs which have appeared in the different scientific periodicals for the last few years. The most recent discoveries in organic chemistry are here embodied.

T. STERRY HUNT.

MONTREAL, CANADA EAST, *July*, 1852.]

INTRODUCTION.

Nature of Organic Bodies.

637. *Definition.*—The name of Organic Chemistry is used to designate that branch of the science which investigates the phenomena and results of organic life, examines the chemical relations of animals and plants, and the properties and

transformations of the peculiar bodies which they afford. The constituents of organic bodies are comparatively few in number. Carbon with oxygen, hydrogen, and nitrogen, form all the combinations peculiar to organic substances. In addition to these, however, sulphur, phosphorus, and iron sometimes occur in small quantities in organic products; and the results of their decompositions and transformations under the influence of different reagents, give rise to an immense number of compounds, in which, with the four organic elements already mentioned, are often united sulphur, phosphorus, arsenic, antimony, chlorine, bromine, iodine, and the metals.

638. It was formerly supposed that the production of the so-called organic substances was exclusively the prerogative of life. But later discoveries have shown that it is possible so to combine the organic elements as to form many of the products which were formerly obtained only through the medium of plants and animals. Hence the distinction between organic and inorganic chemistry is no longer so well defined as before. But as in organic bodies carbon is always present, and is the only constant element, we may define organic chemistry as *the chemistry of the compounds of carbon.* We may distinguish in mineral chemistry many such classes of compounds; as *the nitrogen series*, in which nitrogen is a constant and characteristic element; *the silicon series*, including all the silicious compounds: so in studying the chemistry of organic bodies, we find that they may all be reduced to one, *the carbon series.*

639. Among the organic matters which make up the structure of living beings, we must distinguish two classes: first, *organized substances*, which show either to the naked eye, or under the microscope, a peculiar structure, entirely different from that of crystallization, and never exhibited except in those matters which have been formed under the influence of the *vital force:* such are the woody and muscular fibres, the cellular and vascular tissues, the globules of blood and of starch (which see). These are not always homogeneous chemical compounds, and art, even could it imitate their chemical constitution, will never succeed in giving them their organized forms. The power which effects this must ever remain one of the secrets of life.

The second class of organic substances includes those which are either produced by the destruction of organized bodies, or are the secretions or excretions of organized beings. They are subject to the same laws of form as inorganic bodies, and are liquid, solid, or gaseous, crystallized or amorphous. It is this second class of organic substances which we are able to form artificially, and which are properly in the domain of the chemist; among these are included the various alcohols, oils, acids, resins, sugars, gums, alkaloids, and coloring matters.

640. The immediate effect of chemical agencies upon organized bodies is to produce disorganization, and to convert them into substances which belong to the second class. Hence the study of organized structures belongs to the physiologist, and it is only where he leaves them that the chemist begins. The effect of strong heat upon organic bodies is peculiar. They are completely decomposed into a variety of products, among which are water, carbonic acid gas, carburets of hydrogen, and, if nitrogen be present, ammonia. The carbon, which is generally present in larger quantity than is required to form these compounds, remains in the form of charcoal; hence organic bodies are always more or less combustible, and, unless volatile, generally char or blacken by heat.

641. In addition to the bodies of the carbon series, both animals and vegetables contain salts of potash, soda, lime, magnesia, and iron, with sulphuric, phosphoric, and silicic acids, chlorine and fluorine. Animals also secrete phosphate and carbonate of lime to form their bones, as in vertebrates, and their external coverings, as in the mollusca. These salts have been already described under their proper heads, in the Inorganic Chemistry, and their relations to life will be considered in the section on the nutrition of animals and plants.

Laws of Chemical Transformations.

642. The various changes met with in the study of organic substances, resulting in the destruction of existing combinations, and the formation of new ones, may conveniently be reduced to two classes; first, *equivalent substitutions*, and second, *direct union*. It will be shown that, in the first case, decomposition and recomposition are reciprocal and simultaneous, so that the one implies the other, and we investigate at once the laws of both. In the second case, this relation apparently does not exist; but there is a *direct*

decomposition, which is the converse of direct union, and consists in the partition or dissection of a compound into two or more compounds having a lower equivalent.

Equivalent Substitution.

643 The law of substitution is, that one or more atoms of an element in a compound may be replaced by any other element, or group of elements, which are equivalent in their chemical relations; and the chemical constitution of the compound remain unchanged. Thus acetic acid $C_4H_4O_4$ may lose three atoms of hydrogen and take in their place three equivalents of chlorine, which last are substituted for the hydrogen, without changing the acid constitution of the body; the new compound, *chloracetic acid*, $C_4(HCl_3)O_4$ closely resembles acetic acid in its properties. Here 35·5 parts of chlorine are equivalent to 1 of hydrogen, and Cl_3 is equivalent to H_3, and may be substituted for it without altering the *type* of the compound. Bromine and iodine, and perhaps fluorine, may replace hydrogen in a similar manner.

644. In the foregoing reaction $C_4H_4O_4$ and Cl_6 are concerned, and $C_4(HCl_3)O_4$ and $3(ClH)$ are the results. We shall show farther on, from a consideration of their combining volumes, that as the equivalent volume of chlorohydric acid is (HCl), that of hydrogen is (HH), and that of chlorine (ClCl). In the reaction between acetic acid and chlorine, there are then but three equivalents or volumes of chlorine, $3(ClCl)$, and each successive volume exchanges one of its atoms for one of hydrogen: thus, $(C_4H_4O_4)+(ClCl)=(C_4H_3ClO_4)+(ClH)$—and so on with a second and third volume of chlorine. In many instances we can trace the successive steps by which atom after atom of hydrogen is replaced by chlorine, a corresponding equivalent of hydrochloric acid being simultaneously formed. The law of equivalent substitution is then reducible to that which has been called *double elective affinity*, and always supposes the reaction of two complex bodies, which give rise to two new ones.

645. As hydrogen is replaceable by Cl, Br, and I, so oxygen is capable of being replaced by sulphur, selenium, and tellurium. This can seldom be effected directly, as in the case of chlorine and hydrogen, but it is obtained by indirect decompositions. *Alcohol*, which is $C_4H_6O_2$, gives *sul-*

phur alcohol, $C_4H_6S_2$, and the selenium compound will be $C_4H_6Se_2$. Mineral chemistry affords similar instances; sulphate of soda is $2SO_3+2NaO$, or $S_2Na_2O_8$, while the hyposulphite of soda is $S_2Na_2(O_2S_2)$, and another salt is $S_2Na_2(O_4S_4)$. These different sulphates crystallize with the same amount of water, have the same form, and the same solubility.

Nitrogen, phosphorus, arsenic, and antimony, which form a natural group, may also replace each other, equivalent for equivalent; thus, *glycocoll*, which is $C_4H_5NO_4$, has a corresponding arsenical compound, *alkargene*, $C_4H_5AsO_4$.

646. When any acid, like chlorohydric or acetic acid, acts upon a metal such as zinc, hydrogen is evolved, and a chlorid or acetate of zinc is formed, in which Zn has replaced the hydrogen, $HCl+Zn=H+ZnCl$, and $C_4H_4O_4+Zn=C_4H_3ZnO_4+H$. If chlorine (ClCl) acts upon zinc, we obtain the same chlorid as with chlorohydric acid, $(ClCl)+Zn_2=2(ZnCl)$, and when chlorine combines with hydrogen, it is $(ClCl)+(HH)=2(HCl)$. Now as the action of HCl upon zinc evolves hydrogen (HH), all these analogies lead us to conclude that the equivalent of zinc is $Zn_2=(ZnZn)$, and hence that in the case of acetic or chlorohydric acids, an equivalent of zinc reacts with two equivalents of the acid. Acetic acid $C_4H_4O_4+ZnZn=C_4(H_3Zn)O_4+(ZnH)$, but ZnH with another equivalent of $C_4H_4O_4$ yields a second equivalent of acetate and one of hydrogen (HH). The hydrates of metals like ZnH are seldom stable, and as they decompose water and acids very readily, are difficult to be isolated. The replacement of the hydrogen in acids by a metal is then analogous to that of its substitution by chlorine.

647. When an acid is brought in contact with a metallic oxyd, double decomposition ensues in the same manner, but with the formation of an oxyd of hydrogen; acetic acid $C_4H_4O_4+ZnO=C_4H_3ZnO_4+HO$. But with the equivalents here proposed, the composition of oxyd of zinc must be written Zn_2O_2, and that of water H_2O_2, so that as in the reaction with metallic zinc, two equivalents of the acetic acid react with Zn_2O_2. If we represent the actions as consecutive, the first result will be $(ZnH)O_2$, or the hydrated oxyd of zinc, corresponding to ZnH, which with another equivalent of acid exchanges its Zn for H, forming water, (H_2O_2).

648. All the metals proper are capable of replacing in this

manner a portion of the hydrogen of acids to form salts A great number, like acetic acid, have only one atom of hydrogen which can be replaced by a metal, but in others two and three atoms may be in a similar manner replaced. These are called *bibasic* and *tribasic acids;* while such as acetic acid are said to be *monobasic*. Tartaric acid is bibasic; its composition is represented $C_8H_6O_{12}$, or $C_8H_4(H_2)O_{12}$; the two equivalents of hydrogen may be replaced by two equivalents of some metal as $C_8H_4Zn_2O_{12}$; by two different metals as in $C_8H_4(KNa)O_{12}$, or but one equivalent may be replaced as in $C_8H_4(HK)O_{12}$. The latter still retains acid properties, and is called an *acid salt*. The salts of tribasic acids may contain either one, two, or three equivalents of hydrogen replaced by a metal; the first two of these salts will be acid, and the last neutral.

The monobasic acids are almost always volatile, while the bibasic and tribasic acids are never volatile without decomposition.

649. The sesquioxyds, which have been represented in treating of mineral chemistry as composed of two equivalents of a metal combined with three of oxygen, offer a peculiar case in the formation of salts. If we take, for example, the peroxyd of iron, Fe_2O_3, we find that it saturates, not two equivalents of acetic acid, but three, and that while in the acetate of the protoxyd of iron FeO replaces H, in the acetate of the peroxyd two-thirds of an equivalent of iron sustain the same relation; if then we would represent the acetate of the peroxyd, we must write it $C_4H_3Fe\frac{2}{3}O_4$. In other words Fe_2O_3 has reacted as if it were $3(Fe\frac{2}{3}O)$. But if we examine these two salts still farther, we find that in their chemical reactions they differ from each other as widely as the salts of two distinct metals, and that we have in the salts of the peroxyd, iron with two-thirds its ordinary equivalent, and with peculiar and distinct properties. We may designate the iron in the proto-salts as *ferrosum*, with an atomic weight of 28 and the symbol Fe, and the iron in the persalts as *ferricum*, with an atomic weight of 18·6, and write its symbol, fe. The sesquioxyd of iron, Fe_2O_3, is then 3(feO) and the corresponding *acetate* of *ferricum* $C_4H_3feO_4$.

This same view is to be extended to the proto and sesqui-salts of chromium and manganese, and to the salts of alumina, which is a sesquioxyd; also to the salts of mercury and of tin, in which the equivalents of the two forms are to each other as 1 : 2. We have *chromosum* and *chromicum*, *aluminicum*, *stannosum* and *stannicum*, *mercurosum* and *mercuricum*; the second form of the metal is distinguished by writing its symbol with a small letter as Cr, cr, al, Sn, sn, Hg, hg, &c.

650. We have seen that acetic acid may exchange three equivalents of hydrogen for chlorine, and but one equivalent for a metal, so that in chloracetate of silver, $C_4Cl_3AgO_4$, all the hydrogen is replaced. There are many acids in which we cannot effect the substitution by chlorine, nor can the fourth atom of hydrogen in acetic acid be thus replaced; it can be removed only by substituting a metal. Thus the hydrogen which is replaceable by chlorine is distinct from that which is equivalent to a metal. It will be shown farther on, however, that there are some bodies in which this distinction appears to be lost, and in which all the hydrogen may be replaced either by chlorine or a metal.

651. In treating of the action of chlorine upon acetic acid, we have considered the process only with reference to the acid; but the substitution is reciprocal, and there is mutual decomposition. To make the question more simple, we will select a case where but one atom of hydrogen is replaced. The essence of bitter almonds, *benzoilol*, has the composition $C_{14}H_6O_2$; by the action of chlorine, hydrochloric acid is formed, and one atom of hydrogen is replaced by chlorine, $C_{14}H_6O_2+(ClCl)=C_{14}H_5ClO_2+HCl$. Now if we consider only the oil, it will be said that an equivalent substitution has taken place of Cl for H; but it is equally correct to say, that the benzoilol *minus* H has replaced Cl in the equivalent of chlorine (ClCl); in other words, that the essence has ceded H to form hydrochloric with Cl, and that the *residue* has replaced the eliminated atom of chlorine.

When the constitution of the bodies becomes more complex, the action is still the same; benzoilol reacts with nitric acid, which is NHO_6, and yields water and a new substance containing the elements of the essence and the acid, *minus* an equivalent of water; $C_{14}H_6O_2+NHO_6=C_{14}H_5NO_6+H_2O_2$. An examination of this reaction leads to the conclusion that the acid has furnished H and the essence HO_2 to form the equivalent of water; so that the *residues* $C_{14}H_5$ and NO_6 unite to form the new product; and it may be said that $C_{14}H_5$ replaces H in the nitric acid, precisely as $C_{14}H_5O_2$ replaces Cl in the equivalent of chlorine.

652. The monobasic nitric acid has fixed the elements of a neutral body in place of its atom of hydrogen, and the *nitrobenzoilol* is hence neutral. But if benzoic acid, which is monobasic, be substituted for the essence, it preserves even in combination its saline character; and hence the compound has the monobasic character which pertains to the benzoic acid. And even if this nitrobenzoic compound replaces the hydrogen of a second atom of nitric acid, the monobasic character is still preserved in the resulting compound. A bibasic acid, like the sulphuric, will form with one equivalent of a neutral substance a monobasic acid; and with two, a body which shall itself be neutral; because in these cases, one and two atoms of hydrogen have been removed from the acid. But if an equivalent of a monobasic acid reacts with sulphuric acid, it still retains its saline power in combination, and the result is bibasic: in like manner, with another bibasic acid, sulphuric acid yields a compound which is tribasic. In all these reactions, as in the formation of nitrobenzoilol, corresponding equivalents of H_2O_2 are eliminated, and the derived bodies are often designated as *coupled acids*.

653. Some writers have distinguished these cases from the simpler instances of equivalent substitution, and have designated them as *substitutions by residues*. But this distinction originates in a too much restricted idea of the meaning of an equivalent. In an early period of the science, the equivalent of a metal was fixed from the proportion of hydrogen it replaces, or in other words from the composition of its salts; but we have since learned that although 28 parts of manganese are generally equivalent to 1 of hydrogen and 35·5 of chlorine, there are cases where, as in permanganic acid, which corresponds to perchloric acid, 56 parts of manganese are equivalent to 35·5 of chlorine; and in the sesqui-salts of the metal, 18·6 of manganese become equivalent to H; so 31·7 parts of copper are at one time equivalent to one of hydrogen, and 63·4 parts at another time. Hence the numbers assigned as the equivalents of the elements are changeable as these elements change their functions, and, as in the case of benzoilol, groups of carbon and hydrogen, or carbon, hydrogen, and oxygen, may become *equivalent* to a single atom of chlorine of hydrogen or a metal, and may replace it in combination.

These groups which replace the metals on the one hand, and chlorine and bromine on the other, have been described by some authors by the name of *compound radicals*, and have served as the basis of a system of organic chemistry and of nomenclature. But as we conceive that the system is liable to great objections, and tends to perpetuate false notions of the science, the language of the compound radical theory will not be employed in these pages.

654. *The law of direct union* is much more simple. A salt may assimilate the elements of water, or of a metallic oxyd, or ammonia may combine with an acid, as with hydrochloric acid, to form sal-ammoniac; $NH_3+HCl=NH_4Cl$. A carbon compound, like olefiant gas, C_4H_4, may also unite directly with Cl_2, to form $C_4H_4Cl_2$. In these and similar instances there is only one product, a character by which such reactions are distinguished from those of the first class. On the other hand, a body may eliminate the elements of water or of hydrogen, or some similar substance, and thus resolve itself into two; for instance, alcohol $C_4H_6O_2$, under the influence of certain reagents, may lose H_2, and in some of its combinations is resolved by heat into C_4H_4, and H_2O_2. Many ammoniacal salts which are formed by direct union of the acid and ammonia, separate under the influence of heat into water, and new compounds called amids, which, when placed in contact with water, under proper conditions, combine with that substance, and regenerate the original salts.

655. The compounds formed by direct union may then divide in a manner different from that of their composition, and thus produce two new compounds unlike the parent ones, precisely as in the reactions of the first class. We hence arrive at the conclusion, that the phenomena of the second class represent only an intermediate step in the process of equivalent substitution; and that if we could arrest the latter process, we should always find it to consist of two parts, composition and decomposition, resulting in a mutual substitution. As an illustration, may be cited the compound formed by the direct combination of chlorine with olefiant gas, which is $C_4H_4Cl_2$, but under certain circumstances is decomposed into HCl and C_4H_3Cl; the latter is a substitution product from olefiant gas, and we are here enabled to see the intermediate step in its formation.

The two classes into which we have for convenience divided the phenomena of chemical transformations, are then reducible to one simple formula; $a+b$ and $c+d$ may unite to form $a+b+c+d$, and may afterward be rearranged so as to form $a+c$ and $b+d$, as in the first, or $a+b$ and $c+d$, as in the second case.

On Combinations by Volumes.

656. The law of combination by volumes has already been given in the first portion of this work (257); but we refer to it again to explain the density of vapours, and the equivalents of organic substances.

The proportions in which oxygen and hydrogen unite to form water are one volume of the former to two volumes of the latter, and these three are condensed into two volumes of the vapor of water at 212° F. As these proportions have been assumed to correspond to one equivalent of each, the composition of water is written HO, having an equivalent number of $1+8=9$, and corresponding to two volumes of vapor.

The specific gravity of hydrogen has been found by experiment to be 69·2, air being 1000, while oxygen is 1105·6. Then

2 volumes of hydrogen $2\times 69{\cdot}2$	138·4	
1 " of oxygen	1105·6	
yield 2 volumes of vapor water		1244·0
1 " of do. do		622·0

Experiment gives for the density of water vapor 620·1.

657. *Density of Carbon Vapor.*—In calculating the atomic volume of bodies of the carbon series, it becomes necessary to fix upon the density of carbon vapor; but as carbon is not known in a gaseous form, we must deduce its density from that of some one of its compounds.

When carbon is burned in oxygen gas, this is converted into carbonic acid gas without change of volume. If we subtract from the weight of the new compound that of the oxygen, we shall then have the weight corresponding to the carbon vapor. Experiment has given for the density of

Carbonic acid gas (air $=1000$)	1529·0
Deduct that of oxygen	1105·6
Gives for the density of carbon vapor	423·4

If we suppose the gas to consist of two volumes of carbon vapor and two of oxygen condensed one-half, the equivalent volume of carbon will be the same as that of hydrogen, and its weight represented by the above number. But if it may, with as good reason, be regarded as formed by the con densation of two volumes of oxygen and one of carbon vapor into two volumes, the density of carbon vapor will be twice the number calculated, or 846 8.

The experimental density of carbonic acid is, however, not very exact, and the density of carbon vapor may be more accurately calculated from the well-determined density of oxygen. Carbonic acid consists of oxygen 72·73 and carbon 27·27 parts, and the observed density of oxygen is 1105·6; we have then this proportion:

$$72{\cdot}73 : 27{\cdot}27 :: 1105{\cdot}6 : x.$$

in which $x = 829$, which we shall adopt as the most correct number for the density of carbon vapor.

658. Hence, if we know the composition and equivalent of any body, we can calculate its density; or, having the density and composition given, can fix its equivalent. For example, the density of olefiant gas, as found by experiment, is 967·4. It consists of equal equivalents of carbon and hydrogen, and one volume of it contains

2 volumes of hydrogen = 1 eq. 2×69·2	138·4
1 " of carbon vapor = 1 eq.	829·0
Yield 1 volume of olefiant gas	967·4

If now the equivalent of olefiant gas be like that of water represented by two volumes, the formula will be C_2H_2; but most writers have assumed four volumes as representing the equivalent of organic compounds; while water is written HO, and corresponds to but two volumes of vapor. Thus the the formula of olefiant gas is generally written C_4H_4 = four volumes of vapor; to be compared with this, water must be H_2O_2. Some of the French chemists, choosing to preserve the old equivalents of organic bodies, have doubled in this manner that of water; while others have preferred to divide the formulas of organic substances, and reduce all to the standard of two volumes, oxygen being one; or, in other words, to take the volume of the atom of hydrogen as unity. We shall in these pages regard H_2, which is equivalent to four volumes, (O being one volume,) as unity, and write the formula of water H_2O_2, with an equivalent of 18.

On the Law of the Divisibility of Formulas.

659. The researches of Gerhardt and Laurent have established a very important law which prevails in the grouping of elements in compounds, not only in those of the carbon series,

but also in mineral chemistry. It is, that in all compounds of carbon, hydrogen, and oxygen, represented by an equivalent of four volumes of vapor, the number of atoms of carbon and oxygen is always divisible by two, and that of the atoms of hydrogen by the same number. If the oxygen is wholly or in part replaced by sulphur or selenium, the substitution is always atom for atom, so that the same divisibility is maintained; and if the hydrogen is replaced in whole or in part by chlorine, iodine, or bromine, by nitrogen, phosphorus, arsenic, or antimony, or by any of the metals, the sum of the number of the atoms will always be a multiple of two.

On Isomerism.

660. We have seen, in treating of substitution, that a number of the atoms of any element in a compound may be replaced by another element, and the constitution of the body remain unchanged. From this, and from other facts, we conclude that the properties of compounds depend rather upon the peculiar arrangement, than upon the species of their constituent atoms; and, moreover, that a different arrangement of the same elements may form compounds very different in their properties. Such bodies are frequently met with among the carbon series, and are denominated *isomeric compounds*, (from *isos*, equal, and *meros*, measure.) We have an instance in the essence of *spiræa ulmaria*, and benzoic acid, both of which are represented by the formula $C_{14}H_6O_4$, but are very distinct in their characters. The relation of such as have not only the same proportional, but the same actual composition, may be distinguished by the term *metamerism*, (from *meta*, by, and *meros*, measure.)

Another form of isomerism is that in which the relative proportions of the elements being the same, the equivalent of the one is a multiple of the other. Thus, olefiant gas C_4H_4, butyrene C_8H_8, naphtene $C_{16}H_{16}$, and cetene $C_{32}H_{32}$, have the same proportions of carbon and hydrogen, though each has a density and equivalent double that of the preceding; such bodies are said to be *polymeric*, (from *polus*, many, and *meros*.)

The phenomena which in mineral chemistry have been characterized under the names of *dimorphism* and *allotropism* are instances of isomerism which is often polymeric, and are met with even among bodies which are considered as elementary.

On Chemical Homologues.

661. The carbo-hydrogens just mentioned, whose composition is represented by a multiple of C_4H_4, are possessed of similar chemical affinities, and form with other substances similar compounds. Two of them, the first and last, are artificially formed from compounds which have the formulæ $C_4H_6O_2$ and $C_{32}H_{34}O_2$, and differ from their respective hydrocarbons only by the elements of water.

These compounds are two terms of a series of bodies which are known as *alcohols*, from common alcohol, which was the first known of the series. The first one has the formula $C_2H_4O_2 = C_2H_2 + H_2O_2$, and the next $C_4H_6O_2$, each one differing from the last by C_2H_2; so that representing by n any number divisible by two, the general formula of the series will be $C_nH_n + H_2O_2$, or $C_nH_{n+2}O_2$. Bodies thus related are designated *homologues;* and the study of this relationship, which was first pointed out by Gerhardt, is of the highest importance to the science.

The bodies of an homologous series generally undergo similar changes by like reagents, and the products resulting are also homologous. Thus, wine alcohol, by oxydizing agencies, loses H_2, and forms the body $C_4H_4O_2$; by further oxydation it yields acetic acid $C_4H_4O_4$; and every alcohol in like manner yields an acid homologous with the acetic acid: the general formula of the series being $C_nH_nO_4$. The intermediate body $C_nH_nO_2$ has not, however, in all cases been obtained.

The alcohols also yield a series of homologous alkaloids, whose common formula is $(C_nH_n)H_3N$ or $C_nH_{n+3}N$.

662. In many homologous series the number of equivalents of hydrogen is not equal to that of the carbon, and the formula must be written differently. Thus, benzoic acid $C_{14}H_6O_4$ and cuminic acid $C_{20}H_{12}O_4$ are homologous, and differ from each other by $(C_2H_2)_3$, and we may express them by the general formula $C_nH_{n-8}O_4$, the number of equivalents of hydrogen being less by eight than that of carbon: by this it will be seen that the lowest term of the series will be that in which $n-8=2$, or $C_{10}H_2O_4$; for if $n-8=$ *zero*, the compound will contain no hydrogen, and hence want the characteristic properties of an acid which belong to the series. If, however, the hydrogen be present in excess, the case will be different. In the formula of the alcohols, if $n=$ *zero*, the representative of the type, is H_2O_2, or water, which is the

prototype of the alcohol series; and in the alkaloids of the same group, when $n = zero$, we have NH_3, or ammonia, which is equally their prototype.

It will be seen from what we have said of isomeric bodies that there may be two or more series of homologous bodies, which shall be metameric of one another, and hence similarity of chemical characteristics is necessary to constitute a homology. In an homologous series of chemically allied compounds, then, while the oxygen and nitrogen always remain the same, the proportions of hydrogen and carbon vary by a simple and constant ratio.

Temperature of Ebullition.

663. A simple relation between the boiling points of different members of an homologous series has been pointed out, which may often serve an important end in deciding the equivalent of a compound. The boiling point of the volatile acids of the formula $C_nH_nO_4$ is found to increase about 36° F. for each addition of C_2H_2.

ANALYSIS OF ORGANIC SUBSTANCES.

664. The ultimate analysis of organic substances is of great importance: for as we are unable to form them by a direct combination of their elements, a correct understanding of their composition, and of the nature of the changes which they undergo, must depend entirely on the results of their analysis. The equivalent of many substances is so large, that a change of one-hundredth part in the proportions, gives to the compound entirely distinct properties. Great refinement is consequently necessary in analysis, to enable us to detect the minute differences in composition; and such have been the care and skill with which the subject has been studied, that we have now arrived at very great accuracy in operations of this kind.

665. In theory, the process of organic analysis is exceedingly simple. If any organic substance, as sugar, for example, is heated with a body capable of yielding oxygen, such as the oxyd of copper, of lead, or any other easily reducible metal, it is completely decomposed; the carbon and hydrogen take oxygen from the metallic oxyd, and are wholly converted into carbonic acid and water. From the weight of these, it is easy to calculate the amount of carbon and hydrogen in the body, and if it contains no other element

except oxygen, this is known by the loss. But notwithstanding the theoretical simplicity of the process, its accurate execution is exceedingly difficult, and very many precautions are necessary to insure accuracy. It is not the object of this work to explain all the precautions necessary to the successful performance of analytical operations, but merely to give an outline of the method pursued, and a general idea of the means employed. For more particular information, the student is referred to an excellent memoir on this subject, by Liebig.

666. The operation is performed in a *combustion tube* of hard glass, from 12 to 18 inches in length, and from $\frac{4}{10}$ to $\frac{5}{10}$ of an inch in diameter. One end is drawn out to a point, turned aside and sealed. Oxyd of copper, prepared from the nitrate, is generally employed for the combustion. Just before using it, it is heated to redness, in order to expel the moisture which it readily attracts from the atmosphere; the combustion tube is then about two-thirds filled with the hot oxyd. The substance to be analyzed having been care-

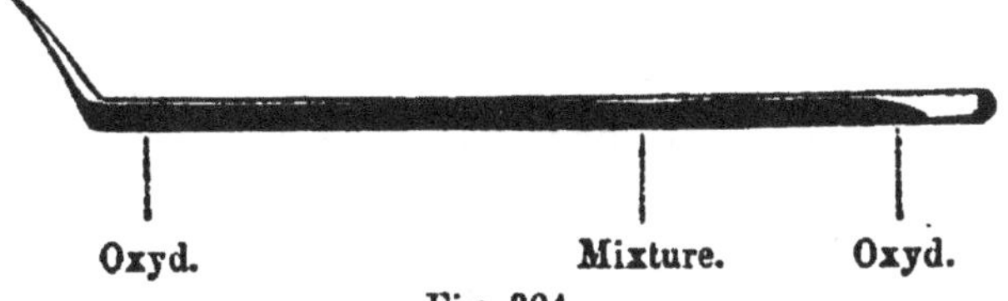

Fig. 394.

fully dried, five or six grains of it are weighed out in a tube with a narrow mouth, in order to prevent the absorption of moisture. It is then rapidly mixed in a warm and dry porcelain mortar, with the greater portion of the oxyd from the tube, to which it is again transferred, and the tube is then nearly filled up with pure oxyd. The relative portions of the oxyd and mixture are shown in fig. 394.

667. However carefully the mixture has been made, a little moisture will have been absorbed from the air, which must be removed by the following arrangement:—To the end of the combustion tube is fitted, by means of a cork, a long tube filled with chlorid of calcium, and to this is attached a small air-pump, fig. 395. The combustion tube is covered with hot sand, and the air slowly exhausted. After a short time, the stopcock is opened, and the air allowed to enter, thoroughly dried by its passage over the chlorid of calcium. It is again exhausted, and this process repeated four or five times, by which the mixture is completely dried.

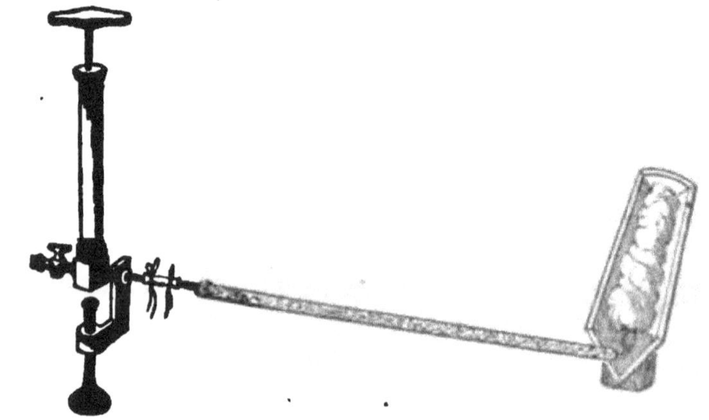

Fig. 395.

668. The tube is now ready for the combustion, and is placed in the furnace, figure 396. This is constructed of sheet iron, and fitted with a

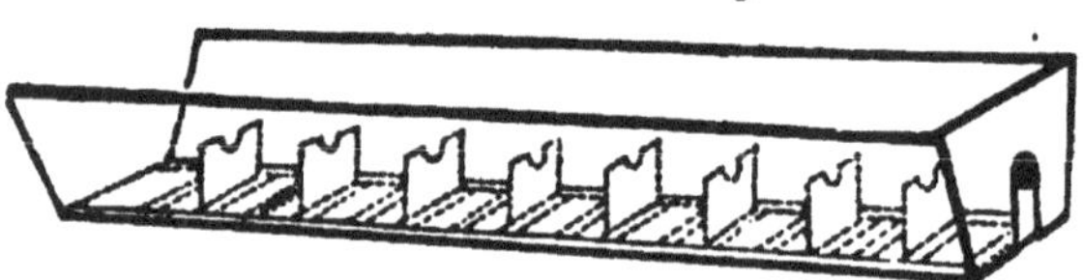

Fig. 396.

series of supporters at short distances from each other, to prevent the tube from bending when softened by heat. The furnace is placed on a flat stone, or tile, with the front slightly inclined downward. The quantity of water formed in the process is estimated by a light tube, fig. 397, which is filled with fragments of chlorid of calcium, and, after having been very carefully weighed, is attached by a well-dried and closely fitting cork, to the end of the combustion tube. To determine the carbonic acid, a small five-bulbed tube of peculiar form is used, called Liebig's

Fig. 397.

potash bulb tube, fig. 398. It is charged for this purpose with a solution of caustic potash of a specific gravity about 1·25, with which the three lower bulbs are nearly filled. Its weight is determined with great exactness, and it is then attached to the chlorid of calcium tube, by a little tube of gum elastic, which is held fast by a silken cord. The whole arrangement is shown in fig. 399. The tightness of the junction is ascertained by drawing a few

Fig. 398.

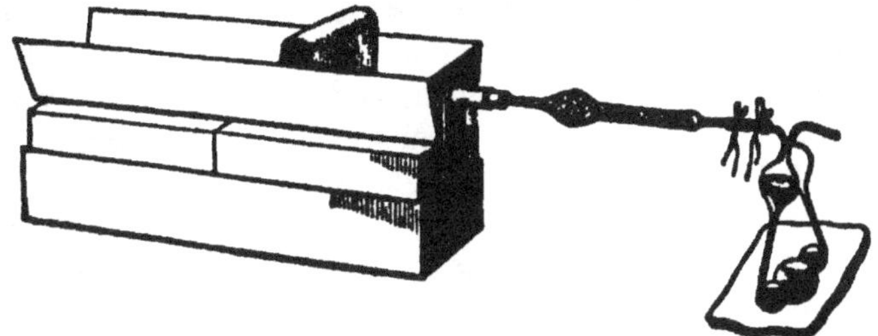

Fig. 399.

bubbles of air through the end of the potash tube, so that the liquid will be raised a few inches above the level on the other side; if this level remains the same for some minutes, the whole apparatus is tight.

669. Heat is now applied by means of ignited charcoal placed around the anterior portion of the tube, and when this is red-hot, the fire is gradually extended along the tube, by means of a movable screen, represented in the figure. This must be done so slowly as to keep a moderate and uniform flow of gas through the potash solution. When the whole tube is ignited, and gas no longer escapes, the closed end of the combustion tube is broken off, and a little air drawn through the apparatus to remove all the remaining products of combustion. The tubes are then detached, and from the increase of weight in the chlorid of calcium tube, the amount of water, and thence that of hydrogen, is deduced. The carbon is determined from the increase in weight of the potash bulb tube, by a simple calculation.

670. Volatile liquids are analyzed by enclosing them in a narrow-necked bulb of thin glass. The weight of the empty tube is first ascertained; the liquid is introduced, the neck sealed, the weight being again ascertained, and the difference gives the weight of the substance. The neck of the bulb is then broken by a file mark at *a*, (fig. 400,) dropped into the closed end of the combustion tube, and covered with oxyd of copper, which should nearly fill the tube. When this is heated to redness, a gentle heat applied to the portion of the combustion tube containing the volatile fluid, sends it in vapor over the ignited oxyd, completely burning it. The products of its combustion are estimated as before.

Fig. 400.

671. Fatty bodies, and others which contain much carbon and a small quantity of hydrogen, are more perfectly burned by employing chromate of lead instead of copper. This substance does not readily attract moisture from the atmosphere, like oxyd of copper, and is consequently better when the hydrogen is to be determined accurately. The chromate of lead is prepared for use by heating it until it begins to fuse, and when cool reducing it to powder.

672. When nitrogen is a constituent of organic bodies, it is determined by placing in one end of the combustion tube about three inches of carbonate of copper, secured in its place by a plug of asbestus; and then the nitrogenous body is introduced, mixed with oxyd of copper. The remaining space in the combustion tube is filled with turnings of metallic copper. The air is then withdrawn by an air-pump, and a gentle heat applied to the carbonate of copper, which evolves carbonic acid, and drives out all remaining traces of common air. The tube is now heated as usual, and the gases evolved are collected in a graduated air-jar, over mercury. When the combustion is finished, heat is again applied to the carbonate of copper, and another portion of carbonic acid expelled, which drives out all the nitrogen from the tube. The use of the copper turnings is to decompose any traces of nitric oxyd which may be formed in the process. The carbonic acid is removed from the air-jar by a strong solution of potash, and pure nitrogen remains, which is measured with the usual precautions, and from its volume the weight is easily determined.

673. Another and a preferable mode of determining nitrogen, is that of Will and Varrentrapp, which is founded on the fact that when a body containing nitrogen is heated with an excess of caustic potash, or soda, all the nitrogen is evolved in the form of ammonia, and may be thus estimated, by conducting it into hydrochloric acid, and forming, with chlorid of platinum, the double chlorid of platinum and ammonium.

674. Chlorine is determined in the analysis of organic compounds, by passing the vapor over quicklime heated to redness in a combustion tube; chlorid of calcium is formed, which is afterward dissolved in water, and the chlorine precipitated by nitrate of silver. From the weight of the chlorid of silver, the amount of chlorine is calculated.

675. Sulphur is a rare constitutent of organic compounds. Its presence is detected by fusion with nitre and carbonate

of soda, or by digestion with nitric acid. Sulphuric acid is thus formed, and is precipitated as sulphate of baryta, from the weight of which that of the sulphur is determined. In the analysis with oxyd of copper, a small tube of peroxyd of lead is introduced between the chlorid of calcium tube and the potash apparatus, to absorb the sulphurous acid which is evolved.

Density of Vapors.

676. The determination of the destiny of vapors is of great importance; in the case of some volatile organic compounds which form no combinations with other substances, it is the only means of ascertaining their constitution and equivalent. The process is very simple, and the method employed in the case of gases has been already described, (49.) When the substance is a liquid or solid, it is introduced into a narrow-necked glass globe, of the form represented in fig. 401, the weight of which is carefully ascertained. The globe is held by means of a handle firmly attached by a wire, beneath the surface of an oil or water-bath, and then heated to some degrees above the boiling-point of the substance. When this is all volatilized and the globe is filled with the vapor, the open and projecting end of the globe's neck is sealed by the flame of a spirit-lamp: at the same time the temperature of the bath is noted. When the globe is cooled it is again weighed, and the end of the neck broken off beneath the surface of mercury, which rushes up and fills the empty vessel. The mercury is then carefully measured. The capacity of the vessel and its weight being thus ascertained, we can find the weight of a volume of vapor at the observed temperature, and by an easy calculation can determine what would be its volume at the ordinary temperature, (88:) its weight compared with that of the same volume of air gives the specific gravity required.

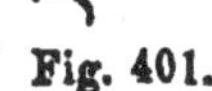

Fig. 401.

677. It is proposed, before commencing the study of those bodies of the carbon series which we have included under the head of Organic Chemistry, to consider briefly the principal products of the ultimate decomposition of this class of substances. These are water, ammonia, and carbonic

acid gas. The latter only strictly comes within our limits, and all of them have been described in the first part of this work; but we shall bring them up again to illustrate certain laws of substitution, which will help to explain the history of the more complex organic compounds.

We shall then treat of starch and sugar, and some other bodies of high equivalents, whose history is comparatively simple, and proceed to the products of their decomposition by fermentation and other means, among which are different alcohols and acids.

Water.

678. In the first part of this volume, water has been described as having the formula HO, and as composed of two volumes of hydrogen and one of oxygen, condensed into two volumes of vapor of water; we have already given the reasons which lead us to adopt four volumes as its equivalent, and to write its formula H_2O_2.

We shall now speak of the products of substitution derived from water. If the oxygen be replaced by sulphur we have sulphuretted hydrogen: the selenium and tellurium compounds have a similar composition. One or both atoms of the hydrogen may be replaced by a metal. Hydrate of potash KO.HO is water in which one equivalent of H is replaced by potassium: it is $(KH)O_2$, and anhydrous potash will be K_2O_2. The hydrated oxyds result from the replacement of one equivalent of hydrogen by a metal, while in the anhydrous oxyds both are thus replaced. Water thus resembles a bibasic acid, and the hydrated oxyds may be compared to acid salts, while the anhydrous oxyds are like neutral salts.

679. The so-called suboxyds are illustrations of the change of equivalent upon which we have insisted. The red oxyd of copper is Cu_2O, or rather Cu_4O_2, but copper here unites in twice its ordinary equivalent weight, and in this form, which we may designate as *cuprosum*, with the symbol cu, is strictly equivalent to H and to Cu, so that the red oxyd is cu_2O_2. The peroxyds, like those of hydrogen or barium, may be either oxyds which have combined with an additional amount of oxygen, and thus increased their equivalent weight, being H_2O_4 and Ba_2O_4, or they may be regarded as sustaining to the ordinary oxyds the same relation that the black oxyd of copper does to the red oxyd,

being compounds in which barium and hydrogen unite in one-half their ordinary equivalent: thus, $(Ba_{\frac{1}{2}})_2O_2$, &c. The same views apply to the persulphuret of hydrogen and other persulphurets. From the volumes of the corresponding bodies of the carbon series, the first view is probably the true one.

680. We have shown that in the group H_2, chlorine may replace H to form chlorohydric acid, and we may here refer to an example in which an atom of the hydrogen is replaced by a metal. It is a product of the action of hypo-phosphorous acid upon a salt of copper, and is a yellow powder containing Cu_2H, which corresponds to cuH. Chlorohydric acid dissolves it with the evolution of hydrogen and the formation of a chlorid of cuprosum, cuH+HCl=cuCl+HH, the hydrogen of both being evolved.

It has already been remarked that there are examples of bodies in which all of the hydrogen may be replaced either by chlorine or by a metal, and water is such a body; hydrated hypochlorous acid ClO,HO is $(ClH)O_2$, or water in which Cl replaces H: the second equivalent of hydrogen may be replaced by a metal to form a hypochlorite, as in ClO.KO, which is $(ClK)O_2$. But this second equivalent may also be replaced by chlorine, and we have the so-called anhydrous hypochlorous acid, which is Cl_2O_2, or water in which chlorine has been substituted for the whole of the hydrogen.

Ammonia.

681. Ammonia is composed of six volumes of hydrogen and two of nitrogen (O being represented by one volume,) condensed to one-half, or to four volumes: its formula is then NH_3. Its properties have already been described, and we have only to notice some of its derivatives. Like water, the whole of its hydrogen may be replaced either by chlorine or by a metal. The direct action of chlorine decomposes it; the hydrogen forms hydrochloric acid, and the nitrogen is set free in the form of gas; but with a solution of a salt of ammonia, like the muriate or sal-ammonia, the action is different; the chlorine is slowly absorbed and a heavy yellow oil separates, which is a most dangerous compound, exploding with great violence by a gentle heat, by the contact of phosphorus, fat oils, and many other substances. It is composed of NCl_3, and by the explosion is resolved into these elements. The name of *chlorid of nitro-*

gen has been given to it, but it is ammonia in which the hydrogen has been replaced by chlorine, and may be called *trichloric ammonia*. The action of iodine upon ammonia is more moderate than that of chlorine: if it is triturated with a solution of ammonia or mixed in an alcoholic solution, a black powder is obtained which explodes when dry by the slightest friction, but less violently than the chlorid. Its composition is NI_2H, and it is therefore *biniodic ammonia*. The chlorine compound is indifferent to acids, but the iodic species still exhibits feebly basic properties: it is dissolved by dilute acids and precipitated again by a solution of potash.

682. When potassium is heated in ammoniacal gas, one equivalent of hydrogen is displaced, and an olive-green compound is obtained, which is $N(H_2K)$, and is decomposed by water into hydrate of potash and ammonia $N(H_2K)+H_2O_2=(HK)O_2+NH_3$. When ammonia is passed over heated oxyd of copper, water is formed, and a compound which contains Cu_6N. It corresponds to the red oxyd of copper, or oxyd of cuprosum cu_2O_2, and is Ncu_3, or ammonia in which all the hydrogen has been replaced by cuprosum. It is formed at a temperature of 480° F., and is decomposed into its elements with evolution of light at 540° F.

683. The salts of ammonia next claim our notice. Their characters and preparation, and the theory of ammonium have already been described, (518.) The mode of their formation is different from that of ordinary salts of metals: these, we have shown, whether the metals or their oxyds are employed, are produced by an equivalent substitution with the elimination of hydrogen or water, while ammonia and the acids unite directly to form salts, without the production of any second body. Thus ammonia and chlorohydric acid NH_3+HCl yield sal-ammoniac NH_4Cl; and sulphuric acid, which is bibasic and must be written $2SO_3.H_2O_2=S_2H_2O_8$, fixes directly $2NH_3$ to form sulphate of ammonia. But these salts, notwithstanding their different mode of formation, are closely analogous to the salts of potassium and even isomorphous with them; and while chlorid of potassium is KCl, the NH_4 in sal-ammoniac is perfectly similar in its relations to K; and hence sal-ammoniac is often regarded, not as the hydrochlorate of ammonia $NH_3.HCl$, but as the chlorid of a *quasi-metal*, ammonium, which unites with Cl like potassium, and, like this metal,

may even form an amalgam with mercury; for $(NH_4)Hg$ evidently corresponds to KHg, and ZnHg. Ammonium, NH_4, is then a group which, although it cannot be isolated, may replace hydrogen, and is equivalent to it. The neutral sulphate of ammonia is $S_2(NH_4)_2O_8$, as sulphate of potash is $S_2(K_2)O_8$, and the acid sulphate $S_2(H.NH_4)O_8$, corresponding to $S_2(HK)O_8$. The group NH_4 may be represented by the symbol Am.

684. The compound corresponding to a metallic oxyd in which NH_4 replaces H, like $(KH)O_2$, probably exists in the aqueous solution of ammonia: it will be $(NH_4.H)O_2$ or $(AmH)O_2$; but the ammonia is readily evolved by heat, the compound being like some salts of ammonia, very unstable. We shall see hereafter that there are homologues of ammonia which form more fixed combinations. A compound of $(NH_4)_2O_2$, or Am_2O_2, corresponding to an anhydrous oxyd, is also possible; like oxyd of zinc, (Zn_2O_2) it would evolve an equivalent of water in combining with an acid.

685. In the same way that ammonia combines directly with acids it may unite with metallic salts; for example, with chlorid of copper $CuCl+NH_3=(NH_3Cu)Cl$, and with sulphate of silver $S_2Ag_2O_8+2NH_3=S_2(NH_3Ag)_2O_8$: in these compounds one equivalent of hydrogen in the ammonia is replaced by copper and silver, and the groups may be designated *cuprammonium* and *argentammonium.* The white precipitate of mercury obtained by adding ammonia to a solution of chlorid of mercury is a body of this class, and is represented by $(NH_2Hg_2)Cl$: when this is boiled in a solution of sal-ammoniac, another compound is obtained, which is $(NH_3Hg)Cl$. Here one and two equivalents of hydrogen are replaced by mercury.

With the chlorid of platinum a similar chlorid is obtained, which is known as the *green salt of Magnus*, and is $(NH_3Pt)Cl$. But the group NH_4 may replace an equivalent of H in the last, and we have a salt described by Gros and Reiset, which is $N(AmH_2Pt)Cl$ or $(N_2H_6Pt)Cl$. Still another one has an equivalent of hydrogen replaced by Cl, and is $(N_2H_5ClPt)Cl$. All of these correspond to chlorid of ammonium, and it will be observed that the sum of their atoms is always divisible by two. They combine with the oxygen acids like ammonia, and their sulphates, when decomposed by baryta, give the hydrated oxyds corresponding to $(KH)O_2$, and, like it, caustic and alkaline. Cobalt and some other metals yields analogous compounds.

686. The decomposition of ammoniacal salts to form water and amids has already been alluded to, (654.) An ammoniacal salt eliminates one equivalent of water for each equivalent of ammonia which it contains, and the salt, if neutral, yields a neutral amid; but if the salt is acid, that is, if a bibasic acid has combined with one equivalent of ammonia, and has still an atom of hydrogen replaceable by a metal, this is preserved in the amid, which is then a monobasic acid. These compounds are often directly formed by the action of heat upon the several salts, and sometimes by distilling them with anhydrous phosphoric acid, which combines with the water. Amids may sometimes lose the elements of another equivalent of water, and form a class of bodies known as *anhydrid amids*, or *nitryls*. Acetate of ammonia $C_4H_4O_4+NH_3=C_4H_7NO_4-H_2O_2=C_4H_5NO_2$, or *acetamid*, from which if H_2O_2 be again abstracted, there remains *acetonitryl* C_4H_3N.

687. Nitrous oxyd, which is NO, or rather N_2O_2, is formed from nitrate of ammonia $NHO_6.NH_3$, by the abstraction of $2H_2O_2$, and is a true nitryl. Like all the other bodies of this class, it can reassume the elements of water and regenerate the acid and ammonia; when passed over heated hydrate of potash, a nitrate is formed, ammonia escaping.

Phosphoric acid forms not less than three anhydrid amids, corresponding to different salts of the different modifications of the acid. They are all white insoluble powders, which, under the influence of strong acids or alkalies, yield phosphoric acid and ammonia. The one corresponding to nitrous oxyd is $(PN)O_2=PO_5.NH_4O-2H_2O_2$.

The points of interest with regard to the amids of the organic acids will be considered in their proper places.

Carbonic Acid.

688. This compound has already been described, but we again refer to it to speak of its equivalent, which, to correspond to those adopted for organic substances, must be written C_2O_4 in its anhydrous state. The gas fixes H_2O_2 when it takes the acid form; and carbonic acid, such as it exists in solution, is consequently $C_2H_2O_6$, in which one or both equivalents of hydrogen may be replaced by a metal, form-

ing neutral and acid carbonates, or bicarbonates, as they are often called.

Carbonic acid is very readily separated from its aqueous solution, or decomposed into carbonic acid gas and water, in which it differs from more fixed bibasic acids, which sometimes require a high temperature to effect such a division.

689. *Carbonic oxyd*, which we write C_2O_2, is interesting from its action with chlorine in the formation of *phosgene gas.* It directly fixes 2Cl to form $C_2Cl_2O_2$, which evidently corresponds to an hydrogen compound C_2H_2O. This group, of which *phosgene* is the chlorinized species, is the prototype of an important class of organic compounds, the aldehydes $C_nH_nO_2$.

SUGAR, STARCH, AND ALLIED SUBSTANCES.

690. Under this head is included a class of substances of vegetable origin, which agree in containing carbon with oxygen and hydrogen in the proportions which form water. When soluble, they are insipid, or have a sweet taste, and are generally nutritious. They are not volatile, and are readily decomposed by heat and many other agents.

691. *Sugars.*—These bodies are soluble in water, have a sweet taste, and most of them by the process of fermentation yield alcohol and carbonic acid.

Cane Sugar, $C_{24}H_{22}O_{22}$.—This occurs in the juices of many plants, as the sugar-cane, maple, beet-root, and Indian corn. It is obtained by evaporating the juice to a syrup, when the sugar crystallizes in grains of a brownish color, and is rendered pure and white by redissolving it, and filtering the solution through animal charcoal, (337.) By the slow evaporation of a concentrated solution, it is obtained in fine transparent crystals, which are derived from an oblique rhombic prism; in this state it constitutes *rock-candy.* It fuses at 356°, and forms, on cooling, a vitreous mass well known as *barley sugar:* this gradually becomes opaque and changes into a mass of small crystals of ordinary sugar. Sugar is soluble in about one-third its weight of water, forming a thick syrup. It is insoluble in pure alcohol.

692. *Grape Sugar; Glucose*, $C_{24}H_{24}O_{24} + 2H_2O_2$.—This sugar is found in the grape and many other fruits, and in honey. It is formed when cane sugar or starch is boiled with dilute sulphuric acid, and is a product in many other trans-

formations. The urine in the disease called *diabetes mellitus* contains a large quantity of grape sugar, which is formed from the starch and similar substances taken as food.

Grape sugar is generally obtained as a white granular mass, which requires one and a half parts of cold water to dissolve it: it is less sweet to the taste than cane sugar, and about two and a half times as much are required to give an equal sweetness to the same volume of water. When heated to 212°, the two equivalents of water are expelled. With sulphuric acid, grape sugar forms a coupled acid, the sulphosaccharic. It forms with chlorid of sodium, a crystalline compound, which is $C_{24}H_{24}O_{24}.NaCl.H_2O_2$. The water is lost by heat. If a solution of grape sugar is mixed with a solution of potash, and then with a little sulphate of copper, the liquid becomes dark, and soon deposits suboxyd of copper in the form of a red powder; cane sugar yields no precipitate until the solution is boiled. This test enables us to detect the $\frac{1}{10000}$ part of grape sugar in a liquid. *Honey* is a mixture of crystallizable grape sugar, with an uncrystallizable syrup identical with it in composition.

693. *Sugar of Milk; Lactose*, $C_{24}H_{20}O_{20}+2H_2O_2$.—This is found only in the whey of milk, and is obtained by evaporating it, and purifying the product by crystallization. Lactose forms semi-transparent prisms, soluble in six parts of cold water, and two and a half of boiling water; it is much less sweet than cane or grape sugar. By a heat of 212° its water is expelled; when boiled with dilute sulphuric acid, it combines with the elements of two equivalents of water, and is converted into grape sugar.

Mannite, $C_{12}H_{14}O_{12}$.—This substance is not properly a sugar, as it does not contain oxygen and hydrogen in the proportions to form water, and is not susceptible of fermentation. It exists in the juice of celery and many sea-weeds, and constitutes the principal part of the manna of the shops, which is the concreted juice of a species of ash-tree. When this is dissolved in hot alcohol, mannite is deposited on cooling in delicate silky crystals, which are sweet, and very soluble in water and alcohol.

Mannite dissolves in a mixture of fuming nitric and sulphuric acids, and water precipitates from the mixture a white matter, insoluble in water, which may be crystallized by dissolving in hot alcohol. It is formed by the fixation of the elements of nitric acid and the elimination of those of water, and is represented by $C_{12}H_8N_6O_{36}$. We may represent NO_4 as replacing hydrogen, and designate it by X The new compound, which is called *nitro-mannite*, will be then $C_{12}H_8(NO_4)_6O_{12} = C_{12}H_8X_6O_{12}$. This mode of notation is convenient, but, agreeably to the views laid down in the introduction, we must suppose successive substitutions, in the first of which $C_{12}H_{14}O_{12} - HO_2$ replaces H in nitric acid NHO_6, yielding $N(C_{12}H_{13}O_{10})O_6$ and H_2O_2; this product then reacts with a new equivalent of nitric acid, and so on. From the large portion of oxygen which it contains, nitro-mannite is very combustible, and it explodes spontaneously when struck with a hammer.

Products of the Decomposition of the Sugars.

694. *The Vinous Fermentation.*—When the juice of grapes or other fruits containing sugar is exposed to the air, a peculiar decomposition ensues, in which the sugar is resolved into carbonic acid gas and alcohol. A solution of pure sugar is not changed by exposure to the air; but if there is added to it a little yeast, or the juice of any fruit in the state of fermentation, decomposition takes place, and carbonic acid and alcohol are formed. Many substances besides yeast will effect this change, as blood, albumen, or flour paste in a state of decomposition. It appears that the influence of a ferment depends on the condition rather than on the kind of matter. Any nitrogenized substance capable of undergoing putrefaction produces the same effect, and we are to attribute this change in the juice of fruits, to a small portion of albuminous matter present. The mode in which these substances act is not understood, but it is supposed that when in a state of decomposition, they are able to induce a similar state in other substances with which they are in contact; the equilibrium of the atoms in the compound is thus disturbed, and the elements arrange themselves in new forms. It is interesting to know that the fermentation of sugar takes place only in immediate contact with the ferment. This is readily shown, as in figure 402, by placing a solution of sugar in the bottle A, and some beer yeast in the tube *ab*, the lower end of which is covered with porous paper. The sugar solution passes through the paper into the tube, where an active fermentation is set up with an abundant

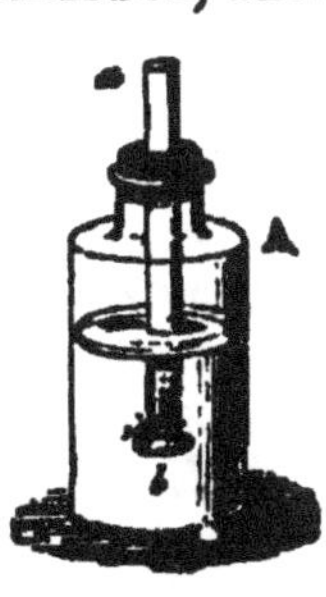

Fig. 402.

evolution of carbonic acid. Meanwhile no change occurs in the solution in the bottle, which may be preserved unaltered for any length of time.

695. The act of fermentation is always accompanied by the appearance of a peculiar microscopic vegetation, which is formed when solutions containing albuminous matters are abandoned to putrefaction. The solution becomes turbid, and a gray deposit is gradually formed in it, consisting of ovoidal bodies variously grouped, whose development has been carefully studied under the microscope. Figures 403 to 407 show the various stages of this fungus growth. The

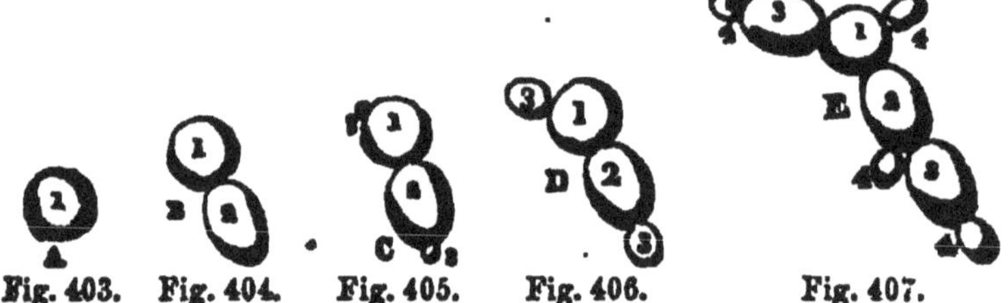

Fig. 403. Fig. 404. Fig. 405. Fig. 406. Fig. 407.

original globule (1) A, fig. 403, in about six hours produces another, (2,) fig. 404, B, like itself; the two again each germinate a third, as seen at 3, C and D, fig. 405; and in like manner the germination proceeds, as in E, (4,) fig. 406, until, in about three days, thirty globules are formed about the original cell. The development then ceases. The several globules are coherent, but appear to be distinct and complete in themselves.

696. The conversion of grape sugar into alcohol and carbonic acid is very simple: one equivalent of dry grape sugar $C_{24}H_{24}O_{24}$ divides so as to form four equivalents of alcohol and four of carbonic acid gas.

4	equivalents of alcohol	$4 \times C_4H_6O_2$.........	$= C_{16}H_{24}O_8$
4	"	of carbonic acid gas $4 \times C_2O_4$	$= C_8 \quad O_{16}$
1	"	of grape sugar....................	$= C_{24}H_{24}O_{24}$

Grape sugar is the only kind which is capable of this fermentation; and, although the others readily yield alcohol and carbonic acid, it is found that the first effect of the ferment is to transform them into grape sugar, by the assimilation of the elements of water.

697. Weak alcoholic liquors often become acid when exposed to the air, from oxydation of the alcohol and the formation of acetic acid; but this acid is sometimes directly

formed from the decomposition of the sugar, independent of the action of the air, and is the cause of the *souring* of such wines as contain considerable sugar, but are very weak in alcohol. If a solution of sugar is mixed with cheese curd and exposed for some weeks to a temperature of about 68° F., the air being excluded, it becomes acid, and a portion of the sugar is converted into acetic acid $C_4H_4O_4$. An equivalent of grape sugar contains the elements of six equivalents of this acid. The presence of cheese curd under conditions modified by temperature and the presence of earthy bases, causes other fermentations and different results. At a temperature of from 95° to 104° F. the products are lactic acid $C_{12}H_{12}O_{12}$, and a viscous substance analogous in composition to sugar. Such a decomposition takes place in the juices of beets and carrots at a high temperature, and has been called the *viscous fermentation*. Mannite sometimes appears as a secondary product. If carbonate of lime is added to saturate the lactic acid as soon as formed, the decomposition proceeds at a lower temperature, and the lactate of lime is almost the only product. An equivalent of grape sugar $C_{24}H_{24}O_{24}$ breaks up into two equivalents of lactic acid $C_{12}H_{12}O_{12}$.

698. The action of the curd of milk in a more advanced state of decomposition gives rise to the vinous fermentation: milk at the ordinary temperature becomes sour from the conversion of its sugar into lactic acid, but when kept at about 100° the grape sugar at first formed is converted into alcohol and carbonic acid gas. In this way the Tartars prepare a spirit from mare's milk; an elevated temperature promotes the decomposition of the curd and enables it to effect this transformation.

699. *Lactic Acid*, $C_{12}H_{12}O_{12}$.—This acid may be obtained from sour milk, but is more easily prepared by the fermentation of sugar with caseine. Fourteen parts of cane sugar are dissolved in sixty of water; to the solution is then added four parts of the curd from milk, and five parts of chalk to neutralize the acid as it is formed. This mixture is kept at a temperature of 80° to 95° F. for eight or ten days, or until it becomes a crystalline paste of lactate of lime. This is pressed in a cloth, dissolved in hot water, and filtered; the solution is then concentrated by evaporation. On cooling, it deposits the salt in crystals, which may be purified by recrystallization. The lactate of lime may be decom-

posed by the careful addition of oxalic acid, which precipitates the lime, and the solution of lactic acid thus obtained is concentrated by evaporation, and purified by solution in ether. It is a syrupy liquid, of specific gravity 1·215, and is strongly acid to the taste.

700. When lactic acid is heated to 482°, a white crystalline substance sublimes, which is called *lactide:* it is derived from the acid by the abstraction of the elements of two equivalents of water, and has the formula $C_{12}H_8O_8$. It is soluble in alcohol, but scarcely soluble in water: by long continued boiling with it, however, it is converted into lactic acid. This acid is bibasic, and its salts are generally soluble and crystallizable. The *lactate of lime* $C_{12}H_{10}Ca_2O_{12}$ crystallizes in fine prisms, with six equivalents of water. The *lactate of zinc* is obtained by decomposing a hot concentrated solution of lactate of lime by chlorid of zinc: the salt crystallizes in cooling in beautiful colorless prisms. The *lactate of iron* $C_{12}H_{10}Fe_2O_{12}$ is sparingly soluble in cold water, and may be prepared by a similar process: it is employed in medicine. A double lactate of lime and potash, and acid lactates of lime and baryta have been obtained; the latter is $C_{12}(H_{11}Ba)O_{12}$. If the crystalline paste of caseine and lactate of lime is kept for some time at a temperature of about 95°, the salt gradually redissolves, hydrogen and carbonic acid gases escape, and when, after a few weeks, this new fermentation has subsided, there remains only a solution of the lime salt of a new acid, *butyric acid,* $C_8H_8O_4$. In this *butyric fermentation,* the lactic acid is decomposed into carbonic acid, hydrogen and the new acid, $C_{12}H_{12}O_{12} = 2C_2O_4 + 2H_2 + C_8H_8O_4$.

701. Under certain circumstances not well understood, there appears as an accessory product to the vinous fermentation, an oily liquid, which is homologous with alcohol and has been named *amylol.* It is represented by $C_{10}H_{12}O_2$, and is supposed to be formed from sugar by a process which may be called the *amylic fermentation,* in which, as in the butyric, hydrogen and carbonic acid will be disengaged.

The action of dilute nitric acid with cane or grape sugar yields *saccharic acid* $C_{12}H_{10}O_{16}$, which is bibasic: strong nitric acid converts sugar into oxalic acid, and chromic acid into formic acid. All of these derivatives will be described in their proper places.

702. When sugar is added to a concentrated solution of three times its weight of hydrate of potash, and heated, the

mixture becomes brown, and hydrogen gas is evolved. When the action ceases and the mass is cooled, dissolved in water, and distilled with dilute sulphuric acid, it yields formic and acetic acids, with a new acid, the *metacetonic*, which is obtained as a volatile liquid, with a pungent acid odor. It is monobasic, and has the formula $C_6H_6O_4$.

A mixture of sugar and quicklime, when distilled, affords acetone and an oily liquid called *metacetone* which yields metacetonic acid when distilled with a mixture of bichromate of potash and sulphuric acid. Mannite, starch, and gum afford the same results with hydrate of potash and lime.

703. *Gum*, $C_{24}H_{20}O_{20}$.—This substance is best known in *gum arabic:* the gums which exude from the cherry and plum, the mucilage of flaxseed, and of many other plants, are identical with it. Gum is soluble in water, and forms a viscid solution, from which alcohol precipitates it unchanged.

When boiled with dilute sulphuric acid, it is converted into grape sugar. With nitric acid, gum and lactose yield the mucic acid, which distinguishes them from all the other bodies of this class. The mucic acid is a white crystalline powder, which is sparingly soluble in water: it is bibasic, and is represented by the formula $C_{12}H_{10}O_{16}$. It is consequently metameric with the saccharic acid, although quite different in its properties.

704. The *pectic acid*, which is extracted from many fruits, appears to be nothing but a modified form of gum, and yields grape sugar with dilute acids. It combines with lime and some other bases to form compounds, which have been described as pectates. Both gum and sugar have also the property of exchanging one or two equivalents of hydrogen for lead, barium, or calcium, to form similar combinations.

705. *Starch*, $C_{24}H_{20}O_{20}$.—This substance exists in a great variety of vegetables. It is found in all the cereal grains, in the roots and tubers of many plants, as the potato, and in the bark and pith of various trees. It is obtained by bruising wheat and washing it in cold water, which holds the starch in suspension, and deposits it on standing. Potatoes furnish a large portion of starch by a similar process The substances known as *arrow-root*, *salep*, *sago*, and *tapioca*, are varieties of starch, obtained from different plants, and sometimes altered by the heat employed in drying.

When examined by the naked eye it is a white shining

Fig. 408.

powder, but under the microscope is seen to consist of irregular grains, which have a rounded outline, and are composed of concentric layers, covered with an external membrane. The diameter of the grains of potato starch is about $\frac{1}{200}$ of an inch.

Starch is insoluble in cold water, but if the mixture is heated, the globules swell, burst their envelopes, and form a transparent jelly, which is characterized by producing a deep blue color with a solution of iodine.

When the solution of starch is mixed with a little acid, or an infusion of malt, and gently heated, it becomes very fluid, and is changed into *dextrine.** This has the same composition as starch, but is very soluble in cold water, and is not colored blue by iodine. If starch is heated to 300° or 400°, it is rendered soluble in water, and possesses all the properties of dextrine. In this state it is used in the arts as a substitute for gum, under the names of *British gum* and *leiocome.* When dextrine is boiled for some time with dilute sulphuric acid, it is converted into grape sugar. It has been mentioned that grape sugar is formed in this way from starch; but its formation is always preceded by that of dextrine. One part of starch may be dissolved in four parts of water, with about one-twentieth of sulphuric acid, and the mixture boiled for thirty-six or forty hours. The liquid is then mixed with chalk to separate the acid, and by evaporation and cooling affords pure grape sugar. Oxalic acid may be substituted for the sulphuric, with the same result. Starch sugar is extensively manufactured in Europe, and is often used to adulterate cane sugar. In this process the starch combines with the elements of two equivalents of water, $C_{24}H_{20}O_{20}+2H_2O_2=C_{24}H_{24}O_{24}$: the acid is obtained at the end of the process quite unaltered, and one part of acid will saccharify one hundred of starch by long continued boiling. Starch or dextrine unites with sulphuric acid to

* So named, because when a beam of polarized light is passed through the solution, it causes the plane of polarization to deviate to the *right hand.*

form a coupled acid; and it is probable that this is first formed and then destroyed by boiling: at the moment of decomposition, the liberated dextrine takes up the elements of water necessary for the formation of sugar. A small portion of the coupled acid is always found in the solution.

706. The action of an infusion of malt upon sugar is peculiar: this substance is prepared from barley, by moistening the grain with water, and exposing it to a gentle heat till germination takes place, when it is dried in an oven at such a temperature as to destroy its vitality. The grain now contains a portion of starch sugar, and a small portion of a substance called *diastase*,* to which its peculiar properties are due. It is precipitated by alcohol from a concentrated infusion of malt, as a white flaky substance, which contains nitrogen, and is very prone to decomposition. When a little diastase is added to a mixture of starch and water, at a temperature of from 130° to 140°, the starch is soon converted into dextrine, and in a few hours into grape sugar. The action of an infusion of malt is due solely to the presence of a minute portion of this substance, one part of which will convert two thousand parts of starch into sugar. This effect appears to be due to a peculiar state of the diastase, which is a portion of the azotized matter of the grain in a modified form, and is analogous to the ferments, already alluded to.

707. *Woody Fibre; Cellulose*, $C_{24}H_{20}O_{20}$.—This substance is the solid insoluble part of vegetables, and remains when water, alcohol, ether, dilute acids, and alkalies have extracted from wood all its soluble portions. It is nearly pure in cotton, paper or old linen. The tissue of vegetables is formed principally of cellulose. The *cellular tissue* is seen almost pure, constituting the cell walls of young plants. These cells are sometimes spherical, or rounded in form. In other cases the woody tissue forms oblong cells, communicating by their extremi-

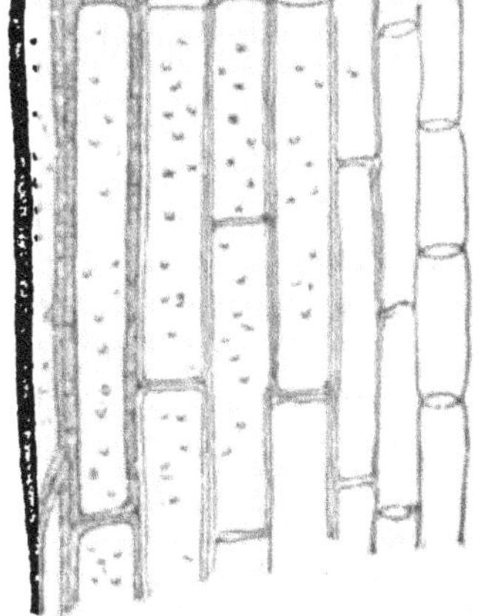

Fig. 409.

* From the Greek *diistemi*, to separate, because it separates the insoluble envelopes of the starch globules.

ties, as seen in figure 409, which is a section of asparagus, and also in figure 410, which shows a fibre of flax much magnified. The cellulose in this form receives the name of *vascular tissue*. In the course of time the walls of the cells become lined with an incrusting matter, which grows thicker with the age of the plant, finally leaving only minute pores or conduits for the circulation of the sap. This

Fig. 410.

incrusting matter which forms a part of ordinary wood, is named *lignin*. It is chemically different from cellulose, but has been little studied. Figure 411 shows the structure of wood as seen in the transverse section of a piece of oak, under the microscope. The black spaces are the ducts, for the circulation of the sap, of which *a a a* are remarkable examples. The white lines mark the outline and comparative thickness of the original cells, such as are seen in the vertical section of asparagus, fig. 409. These have been filled with lignin, which is more dense and hard near the centre of the tree than at the exterior. The albuminous matters, which are the principal cause of the decay of wood, are also more abundant in the outer than in the inner cells. The coloring and resinous matters are deposited with the incrusting material.

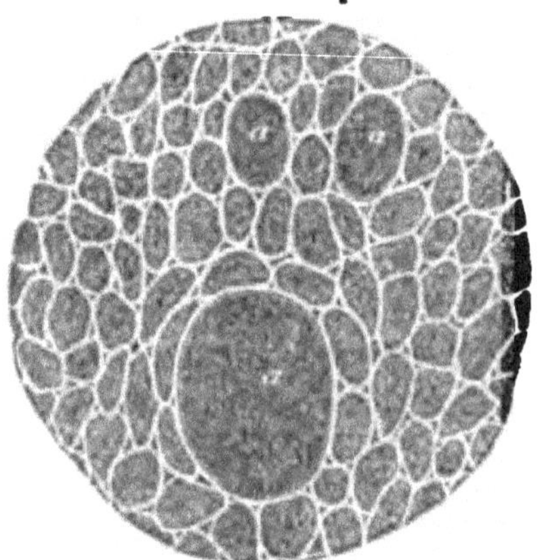

Fig. 411.

Cellulose is identical in composition with starch and dextrine, and by the action of strong sulphuric acid is dissolved and converted into that substance. This experiment is easily made with unsized paper or cotton: to two parts of this, one part of the acid is very slowly added, taking care to prevent an elevation of temperature, which would char the mixture. In a few hours the whole is converted into a soft mass, which is soluble in water, and is principally dextrine. If the mixture is now diluted with water and boiled for three or four hours, the dextrine is completely converted into grape sugar, which is obtained by neutralizing the acid with chalk, and evaporation. By this process paper or rags will yield more than their weight of crystallizable sugar.

708 The mutual convertibility of these different substances is interesting in relation to many of the phenomena of vegetable life. The starch in the germinating seed is changed by the action of diastase into sugar, in which soluble form it seems better fitted for the nourishment of the embryo plant. In the growth of this, we have an example of the formation of cellulose from sugar, in which this substance assumes a structural form under the action of the vital force. This is a transformation from the unorganized to the organized, which mere chemical affinity can never effect.

709. Many unripe fruits, as the apple, contain a large quantity of starch, but no sugar. After the fruit is fully grown, the starch gradually disappears, and in its place we find grape sugar. This change constitutes the ripening of fruits, and, as is well known, will take place after they are gathered. In this process we have clearly a conversion of the starch into sugar, by the agency of the vegetable acids present in the fruit—a change which is the reverse of the previous one, and is probably independent of life.

710. *Xyloidine, Pyroxyline.*—The action of strong nitric acid upon starch yields a compound very similar to nitromannite, which is insoluble in water and very combustible: if we represent NO_4 by X, the formula of this body, to which the name of *xyloidine* has been given, will be $C_{24}H_{18}X_2O_{20}=C_{24}H_{18}N_2O_{28}$. With sugar a similar substance may be formed.

The action of strong nitric acid, or a mixture of nitric and sulphuric acids, upon woody fibre, such as paper, cotton, or sawdust, gives rise to an interesting substance, which has been named *pyroxyline*, or *gun-cotton*, as that form of cellulose yields the purest product. The following is an outline of the process:—one hundred grains of clean cotton are immersed for five minutes in a mixture of an ounce and a half of nitric acid of specific gravity 1·45 to 1·5, with the same measure of strong sulphuric acid; it is then removed, carefully washed in cold water from every trace of acid, and dried at a temperature which should not exceed 120°. As thus prepared, it preserves the form of the cotton unaltered, but has less strength than the original fibre. It inflames by a very gentle heat: sometimes, under circumstances not well understood, it has been observed to take fire at 212° F. Its combustion is instantaneous, accompanied by an immense volume of flame, and it leaves not the slightest residue. When ignited in a confined space it explodes with great violence: one-tenth of a grain is sufficient to shatter the strongest glass tube. Its power in propelling balls is about eight times greater than that of gunpowder; its tremendous energy depends upon the fact that it is completely resolved, by its combustion, into aqueous vapor and permanent gases, which are carbonic oxyd, carbonic acid, and nitrogen. As these are much less noxious than the gases resulting from the combustion of gunpowder, the gun-cotton will be found of great use in mining. Its composition is analogous to that of nitro-mannite. There appear to be two species, one of which is soluble in a mixture of alcohol and ether, and the other insoluble; both are generally present in gun-cotton. They are substitution products from cellulose, and, representing NO_4 by X, the insoluble form is $C_{24}H_{16}X_4O_{20}$, and the soluble $C_{24}H_{14}X_6O_{20}=C_{24}H_{14}N_6O_{44}$. It will be seen that they are formed from the action of nitric acid with the elimination of H_2O_2 for each equivalent of the acid. Thus, $C_{24}H_{20}O_{20}+6NHO_6=C_{24}H_{14}N_6O_{44}+6H_2O_2$.

The ethereal solution dries rapidly and leaves a tenacious transparent film of pyroxyline: it is used in surgery for covering wounds and abraded surfaces from the air, and is known by the name of *collodion.*

Transformation of Woody Fibre.

711. By the action of atmospheric air and moisture, wood undergoes a slow decay, dependent on the absorption of oxygen, to which Liebig has applied the term *eremacausis.** The carbon is converted into carbonic acid, while the oxygen and hydrogen of the lignine unite to form water. The residue is still found to contain oxygen and hydrogen in the original proportions, but the relative amount of carbon is continually increasing. For each equivalent of carbonic acid two of water are evolved. The final result of this process is a brown or black residue, which constitutes *vegetable*

* From *erema*, slow, and *kausis*, combustion, a term by which that chemist denotes those changes which take place in organic bodies from the gradual action of oxygen.

mould. Different products of this decomposition have been described under the names of *humus, geine, ulmine, humic* and *ulmic acids.*

Nearly all of these bodies contain ammonia, for which they have a strong affinity: this is in part absorbed from the air, but the experiments of Mulder seem to show that they have the power of forming ammonia from the nitrogen of the atmosphere. Pure humic acid moistened and placed in a close vessel filled with air, is found after some months to contain a considerable quantity of ammonia. The hydrogen, evolved by a slow decomposition of the water, is brought into contact with nitrogen under such conditions that they combine and produce the alkali.

712. The decomposition of wood, when buried in the ground and excluded from the action of the air, is very different. The oxygen which it contains gradually combines with the carbon to form carbonic acid, and substances are obtained in which the proportion of carbon and hydrogen is greater than in the original fibre. *Peat, lignite,* and *bituminous coal* are products of this decomposition. The carbon and hydrogen in coal combine in various ways, and often generate vast quantities of gaseous carburets of hydrogen, (450.) *Anthracite* has resulted from the action of heat on bituminous coal, which has expelled all the volatile ingredients, and left a residue of nearly pure carbon.

Destructive Distillation of Wood.

713. The principal products of the decomposition of wood by heat are carbonic acid gas, water, and gaseous carburets of hydrogen. With the water are mixed several other bodies, among which are acetic acid and pyroxylic spirit, presently to be described, and a quantity of oily, tar-like substance, containing several interesting bodies, which we shall mention. These products are obtained on a large scale by distilling wood in iron cylinders; the quantity of acetic acid is so considerable that the process has become important in the arts.

Kreasote.—This substance occurs dissolved in the crude acetic acid from wood, and is separated and purified by a complicated process It is a colorless oily fluid, which boils at 397°, and has a specific gravity of 1·037. It has a peculiar and very persistent odor, resembling that of smoke, and a powerful burning taste. It is soluble in about 100 parts of water, and the solution possesses powerful antiseptic qualities. Meat which has been soaked in it is incapable of putrefaction,* and acquires a delicate flavor of smoke. The power of wood-smoke to preserve flesh is due to the presence of kreasote. It is a corrosive poison when taken in any quantity, but a dilute solution is used medicinally, both internally and externally, as a styptic and antiseptic. The composition of kreasote is $C_{14}H_8O_2$. It combines with the alkalies to form crystalline compounds.

714. *Wood-tar* contains several carburets of hydrogen, one of which, called *eupion*, is an oily, fragrant liquid, of the specific gravity ·655, being the lightest liquid known. Its formula is, probably, C_6H_6.

Paraffin.—This is a white crystalline substance, obtained from the less volatile portions of wood tar. It crystallizes in delicate needles, which fuse at 110°; it is soluble in alcohol and ether. Its formula is $C_{48}H_{50}$. Paraffin is obtained in large quantities by the dry distillation of beeswax.

715. *Coal-tar* consists principally of a mixture of various hydrocarbons; some of these are liquid and very volatile, constituting what is called gas naphtha. Among the less volatile products are two solid carburets of hydrogen, *naphthalen*, and *paranaphthalen*, or *anthracen*. The first of these is formed by the decomposition of many organic matters by heat. Its formula is $C_{20}H_8$: it is volatile, and forms beautiful pearly crystals of a fragrant odor. The action of chlorine, bromine, and nitric acid on naphthalen, gives rise to a great number of compounds. They are formed by successive substitutions of the hydrogen by one or more of these substances, and many metameric modifications of these bodies exist. Thus, the bichlorinized naphthalen $C_{20}H_6Cl_2$ occurs in seven modifications, which are perfectly distinct in their characters. We are led to suppose that these compounds owe their different properties to a different arrangement of their constituent atoms, and it is easy to see that, in this way, the number of possible combinations will be immense. More than twenty substances have been described, in which chlorine is in part substituted for the hydrogen of the naphthalen. The final product of the action of chlorine is $C_{20}Cl_8$, being a chlorid of carbon, which preserves the type of naphthalen. In addition to these, coal-tar contains a consider-

* Hence the name, from the Greek *kreas*, flesh, and *soto*, I preserve.

able proportion of a body named *phenol*, and several organic alkaloids. The watery products of the distillation of coal hold a large quantity of ammonia in solution, often combined with hydrosulphuric and hydrocyanic acids.

716. *Petroleum.*—In many parts of the world an oily matter exudes from the rocks, or floats on the surface of springs. The principal sources of this substance are Amiano in Italy, Ava, and Persia, but it is found in many places in our own country. The well known *Seneca oil* is an instance of this kind. Petroleum is a variable mixture of several bodies. By distillation, it yields a colorless liquid, called *naphtha*, which is very light, volatile, and combustible. Its formula is, probably, $C_{12}H_{10}$. Naphtha occurs nearly pure in Italy and Persia, and is used for illumination.

Petroleum contains a variety of other bodies, among which are *paraffin*, and several resinous matters, formed, perhaps, by the oxydation of naphtha. These substances are probably derived from coal or other matters of vegetable origin.

ALCOHOLS.

717. This series of compounds has already been alluded to in explaining the principle of homology. The alcohols may be represented by $C_nH_{n+2}O_2$, n being a number divisible by two: all of them by oxydizing agents lose H_2 and combine with O_2 to form monobasic acids, whose general formula is $C_nH_nO_4$. Of these acids we have now nearly a complete series up to the stearic acid, in which $n=38$. But a few of the corresponding alcohols are known; the principal are *methol* $C_2H_4O_2$, *wine alcohol* $C_4H_6O_2$, *amylic alcohol* or *amylol* $C_{10}H_{12}O_2$, and *cetic alcohol* or *cetol* $C_{32}H_{34}O_2$. We shall first describe the alcohol of wine, to which we may conveniently give the name of *vinol*: it is the best known and most important of the series, and will serve to illustrate the history of the others.

Vinol—Common Alcohol, $C_4H_6O_2$.

This substance has long been known under the name of alcohol, or *spirits of wine*. We have already explained the manner in which it is obtained as a result of the fermentation of sugar. The vinous fermentation in the juice of the grape and other fruits, in an infusion of malt, or in the syrup of the sugar-cane, always results in the conversion of the sugar which it contains, into alcohol and carbonic acid gas. When the fermentation is arrested before all of the sugar is decomposed, the wine is sweet; if the liquor is bottled before the action is finished, the excess of carbonic acid remains in solution, and gives an effervescent and sparkling property, as in bottled beer and champagne.

When these fermented liquors are distilled, the alcohol, boiling at a lower temperature than water, passes over first. By repeated distillation in this way, a liquid is obtained which contains 85 parts of alcohol in 100. To obtain it free from water, it is digested with quicklime, or better with fused chlorid of calcium, which combines with the water. The mixture is then distilled in a water-bath, and pure alcohol passes over. A convenient apparatus for condensing the vapor of alcohol, ethers, and other volatile substances, is shown in figure 412.

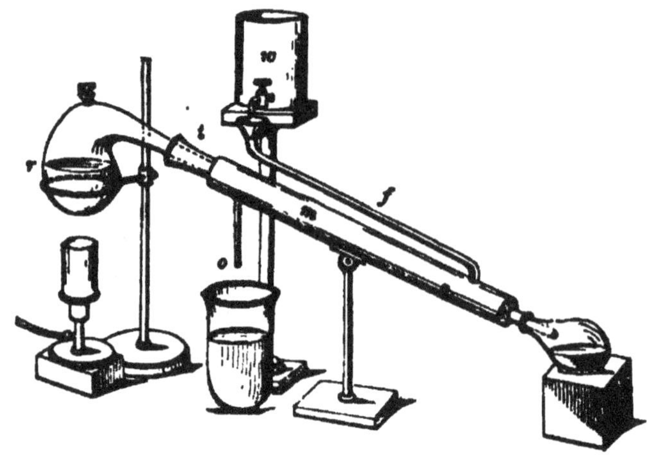

Fig. 412.

The retort *r* is connected with a glass condensing tube *t*, about which a metallic tube *m* is secured by corks at the ends, leaving a water-tight space between the two. A funnel tube *f* conducts cold water from the tank *w* to the lower end of the condenser. This escapes at the upper orifice *o*, thus maintaining a constant current of cold water, by means of which the vapors of even very volatile liquids are easily condensed.

718. *Pure* or *absolute alcohol* is a colorless fluid, with a specific gravity of about ·800, and boils at 173° F. Its den-

sity varies very much with its temperature, (102;) thus at 32° it is 0·815; at 50°, ·8065; at 59°, ·8021; at 68°, ·7978; and at 77°, ·7933. It has a pungent and agreeable taste and a fragrant odor. It is very combustible, and burns with a pale blue flame without smoke, which renders it very useful as a source of heat in chemical processes. The action of alcohol on the system is well known as that of a powerful and dangerous stimulant. It is largely used in the operations of the arts, the preparation of medicines, and the processes of chemistry. Its solvent powers are very great: the volatile oils and resins are dissolved by it, as well as many acids and salts, the caustic alkalies, and a large number of other substances.

The density of alcohol vapor is 1589·4, and its equivalent is represented by four volumes, oxygen being one volume; thus—

4 volumes of carbon vapor	4 ×	829.	=	3316·0
12 " " hydrogen	12 ×	69·2	=	830·4
2 " " oxygen	2 ×	1105·6	=	2211·2
				6357·6
Equal 4 volumes alcohol vapor, of which 1 volume weighs....				1598·4

719. Pure alcohol dissolves several salts, as the chlorid of calcium and the nitrates of lime and magnesia, and forms with them crystalline compounds, in which the alcohol takes the place of the water of crystallization, by virtue of the homologous relation which it sustains to water. When potassium is added to alcohol free from water, hydrogen is evolved and a crystalline compound formed, in which the metal replaces hydrogen. It is $C_4H_5KO_2$, and by the action of water is decomposed into alcohol and hydrate of potash, $C_4H_5KO_2+H_2O_2=C_4H_6O_2+(KH)O_2$. By an indirect process, a compound is obtained in which the oxygen of alcohol is replaced by sulphur, and which is $C_4H_6S_2$. It is a colorless very volatile liquid, having a strong odor resembling that of onions. Like the oxygen species, it may exchange H for a metal; with oxyd of mercury it forms water and a crystalline compound $C_4H_5HgS_2$: from the violence of the action it has received the fanciful name of *mercaptan*, (from *mercurium captans.*)

Action of Acids upon Alcohol.

720. It has been shown that when *n* in the general formula of the alcohols becomes equal to *zero*, we have

water H_2O_2, which may be regarded as their homologue and prototype. We have farther pointed out the fact that a group of elements is often found to be equivalent to an atom of hydrogen, and capable of replacing it in combination: such is NH_4 in the ammonia salts; and in the compounds of vinic alcohol, the group C_4H_5 will be found to sustain similar relations. In water, which is $(HH)O_2$, one atom of hydrogen may be replaced by this group, and we have then $(C_4H_5.H)O_2$, which is alcohol. In the potassium compound just described, the second atom of hydrogen is replaced by a metal, and we shall presently describe a compound in which both atoms of the hydrogen are replaced by the organic group: it is $(C_4H_5.C_4H_5)O_2=C_8H_{10}O_2$. This same group may also replace the hydrogen in acids; a monobasic acid reacts with one equivalent of alcohol and eliminates an equivalent of water, forming a compound in which C_4H_5 replaces H in the acid, and renders it neutral. Such compounds are called *ethers* of the various acids. With bibasic and tribasic acids, two and three equivalents of alcohol combine to form *neutral ethers*, and eliminate two and three equivalents of water. But when a bibasic acid reacts with but one equivalent of alcohol, only one atom of its hydrogen is replaced, and the second atom remains as before, capable of being exchanged for a metal. Such compounds are *acid ethers* or *vinic acids*.

721. Although the ethers are thus analogous to salts in their constitution, they are less readily decomposed than the corresponding metallic salts; they frequently require the aid of heat to effect the breaking up of the combination, and are generally more stable as their equivalent is more elevated.

The neutral ether containing sulphuric acid, for example, does not precipitate salts of baryta, and the corresponding vinic acid forms a soluble salt with that base. In these, and many other instances, the properties of the acids seem masked in their ethers, but similar cases are met with in the salts of inorganic bodies.

722. The action of chlorohydric acid, and other acids containing no oxygen, upon alcohol, requires a little explanation. We have seen that when HCl acts upon a metal, the compound eliminated is of the type H_2; but when the hydracid acts upon a hydrated oxyd, as $(KH)O_2$, the same chlorid is formed, and H_2O_2 is evolved; so it is with alcohol, which with hydrochloric acid yields water and a body

C_4H_5Cl. As C_4H_5 is equivalent to H, the new ether represents chlorohydric acid, and is evidently the chlorinized species of a hydrocarbon C_4H_6, which should yield with (Cl_2) the same product, as a result of direct substitution. As water H_2O_2 is the prototype of the alcohols, so (H_2) is the prototype and homologue of the carbohydrogens like C_4H_6, whose formula is $C_nH_{n+2} = C_nH_n + H_2$; and chlorohydric acid HCl is the type of the chlorohydric ethers.

As the ethers of alcohol contain C_4H_5, replacing H in the acids, and consequently differ from the latter by $(C_2H_2)_2$, it follows that the ethers are always homologous with their parent acids.

In describing these compounds, we shall often designate the group C_4H_5 by the symbol Et, and write alcohol $(EtH)O_2$.

Ethers.

723. *Chlorohydric Ether*, $C_4H_5Cl = EtCl$.—When alcohol is saturated with chlorohydric acid gas, and heated, it is converted into water and this ether, $(EtH)O_2 + HCl = EtCl + H_2O_2$. By distillation it is obtained as a pungent aromatic liquid, slightly soluble in water, and boiling at 52° F.: at a temperature of —4° it crystallizes in cubes: its specific gravity is ·873.

By distilling alcohol with hydrobromic acid, or a mixture of phosphorus and bromine, which evolves the acid, *hydrobromic ether* EtBr, is obtained as a volatile liquid heavier than water; and by substituting iodine for bromine, *hydriodic ether* EtI is found. It is a colorless liquid, with a specific gravity of 1·920, and a boiling point of 160° F. These ethers are all decomposed by an alcoholic solution of hydrate of potash into alcohol and a potassium salt, $EtCl + (KH)O_2 = (EtH)O_2 + KCl$. By the action of potassium upon chlorohydric ether, a compound is obtained in which K replaces Cl. It is C_4H_5K or EtK: this is decomposed by water into hydrate of potash and a volatile oily substance C_4H_6, to which the name of *acetene* has been given. It is the hydrocarbon corresponding to H_2, and may be written EtH. Another product has been formed, which is C_8H_{10}, in which the second atom of hydrogen is replaced by C_4H_5: it is EtEt, and has a density corresponding to four volumes of vapor. The binary grouping which prevails throughout all compounds is such as to forbid the isolation of the elements C_4H_5, which are always grouped with a metal, chlorine, or even another equivalent of themselves, so that the law of divisibility is never violated.

724. *Nitric Ether* $N(Et)O_6 = N(C_4H_5)O_6$.—The action of alcohol and nitric acid is violent and irregular, the alcohol being oxydized at the expense of the oxygen of the acid, and several compounds formed; but the addition of a little urea or nitrate of ammonia to the mixture of the acid and alcohol prevents this, and the ether is then formed and distilled over by the aid of heat; water being the only other product. Nitric acid $NO_5HO = NHO_6 + (EtH)O_2 = NEtO_6 + H_2O_2$. It is a colorless liquid of a sweet taste, is heavier than water, in which it is insoluble, and boils at 185° F. Its vapor explodes by heat.

725. *Nitrous Ether, or Hyponitric Ether*, $N(Et)O_4 = C_4H_5NO_4$.—When nitric acid acts upon starch, copious red vapors are evolved, which are anhydrous hyponitric acid NO_3: they are rapidly absorbed by dilute alcohol, with the production of sufficient heat to cause the new ether to distil over, when it is condensed by means of ice. Hyponitric acid $NO_3HO = NHO_4 + (EtH)O_2 = N(Et)O_4 + H_2O_2$. The hyponitric ether is a pale yellow liquid, having a fragrant odor of apples: it boils at 62°, and has a specific gravity of ·947. It is one of the products of the action of nitric acid with alcohol, when urea is not added; and a solution of the impure product in alcohol, obtained by distilling alcohol with nitre and sulphuric acid, constitutes the *sweet spirits of nitre* of the old chemists, which is still used in medicine. If a mixture of nitric acid and alcohol is distilled with the addition of turnings of metallic copper, pure nitrous ether may be obtained. Nitrous ether undergoes a remarkable decomposition by the action of sulphuretted hydrogen: the gas is rapidly absorbed, with the separation of sulphur, and alcohol, water, and ammonia are formed; $C_4H_5NO_4 + 3H_2S_2 = S_6 + H_2O_2 + C_4H_6O + NH_3$.

Perchloric ether is obtained by an indirect process as an oily liquid, heavier than water, having a sweet, pungent taste, like oil of cinnamon. It explodes by slight friction, heat, or percussion, with fearful violence. Perchloric acid being $ClO_7HO = ClHO_8$, the ether is $Cl(C_4H_5)O_8$. Like the nitric and hyponitric ethers, it is decomposed by an alcoholic solution of hydrate of potash into alcohol and a perchlorate.

Sulphovinic Acid.

726. When sulphuric acid, mixed with its weight of alcohol, is heated to boiling, combination ensues with the

elimination of water, and sulphovinic acid is formed; sulphuric acid $S_2H_2O_8+(EtH)O_2=S_2(EtH)O_8+H_2O_2$. By diluting the mixture with water and saturating it with carbonate of lime, the free sulphuric acid is converted into insoluble sulphate of lime, and the soluble sulphovinate is obtained by evaporating at a gentle heat and cooling, in colorless prisms. As the carbohydrogen elements have replaced one equivalent of hydrogen in the sulphuric acid, the new acid is monobasic, and the lime salt is $S_2(EtCa)O_8+H_2O_2$: this water of crystallization is lost in a dry atmosphere. By substituting carbonate of baryta for lime, the baryta salt $S_2(EtBa)O_8$ is obtained in fine crystals; from this salt, by double decomposition, the sulphovinates of other bases may be obtained. Dilute sulphuric acid precipitates all the baryta from the baryta salt, and sulphovinic acid, $S_2(EtH)O_8$ is obtained in solution: when concentrated *in vacuo* it forms a syrupy liquid, which is decomposed by heat into alcohol and sulphuric acid, by taking up the elements of water. The lime and baryta salts undergo, in part, a similar decomposition by boiling, and after several years, even at the ordinary temperature, are changed into sulphates and alcohol.

With hydrate of potash a similar change takes place by heat, and alcohol and a sulphate are formed. Sulphovinate of potash $S_2(KEt)O_8+(KH)O_2=S_2K_2O_8+(EtH)O_2$; or neutral sulphate of potash and alcohol. If the hydro-sulphuret of potash $KS.HS=(KH)S_2$ is employed, *sulphur-alcohol* $(EtH)S_2$ is formed by a similar reaction; and with any salt, like the acetate of potash $C_4H_3KO_4$, a compound is obtained, in which Et replaces K: it is $C_4H_3(Et)O_4$, or acetic ether. In this way the perchloric and many other ethers are formed by double decomposition.

727. When carefully dried sulphovinate of potash is distilled with a mixture of potassic alcohol $(EtK)O_2$, sulphate of potash is formed, and a volatile liquid distils over, in which the second atom of H is replaced by the elements C_4H_5. $S_2(EtK)O_8+(EtK)O_2=S_2K_2O_8+(EtEt)O_2$. This compound is also obtained when, within certain limits of temperature, sulphovinic acid acts upon alcohol; $S_2(EtH)O_8+(EtH)O_2=S_2H_2O_8+(EtEt)O_2$ being the products. The result of this complete substitution may be conveniently designated as *hydrovinic ether*, precisely as alcohol is *hydrovinic acid*. It has long been known in the history of the

science under the simple name of *ether*, which has since been extended to a great number of allied products, and has become a generic term. It is a colorless, limpid, volatile liquid, and as its vapor is very combustible, should never be brought near a flame. It has a specific gravity of ·725, and boils under the ordinary pressure of the atmosphere at 96° F.: by its rapid spontaneous evaporation it produces great cold. It is sparingly soluble in water, and the ether of the shops, which often contains alcohol, may be purified by agitation with its volume of water, which dissolves the alcohol, while the ether floats upon the surface. Although in the liquid state it is lighter than alcohol, its vapor is much heavier. The density of ether vapor is 2556·3; four volumes then equal 10227·2, and contain two equivalents, or eight volumes of alcohol, minus one equivalent, or four volumes of water:

2 equivalents of alcohol vapor, 2 × 6357·6	=	12715·2
1 equivalent of water H_2O_2	—	2488·0
1 equivalent, or four volumes of ether vapor	=	10227·2
1 volume of ether vapor		2556·3

Its equivalent is therefore $2C_4H_6O_2 = C_8H_{12}O_4 - H_2O_2 = C_8H_{10}O_2$, or Et_2O_2.

728. Ether is used in the arts and in many chemical processes as a solvent; and in medicine, internally as a stimulant, and externally as a refrigerant, from the cold produced by its evaporation. An important application was some years since pointed out by Dr. Charles T. Jackson, of Boston, and introduced into practice by Mr. Morton, a dentist of that city: it depends upon the fact that the vapor of ether, when mixed with atmospheric air and inhaled, produces a kind of intoxication, followed by a state of stupor, in which it was found by these gentlemen that the subject is so far insensible to external impressions, as to undergo the most difficult surgical operations without pain. This important discovery has been very extensively applied both in this country and in Europe;* and the vapor of several other liquids has been found to produce similar effects.

729. In the manufacture of ether on a large scale, the reaction of sulphovinic acid and alcohol is employed. When

* The French government, in token of the high importance of the discovery, has bestowed upon Dr. Jackson the Cross of the Legion of Honor.

the mixture of alcohol and sulphuric, acid containing sulphovinic acid and water, is diluted, so as to boil much below 300° F., it is, as we have already shown, decomposed again into sulphuric acid and alcohol; but at about 300° F., the sulphovinic acid reacts upon a second equivalent of alcohol instead of an equivalent of water, and yields sulphuric acid and ether. By an ingenious method, the alternate formation and decomposition of sulphovinic acid may be made to furnish an unlimited supply of the new product. The arrangement is represented in the fig. 413.

A mixture of five parts of alcohol of 90 per cent. and

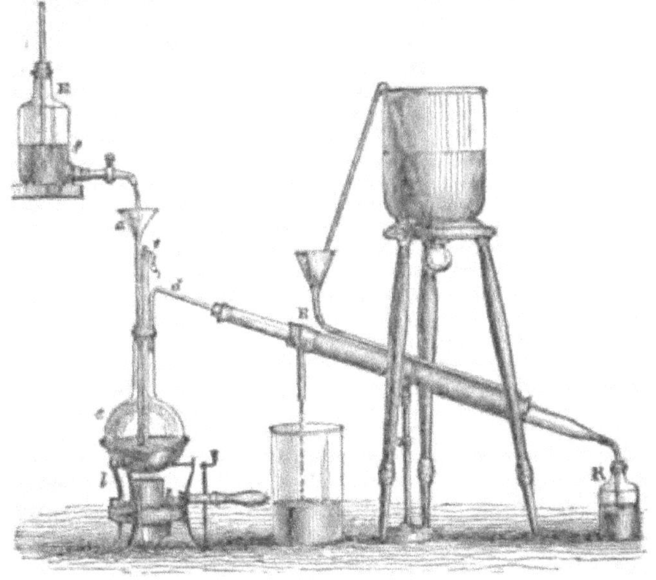

Fig. 413.

eight parts of ordinary sulphuric acid is placed in the flask *e*, through the cork of which passes a thermometer *t*, and two tubes, one of which *d*, conveys the vapors away to a condenser B, while the other *a*, which dips below the surface of the liquid, is arranged to supply pure alcohol from a reservoir E. The mixture is now raised to its boiling point, which is about 300° F., and carefully maintained at that temperature, so as to be in constant ebullition. Alcohol is slowly admitted through the cock *f*, in sufficient quantity to preserve the original level of the liquid in the flask. In this way, as the sulphovinic acid meets with the alcohol, it is decomposed into ether and sulphuric acid, but this reacting upon another portion of alcohol, forms water, which is volatilized, and a new portion of sulphovinic acid, to be decomposed in its turn. The ether and water distil over and are condensed together; and the same portion of sulphuric acid will serve to convert an indefinite quantity of alcohol into water and ether; a trace only of the sulphuric acid passes over. The ether is decanted from the water, and purified by distilling from a small quantity of hydrate of potash.

730. As it has long been obtained by the distillation of sulphuric acid with alcohol, it was formerly called *sulphuric ether*, a name which is still sometimes retained. The true sulphuric ether, which corresponds to the other neutral ethers, is obtained by the action of anhydrous sulphuric acid upon hydric ether. It is a neutral, dense, oily fluid, and differs from sulphovinic acid in having the second equivalent of H replaced by Et, its formula being $S_2(Et_2)O_8$. By heat it is decomposed, in the presence of water, into sulphovinic acid and alcohol.

731. Compounds have been obtained which correspond to ether in which O_2 is replaced by sulphur, selenium, and tellurium. The sulphur compound is $C_8H_{10}S_2$ or Et_2S_2, and is obtained by the action of hydrochloric ether upon sulphuret of potassium $2EtCl+K_2S_2=2KCl+Et_2S_2$: with bisulphuret of potassium, a compound is obtained which is Et_2S_4, and corresponds to persulphuret of hydrogen H_2S_4. These are volatile liquids, insoluble in water, and having a strong odor like garlic.

732. Phosphoric acid yields several compounds containing the elements of alcohol. The tribasic acid is $PO_5.3HO$ $=PH_3O_8$, and the neutral phosphoric ether is $P(Et_3)O_8$. The other two compounds are $P(Et_2H)O_8$ and $P(EtH_2)O_8$, and are respectively monobasic and bibasic vinic acids. Carbovinate of potash is obtained when carbonic acid gas is passed into a solution of hydrate of potash in pure alcohol. The acid being $C_2H_2O_6$, the new salt is $C_2(EtK)O_6$. The acid has not been isolated. The true carbonic ether is $C_2(Et_2)O_6=C_{10}H_{10}O_6$. By substituting bisulphuret of carbon for carbonic acid gas in the above process, carbovinates are obtained in which the oxygen is in part replaced by sulphur. The acid is obtained in a separate form, and is

$C_2(EtH)(O_2S_4)$; from the yellow color of some of its salts, it has been called *xanthic acid.*

733. *Silicic Ethers.*—The action of chlorid of silicon upon alcohol yields two silicic ethers. They are odorous, pungent, and volatile liquids, which are rapidly decomposed by alkalies, like the other ethers, and slowly by water alone; when exposed to moist air, in imperfectly closed vessels, they evolve alcohol and are gradually decomposed, leaving hydrated silicic acid in beautiful transparent masses, resembling rock crystal. The formula of one is represented by $C_{12}H_{15}SiO_6$ which corresponds to a tribasic silicic acid $SiO_3.3HO = SiH_3O_6$, and is $Si(Et_3)O_6$. The other is $C_8H_{10}Si_4O_{14}$, which represents a bibasic acid $4SiO_3 + H_2O_2 = Si_4H_2O_{14}$; the ether being $Si_4Et_2O_{14}$.

Chlorid of boron with alcohol yields two similar ethers: they burn with the fine green flame characteristic of boracic acid. Boracic ether is formed when alcohol is distilled from boracic acid, and is the cause of the green flame of an alcoholic solution of the acid.

734. *Olefiant Gas,* C_4H_4.—When alcohol is mixed with so much sulphuric acid that the mixture does not boil below 320° F., the sulphovinic acid which is formed, undergoes a decomposition different from those already described; it breaks up directly into sulphuric acid and olefiant gas, $S_2(C_4H_5H)O_8 = S_2(H_2)O_8 + C_4H_4$.

A more elegant way of preparing it is by an arrangement similar to that used for producing ether. Sulphuric acid is diluted with nearly one-half its weight of water, so that its boiling point is between 320° and 330°, and being heated in the flask *a* (fig. 414) to ebullition, the vapor of boiling alcohol is introduced from the flask *d* by the tube *b*, which dips a little way in the acid. In this process, we may suppose that sulphovinic acid is formed with the escape of an equivalent of water in vapor, and is then immediately decomposed into sulphuric acid and olefiant gas; an equivalent of alcohol yields $C_4H_4 + H_2O_2$. The gas is thus

Fig. 414.

obtained quite pure, and the process may be continued for any length of time. This compound is a product of the destructive distillation of many organic substances, and is abundant in the gases for illumination prepared by the decomposition of coal and the fat oils.

735. When mingled with its own volume of chlorine combination ensues, and the product condenses as a heavy oily liquid of a sweet pungent taste. It was discovered by an association of Dutch chemists, who, from this reaction, gave to the carbohydrogen the name of *olefiant gas*. It is $C_4H_4Cl_2$, and corresponds to a carbohydrogen C_4H_6, identical in composition with aceten. By the action of chlorine a series of compounds is formed by successive substitutions; we have $C_4H_3Cl_3$, $C_4H_2Cl_4$, C_4HCl_5 and C_4Cl_6. A similar series of compounds is obtained from chlorohydric ether, which, though represented by the same formulas, are unlike in their properties: the two series afford an interesting case of metamerism.

The final product of the action of chlorine upon both series of compounds is the chlorid of carbon C_4Cl_6. This is a white crystalline solid, with an aromatic odor, like camphor; it melts at 320°, and, at a temperature a little above this, may be distilled unaltered. It is scarcely combustible, and is unchanged by acids or alkalies. When its vapor is passed through a porcelain tube heated to redness, it is resolved into chlorine gas and a new compound C_4Cl_4, which is a volatile liquid, of the specific gravity of 1·55. If the vapor of this compound is passed repeatedly through a tube at a bright red heat, it is decomposed into chlorine and C_4Cl_2. This body forms soft, silky crystals, which are volatile and combustible.

The name of *etherilen* has been applied to the type C_4H_6, metameric with aceten, and *etheren* to olefiant gas. The derivatives will be *monochloric*, *bichloric etheren*, &c.

Bichloric etherilen, by the action of an alcoholic solution of hydrate of potash, yields chlorid of potassium and monochloric etheren C_4H_3Cl: the same way, trichloric etherilen gives $C_4H_2Cl_2$; and sexchloric aceten C_4Cl_6, with hydrosulphuret of potassium, yields C_4Cl_4.

Products of the Oxydation of Alcohol.

736. *Aldehyd or Acetol*, $C_4H_4O_2$.—The action of oxydising substances removes H_2 from alcohol and yields

aldehyd.* It is formed, together with nitrous ether, when nitric acid acts upon alcohol. One equivalent of nitric acid $NHO_6+C_4H_6O_2=H_2O_2+NHO_4+C_4H_4O_2$; besides aldehyd, water and nitrous acid are the products, the latter of which forms an ether with another portion of alcohol. Aldehyd is best obtained by the aid of chromic acid acting upon alcohol. For this purpose an apparatus may be constructed like fig. 415, entirely of glass, which will be

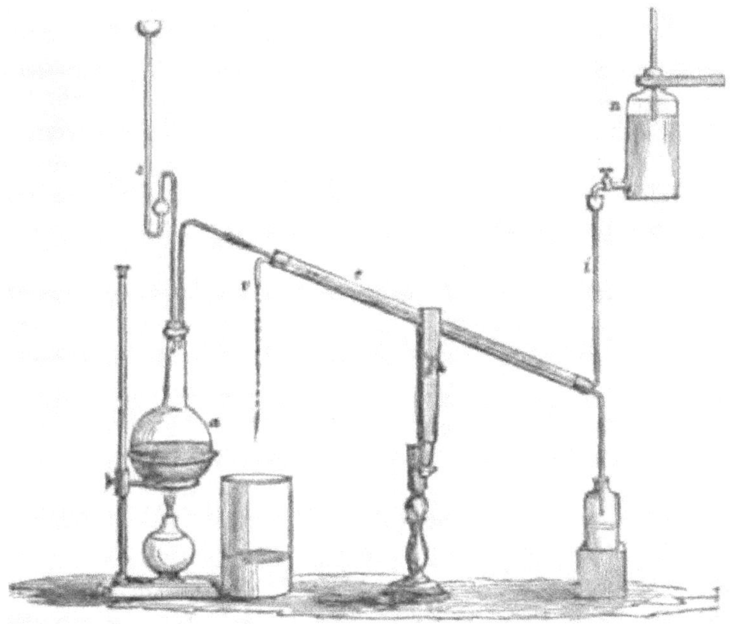

Fig. 415.

found very useful for the distillation of numerous volatile products in organic chemistry. Equal weights of powdered bichromate of potash and strong alcohol are introduced into the flask *a*, and 1½ parts of sulphuric acid are gradually added by the safety tube *s*. Much heat is produced by the mixture, and the distillation commences at once, but is continued by a gentle lamp-heat under the sand-bath of *a*. The condensing tube *t* is of glass, and iced water from the reservoir *n* enters and escapes by the two glass tubes *i*, *v*, the former of which has a funnel mouth.

The impure product is mixed with ether and satu-

* Whence its name, from *alcohol dehydrogenatus*.

rated with ammonia, when a compound of aldehyd and ammonia separates in fine crystals. This, decomposed by dilute sulphuric acid, affords pure aldehyd, as a colorless liquid having a suffocating ethereal odor. It boils at 70° F., and has a specific gravity of ·790: it mixes readily with water, and, when heated with a solution of potash, becomes brown and deposits a resinous substance.

The abstraction of H_2 seems to have been made from the group C_4H_5, and C_4H_3 appears in acetol to play the same part as C_4H_5 in alcohol. Thus, with potassium a compound is formed which is $(C_4H_3.K)O_2$, and the crystalline compound with ammonia is $C_4H_4O_2+NH_3=(C_4H_3.NH_4)O_2$, in which NH_4 replaces H. When a solution of aldehyd is added to one of ammoniacal nitrate of silver, the metal is reduced and lines the vessel with a brilliant film of silver. A similar process has been successfully applied to the manufacture of mirrors.

737. Aldehyd cannot be preserved unchanged, even in sealed tubes, but is slowly changed into two polymeric compounds. One of these, *elaldehyd*, is a dense oily fluid, which has none of the properties of aldehyd. The density of its vapor is three times that of aldehyd; and its formula is $3C_4H_4O_2=C_{12}H_{12}O_6$. The other body, *metaldehyd*, forms hard white prisms; it is formed by the union of four equivalents of aldehyd, and is $C_{16}H_{16}O_8$. Aldehyd is also obtained as a product of the decomposition of lactic acid or lactate of copper by heat, and is formed in large quantity when a lactate is distilled with binoxyd of manganese and sulphuric acid. When the isomerism of lactic acid with glucose is considered, it is easy to understand that while the latter is decomposed by fermentation into carbonic acid and alcohol, lactic acid by oxydation may yield carbonic acid and aldehyd. We shall see, farther on, that it is possible to reproduce lactic acid from aldehyd.

738. *Chloral.*—By the prolonged action of chlorine upon alcohol a liquid is obtained, to which the name of *chloral* has been given. It is aldehyd in which chlorine replaces H_3, and is represented by $C_4(HCl_3)O_2$.

Sulphur aldehyd $C_4H_4S_2$ has also been obtained, and both the trichloric and sulphuretted species yield polymeric modifications similar to those of normal aldehyd. The action of sulphuretted hydrogen upon an aqueous solution of aldehydate of ammonia produces large transparent crystals of an organic base, named *thialdine*. It is slightly soluble in water, but dissolves readily in alcohol and ether: the crystals are very fusible and volatile, and may be distilled with the vapor of boiling water. The formula of thialdine a $C_{12}H_{13}NS_4$: it corresponds to an amid of the trimeric modification of sulphuretted aldehyd $C_{12}H_{12}S_6$. This base has no alkaline reaction, but forms beautifully crystalline salts. A corresponding compound, in which selenium replaces sulphur, has been formed, but is very unstable.

A mixture of bisulphuret of carbon with an alcoholic solution of aldehydate of ammonia deposits sparingly soluble crystals of a new base, called *carbo-thialdine*, which is represented by $C_{10}H_{10}N_2S_4$. It contains the elements of two equivalents of aldehyd, and its formation is thus represented: $2C_4H_7NO_2+C_2S_4=2H_2O_2+C_{10}H_{10}N_2S_4$.

739. *Acetic Acid*, $C_4H_4O_4$.—When aldehyd is exposed to the air it absorbs O_2 and is converted into acetic acid $C_4H_4O_2+O_2=C_4H_4O_4$. If a mixture of hydrate of potash and lime be moistened with alcohol and exposed to heat, hydrogen gas is evolved, and an acetate formed, $C_4H_6O_2+KHO_2=C_4H_3KO_4+H_4$.

740. Pure alcohol undergoes no change when exposed to the air alone; but if its vapor mixed with air is brought into contact with platinum-black, it slowly unites with oxygen to form aldehyd, which readily absorbs another portion of oxygen and produces acetic acid. The oxydating power of finely-divided platinum has been before alluded to; it absorbs or condenses great quantities of gases and vapors in its pores, where they appear to be brought together in such a state that they readily react upon each other.

741. The formation of acetic acid may be beautifully shown by placing a little platinum-black in a watch-glass, by the side of a small vessel of alcohol, covering the whole with a bell-glass, and setting it in the sunlight. In a short time the vapor of acetic acid will condense on the sides of the glass, and run down in drops; and if we occasionally admit fresh air by raising the bell-jar, the whole of the alcohol will be acidified in a few hours.

In the ordinary process for vinegar, alcoholic liquors, as wine and cider, are exposed to the air in open vessels. Although a mixture of pure alcohol and water does not absorb oxygen from the air, a small portion of any ferment;

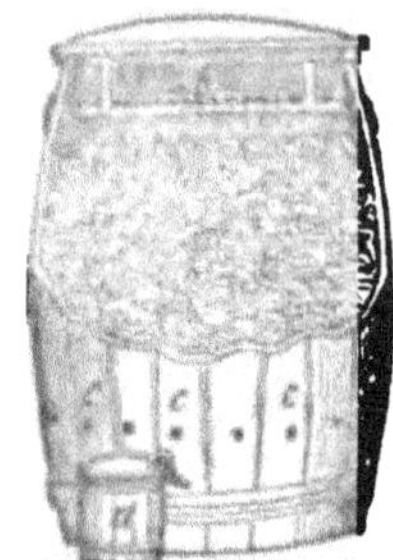
Fig. 416.

as vinegar, already formed, or the fungus plant called *mother of vinegar*, enables it to combine with oxygen. In this process the essential thing is a free supply of air and a proper temperature. In the manufacture of vinegar on the large scale, this is secured by causing the liquor (*b*, fig. 416) to trickle from threads of cotton drawn through holes, over shavings of beech-wood previously soaked in vinegar, and contained in a large cask with holes in its sides, (*c c c c*,) so as to admit a free circulation of air. In this way a vast surface is exposed, and the absorption of oxygen is very rapid, causing an elevation of 20° or 30° in the temperature. The liquid is passed through this apparatus four or five times in the course of twenty-four hours, in which time the change of the alcohol into vinegar is generally complete. The product is collected in the vessel *a*.

742. Acetic acid is also obtained by distilling wood in close vessels, (712,) a process employed on a large scale for the preparation of the acid. The products are, besides carbonic acid and carburetted hydrogen, a large quantity of acetic acid mixed with oily and tarry matters, from which it is separated mechanically. The acid thus prepared is known as *pyroligneous acid*, and is largely used in the arts of dyeing and calico-printing; but being contaminated by empyreumatic oils, is not fit for the purposes of domestic economy. By combining it with bases, salts are obtained, which, when decomposed, afford a pure acid.

743. By distilling dried acetate of soda with strong sulphuric acid, a very concentrated acid is obtained, which, when exposed to cold, deposits crystals of pure acetic acid $C_4H_4O_4$. The pure acid is solid below 60° F.; when liquid, it has a specific gravity of 1·063, and boils at 248°. It is perfectly soluble in water, alcohol, and ether; it has a pungent fragrant odor and a very acid taste, and, when applied to the skin, is highly corrosive. The acid is monobasic; all its salts are soluble in water.

Acetates.

744. *Acetate of potash* $C_4H_3(K)O_4$ is easily prepared by neutralizing acetic acid with carbonate of potash. It is a very soluble deliquescent salt, and is employed in medicine.

Acetate of soda $C_4H_3(Na)O_4$ forms large crystals with six equivalents of water. It is prepared in large quantities from pyroligneous acid; the salt is heated to destroy the oily matters, and then affords by its decomposition a pure acid. *Acetate of ammonia* $C_4H_4O_4+NH_3=C_4H_3(NH_4)O_4$ is used in medicine by the name of the *spirit of Mindereus.* It is prepared by saturating acetic acid with ammonia, and is exceedingly soluble and volatile. The *acetate of zinc* is a beautiful white salt, and is employed as a tonic and astringent. The *acetate of alumina* $C_4H_3(al)O_4$ is much used in dyeing; it is obtained by decomposing a solution of alum by one of acetate of lead; sulphate of lead precipitates, and acetate of alumina with acetate of potash remains in solution. The *protacetate* and *peracetate of iron* are prepared in a similar manner, and are largely employed in calico-printing and dyeing. They are represented by $C_4(H_3Fe)O_4$, and $C_4H_3feO_4$. (See § 649.)

745. *Acetate of Lead,* $C_4H_3(Pb)O_4$.—This salt is well known under the name of *sugar of lead.* It is prepared by dissolving oxyd of lead (litharge) in acetic acid, and crystallizes with three equivalents of water, which are expelled by gentle heat. It is a white salt, with a very sweet and astringent taste, and is often employed as a medicine; but is poisonous, and should be used internally with caution.

The acetate of lead has a great tendency to combine with oxyd of lead, with which it forms several definite compounds. These are generally designated as *basic salts,* but should be carefully distinguished from the salts containing more than one equivalent of base, which are formed by bibasic and tribasic acids. In these last, the metal replaces the hydrogen of the acid, but in the basic acetates the neutral salt combines directly with the oxyd. To distinguish them, the term *surbasic* is applied, and the compound of the acetate with an equivalent of oxyd of lead is called the *surbasic acetate of lead.* Three of these compounds are known, in which the acetate is combined with one-fourth, one, and two and a half equivalents of oxyd. The second is the only one of importance.

746. *Surbasic Acetate of Lead,* $C_4H_3PbO_4+Pb_2O_2$.—This salt, commonly called the tribasic acetate, is obtained by digesting a solution of six parts of the acetate with seven of litharge; the oxyd is dissolved, and the liquid affords, by evaporation, a salt crystallizing in long needles. It is also

slowly formed when metallic lead is digested in an open vessel with a solution of the acetate, oxygen being absorbed from the air. The salt is very soluble in water, and its solution has an alkaline reaction; it is known in pharmacy as *Goulard's extract*, or *solution of lead*. When exposed to the air, it absorbs carbonic acid, and the equivalent of oxyd of lead is precipitated as a carbonate. This reaction enables us to explain the formation of white-lead.

747. A process frequently employed is to mix litharge and about $\frac{1}{100}$ of sugar of lead into a thin paste with water: the mixture is gently heated, and a current of carbonic acid is passed through it. The acetate of lead dissolves a portion of the oxyd to form the tribasic salt; this is immediately decomposed by the carbonic acid, which precipitates carbonate of lead, and leaves the acetate free to dissolve a new portion of oxyd. In this way the smallest quantity of the acetate is able to convert a large portion of the oxyd into carbonate, and at the end of the process to remain unaltered.

748. In the ordinary process, the plates of lead are exposed to the action of acetic acid, moisture, air, and the carbonic acid from fermenting tan, (588.) The lead immediately becomes covered with a film of oxyd by the action of the air. This is dissolved by the vapor of the acetic acid, and forms a solution of neutral acetate, which moistens the plates and gradually acts upon them, forming, by the aid of the atmospheric oxygen, the basic acetate, which is decomposed by the carbonic acid, in the same manner as in the last process, and the neutral acetate is again set free to act upon the metallic lead; the process goes on until all the lead is carbonated. In this way a small quantity of acetic acid will, under favorable circumstances, convert a hundred times its weight of lead into carbonate in a few weeks.

749. *Acetate of Copper*, $C_4H_3(Cu)O_4$.—This salt is very soluble, and forms beautiful green crystals of the monoclinic system, containing one equivalent of water. The acetate of copper forms several surbasic salts which are insoluble in water. The fine green pigment called *verdigris* is a mixture of two or more of these: all of these copper salts are very poisonous. The *acetate of silver* $C_4H_3(Ag)O_4$ crystallizes in white scales, and is the least soluble of the acetates.

750. *Chloracetic Acid*, $C_4Cl_3(H)O_4$.—We have already mentioned this product of the action of chlorine upon crystallizable acetic acid; one equivalent of the acid and

three of chlorine yield three of chlorohydric acid and one of the new compound, $C_4H_4O_4+3Cl_2=C_4Cl_3(H)O_4+3HCl$. The chloracetic acid is very soluble, but may be obtained in fine rhombohedral crystals; its salts resemble the ordinary acetates. When an amalgam of potassium is added to a solution of chloracetate of potash, chlorid of potassium, hydrate of potash, and the normal acetate of potash are formed. In this reaction water intervenes, and we may suppose that the alkaline metal, decomposing water, forms $3(KH)O_2$ and 3KH, which last, reacting with the chloracetate, would form chlorid of potassium, leaving H_3 in place of the chlorine.

Acetic Ether, $C_4H_3(Et)O_4=C_8H_8O_4$.—This ether is formed by the direct action of acetic acid upon alcohol, but is best obtained by distilling a mixture of five parts of acetate of soda, eight of sulphuric acid, and three of alcohol. It is a very fragrant and volatile liquid, soluble in seven parts of water. The odor of wine-vinegar is due to the presence of a little acetic ether. It contains, like the ethers of other monobasic acids, the elements of the acid and the alcohol minus an equivalent of water H_2O_2. The ethers like this, formed by the acids of the type $C_nH_nO_4$ with their respective alcohols, are polymeric of the corresponding aldeydes; acetic ether equals $2\times C_4H_4O_2$.

Acetic ether is dissolved by a concentrated solution of ammonia, and the solution affords by evaporation a white crystalline substance, very volatile and fusible, to which the name of *acetamid* has been given; it is the amid of acetic acid, and contains the elements of acetate of ammonia less an equivalent of water: $C_4H_3(NH_4)O_4=C_4H_7NO_4=H_2O_2+C_4H_5NO_2$, which is the formula for acetamid. In its formation from the ether, alcohol is set free; acetic ether $C_8H_8O_4+NH_3=C_4H_6O_2+C_4H_5NO_2$. The ethers of almost all acids yield amids by a similar reaction. When heated gently with potassium, acetamid evolves a gas and yields cyanid of potassium C_2KN.

If acetamid is distilled with anhydrous phosphoric acid, the elements H_2O_2 are abstracted from it, and a volatile liquid is obtained, which is $C_4H_5NO_2-H_2O_2=C_4H_3N$. It has received the name of *acetonitryl*. By the action of strong acids and alkalies both of these compounds regenerate ammonia and acetic acid.

751. When an acetate is heated with an excess of hydrate

of potash, it breaks up into carbonate of potash and a carbohydrogen C_2H_4. Acetate of potash $C_4H_3KO_4+(KH)O_2=C_2K_2O_6+C_2H_4$. It has already been described under the name of *marsh gas*, from its occurrence in marshes, as a product of the decomposition of vegetable matter. To indicate its relations in the organic series, the name of *formen* has been given to it. The chloracetates undergo a similar decomposition, and yield *trichloric formen* C_2Cl_3H, in which Cl_3 replaces H_3. The chloracetate of ammonia is decomposed by boiling with an excess of ammonia, into carbonate and this chlorinized species.

752. When an acetate is decomposed by heat, or when the vapor of acetic acid is passed through a red-hot tube, the acid undergoes a peculiar decomposition; two equivalents of it unite with the elimination of one equivalent of carbonic acid, $C_2H_2O_6.2 \times C_4H_4O_4=C_8H_8O_8-C_2H_2O_6=C_6H_6O_2$ To this liquid the name of *aceton* has been given; by oxydizing agents, like chromic acid, it yields acetic acid. We have already mentioned aceton as a product of the distillation of sugar with lime: it is accompanied with an analogous compound, to which the name of *metaceton* has been given, and which corresponds to a new acid homologous with acetic acid, to which the name of *metacetonic* or *propionic acid* has been given. It is $C_6H_6O_4=C_4H_4O_4+C_2H_2$, and is very much like acetic acid in its properties. When a paste of wheat flour is fermented with fragments of white leather and a quantity of chalk, propionate of lime is formed in large quantity. The fermentation is probably analogous to that which yields butyric acid. The decomposition of the salts of propionic acid by heat furnishes directly *propion* or *metaceton*, in the same way as butyric acid furnishes the homologue *butyron*. By the action of nitric acid upon butyron, a coupled acid is obtained, which is nitropropionic acid $C_6(H_5NO_4)O_4=C_6H_5NO_8$.

Methol, $C_2H_4O_2$.

753. *Wood-spirit, Pyroxylic Spirit, Methylic Alcohol.**—This substance has already been mentioned as a product of

* Pyroxylic spirit, from *pur*, fire, and *xulon*, wood. Methylic alcohol, from *methu*, wine, and *hule*, wood; signifying the wine or alcohol of wood. In names like kakodyl, and the terms ethyle, amyle, in the language of the compound radical theory, the same syllable is derived from *hule*, in its more extended sense of matter or principle.

the destructive distillation of wood. The acetic acid of the crude product being saturated with lime, impure methol is obtained by distillation, and is afterward purified by repeated rectifications. It is a colorless liquid, of a peculiar and somewhat unpleasant odor, and a hot, pungent taste. It has a specific gravity of ·798, and boils at 152°; it is very combustible, and burns with a pale blue flame. Like alcohol, it mixes in all proportions with water. It is occasionally used in the arts for dissolving resins and making varnishes, and the pure wood-spirit has lately acquired some celebrity in the treatment of phthisis, under the name of *wood-naphtha*. Like vinic alcohol, methol forms crystalline compounds with several salts and with baryta. It furnishes derivatives in which H is replaced by K, and O_2 by S_2. The nitric ether of methol is obtained by the direct action of the acid upon the alcohol, and resembles the vinic compound. The chlorohydric ether C_2H_3Cl is a colorless gas.

The hydrobromic and hydriodic methylic ethers, obtained by processes similar to those described for the corresponding vinol compounds, are liquids at the ordinary temperature. In the bodies of this series, which is homologous with that of vinic alcohol, C_2H_3 plays the same part that we have assigued to C_4H_5. This group may be designated by Me, and wood-spirit will be $(MeH)O_2$, while the chlorid is MeCl and the nitrate $N(Me)O_6$. These ethers are decomposed by a solution of hydrate of potash, with the formation of potash salts and methol.

754. The *sulphomethylic acid* is prepared in the same manner as the sulphovinic; and like it, is an acid ether. It is $S_2(MeH)O_8$. It is more stable than the sulphovinic acid, and may be obtained in crystals. The neutral sulphuric ether is prepared by distilling wood-spirit and sulphuric acid, and is $S_2(Me_2)O_8$; by boiling water it is converted into sulphomethylic acid and methol; $S_2(Me_2)O_8+H_2O_2=S_2(MeH)O_8+(MeH)O_2$. With ammonia it undergoes a partial decomposition, and yields *sulphamethane* and wood-spirit; $S_2(Me_2)O_8+NH_3=C_2H_4O_2+S_2(C_2H_5N)O_6$. The nature of the action will be understood by referring to what has been said of acetamid; it is the amid of sulphomethylic acid, and by hydrate of potash is decomposed into a sulphate, methol, and ammonia.

When sulphomethylic acid is decomposed by heat, *methylic*

ether is obtained as a colorless gas. The principles involved in its formation are the same as those which have already been explained in speaking of the ether of spirits of wine. Its formula is $C_4H_6O_2 = Me_2O_2$, and it is consequently metameric with vinic alcohol.

755. The chlorohydric ether of alcohol has been shown to correspond to a carbohydrogen aceten, $C_4H_6 = (C_2H_2)_2H_2$; in the same manner the methol compounds are derivatives of a homologous hydrocarbon $(C_2H_2)H_2 = C_2H_4$, which is formen or marsh gas, already described as a result of the decomposition of the acetates. By the action of chlorine the atoms of hydrogen may be successively replaced, and the final result is C_2Cl_4, a chlorid of carbon. The trichloric species C_2HCl_3 is of some interest, and is commonly known by the name of *chloroform*. Its formation by the decomposition of chloracetate of ammonia has already been mentioned, but it occurs as a product of the action of chlorine or hypochlorites upon many organic substances. When alcohol or wood-spirit is distilled with a solution of two or three parts of chlorid of lime in twenty of water, chloroform is the principal product; it is a dense oily liquid, having a specific gravity of 1·480, boils at 141° F., and is nearly insoluble in water. It has a pleasant aromatic odor and a very sweet pungent taste. An alcoholic solution of it, prepared by distilling chlorid of lime with an excess of alcohol, has long been known in medicine by the incorrect name of *chloric ether*. Its vapor, when mixed with atmospheric air and inhaled like ether, produces insensibility; as it is more agreeable to the senses and more potent in its operation, chloroform has, to a considerable extent, replaced ether as an anæsthetic agent in surgical practice.

The action of potash upon an alcoholic solution of iodine produces a yellow crystalline substance, which is *iodoform*, the iodine compound corresponding to chloroform, and is C_2HI_3. These compounds with an alcoholic solution of hydrate of potash are decomposed into formate, with chlorid or iodid of potassium, and water; $C_2HCl_3 + 4(HK)O_2 = C_2(HK)O_4 + 3KCl + 2H_2O_2$. The hydrocarbon C_2H_2, corresponding to olefiant gas, is not known in this series, but the final action of chlorine upon chloroform produces C_2Cl_4, which is a dense liquid; at a red heat it loses Cl_2 and is converted into a crystalline chlorid C_2Cl_2 which is the perchloric species of the unknown C_2H_2, or perhaps polymeric of it.

Oxydation of Methol.

756. When the vapor of methol mixed with air, is exposed to the action of platinum black, oxygen is absorbed, and water is formed with a new acid, which is homologous with acetic acid, $C_2H_4O_2 + O_4 = H_2O_2 + C_2H_2O_4$. The intermediate product $C_2H_2O_2$, corresponding to aldehyd, has never been obtained. The action of heated hydrate of potash upon wood-spirit evolves hydrogen, and forms a salt of the new acid, to which the name of *formic acid* is given. It is secreted by a species of ant, (*Formica rufa*,) from whence it derives its name, and by the stinging nettle, (*Urtica urens*;) it is also the result of the action of oxydizing agents, upon many organic substances, as sugar and alcohol, and may be advantageously prepared by the following process:—800 grains of bichromate of potash and 300 of sugar are dissolved in seven ounces of water. The mixture is placed in a retort, and one measured ounce of sulphuric acid very gradually added; it is then distilled (fig. 415) with a gentle heat, until three ounces of liquid are obtained. This is dilute formic acid, and may be used to form salts, which, when decomposed, afford a strong acid.

The pure acid is obtained by passing sulphuretted hydrogen gas over dry formate of lead; sulphuret of lead and formic acid are produced. The action is aided by a gentle heat, and the acid distils over. It is a colorless liquid, of specific gravity 1·168, which boils at 212°, and at 32° crystallizes, like acetic acid, in shining plates. It fumes in the air, and has a very pungent odor, resembling that of ants; it is powerfully acid and corrosive, instantly blistering the skin. When this acid or its salts are heated with strong sulphuric acid, it is decomposed with the evolution of pure carbonic oxyd gas: $C_2H_2O_4 = C_2O_2 + H_2O_2$. The formates resemble the acetates. The formate of silver $C_2(HAg)O_4$ is decomposed when its solution is boiled; the silver is precipitated, while carbonic acid and carbonic oxyd gases escape, $2C_2(HAg)O_4 = Ag_2 + H_2O_2 + C_2O_4 + C_2O_2$.

757. Formic acid yields with alcohol an ether which is $C_2(HEt)O_4 = C_6H_6O_4$. The acetic ether of methol has the same composition $C_4(H_3Me)O_4 = C_6H_6O_4$. These two ethers are similar in their general physical characters, but by the action of hydrate of potash, one yields a formate and alcohol, and the other an acetate and methol. The formic

ether of methol is $C_2(HMe)O_4 = C_4H_4O_4$: it is metameric with acetic acid. All of these ethers by the action of chlorine exchange their hydrogen in whole or in part for that element. The final result of the substitution in formo-methylic ether is $C_4Cl_4O_4$. We have already shown that such ethers are polymeric of the corresponding aldehyds. The chlorinized ether by heat is resolved into two equivalents of phosgene gas $C_4Cl_4O_4 = 2C_2Cl_2O_2$; phosgene gas is, in fact, the chlorinized derivative of methylic aldehyd, which will be $C_2H_2O_2$.

AMYLOL, $C_{10}H_{12}O_2$.

758. *Amylic Alcohol.*—We have already alluded to this compound as a product of fermentation under certain circumstances. In the rectification of the crude spirit obtained by the fermentation of potatoes, it separates as an oil, which comes over with the last portions of the spirit, and is insoluble in water: the distillers give to it the name of *fousel oil*, or *potato oil:* it is sometimes observed in the spirit from other sources, and seems to be a product of the transformation of starch or sugar, under conditions not well understood. When pure, it is a colorless liquid, which is insoluble in water, has a specific gravity of ·818°, and boils at 269° F. It has a burning taste, and a pungent odor which excites coughing and often nausea.

In its chemical relations it is precisely similar to alcohol, and methol, with which it is homologous; its formula is $C_{10}H_{12}O_2 = (C_{10}H_{11}.H)O_2$; it forms ethers in which $C_{10}H_{11}$, corresponding to C_2H_3, to C_4H_5, and to H, replaces hydrogen; we shall represent this group by the symbol Ayl.

The chlorohydric amylic ether is formed by the action of the acid upon amylol, and is $C_{10}H_{11}Cl = AylCl$. The bromine and iodine compounds are similar, as also the nitrous and nitric ethers, the latter being $N(C_{10}H_{11})O_6$, or nitric acid in which Ayl replaces hydrogen; as in all similar reactions, H_2O_2 is eliminated in its formation, and it regenerates a nitrate and amylol by the action of an alcoholic solution of hydrate of potash. With sulphuric acid, *sulphamylic acid*, corresponding to the sulphovinic, is formed, which is monobasic; by its decomposition, *amylic ether* $C_{20}H_{22}O_2$ is obtained, which corresponds to the hydric ether of alcohol, and is Ayl_2O_2, or water in which the group $C_{10}H_{11}$ has replaced both equivalents of hydrogen. By the action of an excess of sulphuric acid, the carbohydrogen $C_{10}H_{10}$, corresponding to olefiant gas, is obtained: the alcohol breaks up into $C_{10}H_{10}$ and H_2O_2.

759. *Oxydation of Amylol.*—By the action of platinum black, amylol combines with oxygen and is converted into an acid homologous with the acetic and formic acids: when heated with hydrate of potash, hydrogen is evolved, and a salt of the same acid is formed, $C_{10}H_{12}O_2+(KH)O_2=C_{10}(H_9K)O_4+H_4$. By distilling the potash salt with sulphuric acid, the new acid $C_{10}H_{10}O_4$ is obtained. It is identical with that previously known to exist in the root of the *Valeriana officinalis*, and hence called *valeric* or *valerianic acid.* It is also found in several other plants, and decaying cheese sometimes owes its peculiar flavor to a proportion of valeric acid. It is a colorless oily liquid, which is soluble in a large quantity of water, is strongly acid and caustic, and has the characteristic odor of valerian root; it boils at 347°, and has a specific gravity of ·937. Its salts are all soluble in water and monobasic; they have a slight odor like the acid. The valerate of zinc crystallizes in white scales, and is employed in medicine as a substitute for valerian, the medicinal properties of which it possesses in a high degree. The action of chlorine upon the acid affords a product similar to chloracetic acid.

The valeric acid yields with amylic alcohol an ether which has, when pure, an agreeable flavor, like apples. The *acetic ether* of *amylol* has a no less striking resemblance in its odor to jargonelle pears; the flavors are not however developed until the ethers have been diluted with alcohol. These ethers are obtained by distilling mixtures of amylol and acetic or valeric acid with sulphuric acid, and are used to give the peculiar flavors of the fruits in perfumery and confectionery.

760. In ascending the series of alcohols, in proportion as the amount of carbon and hydrogen is greater, the bodies become more insoluble in water, and assimilated to the oils and fats and to the different species of wax, to which they have intimate relations. These bodies are generally ethers of acids, which are for the most part homologous with acetic and valeric acids; or *glycerids*, a class of compounds analogous to ethers in their composition. From them several new alcohols are obtained, and a still greater number of

acids pertaining to the alcohol series. We shall first notice those which belong to the class of compound ethers.

Spermaceti.—This substance occurs mixed with oil, filling large cavities in the head of the sperm whale, (*Physeter macrocephalus.*) The oil is removed by pressure, and finally by washing in a dilute solution of potash, and the spermaceti is obtained as a white solid, which fuses at 120°, and crystallizes on cooling in beautiful broad pearly plates. It is soluble in alcohol and ether, but insoluble in water, and is used in pharmacy and in the fabrication of candles. Spermaceti has the composition of a compound ether, and, when gently heated with hydrate of potash, is decomposed into the potash salt of a new acid $C_{16}(H_{15}K)O_4$, and the alcohol of that acid $C_{16}H_{18}O_2$. The acid has been called *ethalic acid*, and the alcohol *ethal* or *ethol;* spermaceti corresponds to the acetic acid of vinic alcohol, and contains the elements of the acid, and the alcohol minus H_2O_2. Both of these are white crystalline volatile substances, analogous in physical properties to spermaceti. Ethalic acid melts at 131°; it yields with other alcohols, ethers which are fusible and crystalline. Ethal forms with sulphuric acid the *sulphethalic acid*, corresponding to the sulphovinic, and when heated with hydrate of potash to 400°, evolves hydrogen, and is converted into ethalate of potash.

761. *Wax.*—This substance has been supposed to be a vegetable production, and to be collected by bees from the plants upon which they feed; but experiments have shown that they yield wax even when fed upon pure sugar or honey, and that it is a secretion of the insects themselves.

A species of wax brought from China is very analogous to spermaceti in its composition, and when decomposed by hydrate of potash, yields the salt of a new acid, called the *cerotic acid*, and the corresponding alcohol *cerotol*. The acid has the formula $C_{54}H_{54}O_4$ and the alcohol is $C_{54}H_{56}O_2$. These compounds are less soluble and fusible than the ethalic series; the wax fuses at 182° F., and the alcohol at 174°. The alcohol yields with sulphuric acid a coupled monobasic acid, and with chlorine a product which corresponds to a chlorinized aldehyd. Heated with hydrate of potash, cerotol evolves hydrogen and is converted into cerotate of potash. It cannot be distilled without partial change, being converted into water and carbohydrogens polymeric with olefiant gas.

Common beeswax is separated by boiling alcohol into a soluble portion, and a residue comparatively insoluble. The soluble part consists principally of cerotic acid in a free state. The insoluble part is decomposed by potash into *ethalic acid*, and a new alcohol, *mellisol*, which is represented by $C_{60}H_{62}O_2$: it is crystallizable, and melts at 185°. When fused with potash it yields *mellisic acid* $C_{60}H_{60}O_4$.

GLYCERIDS.

762. Under this title may be included a number of neutral fats and oils, which, by the action of bases, are converted into salts of fatty acids, with the separation of a substance to which the name of *glycerin* has been given, in allusion to its sweet taste, (from *glukus*, sweet.) Glycerin is prepared by heating a mixture of olive-oil, oxyd of lead, and water. The oil is decomposed, and the acids form insoluble salts with the lead, while the glycerin is dissolved in the water; the solution is treated with sulphuretted hydrogen to precipitate a little dissolved oxyd of lead, and evaporated in a water-bath. It is formed in large quantities as a product of the saponification of fats by boiling with hydrate of lime and water. The liquid which separates from the insoluble lime salts is a watery solution of glycerin containing a little lime; this may be separated by carbonic acid, and the glycerin is then obtained by evaporation.

The formula of glycerin is $C_6H_8O_6$. It is a colorless, syrupy liquid, with a specific gravity of 1·280, of a very sweet taste, and is readily soluble in water and alcohol; it is not volatile, but when strongly heated is decomposed, evolving acetic acid and other products, the most important of which is *acrolein*.

763. Acrolein is also produced when the glycerids are decomposed by heat, and is best obtained by distilling glycerin with anhydrous phosphoric acid. The glycerin loses the elements of two equivalents of water: $C_6H_8O_6-2H_2O_2=C_6H_4O_2$, which is the formula of acrolein. It is a colorless, very volatile liquid, with a peculiar acrid, penetrating odor, which is perceived when the fat oils are strongly heated; it is lighter than water, and sparingly soluble in that liquid. With potash it reacts like aldehyd, and it reduces oxyd of

silver with the formation of a new acid, the *acrylic*, which is $C_6H_4O_4$. It resembles the acetic acid in its properties, and under the influence of alkalies is converted with oxydation into a mixture of formic and acetic acids; $C_6H_4O_4 + 2(HK)O_2 + O_2 = C_4(H_3K)O_4 + C_2(HK)O_4 + H_2O_2$.

764. The constitution of the glycerids is such, that in decomposition they combine with the elements of $3H_2O_2$, and produce two equivalents of a fatty acid and one of glycerin. All of them undergo this change when heated with a solution of hydrate of potash or soda, or with oxyds, like oxyd of lead and lime. The salts thus formed are *soaps;* and different kinds of soaps are produced, according to the nature of the fatty acid and the alkali. Those of potash are very soluble and remain mixed with the water, glycerin, and excess of alkali employed in their preparation; they form *soft soaps*, while those of soda are less soluble and more easily separated from the liquid, and constitute *hard soaps*. Those of lime, lead, and other bases are insoluble in water, and the *lead-plaster* or *diachylon* of surgeons is a lead soap. When a solution of a soap with an alkaline base is mixed with a salt of any other base, double decomposition ensues, and an insoluble earthy or metallic salt is precipitated; it is the presence of salts of lime or magnesia in natural waters; which gives them the power of decomposing soaps, and constitutes what is called *hardness* in water. Strong acids in the same way decompose soaps, and separate the fatty acid in an oily form. Strong sulphuric acid decomposes the glycerids like an alkali, and liberates the fatty acids, forming with the glycerin an acid analogous to the sulphovinic, to which the name of *sulphoglyceric acid* is given.

Butter consists of several glycerids which are difficult of separation. When saponified, and the soap decomposed by distillation with sulphuric acid, it yields four volatile acids, homologous with the acetic. They are called the *butyric*, *caproic*, *caprylic*, and *capric* acids. Of these the first is best known: the others are separated from it, and from one another, by the different solubility of their baryta salts.

Butyric acid is more easily obtained by the fermentation of sugar under certain conditions, which have already been explained, (700.)

The butyrate of lime is decomposed by a solution of carbonate of soda, and the soda salt being concentrated by evaporation is mixed with an excess of sulphuric acid, when the butyric acid rises to the surface as an oily layer, which is separated and purified by distillation. It is a colorless liquid, which boils at 327° F., and is lighter than water. It mixes with pure water and alcohol in all proportions. The odor of butyric acid is strong and disagreeable, resembling that of vinegar and rancid butter; it is powerfully acid and caustic. The salts of butyric acid are all soluble in water; the butyrate of lime $C_8(H_7Ca)O_4$ is less soluble in hot water than in cold, and separates almost entirely by boiling, in transparent prisms, which redissolve as the liquid cools.

765. By mixing together alcohol, butyric acid, and strong sulphuric acid, the heat evolved is sufficient to cause the formation of *butyric ether*, which is precipitated on adding water to the mixture, being insoluble in it. It is a colorless liquid, soluble in alcohol, to which it gives the flavor of pine apples; the solution is used by confectioners to flavor syrups, and by distillers in the fabrication of spirits.

766. When a mixture of glycerin and butyric acid is heated with sulphuric acid, an oily liquid is obtained, which is supposed to be the *butyric glycerid*, to which butter owes its peculiar flavor. It is the only glycerid which has been formed artificially; by alkalies it yields glycerin and a butyrate like the natural glycerids; its composition, agreeably to the rule which we have stated, will be $2C_8H_8O_4+C_6H_8O_6-3H_2O_2=C_{22}H_{18}O_8$.

The distillation of butyrate of lime affords *butyron* corresponding to *aceton*, and a volatile liquid, *butyral* $C_8H_8O_2$; it absorbs oxygen from the air, yielding butyric acid, and is the aldehyd of the butyric series.

The oil of the porpoise (*Delphinus phoca*) contains a glycerid, to which the name of *phocenin* has been given: it is the glycerid of valeric acid, which has been described by the name of *phocenic acid*. The action of nitric acid upon castor-oil yields a volatile oily acid with a fragrant odor, to which the name of *enanthylic acid* has been given; it is $C_{14}H_{14}O_4$; and the distilled water of the rose-geranium (*Pelargonium roseum*) contains another, *pelargonic acid*, $C_{18}H_{18}O_4$.

The peculiar flavor or *bouquet* of wine is due to a small portion of a peculiar ether, which is obtained when great quantities of wine are distilled, and possesses, in a high degree, the vinous flavor. By hydrate of potash it is decomposed into alcohol and a volatile acid, which has the composition of pelargonic acid, and is probably identical with it.

The foregoing acids are all odorous, more or less soluble in water, and may be distilled over with its vapor; their boiling points, however, become gradually higher, and their lime and baryta salt less and less soluble. Beyond capric acid $C_{20}H_{20}O_4$, they are solid at the ordinary temperature, no longer volatile with the vapor of water, and yield with lime and baryta insoluble salts, and with the alkalies proper soaps. Among these the *ethalic*, *cerotic*, and *melissic* have already been mentioned. We shall notice a few of the more important ones remaining.

767. The palm-oil which is expressed from the nuts of the *Elais guinensis* is composed of a fluid fat, *olein*, and a solid crystalline substance to which the name of *palmatin* has been given; it is the glycerid of ethalic acid, which is sometimes named *palmitic acid.* The fat of animals is composed in like manner of a liquid fat and a solid crystalline material. By careful pressure in the cold, this separation may be in part effected, and if the fats have been kept for a long time in fusion, the solid portions crystallize out more or less perfectly on cooling. It is by taking advantage of this property that *lard-oil* is made. The solid portion may be purified by crystallization from ether. That obtained from beef and mutton consists principally of two substances, to which the names of *margarin* and *stearin* have been given. The former is readily soluble in ether, and fuses at 116° F.; stearin, on the contrary, is very little soluble in cold ether, and melts at 130°. By saponification they yield *margaric* and *stearic* acids, one fusing at 140°, and the other at 168°. Although thus distinguished, these bodies have the same composition: they are both monobasic and have the formula $C_{34}H_{34}O_4$. The margaric has been distinguished by the name of *para-stearic acid.* The action of heat and of acids under certain conditions converts stearic acid into this isomeric modification. While margarin and stearin are mingled in beef and mutton fats, the oils, like olive-oil, consist of margarin and olein. Human fat yields by saponification a large amount of palmitic acid, with some margaric, and a new acid, which is probably $C_{38}H_{36}O_4$.

768. The olein of lard, of olive-oil, and of almond-oil, yields by saponification an acid which is called *oleic acid*,

and, like olein itself, is a colorless liquid, insoluble in water. It has a slightly acrid taste, and its alcoholic solution has an acid reaction. Its composition is represented by $C_{36}H_{34}O_4$. Oleic acid does not therefore belong to the series of homologous acids already described, but is one of a new series, of which acrylic acid $C_6H_4O_4$ is also a member; in this series the number of equivalents of oxygen is four, and that of the equivalents of carbon is always two more than the number of the hydrogen.

769. When the vapor of nitrous acid is passed through oleic acid, this is rapidly transformed into a crystalline substance, which is *elaidic acid*, and is an isomeric modification of the oleic acid. The action of the nitrous vapor upon olein produces a corresponding modification of the glycerid. Elaidic acid, like oleic, is monobasic, and forms beautiful crystals, which melt at 112°. When these acids are fused with hydrate of potash they undergo a remarkable transformation; their homologue, acrylic acid, gives acetic and formic acids, while the oleic and elaidic yield acetic and ethalic acids with the evolution of hydrogen: $C_{36}H_{34}O_4 + 2(KH)O_2 = C_{32}(H_{31}K)O_4 + C_4(H_3K)O_4 + H_2$.

The acid from the saponification of a variety of whale-oil has been found to have the formula $C_{38}H_{36}O_4$, and another from the vegetable oil of the *Moringia aptera* $C_{30}H_{28}O_4$, while the olein from human fat has yielded *anthropic acid* $C_{34}H_{32}O_4$. All of these are monobasic and are homologues of acrylic acid and oleic acid. Their decomposition by hydrate of potash will probably yield corresponding acids of the acetic series. Thus, $C_{38}H_{36}O_4$, to which the name of *dœglic acid* has been given, should yield stearic and acetic acids.

770. Castor-oil from the seeds of *Ricinus communis* is distinguished from other fixed oils by its ready solubility in alcohol. The solid fatty acids which it yields, appear to be margaric and palmitic; the olein affords by its saponification an oily acid, which, while containing carbon and hydrogen in the same proportion as in the last series, has six equivalents of oxygen. Different experimenters have apparently obtained from different specimens of oil two homologous acids, to which they have ascribed the formulæ $C_{38}H_{36}O_6$ and $C_{36}H_{34}O_6$. To both of these the name of *ricinoleic acid* has been given. With nitrous vapor, castor-oil yields a crystalline glycerid like olive-oil.

771. We have then three homologous series among the fatty acids; the first and most complete is that homologous with acetic and ethalic acids; the second is that of oleic acid; the third that of ricinoleic acid.

The first has the general formula $C_nH_nO_4$, the second $C_nH_{n-2}O_4$, and the third $C_nH_{n-2}O_6$.

The series of the first, as far as known, is here given:—

1. Formic	$C_2H_2O_4$	16. Ethalic	$C_{32}H_{32}O_4$
2. Acetic	$C_4H_4O_4$	17. Stearic	$C_{34}H_{34}O_4$
3. Propionic	$C_6H_6O_4$	18. Bassic	$C_{36}H_{36}O_4$
4. Butyric	$C_8H_8O_4$	19. Balenic	$C_{38}H_{38}O_4$
5. Valeric	$C_{10}H_{10}O_4$	20.	
6. Caproic	$C_{12}H_{12}O_4$	21.	
7. Enanthylic	$C_{14}H_{14}O_4$	22. Behenic	$C_{44}H_{44}O_4$
8. Caprylic	$C_{16}H_{16}O_4$	23.	
9. Pelargonic	$C_{18}H_{18}O_4$	24.	
10. Capric	$C_{20}H_{20}O_4$	25.	
11. Margaritic	$C_{22}H_{22}O_4$	26.	
12. Lauric	$C_{24}H_{24}O_4$	27. Cerotic	$C_{54}H_{54}O_4$
13. Cocinic	$C_{26}H_{26}O_4$	28.	
14. Myristic	$C_{28}H_{28}O_4$	29.	
15. Benic	$C_{30}H_{30}O_4$	30. Melissic	$C_{60}H_{60}O_4$

772. We have already described the alcohols of the 1st, 2d, 5th, 16th, 27th, and 30th acids, and we have to add that of the 16th. In this group there is a regular transition from formic acid, through the propionic, butyric, and other sparingly soluble oily acids, to the insoluble ethalic and stearic. In the first ten, which are liquid at ordinary temperatures, and distil without any change, there is a progressive increase of about 36° F. in the boiling point of each acid. Thus, the formic boils at 212°, the acetic at 212°+36°=248°, and the propionic at 248°+36°=284°. The fusing point of the solid acids rises in a similar manner, but with less apparent regularity.

The fact that the acids are less fusible than their glycerids has led to their use in the manufacture of candles, which are sold under the name of *stearine*, *adamantine*, or *Belmont sperm*. The tallow is commonly saponified by heating it in vats by steam, with a mixture of lime and water; an insoluble lime salt is formed, and the glycerin remains dissolved in the water. This salt is decomposed by diluted sulphuric or chlorohydric acid, with the aid of heat, and the mixed acids, which rise to the surface, are, when cold, submitted to pressure, by which the oleic acid is removed, and the stearic and margaric acids are obtained nearly pure. The crystalline tendency of the fused acid is corrected by adding a little pulverized gypsum to the mass for the fabrication of candles.

The decomposition of the glycerids by sulphuric acid, already described, is sometimes employed for this purpose. The higher acids of the series may be distilled without change *in vacuo* or in a current of steam, but undergo a partial decomposition when distilled in the ordinary manner. These acids may be distinguished from stearin, from wax, and spermaceti, for which they are often substituted, and with which the latter are frequently adulterated, by their ready solubility in alcohol, and in a heated solution of carbonate of soda.

773. The action of nitric upon oleic acid yields the volatile acids of the above series, from the acetic to the capric inclusive; the other fatty acids yield similar results, and the stearic acid is the first product of the action of nitric upon oleic acid. The residue of the action of nitric acid contains four soluble crystallizable bibasic acids—the *succinic*, $C_8H_6O_8$, *adipic*, $C_{12}H_{10}O_8$, *pimelic*, $C_{14}H_{12}O_8$, and *suberic*, $C_{16}H_{14}O_8$; they correspond to homologues of oleic acid, which have fixed O_4, and are represented by $C_nH_{n-2}O_8$. The succinic acid was originally obtained by distilling amber, a fossil resin which occurs in recent geological formations. Succinic acid is soluble in water and alcohol; when heated it fuses, and is decomposed into water and a neutral crystalline substance called *succinid* $C_8H_4O_6$, which, when boiled with water, is gradually reconverted into succinic acid. The other acids are of but little importance; the suberic is a product of the action of nitric acid upon cork. When olein or oleic acid is distilled, *sebacic acid* is obtained; it is crystallizable, volatile, and soluble in water, and has the formula $C_{20}H_{18}O_8$, being homologous with those just mentioned. When fused with hydrate of potash, these acids are decomposed, and yield members of the acetic series. Thus, the pimelic forms valerate of potash, and, instead of the acetic acid and hydrogen which the homologues of oleic acid would yield, carbonic acid and water are obtained.

774. Castor-oil and ricinoleic acid, like olein, yield sebacic acid by distillation. When ricinoleic acid is distilled with an excess of a strong solution of hydrate of potash, sebacate of potash is formed, and hydrogen is evolved, with a peculiar oily liquid, having the formula $C_{16}H_{18}O_2$. The reaction may be thus represented: $C_{36}H_{34}O_6 + 2(KH)O_2 = C_{20}(H_{16}K_2)O_8$

$+C_{16}H_{16}O_2+H_2$. The new volatile product is the alcohol corresponding to caprylic acid, and may be named *caprylol.* It is insoluble in water, has an agreeable aromatic odor, a specific gravity of ·823, and boils at 356° F. With sulphuric acid it forms a vinic acid, and with acetic and chlorohydric acids, ethers similar to those of ordinary alcohol; by oxydation it yields caprylic acid $C_{16}H_{16}O_4$.

775. The different animal fats generally yield, by saponification, small portions of one or more of the volatile acids already described, and many of them are met with in the distilled water of various plants. Many glycerids appear to undergo a slow, spontaneous decomposition when moist; glycerin is liberated and may be removed by water, while the acids are found in a free state. The alcoholic ethers of all these fatty acids may be obtained by passing chlorohydric acid gas through their alcoholic solutions, or by heating the same solutions with sulphuric acid: they are, like the glycerids, neutral, fusible, fatty bodies, and have the same constitution as their homologue, acetic ether. When a glycerid is dissolved in alcohol and treated with chlorohydric acid, the ether is formed in the same way, and may be precipitated by adding water, which will be found to retain glycerin in solution. The action of ammonia alike upon the ethers and glycerids enables us to obtain the amids of the fatty acids with the separation of alcohol or glycerin. They have the same constitution as acetamid, and are all decomposed by hydrate of potash, with the formation of a salt of the acid and ammonia. Those of the higher acids are solid insoluble fatty bodies.

Alkaloids of the Alcohol Series.

776. The relations between hydrogen represented as H_2, water, and ammonia have already been considered, and we have shown that the alcohols may be viewed as compounds in which the groups C_2H_3, C_4H_5, $C_{10}H_{11}$, &c. replace H in water. These same groups may replace the successive equivalents of hydrogen in ammonia and oxyd of ammonium, giving rise to an interesting class of bodies which are perfectly analogous to ammonia in their chemical relations, and are called *organic alkalies* or *alkaloids.* Besides these obtained from the alcohols, there are many other alkaloids, products of dif-

ferent transformations of organic bodies; others exist ready formed in plants. We shall in this place consider only the first class.

777. When chlorohydric, or better bromohydric ether, is digested with a concentrated solution of ammonia, it slowly dissolves. This operation is accelerated by heat, and is best effected by exposing the ether and ammonia hermetically sealed in glass tubes, to the heat of boiling water. The solution is soon effected, and the mixture, on cooling, is found to contain a salt of the new ether-ammonia: hydrobromic ether, $EtBr+NH_3=NH_3Et.Br$, *bromid of ethammonium*, or $NH_2Et.HBr$. When decomposed by lime or potash in the same way as sal-ammoniac, the new alkaloid NH_2Et, which is named *ethamine*, is obtained as a very volatile liquid, with a specific gravity of ·696. It has a powerful odor resembling that of ammonia, and its solution is very caustic, acting like a strong alkali with acids and metallic salts. It is soluble in all proportions in water and alcohol.

778. If a hydracid ether of methol be substituted for the vinic ether, a corresponding methylic ammonia, or *methamine*, may be obtained, which is $NH_2(C_2H_3)$ or NH_2Me. It is a colorless gas, which at a low temperature may be condensed into a liquid, and is very soluble in water, which dissolves in the cold 1154 times its own volume of the gas. The solution is powerfully acrid and caustic, and in its odor and chemical properties closely resembles ammonia; the gas is combustible. The salts of these new bases are like those of ammonia, but are more soluble.

When placed in contact with a new equivalent of the ether, these alkalies react with it precisely like ammonia itself, and salts of new alkaloids are obtained, in which two and three atoms of hydrogen are successively replaced by the carbohydrogen elements. In this way $NHEt_2$ and $NEt_3=NC_{12}H_{15}$ are obtained; and by using successive different ethers, mixed alkaloids may be formed, such as NHEtMe and NMe_2Et. The amylic and cetylic ethers yield perfectly analogous compounds. *Amylamine* is $NH_2Ayl=NH_2(C_{10}H_{11})$. It is a very mobile liquid, having a specific gravity of ·750, and boiling at 203°; it has at the same time the odor of ammonia and of the amylic compounds, and is very caustic and alkaline. We may even have N(Me.Et.Ayl), in which the elements of three different alcohols are united. These higher alkaloids are liquids, which have still the characters of ammonia, but are less volatile and caustic than those of lower equivalents.

779. When *triethamine* NEt_3 is brought in contact with another equivalent of hydriodic ether, it no longer decomposes it, but unites directly with it to form a salt. This ether EtI, as we have already shown, corresponds to HI, and the ammonia unites with it as it would with the acid: in the latter case a simple ammonia would form iodid of ammonium NH_4I, and the trivinic ammonia $N(Et_3H)I$; but with the ether it forms $NEt_3.EtI = NEt_4I$, or the iodid of vinic ammonium NEt_4. The new iodid forms fine crystals, which have all the reactions of an ordinary iodid with metallic salts. With recently precipitated oxyd of silver, double decomposition ensues, giving rise to iodid of silver and oxyd of vinic ammonium: $2NEt_4I + Ag_2O_2 = 2AgI + (NEt_4)_2O_2$; but as anhydrous lime with water produces a hydrate $(CaH)O_2$, so the new oxyd forms with it two equivalents of a hydrate $(NEt_4.H)O_2$, which corresponds to $(KH)O_2$. It is obtained by evaporation as a very soluble, deliquescent substance, alkaline and corrosive like hydrate of potash, which it closely resembles in its chemical reactions. As we have supposed ammonia to unite with water and form a hydroxyd of ammonium, so in this compound the trivinic ammonia is united with vinic water or alcohol. The aqueous compound of ammonia is readily decomposed by heat; and in like manner, if the new oxyd is exposed to the heat of boiling water, it is decomposed into trivinic ammonia, and alcohol, which latter breaks up into olefiant gas and water; $C_4H_4 + H_2O_2$.

780. The methylic compound is quite similar to the last. When the hydriodic ether of methol is digested with ammonia, the hydriodate of methamine is for the most part transformed into the iodid of ammonium, and the iodid of methic ammonium; $4N(H_3Me)I = 3NH_4I + N(Me_4)I$. The new iodid forms sparingly soluble crystals, which yield a hydroxyd very alkaline and caustic.

The amylic and complex ammonium salts are analogous in their characters. Ethamine and methamine have been obtained by several other processes, and are found in the products of animal decomposition.

781. By the action of an alloy of potassium and antimony upon the hydriodic ethers, compounds are obtained representing ammonias, in which antimony replaces nitrogen, (645.)

They are $SbMe_3=SbC_6H_9$ and $SbEt_3=SbC_{12}H_{15}$. By oxydizing agents they lose H_2, and the resulting compounds constitute alkaloids which form a class of salts.

Stibethic ammonia unites with hydriodic ether to form $SbEt_4.I$, analogous to the nitrogen compound, and this, with oxyd of silver, yields a hydroxyd which is a strongly alkaline base. In like manner, $SbMe_4I$ and $Sb(Me_2Et)I$ may be obtained; all corresponding to the iodids of ammonium and potassium. The action of chlorine or nitric acid upon stibethic ammonia removes H_2 and gives rise to salts of a new alkaloid $SbC_{12}H_{13}$, which is called *stibethine.*

782. When a mixture of acetate of potash and arsenious acid is distilled at a low red heat, there is obtained, among other products, a volatile liquid, somewhat soluble in water, to which the name of *alkarsine* has been given. It is an organic base, related to those just described, in which arsenic replaces nitrogen. It contains $C_8H_{12}As_2O_2$, and corresponds to the oxyd of an arsenic ethamine, from which H_2 has been eliminated, as in stibethine; $As(EtH_2)=AsC_4H_7-H_2=As C_4H_5$, which combines with chlorohydric acid like ammonia: the anhydrous oxyd $(AsC_2H_5)_2.H_2O_2=(AsC_2H_6)_2O_2$ is *alkarsine,* or *oxyd of arsinum.* With chlorohydric acid it yields a liquid chlorid $(AsC_2H_6)Cl$, to which the name of *chlorarsine,* or *chlorohydrate of arsine,* has been given. It is a true salt, like chlorid of ammonium, and by double decomposition yields different salts, which are also formed by the action of acids upon alkarsine. The chlorid is decomposed by metallic zinc; chlorid of zinc is formed, and the organic elements are set free; but two equivalents of arsinum unite to form a compound, which is $C_8H_{12}As_2=(AsC_2H_6)_2$. It is a compound *quasi-metal,* and corresponds to Zn_2 and H_2. It combines directly with chlorine to form anew the chlorid; like alkarsine, it is a volatile liquid, which, when exposed to the air, fumes and takes fire even at the ordinary temperature. All of these compounds have a disgusting odor, and are fearfully poisonous. The oxyd, alkarsine, is like an alkali, acrid and corrosive. M. Bunsen, to whom we are indebted for a knowledge of these bodies, gave to the compound *quasi-metal* the name of *kakodyl,* (from *kakos,* evil, and *hule,* principle.)

783. When kakodyl is covered with water, it slowly absorbs oxygen from the air and yields alkarsine: if to the

alkarsine, oxyd of mercury is added under water, the metallic oxyd is reduced, and a new compound remains in solution, formed by the oxydation of the alkaloid arsine, which combines with the oxygen and forms $AsC_4H_5O_4$, which is the formula of the new body, *alkargen*. The solution yields by evaporation large rhombic prisms of the new substance, which is inodorous, has but little taste, and is not at all poisonous. Deoxydizing agents, like sulphurous acid, converts it into alkarsine. Alkargen combines with acids to form crystalline compounds like arsine; but by its combination with oxygen the alkaloid seems to have become more feebly basic than before; as in ammonia, one atom of hydrogen in alkargen or its salts is replaceable by a metal, so that we may have a compound like $AsC_4(H_4Cu)O_4.HCl$, or chlorohydrate of cupric alkargen. By the action of sulphuretted hydrogen, the oxygen in this alkaloid is replaced by sulphur, and crystals obtained which are $AsC_4H_5S_4$.

784. Succeeding the alcohols and their derivations may be considered a class of volatile liquids, many of them essential oils, which have analogies with alcohols or aldehyds, although not homologous with the preceding series. We shall mention briefly some of the more important. Their history is now nearly as complete as the alcohols, and scarcely less interesting, but the limits of this work will not permit us to speak of them at length.

Bitter-Almond Oil, $C_{14}H_6O_2$.

785. *Benzoilol, Essential Oil of Bitter Almonds.*—This oil does not exist ready formed in the almonds, but is produced by the reaction of certain principles contained in the kernel, when aided by the presence of water. It is obtained by bruising bitter almonds into a paste with water, and distilling the mixture, when the oil passes over, with hydrocyanic acid and other impurities. It is purified by redistilling it from a mixture of protochlorid of iron and lime, and is a colorless oily liquid, of a pungent burning taste, and very fragrant odor, like that of bruised bitter almonds. It boils at 356°, but its vapor distils over with that of water at 212°: its specific gravity is 1·073. It is often used in flavoring articles of food, but the crude oil which is sold for

this purpose is exceedingly poisonous; the pure oil is comparatively harmless.

By the action of hydrosulphuret of ammonia upon bitter-almond oil, its oxygen is replaced by sulphur, and an insoluble powder is obtained of the formula $C_{14}H_6S_2$. Its decomposition by heat gives rise to a variety of new and curious products.

786. *Chlorinized Benzoilol*, $C_{14}H_5ClO_2$.—This is obtained by the action of dry chlorine gas upon the oil of bitter almonds. It is a colorless liquid, which is decomposed by alkalies, yielding a chlorid and a benzoate. By distilling this with bromid or iodid of potassium, similar compounds are obtained, in which bromine or iodine replaces an equivalent of hydrogen.

The action of dry ammonia upon the chlorinized benzoilol yields chlorohydric acid, and a new substance, *benzamid*, $C_{14}H_5ClO_2+NH_3=C_{14}H_7NO_2+HCl$. It is soluble in water, and crystallizes in beautiful prisms.

787. *Hydrobenzamid.*—When bitter-almond oil is placed in a concentrated solution of ammonia, it is gradually converted into a white crystalline mass of this substance. It is formed from three equivalents of benzoilol and two of ammonia by the abstraction of the elements of three equivalents of water; $3(C_{14}H_6O_2)+2NH_3=C_{42}H_{18}N_2+3H_2O_2$. In this reaction the ammonia loses the whole of its hydrogen, which unites with the oxygen of the oil, and the residue (N_2) is substituted for O_6. By the action of chlorohydric acid it takes up the elements of water, and regenerates the oil and ammonia; the latter combines with the acid to form sal-ammoniac. When boiled in a solution of potash, it is converted into a metameric modification, which is no longer decomposed by acids, but unites directly with them and neutralizes them. This substance, which is an alkaloid, is also formed when ammonia is passed through an alcoholic solution of the oil of bitter almonds; it is called *benzoline* or *amarine*.

When the crude oil of bitter almonds is mixed with an alcoholic solution of potash, it is gradually converted into a white crystalline substance, which is called *benzoine*. It is polymeric of the oil, and is formed by the union of two equivalents of it; its formula is consequently $C_{28}H_{12}O_4$. When the vapor of benzoine is passed through a red-hot tube, it is reconverted into bitter-almond oil. By the action of chlorine upon fused benzoine, H_2 is removed in the form of 2HCl, and a crystalline compound remains, which is called *benzile*, and is $C_{28}H_{10}O_4$.

788. When bitter-almond oil is exposed to the air, it rapidly absorbs oxygen, and is converted into a white crystalline substance, which is *benzoic acid;* this is formed by the combination of two atoms of oxygen; the oil is the aldehyd of the acid. The same effect is produced when the oil is heated with hydrate of potash; hydrogen gas is evolved, and benzoate of potash formed. A more abundant source of benzoic acid is found in benzoin, a fragrant resinous substance which is obtained from the *Laurus benzoin.* This contains a large quantity of the acid, which may be procured by exposure to a gentle heat, when the acid is volatilized, and condenses as a white sublimate. It is also obtained by boiling the benzoin with lime, which forms benzoate of lime; chlorohydric acid added to the previously concentrated solution, precipitates the pure acid in crystalline plates. Benzoic acid forms light silky crystals of a pearly whiteness, and has a pleasant aromatic taste, very slightly acid. When pure it is inodorous, but generally has a little volatile oil adhering to it, which gives it a fragrant odor, like vanilla. It is volatile at a gentle heat, evolving a suffocating vapor, which condenses unchanged. It is very slightly soluble in cold, but more easily in hot water.

The formula of benzoic acid is $C_{14}H_6O_4$: it is monobasic, and forms a large class of salts, which are of but little importance. The benzoic vinic ether is obtained by passing chlorohydric acid gas through an alcoholic solution of benzoic acid, and is $C_{14}(H_5Et)O_4 = C_{18}H_{10}O_4$. It is a fragrant volatile liquid, which in its chemical reactions resembles the other ethers; with ammonia, it affords *benzamid* and alcohol. Benzamid is the amid of benzoic acid, and with H_2O_2 yields benzoic acid and ammonia. It is volatile, but at a high temperature loses a second equivalent of H_2O_2 and becomes $C_{14}H_5N$. This is a liquid to which the name of *benzonitryl* is given; with $2H_2O_2$ it regenerates benzoic acid and ammonia.

With strong nitric acid, benzoic acid yields a crystalline compound, with the elimination of H_2O_2; it is the nitrobenzoic acid which has already been alluded to, (652,) and from its mode of formation is monobasic. When heated with a mixture of nitric and sulphuric acids, a second equivalent of nitric acid is fixed, and binitrobenzoic acid is formed.

The atom of hydrogen in each case is eliminated from the nitric acid, and its saline capacity destroyed, but the benzoic elements still retain the original atom of H, replaceable by a metal, and thus each of the new acids is monobasic. The decompositions of the ethers and amids of these acids yield a variety of curious compounds.

789. *Benzen.*—The vapor of benzoic acid passed through a red-hot gun-barrel, is decomposed into carbonic acid and a new substance named *benzen*, *benzol*, or *phene*, which is $C_{12}H_6$. $C_{14}H_6O_4 = C_2O_4 + C_{12}H_6$. Benzen is more easily obtained by distilling benzoic acid with slaked lime, which combines with the carbonic acid. It is a colorless, fragrant liquid, which boils at 187°, and has a specific gravity of ·830; at 32° F. it forms a white crystalline mass. Benzen is formed when the fat oils are decomposed at a red heat, and is obtained in the manufacture of oil-gas for illumination. With fuming sulphuric acid, benzen yields a monobasic acid, the *sulphobenzenic*, and a neutral crystalline body, *sulphobenzid*. They are analogous to sulphovinic acid and sulphuric ether.

The phenic alcohol or *phenol* $C_{12}H_6O_2$ is obtained by the decomposition of salicylic acid, which contains two atoms more of oxygen than benzoic acid. The name of *carbolic acid* is also given to it, and it occurs as a natural product in the secretion of the beaver, called *castoreum*, which owes its peculiar odor and probably its medicinal properties to a small portion of phenol; it is also contained in the oil of coal-tar. Phenol forms colorless crystals, which are liquified by moisture, although but slightly soluble in water. Its aqueous solution has an acrid taste, and an odor like wood-smoke or creasote, which it also resembles in being poisonous, and a powerful antiseptic. Kreasote is probably an homologue of phenol.

790. The derivatives of phene and phenol may be represented as compounds in which $C_{12}H_5$ replaces H, precisely as the group C_4H_5 in those of vinic alcohol. With sulphuric acid, phenol yields *phenosulphuric acid* $S_2(C_{12}H_5.H)O_8$. That formed by benzen is $S_2(C_{12}H_5.H)O_6$, and is *phenosulphurous acid:* sulphurous acid, $2(SO_2.HO) = S_2H_2O_6$. With nitric acid, phenol yields three successive products, in

which one, two, and three equivalents of NO_4 may be represented as replacing hydrogen. The view of the constitution of such bodies, given under nitrobenzoic acid, is, however, to be preferred. Phenol has, like alcohol, an atom of hydrogen, replaceable by a metal, and all these derived compounds have acid characters and are monobasic. The *trinitric phenol* is interesting as the final result of the action of nitric acid upon many organic substances, and has been described under the names of *picric*, *nitropicric*, *carbazotic*, and *nitrophenisic* acids. It is $C_{12}H_3(NO_4)_3O_2 = C_{12}H_3N_3O_{14}$, and forms yellowish-white crystalline scales, which dissolve in a large quantity of water, yielding a deep-yellow solution, with an intensely bitter taste. Its salts are yellow, and explode when heated. That of potash $C_{12}(H_2K)N_3O_{14}$ is a crystalline salt, very sparingly soluble in water.

791. The action of nitric acid upon benzen yields a dense oily liquid, which has a very sweet taste, and an odor like the essence of bitter almonds, for which it is substituted in perfumery. It contains $C_{12}H_5NO_4$, and, by the further action of a mixture of nitric and sulphuric acid, fixes a second equivalent of the nitrous elements, and yields $C_{12}H_4N_2O_8$. Nitrobenzen is to nitrophenol what nitrous ether is to nitric ether, and is the nitrous ether of phenol, or $N(C_{12}H_5)O_4 = C_{12}H_5NO_4$, and the second product may be regarded as $N(C_{12}H_5.NO_4)O_4$, still corresponding to $N(H)O_4$.

792. Phenol combines with ammonia and forms $C_{12}H_6O_2$, NH_3. When this compound is heated in a sealed tube, it is converted into water, and a new alkaloid: $C_{12}H_6O_2 + NH_3 = H_2O_2 + C_{12}H_7N$. This is an ammonia in which $C_{12}H_5$ replaces H, and is $N(C_{12}H_5.H_2)$. The same group may replace an atom of hydrogen in the alcohol-ammonias, and mixed ammonias containing the different alcoholic and phenic carbohydrogens, are thus obtained. To this new alkaloid the name of *aniline* is given: it is a colorless, oily liquid, with a pleasant vinous odor, a burning taste, and is poisonous: it boils at 328°, and has a specific gravity of 1·028. Aniline is slightly soluble in water; it decomposes metallic solutions, and with acids acts the part of a strong alkali, forming crystalline salts. These salts by heat yield compounds analogous to the amids, which are called *anilids*. They are amids in which $C_{12}H_5$ replaces H. The presence of aniline is readily detected by a solution of hypochlorite

of lime or bleaching-powder, which produces a beautiful violet-blue with a solution of the alkaloid. It occurs as a product of the destructive distillation of many organic matters, and is associated with phenol in coal-tar.

When an alcoholic solution of nitrobenzen is mixed with sulphuric acid and a fragment of zinc, the hydrogen evolved by the decomposition of the acid reacts with the nitrobenzen to form aniline and water, $C_{12}H_5NO_4+3H_2=C_{12}H_7N+2H_2O_2$. Sulphuretted hydrogen produces a similar effect, sulphur being separated. When binitric benzen is thus treated, an alkaloid is obtained, which is *nitric aniline*, in which one equivalent of the nitric elements enters into the alkaloid; it is $C_{12}H_6(NO_4)N$.

By indirect processes, alkaloids are obtained which correspond to aniline, in which H and H_2 are replaced by chlorine and bromine. Their basic powers are less strong than the normal aniline, and the trichloric species $C_{12}H_4Cl_3N$ is no longer an alkaloid. When by double decomposition we endeavor to obtain a hyponitrite of aniline, the salt is at once decomposed into phenol, nitrogen gas, and water, $C_{12}H_7N+NHO_4=C_{12}H_6O_2+H_2O_2+N_2$.

793. When benzoate of lime is submitted to distillation, the principal product is a body corresponding to the aceton of acetic acid; two equivalents of benzoate $2C_{14}(H_5Ca)O_4=C_2Ca_2O_6+C_{26}H_{10}O_2$. The new compound is fusible, volatile, and crystallizes in large prisms, which are soluble in alcohol and ether; fused with hydrate of potash, it is decomposed into benzoate and benzen, $C_{26}H_{10}O_2+(KH)O_2=C_{14}(H_5K)O_4+C_{12}H_6$. From this relation to benzoates and benzen or phene, it has received the name of *benzophenon*: with chemical agents it affords several new and curious compounds.

Benzoilol is one of a group of aldehyds which are represented by the general formula $C_nH_{n-8}O_2$, and yield volatile monobasic acids with O_4, decomposable into C_2O_4 and carbohydrogens C_nH_{n-6}, which form alkaloids $C_nH_{n-5}N$. The essence of the seeds of cumin (*Cuminum cyminum*) consists of such an aldehyd, *cuminol* $C_{20}H_{12}O_2$, and a carbohydrogen homologous with benzen, *cymen* $C_{20}H_{14}$. The distillation of *cuminic acid* with baryta affords another homologue, *cumen* $C_{18}H_{12}$. This with strong nitric acid yields nitrocumen, but, by long boiling with dilute acid, it is converted into benzoic acid In the same way cymen gives rise to a new acid, called *tolulic acid*, which is $C_{16}H_8O_4$, and homologous with benzoic and cuminic acids; with baryta it yields *toluen* $C_{14}H_8$, which is also obtained by the distillation of *tolu balsam*. Alkaloids homologous with aniline have been formed from all these hydrocarbons. The action of nitric acid upon benzen has failed to yield an acid lower in the series than the benzoic.

Phenol belongs to another group of what may be termed alcohols, which are represented by the general formula $C_nH_{n-6}O_2$. There is still another class of aldehyds, represented by $C_nH_{n-8}O_4$, which are consequently metameric with the acids of the benzoic group, and which form acid with O_2. Such is *salicylol*, the essential oil of *Spirea ulmaria*, (queen of the meadow.)

Salicylol, $C_{14}H_6O_4$.

794. This is obtained by distilling the flowers of spirea with water; the oil does not pre-exist in the plant, but is formed during the process, like benzoilol, by the reaction of principles in the plant which have not yet been examined. It may also be formed from *salicine*, a vegetable principle extracted from several species of *Salix*, to which both substances owe their name. Salicylol is a colorless liquid, heavier than water, in which it is somewhat soluble, and has the fragrant odor which is perceived when the flowers of spirea are bruised. Its composition $C_{14}H_6O_4$ is identical with that of benzoic acid. One atom of hydrogen in it may be replaced by chlorine or bromine, and an atom of hydrogen is also replaceable by a metal yielding compounds like $C_{14}H_5KO_4$. It forms a crystalline compound with ammonia, which soon changes into an amid like hydrobenzamid.

Heated with hydrate of potash, hydrogen is evolved and a salt of *salicylic acid* is formed. The acid is $C_{14}H_6O_6$. It crystallizes in delicate white prisms, and is volatile and sparingly soluble in water. Salicylic acid is monobasic, and has considerable resemblance to the benzoic; it forms a coupled acid with nitric acid.

795. The ethers of salicylic acid are easily formed: that of methol is interesting, because it constitutes the principal part of the fragrant essential oil of winter-green, *Gaultheria procumbens*, obtained by distilling that plant with water.

The ether is readily decomposed by an alcoholic solution

of hydrate of potash, and yields wood-spirit and salicylate of potash. If to the hot solution of the salt an excess of chlorohydric acid is added, the salicylic acid crystallizes on cooling. Ammonia converts the ether into a crystalline mass of *salicylamid*, which has the composition of salicylate of ammonia minus H_2O_2.

When the salicylic acid is rapidly distilled, it is decomposed into carbonic acid and phenol $C_{14}H_6O_4 = C_2O_4 + C_{12}H_6O_2$. If strong nitric acid is added to the oil of winter-green or salicylic acid, and the mixture boiled so long as red vapors appear, a large quantity of *trinitric phenol*, nitropicric acid, is obtained on cooling.

The essences of anise, fennel, and some other plants, consist principally of an oil, to which the name of *anethol* has been given. It is $C_{20}H_{12}O_2$: by oxydizing agents, such as nitric acid, it is converted into oxalic acid, and a new acid resembling the salicylic and homologous with it, which is called *anisic acid* $C_{16}H_8O_6$. Its decomposition yields carbonic acid and *anisol* $C_{14}H_8O_2$, a homologue of phenol.

Other Essential Oils.

796. The essences just described are types of a large number of essential oils, which, although not all homologous with the classes named, sustain the relation of aldehyds or alcohols to corresponding acids. Such is the oil of *cinnamon*, which is $C_{18}H_8O_2$, and yields by oxydation *cinnamic acid* $C_{18}H_8O_4$. This acid is associated with the benzoic, which it resembles, in its properties, in the *balsam of tolu*: by nitric acid it is oxydized and yields benzoic acid. When distilled with baryta it is decomposed into carbonic acid and a carbohydrogen, *cinnamen* $C_{16}H_8$.

Both cinnamol and cinnamen appear to exist in the balsams, such as *styrax*, *benzoin*, *tolu*, and the *balsam of Peru*. These consist of resinous matters, apparently formed by the oxydation of essential oils, and mixed with cinnamic or benzoic acids, or with both.

797. The oxygenized essences already described are, as in the case of cuminal, often associated with other oils, which, like cymen, contain no oxygen, and these carbohydrogen oils sometimes constitute the only product of the distillation. The most important of this class has the formula $C_{20}H_8$, and is best known under the form of *oil of turpentine*. It is obtained by distillation from the crude turpentine which

exudes from many species of *Pinus*, and is a mixture of the volatile oil and a resin. Its taste and odor are well known; it has a specific gravity of ·865, and boils at 312°. It is insoluble in water, but soluble in alcohol. Oil of turpentine is of great use in the arts, for the preparation of varnishes and paints, and is used for illumination, under the names of *camphene* and *pine-oil*. The liquids sold for the same purpose, under the names of *burning-fluid* and *spirit-gas*, are solutions of camphene in highly rectified alcohol, and, from their great volatility and inflammability, are very liable to explosion and dangerous accidents.

798. The oils of *juniper*, *pepper*, *caraway*, *parsley*, *citron*, *lemon*, *orange*, and *bergamot* are carbohydrogens, identical in composition, density, and boiling point with oil of turpentine, and may be included under the general name of camphen. They absorb chlorohydric acid gas, and yield a crystalline compound, which is $C_{20}H_{16}.HCl = C_{20}H_{17}Cl$, and has all the characters of a substitution product from $C_{20}H_{18}$. The liquid portion of the oil which has been treated with the gas has the same composition as the solid. This is crystalline and volatile, and has an odor like ordinary camphor. The essence of citron, unlike the others, fixes 2HCl, and yields a compound $C_{20}H_{18}Cl_2$. These chlorinized bodies are decomposed when distilled with lime, and yield modifications of camphen, distinguishable principally by their odors and their different action upon polarized light.

799. When moist oil of turpentine is exposed to cold, it often deposits a crystalline compound: a similar substance is slowly separated from a mixture of the oil with alcohol and nitric acid. It crystallizes in beautiful prisms, and is volatile, very soluble in alcohol, and sparingly soluble in water. The composition of this new body is represented by $C_{20}H_{20}O_4$, and it is therefore formed by the fixation of $2H_2O_2$; it crystallizes with an additional equivalent of water, which is expelled by heat: the name of *terebol* is given to it. When dissolved by boiling, in water acidulated with sulphuric or chlorohydric acid, it is completely decomposed into water and a volatile liquid, *terpinol*, which is obtained by distillation and has an odor of hyacinths: it is $C_{40}H_{34}O_2$. Chlorohydric acid gas expels water from fused terebol, and yields $C_{20}H_{18}Cl_2$, a crystalline body identical in composition with that obtained from lemon camphen.

The odors of these different varieties of the same carbohydrogen depend upon differences in constitution not yet understood; they are apparently independent of the presence of any oxygenized compound, as the different essences may be distilled from hydrate of potash or potassium, with no other effect than that of refining their odors. The *oil of roses* is a carbohydrogen of different composition, probably $C_{20}H_{20}$.

800. Many of the oxygenated volatile oils deposit, by cold, crystalline compounds which are often isomeric with the oils themselves, and are distinguished by the general name of *stearoptens*, or *camphors* of their respective oils, from their resemblance to common camphor. This substance is obtained by distilling the wood of the *Laurus camphora* with water, and is crystalline, very volatile, fragrant, and soluble in alcohol, but insoluble in water. Its formula is $C_{20}H_{16}O_2$; heated with hydrate of potash under pressure, it combines directly with it and forms a salt, *campholate of potash* $C_{20}(H_{17}K)O_4$. With strong nitric acid it yields *camphoric acid* $C_{20}H_{16}O_8$, which is bibasic.

801. The *Drybalanops camphora* of Borneo yields a solid fragrant essence, which is known as *Borneo camphor*, and is much valued in the East: it also exists in the essential oil of valerian. This camphor has the formula $C_{20}H_{18}O_2$, and, when heated with nitric acid, loses H_2 and yields laurel camphor. When distilled with anhydrous phosphoric acid, it yields a form of camphen which exists with the camphor in the plant, and fixes H_2O_2 to form it. When laurel camphor is thus distilled, a carbohydrogen $C_{20}H_{14}$ is obtained, which is *cymen*.

802. The essential oil of black mustard-seed *Sinapis nigra*, is obtained by distilling the bruised seeds with water. It is heavier than water, pungent and acrid, and contains sulphur. It is represented by the formula $C_8H_5NS_2$. With ammonia it combines and forms a crystalline alkaloid, *thiosinamine* $C_8H_8N_2S_2$, which, when heated with oxyd of lead, loses H_2S_2 and forms sulphuret of lead and water, together with a new alkaloid $C_8H_6N_2$, called *sinamine*, which is crystalline, and is a strong base.

The essential oil of horse-radish, *Cochlearia officinalis*, is identical with that of mustard. The oil of asafœtida contains carbon, hydrogen, and sulphur: it is probably $C_{12}H_{12}S_2$, and seems allied to a sulphuretted ether or alcohol: with chlorid of mercury it forms a crystalline compound which contains the elements of the oil with those of the mercurial salt. When mixed with sulphocyanid of potassium, a decomposition ensues which gives rise to the essential oil of mustard. The oil of garlic belongs to the same series, which is very interesting from its curious and as yet imperfectly known relations.

The odorous secretion of the polecat, *Mephitis putorius*, contains sulphur, and perhaps belongs to the same class.

803. *Resins.*—These substances are vegetable products, and seem to have been generally formed by the oxydation of essential oils; they are insoluble in water, but soluble in alcohol and ether, and many of them are used in pharmacy and in the arts. Among them are *copal, mastic, elemi, guiacum*, and *colophony* or *pine resin*. In their crude state they are often mixed with volatile oils, which may be separated by distillation with water, as those of turpentine and elemi, or with soluble acids, like the benzoic and cinnamic, as in the balsams, and often with gums and other principles soluble in water, constituting what are called in the *materia medica, gum resins*, like asafœtida and gamboge. The true resins are many of them acids, and form distinct salts with bases. The resin of the pine may be obtained by careful management from its alcoholic solution, in crystalline crusts, very soluble in ether and sparingly soluble in alcohol. Exposed to heat, it distils over and condenses in an isomeric modification, distinguished in its crystallization and solubility. Under certain circumstances, both varieties may be converted into an amorphous form. They have been denominated *pimaric* and *sylvic acids*, and are both monobasic, and represented by $C_{40}H_{30}O_4$. Two equivalents of oil of turpentine and O_6, yield H_2O_2 and an equivalent of pimaric acid. The resins of *copaiva, elemi*, and *anime* belong to one or another of the modifications of this acid.

804. *Caoutchouc, Gum-Elastic.*—This curious substance is found in the juices of many plants, but is principally obtained from the *Hevea guianensis*, and *Iatropha elastica*. Its ordinary properties are well known: it is insoluble in water and alcohol, but dissolves in ether and many volatile hydrocarbons: when softened by these solvents, it is wrought into a great variety of curious and useful articles. Small tubes of gum-elastic are very useful in the laboratory, to join glass tubes and form flexible joints. They are easily made from sheet caoutchouc by cutting the folded edges of the

sheet with clean scissors over a glass tube, as seen in figure 417. Caoutchouc is very combustible, and burns with a bright smoky flame. It contains carbon and hydrogen only, and probably in equal equivalents, but it furnishes no reactions by which we may fix its formula or even determine whether it is chemically homogeneous. When exposed to heat it is decomposed, and yields several volatile hydrocarbons homologous with olefiant gas: among them are said to be C_8H_8, $C_{10}H_{10}$, and $C_{40}H_{40}$. These mixed liquids are used as a solvent for caoutchouc; the volatile oils from coal-tar are also employed for the same purpose.

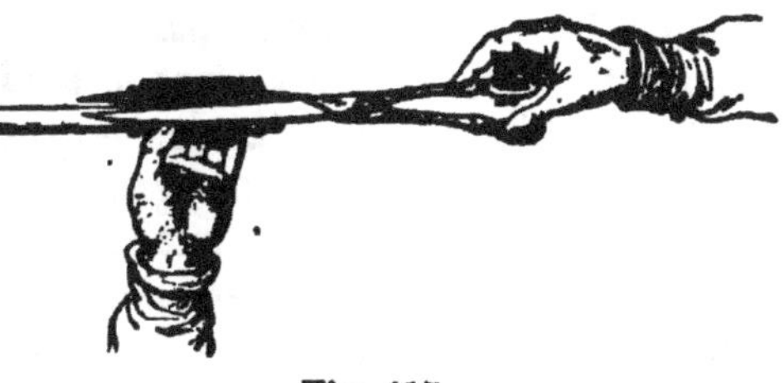

Fig. 417.

When caoutchouc is immersed in a bath of melted sulphur, or when sulphur is added to its substance and the material afterward exposed to a considerable heat, (280°,) the caoutchouc undergoes a peculiar change. It becomes much firmer and stronger, and less liable to be softened by heat or rendered rigid by cold; in this form it is known as *vulcanized gum-elastic*, and is extensively used in the arts, in preference to the unaltered caoutchouc. This is Goodyear's patent.

805. *Gutta Percha.*—This substance exudes from the *Isonandra gutta*, a tree common in the Malaccan peninsula, and forms a tough and elastic mass at ordinary temperatures, which becomes ductile and plastic when warmed by immersion in hot water. Gutta percha (pronounced *pertcha*) is a mixture of several resins, which are separable from each other by means of their different solubility in alcohol and ether. The greater portion of it consists of a resin which softens at 104° F., and is but little soluble in cold ether when pure. It contains a greater amount of oxygen than pimaric acid. Gutta percha is readily dissolved by chloroform and sulphuret of carbon, which deposit it unchanged by evaporation. It is capable of being moulded into a great many articles of utility and ornament.

VEGETAL ACIDS.

806. Besides the acids which we have described as derived from bodies of the alcohol group, or from the various essential oils, and which are generally monobasic, volatile, and

when of high equivalents, sparingly soluble in water, there remains to be described a class of acids of high equivalents, which are bibasic or tribasic, very soluble in water, and contain a large amount of oxygen, having analogies with the lactic acid. Such are the oxalic, citric, tartaric, and malic acids, and some others of less consequence.

807 *Oxalic Acid*, $C_4H_2O_8$.—The salts of this acid exist in many vegetables: the agreeably sour taste of the wood-sorrel, *Oxalis acetosella*, of the common sorrel, a species of *Rumex*, and many other plants, is due to the acid oxalate of potash which they contain, and from which the acid may be extracted. It is also a product of the action of nitric acid upon alcohol, upon sugar, starch, lignin, and many other organic substances. To prepare it, one part of sugar is heated with eight parts of nitric acid, specific gravity 1·25. A violent action ensues, and much nitrous acid is evolved; when this ceases, the solution is concentrated by evaporation, and on cooling yields a large quantity of crystals of oxalic acid, which are purified by washing in a little cold water and recrystallization.

808. Oxalic acid forms colorless crystals, which are $C_4H_2O_8+2H_2O_2$; by a gentle heat the water is expelled, and the dry acid remains as a white powder, which, at a higher temperature, is in part sublimed unchanged, and partly decomposed into formic acid, water, carbonic acid and carbonic oxyd gases. The acid is very soluble in water, has a strongly acid taste, and is poisonous. When the acid or one of its salts is heated with strong sulphuric acid, it is decomposed without blackening, a character by which it is distinguished from the succeeding acids, and evolves equal volumes of carbonic acid and carbonic oxyd gases; $C_4H_2O_8=C_2O_4+C_2O_2+H_2O_2$.

Oxalic acid is bibasic; the neutral oxalate of potash is a very soluble salt, and is $C_4(K_2)O_8$; the acid oxalate $C_4(KH)O_8$ is less soluble, and has a pleasant acid taste. It is known under the name of *binoxalate*, and as it was formerly obtained from the wood-sorrel, is often sold as *salt of sorrel*, for the purpose of removing iron-stains from linen, which it does by forming a soluble salt with the iron oxyd. The acid oxalate crystallizes with another equivalent of oxalic acid to form a salt which is called a *quadroxalate*, and contains $C_4H_2O_8+C_4(HK)O_8$, or one-fourth the amount of potash that is in the neutral oxalate. The acid might hence be regarded as quadribasic, and be $C_8H_4O_{16}$, but its other reactions lead to the conclusion that it is properly bibasic. The second equivalent of acid may be regarded as holding a place analogous to that of the crystal-water in other salts. The oxalate of ammonia $C_4(NH_4)_2O_8$ crystallizes in fine prisms; when decomposed by heat it loses $2H_2O_2$, and yields the amid of oxalic acid, *oxamid*, which is $C_4H_4N_2O_4$. It is a neutral insoluble body, and by the action of acids is reconverted into oxalate. The acid oxalate of ammonia yields in like manner an acid amid, *oxamic acid*, $C_4H_2O_8+NH_3=C_4H_5NO_8-H_2O_2=C_4H_3NO_6$. It is monobasic, and forms a series of salts: when its solution is boiled it is changed into acid oxalate of ammonia.

The oxalate of lime crystallizes with $2H_2O_2$; it is a very insoluble salt, and occupies an important part in the vegetable economy, being secreted by a large number of plants, in the cells of which the microscope reveals a great number of beautiful crystals of this substance; this appearance is represented in figure 418, of a vessel from the bark of *Torreya taxifolia*. In many of the lichens, the oxalate of lime appears to replace the woody fibre, and to be somewhat allied in its functions to the carbonates and phosphates of lime in the animal kingdom. The oxalates of the metals are generally insoluble.

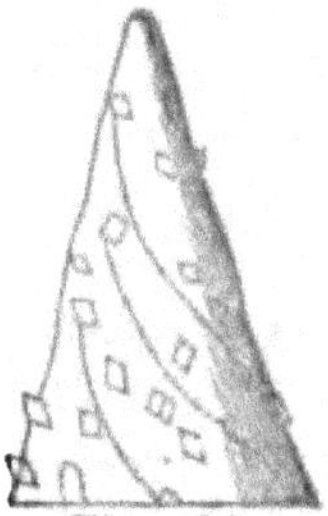

Fig. 418.

With two equivalents of the alcohols, oxalic acid forms neutral ethers; and with one, vinic acids. The oxalic ether of wood-spirit is obtained in fine crystals; it is $C_4(Me_2)O_8$: mixed ethers of the different alcohols may be obtained, such as $C_4(EtMe)O_8$. When ammonia in excess is added to oxalic ether, oxamid is obtained; but if the ammonia is cautiously added, a beautiful crystalline substance is formed, which is named *oxamethane*, and regenerates an oxalate, alcohol and ammonia, by fixing $2H_2O_2$. It corresponds to *sulphamethane*, and is at once the amid of oxalovinic acid, and the ether of oxamic acid. Oxalic acid pertains to the series already described under oleic acid, including succinic and suberic acids, and represented by $C_nH_{n-2}O_8$; when fused with hydrate of potash it yields a formate.

809. *Tartaric Acid*, $C_8H_6O_{12}$.—This acid exists in the juices of many fruits, particularly that of the grape, as an acid tartrate of potash. As this salt is almost insoluble in dilute

alcohol, it is deposited, during the fermentation of wine, as crystalline crusts, known as *crude tartar*, or *argol*. It is decomposed by chalk to form a tartrate of lime; this is mixed with an equivalent of sulphuric acid, which forms a sulphate, and liberates the tartaric acid. From a concentrated solution it crystallizes in fine rhombic prisms, very soluble in water and alcohol, and having a pleasant acid taste. Tartaric acid is bibasic. The acid tartrate of potash $C_8(H_5K)O_{12}$ is prepared by refining the crude tartar by crystallization, and generally appears as a crystalline powder, sparingly soluble in water, and feebly acid to the taste. It is known in pharmacy as *cream of tartar*. The neutral tartrate is mu h more soluble in water, and is commonly called *soluble tartar*. It is $C_8(H_4K_2)O_{12}$. By saturating cream of tartar with carbonate of soda, a double salt is obtained which is $C_8(H_4KNa)O_{12}$: it forms very large transparent prismatic crystals, and is known as *Rochelle salt*.

810. When cream of tartar and oxyd of antimony are boiled together in water, solution takes place, and, on cooling, transparent crystals of a double salt are deposited, which is known in medicine by the name of *tartar emetic*.

The part which the oxyd of antimony plays in this compound is peculiar. We may represent two equivalents of oxyd of antimony $2SbO_3 = Sb_2O_6$ as $(SbO_2)_2O_2$, corresponding to H_2O_2, and the group SbO_2 will then be equivalent to H, and may replace it in combination. The salt in question is such a compound, and the acid tartrate being $C_8H_4(HK)O_{12}$, tartar emetic dried at 212° is $C_8H_4(SbO_2.K)O_{12}$. The crystals at the ordinary temperature contain H_2O_2 as water of crystallization, but lose it by a gentle heat. If the dried salt is heated to 428°, it breaks up into water H_2O_2, and a salt which is $C_8H_2(SbK)O_{12}$: in this compound antimony in one-third its ordinary equivalent may be supposed to replace hydrogen as in the analogous compounds of the sesqui-oxyds: if we call this Sb⅓, *stibicum*, and represent it by sb, the dried salt then becomes $C_8H_2(sb_3K)O_{12}$: it is then, however, quadribasic. Oxyd of uranium UO_2 may in the same way replace H in a tartrate, and by heat U⅓, corresponding to sb, and represented by ur may be obtained in combination, replacing H: in this way all the hydrogen is removed and a compound obtained which is $C_8(ur_3sb_3)O_{12}$. Arsenious acid AsO_3 and boracic acid BoO_3

afford, with bitartrate of potash, compounds analogous to these salts of oxyd of antimony.

Tartaric acid dissolves peroxyd of iron and forms a very soluble salt: in this, as in the preceding compounds, the metal is not precipitated by solutions of potash or ammonia. The decomposition of tartaric acid by heat produces several new acids, which have not yet been thoroughly studied.

811. The crude tartar obtained from the wine of the Vosges some years since, was found to contain an isomeric modification of tartaric acid, which is less soluble than the ordinary acid, and crystallizes with an equivalent of water, while the common form is anhydrous: the new acid precipitates solution of the salts of lime, and in the chemical characters of several of its salts is distinguished from the ordinary tartaric acid, with which however it is metameric: it has received the name of *racemic acid*. The replacements of the crystals of tartaric acid and of its salts are upon alternate angles, constituting what is called a hemihedral modification, and the order of the replacements is from left to right: a solution of tartaric acid or of any tartrate acts upon polarized light, and causes the ray to rotate in the same direction. Racemic acid and its salts are not hemihedral, and do not affect in any way the ray of polarized light. When, however, a solution of the double racemate of potash and ammonia is crystallized, two sets of crystals are obtained in equal quantities: the one are hemihedric to the right, and identical in all respects with the ordinary tartrate of these bases: the others have left-handed hemihedrism, and cause the beam of polarized light to deviate to the left; and these two salts contain two tartaric acids which are distinguished from each other only by their opposite hemihedral modifications and their action upon polarized light. The right-handed acid is ordinary tartaric acid, and the left-handed a new and a distinct modification; and these two are not by any known means convertible into one another. The forms of the two crystals are to each other as the image in a mirror is to the object. When saturated solutions of the two acids are mixed, they become warm, and deposit crystals of the racemic acid, in which their mutual influence upon polarized light is neutralized.

812. *Malic Acid*, $C_8H_6O_{10}$.—This acid exists in the juices of many sour fruits, particularly in the apple and the berries of the mountain ash, *Sorbus aucuparia*: the stems of

the garden rhubarb also contain a large quantity of it It is very soluble in water and alcohol, and crystallizes with difficulty; its solution has a pleasant eour taste. The malic acid is bibasic, and the malates of the alkaline bases are very soluble. The acid malate of ammonia $C_8(H_5NH_4)O_{10}$ forms large transparent crystals. The neutral malate of lead $C_8(H_4Pb_2)O_{10}$ is obtained as a white readily fusible precipitate, which in an acid liquid slowly changes into delicate crystals. Malic acid is not volatile, but is decomposed by heat into water and new acids, which are described in the larger works.

813. When tartaric and malic acids are heated with anhydrous alcohol, vinic acids are obtained corresponding to the sulphovinic. The neutral ethers are more difficult of preparation, as they are soluble in water and not volatile: by passing hydrochloric acid gaa, however, through the alcoholic solutions of the acids, neutralizing the excess of acid with carbonate of soda, and agitating the mixture with hydric ether, the ethers of the acids are dissolved out, and may be obtained by evaporating the solution at a gentle heat. They are converted by ammonia into amids and ethers of amidic acids: in this way *tartramic acid* and *tartramid* may be obtained.

814. Malic ether yields *malamid*, which has the composition of and appears to be identical with *asparagine*, a peculiar nitrogenized principle found in the juices of the asparagus, mallows, and particularly in the young shoots of vetches which have vegetated in the dark. It forms large crystals, sparingly soluble in cold water, and contains $C_8H_8N_2O_6$, corresponding to malate of ammonia from which the elements of water have been abstracted, $C_8H_4(NH_4)_2O_{10}-2H_2O_2=C_8H_8N_2O_6$: by the action of alkalies or acids i' loses ammonia and yields *aspartic* acid $C_8H_7NO_8$, which is now found to be identical with *malamic acid*, and to be formed from acid malate of ammonia as oxamic acid is from the acid oxalate.

The ordinary action of acids or alkalies does not further decompose this acid; but when nitric oxyd is passed into a solution of asparagine or aspartic acid in nitric acid, the hyponitrous acid formed, decomposes the aspartic, yielding malic acid, nitrogen, and water, by a decomposition similar to that described under aniline: $C_8H_7NO_8+NHO_4=C_8H_8O_{10}+N_2+H_2O_2$.

Citric Acid, $C_{12}H_8O_{14}$.—This acid exists in the juices of many fruits, often associated with the tartaric and malic, and is the acid of lemons. It is obtained by saturating lemon-juice with chalk, by which an insoluble citrate of lime is formed; this is decomposed with an equivalent of sulphuric acid, which forms sulphate of lime, and the citric acid is obtained by evaporation and crystallization. It forms large crystals belonging to the trimetric system; it is very soluble in water, and has a strong but agreeable acid taste. The citric acid is tribasic, and forms with potash three salts, in which one, two and three atoms of hydrogen are replaced by potassium : the first two salts are acid, and the last, which is $C_{12}(H_5K_3)O_{14}$, is neutral. In the same way it yields a neutral ether with three equivalents of alcohol, and vinic acids with one and two equivalents.

When exposed to heat, citric acid is decomposed into H_2O_2 and $C_{12}H_6O_{12}$; this is a new acid, which is also found combined with lime in the *Aconitum napellus*, and is hence called *aconitic acid;* it is tribasic and very soluble in water: when the action of heat is carried still further, the aconitic acid is decomposed into C_2O_4 and $C_{10}H_6O_8$; this last is called *citraconic acid*, and is bibasic, soluble, and by heat distils in part unchanged: a higher temperature decomposes it into water, and a neutral liquid $C_{10}H_4O_6$. This substance, which is called *citraconid*, slowly dissolves in water, and combines with H_2O_2 to form an acid isomeric with citraconic acid.

815. *Tannic Acid, Tannin.*—Many plants contain a peculiar principle, characterized by an astringent taste, and by precipitating animal gelatine from its solutions, forming with it an insoluble compound, upon the production of which depends the prosess of tanning leather. The barks of oak and hemlock, and gall-nuts, which are excrescences resulting from the puncture of insects upon the branches of a species of oak, contain a large portion of this principle, which is named *tannic acid*, and are used in the preparation of leather: they are also employed with persalts of iron in dyeing black, and in the formation of writing-ink. The vegetable extracts called *kino* and *catechu*, and many other vegetable substances, contain a principle analogous to the tannin of the oak. Tannic acid is obtained in a pure state from gall-nuts, which yield about one-third of their weight, by the following process:—They are reduced to a coarse pow-

der, and placed in the upper part of a vessel like that represented in the figure, the mouth of which is previously stopped with a piece of linen, and a quantity of hydric ether is then poured over them, which slowly filters through, and collects in the lower vessel, where it separates into two layers. Ordinary ether contains about one-twelfth of water, which dissolves the tannic acid to the exclusion of all other substances, and forms a solution that does not mix with the ether, which dissolves a portion of coloring matter from the gall-nut. The dense aqueous solution is separated, washed with a little ether, and finally evaporated in shallow vessels by a gentle heat. It forms a brilliant porous mass, which has generally a light yellow tint; it is very soluble in water and has a purely astringent taste. Sulphuric, nitric, chlorohydric and phosphoric acids give copious precipitates with its solution, which are combinations of the two acids. The tannic is a feeble acid, and is bibasic or polybasic. The alkaline tannates are soluble; those of the metals are generally insoluble, and often colored. The pertannate of iron is the basis of black dyes; and of writing-ink: it is insoluble in water, but when the solutions are dilute, the precipitate remains a long time suspended, especially if a little gum is added, as in the fabrication of ink. When a solution of tannic acid in potash is heated, a salt of gallic acid is formed, with the production of a brown matter. Similar results are obtained when strong acids act upon tannin, and the powder of nut-galls mixed with water undergoes a sort of fermentation, which also yields gallic acid. When boiled for some time with dilute sulphuric acid, tannin is converted into gallic acid and grape sugar. The brown products obtained with strong acids and alkalies, result from the decomposition of the sugar which is produced. The probable formula of tannic acid is $C_{52}H_{24}O_{32}$; two equivalents of it with $6H_2O_2$ yield one of glucose, $C_{24}H_{24}O_{24}$, and two of gallic acid, $C_{14}H_6O_{10}$.

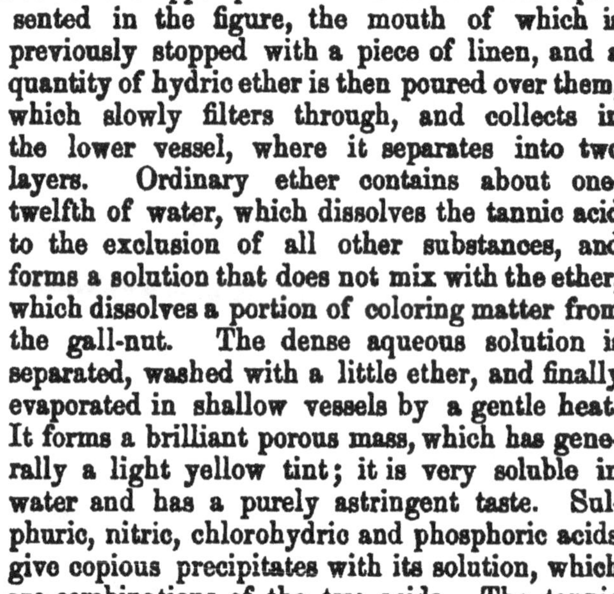
Fig. 419.

Gallic Acid, $C_{14}H_6O_{10}$.—This acid exists ready formed in the seeds of the mango: it is most easily prepared by the process of fermentation already described; it is dissolved out of the mixture by boiling water, and separates on cooling in small silky crystals, which require 100 parts of cold water for their solution, and have an acid and astringent taste. Gallic acid does not precipitate gelatine, and the black color of the pergallate of iron is destroyed by boiling. Gallic acid is bibasic: its salts have been but little studied. When carefully heated, it is decomposed into C_2O_4 and a crystalline sublimate, which is *pyrogallic acid*, and is $C_{12}H_6O_6$. It is very soluble in water and alcohol, and when dissolved in a solution of hydrate of potash, absorbs oxygen so rapidly from the air as to be employed in eudiometry.

Both gallic and pyrogallic acids reduce the salts of platinum, gold, and silver. An application of this is made for the purpose of coloring the human hair, which is first wet with a solution of gallic acid, and then, after drying, moistened with an ammoniacal solution of a salt of silver. The reduced metal imparts a fine black or brown color to the hair, which is permanent.

For a large number of other vegetable acids, many of which are yet but imperfectly known, the student is referred to more extended treatises.

VEGETAL ALKALOIDS.

816. The artificial organic alkaloids which we have described under different heads in the preceding pages, have been considered as derivatives of ammonia in which one or more atoms of hydrogen are replaced by the elements of some carburet of hydrogen; such are aniline and methamine. We have pointed out how these, like ammonia, may fix the elements of water, and form compounds analogous to hydrate of potash, such as the hydroxyd of vinic ammonium $(NEt_4.H)O_2$; but when these combine with an acid, the oxygen is eliminated in the equivalent of water which is formed, and it is but the group NEt_4, which replaces hydrogen in the acid. There are, however, a large number of organic bases occurring in different vegetable substances, which, like aniline and ammonia, combine directly with acids without the formation of water, and which contain oxygen. All of these alkaloids contain one and sometimes two atoms of nitrogen, and may be regarded as derivatives of ammonia in which the group of elements replacing hydrogen contains oxygen. They are commonly crystalline and not volatile

without decomposition, and generally possess active medicinal powers. Those of opium, cinchona, hellebore, and many others constitute the active principles of these drugs. When exposed to heat, especially in the presence of caustic alkalies, they are decomposed, and generally evolve volatile alkaloids without oxygen; among these, methamine and aniline are met with. Several other volatile alkaloids obtained by the action of a solution of hydrate of potash upon plants, are supposed to be the result of a similar decomposition.

817. Many of the vegetal alkaloids are strong bases, and completely neutralize acids; others are comparatively feeble, and their salts are even decomposed by a gentle heat.

They combine with chlorid of platinum to form double salts, which are generally sparingly soluble, and analogous to the chlorid of platinum and ammonium: some of them unite with one, and others with two equivalents of the chlorid, and in like manner they frequently form two chlorohydrates by fixing one and two equivalents of chlorohydric acid, thus giving rise to neutral and acid salts. The alkaloids combine with metallic salts in the same way as ammonia, and yield compounds with nitric acid, and with nitrate of silver. They generally form combinations with chlorid of mercury, which have a similar composition with the ammonia salts. We shall first describe some of the more important of the oxygenized alkaloids, and then proceed to speak of those analogous to aniline.

818. *Alkaloids of Cinchona, or Peruvian Bark.*—The barks of several species of cinchona owe their medicinal properties to the presence of two alkaloids, which are named *quinine* and *cinchonine*. They are extracted by digesting the bark in a dilute acid, and adding to the infusion a solution of carbonate of soda, which precipitates the alkaloids in an impure state. The precipitate is washed and dissolved in boiling alcohol; a little animal charcoal is added to remove some coloring matter, and the filtered liquid, on cooling, deposits crystals of cinchonine, while the more soluble quinine is obtained by evaporation. Quinine is a white crystalline substance, sparingly soluble in water, but readily so in alcohol and ether.

The formula of this alkaloid is $C_{38}H_{22}N_2O_4$. It is readily soluble in acids, forming crystallizable salts, which have a very bitter taste. These are two chlorohydrates, one $C_{38}H_{22}N_2O_4$.HCl, which if we would compare it with chlorid of ammonia, must be written $(C_{38}H_{23}N_2O_4)Cl = QuCl$, and a second acid salt QuCl.HCl, or $C_{38}H_{22}N_2O_4.2HCl$; the platinum double salt corresponds to this acid chlorohydrate: there exists, in like manner, two sulphates of quinine, which with several other salts of this base are employed in medicine. Cinchonine is represented by $C_{38}H_{22}N_2O_2$; it differs from quinine only by O_2, and resembles that base in its characters, but is less soluble in alcohol and ether. Its salts are similar to those of quinine, and are often substituted for the latter in medical practice.

819. In the preparation of these alkaloids, a portion of quinine is often obtained as an uncrystallizable resinous mass, which is, however, identical in chemical composition and medicinal properties with the crystalline base. It is called *quinoidine.* The cinchona known in commerce as *pale bark* contains principally cinchonine; the *yellow bark* quinine, and the *red bark,* a mixture of both. Different varieties of cinchona have furnished two or three other bases very similar to these; to which the names of *aricine, chinovatine,* and *quinidine* have been given.

These bases are accompanied with a peculiar acid, called *quinic* or *kinic* acid; it forms large crystals resembling tartaric acid, and is bibasic: its composition is represented by $C_{14}H_{12}O_{12}$. The results of its decomposition form a very interesting series.

By the action of chlorine and bromine upon solutions of chlorohydrate of cinchonine the hydrogen of the alkaloid is in part replaced, and *bichloric* and *bibromic cinchonine* are obtained; the former is $C_{38}H_{20}Cl_2N_2O_2$, and is isomorphous with the normal alkaloid.

When cinchonine is distilled with hydrate of potash, a carbonate is formed and hydrogen gas escapes, with a new volatile base named *chinoline* or *quinoline,* which is an oily liquid and resembles aniline in its properties. Its composition is represented by $C_{18}H_7N$: $C_{38}H_{22}N_2O_2 + 2(KH)O_2 = 2C_{18}H_7N + C_2K_2O_6 + 5H_2$. Quinine and strychnine yield chinoline by a similar process.

Alkaloids of Opium.—This substance is the inspissated juice of the capsules of a species of poppy, *Papaver somniferum,* and contains several organic bases. The most important of these, and the one to which it owes its power as an anodyne, is *morphine*. It is prepared by precipitating a solution of opium by carbonate of soda, as in the process for quinine; the impure morphine is digested in cold alcohol to remove some other alkaloids present, and finally dissolved in dilute acetic acid. The cautious addition of ammonia to the acetate thus formed, precipitates the morphine, which is dissolved in hot alcohol, and crystallizes on cooling. It forms brilliant rectangular prisms, which are sparingly soluble in water, readily so in hot alcohol, and insoluble in ether; it has a persistent bitter taste. Its formula is $C_{34}H_{19}NO_6$. Morphine forms crystalline salts, some of which, as the chlorohydrate, sulphate, and acetate, are employed in medicine. The best opium contains six or eight per cent. of this alkaloid.

820. *Codeine* is a base which occurs in small quantities with morphine; it is more soluble in water than that alkaloid, and dissolves readily in ether: it seems allied to morphine in its effects upon the animal system. The formula for codeine is $C_{36}H_{21}NO_6$. When heated with sulphuric acid, codeine yields a compound which is derived from the sulphate by the elimination of $2H_2O_2$, and corresponds to an amid: morphine and some other alkaloids yield similar compounds. Bases have been obtained from it in which portions of the hydrogen are replaced by chlorine, bromine, and the nitric elements. When heated with potash it evolves volatile bases, among which are ammonia and methamine.

Narcotine is another alkaloid, which occurs in considerable quantity in opium, and is separated from the morphine by being very soluble in ether and insoluble in water. It forms brilliant transparent crystals, and has the formula $C_{46}H_{25}NO_{14}$. Narcotine is but a feeble base: by oxydizing agents it is decomposed, and yields a peculiar acid called the *opianic* $C_{20}H_{10}O_{10}$, and a new alkaloid, *cotarnine* $C_{26}H_{13}NO_6$. In addition to these there have been observed several other bases in smaller quantities in opium: such are *narceine, papaverine*, and *thebaine*; they are but little known. Opium contains also a peculiar tribasic acid, the *meconic* $C_{14}H_4O_{14}$. It is not improbable that in certain seasons and conditions of soil and climate, different alkaloids may be formed in the same plant, and to an extent replace each other; that such is the case with different species of a genus is shown by the history of cinchona and some other plants.

821. *Strychnine.*—This alkaloid is found in the *Strychnos nux-vomica,* and several other plants of the same genus. It is prepared by digesting the nux-vomica with water acidulated by sulphuric acid, and precipitating the solution by caustic lime. The impure precipitate is boiled with alcohol and animal charcoal, and the liquid on cooling deposits the strychnine in crystals. It is almost insoluble in water, absolute alcohol, and ether, but dissolves in dilute alcohol: its salts are crystallizable, intensely bitter, and highly poisonous. Strychnine and its compounds produce a spasmodic affection of the muscles of voluntary motion; they are used in minute doses in cases of paralysis. The poison of the celebrated *upas* is the product of the *Strychnos tieute,* and owes its activity to strychnine. The formula for strychnine is $C_{42}H_{24}N_2O_4$.

Brucine is another organic base, which is associated with the last, in several species of *Strychnos.* It resembles strychnine but is more soluble in water and alcohol, and although similar in its action upon the animal system, is less potent. Its formula is $C_{46}H_{26}N_2O_8$. Both of these bases yield products in which the hydrogen is in part replaced by chlorine and bromine.

822. *Piperine* is a crystalline alkaloid extracted from black pepper, and is a feeble base: the formula $C_{70}H_{38}N_2O_{10}$ is assigned to it. When heated with a mixture of hydrate of potash and quick-lime it disengages two volatile bases, one of which appears to be *picoline,* an alkaloid which is metameric with aniline, and is obtained as a product of the distillation of bones. The other, to which the name of *piperidine* is given, has the formula $C_{10}H_{11}N$: it boils at 212° F., is soluble in water, caustic, and has a strong odor of ammonia. Piperidine is homologous with arsine and stibethine, having the general formula $C_nH_{n+1}N$; N being replaceable by As or Sb. These are alcoholic ammonias which have lost H_2, and may have one, two, or three atoms of the hydrogen in NH_3 replaced by the alcoholic elements. Thus arsine has but one, and stibethine three equivalents of the carbohydrogen, while the new base has two, which may correspond to the vinic and propionic, C_4 and C_6; or to the butyric and methylic, C_8 and C_2. Piperdine, with one equivalent of hydriodic ether, exchanges H for C_4H_5, to form a new base; but with a second yields an iodid, which

is $NC_{10}H_{10}Et_2.I$, and corresponds to the iodid of vinic ammonium.

823. *Theine; Caffeine*, $C_{16}H_{10}N_4O_4$.—This organic base is found in *coffee*, *tea*, the fruit of the *Paulinia sorbalis*, and the *Ilex paraguayensis*, which affords the *matte*, or Paraguay tea. It is most abundant in green tea, which contains from two to five per cent.; the best coffee does not yield one per cent. To obtain it, a strong decoction of tea is mixed with a solution of the surbasic acetate of lead, as long as a precipitate is formed; to the clear solution a little ammonia is added to precipitate the excess of lead, and the liquid by evaporation furnishes theine in delicate silky crystals. It is readily soluble in hot water and alcohol, and may be volatilized without decomposition; its taste is slightly bitter. Theine is a feeble base, and its salts are easily decomposed: the chlorohydrate crystallizes beautifully. With nitrate of silver it yields a salt in fine crystalline groups, which is $C_{16}H_{10}N_4O_4 + NAgO_6$.

It is worthy of notice, that the plants which furnish this alkaloid are used by different nations to prepare a grateful and gently stimulating beverage. As these substances resemble each other only in containing theine, it is probable that they owe their common properties to the presence of this principle, and that, in some unknown manner, it promotes digestion and the other vital functions. The Brazilians prepare from the fruit of the *Paulinia sorbalis* an extract called by them *guarana*, which is much esteemed as a remedy in dysentery and nephritic complaints; it contains a considerable quantity of theine.

824. The seeds of the *Theobroma cacao*, from which chocolate is prepared, yield an alkaloid *theobromine*, which resembles caffeine and is homologous with it: it is $C_{14}H_8N_4O_4$, and the common formula of the two is therefore $C_nH_{n-6}N_4O_4$. With chlorine and oxydizing agents these alkaloids yield a series of interesting bodies, to which we shall again advert.

825. *Solanine*, from the *Solanum nigrum*, and several other species,—*hyoscyamine*, from *Hyoscyamus niger*,—*atropine*, from *Atropa belladonna*, and *daturine*, from *Datura stramonium*, are alkaline principles which possess in great perfection the poisonous properties of the plants from which they are derived. They are obtained by somewhat complicated processes, and are crystalline and volatile. Their salts are

employed in medicine. *Veratrine* is found in the *Veratrum album*, or white hellebore; it forms a white crystalline powder, which is insoluble in water, but soluble in alcohol. It is a powerful acrid poison, but is used medicinally in neuralgia with beneficial results. *Aconitine* is obtained from the *Aconitum napellus*, and resembles veratrine in its properties. *Sanguinarine* is an alkaloid which exists in the blood-root, *Sanguinaria canadensis*, and to which this plant owes its active properties. *Emetine*, the emetic principle of *ipecacuanha*, is also an organic alkaloid. There are many other oxygenized bases which have been artificially formed. Such are *benzoline*, which has been described as an isomeric modification of hydrobenzamid, and many more, which the limits of this treatise will not permit us to notice.

826. Of the volatile bases analogous to aniline and chinoline, obtained from plants, but two have been much studied, nicotine and conine. *Nicotine* is the alkaloid of tobacco, and is obtained by distilling a concentrated infusion of the plant with lime or hydrate of potash. The recent plant contains a peculiar crystalline body, called *nicotianine*, which affords nicotine by the action of caustic potash; but in the prepared tobacco, nicotine exists ready formed, and can be extracted by the action of ether to which a little ammonia has been added. When tobacco is smoked in a German pipe, the liquid which condenses in the well contains a large quantity of this alkaloid. The strongest Virginia tobacco affords, when dry, six or seven per cent. of the alkaloid, and mild Havanna tobacco no more than two per cent.

The formula of nicotine is $C_{20}H_{14}N_2$. It is an oily liquid heavier than water, in which it is somewhat soluble. It distils at a high temperature unchanged. The taste of nicotine is very acrid, and its odor recalls that of tobacco; it is extremely poisonous. This base is strongly alkaline and forms very soluble salts; it fixes 2HCl to form a deliquescent chlorohydrate.

827. *Conine* is obtained from the hemlock, *Conium maculatum*, by distilling any part of the plant with a dilute solution of hydrate of potash. Like the last, it is an oily liquid, which is slightly soluble in water, and possesses in a high degree the smell, taste, and poisonous properties of the hemlock. It is strongly alkaline, and yields a series of deliquescent salts; the formula of conine is $C_{16}H_{15}N$.

There still remain to be described a number of other

vegetable substances which are not included under any of the previous classes. Among them are some neutral bodies, like amygdaline, salicine, and populine, which are interesting from the peculiar metamorphoses of which they are susceptible; and besides these, several substances used in coloring, among the most important of which, in regard to its chemical history, is indigo.

828. *Amygdaline.*—This substance exists in the proportion of four or five per cent. in bitter almonds; it is also met with in the kernels of peaches and cherries, and in the leaves and young shoots of many species of *Sorbus*, *Prunus*, and others of the *Pomaceæ*. It is obtained from bitter almonds from which the fat oil has been removed by pressure between heated plates, by boiling the residue in strong alcohol. The alcohol is then distilled off in a water-bath, and the syrupy residue, mixed with a little yeast, is set aside to ferment: by this treatment a portion of sugar which the almonds contain is destroyed. The clear liquid is again evaporated to a syrup and mixed with ether, which precipitates the amygdaline in a crystalline powder. It is readily soluble in alcohol and water, and crystallizes from the latter in large prisms, with three equivalents of water; it has a bitter taste. The formula of amygdaline is $C_{40}H_{27}NO_{22}$: when boiled with solution of baryta, it takes up the elements of one equivalent of water, and is converted into ammonia and *amygdalic acid*, which remains dissolved as amygdalate of baryta. Amygdaline may be regarded as the amid of this peculiar acid, which is $C_{40}H_{26}O_{24}$.

Bitter almonds contain, besides amygdaline and a fat oil, a large portion of a nitrogenous substance, to which the name of *emulsine* is given; it constitutes the principal part of sweet almonds, which contain no amygdaline. When bitter almonds are bruised with water, or when an aqueous solution of amygdaline is mixed with a small portion of emulsine from sweet almonds, a peculiar decomposition ensues. The solution acquires the odor of the essence of bitter almonds, and the amygdaline is found to be converted into prussic acid, benzoilol, and grape sugar. Amygdaline, with two equivalents of water, contains the elements of these three compounds; $C_{40}H_{27}NO_{22}+2H_2O_2=C_2NH+C_{14}H_6O_2+C_{24}H_{24}O_{24}$. Amygdalic acid, when distilled with sulphuric acid and peroxyd of manganese, yields also bitter-almond essence, with carbonic and formic acids. The action of emulsine in producing this curious change may be compared to that of diastase, to which emulsine has a certain resemblance. If its solution is heated to 212° F., it is precipitated in an insoluble form, and has no longer any action on amygdaline.

829. *Salicine.*—This principle exists in the bark of those species of willow which have a bitter taste. The decoction of the bark is mixed with the surbasic acetate of lead as long as a precipitate is formed; to the filtered liquid dilute sulphuric acid is added to precipitate the dissolved lead, carefully avoiding an excess. The solution is then decolorized by animal charcoal, and, by evaporation and cooling, deposits pure salicine. It is so abundant in the bark of some willows as to separate in crystals when a concentrated decoction is cooled. Salicine forms small white crystals, readily soluble in alcohol and water; it has a very bitter taste, and is employed in medicine as a febrifuge and tonic. Its formula is $C_{52}H_{36}O_{28}$.

When a solution of salicine is mixed with a small portion of the emulsine of sweet almonds, and heated for some hours to 105° F., it is completely decomposed into grape sugar, and a new compound which separates in fine rhombohedral crystals, and is named *saligenine*. It contains $C_{14}H_8O_4$, and its formation from salicine is thus represented: $C_{52}H_{36}O_{28}+2H_2O_2=C_{24}H_{24}O_{24}+2C_{14}H_8O_4$. Saligenine is readily soluble in water, alcohol, and ether; by the action of dilute acids it loses H_2O_2, and is changed into a white substance insoluble in water, called *saliretine*. When a solution of salicine is heated with dilute chlorohydric or sulphuric acid, it is at first decomposed into grape sugar and saligenine, but the further action of the acid converts the latter into saliretine, which separates in white flakes. When a solution of saligenine is mixed with chromic acid or oxyd of silver, these are reduced, and the oxygen combining with the saligenine forms *salicylol* and water; $C_{14}H_8O_4+Ag_2O_2=C_{14}H_6O_4+H_2O_2+Ag_2$. Salicine, when distilled with a solution of bichromate of potash and dilute sulphuric acid, yields a large amount of salicylol, identical with the essence of spirea ulmaria.

830. Dilute nitric acid by heat decomposes salicine with oxydation into grape sugar and salicylol, which, by oxydation, yields salicylic and nitrosalicylic acids; the final product, with a concentrated acid, is nitropicric acid. If sali-

cine is dissolved in dilute cold nitric acid, a new compound is obtained, which is formed from salicine by the fixation of oxygen and the separation of water; $C_{52}H_{36}O_{28}+O_4=C_{52}H_{34}O_{30}+H_2O_2$. This substance, which separates from the solution in crystals, is called *helicine*, and, by the action of emulsine or dilute acids, is decomposed into grape sugar and salicylol, $C_{52}H_{34}O_{30}+H_2O_2=C_{24}H_{24}O_{24}+2C_{14}H_6O_4$.

831. *Populine.*—This is a crystalline substance which is obtained from the leaves and bark of the aspen-tree, *Populus tremula*. It resembles salicine, but is less soluble, and has a sweetish taste. With acids it yields benzoic acid, grape sugar and saligenine, and when boiled with a solution of baryta, is completely decomposed into salicine, and benzoic acid, which combines with the baryta. Populine is represented by $C_{80}H_{44}O_{32}$, and by fixing H_2O_2 is converted into salicine and benzoic acid, $C_{80}H_{44}O_{32}+2H_2O_2=C_{52}H_{36}O_{28}+2C_{14}H_6O_4$. To indicate this relation, the name of *benzosalicine* has been proposed for the principle. When dissolved in cold nitric acid, a new substance is obtained, which is termed *benzohelicine*, and by boiling with magnesia is decomposed into a benzoate and helicine. Neither of these compounds is affected by emulsine, but the action of acids and alkalies converts benzohelicine into grape sugar, and the metameric bodies, benzoic acid and salicylol.

832. *Phloridzine.*—This substance is contained in the root-bark of the apple, pear, cherry, and some other trees. When a concentrated decoction of the bark is cooled, it is deposited in a crystalline powder, which, when purified, forms delicate silky crystals, sparingly soluble in cold water, but readily in alcohol. It has a slightly bitter taste, and is supposed to possess febrifuge properties. The probable formula of phloridzine is $C_{48}H_{28}O_{24}$, but it crystallizes with $2H_2O_2$. When boiled with dilute acids, it is decomposed like salicine into glucose and a crystalline insoluble substance called *phloretine* $C_{24}H_{12}O_8$. When exposed to the action of moist air and ammoniacal vapors, phloridzine is converted into a dark-blue mass, very soluble in water, from which acetic acid precipitates a red powder that dissolves in ammonia with a magnificent blue color. It is called *phlorizeine*, $C_{48}H_{28}O_{24}+O_6+2NH_3=C_{48}H_{32}N_2O_{30}+H_2O_2$. The ammoniacal solution of phlorizeine is rendered colorless by protosalts of tin, sulphuretted hydrogen, and other deoxydizing agents, but on exposure to the air reassumes its color by

the absorption of oxygen. This substance acts the part of a feeble monobasic acid, and gives splendid colored precipitates with metallic salts. If a salt of alumina or hydrated alumina is added to the ammoniacal solution, it combines with all the coloring matter and forms a blue precipitate, leaving the solution colorless.

The action of phlorizeine with alumina is analogous to that of many dye-stuffs, which form with oxyd of tin or alumina insoluble colored compounds. This property of alumina has already been alluded to; when a tissue of cotton is first impregnated with a solution of the acetate of this base, then dried and immersed in a hot solution of a coloring matter like phlorizeine, this is precipitated, and the insoluble colored compound is fixed in the tissue.

833. There are several other principles obtained from plants or animals, which are characterized by this property of forming insoluble colored compounds with metallic oxyds, like oxyd of tin or alumina, and are hence employed in the art of dyeing as *coloring matters*. We shall briefly notice the more important of those which have already been investigated. In some instances, the plants contain principles which generate the coloring matters by decompositions, such as we have seen in the case of phloridzine. Such is the origin of the colors of the lichens and of madder.

834. Several species of lichen, as the *Roccella tinctoria* of South America and the Cape of Good Hope, the *Lecanora tartarea* of Northern Europe, and some others, are used for the fabrication of a blue or purple dye-stuff, known by the different names of *archil*, *litmus*, *cudbear*, and *tournsol*. When these lichens are digested in the cold with milk of lime, the solution yields with acids a white precipitate, which may be crystallized from alcohol and from its solution in boiling water. It is an acid, and forms crystallizable salts. The names of *lecanorine*, *lecanoric acid*, and *orsellic acid* have been applied to it by different investigators; its composition is represented by $C_{32}H_{14}O_{14}$. When a solution of lecanoric acid is heated to ebullition with an excess of lime or baryta, a new acid is formed by the fixation of the elements of water; $C_{32}H_{14}O_{14}+H_2O_2=2C_{16}H_8O_8$, which is the formula of the new acid, to which the name of *orsellinic* or *lecanorinic* has been given. It is crystalline and more soluble than the lecanoric acid; when its alcoholic solution is treated with chlorohydric acid, or even when simply

boiled, the crystallizable ether of the acid, $C_{16}H_7(C_4H_5)O_8$ is obtained, which has also been described under the names of *pseuderythrine* and *lecanoric ether.*

When this ether is boiled for some time with baryta water, it is decomposed with the evolution of alcohol, into carbonic acid and a new substance, *orcine;* the same body is obtained by a similar process from the two acids, and by the dry distillation of lecanorine. The lecanorinic acid breaks up into carbonic acid and orcine; $C_{16}H_8O_8 = C_2O_4 + C_{14}H_8O_4$, which is the formula of orcine. It forms large colorless prismatic crystals of a sweet taste, which are very soluble in water, and volatile without decomposition. When orcine is moistened with ammonia and exposed to the air, it absorbs oxygen, and is converted into a splendid purple coloring substance, which resembles the analogous product from phloridzine, and is named *orceine.* Its probable formula is $C_{14}H_9NO_8$: orsellic and orsellinic acids also yield orceine when their ammoniacal solutions are exposed to the air.

835. The lichen, called *Evernia prunastri*, yields *evernic acid*, which appears to be homologous with lecanoric acid, and to be $C_{34}H_{16}O_{14}$: when boiled with an alkali it is decomposed into orcine, and a new acid homologous with lecanorinic, which is called *everninic acid* $C_{18}H_{10}O_8$. The *Gyrophora pustulata*, known in Canada as *tripe de roche*, and many other species, contain analogous substances, all of which are available for the manufacture of archil. For this purpose the lichens are ground to a paste with water, a solution of ammonia and sometimes urine is added, and the whole frequently stirred, until, by the action of the air, the whole of the orsellic acid is converted into orceine, when the mixture assumes a magnificent purple color. Further exposure to the air turns it blue, and forms what is known in commerce as *litmus.* When the proper colors have been developed, lime and plaster of Paris are added to the mass, to give it bulk and consistency, and the whole is dried. Archil is used with solution of tin, especially in the dyeing of silks. Litmus colors the common test-paper for acids, which, decomposing the blue compound with lime or ammonia, set free the red orceine. Many salts which are capable of decomposing this feeble combination, restore the red color of litmus, and are thus said to possess an acid reaction.

836. The roots of madder, *Rubia tinctoria*, contain in their

recent state, according to the latest investigations, a yellow crystalline substance, called *xanthine* or *ruberythric acid*, which, when boiled with acids or alkalies, is decomposed into glucose and an orange-red volatile crystalline substance, sparingly soluble in water, to which the name of *alizarine* is given. The formula $C_{20}H_{16}O_{10}$ has been assigned to it. Several other compounds have been described as obtained from madder, but alizarine appears to be the true coloring principle. Madder is used in giving to cotton the much valued Turkey-red dye, which is produced by the conjoined action of a salt of tin, alumina, and alizarine: the combination of the coloring principle with alumina forms the red pigment called *madder lake.*

837. The red coloring matters of *alkanet* or *anchusa*, of *sandal-wood*, and of *carthamus* are insoluble in water, but soluble in alkalies, and appear to possess acid properties. The latter, *carthamine*, is the coloring principle of the *pink saucers* used in dyeing flowers and feathers. On the addition of acetic acid to its alkaline solution, it is precipitated in an insoluble form, and then fixes itself on the tissue without the intermedium of a metallic oxyd. *Hematoxyline* is obtained from *logwood;* it is very soluble and forms yellow crystals: its solutions are rendered blue by alkalies and red by acids, and give a violet color with alum; and a black with salts of iron.

The coloring principle of the cochineal insect is a purple body, very soluble in water and alcohol; it forms beautiful lakes and scarlet dyes with salts of tin and alumina, and has been called *carminic acid;* the formula $C_{28}H_{14}O_{16}$ is assigned to it. The pigment known as *carmine* is a lake obtained from cochineal with alumina.

838. The yellow coloring matters of plants are generally non-azotized substances. Among the most important are *quercitrine*, the coloring principle of the *Quercus tinctoria*, and *luteoline*, from the *woad, Reseda luteola*, both of which are soluble and crystalline. The yellows of *turmeric* and *gamboge* are of a resinous nature. Others employed in dyeing are *morine*, from the *Morus tinctoria*, and *annatto.*

The leaves of plants contain a green resinous matter, which is soluble in alcohol and ether, and seems to possess acid properties; it is called *chlorophyll.* The blue and red colors of flowers are very perishable, and have not been accurately examined. Those of the violet, iris, dahlia, and many other flowers, are turned red by acids and green by alkalies. A most delicate test-paper is prepared with an alcoholic infusion of the petals of purple dahlias.

839. *Indigo.*—This important coloring substance is obtained from a great number of plants, the principal of which are the *Indigofera tinctoria* and *I. anil*, with some species of the genera *Isatis*, *Nerium*, and *Polygonum*. The juices of these contain a peculiar colorless principle in solution, which, when exposed to the air, absorbs oxygen, and is converted into indigo. In the manufacture of this substance, the plants are steeped in water, and made to undergo a kind of fermentation; the clear liquid is then exposed to the air, and frequently agitated to facilitate the absorption of oxygen; by this process it gradually becomes blue, and deposits the insoluble indigo.

840. Indigo is obtained in strongly cohering masses of a deep blue, which assume, when rubbed, a coppery metallic lustre. That of commerce is never pure, but is mixed with various foreign matters. Indigo is insoluble in water, alcohol, oils, dilute alkalies, and chlorohydric acid: when cautiously heated it is volatilized as a purple vapor, which condenses in delicate crystals. The composition of indigo is expressed by $C_{16}H_5NO_2$.

In contact with water and de-oxydizing agents, indigo is converted into a colorless substance, which is soluble in alkaline liquids; this is generally effected by a mixture of lime and sulphate of iron: one part of indigo in fine powder, four parts of quicklime, and three of protosulphate of iron are digested with a large quantity of water. The protoxyd of iron formed by the action of the lime, reduces the indigo, which in this form is dissolved by the alkaline solution, forming a yellow liquid. If this is exposed to the air, oxygen is absorbed, and the indigo is separated in its original color and insolubility. It is by impregnating cloth with this solution, and precipitating the indigo in its texture by the action of the air, that the fine indigo-blue colors are produced.

841. Chlorohydric acid added to this yellow solution, precipitates the dissolved substance as a gray crystalline powder, which, when moist, rapidly becomes blue by absorbing oxygen, and is converted into indigo.

It is called indigogen, and has the formula $C_{32}H_{12}N_2O_4$: exposed to the air it fixes O_2, and is converted into H_2O_2

and $2C_{16}H_5NO_2$. When indigo is boiled with an alcoholic solution of caustic soda and grape sugar, it is converted into indigogen, while formic acid is produced by the oxydation of the sugar. This alcoholic solution, exposed to the air, deposits pure indigo in crystals.

842. Concentrated sulphuric acid dissolves indigo by the aid of a gentle heat, and forms two acids, (652,) which are produced by the union of one and two equivalents of indigo with one of sulphuric acid, the elements of water being eliminated. They are named the *sulphindigotic* and *sulphopurpuric* acids, and, like their salts, are intensely blue. The first named is the most important: when a solution of sulphindigotic acid is boiled with woollen cloth, it is completely decolorized, the acid being taken up by the cloth; in this way the color called *Saxon blue* is obtained. It resists completely the action of water, but is easily dissolved out by a solution of the carbonate of ammonia, which distinguishes it from the blue color obtained with solutions of indigogen.

843. If powdered indigo is heated with a solution of chromic acid or dilute nitric acid, it dissolves and forms a yellow solution; this, on cooling, deposits beautiful orange-red prisms of a new substance, called *isatine*, which is formed from indigo by the combination of O_2, and is $C_{16}H_5NO_4$: with potash it forms a salt of *isatinic* acid, which, when separated from the alkaline base, is decomposed by a gentle heat into isatine and water. Isatine forms several amids with ammonia. When it or indigo is distilled with caustic potash, a large quantity of aniline is obtained: the intermediate product is formed when indigo is dissolved in a solution of potash; a yellow solution is obtained, which appears to contain reduced indigo, and a salt of isatinic acid, but on evaporating to dryness and fusing the mass, hydrogen is evolved, and carbonic and *anthranilic* acids are formed. Anthranilic acid contains $C_{14}H_7NO_4$. It is soluble, crystallizable, and volatile, but, when mixed with sand and rapidly distilled, is completely decomposed into carbonic acid gas and aniline: $C_{14}H_7NO_4 = C_2O_4 + C_{12}H_7N$.

The action of chlorine upon indigo destroys its blue color, and transforms it into a species of isatine in which one and two equivalents of hydrogen are replaced by chlorine. These resemble normal isatine, and, when distilled with potash, yield species of aniline in which the same substitution exists. Dilute nitric acid converts indigo by long boiling into ammonia, carbonic, and nitrosalicylic acids; with stronger nitric acid it forms nitropicric acid.

THE CYANIC COMPOUNDS.

844. The bodies of this series are obtained as products of a great number of reactions, and are very important in their relations to organic chemistry. A cyanid was first recognised in a product of the action of potash upon dried blood, which was employed for producing, with a salt of iron, a fine blue pigment, known as Prussian or Berlin blue: hence the name, from the Greek, *kuanos*, blue.

The ammoniacal salts of the acids $C_nH_nO_4$ yield, as we have shown, nitryls by the loss of $2H_2O_2$, which regenerate the ammoniacal salt by again assimilating the elements of water. The general formula of these bodies is $C_nH_{n-1}N$. The nitryl of formic acid is C_2HN, and is formed when the vapor of formate of ammonia is passed through a red-hot tube; $C_2(H.NH_4)O_4 = C_2H_5NO_4 - 2H_2O_2 = C_2HN$. This nitryl is the parent of the cyanic series, and is commonly known as *prussic* or *hydrocyanic acid.* The equivalent of hydrogen which it contains may be replaced by a metal, and the salts called *cyanids* thus obtained. The cyanid of potassium is formed when nitrogen gas is passed over a mixture of charcoal and carbonate of potash, heated to the temperature at which potassium is evolved. It is sometimes found as a product in furnaces from the action of atmospheric nitrogen upon the intensely heated mixture of carbon and alkali resulting from combustion: the potassium in this case unites directly with carbon and nitrogen. Cyanid of potassium is also obtained when animal substances, like leather, horn, or dried blood, or the charcoal obtained from them, which contains several per cent. of nitrogen, are heated with carbonate of potash; its separation and purification will be described farther on.

845. Hydrocyanic acid, is easily obtained by distilling cyanid of potassium with dilute sulphuric acid, or by decomposing cyanid of mercury at a gentle heat by sulphuretted hydrogen; $2C_2HgN + H_2S_2 = 2C_2HN + Hg_2S_2$.

To procure the anhydrous acid, the best arrangement is shown in fig. 420. Cyanid of mercury in coarse powder is placed in the tube *a b*, and decomposed by a gentle current of sulphydric acid, evolved from sulphid of iron and

Fig. 420.

diluted sulphuric acid. The sulphydric acid is dried by passing it over chlorid of calcium in the tube *c d*, and the product of the action is collected in the bent tube contained in the freezing mixture C. The operation may be conducted without danger in the open air. Pure hydrocyanic acid is a colorless limpid liquid, which boils at 80° F., and has a specific gravity of ·697; a drop of it let fall upon paper, produces so much cold by its partial evaporation, as to freeze the remainder. Hydrocyanic acid is combustible, and burns with a white flame; it is scarcely acid in its reaction with test-papers: its taste is pungent and aromatic, and its odor very powerful, both recall those of peach blossoms or bitter almonds; the distilled waters of these substances and of the cherry-laurel, owe a part of their flavor to the presence of the acid, which is one of the products of the decomposition of amygdaline by emulsine. When hydrocyanic acid is mixed with an excess of strong chlorohydric acid, it is completely decomposed into sal-ammoniac and formic acid; boiled with hydrate of potash, it is decomposed in a similar manner, and yields ammonia and formate of potash: $C_2HN+H_2O_2+(KH)O_2=C_2HKO_4+NH_3$.

846. Hydrocyanic acid is a most fatal poison; a single drop of the concentrated acid placed upon the tongue of a large dog produces immediate death, and the diluted acid even in very small doses causes giddiness and nausea. It appears to act as a sedative to the arterial system, and the suspension of animation following a large dose of it, does not always result in death, if proper remedies are employed. Ammonia and brandy are considered the most efficient antidotes to its effects. The vapor of the acid is also poisonous when inhaled; but workmen constantly exposed to it in a diluted state appear to become accustomed to it, so as to

experience no deleterious effects. The dilute acid is employed in medicine; when pure, it readily undergoes spontaneous decomposition, yielding ammonia and a brown insoluble matter; but if it is diluted, and a trace of sulphuric acid is present, the acid may be preserved for a long time, especially if secluded from the light.

The *cyanid of potassium* C_2KN is deliquescent and very soluble in water and alcohol; it forms cubic crystals, and has the taste, smell, and medicinal properties of hydrocyanic acid: it is strongly alkaline in its reactions. *Cyanid of ammonium* $C_2AmN = C_2H_4N_2$ is obtained by saturating hydrocyanic acid with ammonia, and is volatile and very poisonous. Hydrocyanic acid dissolves red oxyd of mercury, and the solution yields colorless crystals of a cyanid C_2HgN, which are soluble in water and alcohol, and are poisonous.

Hydrocyanic acid and soluble cyanids throw down from solutions of silver a white curdy precipitate insoluble in acids, and resembling the chlorid; it is cyanid of silver, and is insoluble in ammonia. Salts of palladium decompose even the cyanid of mercury, and form an insoluble precipitate of cyanid of palladium. The other cyanids are obtained by double decomposition: they are generally insoluble in water, but soluble in cyanid of potassium, forming salts, which will presently be described.

The action of chlorine upon hydrocyanic acid or cyanid of mercury, yields a compound in which chlorine replaces the hydrogen of the acid; it is a gas of a very strong odor, and at a low temperature crystallizes in colorless needles: it dissolves in water without decomposition, for the solution does not precipitate salts of silver. Its formula is C_2ClN: the bromic and iodic species are crystalline and very volatile. These compounds are commonly called chlorid and iodid of cyanogen; the name of *cyanogen* being applied to the group C_2N, which plays the same part in the saline combinations as Cl does in the chlorids, and is often represented by the symbol Cy, the hydrocyanic acid being CyH.

847. When the carefully dried cyanid of mercury is heated nearly to redness, it is decomposed into metallic mercury, and a colorless gas which is liquefied by a pressure of four atmospheres. It has a pungent odor, resembling that of prussic acid, and burns with a beautiful violet purple, yielding nitrogen and carbonic acid gas; it is soluble in water and alcohol, and must therefore be collected over mercury. This gas is called

cyanogen: the formula of its equivalent of four volumes is C_4N_2. It is therefore not the hypothetical compound represented by Cy, but sustains the same relation to it that the equivalent of four volumes of chlorine, Cl_2 does to the atom Cl which enters into the composition of a chlorid. In its formation, two equivalents of cyanid of mercury react upon each other, $CyHg+CyHg=Hg_2+Cy_2=C_4N_2$. When heated with potassium, combination ensues with combustion, and cyanid of potassium is formed.

Cyanogen corresponds to the nitryl of oxalic acid; oxalate of ammonia, $C_4H_2O_8.2NH_3=C_4H_8N_2O_8-4H_2O_2=C_4N_2$. Its aqueous solution decomposes by keeping, and a variety of products are obtained, among which is oxalate of ammonia, regenerated by a combination of cyanogen with the elements of water. When one volume of cyanogen and two of sulphuretted hydrogen gas are mixed in the presence of water or alcohol, direct combination ensues, and the compound $C_4N_2.H_4S_4$ is obtained, which corresponds to sulphuretted oxamid: it forms orange-red crystals, soluble in alcohol, but sparingly soluble in water. When boiled with a dilute solution of potash, it evolves ammonia, and is completely converted into oxalate and hydrosulphate of potash, $C_4H_4N_2S_4+4(KH)O_2=2NH_3+C_4K_2O_8+2(KH)S_2$. By boiling with chlorohydric acid, the crystals are converted into oxalic acid, ammonia, and sulphuretted hydrogen.

848. *Cyanates.*—The cyanids combine with oxygen to form a new class of salts, called cyanates. Fused cyanid of potassium absorbs oxygen from the air, and reduces oxyd of copper and other metals with ignition, at a temperature below redness. By adding oxyd of lead, in small quantities, so long as reduction takes place, the cyanid is completely converted into cyanate, and the lead separates in a metallic state. The fused mass may be crystallized by solution in boiling alcohol, and is deposited in pearly plates, very soluble in water; $C_2KN+Pb_2O_2=C_2KNO_2+Pb_2$. Strong acids liberate the cyanic acid, but decompose it immediately into carbonic acid and ammonia. Cyanic acid may be considered as the acid nitryl of carbonic acid, derived from bicarbonate of ammonia by the loss of $2H_2O_2$. $C_2H_2O_6.NH_3=2H_2O_2+C_2HNO_2$. Its aqueous solution is readily decomposed, especially in the presence of strong acids and alkalies, into a carbonate and ammonia, and the crystals of cyanate of potash in a moist atmosphere attract water, and, evolving

ammonia, are converted into bicarbonate of potash. Cyanic acid is obtained in a pure form by the distillation of cyanuric acid: it is a colorless, volatile liquid, with an odor like acetic acid, and is very caustic, blistering the skin. It may be preserved in a freezing mixture, but at the ordinary temperature changes very rapidly into a white, solid, insoluble, isomeric modification, called *cyamelid*, which by heat is reconverted into cyanic acid.

849. Cyanic acid combines directly with two equivalents of ammonia, and forms a soluble salt having the reactions of a cyanate of ammonia; but if its solution is boiled, ammonia is evolved, and a substance having the composition of neutral cyanate of ammonia remains in solution; it is an alkaloid, and combines directly with acids. The same compound is obtained as a product of the spontaneous decomposition of an aqueous solution of cyanogen or cyanic acid; the ammonia formed from one portion of cyanic acid, uniting with undecomposed acid, yields $C_2HNO_2.NH_3 = C_2H_4N_2O_2$. This alkaloid exists in human urine, and has hence been named *urea*. When fresh urine is evaporated by a gentle heat to a small bulk, and mixed with an excess of nitric acid, the *nitrate of urea* $C_2H_4N_2O_2.NHO_6$, which is sparingly soluble in the dilute acid, separates in large brilliant plates; these may be washed with iced water and decomposed with carbonate of potash: the urea is then separated from the nitre by alcohol, in which the former alone is soluble.

850. A better process for its formation is by cyanate of potash: the salt known as the yellow prussiate of potash contains the elements of cyanid of potassium and cyanid of iron. It is dried at 212° F., and eight parts of it are mixed with three of dry carbonate of potash, and the mixture fused at a low red heat in an iron crucible: the iron separates in a spongy metallic form, and a white crystalline mass is obtained, which is cyanid of potassium, mixed with about one-fourth of cyanate, and is known in the arts as Liebig's cyanid of potassium. If to this mass, still in fusion, fifteen parts of red-lead are gradually added, the whole is converted into pure cyanate of potash. It is to be dissolved in cold water, mixed with a solution of eight parts of sulphate of ammonia, and evaporated to dryness. The cyanate of ammonia, formed by double decomposition, is thus converted into urea, which is separated from the accompanying sul-

phate by boiling the residue in alcohol. It crystallizes, on cooling, in transparent, colorless prisms, readily soluble in water and alcohol, and having a fresh, sharp taste, like nitre. It is a weak base, but forms compounds with oxalic and chlorohydric as well as with nitric acid; concentrated sulphuric acid and hydrate of potash, by the aid of heat, convert it into carbonate and ammonia. When urea is evaporated to dryness with a solution of nitrate of silver, the elements arrange themselves so as to form nitrate of ammonia and an insoluble crystalline cyanate of silver, which explodes by heat. A solution of urea heated in a sealed tube to 284° F. is converted into carbonate of ammonia $C_2H_4N_2O_4+2H_2O_2=C_2H_2O_6.2NH_3$. The urea in urine undergoes the same change by boiling or by putrefaction. Nitrous acid at once decomposes it into water, nitrogen, and carbonic acid gases, $2NHO_4+C_2H_4N_2O_2=3H_2O_2+C_2O_4+N_4$.

851. *Sulphocyanates.*—Fused cyanid of potassium reduces sulphurets in the same way as oxyds, and combines directly with sulphur to form a cyanate C_2KNS_2, in which sulphur replaces oxygen. If a mixture of dried prussiate of potash is fused with sulphur and carbonate of potash in a covered crucible, and the heat gradually raised to redness, until the mass is in quiet fusion, there is obtained a mixture of sulphocyanate of potash and sulphuret of iron. The salt is dissolved out by boiling water, and crystallizes on cooling. The best proportions are 46 parts of the dried prussiate, 17 of dry carbonate of potash, and 32 of sulphur. Sulphocyanate of potash forms colorless prismatic crystals, having a taste like nitre; they are deliquescent, and soluble both in water and alcohol. The *sulphocyanic acid* C_2HNS_2 is obtained in solution when the lead salt is decomposed by dilute sulphuric acid, and is a colorless liquid acid, with an odor like vinegar. These compounds are all more stable than the oxycyanates. Sulphocyanate of ammonia $C_2(NH_4)NS_2$ is obtained by a peculiar reaction; a solution of cyanid of ammonium separates the excess of sulphur from persulphuret of ammonium, and if a mixture of the two salts in solution is digested with finely divided sulphur, the sulphur is dissolved by the sulphuret and transferred to the cyanid, which is wholly converted into sulphocyanate: by boiling the solution, the volatile sulphuret of ammonium may then be expelled, and the sulphocyanate obtained in crystals. The

soluble sulphocyanates are characterized by forming a deep blood-red liquid with persalts of iron, which is due to the formation of a persulphocyanate of that metal; this reaction affords a very delicate test both for salts of iron and sulphocyanates.

852. When a solution of sulphocyanate of potash is heated with nitric acid, or when chlorine is passed through its solution, a yellow substance separates, which contains the elements of cyanogen, sulphur, oxygen, and hydrogen, and has been called *cyanoxsulphid;* its nature is not well understood. Exposed to heat, it yields sulphur and sulphuret of carbon among other products, and leaves a yellow residue named *mellon,* which is probably $C_{12}H_3N_9$, and by a strong red heat is decomposed into cyanogen, nitrogen, and hydrogen gases. Mellon decomposes fused sulphocyanate of potassa, and yields a salt called *mellonid of potassium* $C_{12}HK_3N_9$. When this salt or mellon is boiled with a solution of hydrate of potash, ammonia is evolved and a salt obtained, to which the name of *cyamellurate of potash* is given; it is $C_{12}HK_3N_8O_2$: the corresponding acid is sparingly soluble in water.

Polycyanids.

853. The cyanids exhibit a great tendency to polymerism, and form compounds in which two, three, and six molecules of simple cyanid are condensed into one. The mellon series is an instance of such a polymerism. When cyanogen is obtained by the decomposition of cyanid of mercury, a portion of a black carbon-like body is always formed, which is represented by $C_{12}N_6$, and is named *paracyanogen.* It contains the elements of three equivalents of cyanogen, and is entirely converted into it when heated in a current of carbonic acid gas; $C_{12}N_6 = 3C_4N_2$. Heated in hydrogen gas, it yields hydrocyanic acid, ammonia, and carbon; $C_{12}N_6 + H_{12} = 3C_2HN + 3NH_3 + C_6$. The brown substance formed by the spontaneous decomposition of an aqueous solution of cyanogen or of hydrocyanic acid, is similar in its nature.

854. When boracic acid or a borate is heated with a cyanid, a compound of boron and nitrogen is obtained: it is, however, best prepared by igniting calcined borax with twice its weight of sal-ammoniac; the mass washed with water and dilute acids, leaves a white insoluble powder, which burns at a high temperature with a green flame, and when heated

with hydrate of potash or strong sulphuric acid, is decomposed into a borate and ammonia: the same decomposition is produced when it is heated in aqueous vapor. It reduces oxyds of lead, copper, or mercury, at a temperature below redness, with the evolution of nitric oxyd gas. The proportions of its elements are represented by B_4N_2, but, from its fixed nature, it is probable that it has a higher equivalent, corresponding perhaps to paracyanogen.

855. The action of chlorine upon an aqueous solution of hydrocyanic acid, the latter being in excess, yields a volatile liquid, which is $C_6HCl_2N_3$, and corresponds to a triple molecule of cyanid in which two atoms of hydrogen are replaced. By the further action of chlorine the third atom is removed, and the *perchloric tricyanid* $C_6Cl_3N_3$ is obtained: this is also formed when dry chlorine acts upon paracyanogen, or upon the cyanid of mercury, with the aid of sunlight, and, unlike the monocyanid, is a crystalline solid, which is volatile at above 300° F. When the bichloric tricyanid above mentioned is digested with oxyd of mercury, cyanid of mercury and water are formed, with a pungent volatile liquid, boiling at 61° F., which is $C_4Cl_2N_2$, or a *perchloric dicyanid*, containing the elements of two equivalents of the monocyanid. It is not decomposed by water, but with hydrate of potash yields chlorid of potassium, and the products of the decomposition of cyanic acid, ammonia, and a carbonate.

856. The solid tricyanid is decomposed by water into chlorohydric acid, and *cyanuric acid*, which is polymeric of the cyanic, and is $C_6H_3N_3O_6$. The same acid is formed when a solution of cyanate of potash is mixed with a small quantity of acetic or nitric acid insufficient for its complete decomposition; cyanurate of potash is deposited. When the compound of chlorohydric acid and urea is heated, sal-ammoniac sublimes and cyanuric acid remains; $3C_2H_4N_2O_2.HCl = 3HCl.NH_3 + C_6H_3N_3O_6$; and urea, when heated alone until it ceases to evolve ammonia, is converted into a grayish mass, which is an amid of cyanuric acid. This is dissolved in concentrated sulphuric acid, the solution decolorized by a little nitric acid, and mixed with its bulk of water; the cyanuric acid separates, on cooling, in prismatic crystals, feebly acid to the taste. It may be crystallized unchanged from a boiling solution in nitric or chlorohydric acid, but by long continued ebullition with them, is slowly decomposed like cyanic acid, into carbonic acid and ammonia. When

exposed to a strong heat it is decomposed into cyanic acid, which is thus obtained pure, $C_6H_3N_3O_6=3C_2HNO_2$.

857. Cyanuric acid is tribasic, and forms both neutral and acid salts. The cyanuric ether of alcohol, obtained by distilling a sulphovinate with alkaline cyanurate of potash, forms beautiful crystals sparingly soluble in water, which are fusible, volatile, and have the formula $C_6(C_4H_5)_3N_3O_6$.

When sulphocyanate of ammonia is decomposed by heat, a residue is obtained consisting of mellon and an amid of cyanuric acid, to which the name of *melamine* is given. It is dissolved from the crude product by a dilute boiling solution of hydrate of potash, and separates, on cooling, in colorless rhombic octahedrons. It is $C_6H_6N_6$, and differs by $3H_2O_2$ from the neutral cyanurate of ammonia. Melamine is a strong organic base, and forms crystalline salts. When boiled with strong acids or alkalies, it is slowly decomposed into ammonia and a cyanurate. The intermediate steps in the decomposition are the amids, corresponding to cyanurates with one and two equivalents of ammonia, and are called *ammelid* and *ammeline*. The latter is $C_6H_5N_5O_2$ and is a weak base. By heat melamine is decomposed into mellon and ammonia; $2C_6H_6N_6=C_{12}H_3N_9+3NH_3$.

858. *Fulminates.*—The salts which from their explosive character have received this name, correspond to the dicyanid $C_4Cl_2N_2$ already described, and contain the elements of two atoms of cyanate. When nitrous vapour is passed into a solution of nitrate of silver in alcohol, the fulminate of silver $C_4Ag_2N_2O_4$ is deposited. The same salt is formed when a solution of silver in a large excess of nitric acid, is added to alcohol; the action is complex; besides the fulminate, aldehyd, acetic and formic ethers are formed by the oxydizing power of the acid, and by a polymerism of the alcoholic molecule, an acid which is homologous with lactic acid and is $C_8H_8O_{12}$. The action of nitric acid upon alcohol yields aldehyd and nitrous ether, and the deoxydation of another portion of the acid giving rise to nitrous acid, this may react with the ether and form fulminic acid and water, $NHO_4+C_4H_5NO_4=C_4H_2N_2O_4+2H_2O_2$. The silver salt is sparingly soluble in water, and forms delicate white crystals, which explode with terrible violence by friction with any hard body, even under water. The products of the decomposition are carbonic acid and nitrogen gases, and a mixture of cyanid with metallic silver. The fulminate

of mercury is less explosive than the silver salt, and is the material used in the preparation of percussion caps. To prepare it, one ounce of mercury is dissolved by a gentle heat in eight and a-half ounces by measure of nitric acid, of specific gravity 1·4, and the solution is poured into ten measured ounces of alcohol, specific gravity ·830; action soon ensues, with the evolution of copious white fumes, and the fulminate is deposited in white crystalline grains, which are washed with cold water, and dried at a very gentle heat. The salt is somewhat soluble in boiling water, and crystallizes on cooling; it explodes violently by a heat of 390° F., by friction, percussion, and by contact with strong acids. Its formula is $C_4Hg_2N_2O_4$. When fulminate of silver is dissolved in nitric acid, one-half of the silver is removed and an acid salt separates, which is $C_4HAgN_2O_4$; chlorid of potassium precipitates only one-half the silver and yields $C_4KAgN_2H_4$. Metallic copper separates the whole, and forms a copper salt. The double fulminate of copper and ammonia is decomposed by sulphuretted hydrogen into urea, sulphocyanic acid, water, and sulphuret of copper. It may be said to separate into cyanate of ammonia, which changes to urea, and cyanate of copper, which yields sulphuret of copper and cyanic acid; this, with an equivalent of H_2S_2, is converted into water and sulphocyanic acid.

859. The relations of the cyanids to the bodies of the series of alcohols are full of interest. When a sulphovinate is distilled with cyanid of potassium, hydrocyanic ether is obtained as a liquid sparingly soluble in water and boiling at 176° F. It is $C_2(C_4H_5)N$ or C_6H_5N, and is homologous with hydrocyanic acid. When heated with hydrate of potash, it is not decomposed like other ethers, but evolves ammonia, and produces a salt of propionic acid $C_6H_6O_4$ homologous with formic acid. The hydrocyanic ether of wood-spirit C_4H_3N yields in the same way acetic acid, $C_4H_3N+2H_2O_2=NH_3+C_4H_4O_4$. These ethers are identical with the nitryls obtained by distilling the ammoniacal salts of these acids with anhydrous phosphoric acid; the amylic ether is the nitryl of caproic acid, $C_{12}H_{12}O_4$. The vinic cyanic ether, with potassium, evolves a gas which is C_4H_6, and the residue yields to water cyanid of potassium. A substance remains which may be crystallized from boiling water, and is an organic base to which the name of *cyanethine* has been given. Its formula is $C_{18}H_{15}N_3$ correspond-

ing to three atoms of hydrocyanic ether, and it pertains to the type of the tricyanids.

860. When the crystalline compound of aldehyd and ammonia is dissolved in water with a mixture of hydrocyanic and chlorohydric acids, and evaporated to dryness, sal-ammoniac is obtained, and the chlorohydrate of a new base, which is formed from the elements of aldehyd, hydrocyanic acid and water, $C_4H_4O_2+C_2HN+H_2O_2=C_6H_7NO_4$. The name of *alanine* is given to this new substance, which is crystalline, soluble in water and dilute alcohol, and has a sweet taste; an atom of hydrogen in it may be replaced by a metal, so that, like ammonia, it combines both with acids and metallic salts. By the action of nitrous acid, alanine is converted into lactic acid, nitrogen and water, $2C_6H_7NO_4+2NHO_4=C_{12}H_{12}O_{12}+2H_2O_2+N_4$.

861. A cyanic ether is obtained by distilling a sulphovinate with cyanate of potash; it is $C_2(Et)NO_2=C_6H_5NO_2$, and is a very volatile liquid, which combines with ammonia and forms a body crystallizing in beautiful prisms, and soluble in water and alcohol. It is $C_6H_8N_2O_2$, and is *vinic urea*, differing from ordinary urea by $2C_2H_2$; when decomposed by hydrate of potash, it yields carbonic acid, and one equivalent of ammonia, with one of ethamine, or vinic ammonia, $NH_2(C_4H_5)$. In the same way vinic cyanic ether, which is homologous with cyanic acid, is decomposed, carbonic acid and ethamine being the only products. The cyanic ethers of the other alcohols yield similar results.

862. When the vapor of cyanic acid from the distillation of cyanuric acid is passed into alcohol, crystals are deposited which contain the elements of one equivalent of alcohol and two of the acid, $C_4H_6O_2+2C_2HNO_2=C_8H_8N_2O_6$. This compound is decomposed by distillation into alcohol and cyanuric acid, but with a solution of baryta, alcohol is set free and the baryta salt of a new acid is formed, which is called *allophanic acid*, and contains the elements of two equivalents of a cyanate with one of water, being $C_4H_4N_2O_6$; it differs from fulminic acid by H_2O_2, and is monobasic. When acids are added to its salts, or when a solution of its baryta salt is boiled, it is decomposed into a carbonate and urea; allophanic acid contains the elements of urea and carbonic acid, $C_4H_4N_2O_6=C_2H_4N_2O_2+C_2O_4$.

The vapors of cyanic acid are absorbed by aldehyd.

and a sparingly soluble crystalline compound is formed, to which the name of *trigenic acid* is given. The formula $C_8H_7N_3O_4$, representing a monobasic acid, is assigned to it, but its equivalent is probably more elevated.

863. When cyanogen gas is passed into an alcoholic solution of aniline, sparingly soluble crystals of a new base separate. It has received the name of *cyaniline*, and is formed by the combination of one equivalent of cyanogen and two of aniline, $C_4N_2+2C_{12}H_7N=C_{28}H_{14}N_4$. Its salts readily separate into aniline, and products of the decomposition of cyanogen. Aniline absorbs the gaseous chlorid of cyanogen, and the chlorohydrate of a new base is formed, $C_2ClN+2C_{12}H_7N=ClH.C_{26}H_{13}N_3$. The new alkaloid is called *melaniline*; it is crystalline, and its salts are more stable than those of cyaniline. It combines directly with cyanogen to form a base analogous to cyaniline, to which the name of *cyamelaniline* is given; it is $C_{30}H_{13}N_5$. These bodies are derived from a compound of two equivalents of aniline, $C_{24}H_{14}N_2$; melaniline is formed from it by the substitution of C_2N for H: and the fixing of $C_4N_2=(C_2N)_2$ or Cy_2, is analogous to the direct combination of Cl_2 and ClH. A reaction similar to the last, in which C_2HN or CyH combines directly, is found in the vegetal alkaloid *harmaline* $C_{26}H_{14}N_2O_2$; when this base is mixed with hydrocyanic acid or its salts with a cyanid, it combines with C_2HN to form a new crystalline base, *cyanharmaline*, $C_{26}C_{14}H_2O_2+C_2HN=C_{30}H_{15}N_3O_2$. This combination is decomposed by heat into prussic acid and harmaline, but forms with acids, salts which are permanent. Many other alkaloids, besides aniline, form compounds with cyanogen and cyanids.

864. By the action of chlorine gas in sunlight upon a hot saturated solution of cyanid of mercury, chlorohydric acid, chlorid of mercury, and sal-ammoniac are formed, together with carbonic acid, nitrogen, and the chloric cyanid, which escape in the gaseous form, while a yellow oily liquid separates, which is heavier than water, and has a pungent odor and caustic taste. The formula $C_{12}N_4Cl_{14}$ is assigned to it; it is soluble in alcohol and ether, but insoluble in water, which however decomposes it into nitrogen, and carbonic and chlorohydric acids. By keeping, it is spontaneously decomposed, with the separation of perchloric acetene C_4Cl_6. This compound is probably derived

from a combination of six molecules of cyanid, of which the normal species will be $C_{12}H_6N_6$, a group which is the type of a large and important class of polybasic salts, much more stable than the ordinary cyanids.* The six atoms of hydrogen are all replaceable by a metal, but two or three atoms of the metallic elements are combined in such a way as not to be recognized by the ordinary reagents, and like the three atoms of hydrogen or chlorine in the acetic acids, form a constant part of the acid. The second atom of silver in the fulminates, and the condition of the metals in some of the tartrates, present analogous instances.

865. *Ferrocyanids.*—These salts may be represented by $C_{12}(Fe_2M_4)N_6$; M being hydrogen or any metal. The two atoms of Fe are so combined as not to be precipitated by alkalies or sulphurets. The *ferrocyanid of potassium* is formed with the separation of hydrate of potash, when metallic iron or its oxyd is digested with a solution of cyanid of potassium, hydrogen being evolved in the former case: $Fe_2O_2+2C_2KN=2C_2FeN+K_2O_2$, which, with H_2O_2, gives $2(HK)O_2$. The cyanid of iron unites with another portion of cyanid of potassium, to form the new salt $C_{12}(Fe_2K_4)N$. This is the ordinary source of all the cyanic compounds. It is prepared on a large scale from the impure cyanid, formed by the calcination of animal matters with carbonate of potash, or by passing heated atmospheric nitrogen over fragments of intensely ignited charcoal, impregnated with the carbonate. In both processes cyanid of potassium is obtained, mixed with excess of the carbonate of potash. It is dissolved in water and digested with oxyd of iron, or a solution of protosulphate of iron is added, until the precipitate at first formed is no longer dissolved by the cyanid. The

---

* Perchloric acetene is decomposed at a red heat into Cl_2, and C_4Cl_4, or perchloric etherene. When this substance is exposed to the combined action of chlorine and water, with exposure to the sun's rays, the compound C_4Cl_6 is regenerated; at the same time, a portion of it forms with the elements of water, chlorohydric and chloracetic acids; $C\ Cl_6+2H_2O_2=3HCl+C_4Cl_3HO_4$. We have seen that by the aid of an amalgam of potassium, the chlorine of a chloracetate may be removed, and the normal acetic acid formed. It has lately been found that when the vapor of acetic acid is decomposed at a red heat, there are obtained, besides carbonic acid gas and acetene, small portions of benzene, phenol, and napthaline. These carbon compounds, high in the organic series, may now by these reactions, be formed, from charcoal, through the cyanids.

filtered liquid is then evaporated, when the ferrocyanid of potassium separates in large translucent lemon-yellow tabular crystals, containing $3H_2O_2$, which is expelled by a gentle heat. It is very soluble in water, but insoluble in alcohol, and is not poisonous. This salt is known in the arts as the *yellow prussiate of potash*, and is employed in dyeing, in the manufacture of prussian blue, and the fabrication of the various cyanids. The preparation of Liebig's cyanid of potassium, of the cyanates and sulphocyanates, by means of this salt, has been already described. When it is carefully dried and fused in a close iron vessel, the cyanid of iron is decomposed into nitrogen and a carburet, and pure cyanid of potassium is obtained, which may be crystallized by dissolving it in boiling alcohol of specific gravity ·900. When two parts of the dried ferrocyanid are heated with one of chlorid of mercury, pure cyanogen gas is evolved, and by boiling two parts of the crystallized salt with three of persulphate of mercury and fifteen of water for a few minutes, cyanid of mercury crystallizes on cooling. Distilled with dilute sulphuric acid, the ferrocyanid yields hydrocyanic acid, which is best prepared by this process.* Heated with an excess of concentrated sulphuric acid, the ferrocyanid undergoes a peculiar decomposition; the hydrocyanic acid evolved in the presence of a strong acid takes up the elements of water and yields ammonia and formic acid; but this last, by concentrated sulphuric acid, is decomposed into carbonic

---

* A dilute acid is readily prepared by distilling a mixture of two parts of ferrocyanid of potassium, one of sulphuric acid, and two of water, and collecting the product in a receiver containing two parts of water, until the liquid amounts to four parts. For this purpose the apparatus shown in figure 415 is well calculated. This acid, from the presence of a trace of sulphuric acid, is not liable to decomposition; it contains fifteen or twenty per cent. of pure acid. To determine the amount of real acid present, a weighed quantity of the distilled acid is added to a solution of nitrate of silver, which should be in excess; the precipitate of cyanid of silver is collected on a filter, dried at 212°, and weighed. Its weight divided by 5 gives the amount of real acid in the specimen. Let us suppose that 70 grains of the acid yield 80 of cyanid of silver, equal to 16 of real acid, $70 : 16 :: 100 : x$, which equals 22·85; it then contains 22·85 per cent. of real acid. But if it is required to reduce it to any standard, as one of three per cent., which is the ordinary medicinal acid, then as this will consist of 97 of water and 3 of real acid, $3 : 97 :: 16 : x$, and $x = 517{\cdot}3$ grains of water, which must be added to 16 of anhydrous acid to reduce it to the standard. But as 70 grains of this acid contain already 54 of water, it is obvious that we have to add $517{\cdot}3 - 54 = 463{\cdot}3$ grains of water to 70 grains of acid to reduce it to the required standard.

oxyd gas and water, and the result is a copious evolution of this gas in a pure state; the residue contains bisulphate of potash, and a double sulphate of ammonia and iron.

866. When a saturated solution of the ferrocyanid is mixed with strong chlorohydric acid and agitated with ether, a white crystalline matter separates, being insoluble in the ethereal mixture; it is washed with ether and dried *in vacuo*, and is *ferrocyanic acid*, $C_{12}(Fe_2H_4)N_6$. Its taste is acid and astringent: it is very soluble in water, and is decomposed by exposure to the air, into hydrocyanic acid and a cyanid of iron. When the potash salt is mixed with solutions of salts of lime, baryta, and zinc, insoluble or sparingly soluble salts are obtained, which are $C_{12}(Fe_2KCa_3)N_6$, &c. The copper salt is analogous in composition; it is insoluble in water, and has an intense red-brown color, which makes ferrocyanid of potassium a delicate test for that metal. With a protosalt of iron a similar compound is obtained, which is greenish-white, and rapidly becomes blue by exposure to the air. With a persalt of iron a characteristic deep blue precipitate is obtained, which is the pigment *prussian blue*: It is $C_{12}(Fe_2fe_4)N_6$, the replaceable iron being in the form of *ferricum*. The iron salt should be added in excess, or the precipitate will contain a portion of potassium, like the preceding compounds. Prussian blue forms a light porous mass of a deep violet-blue color, with a copper-red reflection: it is insoluble in water and dilute acids, but when recently precipitated is very soluble in solutions of oxalic acid and tartrate of ammonia, forming deep blue solutions which are used as writing-inks. Boiled with a solution of hydrate of potash, peroxyd of iron separates, and ferrocyanid of potassium is formed.

867. *Ferricyanids.*—When chlorine is passed into a dilute solution of ferrocyanid of potassium, the gas is absorbed, and the liquid loses the power of precipitating persalts of iron. On evaporating the yellow solution, a new salt is obtained in beautiful deep red transparent prisms, which is known as *red prussiate of potash* or *ferricyanid of potassium*. This salt contains $C_{12}(Fe_2K_3)N_6$, one atom of K having been separated to form chlorid of potassium with the chlorine; but the iron being in the state of ferricum, the salt becomes $C_{12}(fe_3K_3)N_6$, and the acid is $C_{12}(fe_3H_3)N_6$, and is tribasic. It is obtained by decomposing the lead salt with dilute sulphuric acid. The ferricyanid of potassium does not affect

the persalts of iron, but gives with protosalts, a blue precipitate which is $C_{12}(fe_3Fe_3)N_6$; it has a finer hue than the ferrocyanid, and is known as *Turnbull's blue*. When a solution of the red prussiate is mixed with one of potash, in the presence of organic matters, ferrocyanid is formed, and the organic substance is oxydized by the oxygen set free. This process is employed in calico-printing for discharging colors. $2C_{12}(fe_3K_3)N_6 = 2C_{12}(Fe_3K_3)N_6 + 2(KH)O_2 = 2C_{12}(Fe_3K_4)N_6 + H_2O_4 = H_2O_2 + O_2$. Peroxyd of hydrogen appears thus to be the oxydizing agent in this reaction, which is very energetic; oxalates are converted by it into carbonates, and a solution of chromic oxyd in potash, into chromate of potash. The same view may be extended to oxydation by chlorine: $2Cl + 2H_2O_2 = 2HCl + H_2O_4$.

868. *Nitroprussids.*—When a current of nitric oxyd gas (NO_2, or rather N_2O_4,) is passed through a heated solution of ferricyanic acid, a reaction ensues which may be thus represented: $2C_{12}(fe_3H_3)N_6 = 2C_{12}(Fe_3H_3)N_6 + N_2O_4 = 2C_2HN + 2C_{10}Fe_2H_2N_6O_2$; the products being hydrocyanic acid, and a new substance to which the name of *nitroprussic acid* has been given. When either the red or yellow prussiate of potash is heated with nitric acid so much diluted that no nitric oxyd is evolved, nitroprussic acid may be obtained. For this purpose 844 grains of crystallized yellow prussiate are pulverized, and mixed in a capacious vessel with six fluid-ounces of dilute nitric acid, of specific gravity 1·12; the heat of a water-bath is applied until action commences, and is then removed; the salt dissolves, and the liquid assumes a dark coffee color, with a copious evolution of gas, consisting of hydrocyanic acid and cyanogen, with some nitrogen, resulting from a secondary decomposition. When the solution is complete, the heat of a water-bath is again applied until the liquid gives a dark green or slate-colored precipitate with a protosalt of iron. On cooling, nitrate of potash crystallizes, and the liquid is neutralized with carbonate of soda, and boiled; a copious precipitate is formed, and the filtered liquid is of a clear deep-red color, and contains only nitrates of potash and soda, with the nitroprussid of sodium. The nitrates are in part separated by concentration and cooling, and on evaporating the remaining liquid at a gentle heat, the new salt separates in ruby-red prisms, resembling in appearance the red prussiate: its formula is $C_{10}(Fe_2Na_2)N_6O_2$; the crystals contain, besides, $2H_2O_2$,

The potash salt is obtained by substituting carbonate of potash for the soda, but is more soluble. The nitroprussids do not precipitate the persalts of iron, but yield with protosalts a salmon-colored precipitate which is $C_{10}(Fe_2Fe_2)N_6O_2$, and with copper salts a pale green insoluble nitroprussid of copper. This is decomposed by a solution of baryta, and gives a soluble baryta salt, which may be decomposed by sulphuric acid, and the nitroprussic acid obtained in dark red crystals, very soluble in water.*

If a solution of a nitroprussid is mixed with one of an alkaline sulphuret, a magnificent purple liquid is obtained; this reaction is so delicate as to detect the smallest trace of a soluble sulphuret. The color soon fades by standing, and the solution then contains ferrocyanid, sulphocyanid, and a nitrite, while nitrogen, hydrocyanic acid, oxyd of iron, and sulphur are set free. Nitroprussid of sodium forms a crystalline compound with hydrate of soda which is decomposed by boiling; nitrogen gas and peroxyd of iron, with ferrocyanid, nitrite and oxalate are the products.

869. The action of cyanid of potassium upon salts of chromium, manganese, and cobalt, gives rise to salts which correspond to the ferricyanids, the metals being in the same equivalent as in the sesquisalts. The compounds corresponding to ferrocyanid have not been obtained: when protocyanid of cobalt is dissolved in cyanid of potassium, sesquicyanid of cobalt, *cyanid of cobalticum* C_2coN is formed, and potassium is liberated, which, decomposing the water, forms hydrate of potash, evolving hydrogen gas, $4C_2CoN+2C_2KN=6C_2coN+K_2$. The cobaltic cyanid with another

* The formula here given for the nitroprussids is that proposed by M. Gerhardt, and corresponds best with the original analyses of the discoverer, Dr. Playfair, and even with the subsequent results of Mr. Kyd, whose proposed formula for the soda salt, $Cy_5Fe_2Na_2NO$, is not admissible unless it is doubled. There are many reasons for believing that carbon replaces sulphur and oxygen, somewhat as nitrogen does hydrogen, and then O_4N_2 and C_4N_2 become equivalent to each other, while peroxyd of hydrogen H_2O_4 and nitrous acid NHO_4 correspond to cyanic acid, $NH(C_2O_2)$, and hydrocyanic acid C_2HN, to C_2H_2, and to water O_2H_2. The nitroprussids are then ferrocyanids which have lost H_2, becoming bibasic, and under the influence of O_4N_2 have exchanged $Cy=C_2N$ for its equivalent O_2N. The formula will then be written $(Cy_5.O_2N)Fe_2Na_2=(C_{10}O_2)(Fe_2Na_2)N_6$. A similar view may be extended to a great number of compounds; nitrobenzene, for example, is benzoilol in which N replaces H, and O_2 replaces C_2; thus, $(C_{12}O_2)(H_5N)O_2$, corresponding to $C_{14}H_6O_2$.

portion of cyanid of potassium forms the cobalticyanid of potassium $C_{12}(co_3K_3)N_6$.

Platinum has a great tendency to form a platinocyanid, and when the metal in its spongy form is heated to redness with ferrocyanid of potassium, the mass yields to water the new salt, which crystallizes in long transparent rhomboidal prisms, yellow by reflected and blue by transmitted light: it is $C_{12}(Pt_3K_3)N$. By decomposing the mercurial salt with sulphuretted hydrogen, *platinocyanic acid* $C_{12}(Pt_3H_3)N_6$ is obtained; it is very soluble, and crystallizes in golden-yellow prisms, with a copper-red reflection. The baryta salt forms short lemon-yellow prisms, which are greenish by reflected light.

870. The other complex cyanids have been but little studied: one containing silver is obtained when the oxyd, chlorid, or cyanid of silver is added to a solution of cyanid of potassium. The *argentocyanid of potassium* is very soluble, and forms colorless tabular crystals; its composition is represented by $C_{12}(Ag_3K_3)N_6$. It is much less stable than the previous compounds; the silver is not precipitated by chlorids, but strong acids throw down insoluble cyanid of silver, and set free hydrocyanic acid. With a salt of lead, a precipitate is obtained in which lead replaces the potassium. The silver salt is used in electro-plating, and is generally prepared by dissolving oxyd or chlorid of silver in a solution of cyanid of potassium, hydrate of potash or chlorid of potassium being formed at the same time. Oxyd of silver decomposes even the ferrocyanid to form the new double salt. In the process of electro-silvering, the silver being liberated at one pole, the potassium and cyanic elements are set free at the other, and this pole being terminated by a plate of silver, the metal is dissolved as fast as it is deposited at the other pole, thus preserving the strength of the solution.

Oxyd of gold is readily soluble in cyanid of potassium, and yields a double salt which is used in a similar manner to the last for the process of electro-gilding. A solution of cyanid of potassium may be used to remove from the skin or from linen, the stains produced by salts of silver, gold or mercury.

ACIDS OF THE URINE AND BILE.

871. These animal secretions contain several peculiar azotized acids, which are very interesting from their meta-

morphoses: those of urine are named the *uric* and *hippuric* acids.

The hippuric acid is found principally in the urine of herbivorous animals; that of stall-fed horses and cows contains a considerable quantity. To obtain it, the fresh urine may be mixed with chlorohydric acid in the proportion of four ounces of the acid to a gallon, and allowed to stand for some hours in a cool place. A crystalline matter which is deposited is impure hippuric acid: it is separated, redissolved by boiling in water with excess of milk of lime, and a little animal charcoal to decolorize it: the filtered hot solution of hippurate of lime is then mixed with a slight excess of chlorohydric acid, and hippuric acid separates on cooling in beautiful white prisms. The fresh urine may also be heated to ebullition with milk of lime, and after separating the precipitate thus formed, boiled down to one-tenth, and then precipitated by chlorohydric acid: in this way a larger portion is obtained, (from forty to fifty grains from a pound.) Hippuric acid is very soluble in boiling water, but requires about 400 parts of cold water for its solution. It is monobasic and is represented by $C_{18}H_9NO_6$; when boiled with peroxyd of lead it is converted by oxydation into benzamid, carbonic acid and water: $C_{18}H_9NO_6+O_6=C_{14}H_7NO_2+2C_2O_4+H_2O_2$. By the action of nitrous acid, hippuric acid is decomposed like aspartic acid, and yields water, nitrogen, and a new acid called *benzoglycollic acid*: it is $C_{36}H_{16}O_{16}$, two equivalents of hippuric acid being concerned in the reaction. Benzoglycollic acid is bibasic; it is sparingly soluble in cold water, but dissolves readily in boiling water, alcohol, and ether. It fuses below 212° F., and at a higher temperature is decomposed, benzoic acid subliming. When boiled with dilute sulphuric acid, it is decomposed into benzoic acid, and a new bibasic acid called the *glycollic*, $C_8H_8O_{12}$. This is homologous with lactic acid, to which it bears a very close resemblance, and appears to be identical with the acid formed in the preparation of the fulminates. Benzoglycollic acid yields two equivalents of benzoic, and one of glycollic acid: $C_{36}H_{16}O_{16}+2H_2O_2=2C_{14}H_6O_4+C_8H_8O_{12}$.

872. When hippuric acid is boiled with a strong acid, it is decomposed into benzoic acid and a sweet crystalline substance, which was first obtained by the action of sulphuric acid upon glue or gelatine; it has hence received the name

of *sugar of gelatine, glycycoll*, or *glycocine*, (from *glukus* sweet, and *kolla* glue.) It is best obtained by boiling hippuric acid for half an hour, in ten parts of a mixture of sulphuric acid diluted with twice its volume of water. On cooling, benzoic acid separates, and after removing the sulphuric acid by saturating it with carbonate of lime, glycocine remains in solution, and may be purified by crystallization from dilute alcohol. Glycocine forms colorless prismatic crystals which are soluble in four or five parts of water, but are insoluble in pure alcohol; its taste is sweet, like grape sugar. Its formula is $C_4H_5NO_4$, and its formation from hippuric acid is thus represented; $C_{18}H_9NO_6+H_2O_2=C_{14}H_6O_4+C_4H_5NO_4$. It is homologous with alanine, and is, like it, an organic base, forming salts which crystallize beautifully. An atom of hydrogen in it may be replaced by a metal, and species like $C_4(H_4Cu)NO_4$ are obtained, which saturate acids, like the normal glycocine. Alkargen, $C_4H_5AsO_4$, the product of the oxydation of alkarsine, is glycocine, in which arsenic replaces nitrogen. By the action of nitrous acid, glycocine is decomposed and yields glycollic acid: $2C_4H_5NO_4+2NHO_4=N_2+2H_2O_2+C_8H_8O_{12}$.

Benzoglycollic acid may be viewed as a coupled acid, in which two equivalents of the monobasic benzoic have replaced H_2 in the bibasic glycollic acid, with the elimination of $2H_2O_2$; it is therefore itself bibasic. When a mixture of benzoic and lactic acids is fused together, water is evolved and the homologue of benzoglycollic acid, corresponding to lactic acid, is obtained: it is $C_{40}H_{20}O_{16}$, and is readily decomposed by strong acids into benzoic and lactic acids.

873. *Uric* or *lithic acid* exists in the urine of carnivorous animals, and in that of man—in the last associated with hippuric acid. The solid white urinary excretions of birds and serpents are composed almost entirely of urate of ammonia. The urine of the boa or other serpents is dissolved by boiling in a solution of hydrate of potash, ammonia being evolved. A current of carbonic acid gas is then passed through the liquid, which throws down a sparingly soluble acid urate of potash. This is washed with cold water to remove impurities, and redissolved in a hot dilute solution of potash: from the warm liquid chlorohydric acid separates a gelatinous precipitate, which soon changes into a white crystalline powder of pure uric acid. The uric cid may be separated from the dung of pigeons or other

birds by a solution of borax in 100 parts of boiling water: the acid is thrown down from this by chlorohydric acid, and may be dissolved in potash, and purified by the process already described.

Uric acid is soluble in 2000 parts of hot water, and has feeble acid characters: it is represented by $C_{10}H_4N_4O_6$, and is bibasic; the urates, like the acid itself, are sparingly soluble. The products of the decomposition of uric acid are numerous and interesting. When boiled with water and peroxyd of lead, carbonic acid gas is formed, and a substance called *allantoin*, which exists in the amniotic liquid of the cow, and in the urine of young calves. Its formula is $C_8H_6N_4O_6$; allantoin forms brilliant colorless prisms, soluble in 160 parts of cold water. The further action of peroxyd of lead decomposes it into an oxalate and two equivalents of urea, $C_8H_6N_4O_6+2H_2O_2+O_2=C_4H_2O_8+2C_2H_4N_2O_2$. Boiled with acids it fixes the elements of one equivalent of water, and forms one equivalent of urea, and *allanturic acid* $C_6H_4N_2O_6$; this is very soluble and deliquescent. When boiled with baryta-water, allantoin is completely decomposed into an oxalate and ammonia; $C_8H_6N_4O_6+4(BaH)O_2+H_2O_2=2C_4Ba_2O_8+4NH_3$.

874. When uric acid is mixed with warm chlorohydric acid and chlorate of potash is gradually added, the acid is dissolved and oxydized at the expense of the oxygen of the chloric acid. It is converted by this process into urea and a new compound, *alloxan* $C_8H_4N_2O_{10}$. This substance is also formed when uric acid is added in small portions to nitric acid of specific gravity 1·43; it dissolves with the evolution of nitrous fumes, mixed with nitrogen and carbonic acid from a partial decomposition of the urea, and on cooling, alloxan is deposited; $C_{10}H_4N_4O_6+2H_2O_2+O_2=C_2H_4N_2O_2+C_8H_4N_2O_{10}$. Alloxan crystallizes in small colorless brilliant rhomboidal crystals, with a vitreous lustre, which are anhydrous; or in large prisms which contain water, and are efflorescent. It is very soluble in water, and its solution gives to the skin, after some time, a purple stain and a nauseous odor. In contact with bases, alloxan combines with H_2O_2 to form a feeble bibasic acid, called the *alloxanic acid*. Boiled with a solution of baryta or with acetate of lead, alloxan fixes the elements of water and yields urea and a salt of *mesoxalic acid*, which is soluble, quadribasic, and represented by $C_6H_4O_{12}$. If a solution of alloxan is gently

heated with peroxyd of lead, carbonic acid gas is disengaged, and urea remains in the solution, mixed with insoluble oxalate and carbonate of lead. Alloxan, with water and oxygen, yields urea, carbonic acid, and oxalic acid; $C_8H_4N_2O_{10}+H_2O_2+O_2=C_2H_4N_2O_2+C_2O_4+C_4H_2O_8$. The carbonate of lead in the residue results from a further oxydation of a portion of the oxalate by the peroxyd.

875. When sulphuretted hydrogen is passed through a solution of alloxan, sulphur is deposited, together with a white crystalline substance named *alloxantine;* it is $C_{16}H_{10}N_4O_{20}$, and is formed by the combination of two equivalents of alloxan, which fix at the same time H_2. When a solution of alloxan is mixed with chlorohydric acid, and a fragment of zinc is added, the hydrogen from the decomposition of the acid is not evolved, but unites with the alloxan to form alloxantine, which crystallizes upon the zinc. Alloxantine is also formed when a solution of alloxan is boiled with dilute sulphuric or chlorohydric acid, and is deposited on cooling; an equivalent of water is decomposed, and H_2 unites with two equivalents of alloxan to form alloxantine, while the O_2 oxydizes another equivalent of alloxan, as in the case of peroxyd of lead, and forms oxalic and carbonic acids and urea, which last in presence of the acid, is decomposed into ammonia and carbonic acid. The decomposition of water in this reaction is analogous to that of sulphuretted hydrogen in the previous process. This substance is sparingly soluble in water: it appears to possess feeble acid properties, but is at once decomposed in contact with bases. When alloxantine is warmed with twice its volume of water, and a little nitric acid is added, solution takes place, with the evolution of nitric oxyd; the filtered liquid mixed with a few drops of the acid, to oxydize any excess of alloxantine in solution, deposits on cooling pure alloxan; $C_{16}H_{10}N_4O_{20}+O_2=2C_8H_4N_2O_{10}+H_2O_2$. The most advantageous way of preparing alloxan is to dissolve uric acid in warm, somewhat dilute chlorohydric acid, with the aid of one-fourth its weight of chlorate of potash, to precipitate alloxantine by passing sulphuretted hydrogen through the diluted solution, and convert it into alloxan by the above process.

876. A boiling aqueous solution of alloxantine is still further decomposed by sulphuretted hydrogen; sulphur separates, and *dialuric acid* is formed; this is $C_8H_4N_2O_8$, and is monobasic; its ammonia salt is colorless, but becomes

blood-red on drying. Dialuric acid differs from alloxan by O_2, and its potash salt is formed by a process of de-oxydation when cyanid of potassium is added to a solution of alloxan. By exposure to the air, this acid absorbs water and oxygen, and is changed into a dimorphous form of alloxantine. Alloxantine contains the elements of alloxan, dialuric acid, and an equivalent of water; when its solution is mixed with one of sal-ammoniac, alloxan is formed, chlorohydric acid set free, and an insoluble crystalline substance separates, to which the name of *uramile* is given; it is the amid of dialuric acid, being $C_8H_5N_3O_6$. An equivalent of alloxantine, $C_{16}H_{10}N_4O_{20}+HCl.NH_3=C_8H_4N_2O_{10}+C_8H_5N_3O_6+HCl+2H_2O_2$. When a solution of alloxan is heated to boiling with sulphite of ammonia, it deposits, on cooling, brilliant plates of a new salt, the *thionurate of ammonia*. Thionuric acid is bibasic, and contains the elements of alloxan, ammonia, and sulphurous acid; it is $C_8H_7N_3S_2O_{14}$. When its solution is heated to boiling, it is completely decomposed into uramile and sulphuric acid, $C_8H_5N_3O_6+S_2H_2O_8$; but if previously mixed with sulphuric acid and evaporated in a water-bath, dialuric acid and sulphate of ammonia are obtained.

877. The solutions of uric acid in nitric acid are colored of a beautiful purple by ammonia; and alloxantine in an ammoniacal atmosphere, or solutions of uramile in ammonia or hydrate of potash, absorb oxygen from the air, and assume the same purple color. If, to a nearly boiling solution of alloxan, one of carbonate of ammonia is added in slight excess, there is a violent effervescence from the escape of carbonic acid gas, and the liquid assumes so deep a purple hue as to be almost opaque. As it cools, delicate square prisms are deposited, which are garnet-red by transmitted, and golden-green by reflected light; their powder, under a burnisher, assumes a green metallic brilliancy. This beautiful substance is named *murexid*, in allusion to the *murex* which furnished the purple dye of the ancients; it is slightly soluble in cold water, and colors it purple. Crystals of it are also obtained when uramile and oxyd of silver are boiled with water containing a little ammonia; the silver is reduced, and the filtered purple solution deposits murexid on cooling. The probable formula of murexid is $C_8H_4N_4O_4$, corresponding to the amid, or rather nitryl of alloxanic acid. Alloxanate of ammonia, $C_8H_8N_2O_{12}.2NH_3-4H_2O_2=C_8H_4$

N_4O_4. A solution of murexid in hot water gives a red precipitate with nitrate of silver; its solution heated to boiling with sulphuric acid, yields a precipitate of uramile and alloxan, while alloxantine and sulphate of ammonia remain in solution.

When uric acid or alloxan is boiled with an excess of strong nitric acid, carbonic acid gas is evolved and *parabanic acid* formed; it is $C_6H_2N_2O_6$, and is bibasic and very soluble. When its ammonia salt is heated to boiling, it fixes H_2O_2, and is converted into *oxalurate of ammonia.* The addition of chlorohydric acid to a solution of the new salt separates the oxaluric acid as a sparingly soluble powder, which is represented by $C_6H_4N_2O_8$. When its aqueous solution is boiled, it is converted into oxalic acid and urea, $C_6H_4N_2O_8+H_2O_2=C_4H_2O_8+C_2H_4N_2O_2$.

878. The action of chlorine upon the alkaloid caffeine, produces, among other products, a feebly acid crystalline substance, sparingly soluble in water, to which the name of *amalic acid* has been given. It closely resembles alloxantine, and is homologous with it, being $C_{24}H_{18}N_4O_{20}$; the two differ by $4C_2H_2$. When amalic acid is moistened with water and exposed to the action of air and ammonia, it is converted into a reddish-brown substance, which, by solution in hot water, yields red crystals, scarcely distinguished from murexid by their characters. They are named *murexoine,* and are probably the murexid of this series, of which the other members have not yet been studied.

879. *Cholic Acid.*—The bile of animals is a solution of the soda or potash salts of two azotized acids, one of which contains sulphur. When ox-bile is evaporated to dryness and dissolved in alcohol, the careful addition of ether precipitates first the salt of the sulphur acid, and by a further addition of ether, aided by cold, the soda salt of the dissolved cholic acid may be obtained in crystals. On adding sulphuric acid to their aqueous solution, the acid separates after some time in delicate white silky crystals, which have a bitterish sweet taste, and are very sparingly soluble in water. Cholic acid is monobasic, and is represented by $C_{52}H_{43}NO_{12}$. When boiled with a solution of baryta, it is decomposed like hippuric acid into glycocine and a new acid, containing no nitrogen, which is called *cholalic acid,* $C_{52}H_{43}NO_{12}+H_2O_2=C_4H_5NO_4+C_{48}H_{40}O_{10}$, which is the formula of cholalic acid. It forms colorless octahedral

crystals, which require 4000 parts of cold water for their solution, but are very soluble in alcohol. When exposed to heat, or when boiled with strong chlorohydric acid, it is converted successively into *choloidic acid* and an almost insoluble resinous body, *dyslysine*, both of which are formed by the loss of the elements of water; dyslysine is $C_{48}H_{36}O_6$. When cholic acid is heated with a dilute acid, it loses H_2O_2, and yields *cholonic acid*, $C_{52}H_{41}NO_{10}$, which, by boiling, is decomposed into glycocine, and choloidic acid or dyslysine.

880. Acetate of lead precipitates the cholic acid from bile which has been purified by solution in alcohol, but leaves in solution the sulphuretted acid, to which the name of *choleic acid* is given; the bile of sheep, and of some fishes is almost entirely composed of choleates, and that of the dog is pure choleate of soda. Choleic acid resembles the cholic acid, but both it and its salts are more soluble in water. Its formula is $C_{52}H_{45}NO_{14}S_2$; when boiled with a solution of baryta, it is decomposed like the cholic acid, and yields cholalic acid, and in place of glycocine, a neutral body named *taurine*, which is crystalline, soluble in water and alcohol, and contains $C_4H_7NO_6S_2$. The action of acids yields taurine and cholalic acid, and the spontaneous putrefaction of recent ox-bile, which is mixed with the mucus of the gall-bladder, affords similar results; acetic and allied acids, probably from the decomposition of glycocine, accompany the taurine, which is itself decomposed at a later stage of the process, sulphurous and sulphuric acids being formed.

881. The bile of pigs contains a peculiar acid to which the name of *hyocholic acid* is given: it is $C_{54}H_{43}NO_{10}$, and is homologous, not with cholic, but with cholonic acid, differing from this by C_2H_2: boiled with baryta water, it yields glycocine and *hyocholalic acid*, homologous with cholalic acid: by chlorohydric acid it is converted into glycocine and a homologous species of dyslysine: $C_{54}H_{43}NO_{10}=C_4H_5NO_4+C_{50}H_{38}O_6$.

Bile contains, besides these salts, a portion of fat, a yellow coloring matter, and a neutral crystalline body resembling spermaceti in appearance, to which the name of *cholesterine* is given: it often forms concretions in the gall-bladder, known as *biliary calculi*. The formula $C_{52}H_{44}O_2$ is assigned to it.

NUTRITIVE SUBSTANCES CONTAINING NITROGEN.

882. Under this head may be described a class of substances which are common to plants and animals, and sustain a very important part in the economy of nutrition. The seeds and juices of all plants, in addition to the starch, sugar and lignine always present, contain peculiar substances which, although unlike in form and solubility, have a general similarity of composition with each other, and with the muscular tissue of animals. The relations between these bodies may be said to be analogous to those between starch, gum, dextrine, and lignine. In both, the differences are to be considered as in part depending upon organization, and in part upon that molecular arrangement, which constitutes a species of isomerism. As lignine and starch may be converted into dextrine, and as both dextrine and gum, by acids, yield glucose, so these different azotized substances may be converted one into another. To these bodies the general name of *protein* compounds has been given, from *proteuo, I take the pre-eminence*, in allusion to their importance in the vital economy.

883. The muscle or flesh of animals is called *fibrin*, and is an organized form of protein; fibrin also separates from the blood during coagulation, and is, when pure, a white tasteless mass, insoluble in water, and becomes horny and translucent by drying. It dissolves in acetic and dilute chlorohydric acids, in warm solution of sal-ammoniac, nitre, and several other salts, and is separated from them by heat in an insoluble amorphous form.

The serum of the blood and the white of eggs contain in solution a large quantity of a protein compound, which is similar in its characters to dissolved fibrin, and coagulates by a heat of 158° F.: it is called *albumin*, and is nearly pure in the white of eggs. Albumin when coagulated by heat is insoluble in water, and resembles fibrin in its chemical properties; milk contains another soluble form of protein, which is not coagulated by heat, but is at once separated in an insoluble condition by a dilute acid; it has received the name of *casein*, and is nearly pure in the curd of skimmed milk. Casein appears to be insoluble in water when pure, and to be held in solution in milk by a small portion of soda: the albumin of the blood is by the action of a solution of potash converted into a form resembling casein.

884. When a paste of wheat flour is washed with water until all the starch is removed, a tenacious gray substance remains, which dries into a horny mass, and which, though not possessed of the organized structure of muscular fibre, is soluble in acetic acid, and is chemically identical with fibrin: it is called *glutin*. The water from the washing of the paste, from which the starch has separated by repose, and the juices of many vegetables, yield by heat an insoluble protein body, which is *vegetable albumin*. When beans or peas are bruised with water, a large quantity of protein is dissolved, and may be precipitated by the addition of an acid. It is called *legumin*, or *vegetable casein*.

885. When any one of these substances is dissolved in a moderately strong solution of hydrate of potash, and heated for some time to 120° F., the addition of acetic acid in slight excess, separates a white flocculent matter, which when washed with water and dried, is a yellowish brittle mass, soluble in acetic acid, but insoluble in water and alcohol. It is protein in a state of comparative purity, and has nearly the same composition, from whatever source it is obtained. In their natural state, the protein bodies contain variable and often considerable quantities of mineral matter in a state of combination or intimate mixture. The curd of milk yields, when burnt, several per cent. of ashes, consisting principally of phosphate of lime. The different protein compounds also contain small, but variable proportions of sulphur and phosphorus in combination with the organic elements, probably replacing oxygen and nitrogen in a portion of the protein, and the sulphur remains after solution in potash and precipitation by acetic acid. If to a solution of any protein body in potash, a little acetate of lead is added, and the solution is heated to boiling, it becomes black from the formation of sulphuret of lead; but even by ebullition it is difficult to decompose the whole of the sulphur compound. The amount of sulphur generally varies from 1 to 1·5 per cent., but the protein from cows' horns and hoofs contains, according to Mulder, from 3·4 to 4·6 per cent. of that element. The proportion of phosphorus in the different forms of protein also varies from a trace, to ·8 per cent., and in vegetable casein it rises to 2·4 per cent: it is sometimes absent.

886. The facility with which the protein bodies are altered by spontaneous decomposition, and by different reagents, renders it very difficult to fix their exact composition. If

we suppose the sulphur to replace a portion of the oxygen, the formula $C_{24}H_{17}N_3O_8$ may be assigned as expressing very closely the composition of protein. The greatest amount of sulphur present in any variety of protein, scarcely amounts to one equivalent: the normal protein appears to be intimately mixed with a sulphuretted compound, which has probably the same equivalent composition in other respects as protein itself: an analogous case occurs in the two acids of the bile, which can scarcely be separated from each other by any known difference in properties. The phosphorus which is sometimes present, may belong to a body in which that element replaces nitrogen, wholly or in part. There are other organic matters in the brain and the blood, which contain phosphorus in a similar combination; but it is more probable that in the protein bodies, it exists as phosphate of lime.

887. The following numbers give the proportions of carbon, hydrogen, nitrogen, and oxygen, required by the above formula, and the results of an analysis of the protein from albumin, and one of fibrin. The amount of oxygen equivalent to the sulphur present, is given on one side, and added to the quantity of oxygen, for the purpose of comparison:—

	Calculated.	Analyses by Mulder. Protein.		Fibrin.	
Carbon	53·93	53·7		52·7	
Hydrogen	6·36	6·9		6·9	
Nitrogen	15.73	14·4		15·4	
Oxygen	23·98	23·6	24·3	23·5	24·3
Sulphur...........		1·4=0·7		1·2=0·6	
Phosphorus......				·3	
	100·00	100·0		100·0	

The results of different analyses of protein from other sources, show still greater variations in composition, one reason of which is the want of definite chemical characters by which we may be able to separate it from any admixture of foreign bodies. The above formula, however, coincides better than any other, with the analyses of the purest forms of protein: protein is, according to it, an amid, or rather a nitryl, of cellulose; $C_{24}H_{20}O_{20}+3NH_3=6H_2O_2+C_{24}H_{17}N_3O_8$. It should therefore under proper conditions assimilate water, and yield ammonia, and a body belonging to the series of cellulose, dextrine, or glucose; in fact, when protein is dissolved in strong heated chlorohydric acid, it is completely decomposed into ammonia, which forms sal-ammoniac, and a brown insoluble matter identical with that produced by the slow decay of woody fibre, and derived from cellulose by the loss of the elements of water. A similar body is produced from grape sugar by the action of chlorohydric acid.

The muscular tissue is insoluble protein in an organized condition, and sustains a similar rank in the animal structure to that of cellulose in the vegetal, while albumin and casein are soluble unorganized forms of protein, and may be compared to dextrin and gum.

888. The action of hydrate of potash aided by heat, upon the different forms of protein, evolves a great deal of ammonia mixed with hydrogen, and probably several volatile bases, and the residue contains, among other substances, salts of acetic, butyric, and valeric acids, and two crystalline azotized bodies, named *leucine* and *tyrosine*. The former has the formula $C_{12}H_{13}NO_4$; it is homologous with glycocine and alanine, and is an organic base resembling these in its characters. Tyrosine is $C_{18}H_{11}NO_6$. These two bodies are also obtained as products of the action of sulphuric acid upon protein. The protein bodies when mixed with water and kept in a warm place, readily undergo spontaneous decomposition, and evolve a disagreeable odor, becoming putrid. Fibrin is at first converted into a soluble form resembling albumin, hydrogen gas and ammonia are evolved, and there remain in solution ammoniacal salts of butyric and valeric acids, besides leucine and tyrosin, and a portion of undecomposed protein.

889. When any form of protein is distilled with a mixture of bichromate of potash and sulphuric acid, the latter not being in excess, the protein is oxydized by the chromic acid, and a great variety of volatile products are obtained; among them are prussic acid, or formic nitryl, and the nitryl of valeric acid, together with bitter-almond oil, benzoic acid, and the formic, propionic, butyric, and valeric acids. When peroxyd of manganese is substituted for the bichromate, with an excess of sulphuric acid, the nitryls are not obtained, but besides bitter-almond oil, and the acids already mentioned, the acetic and caproic acids, together with the acetic, propionic, butyric, and valeric aldehyds. In the latter process the residue contains salts of ammonia, and the acids may result from the decomposition of previously formed bodies

like leucine: this, when distilled with a mixture of oxyd of manganese and sulphuric acid, yields carbonic acid and valero-nitryl, and the latter by an excess of acid is converted into valeric acid and ammonia.

The destructive distillation of the protein bodies yields a large amount of carbonate of ammonia, and a number of volatile oily bases, some of which are homologous with ammonia, besides water and inflammable gases, and leaves a bulky charcoal very difficult of combustion, which contains several per cent. of nitrogen, and is perhaps a mixture of carbon with something analogous to paracyanogen.

890. When fibrin or casein is kept for some time in a cool, dark, and moist place, it undergoes a decomposition which results in its partial or entire conversion into a fusible fat, resembling butter and easily saponified, which has not yet been minutely examined. It is said to have a sweet taste, and to be readily volatile; if such is the case, it is not improbable that the product is an ether of some fatty acid or acids. This change is observed in the preparation of some kinds of cheese, and may be supposed to consist in the fixing of the elements of water, the separation of the nitrogen in the form of ammonia, and a great portion of the oxygen with some of the carbon, in the form of carbonic acid gas. It is accompanied with the development of a great number of mycodermic plants, or moulds, which appear to be nourished by the evolved gases.

891. The protein bodies not only undergo spontaneous decomposition themselves with great facility, but, under certain conditions, induce changes in a great variety of organic substances. The action of casein in converting sugar into acetic and lactic acids, and this latter into butyric and carbonic acids and hydrogen, and the conversion of sugar into alcohol and carbonic acid have already been described. Diastase which changes starch into sugar, and emulsine which effects the decomposition of salicine and amygdaline, are forms of protein or an allied substance.

If a minute portion of putrefying fibrin is added to a solution of leucine, this substance is decomposed and valerate of ammonia remains dissolved: the spontaneous decomposition of urea, hippuric acids, and the acids of the bile, in the presence of the putrescent animal matters of the secretions, are similar instances. These phenomena may be included under the general name of *fermentations;* although the term should be perhaps more restricted in its signification, and exclude those processes in which diastase and emulsine are the agents.

892. The alcoholic fermentation has been the one most carefully studied; it is produced by decomposing casein or fibrin, as well as by yeast. Yeast, when obtained from fermenting beer, has a chemical composition allied to protein, and resembles it in its properties; it is found under the microscope to be completely organized, and to consist of two minute species of fungus, which seem to be always produced and propagated in a solution of sugar, when undergoing the vinous fermentation: the presence of decomposing protein in a sugar solution, appears to excite fermentation by affording the conditions necessary to the development and nutrition of these fungi. These bodies are figured in § 695. One of the species in yeast appears to be more especially connected with the vinous fermentation, and, being much greater in size, may be separated by filtration from the other, which is regarded as the fungus of the lactic and butyric fermentations; this last also appears in the conversion of casein into fat, and it produces the decomposition of urea into carbonic acid and ammonia, a change which is rapidly effected in the presence of yeast. The acetic fermentation is characterized by a distinct fungus.

The power of yeast or any form of protein to produce these organic changes, is destroyed by boiling water, by chlorid of mercury, arsenious acid, salts of iron, zinc, alkalies, mineral acids, or by oil of turpentine or kreasote. Yeast may be dried at a gentle heat, and regain its activity when moistened with water, but if when dried, it is finely divided by trituration, so as to destroy the fungi, it is inert. It may be said that whatever is fatal to the vitality of the fungi, destroys at the same time the activity of the ferment. The bodies just mentioned are known to act as antiseptics, preventing putrescence, but it is not improbable that all cases of putrefaction belong to the same class of phenomena as these fermentations.

893. From the constant connection between the development of certain fungi and different chemical changes, it is supposed by many chemists that they are the agents in the process of fermentation, which is one essentially vital, and that the fungi decompose the organic bodies, perhaps by a sort of absorption and subsequent excretion.

The action of boiling water and of antiseptics, destroys the power of diastase and emulsine to act upon starch and amygdaline. I am not aware whether in these reactions, the development of fungi has been noticed. The phenomena most analogous to fermentations are such as those in which a small portion of sulphuric acid converts a large amount of alcohol into ether, or olefiant gas, and water, or where the same acid converts dextrine into sugar, or to the spontaneous decomposition of a solution of urea at an elevated temperature: in all these cases, the influence of vitality is evidently excluded. Our knowledge of chemical dynamics appears as yet inadequate to explain the part which fungi play in many processes, or to draw the distinction between those changes which appear to be effected through their agency, and those which are purely chemical.

894. *Gelatin.*—This substance exists in many animal tissues, as the skin, cellular membranes, tendons, and ligaments, and forms the frame-work of the bones; in this organized form it is insoluble in cold water, but by boiling it dissolves, and the solution forms on cooling a firm jelly, which is very characteristic of gelatin; this, when dried, constitutes ordinary glue. The substance known as *isinglass*, is the dried air-bladder of certain fishes, and is a nearly pure gelatinous tissue, which is soluble in boiling water. A solution of gelatin is precipitated by salts of mercury, and yields a copious insoluble precipitate with an infusion of nutgalls, or a solution of tannic acid; the insoluble tissues absorb tannic acid from its solutions to form the same compound, which constitutes leather. The process of *tanning* consists essentially in immersing the prepared skin in an infusion of oak or hemlock bark, by which it is saturated with tannin, and becomes incapable of putrefaction, insoluble in boiling water, firm, elastic, and, to an extent, water-proof.

895. Gelatin undergoes putrefaction like protein, and is susceptible of exciting fermentation; the products of its decomposition, by oxydation, and by the action of acids and alkalies, are the same with those of protein. It however yields, in addition to leucine, its homologue, glycocine $C_4H_5NO_4$, which was first described by the name of *sugar of gelatin*. When a solution of gelatin is boiled for many hours with dilute sulphuric acid, a large quantity of sulphate of ammonia is formed, and the liquid contains sugar, which yields alcohol and carbonic acid by fermentation. This reaction leads to the supposition that, like protein, it is nearly allied to dextrin or glucose, and the formula

$C_{24}H_{20}N_4O_8$, which accords closely with the results of various analyses of soluble and insoluble gelatin, makes it correspond to an amid formed from one equivalent of glucose and four of ammonia by the loss of eight of water. $C_{24}H_{24}O_{24}+4NH_3=C_{24}H_{20}N_4O_8+8H_2O_2$. The decomposition by sulphuric acid will then consist in the assimilation of water, and the regeneration of glucose and ammonia.

The gelatinous substance obtained from cartilage differs somewhat in its composition and properties from ordinary gelatin, and has been distinguished by the name of *chondrin*.

THE BLOOD.

896. This substance when recent is a homogeneous, slightly viscid, red fluid, of a saltish taste and a peculiar odor. When examined under a microscope it is found to consist of a transparent and nearly colorless liquid, in which are floating an immense number of small red bodies, (blood corpuscles,) varying in form and size in different animals, also a small and variable proportion of colorless globules, less in size than the red corpuscles, to which the name of *lymph globules* is given; their real nature is not well understood. Very soon after the blood is taken from the body, it separates into a red mass, called the *cruor* or *clot*, and a yellowish liquid, the *serum*. This change is due to the separation from the liquid of a portion of fibrin, which involves, as in a net, the blood corpuscles, and forms a soft mass distended with serum. If the blood, as soon as drawn, is stirred with a branched stick, the fibrin which separates, adheres in the form of white silky filaments, and the coagulation of the blood is prevented. The same result is obtained if the recent blood is mixed with three or four volumes of a saturated solution of sulphate of soda; this holds the fibrin in solution, and the red corpuscles separate unaltered; they may be separated by a linen filter, and washed from the serum with a solution of sulphate of soda, provided a current of air is kept up through the mixture. These bodies in the blood of most mammiferous ani-

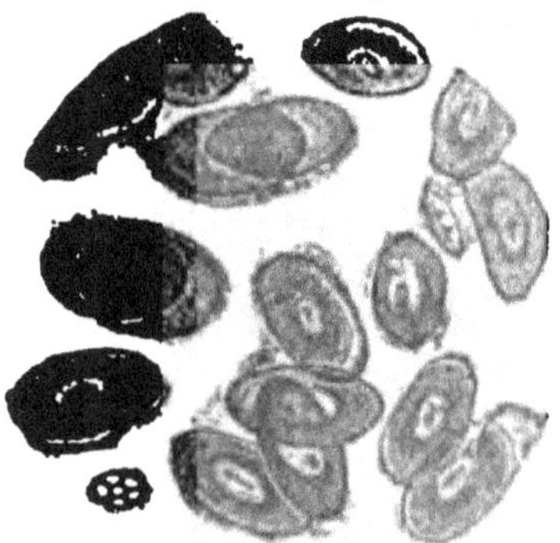

Fig. 421.

mals are red circular discs, with a depressed centre and colorless exterior; those of birds, reptiles, and fishes are elliptical. Figure 421 shows the blood discs of the common frog, as they appear under the microscope. The corpuscles in man are very small, being not more than from $\frac{1}{3000}$ to $\frac{1}{5000}$ of an inch in diameter; those of frogs are three or four times greater in their longer diameter. Figure 422 is a microscopic view of the red globules in the blood of man; they are very similar to those of other mammals; the central portions are less brilliant than the borders. The discs are often seen resting upon each other flatwise, as they are represented at *a a a*, and more frequently edgewise, as at *b b*.

Fig. 422.

897. When placed in pure water, the corpuscles swell, burst, and dissolve into a deep red liquid, which is coagulated by heat, and contains a large portion of protein, analogous to albumin. The coloring matter is separated from this by ammoniacal alcohol, in which it alone is soluble, and is obtained by evaporation as a dark red-brown mass, which is insoluble in pure water, but dissolves with the aid of alkalies, forming a blood-red solution. It constitutes but four or five-hundredths of the dried blood-globules, and is called *hematosine.* It contains a large portion of iron; chlorine separates the iron and renders the matter colorless; an alkaline sulphuret or sulphuretted hydrogen renders it greenish-black, probably from the separation of a metallic sulphuret, and strong sulphuric acid is said to remove the iron, forming a protosalt, and leaving the red color unaltered. The condition of the iron is analogous to that of this metal in some salts, as in the tartrates, in which it is not precipitated by the ordinary reagents. The coloring matter, according to Mulder, affords by analysis,

Carbon	66·49
Hydrogen	5·30
Nitrogen	10·50
Oxygen	11·05
Iron	6·66
	100·00

898. The serum of the blood is alkaline, and contains a large amount of dissolved albumen, which is coagulated by heat; besides this, it holds in solution a considerable amount of salts, which are chlorid of sodium, with sulphates, phosphates, and carbonates of potash and soda, phosphates of lime and magnesia, and peroxyd of iron. The blood contains besides about 1·6 parts in 1000 of fatty substances, consisting in part of ordinary saponifiable fats, and in part of a peculiar fatty acid containing phosphorus, besides cholesterine, and a fat named *seroline.* The following table is by Becquerel and Rodier, and represents the average composition of healthy human blood of both sexes:

	Man.	Woman.
Density of the defibrinated blood	1·0602	1·0575
Density of the serum	1·0280	1·0275
Water	779·000	791·100
Red globules	141·100	127·200
Albumin	69·400	70·500
Fibrin	2·200	2·200
Extractive matters, Salts	6·800	7·400
Total amount of fatty matters	1·600	1·620
Seroline	·020	·020
Phosphuretted fatty matter	·488	·464
Cholesterine	·088	·090
Saponifiable fat	1·004	1·046
Chlorid of sodium	3·100	3·900
Other soluble salts	2·500	2·900
Insoluble phosphates	·334	·354
Oxyd of iron	·566	·541

The existence of alkaline carbonates in the blood has been denied by some chemists, who assert that its alkalinity is due to the presence of tribasic phosphate of soda. Traces of fluorid of calcium, oxyds of manganese, lead, and copper have been detected in the blood of different animals, and silica in that of fowls. Besides these, urea and hippuric acid are found, and uric acid is said to have been detected; in certain cases of disease, the coloring matter of the bile, and its fatty acids, with an increased quantity of cholesterine appear in the blood. After the ingestion of vegetable food, the blood also contains a portion of sugar.

899. The color of arterial blood is bright scarlet, and that of the venous blood is dark red. The blood of the veins acquires the bright red tint in the lungs, and loses it again in the capillary vessels. These variations in color depend upon changes in the form and condition of the blood corpuscles, producing a difference in the reflection of light; those in arterial blood being convex and transparent, while those in the veins have become flattened and semi-opaque. These changes depend upon the action of oxygen; this gas is much more readily and more copiously absorbed by the blood than by water; the arterial blood of a horse contains in a state of solution from $\frac{1}{8}$ to $\frac{1}{10}$ its volume of gas, which contains about four parts of oxygen to one of nitrogen; this oxygen disappears in the capillary vessels, and is replaced in the venous blood, by carbonic acid gas. When venous blood is agitated in contact with atmospheric air or with oxygen, it absorbs this gas, and acquires the bright red color of arterial blood; on the contrary, the corpuscles separated from arterial blood and washed with a solution of sulphate of soda, assume the dark red color of venous blood and become disintegrated, dissolving and passing through the filter, unless supplied with oxygen. If, however, a current of atmospheric air is passed through the mixture upon the filter, the corpuscles preserve their scarlet tint, and remain entire.

900. The globules of the blood appear to be living organisms, which are capable of resisting the dissolving action of a solution of sulphate of soda, so long as life remains, but almost immediately become asphyxiated when deprived of air, and at once lose their bright color, and yield to the dissolving action of the saline solution. The solutions of some salts, as sal-ammoniac and the chlorid of potassium, prevent the aëration of the blood, even in oxygen gas.

The vitality of the blood, a doctrine as ancient as the time of Moses, is thus sustained by these facts. The spontaneous coagulation of the blood, when removed from the body, or in the veins after death, is caused by the separation in an insoluble organized form of a portion of dissolved protein, and seems, like the organization of effused lymph, to be dependent upon an inherent vitality of the fluid, exterior to, and perhaps independent of the blood corpuscles. The proportion of fibrin which thus separates is intimately connected with the state of the vital powers, and affords an index to the state of the system in health or disease. In scrofula and other maladies connected with an asthenic condition of the system, the blood coagulates but feebly, and the amount of fibrin which separates is much less than ordinary; while in inflammatory diseases, where the action of the system is unduly heightened, the blood coagulates firmly and rapidly, and the proportion of fibrin formed is much greater than in healthy blood: fibrin constitutes the so-called *buffy coat* of the blood in inflammatory diseases. The normal quantity of fibrin in healthy blood may be stated at from 2·2 to 2·5 parts in 1000; while in cases of phlegmasia it rises to 6 and 7, and in scrofula and the latter stages of typhus is not above 1·2 or 2. In cases of death by lightning, and by certain poisons, or from a blow upon the stomach, or even from sudden mental emotions, like violent anger, the blood is found to have lost the power of coagulation. The blood corpuscles are found to diminish with the proportion of fibrin, and in some cases of scrofula amount to no more than 64 to 70 parts in 1000; they are at the same time, small, pale, and irregular in shape. The proportion of globules is also diminished after blood-letting or hemorrhages, and while in acute diseases generally, it remains unaltered, is increased in plethoric patients. The proportion of albumin and fibrin taken together, generally remains unchanged, except in what is called Bright's disease, when the amount of albumin is notably diminished, a change dependent upon its excretion in the urine. The mean composition of the blood in the two sexes is seen, by the table already given, to be somewhat different, (§ 898.)

901. *The Flesh Fluid.*—The recent muscular fibre from which the blood has been drained, contains about 80 per cent. of watery fluid, which may be removed by chopping the flesh and washing it with cold water. The liquid thus obtained, unlike the blood, has an acid reaction; when heated, a form of protein resembling albumin coagulates; if the acid liquid is then neutralized by baryta-water, phosphate of baryta and phosphate of magnesia separate, and by evaporation, sparingly soluble, colorless crystals of *creatin* $C_8H_9N_3O_4$, are deposited. This substance is neutral, but when its solution is evaporated with an acid, it loses H_2O_2 and is converted into a crystalline, strongly alkaline, organic base, *creatinine* $C_8H_7N_3O_2$, which under certain circumstances unites with H_2O_2, and regenerates creatin. When boiled with an excess

of caustic baryta, creatin is decomposed, ammonia is evolved, and a carbonate formed, from the decomposition of urea; the liquid affords crystals of *sarcosine* $C_6H_7NO_4$. Creatin with water yields urea and sarcosine, $C_8H_9N_3O_4+H_2O_2= C_2H_4N_2O_2+C_6H_7NO_4$. Sarcosine is metameric with alanine, which it very much resembles in its general characters, and is like it an organic base, but is distinguished from alanine and its homologues, by subliming unchanged at a heat of 212° F. There are evidently two metameric series of bases of the type $C_nH_{n+1}NO_4$, which are represented by alanine and sarcosine; glycocine and leucine appear to pertain to the same series as alanine, while the sulphuretted base thialdine, $C_{12}H_{13}NS_4$ would seem from its ready volatility to belong to the series of sarcosine.

902. The flesh-fluid also affords a peculiar acid, called *inosinic acid*, which is very soluble in water, and has the peculiar flavor of broth. Its probable formula is $C_{20}H_{14}N_4O_{22}$, representing a bibasic acid. The salts of inosinic acid crystallize beautifully; that of baryta is sparingly soluble; and those of potash and soda evolve, when decomposed by heat, a strong and agreeable odor of roasted meat. Besides this, an acid, which appears to be a modification of lactic acid, is obtained from the flesh-fluid. Creatin has been found alike in the flesh of birds, beasts, reptiles, and fishes. Fowls, which contain the largest quantity, furnish about $\frac{3}{1000}$ of creatin, and about half as much of the inosinate of baryta. Creatin and creatinine are also found in the urine, and uric acid has been detected in the muscle of an alligator.

The flesh-fluid contains a considerable amount of salts, principally alkaline phosphates and chlorids; the salts of potassium here predominate, while those of sodium are more abundant in the blood.

903. *Saliva.*—This fluid in its normal state is slightly alkaline, and contains, besides animal matter, small portions of salts, principally chlorids and phosphates of alkaline bases; in that of man a small portion of a soluble sulphocyanate is found.

The *pancreatic juice* is also alkaline, and analogous to the saliva in its composition; both of these secretions contain in solution an azotized organic substance, which may be precipitated by alcohol, and like diastase possesses the power of rapidly transforming a solution of starch into dextrine and glucose. They are supposed in this manner to exercise an important part in preparing these substances for assimilation. The serum of the blood has a similar action upon starch.

904. The secretion of the stomach, called the *gastric juice*, is acid in its reaction, and contains portions of alkaline chlorids, free lactic acid, and an azotized substance similar to that of the saliva. It has the power of dissolving, at the temperature of the body, fibrin, coagulated albumin, and other forms of protein, but has no solvent action upon starch; if however the gastric fluid is rendered feebly alkaline, it no longer dissolves protein, but acts upon starch like the saliva and pancreatic juice. In the same way these, when rendered acid, acquire the power of dissolving protein. The tissue of the pancreas from a dead animal, when cut in pieces and mixed with water, still exerts a solvent power upon starch, and the lining membrane of the stomach, when digested with water slightly acidulated with chlorohydric acid, forms an artificial gastric juice. The animal matter of the gastric juice, which is apparently identical with that of the saliva, has been named *pepsin*, (from *pepto*, I digest,) and like diastase is at once rendered inactive by a boiling heat, and by various antiseptics. It is analogous to the protein bodies in its composition, and like them has, under certain conditions, the power of converting sugar into lactic acid, and thus changing its reaction, so as to become capable of dissolving protein.

905. The *bile* has already been shown (879) to consist essentially of the soda-salts of two azotized acids: besides these, there are small portions of alkaline chlorids and phosphates, and some mucus, the azotized secretion of the mucous surfaces. The substance of the liver generally contains a small portion of sugar. The bile is alkaline in its reactions, and has the power of rendering fats and oils soluble, acting like a soap, and apparently fitting them for the process of assimilation. The same power is possessed by the saliva and pancreatic juice, which with the bile and gastric juice are brought in contact with the food in different parts of the alimentary canal, and by their combined action render the amylaceous, fatty, and proteinaceous portions of the food soluble, and ready to be elaborated in the form of chyle. Such, in the present state of our knowledge, seems to be the nature and result of the process of digestion.

906. *Chyle.*—This fluid in the human body, as taken up by the lacteals from the small intestines, is white and opake, and contains dissolved protein in a form resembling albumen, with small globules of fat, to which its milkiness is due, and a portion of sugar, besides various salts and a portion of iron in a soluble form; when first taken up from the intestines, it yields but very little fibrin, but the chyle from the thoracic duct coagulates like blood, yielding a clot which contains fibrin, and the clear liquid resembles the serum of the blood, to which this liquid is already as it were in a state of transformation, wanting only the red corpuscles.

The solid excrements of animals contain portions of the food, insoluble or unfit for assimilation; those of the herbivora are made up in part of ligneous matter, and those of carnivora contain a portion of an azotized substance, and yield ammonia by their decomposition; phosphates and other salts are present in considerable quantity, in the excrements, and render these substances valuable as manures.

907. *Urine.*—This excrementitious substance is separated from the blood by the kidneys, and removes from the body various salts and azotized matters. The latter are urea and hippuric and uric acids, which have already been described. The urine of birds and reptiles, which is white and solid, is principally urate of ammonia. That of herbivorous mammals is alkaline, and contains in solution, besides urea, a large amount of hippuric acid; while in carnivora this acid is wanting, and a large amount of urea is found, with a little uric acid. This is nearly the composition of the urine of man subsisting upon a mixed diet: the average quantity of urea in healthy human urine is about 3 per cent., and that of uric acid about $\frac{1}{1000}$; it also contains a little hippuric acid. When benzoic acid is taken into the stomach, the urine a few hours afterward is found to contain a large amount of hippuric acid, apparently formed in some way from the benzoic acid. Creatin and creatinine are also found in urine, and that of young calves contains in addition to a considerable quantity of creatinine, a notable amount of allantoin. The saline matters of the urine generally amount to two or three per cent., and consist of chlorid of sodium, with sulphates and phosphates of potash and soda, and traces of ammoniacal salts, besides phosphates of lime and

magnesia. Urine also contains a peculiar organic coloring matter, and a portion of mucus from the bladder, which in a few hours excites a decomposition of the urea, the liquid becoming alkaline from the carbonate of ammonia formed. If this mucus be removed by filtration, the urine may be preserved a long time without change. When putrescent urine is evaporated, the ammoniacal salt forms with the phosphate of soda, the double phosphate of soda and ammonia, which was formerly known as the *essential salt of urine*, or *microcosmic salt*.* If the residue is evaporated to dryness and distilled at a red heat, the acid of a portion of phosphate of ammonia is decomposed by the organic matter present, and a small quantity of phosphorus is obtained; it was by this process that this curious element was first prepared.

The fresh urine of man and the carnivora has an acid reaction, which is ascribed to the uric acid held in solution by phosphate of soda: on adding a little chlorohydric acid to the urine, the uric acid separates after a few hours in small but distinct crystals.

908. In disease the composition of this fluid is sometimes altered, and the elements of the chyle and blood find their way into the urine: in some forms of dropsy and diseases of the kidneys, it contains albumin, while the urea is deficient, and is found in the blood and other fluids of the body. In other cases, all the sugar contained in the food, or formed in the digestive process from starch, is excreted in the urine, under the form of glucose, and constitutes the disease called *diabetes mellitus:* in this disease the urine still contains urea in large quantity.

In some states of the system, the uric acid increasing in quantity, or the solvent power of urine being diminished, this acid is deposited in the form of gravel or *calculus*. Uric acid or urate of ammonia constitutes the most common form of calculus; but phosphate of lime, and the phosphate of magnesia and ammonia, besides oxalate and more rarely carbonate of lime, are also found as urinary concretions.

---

* So named by the older chemists as it was then supposed to be a salt peculiar to man. Man was called the *microcosm*, because in his three-fold nature is repeated in miniature the order of the universe, the great *kosmos* or *macrocosm*.

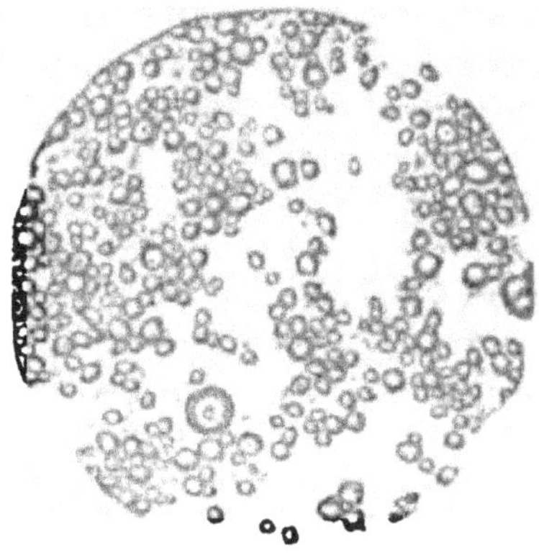

Fig. 423.

909. *Milk.*—This secretion of the female contains in a soluble form all the substances necessary for the nutrition of the young,—protein, fat, sugar, and various salts. When viewed under the microscope, milk is seen (fig. 423) to contain numerous globules of fat suspended in a clear liquid; these globules are butter, and give to milk its opacity. The proportions of its ingredients vary, but the following analysis of cow's milk may be taken as an example:—1000 parts contain,

Water	873·0
Butter	30·0
Casein, and a little albumin	48·2
Milk-sugar, or lactose	43.9
Phosphate of lime, with a little fluorid of calcium	2·3
Chlorids of potassium and sodium	1·7
Phosphate of iron and magnesia, with a little soda combined with casein	·9
	1000·0

Woman's milk contains proportionably more sugar and less casein, and in these respects it resembles asses milk, which also contains but little butter: the milk of carnivora likewise contains a considerable proportion of sugar, even when the animals have been fed for a long time exclusively on flesh. It is in this case probably derived from the transformation of gelatin or protein, in the manner already pointed out; and the lactic acid in the flesh-fluid of carnivora must have a similar origin.

910. When milk is saturated with common salt and filtered, a clear liquid is obtained, which holds in solution the casein, sugar, and salts; while the butter rests upon the filter in the form of globules, which are enclosed in an albuminous membrane, and are insoluble in ether. If, however, the milk is first boiled, the albuminous coating appears to be dissolved, and the whole of the butter is dissolved by agitation with ether, leaving the milk transparent. After a few hours' repose the greater part of the globules rise to the surface in the form of *cream*. In describing casein, (875,) the effect of acids in

producing the coagulation of milk has been already noticed: the whey contains all the sugar, and the soluble salts. The spontaneous coagulation of milk depends upon the formation of a little lactic acid from the sugar: in the preparation of cheese, an infusion of the lining membrane of a calf's stomach, called *rennet*, is added, which causes an almost immediate separation of the casein in an insoluble form; this reaction does not depend upon the formation of lactic acid, but may take place in the presence of an excess of alkali; milk in its recent state has an alkaline reaction. In cheese which has been long kept, there are found several products of the decomposition of casein, among which are salts of butyric and valeric acids, and probably leucine; besides butter from the milk, cheese often contains a portion of fat, from the transformation of the casein already described.

911. *Eggs.*—The white part of the eggs of fowls consists of a solution of albumin, with small quantities of soda and various salts: on boiling eggs, a portion of sulphur, from the albumin, combines with soda to form a sulphuret of sodium, which is recognized by the blackening of a piece of bright silver. The yolk of eggs contains, besides a protein compound, a large portion of oil which consists principally of oleine and margarine, and a peculiar viscous matter which contains ammonia, and yields, by the action of acids, oleic and margaric acids, and a soluble acid which appears to contain the elements of phosphoric acid and glycerine. Besides these, lactic acid and the salts which are found in the blood and flesh-fluid, are present.

912. The *brain* and *nervous substance* are similar in their chemical nature, and the white and gray portions of the brain differ chiefly in their structure; they contain about 80 per cent. of water. The solid matter consists in part of a protein body, and in part of a substance which, by the action of acids, yields products similar to the viscous matter of the yolk of eggs. Besides these there is present a fatty crystalline acid, which contains nitrogen and about one per cent. of phosphorus, and has been named *cerebric acid.* It is but little known, but is probably somewhat analogous to the acids of the bile. It appears to be identical with the phosphuretted fat of the blood; cholesterine is also present in the substance of the brain besides an

oily fat acid, which appears to contain the elements of phosphoric and oleic acids. The solid matter of the brain contains about four per cent. of phosphorus.

913. *Bones.*—The bones consist of a tissue of insoluble gelatine enveloping a large amount of earthy salts. The bones of young animals contain but a small portion of mineral matter, which increases with their growth. A deficiency of the solid ingredients occurs in rickets, and other diseases connected with defective nutrition. The dried bones of adults contain from 30 to 40 per cent. of organic matter, which is almost entirely soluble in boiling water; water also removes small quantities of salts of soda. The remainder, is principally tribasic phosphate of lime $PO_5.3CaO$, with small portions of phosphate of magnesia, carbonate of lime, and fluorid of calcium. The two analyses which follow are of a human femur and the femur of an ox:—

	Man.	Ox.
Phosphate of lime	58·30	59·67
Phosphate of magnesia	2·09	1·21
Carbonate of lime	7·07	6·39
Fluorid of calcium	2·73	2·05
Organic matter	30·58	31·11
	100·77	100·43

When a bone is immersed in a dilute acid, as the chlorohydric, the earthy salts are entirely removed, and the bone becomes translucent and flexible. It then dissolves in boiling water, leaving only a small portion of insoluble tissue, consisting of the blood-vessels which penetrated its substance, and which are composed of protein. The *horns* of the deer are analogous to bones in composition; the tusks of the elephant, which constitute ivory, and the teeth, are very similar: the latter contain less organic matter than bones, and in the enamel of the teeth, which contains a considerable amount of fluorid of calcium, the animal matter is absent.

914. The *horns* of cattle, which, unlike those of the deer, are flexible and softened by heat, are, like the hoofs of animals, composed of a protein body containing a large amount of sulphur. The skeletons of zoophytes and the shells of mollusks contain a small quantity of animal matter, with carbonate of lime and small portions of phosphates of lime and magnesia and fluorid of calcium. Those of many crustaceans consist principally of phosphate of lime with a little magnesia and carbonate of lime.

When the leather-like coating of the *salpæ* and some other tunicate mollusks is digested with a solution of potash, the nervous and muscular portions are dissolved, and the insoluble residue contains no nitrogen, and appears identical in composition to the cellulose of plants.

NUTRITION OF PLANTS AND OF ANIMALS.

915. In the order of nature, the animal creation derives its support from the vegetable, whose products are directly or indirectly the food of the former. A large number of animals subsist upon herbs or grains, and the flesh of these vegetable feeders is the food of carnivorous animals. Plants have the power of forming from carbonic acid, water, and ammonia, those bodies of the carbon series which are necessary for the support of animals. The nutrition of plants may then be properly considered first in order.

916. The organic substances essential to plants are cellulose and protein, to which we may perhaps add starch; these go to make up the simplest vegetable structure, and neither of them are probably ever wanting. In addition to these are sugar, gum, oils, resins, acids, alkaloids, and many other substances, some one or more of which are generally present in different parts of plants. The history of the related series of cellulose, starch, sugar, and gum, and of the protein compounds, has been already given. These bodies in their organized forms always contain small and variable portions of salts of potash, soda, lime, and magnesia, with chlorine, phosphoric, sulphuric, and silicic acids. The juices of plants contain these same salts in solution, sometimes with the addition of those of ammonia, and various vegetable acids, either free or in the form of salts. These mineral ingredients appear essential to healthy development; they perform, however, but a secondary part in the nutrition of plants, whose food consists essentially of water, carbonic acid, and ammonia, from which, as has been already said, they form the various organic substances, by the combination of certain molecules and the elimination of certain others, in a manner similar to that which we have so often illustrated in the preceding pages.

917. Cellulose and the allied substances contain precisely the elements of carbon and water, and may be formed from the elements of carbonic acid gas and water, or rather from hydrated carbonic acid $C_2H_2O_6$, by the separation of oxygen; $12C_2H_2O_6 = C_{24}H_{20}O_{20} + O_{48}$. Protein, which we have shown may be regarded as the amid of cellulose, is formed with the concurrence of the elements of ammonia, in a manner which will be at once understood. Sugar and gum differ from cellulose only by the elements of water, and the various vegetable acids and other matters containing oxygen, hydrogen, and carbon, may be formed in a manner analogous to cellulose from carbonic acid and water, by the separation of oxygen. It is probable that the saline and alkaline matters in the juices exercise peculiar influences upon these processes, and conduce to the formation of the various products.

918. The oxygen set free in all these processes is evolved in the form of gas. If a branch of a green healthy plant is exposed, under an inverted bell-glass filled with water, to the sun's rays, minute bubbles of gas appear upon the leaves, and rise to the top of the vessel. They are pure oxygen, which is constantly evolved by all healthy plants when exposed to the influence of light. In darkness, the action is suspended or imperfectly performed, and the carbonic acid which is absorbed by the roots, is given off from the leaves instead of oxygen; the leaves of plants also exhale large quantities of water. Although it is principally through the roots that carbonic acid, water, and ammonia are taken up, the leaves have also the power of absorbing water and gases for the support of the plant.

If a plant is made to grow in a mixture of oxygen and carbonic acid gases, the latter is gradually absorbed and replaced by pure oxygen. Flowers and fruits, during the period of their growth, however, reverse this process, and absorb oxygen from the atmosphere, while they evolve carbonic acid gas.

919. The atmospheric waters falling upon the earth, contain in solution a portion of carbonic acid and a minute quantity of carbonate of ammonia, two ingredients which are always present in the atmosphere. The water dissolves from the soil a minute portion of earthy and alkaline salts, which are in part set free by the disintegration of the earthy minerals under the influence of water and carbonic acid

In this form the different elements are taken up by the rootlets of the plant, and while the carbonic acid and ammonia are assimilated in the way that we have seen, the sulphates and phosphates furnish the portions of sulphur and phosphorus contained in vegetable protein, while their alkaline bases with the vegetable acids, form salts, which, being decomposed by heat, are the source of the alkaline carbonates, always found in the ashes of vegetables. The bitartrate of potash in the juice of grapes is an example of the occurrence of an organic potash salt.

920. Careful analyses of their ashes have shown that the nature and proportions of saline matters differ greatly in different plants, and that the long-continued cultivation of any species of plant upon the same soil may so far exhaust the soluble mineral matter as to render the soil unfruitful. In such circumstances, its fertility may be restored by the application of mineral manures, such as bone-dust, gypsum, and wood-ashes. A soil which has become unfitted for the growth of one plant may still contain the mineral substances necessary for the support of another, and hence the utility of an alternation of crops in agriculture. The ashes of tobacco contain, for example, a large amount of potash salts, and those of wheat and other cereal grains abound in phosphate of lime, and contain but little potash; so that a soil unfitted for tobacco may still produce good wheat, and *vice versa.* Many plants which grow in the vicinity of the sea contain a large amount of salts of soda; such are those that afford the impure alkali kelp or barilla. The amount of mineral matter in many of the fucoids or sea-weeds is very large, and the quantity of potash which they contain sometimes exceeds that of the soda; a fact which shows the curious power of plants to choose certain elements in preference to others, for the proportion of potash salts in sea-water is very small. The ashes of marine plants are also remarkable for containing salts of iodine, an element which cannot be detected in sea-water, but is contained in considerable quantity in the plants growing therein, and is even present in traces in many fresh-water plants.

921. Fertile soils generally contain a portion of organic matter, derived from the decomposition of roots, leaves, and other vegetable substances, and approaching to what has been named *humus* or *humic acid.* This substance by its slow decomposition constantly evolves carbonic acid, and is

thus a source of carbon to the roots of plants. This organic matter also contains in its substance the various salts necessary for plants, and during its decay, sets them free in a soluble form. It is still further efficient by the power which it possesses, in common with charcoal, clay, and other porous substances, of absorbing the ammonia contained in the air or evolved from the decomposition of azotized matters, and holding it in such a form that it is dissolved out by atmospheric waters, and brought to the roots of plants. It would also appear, from the experiments of Mulder, that humus possesses the power of forming ammonia with the nitrogen of the air.

922. Some chemists maintain that soluble forms of humus are directly absorbed by the roots, and thus constitute their food: there are however no proofs of such an absorption, and many arguments against it. It is well established that, if supplied with atmospheric waters and the proper mineral ingredients, plants will flourish and mature their seeds in a soil destitute of organic matter. Many plants are parasitic, and grow without any connection with the soil; they may be suspended in the air, and will continue to grow for years, absorbing food through their leaves, and generating cellulose, protein, and other organic bodies. The small portion of mineral matter which these plants contain, may be derived from the solution and absorption of the dust floating in the air.

In the process of germination, the albumin of the moistened seed becomes soluble, and its starch is converted into sugar: these substances serve to nourish the embryo plants; but when the roots and leaves are fully formed, the plant begins a new mode of life. Its carbon is derived from carbonic acid, and the decomposing organic matters of the soil serve only as sources of carbonic acid, ammonia, and salts. We have seen how some of the fungi excite the decomposition of protein and sugar solutions, apparently assimilating a portion of the evolved carbonic acid and ammonia, and it is not improbable that the rootlets of the higher orders of plants may act in a like manner upon the organic matters in the soil, thus accelerating their decomposition.

923. Animal matters act beneficially as manures, by the ammonia which they evolve with the carbonic acid, in the process of decay. Bone-dust in addition, affords phosphates; and urine, besides its ammonia, contains a great variety of

earthy and alkaline phosphates, and chlorids. Dilute solutions of sulphate, or other salts of ammonia, act as powerful stimulants to vegetation, and the efficacy of *guano*, which is the decomposing excrement of sea-birds, is due in great part to the ammonia which it yields. In its recent state it contains besides inorganic salts a large portion of urate of ammonia, from which, during decomposition, oxalate and other salts of ammonia are formed. Wheat manured with guano is said to contain a larger proportion of protein than that grown upon the same soil without the manure. The efficacy of gypsum depends in part upon its furnishing lime and sulphates to plants, and in part apparently from its power of condensing and retaining in the form of sulphate, the ammonia from the air and other sources. The ammonia contained as carbonate in atmospheric waters being brought in contact with earthy salts in the soil, must always be brought to the roots of the plants, in the form of sulphate or chlorid, or as a soluble ammonia-magnesian salt.

924. *The food of animals*, whether they feed upon flesh, or upon vegetable substances, consists of protein in its various forms, starch, sugar, gum, and fat, to which, in the case of carnivorous animals, gelatine is to be added. The vegetable feeders convert the protein bodies of their food into muscular fibre, which is afterward the food of the carnivora. These protein compounds, which can alone form blood and muscle, are to be distinguished from the non-azotized portions of the food, and have been called *the plastic elements of nutrition*, in distinction from the latter, which are named *the plastic elements of respiration*, being consumed in that process. Gelatine probably belongs to the latter class; it has never been found in the blood, and is supposed to be converted into sugar and ammoniacal salts.

925. The power of producing from simpler bodies, the complex organic products, does not belong to the animal system. The process of digestion has already been briefly described; the saliva, bile, gastric and pancreatic juices exert upon the food an essentially disorganizing, destroying action, which reduces it to a soluble plastic form, fit for assimilation, in which process the protein assumes an organic structure, and forms blood and muscular fibre, while gelatine is probably formed from a portion of it, by a reaction not well understood. The sugar contained in the food or formed from the starch, appears to be in great part absorbed by

the coats of the stomach and small intestines, in the same way as water and saline fluids, and thus finds its way into the veins, without passing through the chyle-duct. It is directly oxydized in the circulation, and in a few hours after its ingestion disappears entirely from the blood. Alcohol is absorbed in the same way, and oxydized in the circulation, being converted into water and carbonic acid. Acetic acid has been found in the blood as an intermediate product of the oxydation of alcohol, and formic acid is said to have been detected after the ingestion of sugar.

The fat, which, with the protein, passes through the chyle into the blood, is deposited in the adipose tissues: besides that contained in the food, it is probable that fat is formed by some process from the other aliments; its spontaneous production from protein has been already described, and we have seen how fatty acids, like the butyric, valeric, and capric, may be formed from sugar, and by the oxydation of protein. To these considerations may be added some experiments which seem to show that geese, in the process of fattening, secrete a greater amount of fat than is contained in the food which they consume.

926. It has been shown that the blood in the lungs dissolves a large portion of oxygen gas. The cells of that organ are filled with air in the process of respiration, and the minute branches of the pulmonic artery are spread over the walls of the cells. The delicate arterial membrane being permeable to gases, oxygen is absorbed and carbonic acid gas given off through it. The use of the oxygen in the oxydation of sugar and alcohol has already been shown; the whole of the oxygen absorbed, is not given out in the form of carbonic gas, but is in part exhaled as aqueous vapor from the lungs, and from the skin.

There is, in addition to this oxydizing process, a constant action going on in the tissues, which results in their disorganization and conversion into simpler forms. This is effected in the capillary vessels with the concurrence of the dissolved oxygen of the arterial blood; protein is decomposed, with the addition of oxygen, into a set of highly carbonized bodies, the fatty acids of the bile; and of highly azotized substances, urea and uric acid, which are carried by the veins to the liver and kidneys, and are separated from the blood; in the one case to be voided in the urine, and in the other to be returned to the alimentary canal, and there to perform some part in the nutritive process. It is not improbable that the acids of the bile may be converted into ordinary fats, which are thus indirectly formed from the protein tissues. Lactic acid on the one hand, and creatin and inosinic acid on the other, are also products of this metamorphosis, which has been called *the destructive assimilation.* Its relation to the matter of the brain and nerves is not yet well understood.

927. The oxydation of fat, by which it is converted ultimately into carbonic acid and water, does not probably take place in the circulation, as in the case of sugar, but is effected through the capillary vessels, in the tissues where the fat has previously been deposited. When the amount of sugar, and farinaceous food is great, animals grow fat, for the glucose preserves the fatty tissues from the influence of the oxygen, which is consumed in the oxydation of the sugar and the change of the protein tissues. If, however, the supply of farinaceous food is diminished, the fat is removed by oxydation faster than it is deposited, and finally disappears.

928. The object of nutrition, in its wider sense, is to supply the waste of the tissues, and satisfy the demands of the respiratory process, thus preserving the balance of the system. In those animals that feed upon flesh, the fat contained in their food or formed from protein, supplies the wants of the latter process; while in those animals which live upon vegetables, or like man upon a mixed diet, the sugar, alcohol, and farinaceous portions of the food supply more or less completely the demands of the respiratory process, and, if these be in excess, the fat contained in the food often accumulates in the system.

The waste of the muscular, and probably also of the nervous substances, appears to sustain an intimate relation to the amount of muscular and nervous activity of the system,* while the oxydation of the respiratory elements is related to animal heat. Respiration is essential to life, and even in those animals which do not breathe air, the process is effected through oxygen dissolved in the water. We have

* The condition of sleep, in which the muscular and nervous energies are to a great degree suspended, probably sustains an important relation to the nutritive process, particularly as related to the brain and nerves. The different functions of plants in light and darkness suggest an analogy in this connection, which is worthy of consideration.

shown that oxygen is necessary to preserve the life of the blood corpuscles out of the body; and it is the deprivation of air which causes the death of animals, by preventing the aëration of the corpuscles, and destroying the vitality of the blood. The introduction of large quantities of alcohol into the system produces a similar asphyxia, by rapidly consuming the oxygen, and thus preventing the proper aëration of the blood. The presence of phosphuretted fat, mentioned in the analyses of the blood before given, is said to be confined to the venous blood, which contains no soluble phosphates; in the arterial blood the fat is freed from phosphorus, which is found in the form of phosphates in the serum.

929. The oxydation of carbon and hydrogen compounds, converting them into carbonic acid and water, is supposed to be the source of vital heat in animals; the amount of carbon thus thrown off from the lungs of a full-grown man is equal to about seven ounces in twenty-four hours. In some instances of disease, however, where the respiratory function has been suspended for many hours, the heat of the body has remained undiminished. Plants have equally to a certain extent, the power of maintaining a temperature above that of the atmosphere: this is most evident in the leaves and young shoots, where vegetation is most active; but in plants the vital process is accompanied with a constant evolution of oxygen, from an action the very reverse of that which goes on in animals. Heat is a common result of chemical changes, even where oxygen is not absorbed, and there is no difficulty in understanding its production in any of the processes of assimilation.

It is, however, probably true, that in healthy animals the oxydation of carbon sustains a direct relation to the heat evolved. Hence it is that in warm climates, where the loss of animal heat is small, farinaceous matters, containing a large amount of oxygen, and as it were, partly oxydized, are the food of the people, and are found most congenial to the taste; while the inhabitants of arctic regions consume large quantities of fat and oil, less oxygenized species of food, which are found not only agreeable, but necessary to support the demands of the respiratory process, and to resist the intense cold.

930. The elements of the food of plants are taken from the air, earth, and waters, and by the forces of the living organism are formed into woody fibre, starch, sugar, and

protein, which serve for fuel and for the nourishment of animals. By the processes of life, by combustion and decay, these elements are again set free in the forms of water, carbonic acid, and ammonia, and enter once more into the current of organic life. In this way, the results of the decomposition of organic matters are removed from the atmosphere, which would otherwise be vitiated by them, and the carbonic gas which is taken up by plants, is replaced by an equal volume of oxygen gas, so that the purity of the air is preserved.

In the mutual dependence of the great processes of animal and vegetable life and decay, there is seen a system in which no one process is its own end, but is implicated in every other, and can be understood only in its relation to the Universe, and to that Being who is at once the efficient and final Cause of all creation.

APPENDIX,

CONTAINING TABLES OF WEIGHTS AND MEASURES, OF CORRESPONDING THERMOMETRICAL DEGREES, HYDROMETER TABLES, STRENGTH OF ALCOHOL, AND ANALYSES OF WATERS.

WEIGHTS AND MEASURES.

AVOIRDUPOIS, OR IMPERIAL WEIGHT.

						Equivalents in Troy grains.
1 drachm						27·34
16 =	1 ounce					437·5
256 =	16 =	1 pound				7000·
3584 =	224 =	14 =	1 stone			98000·
28672 =	1792 =	112 =	8 =	1 hundred weight		784000·
478440 =	35840 =	2240 =	160 =	20 =	1 ton	15680000·

TROY WEIGHT.

1 grain.			
24 " =	1 pennyweight.		
480 " =	20 " =	1 ounce.	
5760 " =	240 " =	12 " =	1 pound.

APOTHECARIES' WEIGHT.

1 grain, gr.				
20 " =	1 scruple, ℈			
60 " =	3 " =	1 drachm, ʒ.		
480 " =	24 " =	8 " =	1 ounce, ℥.	
5760 " =	288 " =	96 " =	12 " =	1 pound, ℔.

APOTHECARIES', OR WINE MEASURE.

Adopted in the United States and Dublin Pharmacopœias.

	Cubic inches.		Troy grains of pure water, at 60° F.
1 minim, ♏︎	·00376	=	0·95
60 = 1 fluid-drachm, f ʒ	·2256	=	56·95
480 = 8 = 1 fluid-ounce, f ℥	1·8047	=	455.607
7680 = 128 = 16 = 1 pint, O	28·8750	=	7289·724
61440 = 1024 = 128 = 8 = 1 cong.	231·000	=	58317·798

The imperial gallon contains of water, at 60°..... 70,000· grains.
The pint ($\frac{1}{8}$th gallon)........ 8,750· "
The fluid-ounce ($\frac{1}{20}$th of pint)........ 437·5 "

The pint equals 34·66 cubic inches.

The American standard gallon contains of pure water, at 39·83°, 58·372 Troy grains.

The French *kilogramme* = 15434· grains, or 2·679 lbs. Troy, or 2·205 lbs. avoirdupoids.

The *gramme* .... = 15·4340 grains.
" *decigramme* .... = 1·5434 "
" *centigramme* .... = ·1543 "
" *miligramme* .... = ·0154 "

The *mètre* of France........ = 39·37 inches.
" *decimètre* .... = 3·937 "
" *centimètre* .... = ·394 "
" *millimètre* .... = ·0394 "

TABLE OF THE CORRESPONDING DEGREES ON THE SCALES OF FAHRENHEIT, REAUMUR, AND CENTIGRADE, OR CELSIUS.

Fahr.	Reaum.	Cent.	Fahr.	Reaum.	Cent.	Fahr.	Reaum.	Cent.
212	80	100	149	52	65	50	8	10
203	76	95	140	48	60	41	4	5
194	72	90	131	44	55	32	0	0
185	68	85	122	40	50	23	4	5
176	64	80	113	36	45	14	8	10
167	60	75	104	32	40	5	12	15
158	56	70	95	28	35	4	16	20
			86	24	30	13	20	25
			77	20	25	22	24	30
			68	16	20	31	28	35
			59	12	15	40	32	40

HYDROMETER TABLES.

COMPARISON OF THE DEGREES OF BAUMÉ'S HYDROMETER, WITH THE REAL SPECIFIC GRAVITY.

1. *For Liquids Heavier than Water.*

Degrees.	Specific gravity.	Degrees.	Specific gravity.	Degrees.	Specific gravity.	Degrees.	Specific gravity.
0	1·000	20	1·152	40	1·357	60	1·652
1	1·007	21	1·160	41	1·369	61	1·670
2	1·013	22	1·169	42	1·381	62	1·689
3	1·020	23	1·178	43	1·395	63	1·708
4	1·027	24	1·188	44	1·407	64	1·727
5	1·034	25	1·197	45	1·420	65	1·747
6	1·041	26	1·206	46	1·434	66	1·767
7	1·048	27	1·216	47	1·448	67	1·788
8	1·056	28	1·225	48	1·462	68	1·809
9	1·063	29	1·235	49	1·476	69	1·831
10	1·070	30	1·245	50	1·490	70	1·854
11	1·078	31	1·256	51	1·495	71	1·877
12	1·085	32	1·267	52	1·520	72	1·900
13	1·094	33	1·277	53	1·535	73	1·924
14	1·101	34	1·288	54	1·551	74	1·949
15	1·109	35	1·299	55	1·567	75	1·974
16	1·118	36	1·310	56	1·583	76	2·000
17	1·126	37	1·321	57	1·600		
18	1·134	38	1·333	58	1·617		
19	1·143	39	1·345	59	1·634		

2. *Baumé's Hydrometer for Liquids Lighter than Water.*

Degrees.	Specific gravity.	Degrees.	Specific gravity.	Degrees.	Specific gravity.	Degrees.	Specific gravity.
10	1·000	23	·918	36	·849	49	·789
11	·993	24	·913	37	·844	50	·785
12	·986	25	·907	38	·839	51	·781
13	·980	26	·901	39	·834	52	·777
14	·973	27	·896	40	·830	53	·773
15	·967	28	·890	41	·825	54	·768
16	·960	29	·885	42	·820	55	·764
17	·954	30	·880	43	·816	56	·760
18	·948	31	·874	44	·811	57	·757
19	·942	32	·869	45	·807	58	·753
20	·936	33	·864	46	·802	59	·749
21	·930	34	·859	47	·798	60	·745
22	·924	35	·854	48	·794		

TABLES OF ANALYSES

Nos. 1 to 6, inclusive, show the ingredients in 1 American standard and Nos. 9 and

	Ingredients.	(1) Schuylkill River.	(2) Croton River.	(3) Charles River.	(4) Spot Pond.
1	Chlorid of Potassium...	...	...	...	...
2	Chlorid of Sodium.......	·1470	·167	·1547	·3969
3	Chlorid of Ammonium.	...	...	...	...
4	Chlorid of Calcium......	...	·372	·0420	...
5	Chlorid of Magnesium.	·0094	...	...	...
6	Chlorid of Aluminum...	...	·166	...	...
7	Bromid of Sodium......	...	...	...	...
8	Bromid of Magnesium.	...	...	...	...
9	Iodid of Sodium.........	...	...	...	...
10	Sulphate of Potash.....	...	...	...	...
11	Sulphate of Soda........	...	·153	·3816	·2276
12	Sulphate of Lime........	...	·235	·2624	...
13	Sulphate of Magnesia..	·0570	...	...	...
14	Sulphate of Alumina...	...	...	...	...
15	Nitrate of Magnesia....	...	...	...	...
16	Phosphate of Lime......	...	...	...	and iron.
17	Phosphate of Alumina.	...	·332	·0973	·1081
18	Alumina	...	...	...	...
19	Silicic Acid...............	·0800	·077	traces	traces
20	Carbonate of Soda......	...	...	...	...
21	Carbonate of Baryta...	...	...	...	...
22	Carbonate of Strontia..	...	...	...	...
23	Carbonate of Lime......	1·8720	2.131	·1610	·3722
24	Carbonate of Magnesia	·3510	·662	·0399	·1420
25	Carbon. of Manganese.	...	traces	...	...
26	Carbonate of Iron.......	...	...	...	...
27	Fluorid of Calcium.....	...	...	...	...
28	Salts of Soda with the Nitric and Organic Acids..................	1·6436	1·865	·5291	...
	Total..................	4·2600	6·660	1·6680	1·2468
	Carbonic Acid Gas in cubic inches..........	·3879	17·418	·0464	33·79
	Analyzed by.............	Author.	Author.	Author.	Author.

NOTE.—No. 1 is the supply for the city of Philadelphia, No. 2 for New York, and No. 5 for Boston; Nos. 4 and 6 are small lakes in the vicinity of Boston, and No. 3 is a river in Massachusetts, emptying near Boston.

OF NATURAL WATERS.

gallon, (or 58·372 grains.) Nos. 7, 8, and 9 are in one pound Troy, 10 in 1000 parts.

	(5)	(6)	(7)	(8)	(9)	(10)
	Long Pond.	Mystic Pond.	Saratoga C. Spring.	Seltzer Spring.	Sea Water Brit. Chan.	Water of Dead Sea.
1	·0880	·1590	1·6256	·2685	·7660	traces
2	·0323	27·911	19·6653	12·9690	27·9590	78·650
3	...	...	·0326	...	traces	...
4	·0308	·1544	...	...	...	28·220
5	·0764	...	...	...	8·666	50·950
6	...	...	...	...	...	...
7	...	...	·1618	...	...	...
8	...	...	...	...	·0290	7·950
9	...	...	·0046	...	traces	...
10	...	...	·1879	·2978	...	...
11	...	...	...	...	...	...
12	...	1·2190	...	...	1·4060	traces
13	·1020	1·9768	...	...	2·2960	...
14	...	·4478	...	...	...	...
15	...	...	·1004	...	...	...
16	...	...	...	·0007	...	...
17	...	·2810	...	·0020	...	...
18	·0800	...	·0069	...	...	...
19	·0800	·5559	·1112	·2265	...	...
20	...	...	·8261	4·6162	...	...
21	...	...	...	·0014	...	...
22	...	...	·0672	·0144	...	...
23	·2380	·9894	5·8531	1·4004	·0330	...
24	·0630	·1698	4·1155	1·5000	...	...
25	...	...	·0202	...	...	...
26	...	...	·0173	...	...	...
27	...	...	...	·0018	...	...
28	·5295	...	...	...	...	...
	1·2220	82·7671	84·7452	21·2982	35·255	165·770
	10·719	10·318	in 100 114·	c. in. 126·		
	Author.	Author.	Schweitzer.	Struve.	Schweitzer.	Author.

No. 7 is the well-known "Congress Spring." No. 8 is a celebrated German Spa.

No. 10 was collected by J. D. Sherwood, Esq., April, 1848, near the mouth of the Jordan.

ABSTRACT

Of the Table of Löwitz, showing the proportion by weight of absolute or real alcohol in spirits of different densities.

Sp. gr. at 60°.	Per cent. of real alcohol.	Sp. gr. at 60°.	Per cent. of real alcohol.	Sp. gr. at 60°.	Per cent. of real alcohol.
0·796	100	0·881	66	0·955	32
0·798	99	0·883	65	0·957	31
0·801	98	0·886	64	0·958	30
0·804	97	0·889	63	0·960	29
0·807	96	0·891	62	0·962	28
0·809	95	0·893	61	0·963	27
0·812	94	0·896	60	0·965	26
0·815	93	0·898	59	0·967	25
0·817	92	0·900	58	0·968	24
0·820	91	0·902	57	0·970	23
0·822	90	0·904	56	0·972	22
0·825	89	0·906	55	0·973	21
0·827	88	0·908	54	0·974	20
0·830	87	0·910	53	0·975	19
0·832	86	0·912	52	0·977	18
0·835	85	0·916	51	0·978	17
0·838	84	0·917	50	0·979	16
0·840	83	0·920	49	0·981	15
0·843	82	0·922	48	0·982	14
0·846	81	0·924	47	0·984	13
0·848	80	0·926	46	0·986	12
0·851	79	0·928	45	0·987	11
0·853	78	0·930	44	0·988	10
0·855	77	0·933	43	0·989	9
0·857	76	0·935	42	0·990	8
0·860	75	0·937	41	0·991	7
0·863	74	0·939	40	0·992	6
0·865	73	0·941	39		
0·867	72	0·943	38		
0·870	71	0·945	37		
0·872	70	0·947	36		
0·874	69	0·949	35		
0·875	68	0·951	34		
0·879	67	0·953	33		

INDEX.

The references are to the numbers of the sections.

THE END.

CPSIA information can be obtained
at www.ICGtesting.com
Printed in the USA
BVHW041345270622
640732BV00001B/170

9 783375 0571